Shadow Reigns Eternal

Kennedy L. Richard

Thorn & Ember Press

Contents

To the ones who swore they'd never kneel...
you don't need to.
You already offered yourself
the moment you opened this book.

1

The Stranger

Amber's glass tumbled onto the sticky bar top with a soft crash. It was her fourth shot of tequila, but the warmth in her chest hadn't spread far enough to dull the ache. Her heart was still breaking, the pain sharp and relentless. The dim lights around the bar felt oppressive, like a spotlight fixed solely on her.

The place was nearly empty, save for a couple of stragglers shooting pool in the corner and a man slouched a few stools down, nursing his own misery. The neon OPEN sign in the window buzzed faintly, its glow reflected in the smudged glass behind the bar. The counter was damp beneath her arms, sticky from spilled drinks or worse, but Amber didn't care.

She sat slumped forward, her head resting in the crook of her arms. Her gaze flicked lazily toward the bartender as he ambled back in her direction, his movements slow, his expression bored.

"Can I get you another one?" He said, his voice lazy and thick with a country drawl.

Amber shook her head slightly, her response barely audible. "It's not working. I need something stronger."

The bartender nodded, "Whiskey it is," he said, turning away from her and grabbing a glass off the shelf behind him.

Amber watched through heavy-lidded eyes as he dropped a large, square ice cube into the glass and poured a stream of amber liquid over it. *Beautiful*, she thought as she watched the golden cascade roll over the ice, pooling at the bottom like molten gold. It was mesmerizing in its simplicity.

"Thanks," she murmured as he set the glass by her hands.

He didn't linger, just nodded curtly before retreating to the far end of the bar. She noticed how quickly he put distance between them, probably used to these kinds of nights and the women who came with them. Amber didn't mind. She wasn't in the mood to talk anyway.

Slowly, she reached her hand out to the glass, her fingers curling around its soft surface. Gently, she swirled the whiskey, the ice cube clinking softly against the sides. She just listened to the sound for a moment, letting it drown out the buzzing sign and the muffled voices from the corner.

At least this drink was honest, smooth, sharp, and burning. A perfect mirror for how she felt.

Bored of the sound, she slowly sat up and brought the cheap, faux-crystal to her lips. The whiskey was warm and pungent, the sharpness catching her off guard. She winced as she took a small sip and fought to stifle a cough as it burned its way down.

When she finally came up for air, her eyes wandered aimlessly around the bar, landing on the spot where the man had once been slouched over. She blinked. He wasn't where she thought he'd been. Somehow, he seemed closer, as if he'd shifted three stools closer to her without moving. He still sat in the same position, slouched over in the stool.

Amber's grip tightened around the glass as a chill crept up her spine. The man hadn't moved, or at least, she hadn't seen him move, but the distance between them had undeniably shrunk. His slouched figure was eerily still, save for his shoulders' faint rise and fall. She squinted, trying to discern more of his features in the dim light, but his face remained obscured by the shadow of his hat that was tipped over his eyes.

She told herself it was nothing. Just her imagination playing tricks, fueled by the alcohol and the oppressive quiet of the nearly empty bar. Still, she couldn't shake the sense that something about him felt *off*.

She took another sip of whiskey, this time a larger one, and forced herself to look away. The burning warmth steadied her, at least for a moment. Her eyes drifted toward the neon sign buzzing faintly in the window, and the two pool players now laughing softly in the corner, their voices too low to make out.

"Rough night?" The voice, low and gravelly, startled her, cutting through the silence like a knife.

Amber snapped her head around and found the man staring at her now, with only a barstool between them. His eyes were dark and unreadable, but they carried an intensity that made her pulse quicken.

She hesitated, unsure whether to respond. "Something like that," she finally said, her voice quieter than she intended.

He leaned forward slightly, the stool creaking beneath him. "Whiskey's a good choice," he said, nodding toward her glass. "Takes the edge off... eventually."

Amber offered a half-hearted smile and shrugged. "Not really working so far."

The man chuckled, the sound dry and humorless. "That's the thing about whiskey," he said, his voice low and deliberate. "It takes time, but eventually, the fire you feel as it slides down your throat will burn the pain away."

Amber didn't know how to respond. She lowered her gaze to her glass, watching the amber liquid swirl around the melting ice. "Maybe I want to forget," she murmured, the words barely audible, almost as if they weren't meant to be heard.

He tilted his head, studying her with an intensity that made her stomach knot. "Careful what you wish for," he said, his voice a quiet warning, almost swallowed by the hum of the neon sign.

Something about the way he said it made her shiver. She glanced back at him, but his gaze had already shifted, fixed somewhere in the distance.

Amber's unease deepened. She wasn't sure if it was the alcohol or the man's strange presence, but the air around her felt heavier as if the room itself had tilted ever so slightly off balance.

"We don't have to do this," she said finally, her voice cutting through the thick silence.

He didn't respond at first, didn't even look at her. "Do what?" he asked after a moment, his tone as calm and unbothered as if they were discussing the weather.

Without moving, she shifted her eyes to him, but he stared ahead unnervingly still. "This," Amber said, "Talk. I'm fine. I don't need company."

The man finally turned his head toward her, his movements slow and deliberate, like he was savoring the moment. His lips curled into a faint smirk, one that didn't reach his eyes.

"Funny thing about need," he said, leaning in just enough to make her breath hitch. "It doesn't care what you want."

The room seemed to grow impossibly quiet. The faint chatter of the pool players in the corner faded into an oppressive silence, the kind that pressed against her ears and made her heart pound in her chest. Amber's grip on the bar tightened, her knuckles white against the sticky wood.

She refused to look at him as she struggled to keep the tremble out of her voice. "What do you want?"

The man tilted his head again, his smirk widening into something sharper, something almost predatory. "Maybe the better question is..." He paused, letting the silence stretch, his eyes boring into the side of her head. "What do *you* want, Amber?"

Her stomach dropped.

She hadn't told him her name.

Amber froze, her breath caught somewhere between her chest and throat. The whiskey burned hotter now, not just in her throat but in her veins, and her grip on the glass tightened as if it could anchor her to something solid.

Slowly, she turned to look at him, "How do you know my name?" she asked, her voice quieter than she intended, barely above a whisper.

The man's smirk didn't falter. If anything, it deepened. "Names have a funny way of finding me," he said smoothly as if that was any kind of answer.

Amber's pulse raced, her unease sharpening into something close to fear. The bar's dim light seemed to flicker for a moment, though the neon sign continued its steady hum. She glanced around quickly, searching for the bartender, for anyone, but the place was suddenly empty, as though the other patrons had vanished without her noticing.

"You didn't answer my question," she said, trying to keep her voice steady though it wavered at the edges.

The man leaned back on his stool, his posture relaxed as if he had all the time in the world. "What do I want?" he echoed, rolling the words over his tongue like he was savoring them. His dark eyes glittered in the low light. "That depends. What are you willing to give?"

Amber's skin prickled, and she felt the urge to leave, to run, to do anything but stay in this suddenly suffocating space. But her legs didn't move. Her hands stayed rooted to the bar.

"I don't know what you're talking about," she said, though the words came out weak, her confidence unraveling.

"Oh, I think you do," he replied, his tone almost playful, though there was something beneath it, something cold, sharp, and dangerous.

Amber swallowed hard, her mind scrambling for something to hold onto. She looked him over, searching for something mundane to ground him, a name on a jacket, a logo on his cap, but everything about him seemed oddly... blank. Forgettable, in the way shadows could be overlooked until they moved.

"Look, I don't know who you are, but—"

"You will," he interrupted smoothly, his smirk fading into something more serious, his gaze piercing through her like he could see the things she was trying to hide. "And you should stop lying to yourself, Amber. You didn't come here just to drink."

Her stomach clenched, his words hitting harder than she wanted to admit. She wanted to deny it, to snap back at him, but the truth stuck in her throat like a shard of glass.

"What do you mean?" she asked finally, her voice small.

He leaned forward now, resting his elbows on the bar, and the shadows seemed to stretch around him, pulling in closer. "You came here because you're running from something. From someone. And you're hoping the bottom of that glass will hold the answer." He nodded toward the whiskey still swirling in her hand. "But it won't. It never does."

Her mouth opened to argue, to tell him he was wrong, but no sound came out. Because he wasn't wrong.

2

Tremors of Power

"Who are you?" she whispered, the question trembling between them.

The man smiled, slow and deliberate, but this time, there was no humor in it. Only something dark, ancient, and unfathomable.

"Just someone who likes to help," he said, his tone dripping with irony.

Amber stared at him, unease pooling in her chest. She was about to look away when a flash of red raced through his eyes, so brief, so subtle, she almost convinced herself she hadn't seen it at all.

Her heart thudded in her chest, but she forced herself to stay calm. Mustering what little courage she had left, she set her glass down on the sticky bar top and pushed herself to her feet. Her legs trembled beneath her, threatening to betray her, but she steadied herself with a deep breath.

Clearing her throat, she said, "Well, as much as I've loved this conversation, I really need to get going."

The man didn't stop her. He simply watched, his dark eyes unblinking as he lifted his drink to his lips. The way he moved was unsettlingly smooth, almost too deliberate.

Amber grabbed her purse from the back of her stool, her fingers fumbling against the worn leather.

She turned toward the door, ready to exit, when his voice cut through the heavy air like a blade. "Bar's closed. You can't leave."

She froze. Her breath hitched in her throat as a chill raced down her spine. Slowly, she turned her head toward him, her attempt at a nervous laugh faltering before it left her lips. "Very funny," she said, her voice uneven, the words hollow.

He didn't look at her this time. His gaze was fixed ahead, his tone casual, almost bored. "Don't believe me?" he said, swirling his glass lazily. "Take a look at the OPEN sign."

Amber's pulse quickened as her gaze darted toward the neon sign in the window. It still buzzed faintly in the background, casting its familiar red glow. But just as she turned to look, the light flickered and went out, leaving the window in darkness. The hum died with it, plunging the bar into an eerie silence.

Her breathing quickened. "What the hell," she whispered under her breath, her voice barely audible.

Without a second thought, Amber bolted for the door, her sneakers squeaking against the sticky floor. Panic clawed at her chest as she reached for the handle...but her hand met nothing but cold metal. The handle was gone. She clawed at the door, her nails scraping against the surface as her panic grew.

Behind her, the man chuckled softly. The sound wasn't amused; it was dark, low, and filled with something that sent her heart plummeting.

"You can't leave, Amber," he said, his voice smooth as silk, dripping with something that sounded like certainty. "Not until we've finished our little chat."

Her throat tightened, and she pressed her palms flat against the door, willing it to open to give her an escape. But it didn't budge.

She turned her head slowly, trembling as she glanced back toward the bar. The man sat there, as calm as ever, his fingers idly tracing the rim of his glass. His smirk had returned, but his eyes burned now, faintly glowing red in the dim light.

The bar felt smaller, the air heavier, as if the walls were closing in.

"What...what do you want from me?" she stammered, her voice breaking.

The man tipped his head, his smirk widening into something that made her blood run cold. "Oh, Amber," he said, his tone playful. "It's not about what I want."

He leaned forward, his voice dropping to a whisper that seemed to echo in her mind, "It's about what you want...and what you're willing to pay to get it."

He leaned back after he spoke, taking another sip of his whiskey. Then he smiled an easy, casual smile, the kind meant to disarm. But something lurking behind it, something dark and sinister, made her stomach churn.

Come sit.

The words were his, but his lips hadn't moved. Amber froze, her breath catching in her throat. She glanced at his mouth, but it was still curved in that unsettling smile. Yet, she had heard him, clear as day, as though he were speaking directly inside her head.

A tear slipped down her cheek, unbidden, as her chest tightened.

Come sit.

The words echoed again, reverberating through her mind, making her head throb.

I don't bite... much.

He winked, his dark eyes gleaming with amusement, and the stool next to him scraped across the floor with a deafening screech, moving toward her as if it had a mind of its own.

Amber flinched, her knees threatening to buckle. She wanted to run, to scream, but her body refused to obey. Her legs felt rooted to the sticky floor, and her pulse thundered in her ears as the stool came to rest beside him, perfectly still, waiting.

I won't tell you again.

The voice pounded in her head, each word like a hammer against her sanity.

"Who are you?" Amber screamed, her voice cracking under the weight of her terror. "What do you want from me?" Tears streamed down her face, blurring her vision as she stared at the man, desperate for answers.

He tilted his head, his expression as composed as ever. "Well, that's exactly what we'll discuss as soon as you sit." His voice was calm now, unnervingly so, as if this were a routine conversation and not her worst nightmare unfolding.

Amber shook her head violently, her heart hammering in her chest. "No," she whispered, though her body betrayed her. Her legs moved forward, one small, reluctant step at a time, her muscles ignoring every desperate plea from her mind to stop.

"No!" she said louder, panic rising as she felt herself nearing the stool. She strained against the invisible force pulling her, but it was useless. Her hands trembled as they reached out against her will, gripping the back of the chair.

"That's better," the man said, his tone almost soothing, but the malice behind it was unmistakable.

Amber collapsed onto the stool, her body finally obeying her commands to stop, though now it was too late. She sat frozen, her breathing ragged, her hands clenching the bar's edge like it might somehow keep her grounded.

"Let me go," she choked out, her voice trembling.

"Now, now," he said, swirling the amber liquid in his glass. "That's no way to treat someone who's about to help you."

Amber's lips parted, but no words came out. She stared at him, her mind racing. "Help me?" she managed, her voice a strained whisper.

He grinned, setting his glass down with a quiet clink. "That's what I do, Amber. I help people. I give them what they want. Or, more accurately..." His smile widened, his teeth unnaturally white against the dim light. "What they think they want."

Her stomach twisted. "I didn't ask for anything from you," she said, her voice barely audible.

His gaze sharpened, pinning her in place like a predator cornering its prey. "Didn't you?" he asked, his tone suddenly razor-edged. "When you sat here, drowning in misery, wishing to forget. Wishing the pain away."

Her breath hitched as his words struck a chord deep within her.

"I...I didn't mean it like that," she stammered.

"Intent," he said smoothly, "is irrelevant. The wish was made. And I...well, I'm here to deliver."

"You're the Devil," she spat, her voice trembling with a mix of fear and disgust.

He chuckled, unfazed, and raised his hand toward the row of whiskey bottles behind the bar. "Very good," he murmured as if acknowledging a clever remark.

Amber's eyes widened in disbelief as she watched one of the bottles rise from the shelf, floating toward them with eerie precision. It stopped just before their glasses, hovering in midair for a long moment before tilting and pouring the golden liquid into both glasses.

Ice appeared out of nowhere, settling in with a soft clink. The man waved his hand dismissively, and the bottle returned itself to the shelf without a sound.

"Although," he said, his voice casual, as if what had just happened was nothing more than a slight hiccup in their conversation, "I do prefer Lucifer."

He took a sip of his whiskey, his expression entirely at ease, as though the surreal events unfolding were nothing more than a casual exchange. Amber couldn't tear her eyes away from him, her pulse pounding in her ears.

"Devil makes people think of some red fellow with a spiny tail and horns," he continued, his voice smooth, almost amused. "Now, although I can make myself look like whoever or whatever I want, I wish people would stop assuming the monster is my everyday appearance."

Amber stared at him, her mouth slightly agape, her mind struggling to process what he said. When she finally managed to find her voice, it came out as a whisper so quiet, she wasn't sure if she'd even spoken aloud. "I don't... I don't understand."

He chuckled, setting his glass back on the bar with a soft clink. "I know," he said, his smile widening as though the confusion was precisely what he'd expected. "But you will."

He paused then, his dark eyes scanning her, sizing her up with a look that made her feel exposed and small. "Let's play a little game, shall we?" he said. "I'm going to ask you a series of questions, and you're going to answer me as honestly as possible. Don't try to lie to me because I will know. And I do despise liars."

Her stomach twisted. She wanted to protest, to leave, but the weight of his gaze held her in place. She felt the chill in the air like something ancient and unsettling was slowly creeping toward her, suffocating her every instinct to escape.

"First question," he said, not waiting for her to respond. "Why are you really here? What are you running from?"

Amber's breath caught in her throat. The words felt like a weight in her chest, one she wasn't ready to confront. But she knew she couldn't lie to him. The air in the room seemed to thicken, closing in on her as she tried to summon an answer.

"I broke up with my boyfriend," Amber said, her voice small.

He looked at her with patient expectation, waiting for more. "Go on," he drawled, bringing his glass to his lips as if this were all a casual conversation.

Amber took a sip of her whiskey, buying herself a moment to gather her thoughts. "I found him in bed with one of my coworkers," she continued, her voice wavering slightly. "We'd been together for four years. We had just moved in together. I followed him here to be with him and found him with another woman. It hurt, so I left, wanting to numb the pain, and I ended up here."

For a moment, there was nothing but silence between them. Then, a flash of red appeared in his eyes. "No," he said, placing his glass gently on the table.

"No?" Amber repeated, her voice shaky.

"No. That's not why you're here." His voice was colder now, sharper. "That's why you think you're here. What you keep telling yourself is the reason you're here, but there's more to it." He paused, leaning a bit closer, his eyes locked onto hers. "Tell me the real reason you're here."

His words were slow and hypnotic, like a siren's call, and Amber felt herself sinking deeper into his gaze. Without realizing it, she spoke, her words tumbling as if they'd been waiting for this moment.

"I'm here because I thought I was going to marry him, but it's just one failed relationship after another, and I'm terrified that I'm never going to find the one. I want nothing more than to be a mother and a wife. I want the kind of relationship my parents had: kind, loving, and long. But here I am, almost 30, and I just broke up with the only man who's been with me for longer than a fleeting moment. I'm here because I can't help but think that it's me that's faulty. That there's something wrong with me. That I'm the reason these relationships don't last, and I'm sick of feeling that way."

The words poured from her like a river, unstoppable and raw. She hadn't intended to say any of it, but once she started, she couldn't stop.

Suddenly, the Devil blinked, and Amber's hand flew to her mouth as if she could somehow take back every word she had just spoken. He leaned back, adjusting himself on the stool, and a menacing smile spread across his face.

"Much better," he said, his tone darkly satisfied.

Amber's heart hammered in her chest. "How did you...? Why did I...?" She trailed off, her breath steadying as she tried to wrap her mind around what had just happened. "I've never told anyone that before."

He gave a slight, knowing shrug. "People tend to tell me their darkest secrets. Something about me makes them want to talk, I guess." His grin widened, his eyes gleaming with an unsettling understanding. "Now, question number two."

The Devil's voice, smooth and unhurried, filled the space between them once again. "Tell me, Amber, what's one thing you blame yourself for?"

She froze, her breath catching as the question landed like a stone in her chest. Her hand trembled slightly around her glass, the coldness of the whiskey doing nothing to numb the sudden wave of guilt that flooded her. She'd known this question would come, had braced herself for it, but still, it hit her harder than anything she'd expected.

Her eyes dropped to the bar top, tracing the rings left behind by previous glasses, avoiding his gaze. Deep down, she knew that he already knew the answer.

"I...I blame myself for my mother's death," Amber whispered, her voice barely audible, as if speaking the words aloud would somehow make them even more real. She could feel the weight of the silence settling around her like a suffocating fog.

The Devil didn't react immediately, but Amber could feel the power of his gaze on her, and it made her want to shrink into herself, to disappear from the room entirely.

"The car came out of nowhere. There was a fog so thick no one could see the lines of the road, but I shouldn't have been driving that fast; no, I shouldn't have been driving at all. We were always fighting, and she yelled at me that I was driving too fast, so I sped up. Being defiant as always. By the time I noticed the headlights of the other car, it was too late. All I can remember is the sound of glass breaking, and then everything goes dark. The next memory I have is of me being pulled out of the car and my mother, dangling upside down, saying, 'I love you.' I didn't say it back. I should have said it back."

Her voice cracked on the last word, the truth cutting deeper than any blade could.

"And when I think about it and how I failed her... I can't shake the feeling that if I'd just listened to her and slowed down, maybe she wouldn't have died. Maybe I could have saved her."

The words felt like poison as they left her mouth, each one another layer of guilt she could never shake. The room seemed to darken around her, and she closed her eyes for a moment, fighting back the tears that threatened to break free.

The Devil's voice broke through the heavy silence, low and steady. "You really shouldn't be driving when the fog is thick enough to cut." A sly smile crept across his face as Amber stared at him, her heart heavy, her mind spinning with the weight of his words. Part of her wanted to scream, to tell him he didn't understand, but another part of her knew he was right. If she had just waited out the fog, her mother may still be here.

The silence stretched between them, suffocating and thick as they both took a drink.

3

Unraveling Fate

T he Devil leaned in just a little, the faintest glint of amusement dancing in his eyes as he asked the next question. His voice was smooth as velvet, each word dripping with intent.

"What's the worst thing you've ever done, and why did you do it?"

Her stomach tightened at the question, the answer rising like bile in her throat. It wasn't something she liked to think about, let alone speak aloud. But the Devil wasn't going to let her hide from it. The room seemed to close in on her as the weight of his gaze bore down, urging her to answer.

She swallowed hard, forcing herself to meet his eyes. "You mean besides killing my mother?" She paused, her fingers trembling in her lap. She could feel the truth burning, trying to claw its way out.

"I... I sabotaged my brother," she whispered, the weight of the words making her feel small. "He was supposed to have this amazing future. He had everything planned out, straight A's, honors, and acceptance letters lined up from every top school he applied to. He was going to leave, get out of that town, make something of himself."

The Devil's eyes gleamed, his attention unwavering. "And you?" he asked, though his tone made it clear he already knew.

Amber shook her head, her voice breaking. "I wasn't him. I was average. Struggling. Barely scraping by. Nobody looked at me the way they looked at him. I was 'the other one.' The screw-up. The disappointment. And I hated it. Especially after my mother died. My brother was put on a pedestal where everyone was in awe at how well he was doing despite the tragedy. And me? All I got was pity and acceptance that my life should be spiraling out of control."

She took a shaky breath, tears spilling freely now. "When the acceptance letters started coming in, I was the one who checked the mail first. I... I tore them up. I forged rejection letters. I made it look like he didn't get in any-where."

The room seemed to tighten around her, suffocating with the weight of her confession.

"He didn't understand," Amber continued, her voice cracking. "He thought he'd done something wrong and wasn't good enough. Watching him cry, watching his dreams fall apart, it should've killed me. But it didn't. I told myself he deserved it. He'd been handed everything, and it was my turn to win. But I didn't win. I just ruined his life. And mine."

The Devil leaned back, his smile sharp and unrelenting. "Ah, jealousy," he mused, his voice smooth as honey. "A tale as old as time. But tell me, Amber, did it feel good at the moment? Even just a little?"

Amber's face crumpled, shame washing over her. "Yes," she whispered, shaking her head. "At first, it did. Watching him fall felt amazing, but then everything got so much worse. And he got stuck in the town he desperately wanted to escape. I've hated myself ever since."

The Devil's smile widened, his amusement palpable. "Regret," he said, savoring the word. "Such a beautiful, human flaw."

He took another sip of his whisky; his glass always seemed to refill itself, and after a moment, his voice slid out smoothly, like a whisper in the darkness. "You've gotten the hang of my game. Just a few more questions now." Something shimmered in his eyes as he pushed her glass towards her. "If you could get away with anything, Amber," he began, his tone almost playful, "and face no consequences, no guilt or retribution, what would you do?"

Amber's breath hitched at the question. She hadn't expected him to ask something so... open, so dangerous. The idea of being free from consequences was both alluring and terrifying. She searched her mind, the thought of unrestrained freedom opening up something dark within her.

What would she do?

Her first instinct was to recoil from the idea, to push it away. She wasn't that kind of person, was she? The kind who did things without thinking, without fear of the fallout. But the more she thought about it, the more the question lingered, worming its way into her mind.

"I guess..." she started slowly, taking a sip of the whiskey before her, unsure whether she should say the words aloud, "I'd... I'd go after the people who've hurt me. Make them feel the way I did. The way they made me feel."

Her heart pounded in her chest, adrenaline racing through her veins as she spoke. She'd never really allowed herself to think about vengeance, about righting the wrongs in her life by doing harm in return. But now, the idea of it felt almost liberating. The idea of striking back without any fear of the consequences.

The Devil smiled at her response, that dark, knowing smile that made her skin crawl. He didn't speak at first, letting her words hang in the air. Amber glanced at him, her stomach churning at the intensity of his gaze.

"Go on," he encouraged, his voice like honey, sweet but deadly. "What else?"

Amber's mouth went dry, but she continued, the words flowing more freely now. "I'd... I'd probably burn all the bridges. The ones that tie me to people who've kept me stuck. Friends, family... whoever. I'd cut them off and leave it all behind. No more guilt, no more obligations. Just freedom."

She shifted in her seat, her pulse quickening as the weight of her own words settled over her. She had never allowed herself to dream about cutting ties with everything, but now, sitting here with him felt almost intoxicating.

"And... I'd make him regret it," she added, trembling. "My ex. I'd make him see everything he lost. I'd make him wish he had never walked away. I'd... I'd make him feel my pain when I caught him with that girl."

The Devil's smile widened, the approval in his eyes unmistakable. He said nothing, but the silence stretched between them as if he were savoring her vulnerability, enjoying how she revealed herself.

Amber swallowed hard, feeling exposed but also strangely empowered by the words she'd spoken. She could almost see it for a brief, dangerous moment, the power in taking control, in wreaking havoc without fear of what might happen.

The Devil leaned back in his stool, his gaze never leaving her. "You see, Amber," he said softly, his voice a little more serious now, "the real question isn't what you would do if there were no consequences. The real question is... would you be able to live with yourself after?"

The weight of his words hit her like a freight train. Amber blinked, the adrenaline of the fantasy fading as reality started to set in. Could she live with herself if she really did those things? Would the satisfaction of revenge be worth the toll it would take on her soul?

But she didn't have time to think about it for long because his voice broke through her spiraling thoughts. Lucifer's eyes narrowed slightly, his expression almost predatory, as though he could sense the weight of his next question. His voice dropped lower, becoming even more intoxicating.

"Tell me, Amber," he said, his tone smooth as silk, "what's one secret you've never shared? Something you've hidden from everyone, even yourself."

Amber stiffened. Her stomach twisted as if he'd reached right inside her and pulled something dark to the surface. She felt the sting of hesitation before she could even gather her thoughts. Secrets were dangerous, especially the ones she buried deep, which she had never spoken aloud.

Her hands clenched around the edge of her glass, knuckles white, and for a moment, she could hear the rhythmic beat of her pulse in her ears.

"I..." she stopped herself, struggling to find the words. The thick, oppressive silence in the room urged her to speak. Amber's mind raced, flashing through memories and moments, each one containing something she had never dared admit to anyone.

Amber froze, her breath catching in her throat. Her hands gripped the edge of the stool, knuckles white as if holding on for dear life. The words he asked for loomed like a shadow she'd spent years outrunning. She tried to resist, to bury it deeper, but the Devil's presence had a way of loosening the chains around her darkest truths.

Lucifer's voice broke through her thoughts once more, smooth and coaxing. "You know you want to tell me, Amber. I'm listening."

"There was..." Her voice cracked, and she swallowed hard, her gaze fixed on the polished bar top. "There was someone I loved in high school. I thought it was real, that it was everything. But... I got pregnant."

The Devil's expression didn't change, but his unrelenting gaze bore into her, compelling her to continue.

"I panicked," she admitted, her voice trembling. "I was only seventeen. I couldn't tell my father. I was already looked at as a massive screw-up. I couldn't let him hold this over my head, too. And I knew he'd never forgive me, we were barely scraping by as it was. My father didn't need another mouth to feed. So, I... I didn't keep it."

Her voice broke, tears streaming down her face as she clenched her fists in her lap. "I got rid of it. Alone. No one knew...not my boyfriend, not my dad, no one. I told myself it was the only choice I had. But when I got home, my brother had found the positive test in the trash. He was furious, demanding to know who it belonged to."

She choked on a sob, unable to meet his eyes. "I was so scared, so ashamed. I couldn't face the consequences, so I said it was my sister's. I told him she was the one who got pregnant. And he believed me."

The silence between them was suffocating, broken only by Amber's ragged breaths.

"My father grounded her for months," she continued, her voice hollow. "He called her names and told her how disappointed he was. He took her to the doctor for a checkup, and the doctor said she wasn't pregnant, so they just claimed it was a false positive. Still, my father forced her to break up with her boyfriend and kept such a tight leash on her that she barely got to live her own life. And all that time, I let them think it was her. I let her take the blame for my mistake."

The Devil tilted his head, his smile widening. "Ah," he murmured, his tone smooth and indulgent. "The lies we tell to save ourselves. Did you ever tell her the truth?"

Amber shook her head, shame etched into every line of her face. "No. She knows it was me; whose else would it be? But I'll never admit it to her. Our relationship has never been the same since then. No matter what she said to my brother or father about never taking a test and that it was mine, they wouldn't believe her. They would say she was just using me as a scapegoat because it would make more sense if it was mine and I was an easy target after what happened with Mom. My brother even beat up her boyfriend. It was so bad the kid was in the hospital for nearly a week; he almost died. The poor guy had no idea what he was on about and was pissed at my sister because he thought she didn't tell him she was having a baby. I've never dared to admit that it was me."

The Devil leaned forward slightly, his grin sharp and predatory. "Such a delicious secret, Amber. Guilt and betrayal wrapped up so neatly in a single act. I wonder...do you hate yourself for it or simply hate that you got away with it?"

Amber shook her head, "I don't know. Both?"

The air was thick with shame. It felt like a relief and yet a curse. She had spoken the truth, but she couldn't help but wonder if, in doing so, she had just given him more power over her than she ever intended.

Lucifer's gaze never left her as he took a slow sip from his glass. "Don't worry," he murmured. "We're nearing the end of my little game."

The Devil's gaze never wavered, and Amber could feel the weight of his next question settle over her like a dark cloud before it was even said.

"Amber," he said, his voice low and deliberate, "what would you choose? Love or power? The choice is yours... what's more important to you?"

Amber felt a shiver run down her spine as the question's weight pressed down her chest. She opened her mouth, but no words came at first. Love had always been her greatest longing, but power... power was something different. Power was control, security, and influence.

She downed the whiskey in her glass in one gulp, setting it on the table next to her, only for it to fill back up immediately.

She watched the liquid rise from nowhere as her thoughts shouted for attention. She had spent so many years feeling helpless, lost in relationships that left her broken and yearning for more. Love had always seemed like an elusive dream, something to chase but never quite grasp. But power was something that could be held, something she could build. If she had power, she could never be hurt again. No one would have the ability to strip away her strength.

Her thoughts swirled, each option pulling her in a different direction.

"I..." Amber hesitated, her voice faltering as she struggled to find the words. "I want both," she whispered, almost to herself. "I want to be loved, but I also want control. I want to be strong. I don't want to be helpless again. I don't want to be the victim. I want to have it all."

The Devil's smile deepened, and he leaned in slightly, his voice smooth and soothing. "Oh, sweet girl, you can have it all. But the question is, which would you sacrifice? Love or power?"

She swallowed, the words catching in her throat. *Could she genuinely choose between the two? Could she surrender one for the other?*

"Love," she began, her voice trembling slightly as the weight of the decision bore down on her, "has always felt like something that slips through my fingers. Power, though... power feels solid. It feels... real."

The Devil nodded slowly, his eyes glinting with approval. "A wise choice," he murmured, his voice a caress that sent a chill down her spine. "But remember, love can be a powerful tool, and power can be a lonely throne. Choose carefully, Amber. You may find that what you seek could come at a far greater cost than you ever imagined."

Amber's heart raced, her mind spinning as the implications of her answer began to settle in. She had chosen power. And now, in the silence that followed, she wondered if she had made a mistake.

The Devil's smirk never faltered, and she felt something dark twist within her.

He stood, the movement smooth and effortless, as he finished his drink. "We're getting closer now," he said, his voice a low murmur. "You'll learn soon enough the price of your choices."

And with that, the room seemed to grow colder. The silence between them was thick with meaning, and Amber could feel it, a creeping sense that her life was about to take a turn from which there would be no return.

4

Shadows of Power

Lucifer moved to her side and blinked. All the balls disappeared except for the black eight and cue balls. "Far right pocket," he said, lowering himself into the perfect position. In one swift motion, he knocked the cue ball into the eight ball, and with a satisfying thump, the ball rolled into the far right pocket. They both stared at the table briefly before he placed down the cue stick and returned his gaze to her.

She watched as his eyes narrowed slightly as if savoring the moment. The air in the room seemed to thicken as if the very walls were listening for her answer. "Here's my final question for you, Amber?" He paused before licking his lips and continuing, "Would you make a deal with me?" He asked, his voice smooth, coaxing, like a velvet rope tugging her closer to the edge. "A deal that would give you everything you've ever wanted... even if it came with a cost?"

Amber's breath hitched in her chest. The question felt too easy, too simple. And yet, it carried the weight of a thousand decisions, a thousand possible futures.

She felt a shiver run through her, her mind racing with the possibilities. The thought of everything she'd ever dreamed of: love, power, control, everything she'd been longing for in her life, dangling just out of reach, waiting to be claimed. But there was always a cost, *wasn't there? There was always something that had to be paid.*

Her thoughts drilled her head, but the Devil's voice was louder, more insistent, pulling her toward him. "What would you do, Amber? Would you take the chance? Would you risk it all for everything you've ever wanted?"

"I..." Amber started, her voice barely a whisper. "I don't know. I don't know if I could."

The Devil's dark and knowing smile deepened as he leaned in closer, his voice almost a purr. "You already know the answer, Amber. Everyone does. We all make deals. We all pay a price. The question is: Are you willing to face that cost?"

For a long moment, Amber stayed frozen, her mind swirling with the weight of the decision. Could she do it? Could she really choose to have everything she ever wanted if it meant losing something she couldn't get back?

The Devil's gaze burned into hers, waiting, his presence like a shadow that stretched across the room, waiting for her to take that step.

And somewhere deep inside, Amber knew; she'd always known.

"Let me show you what you could have." Lucifer's voice was low and warm, almost inviting. It was intoxicating how he held his hand towards her, promising her everything she ever wanted. "Take my hand and let me show you."

Hesitantly, Amber reached forward and touched his, and in a bright flash, the room around them shifted. The dim bar melted away like smoke, and Amber found herself standing in a gleaming, sunlit kitchen. It was warm and inviting, with polished counters and an oversized window overlooking a perfectly manicured garden. A man's laughter rang out, and Amber turned to see him: a tall, handsome figure with an easy smile, holding a toddler in his arms. The child giggled, reaching for her, and Amber's heart ached with longing.

"That's your husband," the Devil said, his voice echoing in her ear as he appeared beside her. "A man who sees only you, who worships the ground you walk on. And that's your daughter, your family. No more broken relationships, no more empty nights. Just unconditional love."

Amber's breath caught as the man kissed her cheek, and the little girl giggled, calling her "Mommy." The image shifted, dissolving into another scene.

A warm breeze rushed through open car windows, whipping a high school Amber's blonde hair into a wild mess as her sister, Emily, cranked the volume on the stereo. The raspy opening chords of Fleetwood Mac's *"Go Your Own Way"* filled the car, and Emily's fingers drummed enthusiastically on the steering wheel.

Amber watched from the backseat as her younger self glanced at her sister, laughing at how seriously Emily was taking her imaginary drumming gig. "You're gonna blow out the speakers!" Her younger self shouted over the music, grinning from ear to ear.

Emily shot her a mock-offended look. "It's Fleetwood Mac! There's no such thing as too loud!"

With that, Emily belted out the chorus at the top of her lungs, wholly off-key but entirely unapologetic. The younger Amber couldn't help but join in, their voices blending into an absurd harmony of giggles and shouting.

As the song hit the instrumental break, Emily stuck her arm out the window, her fingers slicing through the wind. Amber followed suit, leaning her head back and letting the cool air kiss her skin.

"This is the best!" Amber yelled, her laughter bubbling up uncontrollably.

Emily grinned, her eyes sparkling in the golden glow of the setting sun. "You needed this, Amber," she said, her voice softer but still filled with joy. "Sometimes you just gotta let loose and scream-sing in the car, you know?"

From the back seat, Amber nodded, a lump forming in her throat. "This never happened. Emily and I never had moments like this: carefree, silly, and bursting with love."

The Devil nodded knowingly, "But in this life, you do. You said no to your high school boyfriend. You never got pregnant, so there was no need to pin anything on your sister. You two became inseparable."

Amber smiled at the scene in front of her when suddenly she found herself standing in a space she recognized. It was her childhood home, filled with laughter and joy. Her siblings were there, gathered around a dinner table, her father at the head and her mother beside him, alive and vibrant. Her brother raised a glass in a toast, and her sister laughed, the bitterness and resentment that had once filled their relationship nowhere to be seen.

"You never left your family," the Devil whispered. "Your mother's death? It didn't happen because you waited until the fog lifted. Your brother just received his acceptance letter to the University of Michigan, his dream school, because you weren't bitter. You had no need to tear up the letters."

The scene morphed again, the warmth giving way to cold power. Amber was dressed in an expensive suit in a sleek, high-rise office. People knocked on glass doors to be let in and waited until she was ready for them. Her voice commanded respect, and her presence exuded authority. She was untouchable, a force to be reckoned with.

"You wanted power, didn't you?" the Devil said, stepping towards the bay of dark windows in the scene. "Now, you've got it. No man can break you. No one can hurt you. Every bridge that once tied you down has been burned, and you've risen above it all. You've taken revenge on those who've wronged you, cut the ties that kept you shackled. They fear you now."

Amber's eyes flicked to the hallway where her former boyfriend, whom she thought she was in the bar for, meandered past carrying a mop and bucket. The woman he'd cheated on her with raced into the office with a coffee in hand. The Amber in the scene didn't stop what she was doing; she simply took the coffee out of the woman's hands, tasted it, and, clearly unhappy with the taste, opened the cover and poured the scalding liquid over the woman's head. "Try again." The mighty Amber shouted, and the woman skittered away, terrified.

"Why is it dark outside?" Amber asked, moving her eyes to where Lucifer stood by the windows.

"Because it's night, my dear."

"But I have a baby at home. Shouldn't I be there?"

"Ah," Lucifer smiled as he turned back to Amber, "you chose power over love. You have the man and the family you want, but you're never around. You're too busy building and perfecting your empire. All power comes with consequences. You wanted freedom," he said. "You wanted revenge. No one can stand in your way now. And as for those secrets you've buried..." He waved his hand, and the guilt she'd carried for years evaporated like smoke. The weight was gone, replaced by a chilling sense of lightness.

Amber's breath quickened as the Devil gestured to the scenes around her. "This is the life you can have," he said, his eyes glowing faintly red. "The love, the power, the absolution. No more fear. No more pain. All you have to do is say yes."

Amber's heart pounded as the images swirled together, her dream life shimmering in front of her. It was perfect, everything she'd ever wanted. But as she reached out toward the vision, her hand trembled, her voice faltered, and the scene before her disappeared, returning to the bar.

"What's the cost?" she whispered.

The Devil's smile widened, his teeth gleaming in the low light. "Ah, my dear," he purred, "we'll get to that in time. For now, all you need to do is decide. Will you take what I'm offering, or will you cling to the scraps of the life you've made?"

5

The Thorns of Power

Amber's breath hitched as her eyes darted between the Devil and the empty space where her perfect life had just been. Her mind raced, scrambling for any way out of the situation. Despite the overwhelming fear tightening her chest, she forced herself to stand straighter, her hands clenching at her sides.

"I'll decide," she said, her voice trembling but gaining strength. "But not yet."

The Devil tilted his head, his smile faltering for a fraction of a second. "Stalling won't save you," he said smoothly before flashing back to his previous barstool. "The offer isn't eternal, my dear."

Amber lifted her chin, determination flickering to life in her eyes. "You suggested we get to know each other better, but you already seem to know me," she countered, walking over and sitting back across from him. "So, now it's my turn to get to know you. Allow me the opportunity to ask you anything I want, and if you answer my questions openly and honestly, then I'll accept this new life no matter the consequences, but if I catch you in a lie or you decline to answer, you have to tell me the cost of this life *before* I agree to it."

The Devil's smile returned, more expansive this time, sharp and wicked. "Now, *that* is an intriguing proposal," he said, leaning back and crossing his legs. "You know, Amber, most people don't try to negotiate with me. They simply crumble. I admire your fire."

Amber didn't dare let herself feel relief. Not yet. "Do we have a deal?"

He regarded her for a moment, his gaze sharp enough to cut through steel, "One small change to your game... When I win, I decide if you get the life I showed you or if you simply get the consequences. If we did it your way, there's no point in me playing."

Amber hesitated for a moment, "Deal." She extended her right hand to him.

A smile wide enough to make the Cheshire cat feel inadequate crept across his face as he took her hand. "Ask away, dear."

The coldness of his touch sent a shiver down her spine.

She scanned the shelves, her fingers brushing the cool glass bottles until her gaze landed on the whiskey she'd noticed earlier. It was older than the one she was drinking before, aged for much longer, and much more expensive than she ever could've afforded. But now, the amber liquid glinted under the dim lights, and without hesitation, she reached for it. The chill of the bottle seeped into her fingers, traveling up her arms like icy tendrils.

Setting the bottle on the counter, she grabbed the glass she'd used earlier and poured herself a generous shot. The golden liquid swirled as she lifted the glass to her lips and swallowed it in one go, the burn sliding down her throat like liquid fire. Her hand didn't falter as she poured another.

Her eyes met his, sharp and challenging, as she placed the glass on the bar in front of her. With a quick flick of her wrist, she slid it down the counter toward him, the sound of the glass skimming the wood cutting through the silence.

"Take a shot," she said, her tone steady, daring him with her gaze.

The Devil tilted his head, his lips curving into an amused smirk. The glass was at his lips in the blink of an eye, though she hadn't even seen him reach for it. He drained the whiskey effortlessly, his eyes never leaving hers, and set the glass back on the counter with a deliberate, hollow clink.

"Impressive," he said, his voice low and smooth, laced with something dangerous.

Amber raised a brow, grabbed another glass, and poured herself another, knocking it back just as swiftly. The liquid courage steadied the fire in her chest as she leaned forward on the counter, her voice cutting through the tension.

Amber held his gaze, her breath steady, the fire inside her igniting. "Try me."

The Devil chuckled, a low, rich sound that seemed to reverberate through the room, settling in Amber's chest like a warning.

"Alright, then," he said, his tone deceptively light. "Ask away."

Amber's jaw tightened, but she gave a curt nod, determination flashing in her eyes. "Have you always been the one making the rules?"

The Devil's smile widened, his expression both amused and predatory. He leaned forward, resting his elbows on the counter as his voice dropped, carrying the weight of something ancient and unyielding.

"Once upon a time," he began, "I wasn't the one making deals. I was the one bound by them. I served others, answering their whims, trapped by their desires." He spun the empty glass with one finger, his eyes darkening as memories flickered beneath their surface. "But servitude taught me something, darling. It taught me that power isn't given; it's taken. And when I broke free, I didn't just take power. I took everything."

Amber swallowed, the weight of his words settling heavily in the air between them. But she didn't falter. "What do you mean you were trapped by their desires? Was there not always a devil?"

The Devil's smirk widened, though it didn't quite reach his eyes. For a fleeting moment, something ancient and weary flickered in his expression, a shadow of vulnerability, a glimpse of truths buried deep.

"Ahhh, my dear," he began, his voice soothing and measured, like a lullaby meant to calm a restless child. "Belief is such a funny thing. Humans are fed the same stories, over and over, about what the Devil looks like, who the Devil is, and what Hell must be." He leaned forward slightly, his gaze locking with hers. "But here's the punchline: every storyteller, every preacher, every so-called scholar has one thing in common, they've never been to Hell. They've never met *me* and lived to tell about it."

His words hung in the air like smoke, curling around Amber's thoughts and making her stomach churn.

"The truth," he continued, his voice dropping lower, almost conspiratorial, "is far darker than the stories. The Devil you've heard about? The red-skinned beast with horns and a pitchfork?" He scoffed, shaking his head. "That's a child's nightmare. A distraction. Fiction humans created to make themselves feel braver when they talk about me. As you saw earlier, I can turn into him, but that's not the reality."

Amber's pulse quickened as his words took root in her mind. "So... what's the reality?" she asked, her voice barely above a whisper.

The Devil's smirk faded entirely, replaced by a cold, calculating stare. "The reality," he said, his tone now as sharp as broken glass, "is that Hell isn't fire and brimstone. It's not pits or chains or monsters in the dark." His eyes darkened, and the faintest flicker of something unspoken, pain, perhaps, crossed his face. "It's desires unchecked. Lies we tell ourselves. Choices that feel like freedom but bind us tighter than any chain. Hell is *you*. It's every shadow you fear and every truth you refuse to face."

Amber shivered, her breath catching in her throat. For the first time, she felt the enormity of the thing sitting across from her. Not just a devil, but something older. Something that had witnessed every fall, every sin, every moment humanity refused to look at itself.

"And you?" she pressed, forcing herself to meet his unyielding gaze. "If Hell is all of that, then what are you?"

The Devil smiled again, his sharp teeth glinting faintly in the low light. "I," he said simply, leaning back as though his words were the only explanation necessary, "am the one who shows you the mirror." He paused, sipping his whiskey, "You see, there's always been a devil," he said, his voice soft but sharp, like the edge of a blade. "Just not always *me*." He leaned back against the bar, folding his arms as he regarded her. "Before I was who I am now, there was another. A master. A puppet master, if you will. And I was his favorite marionette."

Amber's brow furrowed, her curiosity outweighing her fear. "You mean someone like you, making deals, controlling the strings?"

He let out a bitter laugh, shaking his head. "Not like me. Worse. Far worse. He didn't just strike deals; he *owned* people. Their souls, their wills, their very thoughts. No room for negotiations, no chance of escape. And me?" He gestured at himself, the movement almost self-deprecating. "I was his enforcer. The one who made sure no one broke their chains."

Amber's stomach twisted, and the thought of the Devil being controlled by something even darker sent a chill through her. "So... what happened?" she asked, her voice quieter now.

His smile was dangerous. "What always happens to tyrants, darling. They get too greedy. Too confident. They underestimate the ones they think are beneath them." He leaned forward again, his eyes blazing like embers. "And I broke free. I didn't just take back my freedom; I took *his* power. His throne. His crown."

Amber blinked, her breath catching in her throat. "So you... you became the Devil by overthrowing him?"

"Precisely." His tone was calm, but his eyes had a dangerous glint. "But here's the thing about power, it doesn't come without a price. I didn't just inherit his throne. I inherited the weight of every deal, every contract, every soul he'd ever claimed. I became the one everyone hated. The villain of the story."

Amber studied him, her mind racing. For the first time, she felt a flicker of something she hadn't expected: sympathy. Not for who he was now but for who he'd been.

"And do you regret it?" she asked softly. "Taking it all? Becoming him?"

The Devil laughed again, but it was quieter, almost wistful this time. "Regret? No. No regret. I'm much more powerful than he ever was," he said, tilting his head, "people fear me more because they don't know the extent of what I'm capable of, and that's where fear lives. The fear is in the unknown."

Amber hesitated, a thousand questions burning in her mind, but before she could ask any of them, the Devil straightened, his demeanor shifting back to the confident, charismatic figure she'd first encountered.

6

The Thorn and the Flame

A smile spread across his face, but it wasn't warm or inviting. Instead, it was cold and predatory, sending a shiver through Amber's body as if even her goosebumps were trying to escape his gaze.

She hesitated, the weight of his gaze pressing down on her. She could feel the danger in his smile, like a coiled snake ready to strike.

"Why do you do it?" Amber asked, her voice steady despite the gnawing unease in her gut. "Why do you play these games with people's lives? What's in it for you?"

The Devil's eyes flickered with amusement like a cat toying with a mouse before the final strike. He swirled his whiskey in his glass, watching the liquid catch the light. "There's nothing in it for me."

Amber blinked, caught off guard by the finality in his words. They weren't emotionless but just simple.

"What...what do you mean?" She stammered.

The Devil tilted his head, his lips curling into a slow, knowing smile. "There's nothing in it for me," he repeated, his voice low and almost contemplative. "Not in the way you think, anyway. It's not about gain or victory for me. I don't play for the prize. I play because I can. Because I can watch you squirm, see how far you'll go when you think you're out of options." He leaned forward slightly, eyes gleaming with a glint of something dark, something that made the hairs on the back of Amber's neck stand up.

"But..." Amber's voice faltered, her confusion growing. "If there's nothing in it for you, then why do you do this? Why the games? What's the point?"

The Devil's smile remained, but his gaze became sharp, cutting through her uncertainty like a knife. "The point? Oh, darling, it's simple. People think they can control everything. They think they can master their fate, that they can dictate what happens next. But you, Amber... you're different." His voice dropped as if he were sharing a secret. "You've always known the truth deep down: control is an illusion."

Amber stepped back, the weight of his words settling in her chest like lead. "Control is an illusion," she echoed, the phrase ringing in her ears. "You... you think I've been playing into your hands this whole time?"

The Devil's eyes gleamed with an eerie satisfaction. "Not just playing, darling. You've been learning." He leaned back, swirling his drink again, his gaze never leaving her.

Amber felt the chill of his words wrap around her, suffocating her. "What do you want from me?" she asked her voice barely a whisper, barely a breath.

The Devil leaned back in his chair, watching her with that predatory smile. "What I want?" he mused, his eyes glinting in the dim light. "I want to see if you'll break. Everyone breaks eventually. The question is how, when, and how much you'll lose in the process." He paused, his smile widening. "And then, once you've lost enough... I want to see what you'll do to get it all back."

Amber's stomach twisted. "You want to watch me suffer," she said, the words coming out with an edge of realization.

The Devil's smile grew even more expansive, cruel, and triumphant. "Not suffer, darling. Evolve. It's all part of the game. You're playing the hardest game of all: one against yourself. And in the end, everyone has a price."

Her breath caught in her throat. She was the prize, the game, the cost.

The clock ticked louder in the silence between them, each beat reverberating in Amber's chest like a countdown. Her pulse hammered, the weight of the moment pressing down on her with suffocating force. But then, something shifted; an idea, a possibility, bubbled up from deep inside her.

Taking a slow, deliberate sip of her whiskey, Amber kept her gaze fixed on him, forcing herself to steady her hand. "Everyone has a price?" she asked, her voice betraying only the slightest quiver.

"Everyone, my dear," the Devil replied smoothly, the words sliding from his lips with dangerous sweetness.

Amber took another sip, savoring the burn as she steeled herself. "What's your price?" she asked, her tone casual, but the question's weight hung heavily in the air.

She turned to face him as she spoke, her eyes locking onto his with a piercing intensity. And for the briefest of moments, something flickered behind his crimson gaze, an imperceptible shift, a tiny crack in his perfect façade. It was subtle, but Amber caught it. He'd slipped. Just for a second, but it was enough.

The Devil froze, the faintest flicker of uncertainty crossing his face before he masked it with his usual impenetrable smile. But Amber knew she'd touched something. She could see it in his eyes.

"Well," he drawled, his voice smooth again, though there was an edge to it now. "That's a question, isn't it? But some things... some things aren't for sale, darling."

Amber leaned in just a little, her eyes narrowing. "You said everything has a price. You said the Devil doesn't lie. So, what's your price?"

The Devil's smile faltered just a fraction, and at that moment, Amber felt a surge of power. She wasn't just playing his game anymore; she was forcing him to play hers.

7

A Dance with Darkness

For the first time, the Devil seemed to hesitate, his calm exterior cracking ever so slightly. His gaze darkened, and something almost like unease flickered through his eyes.

"Not bad, trapping me with my own words," his voice was low and smooth again, but there was an edge to it, a hint of warning.

Amber didn't back down. She leaned forward a bit more, the room's dim glow casting shadows on her face. "I think you're scared of something. I think you have a price and don't want me to know it. But I'm asking anyway. What is it?"

The Devil's lips twitched, and for a moment, his eyes glinted with something like amusement or perhaps frustration. He set his glass down, his hand curling around the rim with a slow, deliberate movement. Then, after a long beat of silence, he spoke again, his voice calm but edged with something more.

"You're right, even I have a price," he said, his words thick with warning. "But... It's not something you'd want to pay."

Amber's pulse quickened. "Try me."

The Devil's grin returned, sharper now, like a predator savoring the chase. "Now, now, I can't just tell you my price," he said, his voice smooth and dark. "No, that would upset the balance of things." He stood up, the stool scraping against the hardwood with a harsh squeal. His gaze turned cold, fixed on her with chilling intensity. "You have no idea what you're asking for."

Amber's heart raced, but she didn't flinch. She knew this was the moment, the tipping point. If she could get him to show his true self, to reveal what it was he truly wanted, she could turn this game around. She could win.

"I'm not afraid," she said, her voice steady despite the adrenaline rushing through her. "What's your price, Lucifer? I want to know."

For a moment, the Devil just stared at her, his gaze flickering into something dangerously close to admiration. But it was gone as quickly as it appeared, replaced by a cold, calculating calm.

Lucifer tilted his head, his lips curling into that smile again, but it was different now, more distant. "Ah, you think you're ready for that answer," he mused, his voice low. "But some prices can't be spoken aloud. They're not something you can *know* until the moment comes. And when it does..."

He paused, savoring the tension, before adding, "Well, let's just say you might wish you had never asked."

Amber's pulse quickened. His words were more than a warning; they felt like a promise. "When will I know?"

The Devil's eyes gleamed with the flicker of something dangerous. "That's for you to discover. But you'll find out soon enough. Don't worry." He gave a small, eerie chuckle. "You'll know when the time comes."

Amber took a deep breath, trying to steady the swirling thoughts in her mind. The weight of his words and the ominous tension of the game made her head spin. But one thing was clear: no matter how much she tried to understand him, there was always more beneath the surface. And that's when she decided to shift the question, to ask something completely different.

She met the Devil's gaze, trying to keep her composure. "Okay, if you can't tell me that then tell me this," she said, her voice quieter now, softer than before. "What happens when you get bored? When all of this..." she gestured vaguely to the space around them, "...loses its thrill? You've been playing these games for how long? Eternity?"

Lucifer raised an eyebrow, the amusement returning to his expression, though it was laced with something darker. "You think I get bored?" he mused. "Eternity isn't quite the same for someone like me. Time is... fluid, you see. It stretches, folds, and bends. And with every passing second, there's always something new to entertain me."

Slowly, he stood and sauntered toward the jukebox in the corner of the room. With a swift, careless kick, the machine hummed to life, and Lucifer, as though it were nothing, pulled a coin from thin air. Amber watched, wide-eyed, as he inserted the coin and began flipping through songs with a casual flick of his fingers.

"You know," he said, his voice light, "I've never even been to Georgia." He paused, his finger settling on a track.

The jukebox crackled, and suddenly, the upbeat notes of *The Devil Went Down to Georgia* poured from the speakers, filling the air with an almost eerie harmony.

In the blink of an eye, Lucifer was back at her side. He moved with a liquid grace, each step a study in control and intent, circling her like gravity itself, inescapable, drawing her in with every breathless beat.

"Boredom doesn't exist for me, Amber," he purred, his voice dripping with an unsettling certainty. "There is always something to be had, something to learn, something to *take*."

Before she could react, Lucifer reached for her hand, his grip firm yet surprisingly gentle. He raised his other hand in a swift, flexible motion, and the entire room shifted with a snap of his fingers. The furniture flew away with the force of a sudden gust, slamming into the walls, leaving an open space where a smooth, polished dance floor appeared. The soft glow of the jukebox light bathed the area in an ethereal glow.

"Shall we?" Lucifer's voice was low, a challenge hidden behind the playful edge, as his eyes locked with hers, daring her to take the next step.

Amber stood there for a moment, the pulsating beat of the song echoing through her veins, her heart racing. This wasn't just a game anymore. It felt like something far more profound, and she had no idea where it would lead.

She nodded so slightly that she almost missed it herself, but as the music flowed through the air, something primal shifted between them. Lucifer, ever the master of control, stepped into her space, close enough that she could feel the warmth radiating from his body, the faint scent of whiskey still lingering on his breath. His eyes sparkled with an intensity that made her pulse quicken, and with effortless grace, he spun them onto the dance floor.

In a single, desperate motion, he caught her against him, as though letting go would undo everything. His grip was firm but never harsh, his hands settling on her waist. The warmth of his palms pressed through the fabric of her clothes, his touch searing like a brand. Without a word, he led her into the rhythm of the song, the smooth melody flowing through their veins like a living thing.

Their steps began in silence, his body pressing to hers with practiced ease, the gentleness in his touch a lie, because beneath the elegance was something coiled and waiting, something feral. Amber's breath caught in her throat as he spun her, guiding her expertly through a series of swift steps and intricate twirls. Each movement seemed to come naturally to him, his feet light but sure, each step calculated with precision, his body weaving in time with the music. The slick wood of the dance floor seemed to hum beneath them as though even the space itself was alive with energy.

Amber's heart thudded in her chest, matching the rhythm of their movements. Her own feet stumbled at first, unaccustomed to the speed and grace of the dance, but Lucifer's hands never wavered in their hold. Every time she faltered, his presence steadied her, his touch almost hypnotic. He was so effortless, so in control, that his every movement drew her deeper into the dance, deeper into the rhythm.

As the tempo quickened, their movements followed suit. Lucifer's hands moved with a strange intensity, guiding her through spins and dips, every motion sharp yet fluid, the lines of his body pulling hers along like a marionette. Amber's breath came faster now, her body slick with sweat, her muscles straining as they twirled and pivoted across the floor. She could feel her heartbeat pounding in her ears, the song's pulse vibrating through her chest like the beat of a drum. The space between them thinned with every breath, their bodies threading past each other in a rhythm that teased more than it gave, like a conversation spoken entirely in silence.

She could see the sheen of sweat on Lucifer's forehead now, his jaw clenched in concentration, his breath coming heavy and deliberate. He was still in control, still the master of the dance, but there was a flicker in his eyes, something raw and primal, something that sent a shiver racing down Amber's spine. His movements grew sharper, hungrier, grace giving way to raw need, every motion a claim, every breath between them charged and electric.

Amber could feel the tension between them, the electricity crackling. Her chest rose and fell with each breath, her muscles burning with the effort of keeping up. Her hands clung to Lucifer, her fingers digging into his shoulders as the pace increased, and their bodies collided and spun in perfect synchrony.

At one point, he pulled her close, so close she could feel his breath on her skin, warm and heavy. The music throbbed around them, the world outside their little bubble falling away. She could hear the faint rasp of his breath, the whisper of his lips against her ear, the rhythm of their bodies locking together in a wild, breathless dance.

The sweat on their skin mingled as they moved, their bodies slick with heat. Amber's legs ached, her feet barely keeping up with the frantic pace of the dance. Her breathing was ragged now, sharp gasps filling the air as she struggled to maintain the dizzying tempo. But the Devil didn't stop. He was relentless, guiding her through the steps, pushing her harder and faster, with every movement sharper than the last.

There was something magnetic in his touch now, something that made her body move without thought, without hesitation. She was no longer thinking about the game, no longer thinking about the rules. She was just... dancing. Just being swept away by the rhythm, by the force of his presence, his body. He spun her again, pulling her close as she stumbled against him, their chests crashing together with the intensity of their movements.

The world seemed to blur, the music crescendoing to a fever pitch, their sweat-slicked bodies tangled in the dance. Their breaths mingled, harsh and heavy, the air thick with the heady mix of their exertion. Lucifer's lips were almost on her ear, his voice a dark purr. "Can you keep up, Amber?" he asked, his words a challenge, a command, as his hands gripped her tighter, pulling her into a final spin.

Her heart pounded in her chest, but she couldn't answer. She could only follow, her body moving on instinct, her legs shaking with exhaustion, but still, she kept dancing. She kept moving, caught in the whirlwind of their shared energy, unable to break free; unwilling to. The music crested, sharp and final, and Lucifer pulled her back with deliberate force, holding her in the charged stillness that followed, as if neither of them dared to speak first. Panting, slick with sweat, they faced one another in the hush that followed, the moment stretched thin, delicate and trembling like glass.

Lucifer, his face flushed with the effort, his breath still heavy in his chest, looked down at her, his grin returning sharp and satisfied. "That was... enjoyable," he said, his voice low, the heat between them still simmering in the space where their bodies had been.

Amber, too breathless to speak, could only nod. She wasn't sure if it was the dance or the proximity to Lucifer that had left her so shaken, but she felt every inch of her being alive with a strange mix of exhilaration and something darker. Something that, for just a moment, made her forget the games, forget the Devil's price, and just... be.

8

Shadows of the Heart

Still riding the high of the dance, the Devil drifted back toward the bar, a satisfied smirk tugging at his lips. Amber remained where he'd left her, the echo of their movements still clinging to her body, her pulse visible in the hollow of her throat. She was a mix of exhaustion and exhilaration, her mind still reeling from the moment's intensity. Ever the picture of ease, Lucifer casually leaned against the counter, watching her with an unreadable expression. He took a small sip of his whiskey, his gaze never leaving her.

Amber's lips curled into a sly smile. *My turn,* she thought

Slowly, she turned and sauntered toward the jukebox, her hips swaying with a newfound confidence. Her voice was soft, but there was a teasing edge to it when she spoke. "Lucifer, darling," she cooed, throwing him a look over her shoulder that was both playful and challenging, "Be a doll and toss me a coin."

A smirk tugged at the corner of Lucifer's mouth, but he didn't speak. Instead, as if on cue, a coin appeared in the air before her, spinning before it landed perfectly in the jukebox's slot. Amber's smile widened, already satisfied with the game she was about to play.

She slowly shifted through the songs, her fingers grazing over the options before settling on one. She hit play, and the hauntingly beautiful opening notes of *I Put a Spell on You* drifted into the air. The sultry melody seemed to wrap around her, and for a moment, she closed her eyes, letting the rhythm take over her body. She swayed her hips gently, a soft smile playing on her lips as the music took root.

Amber stepped back onto the dance floor as the song filled the room, her eyes meeting Lucifer's across the room. She extended her hand to him, the gesture a silent invitation, her posture one of defiance and invitation all at once.

The Devil watched her, his expression unreadable for a moment, before he straightened and began to move toward her. He didn't take her hand immediately, instead he paused just inches from her as if measuring the space between them, savoring the tension.

Amber's pulse quickened as she dared to close the space between them, the music swaying through her veins, urging her to step forward and take control. She tilted her head slightly, waiting, daring him to respond to her challenge.

Lucifer finally extended his hand, but instead of the light touch, she expected, his fingers wrapped around hers with a steady, unyielding grip. His touch sent a shiver through her body, and with a single pull, he led her into the rhythm of the song. The dance was slow this time, the heavy beat of the music wrapping around them like a velvet shroud.

Amber moved against him, her body instinctively aligning with his as they swayed together. The heat from his body seeped into hers, and it felt like the air around them thickened, suffocating in the best possible way. The faint scent of his cologne, mingled with the intoxicating aroma of whiskey and sweat, wrapped around her senses, drawing her further into the moment. Their bodies moved with slow, languid grace, each step deliberate yet effortless, the tension between them building with every subtle shift.

Her breath came in short bursts, mingling with his as they twirled in a slow circle. The dance more intimate, as though every step was a shared secret, a whispered promise between them. Amber could feel the weight of his stare on her, but she refused to let it break her rhythm. Instead, she leaned closer, letting the music guide them both, the world outside fading into nothing.

She whispered, barely above the music's soft hum, "What happens when you run out of things take?" Amber's lips were close to the crook of his neck, her voice laced with curiosity as she tried to peer into his twisted existence. "What does the Devil do when there's nothing left to consume?"

Lucifer didn't answer right away. Instead, he spun her with a sudden, fluid movement, his hand gliding along her waist, before bringing her back in, dipping her low to the floor. For a moment, she was suspended in midair, her breath catching in her chest as his strength held her effortlessly. Slowly, he brought her back up, his eyes locked onto hers, and a dangerous smile stretching across his lips.

"I never run out of things to take, darling," he said, his voice dripping with dark satisfaction. His fingers still gripped her waist, keeping her close as he continued. "You see, I don't just consume, *I create*. Every choice, every sacrifice, every ripple in the fabric of the universe feeds me. I give form to your desires, fears, and regrets; in return, I take from you what you most cherish."

Amber's heart raced in her chest, thundering with the intensity of his words. The music, slow and seductive, swirled around them, but it was the air between them, thick with desire and unspoken truths, that made her pulse quicken. Her body was pressed against his as they danced, the space between them non-existent. She could feel him in every breath, every shift of air between them. The anticipation clung to her skin, alive and pulsing. He was everywhere.

"That's the beauty of it all, Amber," he murmured, his voice low, just for her. He leaned in, his breath brushing against the back of her neck, sending a shiver down her spine. "There is always something new to shape. Something new to twist. And as long as you have something to give, I will always have something to take."

Lucifer's grip on her tightened, pulling her impossibly closer, and Amber's breath caught in her throat. For the first time in this twisted game, she felt truly vulnerable. But there was no fear, only an intoxicating thrill. The Devil's presence was overwhelming and suffocating, but something else kept her rooted to the spot, unable to move away and unwilling to break free.

Her throat went dry, and she swallowed hard, her voice a whisper. "So you're never done? You never tire of it?"

Lucifer let out a soft sigh as he moved with her. His tone becoming almost intimate, his voice brushing against her ear. "Tire? No. The game changes, but it never ends. That's the curse of my existence. And yours, too, if you're not careful."

The weight of his words pressed down on her, settling over her like a dark cloud. It was a warning, a truth, and Amber didn't know if she was ready. Yet, she couldn't help herself. She had to ask. Her curiosity was too dangerous to ignore now.

She pulled back just slightly, her fingers still tangled around his neck as she gazed up at him, her eyes searching for answers. "What about you, then? What do you want to create? If you're so busy taking, is there anything left for you to build? Or are you just waiting for the next soul to devour?"

Lucifer's lips curled into a smile, but it wasn't cruel. It was almost affectionate this time, like an inside joke he wasn't sharing with her. "What I want? Oh, darling, that's the ultimate question, isn't it? And maybe one day... you'll learn what it is."

The music swelled again, the haunting notes of *I Put a Spell on You* growing louder, more urgent, like a pulse that matched the rhythm of their hearts.

Lucifer's gaze shifted past her, and he murmured almost to himself, "It's not about taking or creating, Amber. It's about shaping the world into something far more interesting than you can imagine."

Amber's mind raced, her thoughts tangled as she leaned against his chest, the weight of his words pressing down on her. "So, you just... shape things? And we're all just part of the puzzle?"

Lucifer's grin returned, sharper than ever, its edges cutting through the tension that hung in the air. "Exactly."

Before she could respond, he spun her effortlessly, a flick of his wrist sending her twirling like a leaf caught in a windstorm. Amber barely had time to catch her balance before he pulled her back into him, and for a moment, the world outside the bar seemed to vanish entirely. It was just the two of them, caught in the music, lost in the dance, in the tension that hummed between them like an electric current.

Nothing but the rhythm, the Devil's touch, and the unknown future stretched out before her. And as she danced beneath his hands, Amber couldn't shake the feeling that she was teetering on the edge of something much darker than she had imagined.

9

The Abyss Beckons

Amber didn't know how long they stayed like that, melded in each other's embrace. Her eyes fluttered closed as she inhaled deeply, taking in his scent, an intoxicating mix of spice, smoke, and something darker, something uniquely him. Strangely, it was calming, grounding her despite the chaos she had felt moments before.

The jukebox in the corner had long since fallen silent; *I Put a Spell on You,* now a distant memory. Now, the only sound was the quiet rhythm of her breathing, soft and steady. Then she noticed something peculiar, the Devil's chest beneath her head wasn't rising and falling. Alarm flickered in her thoughts, and she strained her ears, searching for the sound of his breath. Nothing. Only silence. The realization sent a cold shiver down her spine, sharp and cutting despite the heat radiating from his body.

It wasn't until they danced together that she fully registered how devastatingly handsome he was. He was an extraordinary blend of refinement and rugged charm, the kind of beauty that felt dangerous and impossible to ignore. His square-shaped face was a masterclass in symmetry, with strikingly sharp features that showcased an almost unreal jawline. His eyes, when not gleaming crimson, were a deep, expressive coffee brown, warm and piercing all at once. Her fingers curled instinctively into the deep brown, almost black, thick waves of his hair as they rested against the back of his head, marveling at the perfect length and softness.

She had noticed the well-groomed beard framing his face when they first met, but now, in such close proximity, it only added to his allure. He towered over her, his height a subtle reminder of his presence and power. Her head barely reached his shoulders, resting comfortably against his chest as they swayed together in an intimate rhythm. Everything about him, from the confident set of his shoulders to the fluid grace of his movements, exuded strength, elegance, and control. His powerful physique radiated an effortless dominance that made her stomach twist in ways she wasn't prepared to understand.

"Lucifer," Amber said quietly, "You never answered my question."

He stopped swaying, and the air in the room grew heavy, thick with something unspoken.

She waited, holding her breath alongside the rest of the room, before speaking again. "You never told me your price. You declined to answer. I won."

For a long moment, he said nothing. Then, with a slow, measured step, he pulled away from her grasp. "So, my dear," he murmured, a wry smile curling at his lips, "it seems to be that way, doesn't it?"

He looked at her for a long moment, his eyes dark and unreadable, before walking back to the bar. "The game is over. You won, Amber, so I will now honor my word. You now get to know what your perfect life would cost you."

"Thank you," she said, the words feeling strange coming from her lips, but they were true.

Lucifer raised an eyebrow, clearly amused. "Don't thank me yet, little dove. You might just regret it."

But his eyes were softer now, the sharp edges dulled, leaving behind something like... respect.

Amber followed him to the bar, leaning against it casually, "So, what's the toll of my perfect life? What is it that you'd take from me?"

Lucifer's smile faded, replaced by a calculating stillness. He took his time, letting the silence stretch like a weighted curtain between them. Amber's heartbeat quickened the tension building in the air.

Finally, he spoke, his voice slow, deliberate. "Ah, little dove, the price of your perfect life? It's quite simple, really. I'll take your soul. For one month every year, until you die, you will be mine, bound to me in whatever way I choose. When you finally breathe your last, your soul will be mine forever."

Amber's breath caught in her throat. She hadn't expected this; she'd expected some twisted game or sacrifice, but this? This felt final.

"And if I refuse?" she asked, her voice barely above a whisper.

Lucifer smirked, amusement dancing in his gaze. "Refuse, and I'll take more than just your soul. The perfect life you so deeply wish for will disappear, and the life you live now, the one filled with heartbreak and sorrow, will simply get...well, worse." A devilish smile played on his lips as he added, "It's a game, little dove, one you can't win by running away. The cost is always paid, sooner or later."

She exhaled slowly, her hands trembling. This was the truth she'd been waiting for. Could she accept it? Would she ever truly be free, or had she already sold herself into an eternal servitude?

Her mind raced.

"What if I don't want either?" The words escaped before she could stop them, catching both her and the Devil off guard.

The Devil looked at her with curiosity and confusion, a look she hadn't seen before. "I don't see a third option, darling," he said, his eyes gleaming with intrigue. "Do elaborate."

"Well…" she hesitated, glancing between Lucifer and the counter. "The life I live now isn't what I want, obviously. But the 'perfect' life you offered comes at such a high price… What if we just skipped to the end?"

Lucifer tilted his head, intrigued. "Skipped to the end?" he echoed, swirling the dark liquid in his glass. "And what, pray tell, do you mean by that, little dove?"

Amber swallowed hard. She had no idea where the words were coming from; maybe exhaustion, desperation, or something else entirely. But once the thought had taken root, she couldn't ignore it. She lifted her gaze to meet his. "What if I became your partner instead? In whatever capacity you see fit."

For the first time, Lucifer looked genuinely caught off guard. His smirk faltered, replaced by something unreadable.

Then, ever so slowly, a grin crept across his lips. "Oh, Amber," he purred, leaning in just enough for his presence to feel suffocating. "What an absolutely delicious proposition."

The air crackled between them, an invisible current shifting, changing.

"But tell me," he continued, his voice dangerously smooth, "do you have any idea what you're offering?"

Amber inhaled sharply. "No. But I know that the alternative, living a lie only to have you take my soul anyway, sounds worse."

Lucifer chuckled, low and indulgent. "So you'd rather stand at my side than in my debt?"

She nodded once. "I think so."

Lucifer hummed, considering. Then, after a long pause, he reached for his drink and took a slow sip. "Well then, little dove," he mused, eyes locked onto hers with razor-sharp amusement. "Let's talk terms."

Lucifer set his glass down with a soft *clink*, his fingers tapping idly against the counter as he regarded her. His expression was unreadable, sharp amusement tempered by something deeper, something she couldn't quite name.

Amber's heart pounded. What the hell was she doing? She'd just suggested tying herself to the literal devil willingly. And yet… it wasn't fear coursing through her veins. It was something else. Anticipation? Excitement? A sick kind of relief?

Lucifer's voice was smooth, edged with something dangerous. "Very well. Humor me." His eyes gleamed, predatory. "What exactly do you imagine this arrangement entails?"

Amber licked her lips, considering. "You said that if I took the perfect life, I'd belong to you, one month a year until I died, and then forever." She swallowed hard. "But what if, instead, I worked for you? Assisted you. *Learned* from you. Became... something more than just a soul to be owned."

The air around her seemed to thicken as Lucifer's gaze darkened.

"My, my," he murmured, his voice like silk over a blade. "You don't just want to change your fate...you want to escape it."

Amber held his stare. "Yes."

A slow, wicked grin curled his lips. He leaned in close enough that she could feel the heat of his presence and the weight of his words before he even spoke.

"Amber, my dear," he purred, his voice a silken trap laced with amusement and something perilously close to admiration. "This deal wouldn't just change your life; it would *end* it."

Amber took a steadying breath, her pulse a drumbeat in her ears. "I know."

His eyes gleamed, but the amusement faded, replaced by something sharper, heavier. "You'd have to die, Amber. Right here. Right now. No goodbyes. No tying up loose ends. Just *gone*." He snapped his fingers, the sound like a blade slicing through the air. *"Just like that."*

Amber flinched, but she didn't back down.

Lucifer studied her, tilting his head slightly. "Your new existence wouldn't be glamorous. Not at first." He leaned back in his chair, the air between them still charged. "You'd live just above the souls I already own, scraping by, proving your worth until you convince me you're capable of more." His eyes gleamed. "Until you show me you can truly stand at my side."

Amber took a sip of her whiskey, her hands trembling slightly.

"You'd do whatever I asked, whenever I asked. Your tasks would be darker, far beyond that of my average soul. But to truly prove yourself, you wouldn't just exist in my world, Amber. You'd have to *thrive* in it. That means obeying my rules, learning the intricacies of my domain..." A flicker of red flashed through his eyes. "And proving you're worthy."

Amber's throat went dry, but she forced herself to ask, "And if I do?"

Lucifer's grin stretched wider, slow and predatory. "Then, little dove, you'll have power beyond your wildest dreams." His fingers tapped rhythmically against the bar. "You wouldn't be a servant. Not just another soul in my collection. You'd be something *more*."

The weight of his words settled over her, heavy and intoxicating. Her old life, mundane and fragile, was already slipping away. What was left for her there? A perfect life with a terrible cost? Or this, a dangerous unknown where she could carve out something real, something not dictated by fate or cruel bargains?

Amber exhaled slowly. "Once I prove myself, what would you want from me? If I were to be your partner?"

Lucifer chuckled, low and knowing. "In whatever capacity I see fit, wasn't that your offer?" His eyes glowed with amusement, but something else lurked beneath the surface, something unreadable. "You'd have the chance to be my second in command. The Queen of Hell, if you will."

Amber's pulse pounded. Not from fear. From exhilaration.

"And if I fail?" she asked, voice barely above a whisper.

Lucifer's smile sharpened a glint of amusement in his eyes. "That depends," he murmured, as if already thinking ahead.

"On what?" Amber pressed, more curious than afraid.

He leaned closer, his voice brushing against her skin like a whispered promise. "Oh, don't worry about that now," he said smoothly. "Because something tells me... you won't fail."

Amber let out a breath she hadn't realized she was holding. Her choice was made. There was no going back now.

"Then do it," she said, steady despite the storm raging inside her. "End my life. Let me prove myself."

Lucifer's eyes darkened, a flicker of something almost like pride flashing across his face.

"As you wish, little dove," he murmured, and with a snap of his fingers, everything went black.

10

In the Hands of Monsers

I t was the scent that woke her first.

Pungent and laced with something that she could almost taste. The air was thick, choking, and suffocating, pressing against her lungs like an iron weight. But it was the heat that unsettled her most. It clung to her skin like a wet blanket, seeping into her bones and restricting her breathing. Try as she might, her chest wouldn't rise to its full capacity.

She wanted to cough, to scream, *anything*, but no sound came. A single tear slipped down her cheek, only to sizzle away the moment it fell, evaporating into the sweltering air.

Darkness consumed everything, an endless void, and her senses scrambled to piece together the world around her. Then the noise started.

A screeching, high-pitched, and relentless, like nails dragging across a chalkboard, dug straight into her skull. She flinched, instinctively recoiling, but something held her in place.

Invisible bonds coiled around her wrists and ankles, searing into her skin like molten chains. She writhed, but the more she moved, the deeper they burned.

And somewhere in the suffocating blackness, something was watching.

Shapes stirred in the darkness. Twisted figures with elongated limbs and too many joints scuttled into the room, claws clicking against the unseen floor. Their skin glistened, shifting between textures: scaly, smooth, raw.

They spoke in that ear-piercing screech, their words a chaotic jumble of sounds that meant nothing to her. But they understood each other. They laughed, high, shrill bursts of sound that sent a shiver down her spine.

One of them leaned in close, its breath hot and rancid against her face. A guttural noise slithered from its throat, like it was tasting the air around her.

She couldn't understand them. But she knew, with bone-deep certainty, that they were talking about her.

And they were pleased.

She blinked, and suddenly, one was on each side of her.

They moved impossibly fast, flashing around her like lightning, their forms flickering in and out of the shadows. She whipped her head side to side, trying to track them, but the effort was futile. They were everywhere and nowhere all at once.

Then, without warning, one of them leaped onto her bare skin.

It was only then that she realized she was completely naked.

At first, the creature's weight was strange, almost nonexistent, as if it weren't truly there. But then, like the snap of a trap, it changed, becoming a crushing force, suffocating, unbearable.

She couldn't breathe.

The demon cocked its head, watching her struggle, its grotesque features twisting into something like an evil grin. It was enjoying this, relishing her pain.

Slowly, deliberately, it began to walk up and down her body. Each step sent agony ricocheting through her as her bones cracked beneath its unnatural weight. A white-hot, earth-shattering pain consumed her, and she screamed.

To her dismay, the sound only seemed to delight the others.

High-pitched screeches filled the air, their twisted laughter like shattered glass against her mind. They chattered in that strange, incomprehensible language, their voices rising and falling in what almost sounded like excitement.

Then, as suddenly as it had landed, the demon jumped off her. The crushing weight lifted, but the damage was done.

Amber sucked in a ragged breath, her body screaming in protest as she tried to move. She could feel the bruises already forming, deep and brutal, and there were ghostly imprints of clawed footprints burned into her flesh. Her right knee throbbed with sharp, searing pain, pressed too flat against the unseen surface beneath her.

Then, the biting began.

At first, it was small, sharp pinpricks like needles grazing her skin. But the pain deepened, growing more vicious, more hungry. Teeth, jagged and inhuman, sank into her flesh, ripping and tearing.

She thrashed, but unseen hands clawed, bony, and impossibly strong, holding her down.

The chattering turned frenzied, almost gleeful. The demons were feasting.

A fresh scream tore from her throat, but it only fueled them. More teeth, more tearing, more searing pain.

The agony was unbearable.

She was going to die here.

Then, through the haze of suffering, something changed. The air in the room shifted.

The screeching stilled, the chatter cut off, and the biting stopped.

The presence of something else, something far more significant, far more powerful, pressed down on the space around her. The demons hesitated, their clawed hands retreating, their weight lifting as they scuttled back into the shadows.

Amber lay there, gasping, her body broken, her mind reeling.

Then, through the suffocating darkness, a voice.

Low. Smooth. Familiar.

"Now, now," Lucifer murmured, amusement laced with something darker. "You're all getting ahead of yourselves."

A hand, warm, firm, undeniably his, cupped her chin, tilting her face upward, "She's mine."

Immediately, she relaxed at his touch despite every instinct screaming at her not to.

"Dolor. Timor." Lucifer's voice was smooth, unhurried. He watched her as he spoke, but his words weren't meant for her.

The darkness shifted.

At first, it was only movement, something stirring in the shadows, fluid and unnatural.

Then, the creatures emerged, dragging themselves into existence with a slow, dreadful inevitability.

They were wrong.

Where the demons from before had been small, twisted things, these were impossibly tall, gaunt yet massive, their limbs stretched beyond natural proportions, their joints bending in ways that defied anatomy. Their bodies seemed woven from pure darkness, flickering at the edges like smoke struggling to hold form.

And then there were their faces, or rather, the absence of them.

Their heads were smooth, featureless voids, blacker than the rest as if they were holes cut straight into the fabric of existence. Yet somehow, she knew they were staring at her.

The closer they came, the more wrong they became.

Their elongated arms dragged nearly to the ground, their fingers too long and thin, ending in jagged, uneven claws curling inward like grasping talons. Their torsos were impossibly emaciated, ribcages stretching out beneath sickly, pulsing flesh that rippled with something alive beneath it.

A stench clung to them, something ancient and rotting, metallic and bitter, like decayed blood left to fester in the heat. The air around them warped, heavy, and suffocating, pressing against her skin like something tangible.

Then came the sound.

It wasn't a growl. It wasn't a whisper.

It was the creaking of wood ready to splinter, the distant shrieks of something dying slowly, the guttural wheeze of breath forced through a throat that had never learned to breathe.

Suddenly, a terror, unlike anything she'd ever known, slammed into her.

It was primal, raw, all-consuming. This wasn't the fear that sent chills down one's spine or made one's breath quicken. This was absolute. Hopeless.

It lived inside her bones. It clawed at her mind.

She couldn't think. She couldn't rationalize. She couldn't do anything except try to escape, to writhe against the invisible restraints even as agony screamed through her broken body. The force of the fear was so overwhelming, so excruciating, that she wanted to die just to escape it.

But there was nowhere to go.

The creatures floated toward her, moving with a horrifying elegance. They didn't walk; they simply *were*, shifting closer without sound or effort.

One of the creatures loomed closer, its faceless void mere inches from her own. She wanted to shut her eyes, to turn away, but she couldn't. The more she looked, the deeper the blackness became, stretching outward, swallowing everything, swallowing her.

She wanted to vomit.

Her vision flickered, black creeping in at the edges. It was impossible to understand, but she knew everything she had ever feared was in this room with her. She couldn't see them, but they were there, crowding in at the edges of her mind, whispering things she couldn't hear, brushing against her skin with fingers she couldn't see.

And Lucifer, Lucifer did nothing.

He merely watched.

His expression was unreadable. Not amused, not concerned. Just blank.

Finally, he blinked, breaking the unbearable silence, and turned to the darker of the two figures.

"Timor," he said lazily, "spread the word: this particular soul is not to be disturbed by anyone but me. She is not to be moved, touched, or tortured unless by my direct command."

Then he shifted his gaze to the other.

"Dolor, lock down this room. Only I may enter."

The creatures stood motionless. They didn't nod, shift, or acknowledge him in any way. For a moment, it seemed as if they would simply ignore him.

Then, finally, the sound came again.

It wasn't speech; it was something else entirely.

It reverberated through the air, slipping into the very marrow of her bones. A voice that wasn't a voice, something speaking in a way no living thing should be able to.

It came from everywhere and nowhere all at once. She had no idea what they said but Lucifer seemed pleased as they left.

It wasn't a natural movement. They didn't pivot, didn't shift their weight. They simply were, standing before her one moment, gliding away the next, vanishing into the blackness from which they came.

The agony, the soul-crushing fear, it all disappeared with them.

Amber sucked in a ragged breath, choking on the thick air, *grateful* for the simple, familiar pain of her broken bones.

Slowly, she turned her head toward Lucifer, still trembling.

"What is this?" she spat, her voice raw, fractured.

Lucifer smiled, slow and knowing.

"This, my little dove," he murmured, "is the beginning of your deal."

11

Devilish Mercy

For a moment, Lucifer and Amber simply stared at each other. The silence stretched between them, thick and heavy. Then, finally, he spoke.

"I apologize for the *rude* introduction," he said smoothly, though there was no genuine remorse in his tone. "My demons tend to get a little *zealous* when they think a new toy has entered their domain. I hadn't had the chance to tell them to back off yet. Those were just the Liberi anyway. They're still learning; they couldn't have done any real damage."

He paused, his gaze dragging over her slowly, deliberately. His eyes lingered on her bare skin, pausing momentarily on her breasts, then lower, where her legs parted just enough for his eyes to trace places he had no right to look.

Heat flooded her, a slow burn of humiliation, and something else, something almost like cruel desire, swirled in her gut. She instinctively curled in on herself, shrinking beneath his gaze, but she didn't miss the brief flash of red that swept through his irises, a flicker of something *hungry* before he schooled his expression back into indifference.

"Well," he continued, finally meeting her eyes again. "I'm sure you have a *lot* of questions, and I'd be happy to answer them tonight." His lips curled into something almost resembling a smirk. "But for now, Sana will be coming in with Subsidio and Pax to help you prepare."

Amber's throat tightened. "Luci—"

He raised a hand, cutting her off effortlessly.

"Like I said," he murmured, a finality to his tone, "I will answer everything *tonight*."

And with that, he turned and walked away, leaving her alone in the suffocating stillness, the weight of what had just happened pressing against her like a phantom touch.

Amber lay still, her body aching, her breath shallow. She could feel the bruises and fractures knitting together on their own, but it was slow, sluggish, and excruciating. The pain clung to her, unwilling to release its grip just yet.

Then, the air shifted, and once more she realized, she wasn't alone.

From the darkness, they emerged: three figures impossibly smooth in their movements, gliding forward as though they weren't walking at all. Although they moved like the creatures from before, these carried an unsettling grace. Their presence was quiet but charged with something else, something like *anticipation*.

The first was draped in robes that weren't quite fabric, more like mist given form, shifting and swirling even though there was no wind. Their face was featureless, a void of smooth, pale nothingness. And yet, as they moved closer, Amber felt it, an unnatural calm bleeding into her veins, muting the sharpest edges of her agony. It wasn't mercy. It was *functionality*. They weren't here to soothe her; they were here to *prepare* her.

The second was thinner, their body flickering at the edges like they weren't fully *here*. Long, skeletal fingers hovered just inches above Amber's torn skin, tracing the damage without making contact. A quiet hum cracked between them, an energy that coiled tight, waiting to be unleashed. Their hands trembled, not with hesitation, but with excitement. This was their *purpose*. This was what they were *made* for.

And then there was the third. Solid. Unwavering. Their body was carved from something smooth and flawless, like marble brought to life, glowing lines etched into their skin pulsing in a steady rhythm, like a heartbeat, like breath, like *life*. When they touched her, warmth spread through Amber's limbs, slow at first, then faster, an unnatural acceleration of healing that made her muscles seize before they eased. It was intrusive, invasive, but undeniably *effective*.

The three worked in tandem, their movements silent, synchronized. The one in robes stood near her head, their presence pressing down like a weight of forced serenity, ensuring she didn't fight what was happening. The second traced the worst of her wounds, and as they did, the first followed, sealing them shut with an eerie efficiency.

Amber's fingers curled against the surface she lay on, her breath hitching. There was no pain anymore, just the lingering memory of it, an echo that refused to fade completely. They were fixing her, *mending* her, but not out of kindness. This was *a necessity*. Lucifer's orders.

She swallowed hard, forcing her voice through the thick air. "You're... different," she murmured, though she knew they wouldn't answer.

The first tilted their head as if considering her words. The second's fingers twitched. The first's pulse quickened beneath their glowing skin.

They were excited.

Amber shuddered.

The presence of the one by Amber's head seemed to deepen, the calm they exuded pressing down on her like a thick fog. Amber felt the pull of it, the temptation to close her eyes, to surrender to the numbing stillness they brought, but she resisted, keeping herself alert, unwilling to fall into their quiet control.

The marble-like being's touch seemed to guide her with ease, as though her very body *knew* what to do in response to their presence. The bones in her legs groaned in protest, but they healed at such a pace now it was almost dizzying. Still, Amber tensed, unwilling to trust anything in this place.

The three moved without words, without hurry, but each one understood their role in this delicate choreography. The first figure, the one at her head, pressed a hand gently against her shoulder, coaxing her upward. There was no urgency in their movement, no force, just an unspoken certainty that she'd rise. Amber found her body responding almost automatically, her muscles moving with an unnatural smoothness, though they still trembled with the aftershocks of pain.

The flickering presence at her side moved with a sudden burst of energy. Their long fingers reached down to lift her arms, steadying her when her legs faltered beneath her. There was no help in the physical sense, not exactly. But their touch held something more, something tethering her to a strange sense of *purpose*, as though she were simply *meant* to stand.

The third being stepped in front of her, moving in silence as they held Amber's gaze. The glow from their skin was softer now, an eerie warmth that pooled around them, and Amber could feel their presence like an anchor in the storm of her thoughts. The weight of her body felt lighter, as though the air itself were lifting her.

With their combined presence, Amber found her legs steadying, her spine straightening. For a brief moment, she was sure that they had lifted her up without touching her at all.

Then, as if it had been choreographed from the start, the three of them retreated in perfect unison.

There was tension in the room, palpable and thick with silence, before they reappeared, slipping through the shadows like ghosts returning to their realm.

They weren't empty-handed.

One of them held a gown draped over their arms. It shimmered with a dark, ethereal beauty, black as night yet alive with subtle movements as if woven from the very fabric of the night sky. The gown seemed to breathe, the hem shifting in invisible winds, and the fabric rippled with unnatural grace, catching the dim light in a way that almost seemed to *speak*.

The third one, clearly in charge, stepped forward first, holding the gown as though it was fragile, yet Amber could tell that this garment was anything but. The figure extended it toward her, but the gesture had no urgency. Amber felt herself being *guided* into it rather than dressed. She found her arms lifted, her body moving as if on cue, her limbs obeying without question.

The fabric slid over her skin like a second layer of air, cool and smooth, until the gown settled into place. The collar rose high around her neck, the waist tightened just enough to shape her body, and the hem fell to her feet with a fluid motion. The gown clung in places and left others open, the contrast between its lightness and weight both seductive and suffocating.

The second one reached forward, their hands brushing over the gown with absent care, adjusting it, making sure every fold was in place. They didn't speak. There was no need for words; their movements were all that was needed.

Finally, the third stepped back, their gaze flicking over Amber's newly adorned form. The touch of their hand was lingering, just barely skimming over her skin as if measuring her essence, before they gave a subtle nod.

The air was still again, the weight of their scrutiny heavy, but Amber didn't feel as if she was at the mercy of their gaze this time.

For a moment, there was nothing but silence, the kind that presses into ones bones, like the very world was holding its breath. And then, as quietly as they had come, the three figures vanished into the shadows again.

Amber was once more alone, dressed in a gown that could've belonged to a queen, and she realized with a shudder that *nothing* about this world, about *her* now, would ever feel normal again.

12

A Familiar Darkness

Amber had no way of knowing how much time passed. It felt like forever, but maybe it had only been a few minutes before the leader of the three ethereal creatures came back into the room. Again, she didn't speak, but Amber knew to move towards her. The pull was irresistible, that same quiet command that thrummed through the air, guiding her without words. Her gown shifted as she moved, the fabric almost alive against her skin, its weight pressing down like a reminder of her place in this world that wasn't hers.

The creatures flanked her, their presence drawing her forward as though they were tethered to her in some unseen way. They didn't need to guide her hands or feet; Amber walked almost automatically, her body responding as if it were part of a larger, unspoken plan.

As she passed through the doorway, the temperature changed instantly, the air growing heavier and thicker. It wasn't like the suffocating heat from before, but something much colder, an oppressive chill that bit at her skin and sank into her bones, a feeling of decay that clung to her like a shadow.

Amber glanced around, her eyes straining to make sense of her surroundings. The walls were jagged, the stone rough and blackened, veins of red coursing through the cracks like a bleeding wound in the earth. The ground beneath her feet felt uneven, as though the very foundation of this place was in a constant state of decay and reconstruction. It looked like a landscape forgotten by time, a place where everything that lived or once lived had been twisted into a cruel mockery of life.

The ceiling above was just a vast stretch of darkness, dotted with occasional flickers of red light that seemed to come from nowhere, as though the very air itself was made of fire. The flickering gave the illusion of a thousand eyes, unseen and watching, waiting for something, *anything*, to happen. The silence was nearly suffocating, broken only by the echo of their footsteps on the rough stone, a steady rhythm that seemed to reverberate through the very walls.

Amber could feel the weight of this place pressing down on her, its oppressive energy crawling over her skin and through her veins, wrapping her in a coil of unease. The air tasted bitter, sharp, and metallic, like burnt copper. She breathed in, unwilling to show discomfort, but her body betrayed her as a slight shiver ran down her spine.

Ahead of her, the creatures moved with effortless grace, their forms blurring as they floated through the air, never quite touching the ground. They made no sound, but Amber could feel their energy radiating from them like an invisible force, their calm presence sharpening the tension around her.

Then, from the shadows ahead, two demons appeared, their grotesque forms emerging from the darkness like predators materializing from the abyss. One was a towering figure, his charred skin stretched tight over bone, yellow eyes gleaming from hollow sockets, a mouth full of jagged fangs curled into a cruel grin. The smaller one crept forward with a jittering gait, its joints clicking faintly as if something inside had come unhinged. Shredded wings clung to its back like the husk of something long dead. It grinned as it approached, its teeth sharp and unnervingly long, its eyes gleaming with a malicious joy that made Amber's skin crawl.

They didn't speak either, and they were larger than the ones that had tortured her before, but the aura of hostility around them was undeniable. The air grew heavier with their presence, as though the ground beneath Amber's feet threatened to swallow her whole. One of them glanced at the ethereal creatures leading her and, with a sharp hiss, reached to its side, fingers curling around a length of dark metal coiled like a belt. From it, the demon drew a cruelly hooked instrument, slick with something dark and viscous.

The creatures didn't flinch. They moved with unspoken authority, guiding Amber forward without hesitation. It was clear that they were in control of this space, as though they had claimed it as their own. The demons, for their part, didn't challenge them, but Amber could sense the wicked hunger in their gaze, the twisted desire to torment. They fell into line behind Amber and the creatures like bodyguards.

As they moved deeper into the heart of Hell, the environment shifted. Fiery rivers of lava flowed in the distance, their molten tendrils licking the air with an orange glow that cast eerie shadows across the jagged cliffs. Strange, spindly trees grew from the cracks in the earth, their blackened bark twisted and gnarled, while in the far distance, enormous spires rose from the ground like teeth, piercing the sky.

Amber couldn't help but feel small in this vast, overwhelming world. Every inch of the place seemed to pulse with malevolent energy, as though the land was alive, aware of her presence. There were no sounds of life, only the distant echoes of screams, muffled by the thick air and the low hum of some terrible, ancient force that ran through the very core of this place.

One of the demons behind her poked her slightly with something sharp in the back, a quick nudge that urged her onward. Amber stumbled slightly but regained her balance. Her senses heightened, and the weight of the moment sank in. This was her new reality. There was no escape. There was no safety. There was only this cruel, unforgiving world and whatever Lucifer had planned for her next.

They walked for what felt like eons before they rounded a corner. What Amber saw in front of her stole the breath from her lungs. She didn't know how she had missed it. From the pits of the Underworld came the towering structure, constructed from dark grey lava rock, jagged and imposing, rising from the earth like a twisted mountain forged in the depths of some ancient, forgotten war. The castle loomed like a living thing, jagged spires reaching up toward the sky, their tips lost in a swirling red-black mist that seemed to bleed into the atmosphere.

The castle walls were unlike any stone Amber had ever seen, dark, polished, and slick, reflecting the shifting flames and molten rivers that ran through the land like veins. The stones pulsated with a subtle, unnerving glow as though they were alive, breathing in time with the pulse of the Underworld. Embedded in the rock were veins of glimmering, obsidian-like crystals, shimmering with an inner fire, casting sharp shadows across the landscape. It was as if the castle was a living entity, an ancient god carved into the very fabric of Hell, its blackened exterior rippling with endless energy, hungry for souls.

Great, twisted iron gates adorned with chains of pulsing blood-red energy hung open like a dark invitation into the heart of the abyss. The gates didn't creak or groan; they moved like living things, their heavy iron bars swaying slowly with a sickening, metallic hiss, welcoming no one yet allowing all to enter.

The castle's towers twisted impossibly, each one spiraling upward in a helix of black stone, the edges razor-sharp like the claws of some giant beast clawing at the sky. From within, the soft murmur of a thousand whispers seemed to emanate as if the stone itself were alive with the tortured souls of the damned. The windows were jagged and broken, darkened with grime, but Amber could feel the heavy gaze of unseen eyes peering through them, watching her every move, an unseen force observing her with malicious intent.

Above her, the sky had turned an unnatural hue, a swirling mix of crimson and violet, where flashes of lightning lit up the atmosphere in streaks of purple fire. The air was thick with ash, the sky suffocating under a constant storm of jagged, molten rain. The wind screamed through the castle, howling like a chorus of tortured souls, swirling around the spires and crevices, sending jagged flares of fire into the air in sporadic bursts.

Amber felt the weight of the place pressing down on her, wrapping around her like an oppressive cloak. The ground beneath her feet shifted subtly as though the castle itself were settling deeper into the earth, sinking its roots into the very core of Hell.

A staircase of impossible scale loomed ahead, stretching upward in a relentless climb. It had to be at least a thousand steps, each worn smooth, not by time, but by the countless souls forced to ascend before her. The front yard of the castle was enclosed by towering cast iron fencing, each bar twisted and jagged, resembling gnarled fingers clawing at the air. Beyond the fence, twisted trees stood barren and skeletal, their charred limbs stretching toward a sky that offered no mercy. A path made entirely of bones, skulls, femurs, and ribs fused together led the way to the castle's monstrous entrance. The brittle remains crunched beneath Amber's bare feet, yet they didn't break, as though the path refused to crumble under her presence.

As she climbed the steps, she braced herself for the inevitable burn in her muscles, the crushing exhaustion that should've come from such an ascent, but it never did. Her breath remained steady, her legs unfaltering.

The ethereal creatures leading her remained silent, their movements fluid and purposeful, their presence an eerie contrast to the grim scenery around them. The two demons that followed trailed just far enough behind to remind her they were still there, watching.

At the top of the steps, the castle doors loomed before her, two massive slabs of iron, blackened and etched with twisted carvings of tormented faces frozen in eternal agony. Chains as thick as her waist crisscrossed the doors, glowing faintly with ember-like runes that pulsed with a dying heartbeat. Burned into the doors' center was a magnificent emblem: a black crown dissolving into streams of flowing shadow. At its heart lay a seven-pointed star. Amber shuddered at the sight. Encircling the crown were words carved deeply into the metal. Though she couldn't translate the Latin, their meaning resonated through her bones: "Et lux in tenebris non lucet. Umbra regnat in perpetuum." Above the doors, the castle's name shimmered softly in the dim glow: Castellum Umbrae. Suddenly, the doors groaned open, a deafening wail rising from the iron as though the tortured souls carved upon them were crying out in endless torment.

The guardian demons flanking the entrance stepped aside, their burning eyes fixed on Amber, their expressions unreadable. No words were spoken. No gestures were made. The invitation was clear.

The doors yawned open, revealing the darkness beyond.

The floors were marble, black as night, streaked with veins of deep red that glowed faintly, casting blood-colored reflections beneath her feet. Statues of grotesque figures lined the hallway, their faces twisted in eternal expressions of agony, their eyes glowing a sickly yellow that seemed to follow Amber's every step, their stone lips frozen in eternal screams. Torches, burning with a purple flame, hung from the walls, casting long shadows stretching endlessly, reaching toward her, yearning to consume her.

Above, the vaulted ceilings were impossibly high, covered in intricate carvings that seemed to move as Amber's gaze passed over them, the figures twisting and writhing as if alive as if caught in the throes of some eternal struggle. Massive chandeliers made of obsidian and dripping with flickering flames hung precariously, their light casting ominous reflections on the floor below. The entire Castellum Umbrae exuded an air of unholy grandeur, a sickening combination of magnificence and decay. Nothing was beautiful about it; everything was born of torment and darkness. Still, it was breathtaking.

Amber was led forward, her footsteps echoing in the cold, empty halls. The creatures flanked her like shadows, their presence a quiet, unnerving calm amidst the chaos. The demons that followed her, their eyes gleaming like twin suns, seemed out of place in the grand, horrifying scale of Castellum Umbrae. They were like insects in comparison to the towering, ancient might of the structure itself as if they were merely pests in this vast, unholy kingdom.

The deeper they went, the more Amber could feel the pressure of this place closing in around her. It wasn't just the darkness; the weight of history and power had been etched into every inch of this place. The walls seemed to whisper in a language she couldn't understand, but it was ancient, cursed, something older than time itself. And at the heart of it all, Amber knew, was Lucifer. This was his domain, his throne. Castellum Umbrae was his sanctuary, his kingdom, and she'd just stepped into its very bowels.

And yet... even as the enormity of it settled in around her, Amber couldn't help but feel the faintest twinge of awe. There was something impossibly powerful about it all, something that made her feel small and insignificant, and at the same time, it made her feel as though this was where she had always belonged.

13

A Feast for the Dead

E ventually, Amber and her silent escorts entered a grand dining hall, an opulent space that seemed to stretch endlessly. A massive table dominated the center of the room, set for two, though it could've easily seated thirty, perhaps more. The candlelight flickered against towering stone walls, casting long, shifting shadows that made the room feel alive as if unseen eyes lurked just beyond the glow.

Amber's gaze swept over the feast before her, and momentarily, she forgot where she was. The sheer abundance was staggering. Platters of golden-roasted meats, delicate seafood glistening with oil, and fruits so vibrantly ripe that they looked almost surreal. There were dishes from every corner of the world, sumptuous plates of pasta twirled into perfect nests, steaming loaves of bread split open to reveal soft, warm centers, and at the very heart of it all, a pig rested on a silver platter, an apple wedged mockingly between its lifeless jaws.

She stared, entranced by the decadence, the sheer impossibility of it in a place like this.

A sharp jab to her back snapped her from her daze. Amber let out a startled yelp, spinning around to find one of the demons looming behind her, its clawed hand nudging her forward with unmistakable insistence. She hesitated for only a moment before quickly sinking into the chair at the head of the table, the weight of expectation settling over her like a shroud.

The moment she sat, the three ethereal beings vanished.

A rush of unease flooded her; the brief comfort of their presence yanked away so suddenly it left her breathless. Her eyes flickered toward the two demons, but they had already retreated to the back wall, standing still as statues, their burning eyes fixed ahead.

The room fell into a breathless silence, thick and stifling. It wasn't the absence of sound but rather the presence of something else, an invisible force waiting, watching.

And then, slowly, deliberately, the doors at the far end of the hall creaked open.

Amber swallowed hard, her pulse a steady drumbeat in her ears as the doors groaned apart. The sound was excruciatingly slow, an intentional warning rather than a simple entrance. The room seemed to shudder with it, the flames in the sconces along the walls flaring brighter, stretching toward the ceiling as if bowing in reverence.

And then, he entered.

Lucifer moved like he had all the time in the world. His presence filled the room before he even crossed the threshold, a quiet, effortless dominance that sent an involuntary shiver down Amber's spine. He was dressed in black, of course, but the way the fabric clung to him and the way it seemed to absorb the light made him look less like a man and more like something sculpted from the void itself. His hair, dark as ink, was slightly tousled, a studied imperfection that only added to his unnerving beauty.

His eyes, though, that was where the real danger lay.

Amber had seen them burn with amusement, hunger, and the promise of ruin. But now, something else lurked beneath the surface as they locked onto her. Curiosity? Possession? A predator's satisfaction upon finding its prey exactly where it should be?

A slow smile curled at his lips.

"Amber," he murmured, savoring her name like fine wine. "You look…" His gaze flickered over her, taking in every inch of the gown that clung to her form, the bruises still fading from her skin. "Presentable."

The heat of humiliation flared in her chest, but she bit down on her tongue, forcing herself to stay still as he approached. He didn't sit immediately. Instead, he took his time, circling the table like a lion stalking its territory.

"Tell me," he mused, reaching for a goblet filled with deep crimson liquid, wine, she assumed, though in Hell, assumptions could be dangerous. He swirled it lazily before taking a slow sip. "How does it feel? Knowing that from this moment forward, you no longer belong to the world you left behind?"

Amber clenched her fists under the table. She wouldn't give him the satisfaction of an immediate answer.

Instead, she inhaled deeply, steadying herself before meeting his gaze, "Like I never really belonged there in the first place."

Lucifer stilled for just a fraction of a second, the only indication that her words had caught him off guard. Then, his smile widened, dark, knowing, something dangerously close to pleased.

"Good," was all he murmured.

Finally, he sank into the chair opposite her, resting his elbows on the table, fingers steepled beneath his chin.

"Eat, Amber. You'll need your strength."

She hesitated. "For what?"

Lucifer's grin sharpened all teeth and wicked promise, "For what comes next."

Amber hesitated, choosing her next words carefully. "Fine. But you promised me answers."

Lucifer's smirk deepened, slow and deliberate. "Ahh, so I did." He leaned back in his chair, studying her with almost lazy amusement. "Well, little dove, what is it you wish to know?"

"Everything," Amber said without hesitation. "Start at the beginning. How did I die?"

Lucifer exhaled through his nose as if the question amused him. He tapped a single finger against the rim of his goblet, considering. "I could tell you," he mused, his voice rich with suggestion, "but I'd much rather show you." His eyes gleamed like embers in the dim candlelight. "If you're going to be my partner, I need to know that you can handle reality, no matter how gruesome. Do you think you can manage that?"

Amber swallowed the lump in her throat, forcing her nerves into submission. She met his gaze, steady and unyielding. "Show me."

Lucifer's grin sharpened, predatory and pleased. "As you wish, little dove."

With a snap of his fingers, the air before her crackled, distorting like heat rising off scorched earth. Then, in a flash, an image appeared, hovering, shifting, alive.

And Amber saw the truth of her own death.

What she saw wasn't particularly horrific, at least not how she expected. But there was something deeply unsettling about watching herself move as if controlled by unseen hands, her actions no longer her own.

She watched as her former self stepped out of the bar, slipping into the driver's seat of her car with eerie detachment. The drive was short, less than three miles before the vehicle veered off the road and plunged nose-first into the river.

Amber should've panicked. She should've fought, clawed for the surface, struggled for breath. Instead, she saw herself surrendering. Felt the water creeping into her lungs, heavy and cold, filling every inch of her until there was nothing left to resist. The river didn't take her; it embraced her. Welcomed her. And she let it.

The image flickered. A jarring shift.

Now, her body was being pulled from the wreckage, lifeless and pale beneath the harsh glare of emergency lights. Another flicker, and suddenly, she was staring at her own funeral.

The crowd stood solemn around a closed casket. She couldn't hear them, but their grief bled through the silence. Her brother held her sister close, their faces streaked with tears. Her father knelt in front of the casket, hands gripping the polished wood as he wept. Strangers she once knew whispered condolences, their mouths moving soundlessly.

Then, the casket was lowered. The dirt was shoveled. And just like that, she was gone.

The images vanished as quickly as they had appeared, leaving only the dim candlelight and the heavy silence between them.

Amber waited for something, grief, regret, or anger, but there was nothing. There was no sadness, no emptiness, just a quiet, detached acceptance.

Lucifer observed her, waiting for a reaction.

She blinked once, then reached for her plate, selecting a portion of the expertly prepared meats. Without a word, she sliced into it, the knife gliding smoothly through the tender cut. The first bite filled her mouth with rich, decadent flavor, the kind that lingered on the tongue long after it was swallowed. She chased it with a sip of wine, the warmth sliding down her throat with a tingling burn.

Finally, she lifted her gaze and met Lucifer's eyes.

"Now," she said, voice steady, "tell me how it works down here."

14

The Order Beneath the Flame

L ucifer smiled slightly as he took a slow bite of the food before him. "Well, darling, let's start with the rankings. Feel free to interrupt if you have any questions; we'll fill in the blanks as we go."

Amber nodded, continuing to eat, her appetite strangely unaffected by the discussion.

"As I'm sure you've gathered, I am the ruler of this realm. Everyone answers to me. My second and third in command are Timor and Dolor, whom you've already had the pleasure of meeting. They cannot speak, at least not in a language we can comprehend, but they understand me. And they obey only me."

Amber shuddered at the mention of their names, the memory of their oppressive presence pressing in on her like phantom hands.

"They have... unique talents," Lucifer continued, swirling his wine. "Timor can conjure a soul's deepest, most paralyzing fears, while Dolor can inflict excruciating pain without so much as laying a finger on his victim. They are neither human nor demon; they simply are."

He took a measured sip of his wine before continuing. "Below them are the Legatus, the diplomats. They send messages to other places in and out of Hell and assist me when creating new laws or when a problem arrives. They are who I lean on for assistance. After the Legatus, there are the Bellatores, the warriors. They enforce my laws and keep order. They are relentless, disciplined, and built for battle."

Taking a bite of his food, he continued, "After the Bellatores are the Crevits, the fully matured demons. Unlike the younger ones, they have complete control over their forms and can shift into any shape they desire. However, their natural states always bear one of three colors. The red demons radiate heat so intense that a single touch could melt flesh from bone. The blue demons wield the opposite power, freezing anything they touch, causing frostbite to spread instantly. And the yellow demons exude a poison so vile and unpredictable that no two souls react the same. Some break out in boils, others begin bleeding from every orifice."

Amber took another bite, listening intently as he continued.

"Below the Crevits are the Eques, the guardians. You saw them escorting you earlier. They are not truly demons, as they possess no unique powers, but they are unnaturally strong and fast. They exist solely to execute orders and derive immense satisfaction from inflicting pain when someone disobeys. Their entire being is built upon discipline and obedience."

Amber shuddered slightly, remembering the silent, hulking figures that had flanked her on the way to Castellum Umbrae.

"The Eques oversee the Operarios, the workers," Lucifer said. "They handle menial tasks such as cooking, cleaning, and maintaining my kingdom. They are not warriors, nor do they have any real authority, but they serve an important role. The Eques ensure that the Operarios perform their duties with absolute precision."

Amber swallowed, gripping her wine glass a little tighter. "Are they the lowest rank?"

"No, that would be the Liberi," Lucifer said with a smirk. "The young demons. They are still growing and learning what they will become. Curious, mischievous things. When a new soul arrives, they get... excited."

Amber nodded slowly, the memory of their sharp claws and shrieking chatter still fresh in her mind. She took a sip of wine, letting the warmth settle in her stomach before asking, "And what about the ones who led me here?"

Lucifer paused, his expression darkening slightly, not with anger, but with something close to reverence. "Ah, the Sororibus Anima," he said, the name rolling off his tongue like a sacred chant. "They are outside the ranking system. They move freely through my kingdom, untouched by the rules that govern the others. No one harms them without facing severe consequences."

Amber frowned. "Then what are they?"

Lucifer leaned back, his fingers idly tracing the rim of his glass. "The eldest, Sana, possesses the extraordinary ability to heal even the most devastating wounds in moments. She is the leader of the three. Then there's Subsido; her gift is relief. And finally, Pax, who can flood a soul with an overwhelming, irresistible sense of peace. When Subsido and Pax work together, pain becomes almost impossible to feel. I use them when I need a soul healed quickly so the torture can begin again."

Amber set her fork down, glancing toward the empty space where the three beings had stood not long ago. They hadn't spoken or threatened her, but there was something unsettling about them. Not in the way the demons were, but in the way they had touched her, bent her pain to their will so effortlessly.

"Why did you send them to me?" she asked carefully.

Lucifer's smile was slow, deliberate. "Because, my little dove, you are far too valuable to break just yet."

Amber swallowed slowly, a gnawing unease twisting in her stomach as the next question surfaced in her mind. "I... I didn't get tired walking up the stairs to Castellum Umbrae. Am I... am I still human?"

Lucifer studied her for a long moment, his gaze unreadable, as if searching for the right words. "Yes and no," he finally said, his voice smooth but weighted with meaning.

Amber sat frozen, waiting.

"You are no longer who you were," he continued. "The laws and rules that govern life as you knew it do not apply here. You're dead, Amber. There's no soft way to say it." He leaned forward slightly, watching her reaction. "You no longer need to breathe. Eventually, your body will forget the motion entirely. You will never age; time here passes just as it does in the Overworld, but it will not touch you. There is no day, no night, and you don't need sleep. The food you've been consuming? It's unnecessary. You may feel hunger or thirst, but your body doesn't need it. One day, you may even forget what those sensations are."

His words wrapped around her like a vice, suffocating in their finality. She tried to process it, but something didn't add up. "Then why can I feel pain?" she asked, her voice barely above a whisper. "And fear?"

Lucifer's lips curled into something like amusement. "That, my dear, is an excellent question." He swirled the wine in his glass before taking a slow sip. "Because emotions do not die the way the body does. Hunger, thirst, exhaustion, those things are bound to flesh, and flesh is gone. But pain, fear, anger? Those are tied to the soul. And that, my little dove, is the only thing you have left."

Amber's grip tightened around her wine glass as Lucifer's words settled deep in her mind. The only thing she had left was her soul. No body, no aging, no true hunger, just the raw weight of emotions that would never fade.

She swallowed hard. "Then what about this place?" she asked, her voice quieter than before. "Hell. How does it work? What is it, really?"

Lucifer chuckled; the sound was rich and almost indulgent. "Ah, now we're getting to the real questions." He leaned back in his chair, tapping a lazy finger against the rim of his goblet. "Hell is many things, Amber. A prison. A kingdom. A sanctuary for the damned. It exists outside of time and human understanding, and it changes depending on who looks at it."

Amber frowned. "Changes?"

Lucifer smirked. "Hell is not the same for every soul. For some, it is fire and brimstone, an endless pit of torment. For others, it is nothingness, a vast, empty abyss where they are utterly alone. And then, for those like you, it is something else entirely."

"Like me?" she echoed, narrowing her eyes.

Lucifer merely smiled. "You will see soon enough." Then, slowly, deliberately, he set his goblet down and stood. "Come, little dove. I think it's time for a tour."

Amber hesitated but then pushed back her chair, rising to her feet. The two demons guarding the back wall straightened as Lucifer moved, but he ignored them. With a flick of his wrist, the massive dining room doors creaked open, revealing the darkened halls beyond.

Lucifer turned to her, extending a hand. "Shall we?"

Amber didn't take it, but she followed.

As she stepped past the threshold, the air seemed to shift. Castellum Umbrae groaned around her as if it knew she was leaving the safety of its walls. And beyond them... something was waiting.

Something vast.

Something eternal.

Something Hell.

15

Echoes of the Damned

As they left Castellum Umbrae's doors and stepped onto the platform staring down at the steps she'd climbed earlier, Lucifer murmured something to one of the Eques, words Amber couldn't comprehend, but she watched as the creature scuttled off swiftly. A few moments later, a magnificent chariot stopped before them, hovering eerily in mid-air. The beast that drew it was the size and shape of a horse, its muscular frame dark and imposing. But what truly captured Amber's attention was the creature's wings, immense, jet-black, and silent as they beat. Each feather shimmered with a strange, otherworldly beauty, stealing the breath she no longer needed right from Amber's lungs.

"That's Equus," Lucifer remarked casually as one of the Operarios opened the doors to the chariot.

Amber tore her eyes away from the majestic creature, finally looking at the chariot. The vehicle was made of dark black metal with gold accents and intricate designs running along its surface. The interior was deep crimson, a rich velvet lining the seats. She hesitated momentarily before stepping in, sinking into the plush seat as though it was made for her. Lucifer followed suit, settling beside her.

Without missing a beat, one of the Eques left its post and jumped onto the back of the chariot. Lucifer spoke in the strange, unrecognizable tongue again, and with a sharp crack of a whip, the Operario snapped the reins, sending the chariot flying away from Castellum Umbrae.

Amber felt an unsettling shift in the air as the chariot sped away. The further they traveled, the more oppressive the weight of the place seemed to settle around her. It was as if the land was breathing, alive, ancient, and restless. Lucifer remained silent beside her, his gaze unfathomable as they crossed the dark expanse.

Amber's eyes wandered, unable to resist the pull of the view unfolding before her. Not far from Castellum Umbrae, the land abruptly dropped into a vast, turbulent expanse, a massive moat, as if the very core of Hell itself was separated by this churning abyss. Waves crashed violently against the edges, frothing and white-capped like the sea of torment. Amber's breath caught in her throat as the sight deepened her unease, the water's agitated movement reminding her of the chaos beyond.

"What is this?" Amber whispered though she hadn't expected an answer.

Lucifer glanced over at her, a faint smirk on his lips. "That's the dividing line, The River Styx. Beyond it lie the islands, the Gardens of Retribution. Each island and section holds those who have earned their place there."

Amber's eyes followed the dark expanse, landing on the islands scattered like dark jewels in the distance. There were seven islands in total, each looming ominously on the horizon. Each one, she realized, was more than just a patch of land; it was a prison, an eternal sentence for sins too great to be wiped away.

"The first island," Lucifer continued, his voice steady as ever, "is Decrepitus. That's where the souls of those who committed petty sins are cast away. They are punished, but their sins were insufficient to warrant much more. Most obtain righteousness within a matter of days to weeks, provided they choose to change."

Amber looked at the island he was pointing to. It was small and desolate, with barely any signs of life except for the occasional wisp of smoke. The air over the island was thick with a strange, oppressive stillness, as if even the winds feared to disturb the souls who wandered there.

"The second is Enervated," Lucifer said, eyes narrowing as he watched Amber's gaze. "For the souls of those who have committed minor sins such as cowardice, enabling, and passivity. They linger in a state of constant exhaustion, never quite able to rest or escape. Most get redemption within several weeks but for others it may take a month before they earn release."

The next island appeared slightly more twisted; broken trees and skeletal structures littered the land. It seemed like a place drained of vitality, a stark contrast to the raging energy of the water surrounding it.

Amber felt a chill creep up her spine as Lucifer pointed again. "The third is Abominabilis. For those who have committed selfish, cruel, or manipulative acts in moderation. These souls are tormented by self-loathing, constantly faced with their failures. Redemption is possible, but it usually takes months, sometimes up to a year."

She stared at the third island, which appeared shrouded in thick mist. The shadows moved unnaturally across the landscape, creating an eerie distortion that made Amber feel like she might be swallowed whole by the land itself.

Lucifer continued, "The fourth is Languorous, reserved for those whose sins were more formidable such as lust, emotional destruction, and manipulation. It can take a soul here years, or up to a decade, until they can reject the desires that once defined them."

The island that appeared before them now seemed almost suffocating. Amber could make out dark shapes moving slowly across the barren land. Their movements were sluggish and heavy, like the burden of their sins weighed them down.

"The fifth is Pachydermatous," Lucifer's voice grew colder as he spoke. "For severe sinners; those ruled by pride, coldness, and moral rigidity. Their souls are burdened with a weight so crushing, they can't even remember what it was to be free. It often takes decades, sometimes a full century, for one to humble themselves enough to leave."

Amber felt a pang in her chest as she stared at the next island, where giant, dark shapes seemed to move under the thick, roiling air. The ground was parched, ruptured like scorched flesh, and the tortured trees bent beneath the invisible weight of the suffering buried within.

"The sixth is Vehement," Lucifer's words were sharper now, as if the very thought of this place stirred something deeper within him. "It is reserved for those who have committed unspeakable sins. Acts of wrath or destruction; cruelty born of hate. These souls remain for centuries, sometimes even up to a millennium, until they choose peace instead of violence."

The sixth island was the most grotesque. Amber could see dark shapes writhing in the distance, shadows clawing at each other. The land seemed to bleed, dark streams of something foul running through the dirt.

"And lastly," Lucifer's voice turned low and almost contemplative, "Pernicious. For the worst of the worst. Creatures who have committed horrific sins so vile, they are beyond redemption. No one leaves Pernicious. Not ever."

The last island was the most foreboding, a looming, jagged mass of rock and fire. Amber could feel the heat radiating from it, even from a distance. The sky above it burned a sickly shade of red as if the air itself was aflame with the intensity of its inhabitants' suffering.

Amber's gaze lingered on that last island, a sick realization settling in her stomach. It wasn't just a place of punishment; it was a place of eternal, unforgiving torment.

Lucifer's eyes glinted with a subtle, predatory gleam as he watched her reaction. "Each of these islands serves as both a prison and a lesson. A reminder of the consequences of their actions. Each soul is forced to confront the enormity of their sin."

Amber couldn't tear her eyes away from the Pernicious Section. "And what happens to those who end up there?"

Lucifer's smile was slow, dark. "The same thing that happens to all of them. They suffer for eternity. The beauty of Hell is that no soul ever truly escapes their sins."

"Are they tortured in all the same ways?" Amber asked, her voice trembling with disgust and a shameful curiosity.

"Oh no, my dear," Lucifer replied, his voice smooth but laced with dark amusement. "They are tortured very differently depending on the island." He turned to the driver of their chariot, speaking to him in a language Amber couldn't understand. With a sudden jolt, the chariot took a steep dive toward the raging waters below.

Amber gasped, bracing herself for the cold rush of water to engulf them. But instead of plunging into the depths, they leveled out with only a light spray hitting her face.

"Let's take a closer look," Lucifer said, his smirk widening as he looked at her reaction.

As they neared the first island, the air was thick with distant moans, growing louder as they approached. The driver said nothing, but Amber saw tension in the way his knuckles tightened around the reins. When the chariot slowed, he dismounted in silence and opened the door.

Amber stepped out and froze.

A fence circled the island, only it wasn't made of stone or iron, but of bodies.

Each one was impaled from the base of the spine to the base of the neck, held upright by towering black spikes. Their mouths hung open in silent screams, and their eyes, those that still had them, twitched in the direction of every sound.

Seeing her horrified gaze, Lucifer explained calmly, "What you're looking at, my dear, is what we call The Spiked. For eternity, these souls are forced to act as a 'fence,' suffering as they are both prisoners and barriers. Their agony is the price they pay for their sins."

Amber's stomach twisted. She tore her gaze away from the gnarled bodies just as two Eques approached and heaved open the gates. They creaked like bones being pried apart.

The path ahead pulsed with quiet horror.

Bone fragments crunched beneath her boots, crushed and scattered like forgotten whispers. Just ahead, flames rose in slow, steady waves from the feet of impaled souls, Soul Candles, Lucifer called them. Fire crept inch by inch up their bodies, searing slowly, never fast enough to destroy, just enough to consume.

"Does the fire ever go out?" Amber asked, her voice hoarse.

Lucifer's eyes caught the light, sharp and gleaming, "It does go out," he said softly. "And then a red demon lights it again."

He paused for a beat, then added, "Souls cannot die twice, Amber. But they can burn forever."

His voice stayed calm, but there was something beneath it, something darker.

"To live without end, without freedom, reliving the worst moment of your existence again and again, that is the punishment. It's not mercy. It's a curse."

The silence that followed was weighted, deliberate. He let the words settle between them, as if they belonged not just to him, but to the very structure of Hell itself.

Amber felt the weight of his gaze pass over her, assessing, measuring, waiting to see if she flinched.

"Here, death is a cycle, a loop that keeps turning," Lucifer said. "A pulling everything back to the beginning. The soul may shatter. The body may be torn apart. But Hell will put it back together, just to break it again."

He looked out across the scorched land, voice colder now. "It's a twisted kind of immortality."

His gaze hardened.

"The longer they're here, the more pieces go missing. The flesh repairs itself, but the mind? The soul?" A bitter smile touched his lips. "They start to forget. Who they were. What they did. Eventually, all that's left is the pain. And when even that becomes dull, we remind them."

Amber's stomach twisted.

Lucifer exhaled, a slow, quiet sigh. "There's no rest here. No peace. Even in death, you belong to Hell."

They continued walking, and Amber noticed a striking contrast on either side of the path. On the right, a serene-looking lake stretched out before them. On the left, there were boulders piled atop hard, cracked earth.

Squinting, Amber looked closer at the boulders. To her horror, each one wasn't just a rock; it was a soul entombed within the stone, its bodies frozen in a desperate reach toward something just beyond its grasp.

"The souls trapped in those boulders have been condemned for gluttony," Lucifer said, his voice detached. "They clung to excess while others starved. And now they reach, endlessly, for what they never shared."

Amber turned away. To the right, a shimmering lake mirrored a deceptively tranquil sky. Souls stood waist-deep in the crystalline water, surrounded by fruit trees with branches that dipped low, almost too low.

One soul reached up. The wind shifted. The branch recoiled.

Another scooped water into cupped hands, only to watch it spill through invisible cracks. Again. And again.

Amber's stomach twisted at the cruel nature of their torment. "So, they're tortured by hunger and thirst... even though the food and water are right there?" she asked, her voice barely more than a whisper as she watched the souls' desperate, starving screams.

"Yes," Lucifer said softly, his voice almost sympathetic, though his smile never faltered. "Hunger and thirst may be tied to the human body, but we have spells to ensure that a soul always knows longing, always knows need. Even though food and drink are just inches away, they can never taste it, never reach it. It is the cruelty of eternal yearning, Amber. That is the real torment."

Amber's voice cracked. "And they stay here forever?"

Lucifer paused, then smiled, thin and knowing. "Not always. Decrepitus is for the stagnant. The apathetic. The indulgent who never chose anything real. But sometimes..." He gestured to the lake. "A soul reaches not for the fruit, but for another soul's hand. Or turns away from the water entirely and walks toward the flames. That's when we know."

"Know what?"

"That they've chosen something. Anything. To feel, to act, to change. *Intention* is the only thing strong enough to wake a soul from Decrepitus. And once it stirs, Hell lets them go."

Amber's stomach twisted as she watched the souls in the lake, their hands desperately clawing at the air, yearning for something just out of reach. The constant motions of their hands, their futile attempts to grasp the fruit or water, but then she noticed it. One soul, far off, was not reaching. He stood still, eyes shut, unmoving.

Her breath caught.

Lucifer watched her carefully. "You see it, don't you?"

She nodded, unsettled.

"He may still fall back into habit," Lucifer said. "But if he doesn't, if he turns away from want, and toward will, he'll be gone by morning."

The wind shifted and The Spiked groaned softly in unison.

As they moved along the path, Lucifer's tone shifted, growing more conversational. "You see, torment in Hell is not always physical. It's psychological as much as it is corporeal. To want something you can never have, to be surrounded by it, only to have it constantly pulled away from you, that is one of the most intense forms of suffering." He paused, watching her carefully as they passed the souls, reaching for the unattainable.

As she took in the sight before her, a feeling she couldn't quite name swept over her.

"Can we visit all the islands?" she asked, her voice barely above a whisper.

Lucifer hesitated momentarily, his gaze flickering to the horizon, before responding, "Almost all," his tone tinged with something unreadable.

Amber's brow furrowed at his words, but Lucifer motioned for them to head back toward the chariot before she could ask more.

As they made their way to the gate, the air seemed to grow heavier, thick with the weight of unspoken things. The sound of the souls' agony hung like a haunting melody, but Lucifer remained unfazed, his every step measured, deliberate.

Amber's heart raced as she grabbed his outstretched hand and followed him onto the chariot. With one word from Lucifer, they were off to the second island.

16

Beautifully Rotten

The entrance to the second island was the same as the first, just as Lucifer had said it'd be. Upon entering the gates, Amber noticed how the ground before them shimmered with heat. The floor was made of jagged lava rock, glowing with the heat of a thousand buried suns. Pools of boiling lava were scattered across the land, their surfaces rippling with movement.

With each step, the heat clawed at Amber's skin like sharp, invisible fingers that scraped raw across her arms and neck. The air shimmered, thick as oil, choking her lungs with every breath. A chorus of screams twisted through the haze, high-pitched and unending, like metal being dragged across stone. The source drew her eyes to the banks of molten lava, where the landscape seemed to writhe and bleed.

Souls flailed in the molten heat, their forms half-melted, struggling to escape. But just as one neared the edge, another reached out, not to help, but to drag them back under.

"Why are they doing that?" Amber whispered, horrified.

Lucifer stood beside her, his voice low and measured. "Because it's what they did in life. Not with fire or blades, but with silence. With passivity. These are the enablers, the cowards. The ones who watched others suffer and chose safety over justice."

From high above, perched on ledges carved into the blackened rock, red demons lounged like predators at rest. Their skin glowed faintly, like coal that never cooled. They held pitchforks, but didn't use them, not *directly*. Instead, they gestured. Commanded. *Or tempted.*

Amber watched as a demon pointed toward a soul climbing out of the lava. Immediately, another soul flinched and stepped forward, trembling.

"They don't have to obey," Lucifer murmured, "but they almost always do. Fear is a powerful motivator."

The trembling soul shoved the other down. Screams erupted and the red demon laughed, the sound low and knowing, and turned to another.

"They're not torturers here," Lucifer said. "Not exactly. They're provocateurs. They create the dilemma, push or be pushed, betray or burn. And then they watch what the soul chooses."

A soul stood on a narrow ledge nearby, her hands shaking violently as a red demon whispered something in her ear. At her feet, another soul reached out, pleading for help.

"She's been standing there for days," Lucifer said. "Every time she refuses to act, the moment resets. A demon pushes her in, she climbs out and the choice is offered again."

Amber turned toward him. "If she helps... she's freed?"

"If she helps, and it costs her something, yes. This is the only section of Hell where salvation comes not from endurance, but from *bravery*. Not just action, but risk."

The heat gnawed at Amber's skin, but she barely noticed. She was watching the souls, *all* of them. So many just watching, turning away, stepping back. She recognized the fear in their eyes. It wasn't fear of the demons.

It was fear of doing the right thing.

Lucifer's gaze was on her. "This place doesn't punish evil. It punishes *inaction*. Every soul here had a moment in life where they could've spoken, stepped in, done something. And they didn't."

Amber swallowed hard, a chill slithering beneath her skin despite the heat.

"And what about now?" she asked. "What if they never act?"

Lucifer's expression was unreadable. "Then they stay until they do. The longest I've seen a soul stay was about a month, but they can stay forever if they never act."

A soul climbed onto the rocks. His body trembled. He was almost free when A red demon smirked, and pointed.

Another soul began to move toward him.

Amber looked away.

But she heard the splash.

And the scream.

***

The smoke hit Amber first, thick, acrid, smoke that clung the back of her throat like guilt made tangible. As they approached, Amber could hear the unmistakable sounds of agony, screams, cracking bones, and the undeniable rush of a demonic laugh. The land was covered in a muddy, dirt floor, patches of scorched earth mixing with the suffocating fumes that seemed to rise from the ground.

"Welcome to the Abominable Section," Lucifer said, his voice steady as they passed through the gates. "Here, punishment is physical, and it's brutal. But don't mistake the violence for mindless chaos. Each punishment serves a purpose. This is where the selfish come to understand the cost of their choices."

Amber's eyes widened as she took in the scene before her. Souls were scattered across the island, some bound to strange devices, others lying in the dirt, writhing in agony. The harsh sounds of bone breaking, flesh being torn, and wails of torment filled the air.

He gestured toward the nearest display. A towering wheel of blackened wood stood at the center, its spokes charred and smoking. A soul was bound to it, arms and legs spread wide, body already blistering. A demon stepped forward with slow, theatrical purpose and touched flame to the base. The wheel turned.

"The Wheel of Fire," Lucifer said softly. "This man once abandoned a friend to ruin, watched him burn, metaphorically. Now he learns how that fire felt. Not as punishment. As education."

Amber watched as the soul writhed, and suddenly his face changed, not from pain, but from something else. Recognition.

Lucifer smiled faintly. "Ah. There it is."

They moved on.

The next scene was even more brutal. A soul was strapped to a rotating iron wheel while yellow and blue demons took turns breaking every bone in his body with thick iron rods.

"They call it the Bashing Cycle," Lucifer said. "He destroyed people piece by piece, emotionally, financially. Dismantled lives for his own gain. Now he feels what it's like to be dismantled himself. But it won't stop until he *understands* what he's done."

Amber's stomach churned. "And if he never understands?"

"Then he remains."

The third punishment was even worse. "This is the Rack," Lucifer explained, taking a few steps deeper into the island. Amber watched in horror as another soul bound to the ground, limbs stretched taut between four stone pillars. Demons turned thick pulleys with mechanical detachment, pulling until muscles tore and joints dislocated. The soul screamed, but the air didn't carry rage, it carried grief.

Lucifer's voice dropped. "She once betrayed someone who loved her. Traded them for comfort. Trust for survival. Now she learns what it's like to be pulled in two directions and abandoned."

The words hit Amber harder than she expected.

"And at night," Lucifer continued, "they heal. Their bodies knit back together. But their understanding, that's what we're really watching. Not whether they can endure. But whether they *feel*."

Amber could barely comprehend the cruelty she was witnessing. Each soul was being tortured in ways that defied all understanding, suffering unceasingly day after day, only to heal overnight and face the same fate once more. The air was thick with pain and despair, and as they walked through the section, Amber could feel the weight of the torment around her.

She blinked. "So... the punishment only ends when they understand what they did?"

"When they stop asking *why is this happening to me*? and begin to ask *how did it feel for them*? That's when the island lets them go."

A yellow demon walked past, dragging a metal rake across the ground. He glanced at Amber, not cruelly, but almost with curiosity.

"And some never ask that question," Lucifer said. "Because they still believe they were right."

Amber looked back at the wheel. The fire was almost to the top and the man was screaming a name.

Lucifer guided her back towards the waiting chariot toward the fourth island: Languorous. As they approached, Amber felt a sudden chill creep over her skin. The air clung to their skin like oil, dense and unnatural, the darkness so thick it felt alive, swallowing everything in its path. There was no moon, stars, or glimmer of light save for the faint glow of candles placed sporadically on the ground. The faint light flickered in the darkness, casting long, eerie shadows that seemed to dance independently.

Amber shivered as she looked around. She could barely distinguish the tortured souls' shapes in the distance. The only sound she could hear was the constant, ear-piercing wail of agony that echoed throughout the island.

Amber's heart raced as the chariot came to a halt. As soon as they passed through the gates, she could see figures moving through the darkness, stumbling as they dragged their bodies along the ground, their faces twisted in unbearable agony.

Lucifer stepped out of the chariot and extended a hand. "Come, little dove. This place is quieter, but no less cruel."

As they passed the gates, the candlelight revealed twisted, hollow figures curled across the earth. Some tore at their skin with trembling hands. Others bent over themselves in strange, hunched positions, teeth gnashing into their own limbs.

Lucifer's voice was calm. "The first punishment here is hunger. But not for food. For what they once craved most: power, control, devotion. They fed off others in life, used affection like a lure, love like a chain. Now, they can only feed on themselves."

Amber's eyes locked onto one soul gnawing at his wrist, blood soaking his chest, tears running down his cheeks. His mouth never stopped moving.

"The hunger never fades," Lucifer continued. "They gorge on their own flesh, but it doesn't heal until the next 'night.' The cycle begins again. No amount of consumption will satisfy what they destroyed in others."

Amber's throat tightened. "Why not just starve them?"

Lucifer turned to her, a faint smile playing on his lips. "Because starvation teaches nothing. But indulgence, the freedom to choose, that reveals who they truly are."

Amber's stomach churned, her throat tightening as she imagined the horrors of such an existence, when suddenly, movement skittered through the darkness.

Amber flinched as long, slick shapes darted between the shadows. Rats, huge and ravenous, began to swarm toward the curled bodies on the ground.

She stepped back instinctively, but Lucifer held her still.

"The second punishment," he said coolly, "comes not from pain, but from *invitation.*"

The rats approached the souls slowly, waiting.

Then a woman screamed, not in fear, but in desperation. "Please, I'll do anything...just make it stop. Just touch me again."

She collapsed into sobs.

The rats surged forward.

Amber's eyes widened in horror as the rats swarmed her body, crawling between her legs, burrowing upward from within. The woman's scream became a gurgle as blood poured from her mouth, but her hands didn't push them away.

She welcomed them.

"But why?" she whispered, her voice barely audible. "Why this torment?"

Lucifer turned to her, his gaze dark and unfathomable. "Because, she once used her body to manipulate, her voice to seduce, her affection to control. Now, the thing she craved most, intimacy, destroys her from the inside out. And still, she begs for more."

Amber's stomach lurched.

"For the men," Lucifer added casually, "it's often a different arrangement. The rats are trapped beneath baskets set aflame. With nowhere to go, they dig. And they find a way out."

Amber stumbled back, bile rising in her throat. "And they all... chose this?"

Lucifer looked at her then, really looked. "They chose not to stop. In life, they fed their addictions, their need to be worshipped, their hunger for more. Here, they are given the same choice again and again: to indulge or to resist. And only when they choose *absence*, only when they turn away from what they want most, can they be freed."

Amber's gaze darted to a figure in the distance. A man stood still among the chaos, arms at his sides, his face blank. He was surrounded by temptation; visions of lovers, soft whispers, warmth, but he didn't move.

"How long has he been like that?" she asked.

"Almost a year," Lucifer said. "If he lasts until the end of the week, he'll be gone."

Amber watched him in silence. He looked calm. But not at peace.

"I don't understand," she whispered. "If they know it's a trap, why don't more of them stop?"

Lucifer's smile sharpened. "Because for most of them, pain is easier than emptiness. And lust... is the only thing that ever made them feel alive."

Amber swallowed hard. The trials of Hell were more than just physical; they were tests of endurance, strength, and character. To be Lucifer's partner was no small thing. Amber would have to prove that she could survive not just the horrors of this place but the very essence of what it meant to endure Hell itself.

Lucifer's voice was quiet, but firm, "Let's move on."

She followed. But the whispers followed her too.

17

Little Monster

A s the chariot ascended from the darkness of Languorous, Amber's breath remained shallow, her mind still trapped in the echoes of the screams she had left behind. But there was no time to recover. The air shifted again, carrying with it the scent of raw flesh and something metallic: blood.

From above, Amber could see figures bound to wooden frames, their bodies glistening under Hell's unrelenting heat. As they descended, the sight became clearer. The island was barren, void of distractions. No trees, no water, just suffering on full display.

The chariot landed, and Amber stepped down cautiously, her feet pressing into the scorched earth. The silence here was different. There were no loud wails, no hysterical cries. Instead, there was a muted, breathless pain punctuated by occasional gasps and the wet, sickening sound of skin being stripped away.

Lucifer motioned for her to follow, and as she did, Amber's eyes landed on the nearest victim. A soul lay stretched across a wooden frame, limbs bound. A yellow-skinned demon stood above them with long, precise claws. It moved with a strange gentleness, slow and exact, as it made the first incision at the scalp. The soul's mouth opened in a silent scream. Amber flinched as the demon began peeling the skin back from the head with surgical care.

Her stomach twisted.

"This is Pachydermatous," Lucifer said, his voice calm, as if he were giving a casual tour. "A fitting punishment for those whose greatest shield in life was pride."

Amber could see the yellow demons working methodically, their movements practiced. The process was meticulous. Their claws never moved too quickly. Every inch of skin was carefully peeled away, exposing raw muscle and nerve endings. The head was always first, the most excruciating place to begin.

"The skin is the body's protection," Lucifer continued. "It is the boundary between pain and relief, between sensation and numbness. To strip a soul of their skin is to strip them of all comfort, to make them feel every whisper of air, every pulse of agony in its purest form. Those who lived wrapped in self-righteousness and superiority wore their pride like armor. So here, we strip it away."

Amber swallowed hard as she watched a nearby soul writhe in their restraints, the skin hanging from their body in delicate, bloody ribbons. His muscles twitched in the open air, lips pulled back in a grimace of agony. The demon beside him dipped a cloth in brine and began wiping down the raw tissue. The soul didn't even scream anymore. Just trembled.

"And when night falls?" Amber asked though she dreaded the answer.

Lucifer smirked. "The demons leave, and their flesh slowly reattaches itself. By morning, they are whole again, ready to be flayed anew. But it's not the body that matters here. It's the *ego*. And that takes longer to break."

Amber shuddered. The repetition, the endless cycle, it was worse than she imagined. These souls were forced to endure their torment again and again, knowing exactly what was coming, knowing there was no escape from the claws, no relief from the searing pain.

Lucifer followed her gaze. "Humility," he said quietly. "The only thing that frees them. The moment they stop trying to prove they're above pain, above need, Hell lets them go."

Amber blinked. "That's all it takes?"

Lucifer's expression darkened. "You say that as if it's easy. Most of them would rather be torn apart a thousand times than admit they were ever wrong."

She turned back to the soul still being flayed, his lips moved soundlessly, eyes full of hate, not pain. He wasn't crying. He was enduring.

Amber's chest ached.

As they walked, she noticed the group of ethereal creatures from earlier working alongside the demons. Their hands moved with the same precision, and their faces were expressionless as they assisted in the peeling.

"The Sororibus Anima work on the third, fourth, fifth, and sixth islands," Lucifer said, catching her gaze. "If you wish to prove yourself, you will need to learn their craft along with the craft of torture."

Amber stiffened, her body tense. The weight of his words wasn't lost on her. She'd already been forced to endure pain in Hell, but this, this was different. This was inflicting it. This was becoming part of it.

Lucifer stepped close, tilting her chin with two fingers. "Tell me, Amber," he murmured, voice low, "can you make someone beg? Not from pain. From the realization that they're no longer a god in their own story?"

Her breath hitched, her pulse hammering in her ears. She didn't know the answer.

And she wasn't sure she wanted to.

"Come," Lucifer said, releasing her. "We have more to see."

As she turned away, one of the kneeling souls whispered: *I don't want to be right anymore.*

Amber looked back once. And then followed Lucifer toward the next island.

As the chariot soared toward the Sixth Island, Vehement, Amber felt an overwhelming shift in the air like pressure building behind her eyes. Below, the land stretched in every direction like a forgotten battlefield: dusty, cracked, and stained red as if the earth itself had bled dry.

Lucifer's demeanor changed as well. He no longer wore his smirk but instead gazed at the island with something unreadable in his expression, something like anticipation.

As they descended, Amber immediately felt the unnatural weight of the silence. It wasn't just quiet; it was oppressive, pressing against her ears, making her own breath sound deafening.

The moment the chariot landed, Lucifer stepped forward first.

He turned to her, his voice smooth but laced with warning. "Be mindful of the walls here," he said. "They are soundproof, but should one break..." He trailed off, letting her imagination fill in the rest.

Amber stepped down slowly. The ground beneath her feet crumbled like dried blood. Towering walls rose high around them, impossibly smooth, like black glass, unyielding and cold. The stillness here wasn't peace. It was a threat.

Lucifer led her through a narrow passage until they reached an open clearing. There, she saw the first punishment in motion.

A soul lay chained to a massive black rock, their limbs bound by thick, rusted chains. They thrashed weakly, their body stripped bare, their chest rising and falling in rapid, terrified breaths. Above them, a dense swarm of ravens circled like a living storm cloud, their black eyes gleaming hungrily.

Without warning, the first bird dove. Then another. And another.

The ravens tore into the soul's flesh with sharp beaks and talons, carving through muscle and shredding sinew until they reached the liver. The damned screamed soundlessly, mouths stretched in silent torment, their agony suspended in a void where no sound could escape. The silence didn't soften the horror; it sharpened it. Each flinch, each futile twist of the body, played out like a scene in a nightmare where Amber could see everything but hear nothing. It made her want to step back, as if even the air around her had gone wrong.

Lucifer watched, his arms crossed as if observing fine art. "These birds are relentless," he mused. "Each day, they return, feasting on the liver that regenerates overnight. The pain never dulls. The fear never fades." He glanced at her. "Do you think they deserve it?"

Amber didn't answer.

Because she didn't know.

Because part of her thought... maybe.

Lucifer smiled and motioned for her to follow him deeper.

They passed another chamber. Another punishment.

A soul lay face down, their body stretched across a stone platform. A demon stood over them, sharp talons, meticulously slicing into the flesh along the spine. Amber's stomach twisted as she watched the ribs being snapped apart one by one, the bones pried open like a grotesque pair of wings.

The demon reached inside the gaping wound and pulled, slowly extracting the damned's lungs and laying them delicately across their back. The exposed lungs expanded and contracted, glistening with blood, the soul writhing in unbearable agony.

And still, there was no sound.

Amber's breathing was shallow. She felt her knees weaken. Every island had been horrifying, but this, this was cruelty in its purest form. The silence amplified the horror. There were no screams, no pleas for mercy, only suffering beyond words.

Lucifer stepped beside her, his voice smooth, deliberate. "This is where true fear lives," he said. "Pain is one thing. But knowing you will endure it again and again, knowing that nightfall will bring only the promise of another day of torment, that is true despair."

Amber's hands clenched into fists. She wanted to look away, but she couldn't.

Lucifer turned to her, his gaze sharp. "Tell me, Amber," he said, his voice softer now, more insidious. "Could you watch this every day?"

She swallowed hard.

Because she knew the answer, and it wasn't *no*.

There was something in her, something she didn't have a name for, that didn't flinch. A part that stood still amid the screams and fire, curious, almost calm. Not out of cruelty. Not even out of strength. But something deeper. Something ancient. As if Hell wasn't *entirely* foreign to her.

And Lucifer knew. Of course he did.

The truth pulsed inside her, slow and undeniable, like a shadow just beginning to stretch.

Lucifer's smirk deepened, a glint of satisfaction in his eyes, as though he'd felt it stir too.

They moved on, deeper into the island.

Amber noticed something strange in the next clearing.

A soul stood in the center of a circle, surrounded by weapons: blades, spears, iron whips; all laid out before them like an offering. Surrounding the ring, demons chanted silently, their mouths moving without sound.

The soul stared at the weapons. Trembling. Rage in their eyes.

Lucifer's voice dropped. "Some souls are offered tools to fight. If they pick one up, they are given someone to kill. Again and again. Every time, they're told it's for freedom."

Amber watched as the soul grabbed a dagger and turned toward the target.

"But it's a lie," Lucifer finished. "They're only freed when they refuse. When they drop the blade. When they walk away from the fire inside them. That's the test."

Amber's breath caught.

"No one tells them that?"

"No," Lucifer said. "Because if they can't discover peace on their own, if they can't lay down their hatred without being told, it's not real."

She looked at the soul, now mid-fight, eyes blazing with fury.

"He won't leave," she whispered.

"No," Lucifer agreed. "Not for centuries."

***

As they approached the final island, Lucifer's expression lost its playfulness. The space before them wasn't just another section of Hell but something more. The very air shifted, warping like a mirage. The landscape below twisted and flickered, shifting between impossible forms, an ever-changing nightmare that refused to settle.

She leaned forward slightly, trying to get a better look, but Lucifer raised a hand before the chariot could descend. Instantly, the driver halted midair, keeping them just out of reach.

Amber frowned. "Why aren't we landing?"

Lucifer turned to her, his expression unreadable. "Because you're not ready."

Amber's gaze snapped to him. "Not ready?"

Lucifer's smirk returned, though it was laced with something darker this time. "The Pernicious Island is not for the eyes of just anyone, my dear. Even most of my demons aren't allowed here." He gestured toward the shifting landscape below. Unlike the other islands, there were no clear landmarks, no pits of fire or chains, just a swirling mass of distorted shapes and flickering images. Something in it almost called to her, like a whisper just beyond her ability to hear.

"This is where the worst of the worst reside," Lucifer continued. "Their punishments are uniquely tailored, their suffering... personal. Unlike the others, they do not endure mindless torture. They live their sins. Again and again." His gaze remained fixed on the island. "The only place in Hell where suffering is crafted, not assigned."

It was almost worse than the explicit violence of the previous islands. This was personal. Intimate.

Amber swallowed. "So why can't I see it?"

Lucifer chuckled, but there was no warmth in it. "Because seeing it means understanding it. And understanding it means proving you belong."

Amber stiffened. "I don't belong here?"

Lucifer turned to her fully now, his gaze burning into hers. "Do you?"

For a moment, the weight of his words threatened to crush her. But then, with a sharp flick of his wrist, he signaled to the driver. The chariot veered away from the island, leaving the shifting horrors behind.

Amber sucked in a breath, her hands curling into fists. Something about his question made her chest tighten. Because she already knew, deep down, in a place she didn't want to acknowledge that that moment would come.

That one day, she'd step onto that island.

And she'd be ready.

"You have much to learn, my dear," Lucifer said smoothly. "But when the time comes, when you are ready..." He glanced back toward the island as it faded from view, "I will take you inside myself."

18

Ice and Blood

The chariot sliced through the thick, dark sky, gliding away from the islands like a blade through flesh. As they passed over The River Styx, the sprawling inferno of Hell's mainland stretched beneath them, a labyrinth of twisted spires, endless caverns, and rivers of molten gold. It was alive in its own way, thrumming with an energy that coiled beneath Amber's skin like a living pulse.

She exhaled slowly. The horrors of the islands still burned behind her eyes, but there was no time to dwell. This was only the beginning.

Lucifer sat beside her, silent for once, fingers tapping idly against his knee. His expression was unreadable, but Amber felt his gaze studying her, weighing her.

The chariot passed Castellum Umbrae, continuing into the barren landscape. About three hundred yards from the towering fortress, a structure emerged from the wasteland, a massive, sunken coliseum of black obsidian. Its jagged walls jutted from the earth like the fangs of some ancient beast. As the chariot descended, Amber noticed a gathering at the entrance. A mix of demons, some hunched and twisted, others sleek and predatory, stood waiting, anticipation thick in the air.

Lucifer stepped down first, casting Amber an expectant and amused look. "Welcome to your proving ground, my dear."

Amber lifted her chin and stepped out. "What is this?" she asked, hating the slight tremor in her voice.

"This, darling, is Anulum Pugnatum, the Fighting Ring," Lucifer said smoothly. "It's where we asses how far the Liberi have come in their training. The Bellatores, Crevits, and Eques come here when it's time to prove themselves, when drills are no longer enough, and theory gives way to carnage. It's not about learning. It's about surviving."

Amber inhaled deeply. "And what am I doing here?"

Lucifer chuckled, a dark, icy sound. "Simple. You're here to be seen." His eyes gleamed with something unreadable. "I can't have a partner who can't defend herself, or worse, one who clings to mercy."

He stepped closer, voice dropping lower, colder. "This is where you show me you're meant to be more than a soul bound to me. This is where you show *them*."

He paused, just long enough for the weight of his words to settle. "But don't worry. You're not ready for Anulum Pugnatum yet. Tonight, you're only here as a witness."

Amber held his gaze, defiant.

Lucifer smirked, then placed a hand on her back, guiding her forward. "And, of course, there's more," he murmured. "But we'll get to that soon enough."

Lucifer stepped forward like a king returning to his throne, his long coat billowing behind him like a war banner. The gathered demons bowed their heads as he passed, parting in silent reverence. Even those with jagged teeth and wicked grins didn't dare to speak. This was his domain, his battlefield.

The entrance yawned open, leading them through an arched corridor lined with torches that burned with eerie blue flames. The walls were etched with depictions of past battles, scenes of agony and triumph immortalized in black stone. The air carried a heavy musk of sweat, steel, and something darker. Something primal.

Amber felt it in her bones. This was a place of war.

As they moved deeper inside, the distant roar of the crowd thundered above them, shaking the very foundation. The sounds of thousands filled the space, jeering, chanting, the sharp clang of metal against metal. Somewhere, a horn bellowed, deep and guttural, signaling the next fight.

Lucifer motioned for her to follow him as he ascended the grand stairway to the spectator's balcony. The ascent was deliberate and regal as if each step reaffirmed his dominion over this coliseum. The moment he emerged into the open, the crowd erupted in deafening applause, a wave of devotion washing over him. The seats were carved from volcanic stone, stretching in a perfect circle around the pit, where the combatants would soon fight for their lives.

His throne sat at the highest point of the coliseum, an imposing seat of polished black rock adorned with infernal carvings of serpents and flames. He settled into it with the ease of a king watching his chosen warriors battle for his favor.

Amber hesitated at the platform's edge, not allowed to follow him past a row of Eques, her fingers curling into fists as she took in the sight before her. The arena sprawled beneath them, a vast pit of golden sand stained dark from previous battles. The torches lining the upper rim crackled and hissed, their flames flickering with an unnatural life of their own, casting long, wavering shadows across the stands. The crowd, demons of every shape and size, and creatures she didn't recognize, bellowed and shrieked, their voices melding into a discordant hymn of bloodlust and hunger.

She could feel Lucifer's presence looming nearby, his throne an obsidian monolith above her. He leaned back, one arm draped over the carved serpent head of the chair, his expression unreadable. He said nothing, only tilting his chin slightly as if daring her to turn away.

Amber swallowed hard but remained standing. She wouldn't cower, not now.

A metallic groan echoed through the coliseum as the iron gates below rattled open.

The first battle had begun.

Two Bellatores strode into the pit, their heavy footfalls kicking up the sand. Both were monstrous in stature, their skin slick with sweat and the promise of violence. The first, a beast of a man with gnarled, bark-like flesh, brandished twin axes, the blades etched with sigils that pulsed faintly in the torchlight. His opponent, leaner but no less formidable, wielded a jagged sword as dark as the void, its edges glinting wickedly.

A horn sounded a deep, bone-shaking note that signaled the start.

They clashed like titans.

Amber sucked in a sharp breath as the axe-wielder struck first, his weapons whistling through the air in an arc meant to cleave flesh from bone. The swordsman dodged, rolling beneath the blow and retaliating with a sharp upward slash. His blade bit deep into his opponent's side, but instead of blood, a thick, tar-like substance oozed from the wound.

The more enormous warrior bellowed, more enraged than injured. He swung wildly, his axe embedding into the ground as the swordsman danced out of reach. The fight continued, relentless and brutal. Sand turned to mud beneath them as they tore into each other with reckless abandon, their growls and grunts swallowed by the roaring crowd.

Amber's heart pounded. She had seen violence before, but never like this. Never this raw, this primal.

The duel ended in a crescendo of savagery. The swordsman, bloodied and gasping, managed a final, desperate thrust, his blade plunging deep into his enemy's throat. For a breathless moment, the massive warrior staggered, choking on his own blackened lifeblood. Then, with a sickening *crack*, his body crumpled.

The crowd erupted in cheers as the victor ripped his sword free, lifting it in triumph.

Amber exhaled, her limbs taut with tension.

"Impressed?"

She turned sharply at Lucifer's voice. He hadn't moved, though amusement lingered at the edge of his smirk. He had spoken into her mind.

She didn't answer. She wasn't sure she could.

But there was no time to dwell because the second match was beginning.

The ground rumbled as the iron gates groaned open once more. A new figure stepped into the pit.

Amber's breath hitched.

The demon was unlike any she'd seen before.

His skin was a deep, brilliant, shimmering blue, like the depths of the ocean. His form was lean but impossibly strong. His features were sharp and almost ethereal, his piercing white eyes glowing like stars against the darkness of his skin. His hands flexed at his sides, fingers crackling with raw, untamed power as the air around him grew inexplicably colder. The temperature in the arena seemed to drop as he moved, a frosty chill creeping across the sand in his wake.

His opponent, however, was no mere warrior.

From the opposite gate, a beast emerged, a hulking, grotesque creature with too many limbs and jagged tusks protruding from its maw. Its body was stitched together like an abomination, thick slabs of muscle coiling beneath mangled flesh. Its eyes burned a furious crimson, and a gurgling roar reverberated through the coliseum when it opened its mouth.

Amber's stomach twisted.

The horn sounded again and the blue demon didn't hesitate.

He was in motion instantly, moving with a speed that defied logic. His feet barely touched the ground as he darted around the beast, dodging a massive claw that nearly tore the sand apart. Then, with a flick of his wrist, a flurry of snow erupted from his palm, swirling in a chaotic whirlwind that momentarily obscured the creature's vision.

The air around the blue demon shimmered with frost that crept across the arena's edges, making the atmosphere feel like winter had descended in Hell. The ground beneath him froze with each step, ice crystals forming on the sand where his boots had passed.

The beast roared in fury, swiping wildly with its claws, but the blue demon was untouchable. He conjured a spear of jagged ice from thin air, hurling it with deadly precision toward the creature's throat. It sank into the beast's flesh with a sickening crack, but the monster wasn't finished yet.

The creature howled, its body convulsing, but instead of retreating, it surged forward, now more enraged than ever. It swung its massive arms with reckless abandon, smashing the ice spear from its throat, shards scattering into the air like poisonous glass.

The blue demon remained unfazed, his form almost ethereal in the swirling snow that followed him. With a flick of his fingers, a thick, icy wall shot up between them, cutting off the creature's advance. The beast charged again, but the ice shield held firm.

Then, with a guttural cry, the blue demon raised both hands to the sky, as if calling down judgment. The temperature plummeted instantly, and the air itself seemed to freeze. Snow began to swirl around him, gathering into a blizzard that filled the arena. The beast's movements slowed as its massive limbs froze, encased in a thick layer of ice. With a final roar, the creature tried to move, but its body had been completely immobilized, encased in an icy prison.

The blue demon stepped forward, unhurried, and with a single motion, slammed his fist into the frozen chest of the beast. The ice shattered, and with it, the creature toppled. The beast crumpled into the sand, lifeless.

Silence fell over the coliseum.

Then, the crowd *exploded* in praise.

Amber watched, chest heaving, as the demon stood victorious. Frost still lingered in the air around him, his breath visible in the cold that had spread through the arena. He looked down at the fallen beast, then back to the crowd, his icy demeanor unwavering.

Lucifer leaned forward slightly on his throne, his fingers steepled together. "Now *that*," he mused, "is power."

Amber barely heard him.

Because in that moment, watching the warrior stand victorious, she realized something.

She wasn't ready.

But she would be.

Because one day, it'd be *her* standing in that pit.

And she refused to be the one left bleeding in the sand.

19

The Fire Within

The crowd was still cheering as Lucifer climbed to his feet. He lifted a hand, and a thunderclap echoed throughout the Anulum Pugnatum. The entire structure fell silent, and everyone sank to one knee. Amber looked around, confused for a moment before she turned to face Lucifer and realized what was happening.

He didn't look at her, didn't even acknowledge her presence as he spoke, "Spectaculum finit. Redeat unusquisque ad operandum. Solus qui ad disciplinam attinent vel adsunt mundare possunt manere, secus exitus. Nunc."

The language was foreign but there was something almost familiar about it that clug to Ambers mind wrapping around her memories like buried treasure waiting for its key. The crowd bowed as Lucifer descended from his throne. He didn't glance in her direction, his posture regal as ever, his eyes fixed forward. The Bellatores who had fought and the demons who had waited remained kneeling in reverence until he moved past them.

Amber felt the weight of the moment pressing in on her. Even if she didn't fully understand the words, the power behind them was undeniable. It was as if the air itself trembled in response to his command.

The moment he reached her, Lucifer turned and motioned for her to follow, the cold command in his movements leaving no room for hesitation.

Without a word, Amber fell into step behind him, the oppressive silence of the arena thick around them. As they made their way toward the exit, Lucifer's steps were measured as if he had nothing to prove, as if the entire coliseum had bent to his will with the mere gesture of his hand.

And it had.

The chariot was waiting for them just outside the gates. A large, obsidian vehicle gleamed in the dying light of the day, the same infernal chariot that had brought them here. Amber stepped into it first, following Lucifer's sharp gesture. She took her place without question, feeling the cold weight of his silence press on her as they ascended.

They rode in silence for a moment, then Amber spoke, unable to contain her curiosity, "What did you say back there?"

Lucifer laughed, the sound deep and amused. "That was Latin, my dear. Something you'll need to learn if you plan to speak to your subjects."

"But Latin is a dead language."

He laughed a little louder this time, motioning to the world they flew over. "We're in the world of the dead, are we not?"

Amber felt her cheeks turn a crimson red. "What did you say to them?"

Lucifer's gaze shifted back to her, his eyes glinting with amusement, but there was something more beneath the surface, something calculating. "I merely told them that the show was over and that unless they were cleaning or training, they needed to return to their duties."

"And what about the demons that died?"

Lucifer's lips curved into a slow, deliberate smile, his eyes glinting with an almost wicked amusement. "Ahhh, that is a great question. Since everyone in the Underworld is already dead, one cannot die twice."

Amber frowned, "I don't understand. I saw the demon get cut. I saw him die."

Lucifer shook his head slowly, a faint, almost pitying smile curling on his lips. "I guess in a way he sort of did, yes. But 'death' here is different. Death is just the end of one form, not the end of the soul. His body will patch up the injured sections within a few days, and he'll be as good as new. If the Sororibus Anima decides to visit him, which they might, if they deem his injuries brutal enough, he'll heal even faster." He gave her a sidelong glance, eyes narrowing slightly. "It's a strange kind of immortality here. You can feel the pain, experience it, even die, but it doesn't last."

Amber shivered at the thought, her mind racing. "So, you can't really die. You just... keep coming back?"

"Precisely," Lucifer said, his voice low, almost contemplative. "We don't decay. We don't fade. We return. Again and again." His eyes drifted toward the horizon, something ancient flickering in their depths. "Not because we're punished. Because we are."

He looked back at her, the faintest shadow of a smile tugging at his mouth. "To be born of Hell is to belong to it. Death has no claim on us."

The weight of his words settled over Amber like a dark cloud. The horror of it was impossible to ignore. "And you... you control all of this?"

Lucifer's eyes flicked back to her, his smile returning, but this time, it was sharper, more knowing. "I do."

They fell into silence after his words, and the rest of the journey was swift. Soon, the coliseum's sprawling inferno and the crowd's distant roar faded into the blackened horizon. Amber could only focus on the slight chill in the air, the weight of her thoughts, and Lucifer's unwavering presence beside her. The silence between them wasn't uncomfortable but rather heavy with meaning.

When they finally reached the cave, the chariot slowed to a halt. The cavernous opening loomed ahead, dark and mysterious, like the mouth of some great beast waiting to swallow her whole.

Lucifer offered his hand to her as he stepped out of the chariot. "You will remain here tonight," he said simply, his voice devoid of warmth. He didn't wait for her response before climbing back in and motioning for the chariot to rise again.

Amber watched him go, the silence returning as she stepped down onto the cold stone of the cave's floor. The wind howled faintly outside, but it was the only sound now. The battle, the blood, the warriors, all felt distant.

She had watched true power in the coliseum today. She had seen what it meant to stand before an audience and command respect. And though she wasn't there yet, Amber knew this was only the beginning of her own journey, to prove herself, and to become that warrior.

She had no intention of staying in the shadows forever.

20

Wings of Ruin

S he knew that Lucifer had told her there was no need for her to rest, but she still felt exhausted, and eventually, the aching reminder of how good sleep felt won out.

Amber had no idea how long she remained in her cave but she awoke to the chattering of something clicking and running around her. She sat up abruptly, her senses on high alert as she looked around frantically for the source of the noise. A flash of color, deep brown like mud, whizzed by before disappearing into the shadows. Another followed, then another.

Her heart raced, and she froze in place, scanning the dark corners of the room. Then, she noticed the piercing yellow eyes that gleamed from the depths of the darkness, watching her closely.

Liberi, she thought to herself, a small chuckle escaping her lips despite her nervousness.

Cautiously, she climbed down from the bed she had been resting on, her feet meeting the cold stone floor. She settled cross-legged, her posture calm, even though her mind raced. "It's okay," she said softly, stretching her hand out toward the shadows. "I won't hurt you. I just want to see you. Come out from the shadows."

They can't understand me, she thought, but still, she spoke with her most soothing voice, trying to coax them out.

Slowly, one creature stepped forward into the dull light that illuminated only inches past her bed. It was small, brown, and stocky. Its arms were far too long for its body, and its face had a massive overbite that would've been almost cute if its teeth weren't as sharp as a shark's. Amber shuddered involuntarily. The creature recoiled, retreating back into the darkness.

"No, no, wait!" she called, extending her hand as though to beckon it back. "I'm sorry. Come back!" But it was no use; the creatures were already gone, swallowed once again by the shadows.

"They can't understand you, you know," a voice floated towards her from the dark. She thought the only person who could speak to her in this place was Lucifer, but this wasn't his voice. It was higher-pitched, airy, almost musical.

It was female.

Amber's eyes widened, and her hands began to tremble. "Who said that?"

"They've been told not to hurt you, but they're excited," the voice continued, this time a little closer. "It's a training day for them too."

"Who... who's there?" Amber asked, her voice quivering slightly.

Then, out of the shadows, a figure stepped forward. The woman who emerged seemed to glow faintly, pale as if she were made of mist. Her piercing blue eyes locked with Amber's, and her white hair cascaded past her shoulders, flowing like a waterfall down her back. Her limbs were long and thin, moving with a fluid grace.

As the woman drew closer, Amber noticed a dark contrast against her otherwise ethereal appearance. From her back, tattered black wings stretched out, jagged and worn. They starkly contradicted the delicate beauty of the rest of her form.

"My name is Abelia," the woman said, her voice light and melodic. "I'm here to serve you, be your guide, or anything else you might need here."

Amber stood frozen, speechless, staring at the woman in disbelief. Finally, after what felt like an eternity, she shook her head, forcing herself to speak. "But you... you have wings."

Abelia's soft, melodic laugh echoed through the cave, but it was far from comforting. It was a sound that carried an unsettling finality, as though the bell she resembled had already tolled for Amber in some distant past.

"Yes, I do. I'm Angelus Mortis, the Angel of Death." The angel laughed.

Amber's eyes widened as she took in the strange, bittersweet beauty of the woman before her. Her mind raced with questions, but all she could do was stare. The Angel of Death wasn't something you read about in stories; she was something you feared.

Amber's chest tightened. The Angel of Death. The words weighed on her like lead. The woman before her, so serene and poised despite the darkness around her, made it hard to reconcile the truth. How could this ethereal, otherworldly being be the bringer of death? Yet everything about Abelia screamed power, control, and a sense of quiet inevitability.

Amber could only stare, her mind unable to find words. She had always heard of death, stories of a shadow, a figure with a scythe, but she had never imagined it'd look like this. Abelia was no haunting specter; she was real, tangible, and impossible to ignore.

Abelia's icy-blue eyes lingered on Amber with an unsettling intensity, like she could see through every facade Amber had ever built. Her voice came again, smooth and soothing but carrying a weight that made Amber's heart tense.

"You have questions," Abelia said, a hint of knowing in her tone. "I can see it in your eyes."

Amber swallowed, trying to shake the dizzying swirl of thoughts that gripped her mind. The Angel of Death. She had never considered the possibility that death might have a name, a face, a presence. A being who could speak to her so casually, who was the darkness she now found herself surrounded by.

"Why are you here?" Amber's voice trembled, her nerves straining with uncertainty.

Abelia's lips curled slightly, her smile both gentle and chilling. "Because, Amber, you've been chosen. Lucifer believes you have a place here, a purpose that you can only discover if you are prepared. And for that, you will need guidance."

Amber blinked, taken aback. She felt she should've understood something here but was lost, floating in a sea of confusion. "Guidance for what?"

Abelia's gaze deepened, the weight of her eyes holding Amber captive as if they were both privy to some ancient secret. "Training, Amber. The Underworld is not a place for the unprepared. You will be tested, over and over, until there is nothing left but your will to survive." Her voice dropped, her words low and solemn as if she were speaking of a fate inevitable and harsh. "But you won't be alone in this journey. Not entirely."

Before Amber could ask further questions, the air around them shifted. A sudden presence approached. Emerging from the shadows, like creatures born of the Underworld itself, were dark angels, each one more imposing than the last. They were tall, their figures barely visible in the dim light, save for their eyes' eerie, dim glow. The air turned colder as they moved forward, their tattered wings brushing against the walls with a sound that made Amber shudder.

Abelia stepped back, her posture suddenly regal, her wings folding behind her in a graceful arc. "These are the ones who will guide you. They are my crew. My fallen. The Angelus Lapsus are bound here for reasons known only to them. Together, we create the Angeli Tenebrarum, The Angels of Darkness." She motioned to one of the taller figures. "This is Cadeyrn. He is the one you will be working most closely with."

The Fallen Angel named Cadeyrn stepped forward, his wings black as the void, jagged and broken, almost as if the very act of falling had torn him apart. His golden eyes fixed on Amber, assessing, calculating. "I've seen your kind come and go," he said, his voice a low rumble, barely more than a growl. "Most don't survive long in Hell. But we'll see if you're worth the effort."

Amber's heart raced. Her mouth went dry as she tried to focus on him, to understand what was happening. But all she could feel was the heavy weight of the Underworld pressing in on her, the eyes of these angels, these creatures, bearing down on her as though she were already their prey.

Abelia's voice rang through the tension. "Do not mistake their harsh words for cruelty. The training here is necessary. You must learn to wield power and understand your place in this world."

The Fallen Angels moved, their wings brushing the stone walls as they led her through a narrow corridor branching from the cave. Amber followed silently, her mind still spinning from what she'd seen.

The tunnel widened. Then opened.

And suddenly, the world dropped away.

Before them lay a battlefield that was vast, cracked, and scorched, the bones of old wars embedded in the stone. It stretched endlessly, as though Hell itself had carved out this place to test its children. The air was hot, humming with the charge of imminent violence, and the silence carried the weight of a thousand past screams.

Abelia turned to Amber, her wings brushing the stone as she moved. "Welcome to Disciplina Regio. This is where you will begin and learn what it means to fight here. And where you will decide who you truly are." She paused, letting the weight of her words settle. "But know this, everything you do here matters. Everything will either lead you to power... or to oblivion."

Amber swallowed hard, but something stirred deep within her. A fire she hadn't known she possessed.

Abelia gave her one last look, almost as if waiting for something, before turning to the other Fallen Angels. "Get her started. I will return later to ensure her progress."

Amber was left standing at the edge of the arena, the stares of the Fallen Angels heavy on her. The silence that followed was deafening. She could hear the faint echo of her heartbeat, the rumbling of her thoughts.

The training would begin now. And in this place, there was no turning back.

21

Lessons in Flame

"Follow me," Cadeyrn said, his voice cutting through Amber's spiraling thoughts. "I'll take you to where you will begin."

Amber nodded slowly, hesitating only a moment before following the Fallen Angel. As they exited the cave, Cadeyrn's figure glowed faintly in the darkness, like a ghost, leading her deeper into the Underworld.

They walked through winding, narrow corridors that seemed to stretch endlessly. The air was thick with the scent of damp earth and the faintest trace of burning incense, and the further they went, the more Amber felt like she was stepping into the heart of this forsaken realm. She had no idea what awaited her, but the oppressive weight of the Underworld pressed down on her as if every step was an irreversible choice.

Eventually, they reached the entrance to the large open space, that was more of a cavern than a room. Amber's eyes widened at the sight. In the center, a group of figures stood waiting, the rest of the Fallen Angels, who hadn't walked with her and Cadeyrn; they must have flown.

Only then, when they were standing in the open air outside of the cave, she realized how massive the Fallen were. They towered above mortal men, wings warped and skeletal in places, the remnants of feathers clinging like charred silk, their eyes aglow with something unholy. They were their own form of warriors, the ones who had been cast down from grace and now fought for their place in this world.

Cadeyrn stepped into the cavern and gestured to the angels, "These are your trainers, Amber," he said, his voice carrying through the cavern. "They will teach you how to survive, how to fight, how to command the power that runs through you." His eyes hardened, and Amber could feel the weight of his gaze. "You will need it."

Amber's pulse quickened. She had been through much since arriving, but this was different. The Fallen Angels had been here longer. They knew the ways of this place, and they knew what it took to survive. She could sense their power, and the thought of training with them made her stomach twist with anticipation and fear.

Cadeyrn stepped aside, motioning for Amber to move forward. "It's time to begin," he said, his voice echoing in the cavern. As Amber stepped into the center of the training area, the gravity of her new reality settled over her like a second skin. This was her new life now; whether she was ready or not, she'd have to fight her way through it. If she was lucky, she'd survive long enough to learn what it meant to live here.

Amber took a steadying breath. The air thick with heat, and the scent of sulfur and scorched earth filled her lungs. Around her, the Fallen Angels watched in silence, their unreadable expressions making it impossible to tell if they expected her to fail or succeed.

Cadeyrn stood before her, his presence imposing, his golden eyes sharp as he observed her. "We will start simple," he said, rolling his shoulders, the bones of his massive black wings shifting against the air. "You must learn to move before you learn to fight. Balance, endurance, and control. Without them, you won't last a day here."

Amber clenched her fists. "Fine. What do I have to do?"

Cadeyrn's lips curled slightly, something between amusement and a challenge. He turned, motioning toward a jagged rock formation in the distance. "Run," he said simply. "To the peak of that cliff and back."

Amber frowned, glancing up at the looming rock face. It wasn't a far distance, but it looked steep, crumbling, and dangerously unstable. "That's it?" she asked, in mock skepticism.

"Do not mistake simplicity for ease," Cadeyrn warned. "You are in Hell. Everything here is designed to break you."

She swallowed hard and nodded. Fine. Run. How hard could that be?

With a sharp inhale, she took off.

The ground beneath her feet was rough and cracked, shifting unpredictably as she moved. Loose rocks threatened to trip her up, and with every step, the heat seemed to intensify, making her legs feel heavier than they should. By the time she reached the base of the cliff, her muscles were burning.

Amber pressed on, digging her fingers into the jagged stone as she climbed. It was like the cliff was alive, resisting her ascent, the stone crumbling beneath her grasp, forcing her to fight for every inch. Her heart pounded, sweat dripped down her back, and her breathing turned ragged.

This is nothing, she told herself. I can do this.

Halfway up, her grip slipped. Her stomach lurched as she lost her footing, barely catching herself before tumbling back down. She gritted her teeth. Hell no.

When she finally pulled herself over the peak, her limbs trembled with exertion. She took only a second to breathe before turning and starting the descent.

Going down was somehow worse. The incline was treacherous, the rocks sharp enough to slice through her palms. She skidded several times, barely managing to keep control as she forced her aching legs to move.

By the time she made it back to the starting point, she collapsed to her knees, her lungs burning.

Cadeyrn stood over her, arms crossed. "Not bad," he said, though there was no genuine praise in his tone. "But you are slow. Weak."

Amber clenched her jaw. "I..." she sucked in a breath, pushing herself up. "I did it."

"Barely." He turned to the other Fallen Angels. "Again."

Amber's stomach dropped. "What?"

"Again," Cadeyrn repeated, unbothered by the exhaustion apparent on her face. "Until you are faster. Until you are stronger. Until the ground beneath you is nothing but dust."

Amber wanted to argue, to tell him this was impossible. But then she saw how the others were watching her, judging her.

She wouldn't be weak.

As she turned back toward the cliff, a thought surfaced, Lucifer's smooth and taunting voice whispering in the back of her mind: "There is no need for you to rest, my dear. There is no breath to catch, no exhaustion to weigh you down. You are beyond such mortal limitations now. If you feel it, it is only because you believe you should."

Her steps faltered for half a second. Was that true? Was all of this, her burning lungs, the ache in her legs, just in her head?

She clenched her jaw and forced herself forward, pushing past the pain, past the illusion of fatigue.

And she ran.

Amber forced her legs to move, digging her heels into the rocky terrain as she sprinted forward. The incline was brutal, the jagged stones shifting differently beneath her weight, but she didn't stop. Wouldn't stop.

Her muscles screamed in protest, and her chest heaved as if she were gasping for breath, but then Lucifer's words whispered through her mind again: "No breath to catch. No exhaustion to weigh you down. If you feel it, it is only because you believe you should."

She faltered for only a moment, frustration bubbling beneath her skin. Then why did it feel so real?

Her lungs burned. Her legs ached. But did they?

Amber sucked in a breath and listened. Listened to her body, to the way her heart should be hammering against her ribs, but it wasn't. The sharp sting of exertion in her limbs never deepened. The pain never worsened. It didn't build like it should have.

She ran harder, faster, pushing herself until she should've collapsed, but she didn't.

Her feet barely skimmed the loose stone as she drove herself upward faster than before. The heaviness in her limbs was a lie. The burning in her chest was an illusion. She wasn't weak.

She reached the top of the mountain in a rush of movement, skidding to a halt. The wind howled around her, whipping her hair across her face, but she was steady. Her chest wasn't heaving. Her heart wasn't hammering. The exhaustion she had felt before? Gone.

Lucifer had been right.

Amber swallowed, staring down at her own hands, flexing them as she tested this new, terrifying truth. She'd been fighting against nothing but herself.

As Amber made her way back to where the Angelus Lapsus stood, she came to a halt before Cadeyrn. His arms were crossed over his chest, his expression unreadable. The other Fallen Angels had stopped their own training to watch, their eyes flicking between Amber and Cadeyrn as she approached.

For a long moment, he said nothing. He just looked at her, really looked at her. Not with pity. Not with amusement. But with something sharper. Something weighing, measuring.

Then, finally, he smirked, "You fought yourself harder than you fought the mountain."

Amber's jaw tightened, but she held his gaze. She wouldn't let him see that his words had struck something deep inside her.

Cadeyrn stepped closer, tilting his head as if studying an unfamiliar creature. "You think you're bound by the rules of the living, but you're not. Not anymore. You're learning slowly, but you're learning."

22

Through Shifting Ground

Amber nodded, steeling her nerves in front of her trainer, "We'll continue strength and conditioning training in a bit, but now that you've come to terms with the fact that you're not bound to the rules of the Overworld, it's time to understand the terrain," Cadeyrn said, his voice cold but instructive. He gestured to the uneven, cracked earth. "This place is alive in a way, constantly shifting. No battle is ever the same here. You must learn to move with it, not against it."

Amber nodded and stepped forward, feeling the ground tremble slightly beneath her feet as if the earth was testing her balance. The cracks in the ground widened and closed with every shift she made, forcing her to focus on her footing.

Cadeyrn watched her closely. "Good. Now, concentrate. You need to stay aware but not tense. Fight the ground, and it'll devour you."

She shook out her hands and continued forward, trying to keep her steps light. The ground seemed to respond to her, and the shifts became less erratic as she concentrated. After a few moments, Cadeyrn nodded, seemingly satisfied.

The echo of Cadeyrn's voice hadn't even faded before the ground heaved beneath her feet. The cracked earth split apart without warning, forcing her to leap backward as a gaping chasm opened where she had just stood. A blast of searing heat rose from the depths, like the breath of some unseen beast lurking below.

"Lesson two," Cadeyrn called out from the sidelines, his voice even. "Hell is never still. If you hesitate, you die."

The ground moved again before Amber could so much as draw a breath. The heat vanished in an instant, replaced by an icy gust so bitter that frost formed on the jagged stones around her. The sudden shock of cold bit into her skin, but she felt no numbness, no true discomfort. Her body wasn't reacting the way it once had.

She didn't have time to dwell on it, before the ground beneath her feet tilted violently to the side, throwing her off balance. She stumbled, barely staying upright as the stone became sand, shifting like an ocean tide beneath her.

Amber gritted her teeth. Hell was trying to shake her loose.

She tried to steady herself, planting her feet, but the sand was already turning to slick, wet stone beneath her boots. Water rushed up from nowhere, flooding the landscape in seconds. Her footing disappeared entirely as the current dragged at her, pulling her under.

She thrashed for the surface, her instincts screaming at her to panic, but she wasn't drowning.

Amber froze. She was under water, but her body felt... normal. No burning in her lungs, no desperate need to gasp for air.

Lucifer's words echoed in her mind: "You're not bound to the rules of the Overworld."

That meant no exhaustion. No suffocation. No drowning.

The realization clicked into place like a key in a lock.

With a growl of frustration, she stopped struggling. Instead of fighting the water, she pushed off the riverbed, using the current's momentum to propel herself forward. Just as she breached the surface, the water vanished, leaving her gasping on dry, cracked stone.

Amber rolled onto her hands and knees, blinking at the sudden change. She had just been beneath a river, but now... now she was in the middle of a desert. The air wavered with intense heat, the sun beating down from a sky that had no right to be there.

She looked up at Cadeyrn, standing unmoved in the distance, arms crossed.

"Better," he said, his sharp eyes assessing her. "You stopped thinking like a human. But you're still too slow."

Amber forced herself to her feet. Her body should've been aching, shaking, but it wasn't. No exhaustion. No pain.

Her lips curled into a smirk. She could work with that.

"Again," she said.

The ground trembled in response.

***

Days Passed. Maybe Weeks. Time Had No Meaning Here.

Amber had lost count of how many times she had run that course. How many times she had fallen, fought the earth, and cursed the Fallen Angels for their endless, merciless training.

Her body should've been sore all over. Every inch of her should've ached, but it didn't. Her throat wasn't raw from breathing in the thick, hot air.

She was learning, getting better, becoming stronger. She could feel it. Her body was adapting, healing faster, moving sharper.

Learning the terrain and building endurance were only the first steps.

The real pain began when Cadeyrn placed a blade in her hands.

It was heavier than she expected, the hilt rough in her grip. She adjusted her hold, looking up at him warily. "And now?"

"Now," Cadeyrn said, a cruel smirk forming, "we teach you how to yield a sword. Androkles, step forward."

From the row of Angelus Lapsus, a muscular angel came towards Amber and Cadeyrn. He was a towering presence, his broad shoulders and muscular frame making him look more like a warrior sculpted from stone than a Fallen Angel. His skin was a deep bronze, weathered by centuries of battle and covered in faint scars that told stories of wars long past. His face was hard, carved with deep lines that made him appear both ageless and ancient.

His jaw was strong, his nose bent just off-center, not from a single break but the memory of many. As if, over time, his body stopped bothering to heal it right. His dark brown eyes were sharp, always watching, always calculating, with a depth that spoke of a time before the fall.

His black hair was cropped short and streaked with silver at the temples. His massive, tattered wings were once the purest white but had darkened over time, their feathers now a mottled mix of gray and shadowy black.

Androkles radiated discipline and power, a soldier through and through. But there was something else beneath the hardened exterior, a wisdom, a patience that made him more than just a brute with a blade.

He studied Amber for a long moment, then sighed, shaking his head. "You hold it like a frightened child," he muttered, stepping behind her.

Before she could protest, his large hands closed over hers, adjusting her grip on the hilt. His touch was rough and calloused. He'd wielded a sword for centuries, and it showed.

"Too tight, and you'll tire your hands." He loosened her fingers slightly. "Too loose, and you'll drop it in battle."

Amber nodded, swallowing her pride. This was different from any training she'd done before.

"First, your stance," Androkles said. He kicked her right foot outward, forcing her to widen her stance. "You stand like a human, but you're no longer bound by human weaknesses. Keep your feet planted, but always be ready to move."

She adjusted, grounding herself.

Androkles nodded approvingly. "Now, control." He lifted his own blade, demonstrating a simple movement. A slash, precise, controlled, not wild.

Amber copied him, swinging her sword. The weight threw her off, her balance shifting too far to one side.

"Again."

She tried.

"Again."

She swung.

"Again, slower."

Androkles guided her through the movement, adjusting her posture, her grip, and how she followed through.

The hours blurred together, each strike, each correction slowly molding her into something sharper, deadlier.

At one point, she realized she wasn't tired. She'd been swinging this sword for what felt like forever, yet her muscles didn't ache. She didn't gasp for breath.

Lucifer had been right. She was more than she'd been before.

Cadeyrn watched from the sidelines, arms crossed. "You learn quickly," he observed. "Good. Because this was the easy part."

Amber exhaled, rolling her shoulders. The sword no longer felt foreign in her hands.

Androkles smirked. "Tomorrow, we will teach you how to kill with it."

23

Blades Between Allies

The following day, the air in the training grounds was thick with an unnatural stillness. It was as if the very atmosphere knew what was coming. The ground beneath Amber's feet felt more unstable today, the cracks in the earth seeming to widen as though the world itself was bracing for what Cadeyrn had promised.

Amber stood tall, her hand gripping the hilt of her sword. Her muscles had grown from the relentless days of conditioning, and there was a sense of strength around her. The blade was now an extension of her arm, fluid in her grasp, not a clumsy tool.

Androkles stood before her, eyes focused and intense. Yesterday's smile had faded into something far more serious, almost cold.

"Today," he said, his voice low and steady, "you learn how to kill. Not just how to defend yourself. Not just how to fight." He took a step forward, the sound of his boots barely making a sound against the earth. "A true warrior isn't defined by the number of battles they've fought. It's the number of lives they've taken."

Amber's pulse quickened, but she stood firm, meeting his gaze.

Cadeyrn, standing off to the side, spoke up. "You will be taught to fight without hesitation, without mercy. And you'll learn the difference between killing for survival and killing for dominance. Only one of those will serve you here."

Amber barely had time to register his words before Androkles lunged.

She barely dodged the first strike, the rush of air from his swing brushing past her cheek. Her heart jumped into her throat. She tried to step back, but he was relentless, striking again; this time, she managed to block, but the force of the impact nearly knocked the sword from her hands.

"Pathetic," Androkles growled. He struck again, faster.

Amber grit her teeth and swung, aiming to deflect, but he parried easily, twisting his blade and knocking her weapon from her grasp.

She didn't have time to react before he swept her legs out from under her.

Amber hit the ground hard, feeling like the breath had been knocked from her lungs. She gasped, eyes widening as Androkles' blade hovered just above her throat.

He sneered. "You're dead."

Amber clenched her jaw, frustration burning in her chest. "I...I didn't..."

"Didn't what?" Cadeyrn mocked from the side. "Didn't think we would go easy on you?"

Amber pushed herself up, rage bubbling beneath her exhaustion. "Again."

Androkles raised a brow, intrigued. "Oh? You have a death wish, human?"

Amber snatched her sword from the ground, adjusting her grip. Her arms shook, her head screaming not to, but she refused to give in. "Again."

Androkles' smirk deepened.

The fight resumed.

And this time, she refused to fall so easily.

Androkles moved, his speed faster than she could've expected. With a quick strike, he aimed at Amber's midsection. She didn't think just let her instincts push her sword up to block the blow, feeling the impact vibrate through her arms.

"Good," Androkles said. "But blocking isn't enough. You're not just defending. You're taking. Control the fight."

He stepped back, giving her space to breathe. His eyes never left her, his stance predatory. The tension in the air was palpable as Amber adjusted her grip. The sword felt heavier now, the weight of what she was learning pressing down on her.

Cadeyrn's voice rang out, steady and commanding. "Killing isn't just about strength. It's about precision. And purpose. Every strike must be calculated. You can't afford to be sloppy."

Androkles moved again, his blade coming for her neck. Amber instinctively stepped back, but she did more than avoid the attack this time. She twisted the sword, deflecting his strike with a sharp motion that sent a jolt through her body.

"Better," Androkles muttered, eyes narrowing. "You're getting the hang of it. But now, you must strike."

Amber hesitated. Her instincts screamed at her to hold back. This isn't me. This isn't who I am. But she had to push past that.

She lunged, her sword aimed at his chest. But Androkles was ready. He sidestepped, grabbing and twisting her wrist, forcing her to drop the sword.

The sound of her blade hitting the ground was a stark reminder of how far she still had to go.

"Again," he said, his voice cold. He stepped back, giving her space to regain her footing.

Amber picked up the sword, her breath coming faster now. The training was fighting her too, but there was no room for weakness, not here. Not with him.

She adjusted her stance, her feet planted firmly in the shifting ground. She could do this. She had to.

And so, again, she lunged. This time, the strike was faster and more controlled. Androkles didn't step aside; he met her head-on, his sword coming for hers in a brutal clash.

"Better," he said again, his voice thick with approval. "But you're still holding back."

Amber's heart pounded in her chest. *Don't hold back.* She had to kill. She had to stop thinking of it as training and see it for what it was. She couldn't afford mercy.

She attacked again, this time with everything she had.

***

Days bled into weeks, the weight of the training growing heavier with each passing hour. Amber's skin was scraped and bruised from countless encounters with the Fallen Angels. Each fight, each lesson, each relentless strike was an assault on both her body and her mind. But she endured. The environment, the sword, the tactics, all of it was becoming second nature to her. The fluidity of battle had settled within her as if her body understood the dance of war before her mind did.

The Angelus Lapsus were relentless. They were never gentle, never letting up. They didn't hold back like she realized Androkles had done. Each had their own fighting style, from brutal strikes to lightning-fast counters. Every engagement tested Amber's limits. There were moments when she thought she might collapse, when her arms screamed for relief when her mind screamed for respite. But then she remembered that she was more than the mortal she used to be, and the aching ceased. She wouldn't stop. Not now. Not after everything she'd learned.

Every fall was a lesson, and every bruise was a reminder that she was still "alive." The soreness didn't matter; it was in her head. The exhaustion didn't matter; it was a figment of her imagination. What mattered was that she was growing stronger with every battle.

Then, one day, Amber wasn't sure how much time had passed; Cadeyrn stopped her mid-fight, his sharp eyes scanning her from head to toe. He was silent for a long moment, his arms crossed over his chest as he looked her over with that same calculating gaze.

She held herself upright, sword in hand, waiting for his command. Her body felt tired, but she knew it wasn't really.

After what felt like an eternity, Cadeyrn spoke. "You've earned it," he said, his tone curt and cold. "It's time."

Amber's eyes narrowed, unsure of what he meant, "Time for what?" she asked, her voice hoarse but steady.

"The demons," he said, a hint of something like approval in his voice. "You've learned to fight, to survive, and now you need to face something different entirely. It's time you learn how to deal with them."

Amber felt her heart skip a beat. She had been fighting the Angelus Lapsus to prepare, but she had never fought the Liberi before. They swarm like pests, each one a small beast in its own right.

Cadeyrn's voice broke through her thoughts. "Don't think of them as smaller or weaker. Think of them as fast, vicious, and deadly in their own ways. The ones you face now are far from helpless. They are quick. Relentless. You'll need everything you've learned to survive them. Remember, they're in training too. They're learning to kill just like you." He motioned for her to follow him. "Come. You've earned this fight."

They walked away from the shifting, treacherous terrain to a different part of the Disciplina Regio. The ground here was flat, with various rock formations scattered across the landscape, providing obstacles and hiding spots. The air felt heavier, thick with anticipation.

Cadeyrn glanced at Amber, his gaze steely. "These demons are fast. They won't fight with honor. They won't fight with pride. They fight to kill. No rules. No mercy. They'll attack you in packs."

Amber gripped her sword tighter, feeling the weight of what Cadeyrn was saying. Demons were different from Fallen Angels, less controlled and less predictable.

"Are you ready?" he asked.

Amber nodded, her heart pounding in her chest. The sword felt heavier in her hands than ever before, but she didn't let the fear show.

From the far side of the clearing, the Liberi tensed, their bodies vibrating with barely contained energy, ready to act.

"I said," Cadeyrn's voice was steady, commanding, "Are you ready?"

Amber met his eyes, her gaze hardening. "I'm ready."

With a sharp nod from Cadeyrn, the gates at the far end of the Disciplina Regio opened.

The fight had begun.

24

The Whispering Flame

Cadeyrn raised an eyebrow and shouted from where he hovered above her, his massive wings beating soundlessly. "Fear won't serve you here. You'll need to trust your instincts, make them sharper."

At first, she saw only shadows shifting across the field. Then they emerged.

Four Liberi crawled from the darkness at the far end of the arena, their bodies hunched and twitching with anticipation. They were twisted, grotesque versions of the smaller ones she'd glimpsed in passing, barely the size of children but unmistakably demonic. Their eyes glowed like embers, and their limbs moved with unsettling, animalistic coordination. Clawed hands scraped along the stone, jaws snapping in rhythmic bursts like they could already taste her blood.

Amber had no time to breathe before they descended.

Two launched at her without warning, blurs of violence. She blocked the first, her sword catching the blow just in time. The impact jolted her to the bone. She barely turned in time to avoid the second, which grazed her arm and ripped a shallow tear in her skin. Pain flared hot and fast, but she bit it down.

They circled.

The third flanked her left. The fourth disappeared into the rocks.

Cadeyrn's voice echoed above. "They'll play with you first. Don't let them."

The second Liberi lunged again. Amber ducked low, spinning beneath its claws, and drove her blade upward, but the steel barely cut its hide. Furious but unharmed, the creature shrieked and leaped away, regrouping with the others.

She pivoted, heart hammering. Her breath came ragged. She could feel the sting of blood trickling down her side, her pulse roaring in her ears.

Then, the hidden one struck.

It burst from the rocks behind her, claws raking across her back, slicing through her armor like paper. She screamed and dropped to one knee, vision swimming. Another Liberi charged from the front, slamming her flat onto the ground.

"Get up," Cadeyrn barked. His tone was colder now, with no sympathy in it. "This is Hell, Amber. There's no mercy here. Fight, or be torn apart."

Amber gasped, sucking in air laced with sulfur and pain. Her fingers curled into the dirt, but she forced herself upright.

The Liberi came again, fast, all four at once. But something shifted. Her pain sharpened her focus, and her fear morphed into fury.

The first one lunged, and she pivoted hard, letting its momentum carry it past her. She spun with it, driving her sword deep into its spine. It shrieked and crumbled into ash.

The second creature hesitated after seeing the first, too slow. She turned on it, kicking out its leg and plunging her blade through its throat. Another burst of dust.

The third slashed at her, grazing her cheek, but she ducked low and rolled. As it turned, she was already swinging, this time aiming for the soft, unprotected flesh beneath its jaw. The sword found purchase. Another body fell.

The last Liberi, the one that had ambushed her, came at her with a scream, but she was ready. Amber dropped low, sidestepped its charge, and, in a single fluid motion, severed its head. The creature dissolved before it hit the ground.

Silence.

Amber stood alone in the center of the field, trembling, her blade dripping, her breath ragged, but she was alive.

Cadeyrn descended slowly, the wind from his wings rustling the ash around them. His face betrayed nothing, but his voice held weight.

"You've survived your first real fight," he said. "But this is only the beginning. You'll need to be stronger. Faster. More ruthless."

Amber didn't respond. She just nodded, her chest rising and falling as blood trickled down her ribs, but there was a new fire behind her eyes.

"Yes, Cadeyrn, this is all true," an airy voice floated around them as Amber watched Abelia beat her mighty wings and descend into the arena. All of the Angelus Lapsus bowed as their leader came to rest before Amber.

Abelia's pale, translucent skin glowed faintly under the dim, ever-changing sky of the Underworld. Her eyes, those piercing blue orbs, locked onto Amber as she descended. The black and tattered wings on her back tucked neatly behind her back, the air around her shimmering with an otherworldly energy.

"I've been watching," Abelia said, her voice soft yet commanding. "I must admit, I'm impressed."

Amber wiped the sweat from her brow, still panting. "Impressed?"

Abelia nodded. "You've fought well, much better than I expected for someone so new. You've adapted to the harsh environment, handled the demons, and fought without hesitation." Her gaze softened. "You're more than just a survivor. You're a warrior in the making."

Amber stood tall, trying to steady her breath, though excitement coursed through her. "What does that mean? What's next?"

Abelia smiled with a calm and enigmatic expression. "Next, it's time for you to fight in Anulum Pugnatum. The real trials. The demons there will challenge you in ways you can't imagine. But I think you're ready. Anulum Pugnatum is where those who prove themselves worthy go to test their skills." Her smile faded slightly as she added, "If you survive."

Amber's heart raced. The Coliseum was where only the strongest, the fiercest, fought for survival.

"I'll be ready," Amber said, determination in her voice, though she wasn't entirely sure what she was about to face.

Abelia gave a satisfied nod. "I'll be watching, as always. We'll see just how far you're willing to go. For now, rest. The Angelus Lapsus and I will make the necessary preparations."

With that, the Angel of Death turned and walked away, vanishing seamlessly into the shadows.

Amber watched her leave, the weight of Abelia's words settling heavily on her shoulders. She wasn't sure whether she was truly ready for what came next, but she had no choice. The only way was forward.

With a steadying breath, she began the walk back toward the cave, her sword still clutched in her hand. The rush of battle was fading, leaving behind the ghost of exhaustion, not physical, but something deeper, something pressing against her very being.

From the darkness, Abelia lingered, her gaze following Amber as she disappeared into the distance.

The air around her shifted and thickened. A silent but undeniable presence emerged from the void. She didn't flinch as the figure came to her side.

Lucifer.

He stood there, watching Amber's retreating form, his expression unreadable, his presence effortlessly commanding the space between them.

"She's done well," he murmured, his voice rolling like distant thunder.

Abelia remained silent for a moment, her lips curving slightly as she finally spoke. "Yes. She has."

Abelia tilted her head slightly, studying Lucifer's expression. His gaze was fixed on Amber, sharp yet contemplative. He wasn't a creature prone to sentiment nor one to lavish praise without reason. Yet, there was something in the way he watched her, a quiet fascination, an unspoken acknowledgment.

"She's unlike the others," Abelia mused, crossing her arms. "Most would have broken by now. You and I both know that."

Lucifer's lips twitched, not quite a smirk, but close. "Most do break. And yet, she refuses."

"She's not just surviving," Abelia continued. "She's adapting. Learning. There's a fire in her, something raw and unyielding." She glanced at Lucifer from the corner of her eye. "Reminds me of someone else I once knew."

Lucifer finally turned his head, leveling Abelia with a knowing look. "Tread carefully, Angelus Mortis," he warned, though his words had no actual bite.

Abelia smirked. "I only mean that she's proving herself in ways none of us expected. Even you."

Lucifer's jaw tightened, but he didn't deny it. Instead, his gaze flickered back to Amber's retreating form. He'd expected resistance, defiance, perhaps even rebellion. But not this. Not how she threw herself into his world, how she fought, not just for survival, but for understanding.

"She'll fight in Anulum Pugnatum soon," Abelia said after a pause. "The others are eager to see what she's truly capable of."

Lucifer didn't answer immediately. He watched as Amber disappeared into the darkness, her figure swallowed by the winding path back to her cave.

"Let them watch," he murmured at last. "They'll see soon enough."

Abelia chuckled, a knowing gleam in her eyes. "And what about you? What will you see, I wonder?"

Lucifer didn't answer. He simply turned and vanished into the shadows, leaving Abelia alone with the ghost of a smile playing on her lips.

25

Ash Before the Flame

Amber had started to adjust to the cycles of the day. There was no actual sunrise or sunset, no moon or stars to mark the passing of time, yet she could still sense the shift between day and night. The ever-changing skies deepened into rich purples, blues, browns, and blacks when night fell, while the daytime brought a muted brightness.

A peculiar stillness settled over the land at night, except for the skies. That was when they came alive.

Winged creatures took to the air, their flapping wings echoing through the darkness, punctuated by the screeches of ancient birds. One night, Amber found herself outside her cave, watching as they soared, swooped, and dove through the vast expanse above.

No two wings were identical, but she could tell there were separate aerial creature groups.

Some glided effortlessly, feathered wings spreading wide, needing only a few powerful beats to stay aloft. Others flapped hard and fast, working tirelessly against unseen currents. There were smaller creatures with leathery, bat-like wings, their silhouettes darting between the larger ones. And then there were those whose wings defied description, twisting and shifting in ways that didn't seem possible.

The aerial display was mesmerizing.

As Amber watched, she noticed some of the creatures soaring so high that they vanished into the abyss above. Yet, she never saw them return.

The thought lingered in her mind the following day as she set out for a jog. The land remained as harsh and unpredictable as ever, but she'd grown more vigorous, more attuned to Hell's shifting terrain.

Then, as she ran, a presence descended before her.

An Angelus Lapsus she'd never met before.

"Today's the day!" The Angelus Lapsus announced as Amber skidded to a halt just feet from her. The creature practically vibrated with excitement.

Confused, Amber frowned. "The day for what?"

"For your fight, of course!" The angel laughed, eyes gleaming. "My name's Zosime! I'm here to take you to the Anulum Pugnatum!" She bounced on her heels, barely containing her enthusiasm. "I'm so excited! Everyone is going to be there!"

Amber's stomach twisted. "*Everyone?*"

"Of course, silly! No one wants to miss this! Cives are even placing bets!"

"Bets?" Amber's frown deepened. "What kind of bets?"

"I'll tell you all about it on the way! Now, come on, take my hand so we can go!"

Zosime stretched out her hand, and after only a moment's hesitation, Amber took it. The moment their fingers locked, Zosime gave two powerful beats of her wings, and they soared into the air.

Zosime picked up where she left off as soon as they leveled out. "The Cives Inferni, the citizens of Hell, or Cives as we call ourselves, are betting on how long it'll take the beast to take you down. Some say minutes, others up to an hour. But not all the betting is bad! There are a few who've bet that you'll actually survive!"

Amber's grip on Zosime's hand tightened.

"Not that you really have to worry about that," Zosime added breezily. "I mean, you can't die twice. Worst case scenario, you'll fall apart and eventually be put back together again! No big deal!"

Amber's stomach twisted at Zosime's casual tone. "What do you mean, put back together?"

Zosime grinned as if Amber had asked about the weather. "Oh, you know, reformed! If you get torn apart too badly, the Operarios will collect the pieces, and you'll be stitched back up. Well,... not literally stitched. More like... restored. It takes time, though. Some Equis have taken weeks, months, and even years to come back after a bad fight."

Amber hesitated. "And that... works for everyone?"

"Of course. We're born in this place. It's in our bones." Zosime gave her a sideways glance. "You, though... I don't know how it works for you. You weren't made here. You had to die to enter."

The words sank in, slow and heavy.

"I guess if you fall apart, they'll try to put you back together," Zosime went on, tone still too light. "But you might not come back the same. Or at all. Maybe it depends on the Devil."

Amber looked down at her hands. At her scars. At the flesh that no longer bruised like it once did.

Maybe it wasn't that she couldn't die twice. Perhaps it was that if she did... she wouldn't return as herself.

Amber swallowed hard. "And what happens if I win?"

Zosime laughed delightedly, twisting them both in mid-air as they soared over the jagged, shifting terrain below. "Then you'll really have their attention! Fights in the Anulum Pugnatum aren't just about survival, Amber. They're about proving your place here. If you win, you won't just be another soul trying to find her footing. You'll be a contender."

Amber processed that in silence. She'd already fought the Liberi and had already endured grueling training under Cadeyrn and the Angeli Tenebrarum. But this was different. This wasn't training. This was a test.

Her free hand clenched into a fist. She'd win. She had to.

Zosime gave her a side glance and smirked. "You're thinking about it, aren't you? Good. Keep that fire."

They descended sharply, the wind tearing through Amber's hair as Zosime angled them toward the massive structure looming ahead. The Anulum Pugnatum was just as magnificent as she remembered. Its obsidian and brimstone walls jutted out of the ground like broken glass. Strange runes glowed faintly along the archways, flickering between deep crimson and molten gold. The closer they got, the louder the noise became, a dull roar of anticipation, of hunger.

Zosime brought them down near a massive iron gate set into the side of the Coliseum. This was no grand entrance, no fanfare, no torches lining the way. This was completely different from where she'd entered with Lucifer. This was the Bellatores' entrance. A place for fighters to step into the pit without the spectacle of the main doors.

Amber barely had time to steady herself before Zosime clapped a hand on her shoulder. "This is it," she said, her excitement undiminished. "This is where you prove what you're made of."

Amber exhaled slowly, staring at the looming gate. The metal was old, scarred with claw marks and dents from battles fought long before her.

She squared her shoulders, "Let's do this."

Zosime smiled and took to the sky again, and two Eques opened the cast iron gate for Amber. Hesitantly, she stepped inside, and immediately, an Eque, armored in iron and bone, grabbed her arm and pulled her toward a side passage, downward, into the underbelly of the Coliseum.

The underground tunnels were a world of their own, a labyrinth of dimly lit corridors reeking of blood and damp stone. Chains rattled in the distance, and the air was thick with the scent of metal and suffering. Bellatores, some human-looking, others monstrous, moved in the shadows, stretching, sharpening weapons, psyching themselves up for the bloodshed above.

Amber's boots scuffed against the uneven floor as she was led into a chamber with thick wooden bars separating the fighters from the arena. This was the Tenens Cellulam, the holding place for those awaiting their turn.

The ground was stained dark with old blood, and the ceiling dripped condensation from the heat above. The sounds of battle filtered through the narrow openings, grunts of pain, the sickening crunch of bone, and the crowd's roar as another body hit the dirt.

She forced herself to step forward, gripping the bars to peer through.

Two Bellatores were already engaged in brutal combat. Two warriors, clad in nothing but tattered cloth and leather armor, circled each other in the pit. Their movements were sharp and calculated, one wielding a jagged dagger, the other a curved blade. The crowd screamed for blood, their voices merging into one primal entity, demanding entertainment.

The man with the curved blade lunged, slicing across his opponent's shoulder. A burst of crimson painted the sand, but the injured Bellator didn't fall. Instead, he grinned a wicked, blood-streaked smile and drove his dagger into the other's side.

Amber's breath hitched.

The wounded fighter dropped to his knees, gasping as the dagger was twisted deeper. A final, guttural scream tore through the air before his body collapsed into the dust.

The crowd erupted in victory. The victor raised his blood-soaked blade, basking in their applause.

Then, without ceremony, an Operario stepped forward and dragged the body away, leaving only a fresh stain on the ground. The fight was over.

Amber's heart pounded.

She wasn't just a spectator. She was a contestant.

Suddenly, a face appeared before her, clicking in some ancient tongue she couldn't understand. Amber recoiled, pressing herself into the opposite corner of the Tenens Cellulam as fear coursed through her veins. The creature, a hunched, skeletal demon with hollowed-out eyes, unlocked the cell and stepped inside.

Her breath hitched, but then she saw the tattered rags draped over its wiry frame; an Operario.

She exhaled in relief, only for it to shift in a blur of movement.

Before she could react, before she could even scream, the athletic clothes she'd been wearing were ripped from her body and discarded in a pile. She gasped, covering herself instinctively, but the creature was already retreating, leaving behind the garments it had carried. With a final, sharp click of its teeth, it scurried back into the corridor, slamming the cell door shut behind it.

Amber swallowed hard and looked down at what had been thrown at her.

The armor was nothing like the heavy, cumbersome plate she'd seen in history books. This was something far older, something out of ancient warfare. She picked up the first piece: a bronze cuirass molded to fit the torso, with intricate engravings of serpents winding along the metal. It was light in her hands but sturdy, built not for protection but for mobility.

Next, a simple linen chiton, sleeveless and dyed a deep crimson, meant to be worn beneath the armor. The fabric was rough against her skin as she pulled it over her head, its hem ending just above her knees. The Operario also had left pteruges and a skirt of leather strips reinforced with small bronze studs.

She fastened the cuirass over the chiton, securing the straps at her shoulders, then bent down to pick up the greaves. They were solid bronze, shaped to fit her legs perfectly, running from her knees to her ankles. She strapped them on, wincing as the cold metal pressed against her skin.

The last piece was a pair of leather bracers, each laced tightly along her arms' underside. There was no helmet, no shield, just her body and the armor built for war.

Amber clenched her fists.

She was dressed as a warrior.

And soon, she'd have to fight like one.

26

The Matchstick Queen

The air in the underground chamber was thick with sweat, blood, and the acrid sting of burning torches. The walls, carved from dark obsidian, seemed to drink in the dim light, their jagged surfaces slick with condensation. The Tenens Cellulam was a labyrinth of holding cells, some empty, others occupied by fighters waiting for their turn in the pit above. Low murmurs and distant screams echoed through the tunnels, a cacophony of suffering and anticipation.

Amber stood stiffly in her cell, adjusting the leather straps of her pteruges as her breathing steadied. The weight of the cuirass on her chest was unfamiliar, the cold metal pressing against her skin like a second spine.

Then came the roar.

It rumbled from above like thunder rolling across the heavens, only this wasn't the sound of nature's fury. This was the bloodlust of an audience demanding carnage.

Amber turned sharply as a grated door at the far end of the corridor slid open with a groan. Two Bellators stumbled inside from the arena above. Their bodies were slick with sweat and streaked with deep gashes. One collapsed against the wall, his breaths coming in ragged gasps. The other stood victorious, chest heaving as he wiped his blade clean on his opponent's torn chiton.

A tall demon overseer, draped in crimson, barked something in that same ancient tongue Amber had heard earlier. The defeated warrior was seized by two Operarios and dragged away, leaving a crimson smear along the stone floor. The victor simply laughed, his sharpened teeth gleaming in the flickering torchlight.

Amber swallowed, her fingers twitching at her sides.

Then, the overseer turned to *her*.

The moment stretched, thick with expectation. Then, in one swift movement, he lifted a hand and pointed.

Her cell door was unlatched with a deafening *clang*.

Amber's pulse spiked.

This was it.

The Eques gestured for her to move. She took a shaky breath and stepped forward, her sandals slapping against the damp stone floor as they led her up a winding staircase. Each step brought her closer to the deafening roar above.

Then, all at once, she was blinded.

Amber stumbled as the bright, golden light of the torches lining the arena hit her like a slap to the face. The heat was immediate, pressing down on her like a physical force. Sand crunched beneath her feet as she stepped fully into the pit.

The Coliseum was massive, more enormous than she'd realized now that she was standing in the pit. The stands, carved into the natural rock, were packed with demons and Angelus Lapsus of every kind, their clawed hands, and twisted faces alight with a hunger for the spectacle. Massive banners of black and crimson hung from the high walls, bearing the sigil of Lucifer himself, the same black crown dissolving into streams of flowing shadow. At its heart lay a seven-pointed star. Amber shuddered at the sight. She'd seen the sigil at the gates to the castle, and just like there, the crowns on the banners were encircled in Latin. She could now understand: *The light does not shine in the darkness. The shadow reigns forever.*

And there, above it all, sat the King of Hell.

Lucifer lounged atop a raised obsidian throne, his posture lazy but his eyes sharp. One hand rested on the armrest, fingers drumming against the stone. The other cradled a goblet filled with a dark liquid. He looked at her, not with amusement this time, but with something more profound. Something she couldn't name.

Amber barely had time to process it before the opposite gate *slammed* open.

She saw its eyes first. All six of them, burning red like fresh-spilled blood.

The beast was a nightmare-given form, a towering, grotesque amalgamation of muscle, sinew, and jagged bone. Amber looked up at the creature that stood nearly fifteen feet tall. Its body was covered in a thick, obsidian-black hide, cracked in places to reveal molten veins that pulsed like liquid fire. Its hulking frame was supported by four powerful limbs, each ending in razor-sharp claws that gouged deep scars into the stone beneath it with every step.

Its head was a monstrous fusion of predator and demon, with a gaping maw filled with layered rows of jagged teeth dripping with thick, acidic saliva that hissed as it touched the ground. Twin horns curved like a ram's but lined with serrated edges, jutted from its skull, glowing faintly as if smoldering from within.

Each eye roved independently in its sockets, scanning the arena with a hunger that was more than just instinct; it was malice, a deep, insatiable rage. Its breath was thick and sulfurous, pouring from its nostrils in hot gusts, filling the air with the stench of decay and fire.

Every movement was accompanied by grinding bones and snapping sinew as if the very act of existing was an agonizing yet unstoppable force. When it roared, the ground trembled, a deep sound that seemed to reverberate through the soul's marrow, a promise of destruction and death.

This was no mere creature.

Amber's breath hitched as the crowd fell into an expectant hush.

Then, the horn sounded, and the beast lunged.

Amber moved on instinct alone, reaction chasing awareness by mere heartbeats as its claw came crashing toward her skull. She threw herself to the side, rolling across the hot sand as the talon struck the ground with a sickening *crack*. The impact sent grains of sand flying into the air, the force rattling her bones.

She scrambled to her feet, heart hammering.

The monster released a sound eerily similar to laughter, deep and guttural. It lifted its limb and swung again, but this time, she was ready.

Amber ducked, stepping inside its reach before driving her sword into its ribcage. It was like hitting a brick wall, but the force sent it staggering back a step.

The crowd roared in approval.

Lucifer remained still.

Amber clenched her fists.

She *wouldn't* die here.

Her opponent recovered quickly, its lips pulling back into a grin-like look.

He charged again.

And this time, Amber met him head-on.

A dark, clawed limb shot toward her, swiping for her throat. Amber threw herself backward, dodging it by mere inches. The creature steadied itself, its eyes locked onto her with a hunger she didn't understand.

Amber's breath came fast, but she forced herself to focus. The ground was moving beneath her, the air thick with heat, as she realized this thing, whatever it was, was hunting her.

The creature lunged again, and Amber moved. She sidestepped at the last second, letting it stumble forward, and when its balance faltered, she struck. Her sword connected with its neck, but instead of shattering like she expected, the thing barely reacted.

Amber swore under her breath. *If I can't hurt it, how the hell am I supposed to beat it?*

The beast let out a guttural growl, more amused than pained. The slight wound she'd inflicted sealed almost instantly, the molten veins beneath its hide glowing brighter as if feeding off the attack. Amber tightened her grip on the sword, her mind racing. It was healing too fast; it was too strong, too monstrous. She couldn't overpower it.

Think.

The ground trembled beneath her feet as the beast lunged again, faster than something its size should've been able to move. Amber barely managed to twist out of the way, rolling across the cracked earth before pushing herself up. She could feel the weight of the entire Coliseum watching, hundreds, maybe thousands of eyes on her.

Some waiting for her to die.

Some waiting for her to surprise them.

She wouldn't die here.

The beast charged again, its claws carving deep trenches into the stone as it moved. But this time, Amber didn't run. She dropped low at the last second, letting it pass over her, its massive claws raking just above her head. As it landed, she saw her chance.

Its legs.

The thick, armored hide covered most of its body, but the joints, where the molten glow pulsed brightest, were softer and more vulnerable. She had to disable its ability to move.

Gritting her teeth, Amber sprinted toward the beast as it turned, its many eyes flickering with something almost like curiosity. She wasn't running. She was attacking.

She brought the blade down at the back of its knee with all her strength. This time, the sword bit deep. The beast roared in pain, staggering as dark, molten blood sprayed from the wound, sizzling against the stone.

Amber didn't hesitate. She struck again, this time at the other leg. The beast collapsed onto its front knees, its balance thrown.

The crowd erupted into a frenzy, shouting, cheers, and laughter mixing in a chaotic roar.

Amber barely heard it.

She had it down. Now, she just needed to finish it.

But as she lifted her sword for the final blow, the beast's lips curled back again, not in pain, but in something far worse.

Amusement.

Before she could react, its tail, thick and lined with jagged bone, swung around and slammed into her side.

The impact sent her flying.

She hit the ground hard, rolling across the stone until she stopped near the arena's edge. Phantom pain exploded through her body, but before she could even catch her breath, the beast was already rising, molten blood dripping from its wounds, its gaze locked onto her.

Still standing.

Still smiling.

It was healing.

Amber coughed, pushing herself to her feet, ignoring the taste of blood in her mouth.

She wasn't done.

Amber wiped the blood from her mouth, forcing her mind to push out pain. *It isn't real. I can do this. I have to do this.*

The beast moved toward her, slower now, its molten wounds dripping as it stepped. But the amusement in its many eyes remained as if it still believed it'd win.

Not today.

Amber tightened her grip on her sword and ran straight at it. The beast roared, swiping at her, but she ducked under its claws, sliding beneath its body. With a fierce cry, she slashed at the back of its knees again, this time severing the tendons completely.

The beast howled, its body crashing down onto all fours.

Amber didn't hesitate. She climbed onto its back, using the ridges of its spine for leverage. The beast bucked wildly, trying to throw her off, but she held on, raising her sword high.

Then she *stabbed*.

The blade plunged into the first eye, bursting in a thick, dark fluid spray. The beast shrieked, its entire body convulsing in agony. Amber yanked the sword free and struck again, destroying each of its glowing eyes until nothing remained but empty, scorched sockets.

The monster howled, its massive body thrashing blindly. It couldn't see.

Now, to finish it.

Amber leaped off its back, landing on unsteady feet. The beast was furious, snapping its dripping fangs at the air, its acidic saliva sizzling as it hit the ground.

Her mind raced. The molten veins, its life force. The acidic saliva is its weapon.

She had to turn them *against* it.

Amber lunged forward and drove her sword deep into its molten wound, the heat of its blood making the blade glow red-hot. She pulled it free, the metal now scorching, hissing with power.

Then, before the beast could react, she spun and plunged the blade into its gaping mouth.

The sword passed through the acidic saliva, coating it in a burning, hissing layer of corrosive liquid. The metal didn't break; it became deadlier.

Amber took one last steadying breath.

She ran toward the beast's head, dodging blindly swiping claws, and leaped onto its snout. With both hands, she lifted the molten, acid-coated sword high and *drove* it down between its two great horns straight into the soft spot of its skull.

The beast let out a shuddering cry as the blade sank deep, the combined heat and acid burning through flesh and bone alike.

The creature shrieked, a horrible, echoing sound, and then, with a final, heaving breath, it went still.

The arena fell into silence.

Amber stood there, panting, her hands still gripping the hilt of her sword, buried to the hilt in the beast's skull.

And then, the crowd *erupted.*

Cheers, shouts, and roars of excitement thundered through the Coliseum, shaking the ground beneath her feet.

She'd won.

She'd survived.

Amber stepped back, pulling her sword free, her arms trembling. She could feel the weight of countless eyes upon her as she looked up at the towering stands.

Some watching in awe.

Some were in disbelief.

And one, in the highest shadows of the Anulum Pugnatum, was watching with something else entirely.

27

A Door Left Open

Amber had barely stepped out of the arena before hands clapped her back, and voices called out her name.

"Unbelievable," one demon muttered, shaking his head in amazement.

"You fought like a true Bellator," another nodded approvingly.

A third, a Fallen Angel with jagged, broken wings, smirked. "Didn't think you'd last, but you proved me wrong."

She accepted the accolades with quiet nods, still in shock herself. The fight had left her covered in sweat and grime, her clothes torn and stained with the beast's blood. But there was something else beneath the exhaustion. A spark of something dangerous, something *alive*.

Zosime appeared, beaming, and practically dragged Amber away from the lingering crowd. "Come on, let's get you cleaned up. You *reek*."

Amber rolled her eyes but didn't argue.

***

When she stepped inside, the bathhouse was quiet. Most fighters celebrated their victories in the feasting halls, drinking and boasting about their conquests, but Amber preferred the solitude.

She stripped down and lowered herself into the heated water, wincing as the warmth seeped into her muscles that ached with forgotten pain. She closed her eyes, exhaling slowly.

She'd expected pain. Soreness. Maybe even the creeping tendrils of fear.

But instead... she felt *powerful*.

She'd faced the beast and won.

The thought sent a strange shiver through her. A blooming awareness, half pride, half something else.

She reached for the soap, scrubbing the dried blood from her skin. Steam curled around her as she leaned back, tension melting away, muscles loose, thoughts soft.

"You fight like someone who's finally beginning to understand what she is."

Her hand froze.

The voice came from the room's far end, smooth, deep, unmistakable.

She didn't turn right away, but her voice was more sultry than she intended. "You always spy on the ones who bleed for you?"

A pause. "Only the ones worth watching."

Amber turned slowly, water rippling around her. Lucifer stood in the archway, shrouded in shadow, eyes gleaming like molten gold through the steam. There was something dangerous in his gaze, but it wasn't hunger. Not quite.

She didn't cover herself. Didn't shrink. She just met his gaze.

And something passed between them, unspoken and electric.

He stepped forward slowly. Not toward her, not exactly. Just closer.

"Does it feel real yet?" he asked.

Her voice was quiet but steady. "More than I expected."

He tilted his head, studying her like a riddle he wasn't sure he wanted to solve.

"I see it in you," he said. "The change."

Amber let the silence stretch.

Then she said, "Is that what you wanted?"

Lucifer's lips curled almost imperceptibly.

"I wanted you to survive," he said. "But this? This is something else."

His gaze dipped for a moment, just long enough for her to notice. It lingered a heartbeat too long before he forced his attention back to her face.

Amber raised an eyebrow, the corner of her mouth tugging up. "If you're going to stare," she said, "you could at least be useful."

Lucifer didn't move.

"Hand me a towel?" she offered sweetly, tilting her head.

There was a flicker in his expression, something unreadable. Then, without a word, he crossed to the wall, took a towel from the hook, and held it out.

Amber stood, rising from the water with unhurried grace, droplets cascading down her bare skin. She took the towel from his hand without breaking eye contact, then wrapped it around herself in one fluid motion.

Lucifer didn't speak.

He didn't need to.

His silence said enough, but she saw his jaw tick just slightly.

After a moment, he spoke again, his voice smooth and unreadable. "Collect your things. It's been four months. I think it's time."

Amber frowned, turning fully toward him. "Time for what?"

Lucifer met her gaze, his expression impassive. "Your move to Castellum Umbrae."

They stood in silence, the words hanging between them. Amber's heartbeat picked up, though she wasn't sure if it was from excitement, dread, or something in between.

Castellum Umbrae.

Another step deeper into his world.

"Amber! Where are you?" A sing-song voice rang out behind her, breaking the tension.

She turned, catching sight of Zosime emerging from the corridor, her wings fluttering with impatience.

"I'll be right there!" Amber called, but when she turned back, Lucifer was gone.

She hadn't heard him leave. Hadn't felt his presence slip away.

He'd simply vanished.

Amber stood there for a moment longer, staring at the empty space where Lucifer had been. The air still carried the faintest trace of him, sulfur and something darker, something that made her stomach twist in ways she refused to name.

She exhaled sharply, forcing herself to move.

By the time she caught up with Zosime, the Angelus Lapsus was practically vibrating with excitement. "Finally!" Zosime grinned. "I thought you were going to ignore me forever. What were you doing back there, staring at nothing?"

Amber shook her head. "Just... thinking. Lucifer was here."

Zosime raised a brow, looping her arm through Amber's, and tugged her forward. "Lucifer? What did he say?"

Amber hesitated, "He... told me to collect my belongings because he wants me to move into Castellum Umbrae."

Zosime stopped walking and turned to face Amber, "What? You're moving to Castellum Umbrae! Do you know what this means?"

Amber hesitated. "That Lucifer wants to keep a closer eye on me?"

Zosime giggled. "Maybe. Or maybe you've impressed him enough to earn a place by his side."

The words hit harder than they should have.

Amber's breath caught, not because she dismissed it, but because some part of her wanted it to be true and be by his side.

The thought was too big, too loud.

"I... I doubt that," she said, but her voice was softer now, not quite convincing.

Zosime hummed, a knowing little sound, but she didn't press. She just beat her wings, and together, the girls took to the sky, though Amber's heart was still tangled somewhere between fear and something dangerously close to hope.

28

Shadows and Intentions

Amber stood at the mouth of the cave, her meager belongings packed into a small satchel. It was strange, leaving this place behind. It had been her harsh, merciless home for months, but it was a home nonetheless. She'd trained here, fought here, bled here. And now, she was being summoned to Castellum Umbrae.

A sleek black chariot awaited her just beyond the rocky outcrop, its dark metal glinting under the dim light of Hell's ever-changing sky. The same beautiful Equus she'd met before bellowed as it pulled up to her. An Operario jumped down from the driver's seat and opened the door for her.

Amber took a steadying breath and climbed inside, nodding briefly at the Eque, who sat in the back.

The ride was smooth, eerily so. She'd expected something rougher, more chaotic, but the chariot glided through the air without so much as a dip. She kept her hands tight around her bag, watching as the desolate cliffs and molten rivers gave way to the looming structure of Castellum Umbrae. It grew larger and larger until it consumed the horizon.

When they arrived, the doors of the chariot opened by waiting Operarios. Amber stepped out cautiously, her boots clicking softly against the black stone. The entrance to Castellum Umbrae stood before her, massive, unwelcoming, and silent.

No sign of Lucifer.

Instead, a young demon stood waiting at the top of the grand staircase. He was shorter than the Angelus Lapsus but still carried the same air of discipline. His dark horns were smaller and less twisted, and he had no wings to call his own.

The young Operario inclined his head respectfully. "You're expected. Follow me."

Amber did as she was told, stepping past the massive doors and into the grand halls of Castellum Umbrae once more. The air was cooler here, the ever-present heat of Hell dampened by the thick stone walls. The floors gleamed beneath her feet, and the distant sound of movement echoed through the corridors.

The Operario led her deeper inside, his pace brisk but not rushed. "Your quarters have been prepared. If you require anything, you may call upon me."

Amber studied him for a moment. "What's your name?"

The demon blinked, clearly not expecting the question. "Therapon."

Amber nodded. "Thank you, Therapon."

He hesitated, uncertain whether he should acknowledge the gratitude, then simply gave a curt nod before opening the doors to her chambers.

Amber took in the room, vast, imposing, and undeniably fit for royalty. The space would've been a dead giveaway if she hadn't known she was in Hell.

The walls were made of dark, polished obsidian, and their surfaces veined with glowing streaks of deep crimson that pulsed like molten lava trapped beneath the glass. The ceiling arched high above, carved with intricate patterns that seemed to shift when she wasn't looking, twisting and curling like living shadows.

The bed was enormous, draped in rich, black velvet with silken sheets that shimmered like liquid midnight. Carved obsidian posts framed it, each etched with ancient runes that pulsed faintly as if imbued with their own magic. The pillows were impossibly soft, stuffed with something lighter than feathers, and the sheer weight of the blankets carried an odd sort of warmth, comforting yet inescapable, like being wrapped in the night itself.

A grand fireplace dominated one side of the room, but instead of flames, it held smoldering embers that radiated a steady heat, casting flickering shadows across the walls. The mantle was adorned with clawed, golden candleholders, their blackened wax dripping onto the stone like hardened blood.

Across from the bed, floor-to-ceiling windows framed the ever-shifting landscape of Hell. The view stretched for miles, showing molten rivers, jagged peaks, and skies that churned with endless violet and crimson storms. The balcony outside was lined with sharp, wrought-iron railings twisted into the shapes of serpents and wings.

An ornate vanity stood to the side, its surface inlaid with dark gemstones that caught the firelight, glinting like captured souls. The mirror above it wasn't quite normal; its reflection shimmered, sometimes showing her face and sometimes flickering with indistinct figures that disappeared when she tried to focus on them.

The wardrobe was a towering piece of gothic artistry, its dark wood carved with depictions of creatures both celestial and damned. When she pulled it open, rich fabrics of deep reds, blacks, and purples hung inside, clothes designed not just for battle but for ruling.

A door led to an adjoining bath chamber, where an obsidian tub rested on a platform of black marble filled with water that emitted wisps of fragrant steam. Strange, delicate flowers, black with veins of silver, floated atop the surface, their scent a mix of spice and something darker, something unknown.

The entire room felt like a paradox: a sanctuary and a cage. Luxurious beyond measure, yet undeniably Hellish. A place designed for a queen but also for someone who was never meant to leave.

Therapon stood at the threshold, silently watching her take it all. "Shall I bring you anything?"

Amber shook her head. "No, this is fine."

He gave another short nod, "Your Domina in Exspectatione, Korinna, will be here in a few hours to dress and collect you for dinner." With that, he turned to leave, the door clicking softly shut behind him.

Amber stood in the center of the room for a long moment, staring at the space around her. She was here. Back in Castellum Umbrae. Back under Lucifer's roof.

And now, whatever came next was entirely out of her hands.

Amber set her bag down on the bed, walked toward the massive windows, and stepped onto the balcony. From this vantage point, Hell looked almost... beautiful. The ever-changing landscape, the flowing rivers of molten rock, and the shifting skies were darkly artistic. Everything moved with purpose, a flawless machine of suffering and order.

A shiver ran down her spine despite the heat. The realization that this was now her home settled deeper in her bones. No matter how grand Castellum Umbrae was, how luxurious her new chambers were, she was still in Hell.

Turning away from the view, she strode back inside, glancing around the room again. As impressive as it was, it felt too vast, too foreign. She knew so little about Castellum Umbrae itself. If she was going to live here, it was time to explore. No one had told her not to, after all.

She approached the door with quiet steps, pausing as her fingers brushed the cool metal handle. A part of her hesitated: Why did she feel like she was sneaking around? If they wanted her to stay put, they'd have told her or locked her in.

Taking a breath, she opened the door and stepped into the corridor.

The hallway stretched endlessly in both directions, lined with flickering sconces that cast eerie shadows along the obsidian walls. The air smelled of old stone and something faintly metallic, like cooled blood. The silence was thick, broken only by the occasional distant echo, footsteps? Voices? It was hard to tell.

Amber chose a random direction and started walking.

The deeper she went, the more Castellum Umbrae revealed itself to her. She passed intricately carved doors, each unique. Some bore clawed marks as if something had tried to get out, and others had symbols she didn't recognize, glowing faintly when she neared them. One hallway was lined with statues of warriors, their expressions frozen in agony. At the same time, another led her past massive windows overlooking the courtyard below, where lesser demons moved about like an army preparing for war.

Eventually, she came to a grand staircase, its steps carved from a single piece of dark marble, polished to a mirror finish. The banisters were twisting metal, shaped like serpents devouring their own tails.

She descended cautiously, her hand trailing along the railing. The air grew warmer, the distant hum of voices growing clearer.

Castellum Umbrae opened into a grand hall at the base of the stairs. Towering columns stretched toward a ceiling lost in shadows, and massive chandeliers hung like cages of twisted iron, holding flickering blue flames instead of candles. The floor was inlaid with intricate patterns, black stone veined with glowing gold, leading toward a massive set of doors at the far end.

Her boots made little sound as she skittered across the grand hall, the smooth stone floors slick underfoot. Castellum Umbrae seemed even larger up close, its high ceilings and winding corridors whispering with the weight of time and secrets. She couldn't help but feel like a small part of something vast and ancient.

She turned a corner at the end of the hall and immediately found herself in a grand library. Shelves of books lined the walls, their spines aged and worn. Amber's fingers brushed over the spines as she walked deeper into the room, the smell of old paper filling her senses. She pulled a few books off the shelves reading their titles: *Ars Bellica* one read, *Saltare Cum Diaboli* read another. Most she couldn't understand the writing lost to her, but others she could, such as *The Hourglass* and *The Iliad*.

As her hand hovered over a shelf, something caught her eye. A thick, leather-bound book. She pulled it from the shelf, and in that instant, a soft clicking noise echoed in the air. Startled, Amber stepped back as the shelf before her shifted, revealing a narrow, hidden passage. The walls of the passage were different from the rest of Castellum Umbrae. This stone wasn't polished; it was rough and raw as if forgotten.

She didn't hesitate.

Immediately, curiosity won out, and she stepped into the passage, the door sliding shut behind her with a soft thud. The space was narrow and claustrophobic, but the voices she'd heard from the other side of Castellum Umbrae suddenly grew clearer, as if there was an opening somewhere. Amber crept forward, careful not to make a sound, lit only by a dull light coming from the end of the passage. Following the glow, she rounded a bend and found a small, hidden room.

Inside, she could hear the murmur of several voices and one of them, she recognized immediately, was Lucifer's. Her breath hitched, but she pressed closer to the crack where the light was coming from, trying to stay out of view. She peered through to the Magna Aula, where some of the most formidable creatures were seated around a table with Lucifer at the head.

"I'm not sure it's wise to push her this quickly," a voice murmured, its tone heavy with caution. It wasn't Lucifer's, but it sounded ancient, one of his higher-ranking demons.

Another voice, sharp and calculating, answered. "She has to be tested. You know the rules."

"And what of her?" the first voice continued, hesitant. "She's... different from the others. She hasn't broken yet. Is it really necessary to push her so hard?"

Amber's heart raced, and she could feel the hall walls closing in, the air thickening with their words. The tension was suffocating.

Lucifer's voice cut through the silence like a blade. "The moment she set foot in Hell, the clock started ticking. She's here for a reason, and she needs to understand that. She needs to learn her place."

A long, tense silence followed, the weight of his words hanging in the air. Then, another voice, colder, more calculating, spoke. "She could be it, Lucifer. She could seal the deal."

Amber's hand instinctively reached out, gripping the stone wall to steady herself. Seal the deal? The words left her confused, a knot forming in her stomach.

Lucifer's voice was colder now, sharper. "It's not that simple, and you know it. She has to want it... all of it."

"But what about you?" A voice, older and more authoritative, cut in above the murmurs. "The rules are clear on your part as well if you plan to fully cement your place."

"That part of the clause is impossible," Lucifer replied, his tone colder still. "It's why God put it there."

Amber ducked instinctively, heart pounding in her throat. But it wasn't her Lucifer was looking at.

His eyes had lifted, sharp and deliberate, scanning the upper arches of the chamber. The torches along the balcony flickered, shadows stretching around him as his gaze swept the darkness. It was like he'd caught a whisper of something as if he *sensed* them.

Syn stilled beside her.

Below them, Lucifer didn't speak. Didn't move. But the tension in his frame coiled tighter, head tilting ever so slightly as if listening to something no one else could hear.

"Then what's the point of her being here?" A young voice, sharp with frustration, demanded, bringing his attention back to the Archdemons surrounding him.

The room seemed to hold its breath, and Amber's pulse quickened. What were they talking about?

"The point," Lucifer nearly spat at the young demon, his voice thick with disdain, "is that people find it much harder to defeat two people in power than one."

Amber's breath caught in her throat. Power? The word reverberated in her mind. She wasn't just a soul here to face trials but a pawn. The very thing Lucifer was trying to control.

Lucifer's voice broke the silence again, this time colder, more resigned. "We're getting ahead of ourselves. Let her explore. She has nothing to lose. But when the time comes, she'll choose. That's the only way."

"But she doesn't know what she's choosing yet," the older voice said, the sharpness of concern threading through it. "She's still... human in ways you don't even understand."

Lucifer didn't respond immediately. Instead, there was a soft rustle as if he was shifting his weight. "Perhaps. But she won't remain that way for long." His voice grew more confident, more forceful. "And if she's to take the throne, she'll need to make a choice. For better or worse, but first, she needs to prove that she's worthy of making such a choice."

Amber's mind raced. Throne? What throne? She barely understood what had been said, but they were clearly discussing her, her role, and the choices she'd have to make.

And just when she thought the conversation would slip into further murkiness, Lucifer's voice pierced the tension again, hard and commanding.

"Don't worry about her yet. Let her learn. Let her grow. She will make her decision in time. And maybe then, that'll be all the cement we need."

The voices fell silent again. Amber took a hesitant step back, but before she could retreat any further, the older voice spoke again, its words sharp with an air of wisdom.

"Your place will never be cemented, my liege, not unless..."

"I know!" Lucifer roared, his voice seething with fury. Amber turned back just in time to see him close his eyes, forcing himself to regain composure. "I am well aware of what the clause says, and I am well aware that it is not possible." He exhaled sharply, his voice lower now, controlled. "We'll just have to hope that *this,* she, is enough. Together, we can be powerful and defeat whoever dares to challenge the throne."

Powerful? Together? Take the throne? Amber's mind reeled at the weight of what she'd just heard. Footsteps echoed from below, signaling the end of the meeting. The conversation had finished, and the oppressive weight of their words lingered in the air, leaving a deafening silence in its wake.

She stood frozen, absorbing what little she'd overheard. "What decision?" she whispered, her thoughts in a frenzy of confusion and fear. She didn't know exactly what they were talking about, but she could feel the gravity of it pressing down on her.

But the thought that someone, *even Lucifer,* might be watching her, waiting for her to choose, unsettled her more than anything. She was more than just a test. She was the key to something bigger. But what was it? And what would she do when the time came to decide?

29

Control, Thread by Thread

The evening in Castellum Umbrae carried a strange stillness. The kind that made Amber feel like the walls were watching her. After what she'd overheard, she couldn't shake the feeling that something was shifting out of her reach.

She sat before the grand vanity in her chambers, having eaten dinner alone in the grand hall. She'd expected Lucifer to show, but he never did. Her Domina in Exspectatione, a quiet but efficient demoness named Korinna, was brushing through her hair. Korinna was one of the few Operarios she'd encountered who seemed genuinely indifferent toward her presence, neither overly excited nor openly hostile. She simply did her duty, speaking only when necessary.

Amber stared at her own reflection, eyes tracing her face, expecting to see the faint marks of exhaustion, but there were none. The past few months had been grueling, but she'd survived. She'd fought, endured, and learned. And yet, she still felt as if she were missing a crucial piece of the puzzle.

Korinna had just begun braiding a section of Amber's hair when the chamber doors swung open without warning.

Lucifer stepped inside.

The temperature in the room seemed to shift immediately, the air thickening under his presence. Korinna's hands froze for only a second before she resumed her task, though Amber noticed her movements had become more careful, more deliberate.

Lucifer's gaze swept over the room before settling on Amber. He was dressed in black, as usual, but his demeanor was different tonight, something unreadable in how he watched her.

"You look troubled," he observed.

Amber forced herself to hold his gaze, refusing to let him see any hesitation. "I didn't realize you made a habit of walking into rooms unannounced."

Lucifer smirked. "I don't make habits, Amber. I make rules."

Korinna tied off the braid and stepped back, lowering her head slightly. She'd yet to speak, but Amber could feel her discomfort.

Lucifer gestured toward the door. "Leave us."

Without hesitation, Korinna bowed slightly before slipping out of the room, leaving Amber alone with him. The door closed with a quiet *click*, and suddenly, the massive space felt too small.

Amber turned fully to face him. "Where were you tonight?"

Lucifer tilted his head, watching her with an expression that bordered on amusement. "Did you miss me?"

Amber scoffed. "Hardly."

He stepped closer, the soft flicker of candlelight casting shadows over his sharp features. The air between them tightened, charged with an unspoken challenge.

She crossed her arms, refusing to let his casual tone distract her. "But, I thought you might show."

He slowly stepped closer, his presence filling the space between them. "Did you want me to?"

Amber rolled her eyes, but the warmth creeping up her neck betrayed her. "You invited me to stay in Castellum Umbrae; the least you could do was have the decency to share a meal."

Lucifer chuckled, a deep, knowing sound. "Decency? In Hell?"

She exhaled sharply through her nose, unwilling to let him bait her. "You avoided me."

"I was busy."

Amber narrowed her eyes. "Doing what?"

Lucifer didn't answer immediately. Instead, he reached for her, fingers grazing the curve of her shoulder before slipping higher. She stiffened as he found the ribbon in her hair, twining it lazily around his fingers.

"I had things to tend to," he murmured, his voice like silk and smoke. "Things that required my attention."

"I don't?" she challenged, her voice steady even as her pulse thrummed loudly.

Lucifer hummed, amused. "Oh, Amber," he whispered, leaning in just enough that she could feel his heat. "You have more of my attention than you realize."

With that, he gave the ribbon in her hair a slow, deliberate tug, undoing it quickly. Her hair cascaded down her back in soft waves, and his fingers brushed through the light strands with a languid sort of indulgence as if he had every right to touch her.

She swallowed hard, refusing to react. "You didn't answer my question."

Lucifer smirked. "No, I didn't."

Amber clenched her jaw, frustrated by his evasiveness, by the way he always seemed to hold all the cards. "You're infuriating."

He lifted a strand of her hair, twirling it lazily between his fingers before letting it slip away. "And yet, you can't look away."

She hated that he was right.

"You look better this way," he murmured, his voice dipped in something dark and indulgent as he tucked a strand of loose hair behind her ear.

Amber swallowed, willing herself to keep steady. "You have a habit of taking things that don't belong to you."

Lucifer chuckled, the sound low and rich. "And yet, you never stop me."

She clenched her jaw. "Maybe I should."

His eyes glinted in the dim light, a silent dare in their depths.

He stepped closer, and she could see the faint curl of amusement on his lips. "You could try," he said.

The air between them crackled, heavy with something unspoken. Amber hated how aware she was of him and how easily he pulled her into his gravity.

Lucifer then pulled his hand away from her, dragging his fingers against her shoulder. When he held up his hand, she realized he held the ribbon Korinna had used to fasten her braid.

He threaded it between his fingers, inspecting it lazily before meeting her gaze again. "Tell me, Amber," he murmured, voice like silk and sin. "Would you rather I take this... or something else?"

The weight of his words settled between them, teasing, testing.

Amber held his gaze, refusing to back down, "Maybe I'd rather take something from you instead."

Lucifer's smirk widened. "Oh?" He leaned in, his breath a whisper against her skin. "Then, by all means... try."

The challenge hung between them, electric. But before Amber could respond, Lucifer stepped back, the stolen ribbon still twined around his fingers.

"Sleep well, Amber," he said, turning toward the door. "You'll need your strength."

Then, as suddenly as he'd come, he was gone.

Amber exhaled, only just realizing she'd been holding her breath. She stared at the door long after it had closed, her pulse a frantic rhythm beneath her skin.

She wasn't sure what game Lucifer was playing.

But she was confident of one thing.

She'd just become a player.

***

Morning came faster than she anticipated. Not that she slept much anyway. She was finding it easier and easier to go long periods of time between resting. Plus, with the noise of the Volaces, there was no way she was getting any shut-eye.

"Domina Amber?" a small voice crept into her subconscious.

Cracking an eye open, Amber searched for the sound of the voice.

Korinna stood near the doorway, hands folded neatly in front of her, waiting patiently. The demoness's expression was unreadable as always, but there was something softer in how she observed Amber, as if she were taking care not to startle her.

"Domina Amber," Korinna repeated, her voice quiet but firm. "It's time to get ready."

Amber groaned, dragging a hand down her face before forcing herself upright.

"For what?" she muttered, stretching out the stiffness in her limbs.

Korinna stepped forward, already reaching for the wardrobe. "It's your first day of school. I was instructed to prepare you."

Amber froze mid-stretch, blinking at Korinna as if she'd misheard. "...*School?*"

Korinna pulled a long, flowing dress from the wardrobe, deep red with delicate gold accents. "Yes," she said simply, laying it across the bed. "Lucifer has arranged for your education to begin immediately."

Amber stared at her, dumbfounded. "I survived Hell's trials, endured months of torment, and now I'm being sent to *school?*"

Korinna didn't react to her sarcasm. "Knowledge is power, Domina Amber. To survive here, you must understand what you are part of."

Amber let out a humorless laugh, shaking her head. "And what exactly am I supposed to be learning?"

Korinna met her gaze, her dark eyes unreadable. "Everything."

Amber's stomach twisted, but she said nothing as she got out of bed, and Korinna began the familiar routine of dressing her.

"Come," Korinna said, fastening the last tie at Amber's back. "It's time."

Amber took one look at herself before straightening her shoulders and following Korinna out of her chambers.

30

Ghosts of the First

Amber followed Korinna through the winding halls of Castellum Umbrae, her steps slow but deliberate. The idea of school in Hell felt absurd, but something told her this would be nothing like the classrooms she'd known in life.

They descended a spiraling staircase, the stone beneath her feet cool despite the ever-present heat of Hell. The deeper they went, the more Castellum Umbrae seemed to change, less grand and regal, more ominous and ancient. The walls pulsed with a strange energy, faint symbols carved into the obsidian surface.

Finally, they reached an arched doorway that led into a vast chamber. Rows of dark wooden desks filled the room, each adorned with strange artifacts, worn books bound in unfamiliar leather, quills that seemed to move independently, and vials of ink that shimmered unnaturally.

A relatively tall, slender Operario stood near the entrance, bowing slightly. "Domina Amber," she greeted, her voice smooth and articulate. "My name is Smeme, and I am honored to be your first teacher of the day."

Amber nodded, eyes flicking over the strange room before landing back on the woman. "First teacher?" she echoed, tilting her head.

Smeme straightened, offering a knowing smile. "Yes. I will be teaching you Latin." She motioned for Amber to enter fully, nodding at Korinna, who turned and left without a word. Now, it was just the two of them.

"While most lessons here are taught in your tongue, so the Libiri can learn to speak it, there will be times when Latin is used, and it is vital that you understand it."

Smeme gestured toward a grand, dark wood table in the center of the room, pulling out a chair for Amber. She waited until Amber took her seat before settling into her own.

Amber leaned slightly forward. "You mean... you teach the Libiri?"

Smeme let out a soft, almost melodic laugh. "Why, of course! They need to learn why Hell works the way it does... and their place within it." She paused, observing Amber's reaction before adding, "They also have to learn the art of torture somewhere, don't they?" A slow, knowing smile played at the edge of her lips.

Amber fought the instinct to tense. It shouldn't have surprised her; everything in Hell had a purpose, and suffering was part of the design, but hearing it said so plainly was unsettling.

Smeme tapped her fingers against the table, breaking the silence. "Shall we begin?"

Amber exhaled, nodding. "Let's get it over with."

Smeme's smile widened, and with a flick of her wrist, a thick book floated from a nearby shelf, landing with a heavy thud in front of Amber. The cover was worn, the pages edged in gold that had long since faded.

"This," Smeme said, tapping the book, "is where we start. Read the first passage."

Amber opened the book, her eyes scanning the words. The Latin script was unfamiliar, but something stirred deep in her mind.

Amber exhaled slowly and focused on the text in front of her. The letters twisted and looped in ways that should've been indecipherable, but as her eyes traced each word, meaning unfolded in her mind as if she'd always known them.

She read aloud, her voice steady, the syllables rolling effortlessly off her tongue.

Smeme stilled.

Amber barely noticed at first, too caught up in the strange sensation of *understanding*. The words weren't foreign; they belonged to her. She *knew* them.

By the time she reached the end of the passage, an eerie silence had settled over the room.

Slowly, Amber looked up. Smeme was staring at her, eyes alight with something between curiosity and... wariness.

"You've never studied Latin before?" the Operario asked, her voice measured.

Amber shook her head. "No."

Smeme tapped her fingers against the tabletop again, considering. "Then how did you read it so perfectly?"

"I don't know," Amber admitted, her brows knitting together. "It just... made sense."

Smeme studied her for a long moment before letting out a low, approving hum. "Interesting."

She waved a hand, and the book turned its own page. "Try another."

Amber hesitated before reading again, and just like before, the words came easily. The more she spoke, the more natural it felt, like she wasn't learning but remembering.

When she finished the second passage, Smeme leaned back in her chair, lips curving into a knowing smile. "It would appear, Domina, that Latin is in your blood."

Amber swallowed. That phrase, *in your blood*, sent an involuntary shiver down her spine.

Smeme stood, closing the book with a decisive thud as Amber nodded, still unsure how to feel about what had just happened.

Smeme's smile remained as she moved toward the door. "You may go. Your next lesson awaits."

Amber pushed herself to her feet, her mind still swirling. She knew she'd always been quick to learn, but this was different. This felt like something had been waiting inside her, dormant, only to wake the moment she was asked to use it.

She entered the corridor, where Korinna was already waiting to escort her to the next lesson.

"Come," Korinna said simply.

Amber followed, but her thoughts remained behind in that room, replaying the moment over and over.

Something was changing.

And she wasn't sure if she was ready for it.

The halls of Castellum Umbrae were eerily quiet as Korinna led Amber toward her next lesson. The air was thick with the weight of everything she'd just learned, her mind still tangled in the language she'd picked up so easily.

Amber hugged her arms to her chest as they walked, her fingers curling slightly against the fabric of her dress. What did that mean for her? Was she special? Had she always known Latin? Why couldn't she understand it when Lucifer spoke it?

Korinna moved with her usual quiet grace, her steps light but purposeful. Amber had learned by now that her lady-in-waiting spoke only when necessary, which left Amber alone with her thoughts far too often.

Castellum Umbrae seemed to shift as they turned a corner, the flickering torchlight casting long, stretching shadows along the cold stone walls. Amber couldn't help but wonder how many had walked these halls before her and how many had tried to understand the enigma that was Lucifer and failed.

Finally, Korinna stopped before another door, this one different from the last. The wood was dark and polished, the handle shaped like the twisting form of a serpent.

"Your next lesson," Korinna said, reaching for the door and pushing it open.

Amber took a steadying breath before stepping inside.

At the front of the room stood a tall, skeletal figure cloaked in deep purple robes. His hollow eyes settled on Amber the moment she entered.

"You're late," the figure rasped.

Amber uncrossed and recrossed her arms. "Didn't realize there was a schedule."

A few of the other students, demons of varying forms, some humanoid, others more monstrous, chuckled at her remark. The instructor, however, didn't seem amused.

"You must learn, Domina Amber," he mockingly emphasized the title, "that time is not yours to waste."

Amber lifted a brow but said nothing as she found an empty seat.

The instructor moved to the front, his skeletal fingers tracing over the surface of an ancient tome. "Now, students, I am Professor Solon, and today, we begin with the history of Hell."

Amber straightened in her seat. Now, this was something she needed to hear.

Solon tightened his posture, his gaze steady and commanding as he began to speak. "To truly understand the workings of this realm, you must understand its past."

He moved toward the blackboard, his fingers gliding swiftly as he scrawled in Latin across it. Amber squinted, recognizing more than she expected.

"Long ago," he said, pointing to the writing, "the world was created by God, and with it, Heaven. It was a time of peace, meant to last for eternity."

A hand shot up from a demon in the audience. "Yes, Pavlos?"

The young demon hesitated before stammering, "Was... was Hell created then, too?"

Solon's lips curled into a slight smile. "Ah, an excellent question, Pavlos." He turned to address the entire class. "You see, God did not anticipate that by granting humanity free will, they would struggle to control their darkest desires. They would be unable to resist temptation."

Amber's fingers curled against the desk. she'd heard of the first sin, of humanity's fall, but never like this.

"The first sin," Solon continued, "was not merely a fall from grace. It was the birth of something much darker. And with it, the first sinner was claimed. Not simply as a lost soul but as the ruler of Hell. Not by choice, but by consequence."

Amber's gaze remained fixed on the professor as he spoke, a mix of intrigue and dread bubbling in her chest.

"The First Devil, Zagan," Solon went on, his tone growing more solemn, "was not born of Hell. He was once one of God's most favored beings. But the moment the first sin was committed, Hell took shape and needed a ruler. It was not a throne given; it was a sentence carried."

Amber's mind raced. This wasn't the story she knew. Hell wasn't simply a place of punishment; it was built from sin itself, its first king an unwilling prisoner. It made her own predicament feel even heavier.

Solon turned back to the blackboard, his writing coming faster now. "Most of you have heard of Magnum Bellum Tenebrarum."

Murmurs of agreement filled the classroom, but Amber remained silent. She could read the words, but they meant nothing to her.

As if sensing her confusion, Solon glanced at her. "For those who do not know," he continued smoothly, "The Great War of Darkness was the devastating conflict in which Lucifer, our current ruler, overthrew the previous king. It was a war not just for power but for the very soul of Hell itself. There were those who sought to maintain the old order, and those who believed in something... different."

Amber's eyes narrowed. She already knew some of Lucifer's story, the rebellion, and his rise to power. But hearing it like this, as part of a larger narrative, felt different.

Solon cast a look over his shoulder, his gaze piercing. "Lucifer did not simply seize the throne. He inherited the weight of every deal, every soul claimed, every contract signed. He became the villain of the story, the one hated by all, and he carried the burden of Hell's eternity on his shoulders. This is why he is the way he is. Why he will never let go. It is not just about power; it's about survival."

Amber leaned forward slightly, her curiosity piqued. "Won't someone try to overthrow him? Like he did to the last Devil?"

Solon smiled, the edges of his lips curling with a knowing gleam. "Ah, now that is where things become even more interesting." He set the chalk down, turning fully to face them. "Hell is not merely a place of torment; it is a place of balance. And there exists a clause, a condition placed upon it by God himself, that could cement a devil's reign forever. But that condition is nearly impossible to fulfill."

A silence fell over the classroom, each student anxious to learn of the clause.

"Unfortunately," Solon continued, his voice almost amused, "the details of this clause remain known only to Lucifer and his most trusted Legatus. You will not find it in any book, nor will any *mere* Cives Inferni ever learn the truth of it."

Amber clenched her jaw.

"All that being said," Solon finished, "Lucifer is a powerful devil. To challenge his rule would be madness, suicide."

The room remained silent. But Amber's mind was anything but.

Then, finally, a voice rang out from somewhere behind her, "If we can't die twice, what happened to the old devil?"

The room fell into a tense silence. Every gaze turned to Professor Solon as he stood still, his fingers tapping thoughtfully against the desk. He seemed to weigh his words carefully before speaking.

"No one truly knows," he admitted at last. "Ask different souls, and you'll get different stories. Some say Zagan was cast into a place beyond Hell itself, somewhere even darker, where not even demons dare tread." His gaze swept over the class, lingering for a moment on Amber. "But the only thing everyone agrees on is this, wherever he is, it's far worse than Pernicious Island."

A ripple of unease passed through the room. Even the demons, who had murmured so confidently before, now exchanged wary glances.

Amber frowned. "Worse than an island meant for personal suffering?" she asked.

Solon nodded gravely. "There are places in existence that even Hell fears, Domina Amber. The old devil's fate is a cautionary tale. One that keeps even the strongest from daring to challenge the throne."

Amber swallowed. There was always something worse.

"Now," Solon said, clapping his hands together as if to shake off the heaviness in the air, "enough about vanished kings and lost causes. You have much more to learn, and we are only just beginning."

The lesson continued, but Amber's mind lingered on that one haunting thought.

Where could someone go that was worse than Hell?

31

The Devil's Threshold

After the history lesson, Professor Solon swiftly transitioned to what he called Demonologia 101. At first, Amber struggled to focus, her mind still reeling with unanswered questions. It didn't help that Lucifer had already explained the demon hierarchy to her, and as Professor Solon wrote the rankings on the board, she found them identical to what she'd been told:

Lucifer

Timor and Dolor

The Legatus

The Bellatores

The Crevits

The Eques

The Operarios

The Liberi

Professor Solon turned back to face the class, his sharp gaze sweeping across the room. "Now, class, are there any beings that fall *outside* the established hierarchy?"

A moment of silence followed before a few tentative hands rose, including Amber's.

"Domina Amber," Solon called on her, his tone expectant. "Do you know the answer?"

"Yes," she said confidently. "There are two groups that exist beyond the formal ranking system. The first is the Sororibus Anima, who possess the ability to take away pain. The second is the Angeli Tenebrarum, led by Angelus Mortis. Although both factions operate under their own leadership, their highest-ranking members, Abelia and Sana, must answer to Lucifer."

A flicker of approval crossed Solon's expression as he nodded. "Correct. However, the distinction between these groups and the ranked demons is more than just structure. Their very *purpose* within Hell sets them apart. The Sororibus Anima do not torture, nor do they command armies. They serve in a way unlike any other by alleviating suffering, but only when commanded. And the Angeli Tenebrarum..." His voice lowered slightly as if the words themselves carried a weight. "Well, their role is far more... complex."

Amber leaned forward, intrigued despite herself. She'd given the answer but suspected there was still much she didn't know.

Professor Solon paced at the front of the room, his long fingers tracing the edge of his desk as he spoke. "Understanding the hierarchy is not enough. To survive here, you must know how to navigate it. Power in Hell is not just about strength but influence, control, and knowledge. Those who fail to recognize this become pawns in games they don't even realize they're playing."

Amber frowned. That much, she'd already figured out.

Professor Solon turned, his gaze sweeping over the class. "Outside of the ranking order is one group Domina Amber mentioned: The Angeli Tenebrarum. What is most interesting about this group is that they have the ability to travel outside of Hell and to the Overworld. In fact, most of their job demands that they exit Hell. Although not controlled by anyone other than Lucifer and the Angelus Mortis, another entity greatly influences them." He paused for effect. "The Reaper."

A hush fell over the room. Even Amber felt her pulse quicken at the name.

"In the Overworld," Solon continued, "the Grim Reaper is neither good nor evil. He does not belong to Heaven, nor does he answer to Hell. His sole duty is to collect the souls of the dead."

A student near the back shifted uneasily. "But... if he isn't part of Heaven or Hell, where does he take them?"

Solon's lips curled slightly. "He doesn't. The Reaper does not decide where a soul belongs. He only determines who will collect it. That is where Angels and The Fallen come in."

Amber furrowed her brows. "So he's... a messenger?"

"Of sorts," Solon allowed. "When a soul departs from the mortal realm, the Reaper marks it. He alone knows where a soul is meant to go. But he cannot be everywhere at once. He has limits."

He turned, tracing his fingers over an ancient-looking book on his desk. "And so, when a soul passes away, he assigns an Angel from Heaven or a Fallen from Hell to retrieve it." His gaze darkened. "This is where things become... complicated."

Amber exchanged a glance with one of the other students, who was listening intently.

"Complicated how?" she asked.

Solon clasped his hands behind his back. "Because not all collectors are honest."

Solon let the silence settle for a moment before continuing, his voice calm but heavy with implication.

"Most collectors do as they are tasked; Heaven's angels bring the marked souls to paradise, while Hell's Fallen deliver them to damnation. But there are whispers... stories of those who intervene. Who take souls not meant for them."

Amber felt a chill crawl up her spine. "You mean they steal them?"

Solon nodded. "Some Fallen Angels have taken souls meant for Heaven, dragging them into the abyss. And there are rumors, persistent ones, that some of Heaven's Angels have done the opposite, rescuing the damned before they ever reach us."

The room was deathly still.

Not the kind of stillness that followed silence—but the kind that followed *truth*.

Leandros frowned. "But why would the Reaper allow that?"

Solon smiled though there was no warmth in it. "The Reaper allows nothing. He sees all, yes, but he does not interfere. His only role is to mark a soul and send for its collector. What happens afterward..." He spread his hands. "That is left to those who carry out his will."

Amber's stomach dropped.

If that was true, then how many souls had ended up in the wrong place? How many had been snatched by the wrong angel, claimed through manipulation, bribery, and cruelty? How many had suffered damnation... who were never meant to suffer at all? How many were *still* here?

As if reading her thoughts, Solon's expression darkened. "And that, students, is why the hierarchy matters. Power in Hell is not just about control within these walls. It extends beyond into the very fabric of death itself. Every order passed, every soul claimed, every deal made; it all threads through a system most of you don't even realize exists."

His eyes settled on Amber.

"If you do not understand the game being played," he said quietly, "then you are not a player." A beat. "You are a pawn."

Amber shuttered beneath his gaze.

Finally, Solon gestured toward the board again. "Each rank has its own function, its own purpose. The Liberi," he said, lips curling slightly. "That's you lot, save for Domina Amber. You are young demons, still learning, still proving yourselves, and finding your role within Hell. You are dangerous in your own way because many of you have yet to be shaped by its order. Some of you will rise. Others will be consumed by it." He paused, letting his gaze sweep the room. "Each of the ranks above you is a possibility for ascension.

Your goal is to figure out where you fit and how far you're willing to go to get there."

Amber raised her hand before she could stop herself.

"Yes, Domina Amber?" Professor Solon asked, his sharp gaze settling on her.

"I was just wondering; Lucifer told me I will never age, never change physically." She hesitated before continuing, "That souls cannot die twice. Is that not true for every Cive Inferni?"

A brief silence followed before a small, knowing smile crept across Solon's face. "An astute observation, Domina Amber." He turned to address the entire class.

"It is true that souls who enter Hell do not age or die in the way mortals do. However, the same cannot be said for the natural-born Cives Inferni. Aside from Lucifer himself, who is unique in his immortality, the rest of us are bound to a different fate."

Amber listened intently as Solon continued. "Everyone in Hell is, by definition, already dead, so traditional death is not an option. When a demon is gravely injured or destroyed, it can often be restored, healed, or remade. But when the damage is too great for repair, the body is... repurposed."

Amber tensed at the implication, and a few demons nearby chuckled at her reaction.

Solon's expression remained unreadable as he went on. "The remains are ground into a fine powder, which is then used to season everything at a grand feast. This process is necessary, ensuring that our numbers are replenished."

Amber's stomach churned, but Solon was unfazed.

"Every female Crevit is called to partake in this feast," he explained. "Crevits are the only demons capable of carrying offspring. The one who consumes the greatest amount of the powdered body becomes..." he paused, searching for the right word, "...pregnant, in a sense. Unlike in the Overworld, this gestation lasts only about a month. When the Liberi are born, they emerge only needing about a month of guidance before they can survive on their own. But the Crevits are not mothers; the babies are cared for by a special type of Operario."

A few murmurs rippled through the class, but Solon continued smoothly. "From there, their growth follows a pattern somewhat similar to the Overworld, but once their rank in Hell is determined, their aging slows significantly. We do not age in a linear way. We continue on until our bodies become too damaged to be repaired, at which point the cycle begins anew."

Amber swallowed hard but forced herself to keep her expression neutral. She'd come to Hell expecting torment, but this was something else entirely. "Thank you," she managed meekly.

Professor Solon nodded and turned back to the board, pointing to the rank just above the Liberi. "The Operarios. Servants. Laborers. People like me." His expression remained neutral. "We maintain Hell's structure, handling the tasks too menial or insignificant for higher ranks. While not the most powerful, the majority of you will end up in this role. Do not underestimate its significance. A well-placed Operario can be an invaluable asset or a dangerous liability."

Amber thought of Korinna. Was she just another nameless servant? Or did she have influence in ways others overlooked?

Solon continued, moving up the list. "The Eques, Hell's knights and guards. Few in number, but omnipresent. They stand watch over every entrance and exit, tracking who comes and goes. You may not always see an Eque, but rest assured, they see you. They are silent, loyal, and obedient to no one but Lucifer himself."

Amber listened intently. This was more than just a lesson; it was survival training.

Solon's hand slid further up the board. "The Crevits. Many of you will end up here. While the Bellatores rely on brute strength, the Crevits are strategists and tacticians. They rarely engage in physical combat, but that does not make them weak. Their minds are their weapons. Underestimate a Crevit, and you'll be ensnared in a trap before you even realize one was set."

A murmur of excitement rippled through the class.

"Yes," Solon confirmed. "They are the ones who enter the islands and punish the damned."

He moved on. "Above them, The Bellatores. The warriors of Hell. Enforcers of Lucifer's will. They thrive in combat and command the battlefield. They are not patient, but they are relentless." His gaze swept the room. "Would you challenge one in a fight?"

Some students shifted uncomfortably. A voice from the front hesitated before answering, "Not directly. If I had to, I'd find another way."

A pleased smile ghosted across Solon's lips. "Good. You're learning."

His hand tapped the next rank. "The Legatus. Messengers. Diplomats. Spinners of webs. They weave through Hell's politics, brokering deals and whispering secrets. To cross a Legatus is to invite ruin upon yourself. Their words carry far more weight than their fists."

Amber glanced around, wondering how many of her classmates already knew this and how many of them would rise to be among them.

"The final two ranks: Timor and Dolor. They are rarely seen outside of Pernicious Island or Lucifer's side, but when they are, every Cive Inferni fears them. They do not distinguish between soul or demon. If you encounter one, do not make eye contact. Bow. You will still feel the pain and fear they radiate, but they will not direct it at you unless ordered to or if they sense you looking at them."

A shudder ran through Amber. She knew that all too well.

"I will not go into great detail about our Liege, Lucifer." Solon's voice lowered. "You already know who he is. He is at the top of the food chain. He is not to be trifled with. As with Timor and Dolor, you bow when you see him. He will not trouble you if you complete your tasks and follow his rules."

He clasped his hands behind his back. "Power is a currency here, and knowing how to wield it matters more than brute strength. You must learn to read the room to assess who truly holds influence. Do not mistake volume for authority. The most dangerous creatures are often the quietest ones."

Amber absorbed every word. She'd known Hell would be treacherous, but now she saw how layered its dangers were.

From the front of the room, a cautious hand rose.

"Yes?" Solon acknowledged the student.

"Are there any ranks that a Liberi cannot rise to?" the girl asked timidly.

Professor Solon considered the question for a moment before answering. "Yes. Within the ranking system, a Liberi can only ascend as high as a Legatus. Timor and Dolor cannot be overtaken or killed, nor does any other being possess their gifts. They are not demons; they are manifestations of darkness itself. Becoming them is impossible."

He continued, his tone measured. "A Liberi also cannot become something outside of the ranking system. For example, there have never been or will ever be additional Sororibus Anima. As for the Angeli Tenebrarum, they procreate exclusively among themselves, meaning no one can ascend to their rank. To be one, you would have to be born into it."

The girl nodded, satisfied with his response, and Solon turned his attention back to the entire class. "Now," He said, eyes gleaming, "let's talk about weaknesses."

A shiver ran down Amber's spine.

Solon turned back to the board, but instead of writing another rank this time, he simply tapped the chalk against the surface. "Every demon has a purpose. But more importantly, every demon has a weakness."

The murmurs in the classroom stilled.

"A strong warrior is only as good as the flaws his enemies can exploit," Solon continued. "You will need to recognize not only your own weaknesses

but those of your enemies and your allies. If you don't, you won't last long."
He paused, then turned back to the class. "Let's begin. Tell me, what is the
greatest weakness of The Bellatores?"

A student raised a hand. "They're strong but impulsive," he said carefully.
"They fight first and think later."

Solon nodded approvingly. "Precisely. Bellatores are the most physically
powerful demons beneath Lucifer's direct command but lack patience. You
will never outrun them or beat them with strength, but they can be outma-
neuvered if you keep your wits about you. Make them angry, and they will
charge. Make them chase you, and they will follow. But set a trap, and they
will run straight into it."

Amber committed that to memory. She didn't expect to fight a Bellator
anytime soon, but knowing how to outthink one could mean the difference
between survival and destruction.

Solon gestured next to The Crevits. "And what of them?"

A different student hesitated before answering. "They... rely too much on
their intellect?"

"Correct," Solon said. "A Crevit believes they are always the smartest in
the room. If you can force them into a position where they do not have time
to think, you can break them. They do not handle unpredictability well. If you
can outthink them or make them *believe* they've made a mistake, they will
hesitate. And hesitation is a death sentence in Hell."

The lesson carved itself into her bones.

Solon continued down the list. "The Eques, silent, observant, unwavering. They are loyal beyond reason, which means their weakness is simple:
obedience. They will not break rank. They will not question orders. If something falls outside their expectations, it disrupts them. They do not act on
impulse, and that can be used against them."

Amber raised a brow. That made them sound almost... mechanical.

"The Operarios." Solon leaned back slightly. "Servants. Workers. You
might think they are weak, but they are *many*. Their greatest power is their
numbers, their ability to blend in, to move unseen. Their weakness?" He
smiled. "They are often overlooked. If an Operario steps out of line, they are
easy to replace." His voice turned cold. "Do not become forgettable."

The class went silent, observing every word.

"The Liberi." His lips curled slightly. "You are young. You are unpredictable. That makes you dangerous, but it also makes you *reckless*. Many of
you will rise. Many more will fall. Your greatest weakness?" He let his gaze
sweep the room. "You do not yet know who you are."

A few nervous murmurs wafted over the crowd.

Solon's expression grew sharper. "The Legatus. The most cunning of all demons. They do not fight with brute force but with words and influence. Their greatest strength is their ability to turn truth into a weapon." His eyes darkened. "But even the best manipulators have flaws. Their weakness is their *ego*. A Legatus who believes themselves untouchable becomes reckless. If you find one who overestimates their control, you have an opening but be careful. Their tongues are sharper than any blade."

Amber's mind flickered back to the conversation she'd overheard in the hidden room of Castellum Umbrae. How much of their power was built on perception rather than reality?

"Now," Solon said, his voice lowering, "let's talk about Timor and Dolor."

Amber tensed.

Solon's expression darkened. "They are fear and pain incarnate. Unstoppable forces. Most of you will never encounter them outside of the islands, but if you do, you must remember this: *They cannot tell the difference between soul and demon. To them, all things are prey.* Their weakness, if you can call it that, is that they are bound to Lucifer's command. Without it, they follow their nature. Chaos. They are immune to any attack and cannot be killed. If you stand in their way, may our Lord have mercy on you because they will not. You will not survive."

Amber's stomach tightened at the memory of the pain they had inflicted upon her. The agony of their presence alone had nearly shattered her mind.

Then Solon's voice turned sharp. "And what of Lucifer?"

The air in the room grew still. No one dared to speak.

Amber's pulse quickened. She'd seen his cruelty, his power, his indifference. But she'd also seen something else he hadn't intended her to see.

"Domina Amber." Solon's voice sliced through the silence. "You seem to have thoughts."

Amber hesitated. Every instinct told her to stay quiet, but she forced herself to meet his gaze. "He has no weakness," she said carefully.

Solon's eyes gleamed with something almost like approval. "A wise answer," he murmured. "And yet... all things have weaknesses, even Lucifer."

A charged silence hung in the air.

"Lucifer has no equal in Hell. His power is absolute, but absolute power is a heavy burden. His greatest weakness?" Solon's lips curled slightly. "*Obligation.* He is bound by his own laws, his own bargains. And because he must uphold the balance, he cannot always act as he pleases. If you ever think you've found a way to manipulate him, you are gravely mistaken. He sees *everything*, even when you think he does not."

Amber swallowed, gripping the edge of her desk.

"His only weakness is the clause that no one knows." Solon finished.

Amber felt a strange sensation crawl up her spine. She'd always thought of Hell as a place of torment, of suffering. But this, this was something else.

This was a game of survival.

And she'd just learned the rules.

Sloan's gaze lingered on her for a fraction too long before he turned away. "That is all for today. Class dismissed."

Amber remained still as the other students gathered their things and filed out of the room, her mind racing.

32

Vehement Vows

Amber sat frozen at her desk, the echoes of Solon's voice still whispering in her ears like a curse she couldn't shake.

Lucifer had a weakness. An obligation.

The thought pressed down on her chest like a weight, heavy and unfamiliar. She'd seen the Devil's power, witnessed the way he commanded the room, the way shadows bent to his will. But this... this was something different. A thread in the tapestry she hadn't noticed before, something fraying beneath all that control.

The clause no one knew.

Her fingers curled against the edge of the desk, nails digging into the smooth wood as her thoughts spiraled. What did it mean for her? For anyone in Hell? Was there a way to pull at that hidden thread, to unravel the rules that kept her bound?

The scrape of a chair broke the spell.

Amber blinked and looked up, startled to find the classroom emptied. The cold hush had given way to the rising tide of chatter and laughter as the Liberi filtered out, their voices bouncing off the high stone walls. She hadn't even noticed them move.

She stood slowly, her legs stiff from stillness. The corridor beyond the classroom glowed softly, lit by the strange ambient light that poured in from the courtyard. The moment she stepped into the open air, warmth kissed her skin, a gentle contrast to the chill that still lingered inside her.

The Liberi were already scattered across the courtyard, the younger ones tackling each other and chasing the older ones, their faces lit with laughter. They ran, spun, and shouted, some darting past each other in play, others collapsing onto the stone benches in clusters.

Amber lingered at the edge, caught between her thoughts and the surprising sweetness of the scene. She hadn't expected to find joy here. But in their laughter, she caught a glimpse of something fragile and human, something untouched by Hell's cruelty.

One of the young demons caught her gaze and padded toward her. His golden eyes blinked curiously up at her.

"Domina Amber," he said hesitantly.

Amber blinked, caught off guard. "You can speak to me?"

The Liberi seemed almost embarrassed, so Amber quickly corrected herself, "I'm sorry. I didn't mean it like that. I'm just surprised we can understand each other."

The demon tilted his head. "Your Latin is a little broken, but I can understand it."

"My... Latin?" she echoed, confused.

He nodded matter-of-factly. "We learn it. The younger ones, my age and below, we start with our own tongue and pick up Latin later. You're doing fine, though."

Amber's eyes widened slightly. *I've been speaking Latin this whole time?* It hadn't even registered. Somewhere along the line, the language had slipped into her like breath.

"Oh," she said, shaking it off. "Well... do you want to play a game?"

He blinked again, this time slower. "A game?"

She laughed softly. "Something simple. We can play hopscotch. It's a game I used to play in the Overworld when I was younger."

The demon's brow furrowed, but several other Liberi had started to drift closer behind him, their curiosity piqued. Amber crouched down and scraped a grid into the dirt with the toe of her boot. Dust curled in lazy spirals around her ankles.

"You take turns jumping through the squares," she explained, "one foot, then two feet, all while trying not to touch the lines."

They watched her demonstration as if she were casting some kind of spell. For a moment, no one moved. Then, a lanky demon with sharp teeth and curious eyes stepped forward and mimicked her awkwardly, hopping from square to square.

His landing was clumsy, but when he turned to Amber with a triumphant grin, laughter broke out around them like sunlight.

Amber's heart swelled a little as she watched them, feeling a sense of pride she hadn't expected to think in this place. They were learning something more than survival; they were learning joy. For a brief moment, they were just kids.

Their laughter filled the courtyard as they played, and Amber found herself smiling more than she'd in a long time. For a moment, she could almost forget where she was and who she was surrounded by.

A breeze stirred the hair at the nape of her neck, and something shifted. A chill swept over her, quiet but unmistakable. She turned instinctively, her gaze drifting upward.

There, high above the courtyard, standing in the shadowed curve of the balcony, was Lucifer.

He didn't move. Didn't speak. But his eyes were dark and unfathomable and were locked on her.

Amber's breath caught. The warmth in her chest cooled.

He watched her like one might study a puzzle or a threat. And yet... there was something else in his gaze. A flicker she couldn't name. She turned quickly, pretending not to see him, but the weight of his presence anchored her in place.

He didn't look away.

The young demons continued to play, oblivious, their laughter undisturbed. Amber focused on them, kneeling to fix a smudged line in the dirt. But the tension curled tight in her stomach.

She risked another glance; still, he stood there, statuesque and unreadable. Watching her not as an overlord might survey a subject... but as a man might study a flame he couldn't touch.

And for the first time, Amber couldn't help but wonder if she'd caught his attention in a way that was different from before.

A few moments passed when Korinna's voice cut through the moment.

"Domina Amber," she said gently. "Classes have ended for the day. Please come with me."

Amber hesitated. She glanced back at the balcony.

Lucifer was still there. Their eyes met, and in that sliver of silence, something shifted. His expression barely moved, but she could swear there was amusement there. A ghost of a smile.

Then he vanished.

Amber's pulse stuttered.

She followed Korinna in silence, her thoughts tangled like threads knotted tight. The Liberi had accepted her without hesitation. Was it innocence that softened them? Or something else? Could they sense something in her even she didn't fully understand?

But her thoughts broke off as a shadow stretched across the corridor.

A demon stood before them, tall and sharp-edged, his eyes glowing with unnatural heat. He dipped his head in a bow, "Domina Amber. Domina in Exspectatione Korinna. Lord Lucifer requests your presence."

Amber's stomach twisted. "Now?"

"Immediately."

She swallowed, forcing herself to nod. The last time Lucifer had summoned her, it had been for his games. This time, she had no idea what to expect.

Korinna nodded at the demon, and he scurried away. Amber followed Korinna, her footsteps echoing too loudly against the stone. The deeper they went into Castellum Umbrae, the darker it became, walls flickering with firelight, shadows stretching like fingers across the floor.

When they reached the great double doors, two Eques stepped forward and pulled them open without a word.

Lucifer stood before the fireplace, bathed in the glow of embers. He held a glass of deep crimson liquid, swirling it lazily between his fingers.

"You enjoyed yourself today," he said without turning.

Amber tensed. "What do you mean?"

"The young ones," he said, sipping slowly. "You entertained them. Taught them something... new."

Amber shifted, suddenly self-conscious under his scrutiny. "They needed a break," she said simply. "They're still children."

He turned then, gaze settling on her. "And you? Do you see yourself as their teacher?"

"I don't know," Amber admitted. "Maybe. They were kind to me. That's more than I can say for most here."

"Kindness," Lucifer murmured, "is a dangerous trait in Hell."

He crossed the room with easy steps, each one silent despite his presence filling the space. His eyes never left hers.

"You don't follow rules," he said. "That's what makes you interesting."

Amber squared her shoulders. "If I followed the rules, I wouldn't be standing here, would I?"

A dark smile curved his lips. "No. You wouldn't."

He reached out, tracing a single finger along the fabric of her sleeve. His touch was barely there, yet it sent a shiver through her.

"You're learning," he said quietly.

Amber forced herself to hold his gaze. "Is that why you called me here? To test me again?"

Lucifer's expression shifted, something darker flickering behind his eyes. "Not this time."

"Then why?"

Lucifer didn't answer immediately. He stepped back, setting his glass down with a soft clink. "We should dine together."

She blinked. "Tonight?"

"No," he said, voice silk and smoke. "But soon. You were right; I invited you into my castle. It's time I act like a proper host. Unless..." His voice trailed off as he looked her up and down.

Amber's heart beat faster. "Unless I'm afraid."

"Are you?" he asked, stepping close. "Because I think you are."

"I'm not afraid of you."

His smile deepened, eyes gleaming with something too complex to name. "You say that..."

His fingers retraced her sleeve, slow and deliberate, before falling away. "But I wonder what you'd do if I proved it."

Amber couldn't breathe.

Lucifer leaned in, his mouth close to her ear, voice a thread of darkness. "I'll summon you when I've decided. Until then... I want you to wonder."

"About what?" she whispered, breathless.

He stepped back, already fading like mist in firelight, "What you've already started to want."

And then he was gone, leaving only the echo of his words, the taste of heat on her skin, and a fire in her chest that no amount of reason could smother.

33

A Heart in Chains

Amber tried to ignore the tingles that still clung to her skin after Lucifer walked away, but they lingered like fingerprints burned into her for the rest of the day. Imprinted on her skin like tattoos, reminders of a touch that had gone nowhere.

Now, hours later, she couldn't sleep. His touch, scent, and words tormented her every thought, tightening around her like a noose.

The castle around her was quiet, too quiet, as if even the Volaces, who normally shrieked and spun through the upper towers by nightfall, decided to halt their aerial displays.

Annoyed and restless, Amber grabbed a robe from the closet and threw the covers off. She didn't know where she was going, only that she couldn't stay still. Not with her mind like this, not with him pressing into the edges of her thoughts as his words echoed relentlessly:

"What you've already started to want."

Could he really see right through her that easily?

With a heavy sigh, she slipped through a side door that led to the castle's back courtyard. It was one of the only places in Hell that felt truly beautiful, twisted, yes, but still beautiful.

Dark water toppled from the wings of a stone-carved Fallen Angel, landing in a still obsidian basin below. The soft sound of the cascade echoed through the courtyard like a lullaby for the damned. Blood-hued lilies clustered at its base, their petals opening like wounds in the moonlight.

Thick vines of curling, deep, ocean-blue thorns crept along the ground, scaling the stone pillars and coiling around the skeletal remains of what might have once been a wrought-iron trellis. Deep red and black roses spilled between the lilies, their velvety blooms heavy with dew that shimmered like spilled wine.

There was a wildness to it all, something ancient and untamed. Pale bioluminescent blossoms blinked open in the dark corners of the garden, glowing faintly with ghostly light. The air hung heavy with the scent of petrichor and spice as though the garden breathed in time with the darkness.

Above her, vines wove through the crossbeams of the open lattice, their leaves glistening silver-green under the distant stars that never shifted in Hell's eternal sky.

It was beautiful. Terrible. Alive.

And somehow, it felt like it had been waiting for her.

A soft breeze rustled the lattice above her, brushing cold air against her heated skin, and she closed her eyes.

It was then that she felt it.

That familiar, invisible pull.

She turned slowly.

Lucifer stood just outside the pergola, half-shrouded in shadows. Watching.

At first, she wasn't sure if he was really there or just a figment conjured by her restless mind. He didn't speak. Didn't move.

Then, finally, his deep voice echoed around her, curling like smoke. "You're wondering, aren't you?"

Amber's breath caught in her chest, but she turned away from him, forcing her gaze back to the fountain, "No."

For a moment, there was nothing. Then, ever so slowly, he came up behind her, his breath hitting the back of her neck.

"Liar," he whispered so softly she almost thought she imagined it.

Her eyes fluttered shut despite every instinct shouting: *don't react. Don't let him know how deeply he affects you.*

But then, his fingers, light as air, brushed her thigh. They drew delicate circles as they climbed higher, tracing over her robe's silk as though time had slowed. His other hand swept her hair off her shoulder, exposing the vulnerable skin beneath.

And he kissed her.

A single, gentle kiss to the space between her shoulder and neck. Barely there. But it ignited her like nothing else.

She leaned back into him without meaning to, her body betraying her resolve. Her head tilted, giving him more, giving him *everything.*

Another kiss followed. This one higher on her neck but slower. His other hand settled on her hip, grounding her even as she felt she might come undone.

"You want me to test you?" he murmured, his voice threatening and promising. "Fine. Let's see how long you can hold on."

She didn't have time to respond.

His hand slid from her hip to the small of her back, guiding, no, *commanding,* her gently, wordlessly, until her spine met the cold stone of one of the pergola's pillars. She gasped at the temperature, but the chill only heightened the fire coursing through her veins.

Lucifer curled around to her front and pressed in close.

Not enough to trap her. Just enough to *remind* her that he could.

His hand dipped to the tie in her robe. Effortlessly, he tugged it, and the robe opened, revealing the sheer nightgown beneath. His eyes burned a trail across her body as he took her in. Her nipples peaked beneath the light fabric, and for a flash of a second, he squeezed his eyes shut as if trying to maintain his control.

Then his fingers found the hem of her dress and slipped beneath it. Skin met skin, Amber's fingers curled against the pillar behind her, her knees softening as his touch traveled higher. His other hand braced beside her head, caging her in without ever forcing her.

"Still not afraid of me?" he murmured.

Amber's mouth parted, but no words came out, only breath, shaky and shallow.

Lucifer's fingers found the heat between her thighs; he didn't hesitate.

He touched her like he knew her body better than she did. Like he'd imagined this, *rehearsed* this, for far longer than she could ever guess. Each movement was maddeningly slow, intentional, and devastating. Every flick of his fingers drew her closer to that edge, every breath she took caught higher in her chest.

She whimpered. Just once.

And he smiled against her throat.

"Look at you," he whispered, his lips brushing her skin. "Breaking for me."

Her hands gripped his arms now, nails biting through the fabric. She was close, so close, and he knew it.

He always knew.

Her eyes flew shut as she shuttered beneath his gaze.

"Open your eyes," he coaxed, voice low and unrelenting. "I want to see you unravel."

So, she did as she was told.

With a gasp, she opened her eyes and nearly came undone right there, melting into the depths of his unwavering stare. The pleasure, the pressure, the *power* of it all; it was too much.

And then...he stopped.

His hand stilled, the heat of him vanishing all at once as he pulled back just enough to make her feel the loss. Her body trembled, unfinished, desperate, furious.

Instinctively, she reached for him and tugged at him, breathless with disbelief. But Lucifer looked down at her with infuriating calm, his expression unreadable, though his eyes were still burning.

"If I finish this... you'll never walk away." He looked at her like she was already gone, "And I can't take that from you."

His gaze dropped to her mouth, something softer flickering behind his control, "Not you."

Then he stepped back, turned, and disappeared into the shadows again, leaving her alone, shaking, and completely undone.

Infuriated, Amber stormed back to bed. Over and over again, she told herself she hated him, but the truth curled around her like a secret. She knew her body hadn't. But more than that, she knew her heart hadn't, and *that* terrified her most of all.

34

An Invitation to Bleed

The next day, Amber didn't speak to anyone.

She moved through the castle like a ghost, haunted, restless, and aching in places she didn't have names for. She couldn't stop replaying it: the feel of his breath, the heat of his hands, the sharp absence of him when he left.

She had no idea what it meant or if it meant anything at all.

So, she did what she always did when the world didn't make sense: she looked for something she could understand.

Amber found herself seeking solace in the library, curled up with a book, practicing her Latin. The language was coming to her quickly, perhaps too easily. She'd just finished reading and reciting passages in Latin from Macbeth when the soft sound of footsteps pulled her from her thoughts.

Korinna stood at the edge of the room, her expression solemn. "Domina Amber, it is time to prepare you for dinner. Please follow me."

Amber stood, stretching out her legs before silently following Korinna through the winding halls of Castellum Umbrae. The air felt heavier as they ascended the steps to her chambers, a quiet anticipation settling in her chest.

Inside, she barely had a moment to breathe before she was ushered into the closet. Two other Dominarum in Exspectatione were waiting, far more excitable than Korinna. Their eyes lit up the moment they saw her, and without hesitation, they swept forward, already chattering about the dresses they had chosen.

Before her stood three magnificent gowns, each more stunning than the last.

Amber reached out, her fingers grazing the first gown, a black so dark it was like a night without stars. The fabric was cool and impossibly smooth, unlike anything she'd ever touched, almost like liquid shadow woven into silk. Tiny silver threads formed constellations across the bodice and sleeves, twinkling when the light hit them just right. It had long, flowing sleeves draped elegantly past her wrists, almost sheer, giving the illusion of midnight mist curling around her arms. The neckline was high, framing her collarbones, while the bodice hugged her torso before flaring out into a cascading skirt of layered chiffon that trailed behind her like a whisper of darkness. It was mysterious, powerful, almost ethereal.

She let her fingertips slide away, turning to the red gown. This one was bolder, heavier, made from a rich, luxurious velvet that felt almost sinful against her skin. The deep crimson shade caught the candlelight, glowing like embers in a dying fire. It was strapless, with a plunging sweetheart neckline that emphasized the delicate line of her shoulders. The corseted bodice cinched her waist and laced up the back with intricate black ribbon, while the skirt flowed in dramatic waves, the edges tinged with subtle hints of black embroidery that looked like creeping vines. It was the kind of dress that spoke of temptation, power, and danger.

Then there was the gold gown. Lighter than the others, it felt like spun sunlight beneath her fingers, impossibly soft, almost weightless. The fabric was a delicate blend of silk and something else, something unearthly, that shimmered as it moved as if woven with strands of fire. It had an off-the-shoulder design, with delicate golden chains draping across her arms like jewelry. The bodice was structured but not confining, embroidered with intricate patterns that resembled the sun's rays stretching outward. The skirt fell in perfect layers, flowing like molten gold, pooling at her feet in a soft, radiant train. It was warm, regal, almost celestial, meant for someone who belonged in the light, not the darkness of Hell.

Amber swallowed, her fingers curling at her sides. Each dress carried its own presence, its own meaning. No matter what she chose, it'd say something, perhaps even something she wasn't ready to admit.

The attendants watched her, waiting.

Korinna, ever composed, finally spoke. "Domina, which will it be?"

Amber hesitated, staring at the gowns. She'd never worn anything like them before.

"The black one, please."

"Excellent choice, Domina," Korinna said, nodding to the two other demonesses.

Immediately, the three began the process of undressing and redressing her. Amber stood still, her heart racing as the attendants worked swiftly around her. Each movement was deliberate and practiced, as though they had done this a thousand times before. The black dress shimmered as it was pulled over her head, the fabric cool against her skin. It was sleek, fitting perfectly as if it had been made just for her. The deep shade absorbed the light, yet there was an elegance in its simplicity and quiet power.

As Korinna adjusted the bodice, Amber couldn't help but feel exposed. The weight of the dress was both literal and figurative, settling heavily on her shoulders. She wondered what Lucifer would think when he saw her in it. Would it change the way he looked at her? Would he notice the subtle shift in her, the way she was slowly starting to understand the role she was meant to play in Hell?

The attendants finished with a final tug of the fabric, and Korinna stepped back, inspecting her work. "Perfect," she murmured before turning to Amber. "You look... pulchra, Domina."

Amber met her reflection in the mirror, taking in the sight of herself. The woman who stared back seemed both familiar and foreign. This was a version of herself she hadn't expected, potent, poised, and undeniably different from the girl who had arrived in Hell.

Korinna's voice interrupted her thoughts. "The master will expect you soon. He has requested dinner, and we have prepared the ballroom for you both."

Amber nodded, forcing a smile as she turned to face the attendants. "The ballroom?"

Korinna just nodded clearly, not willing to say more.

"Thank you," Amber said, accepting the mystery.

As she left the room, her steps were heavy, not with the dress but with the expectations that now surrounded her. She felt the weight of what she was stepping into, the part she had to play, and a twinge of fear crept in.

Amber walked quickly through the grand hall, her heels clicking sharply against the polished stone floors. The dining room stretched before her, glowing under the soft, golden light of chandeliers that hung from the ceiling like stars. She could hear the faint hum of music, soft but hypnotic, drifting in from a room nearby.

Lucifer was standing near the head of a long, opulent table. His dark suit contrasted sharply with the elegant surroundings, as though he belonged to a world of shadow, always separate from the beauty he ruled. His eyes flicked toward her as she entered, but his expression remained unreadable.

Amber paused at the threshold, uncertain. The air seemed charged with something unspoken between them. She didn't know what to expect, if he was testing her, playing his usual games, or if tonight would be something entirely different.

"Come in, Amber." Lucifer's voice was smooth and quiet, carrying a quiet command. You're late."

She stepped forward, her heart beating a little faster under his gaze. "I'm sorry, my lord," she said softly, unsure if that was correct.

His lips curled ever so slightly, and there was a hint of amusement in his eyes, though there was a flicker of something else, something deeper, beneath the surface. "No need for apologies. You look extraordinary," he said, his gaze lingering on her dress, on how it seemed to shape her in an almost fitting way.

Amber gave a slight nod, her eyes briefly meeting his before she looked away, unsure how to navigate the shifting tension. "Thank you," she murmured, her voice barely above a whisper.

"But it's missing something," he said, a slight smirk playing at the corners of his lips.

"Oh?" Amber's voice was tentative, her curiosity piqued.

Lucifer didn't answer immediately. Instead, he reached into his pocket, his movements slow and deliberate. He pulled out a small black box, its surface gleaming softly in the dim light. With a quiet grace, he made his way around the table, approaching Amber with the box in hand. He opened it slowly, revealing the most exquisite necklace she'd ever seen.

Amber's breath caught in her throat. The clear yet seemingly alive jewels sparkled like stars in the night sky. They were unlike anything she'd ever seen, their brilliance almost otherworldly. Her heart raced, her mind momentarily blank, as she stared at the necklace, speechless.

A soft gasp escaped her lips before she could stop it. The beauty of the piece left her breathless.

With practiced grace, Lucifer lifted the necklace from its velvet bed and set the box gently on the table. He moved behind her with fluid steps, a quiet confidence in every motion. He carefully swept her hair to one side, his fingers brushing her skin as he did so.

He leaned in closer, the heat of his presence undeniable as he slid the collar of her dress back, exposing her neck. Slowly, deliberately, he draped the necklace around her neck, the coolness of the jewels a stark contrast to the warmth of his fingers that lingered for a moment longer than necessary. Amber could feel the delicate pressure of the necklace settle against her skin, its weight being a strange comfort.

The brief touch of his fingers against her skin sent a shiver down her spine, and she swallowed hard, her pulse quickening under his gaze.

His fingers stayed for a heartbeat longer than necessary, the silence between them humming with something neither dared name. Amber could feel the warmth of his breath on her neck, and for a heartbeat, the world seemed to narrow to just the two of them, her pulse, the weight of the necklace, and the faint brush of his fingertips.

He stepped back, his eyes lingering on her for a beat too long, as though studying her reaction in the mirror, though his face remained unreadable.

"There," he said, his voice low and almost velvet. "Now, you are truly *praeclarum*."

Amber's heart raced, her breath coming in shallow bursts. She wanted to say something, to respond in a way that felt appropriate, but the words seemed to stick in her throat. Instead, she turned her gaze into the mirror across from where they stood, where Lucifer had already watched her. They stood there, her just in front of him like something of an ancient painting; a king with his queen.

It was more than just an accessory; it felt like a mark, a claim. It made her look different, stronger, even.

Lucifer watched her reflection for a moment, his eyes dark but unreadable. He stepped back, giving her space to adjust to the moment. "I rarely give gifts," he murmured, almost to himself. "But for you..."

Amber's eyes flicked back to his, meeting his gaze in the mirror. She wasn't sure what to make of his words, but she could sense the weight behind them like there was more to this moment than just the necklace.

"But for me...?" she repeated, her voice steady despite the turmoil she felt inside.

Lucifer smiled faintly, his expression softened but still carefully guarded. "Yes," he said simply. "But don't get used to it."

Amber gave a small laugh, though it felt uncertain. She was caught between tension and the strange pull of something unspoken between them. She turned to face him fully, the weight of the necklace heavy on her chest, the air around them still crackling with the moment's intensity.

Lucifer gave a slight, almost imperceptible nod. "Now," he said, shifting the mood toward dinner. "Shall we eat?"

Amber nodded as Lucifer gestured toward the table, where a feast had been laid out. The dishes gleamed, each more extravagant than the last, an intricate balance of decadence and restraint. "Please," he said, his tone softer, almost coaxing. "I insist. Sit with me."

Amber moved to the table, carefully settling into the chair he indicated. The moment she did, a subtle tension seemed to settle between them, the silence thick with the weight of unsaid things. Lucifer had always been an enigma, but tonight, something was different.

"Tell me," he began after a long pause, his voice cutting through the quiet. "How are you finding Hell, Amber? The trials, the... *adjustment*?"

Amber hesitated, choosing her words carefully. "It's... different," she said slowly, in perfect Latin. "But not as terrible as I expected."

Surprise washed over Lucifer's face for a moment, but it was fleeting, gone as quickly as it had come. His eyes narrowed slightly, studying Amber with renewed interest.

"Perfect Latin," he said, his voice tinged with approval, though his tone remained measured. "I didn't expect you to master it so quickly." There was a subtle edge to his words, a trace of admiration buried beneath the coolness.

He leaned back in his chair, his gaze unwavering as he observed her more calculatingly. "You must have more surprises than I thought," he added, his lips curving into the faintest of smiles. "Tell me, Amber, how did you learn? I doubt it was from any mortal teacher."

Amber met his gaze, an unexpected thrill coursing through her at the challenge in his tone. "You could say it was in my blood," she replied, her voice steady but laced with quiet confidence.

Lucifer's eyes flickered with something unreadable, his smile deepening slightly. "Perhaps you're more of an enigma than I initially thought," he murmured, almost to himself, before leaning forward slightly, his expression softening. "I'll be curious to see what other surprises you have."

Amber couldn't help but feel a strange tension in the air, part curiosity, part something else, something she couldn't quite place. But there was no mistaking it now: she'd captured his attention in a way she hadn't expected.

The conversation hung between them, thick with unspoken tension. Amber didn't know where the conversation was heading or if it was heading anywhere. She leaned in slightly, her voice playful yet laced with challenge. "I'm full of surprises, my liege. You have no idea what I'm capable of."

Lucifer simply regarded her for a moment, his gaze sharp and penetrating. Then, suddenly, a flash of fiery, intense red shot across his eyes. But as quickly as it had appeared, it was gone, replaced by the usual cool, calculating expression he wore so well.

He leaned back in his chair, folding his hands in front of him, his eyes never leaving hers. "Let's eat, Amber," he said, his tone shifting back to something more measured but still holding that undercurrent of intrigue. "I'm curious to see how well you handle the... *indulgence* of Hell."

And with that, they dove into the lavish dinner, the food rich and decadent, a feast for the senses. Amber noticed Lucifer watching her between bites, his gaze intense, but she couldn't quite decipher what he was thinking. There was a battle happening, one she wasn't yet sure she could win. But as they continued their meal, Amber couldn't shake the feeling that this night would be a turning point; either she'd prove herself or find herself caught in Lucifer's web for good.

35

Dancing on the Edge

To her surprise, Amber found herself laughing genuinely, unexpectedly, as the conversation shifted from tense, unspoken moments to more casual exchanges. Lucifer had a way of telling stories that made her forget, for just a moment, where they were, or *who* they were. He spoke of the absurdities of Hell's court in an oddly charming way, poking fun at some of his own demons, and for the first time that night, she found herself laughing with him rather than at the distance between them.

"You know," Amber said, wiping a tear of laughter from her eye, "I never would have pegged you as a fan of practical jokes."

Lucifer raised an eyebrow, a smirk tugging at the corner of his mouth. "You'd be surprised what a little chaos can do for entertainment. You should see the demons when they get wind of a new trick."

She laughed again, this time louder, the sound echoing softly in the room, and Lucifer's expression softened just slightly. There was something almost human at that moment, a crack in his armor she hadn't expected.

The meal continued, and the conversation became lighter and more natural as the tension that had initially lingered between them began to dissipate. There were no more guarded glances, no more weighing each word. The moments of silence felt comfortable, not strained.

When the last course was cleared away, Lucifer gave her a thoughtful look, his eyes still sharp but with a hint of warmth that hadn't been there before. "Well, Amber," he said, his voice smooth, "I believe we've had enough indulgence for tonight."

Amber raised an eyebrow, unsure of what he meant.

He stood, offering her his hand with a slight bow. "Shall we dance?"

Amber's heart skipped a beat, the offer unexpected but intriguing. She placed her hand in his, a slow smile spreading across her face. "Lead the way, my liege."

As Lucifer guided her to the ballroom, Amber felt a strange sense of anticipation settle in her chest. For once, the evening felt less like a battle and more like an unexpected truce, leaving her wondering what this night might bring.

***

The ballroom was breathtaking, bathed in soft golden light. The music grew louder as they entered, and Lucifer guided Amber to the center of the floor. The first song played was an acoustic version of *Skin and Bones*. It was slow and melodic, and as they began to move together, the tension between them shifted once more, this time to something more electric. Their bodies were close, the musical rhythm flowing through them as if they were two parts of a whole. Amber could feel Lucifer's breath against her cheek, and though his touch was steady, his presence was undeniably commanding.

She tried to focus on the dance, on matching his steps, but her mind kept drifting to the way his fingers rested on her waist, the heat of his chest so close to hers. His eyes were intense, flickering with something unreadable, but there was a softness to him in this moment that made her pulse quicken. His touch was careful and deliberate as if he could guide her without forcing anything. Every step felt like a conversation, each movement speaking volumes without uttering a word.

He spun her with practiced ease, perfectly matching their movements to the music. The world around them seemed to blur, and for a few seconds, it was just the two of them moving as one. The music was their heartbeat, and their bodies responded instinctively, perfectly aligned at every step.

She felt weightless, as though the floor beneath them had disappeared, and all that remained was the air, the melody, and the connection between them. It wasn't just the physical closeness; it was something deeper, something intangible, that made her chest tighten and her thoughts scatter. For the first time since arriving in Hell, Amber wasn't entirely sure what she was supposed to be doing. She wasn't focused on proving herself to him or trying to read his every move. For the first time, she was just... with him.

They moved in seamless harmony, her body following his lead with a grace she didn't know she had. Amber felt like they were floating, their feet barely touching the ground, carried by the music and the way Lucifer held her in his arms. More than two people dancing, they had become one with the music.

At that moment, they had an unspoken understanding, a mutual trust that felt almost too fragile, too fleeting to be real. Her breath quickened as Lucifer's hand slid further down her back, pulling her closer, their faces now inches apart. She could see the faintest flicker of something in his eyes, a rawness that took her breath away.

The music slowed, the final notes lingering in the air, and for a brief second, everything seemed to stop. They were suspended in time, their tension palpable, as if the song had woven them into a fragile web neither wanted to break. But when it ended, neither of them moved away, their bodies still swaying gently in the aftermath of the dance, the silence heavy with unspoken words.

Amber's heart was racing. She'd expected this moment to feel like a battle, like everything she did have to be calculated like there was a hidden test she had to pass. But now, in the song's aftermath, it felt more like an invitation.

Lucifer's hand rested on the small of her back, inches above the curve of her rear, steady and unyielding. His gaze didn't waver from hers as the last echoes of the song faded. The distance between them seemed to shrink even more, and Amber felt like they were balancing on the edge of something new, something she wasn't sure she was ready for.

But then, as the song ended, the music abruptly shifted. A sudden jolt of an upbeat tempo filled the room, sharp and jarring compared to the gentle melody they'd been swaying to. Amber paused, surprised, and looked up at Lucifer to find his expression darken almost immediately.

"What is this?" he muttered under his breath, his grip on her tightening slightly, though not in anger, more like frustration. His lip curled in displeasure, and it was clear that the sudden change in pace unsettled him.

Amber, however, couldn't contain the burst of energy that surged through her. She grinned, her eyes sparkling as she kicked off her heels, suddenly feeling free. "Come on, Lucifer! Lighten up!" she teased, her voice playful as she spun in a circle, the sudden rhythm of the upbeat song urging her on. *Devil in a Dress* surged through the speakers, and she laughed at the irony.

Lucifer's brow furrowed for a moment as he watched her, clearly caught off guard by her change in demeanor. But then, something shifted in his expression. The surprise morphed into reluctant amusement, and before Amber knew it, he let out a low, almost incredulous laugh, a rare, so genuine sound that it made Amber's heart skip a beat.

"You really are a wild card, aren't you?" he said, amusement edging his voice.

"Come on!" Amber laughed, pulling him into the rhythm. "Live a little!"

He followed her lead, stepping into the beat, and Amber saw him wholly let go for the first time. The cold, calculating devil she'd come to know was replaced by a man who could laugh and move with the music without thinking about the weight of his role. They twirled and spun, the air between them crackling with energy as they fed off each other's movements.

Amber laughed, spinning away from him, feeling the freedom of the moment. Lucifer followed, and for once, he didn't look like the Devil; he looked like someone enjoying the chaos of the dance and the pure, unfiltered joy of the music.

The song eventually slowed, and as it did, they faced each other again, breathless but with a genuine, unforced shared smile between them.

But as the next song began, something shifted again, *and Love Me Harder* echoed through the speakers. The music became a sultry, intimate rhythm, pulling them back into the quiet, the personal space between them filling with more than just the music. Amber's breath hitched as Lucifer closed the distance, his touch firm but gentle, drawing her back into his embrace. The heat intensified, and the air became thick with something much deeper than the dance they'd shared before.

This time, there were no words, no distractions, only the music and how their bodies moved together, slow and deliberate, drawn by an invisible force. The dance was fierce, almost possessive, as Lucifer spun her effortlessly, the world blurring around them. When he lifted her above his head, the air seemed to hold its breath. His touch had changed, no longer just a guide but a claim, each movement precise, as if he were committing every second to memory. His fingers pressed into her skin, firm and unyielding, sending a shiver down her spine. His gaze locked onto hers, dark and unreadable, the intensity in his eyes like a tether binding her to him in a way that went beyond the dance.

As the music flowed, every step became more intimate, the distance between them shrinking until barely any space left. Lucifer leaned in just enough for Amber to feel the heat of his breath against her lips. For a brief, tantalizing moment, it seemed like the world had stilled around them, leaving only the two of them in the center of the dance floor.

Amber's pulse quickened; she couldn't look away. The song swirled around them, every note heavy with anticipation. This dance, unlike the others, felt like something more, something laden with unspoken desire.

Lucifer's voice, low and husky, broke through the silence. "You've learned how to make everything... interesting, haven't you?"

Amber could barely form words, her body responding to him in ways she hadn't expected. All she could do was nod, her chest rising and falling with each breath.

And with that, they danced. A dance of slow, seductive rhythm, where every moment felt like it was drawing them closer to something neither of them could name.

By the time the song neared its end, their faces were mere inches apart, their breaths mingling. Amber's fingers had found their way into the back of his hair, tangling themselves into the thick mane. His hands had drifted dangerously low on her body, his thumb tracing slow, absent-minded circles against her hip, the touch searing even through the fabric. The record crackled with static, but they didn't stop swaying, lost in a moment that felt suspended in time.

"Lucifer, I..." Her voice was barely a whisper. She didn't even know what she would say; she only needed to say something, acknowledge this pull between them, and make sense of it.

The second the words left her lips, she knew it was a mistake. The moment shattered like glass, the tension snapping so violently it nearly left her breathless.

Lucifer's hands fell away from her as if burned. His expression hardened, and he took a step back. "It's late," he said, his voice even, controlled. "Korinna will meet you in your chambers."

He lingered for only a moment longer, his gaze once again turning hard, before turning on his heel and striding out of the ballroom. He left Amber standing in the silence, the echoes of their dance still lingering in the air.

36

Haunted Hearts

Back in her chambers, Amber dismissed Korinna with a quiet nod, craving solitude to unravel the night's chaos. As the door shut behind her, she exhaled slowly, running her fingers over the necklace draped around her neck. Its beauty was a stark, almost cruel contrast to the storm still raging inside her, the lingering heat of Lucifer's touch, the way his breath had felt against her skin, the way he'd looked at her before he walked away.

She sat on the edge of the bed, the silk sheets cool beneath her fingers. The ballroom still felt wrapped around her, like she'd never left it. The ghost of their last dance clung to her, the weight of Lucifer's hands still imprinted on her body, his absence an ache she wasn't sure she could fill.

Had she imagined it? The way he'd held her, touched her, *wanted* her? Or had she pushed too far, too fast, speaking when she should've let the silence stretch between them a moment longer?

Amber sighed and slipped off her dress, letting it pool at her feet before crawling into the massive bed. The sheets were soft and luxurious, but they felt empty. She pulled the covers around herself, staring up at the ceiling.

She'd survived another night in Hell. More than that, she'd *danced* with the Devil himself, and for a fleeting moment, she'd seen something in him that felt almost... human.

But then he'd left.

Amber closed her eyes, turning onto her side, her fingers brushing absently over the necklace again before removing it and laying it on the nightstand beside her.

Tomorrow, everything will be different. It *had* to be.

But tonight?

Tonight, she let herself remember.

She didn't know why, but a single tear slipped down her cheek as she shut her eyes, willing sleep to take her.

She didn't know that just beyond her door, an entirely different storm was raging.

***

Lucifer *wanted* to knock.

The thought pounded in his skull as he paced the corridor length, his boots striking the floor with each sharp, clipped step. Back and forth. Again and again. His fingers twitched at his sides, curling into fists before relaxing, only to clench again.

It was ridiculous. *He* was ridiculous. The King of Hell, the great Morningstar, the being who'd toppled empires and dragged souls into the abyss, standing outside a woman's door like some lovesick fool, like some mortal *man*.

His jaw tightened. His thoughts were at war with each other, tearing at the edges of his carefully crafted control.

She'd gotten under his skin.

Damn her.

Damn, the way she looked at him, the way she moved in his arms like she *belonged* there. The way she'd said his name was soft and uncertain, as if she *felt it too* like she was offering him something dangerous, something he had no right to take.

He couldn't give her what she needed, what she deserved to have.

He had no right to touch her, no right to *want her*.

For centuries, millennia, he'd been untouchable. The villain. The monster. That was how it had to be. That was what *kept him in control*. And yet here he was, standing outside her chambers, battling the urge to go inside, and,

And *what?*

Hold her? Kiss her? Let himself drown in something he'd spent lifetimes knowing he could never have?

His wings itched beneath his skin, a restless energy crawling through him, pressing against the inside of his ribs.

She just needed to want this for just long enough. Then, they could find a loophole, cementing his power and sending her home.

He exhaled sharply and turned away from the door, every muscle in his body taut with restraint. He could still feel her shape against him, the ghost of her touch lingering where her fingers had tangled in his hair. Her scent clung to him, warm, intoxicating, and utterly *maddening*.

This *had* to stop.

He strode through Castellum Umbrae, his movements rigid and purposeful as if he could walk off whatever *this* was as if he could outpace the thoughts that were clawing at the inside of his skull.

This feeling, this *pull*, was unacceptable. It was reckless. It was dangerous.

He reached his chambers in a blur of wrath and restraint, the doors slamming shut behind him with a force that cracked the stone frame. The walls pulsed with heat, mirroring the storm in his chest.

Without slowing, he crossed the room and threw open the balcony doors, the ancient iron groaning under his violent grip. A rush of scorched air flooded in, carrying with it the ever-burning winds of Hell's sky. Far below, the abyss churned, red and black, endless and alive.

Lucifer stood at the edge, chest heaving, fists clenched at his sides. With a furious snarl, he threw his head back and *roared*.

The sound tore through the castle like an earthquake, shaking the very foundations of Hell. Firelight flickered wildly, shadows stretched and twisted as if cowering from the force of his rage.

The entire realm went silent in the aftermath.

This feeling clawed at him from the inside out.

He was the Devil. The King of the Damned. He did not *yearn*.

And yet...

The shadows at his feet writhed, echoing his unrest. Flames licked at the edge of the balcony as though drawn to his fury, desperate to consume *anything*.

He gritted his teeth and looked out into the distance, where the twisted spires of Hell met the bleeding sky.

But no matter how far he looked, she was all he saw.

His breath heaved, his chest rising and falling in ragged pulls, and then his wings ripped free in a violent snap. Massive and black as the void itself, they stretched wide before curling inward like a shroud. He rarely let them loose, rarely let himself feel like this.

But tonight, he did.

With three powerful beats, he launched himself from the balcony, shooting into the night, higher and higher, until Castellum Umbrae was nothing but a distant glow beneath him.

And still, even as the wind howled around him, the fires of Hell burned below, and even as the night swallowed him whole, he couldn't shake the ghost of her touch.

37

Speaking in Shadows

A few days passed, and Amber hadn't seen Lucifer.

Every morning, she attended class. Every afternoon, she lost herself in the library. And every evening, she arrived at dinner, hoping, *waiting*, to see him. But every night, she was left disappointed.

Still, she refused to let his absence consume her. She'd started forming friendships with some of the Liberi, mainly two older ones, Efrosyni and Leandros, or Syn and Lean for short.

Syn was quiet but fiercely loyal, always willing to go along with whatever reckless idea Lean cooked up. And Lean? He was the troublemaker of the three, far more outgoing than either of the girls and constantly pushing limits just to see how far he could go. He was infuriating at times, but they loved him for it anyway.

The two of them were nearing their Collocatione Ceremonia, where they'd finally learn the roles their years of training had prepared them for. They could be called upon to join a demon rank any day, but until then, they filled their days helping with the younger Liberi, studying in the library, and sparring in the training ring.

Despite everything, Amber found herself enjoying Hell more and more.

However, This morning, enjoyment was the last thing on her mind.

She groaned as the heavy drapes were yanked open, flooding her room with golden-red light.

"Korinna," she mumbled, burying her face in her pillow.

The Domina in Exspectatione said nothing as she moved through the room, pulling an outfit from Amber's wardrobe and laying it out neatly at the foot of the bed.

Amber sighed, rubbing the sleep from her eyes. Another day. Another routine. And still, no Lucifer.

Amber dressed quickly, pulling on the outfit Korinna had chosen without complaint. The fabric was light and comfortable, tailored for movement and formality, and practical yet elegant. She barely glanced at herself in the mirror before grabbing her satchel and heading out the door.

The halls of Castellum Umbrae were already bustling with activity. Operarios and Eques moved purposefully, their footsteps echoing off the stone walls. Amber fell into step with the steady flow of bodies, her mind drifting as she made her way toward the academy.

She'd started to memorize the route now. Down the grand staircase, through the eastern corridor, past the towering obsidian doors that led to the main hall, then out into the open courtyards where the academy loomed in the distance.

She spotted Syn and Lean waiting at the academy's entrance as she walked.

"Took you long enough," Lean teased, crossing his arms. His silver-blue eyes sparkled with mischief, his horns straighter than usual. "I was about to send a search party."

Amber rolled her eyes. "You? Organize a search party? I'd be lost forever."

Syn smirked but said nothing, as usual. The Liberi's dark eyes were sharp, always watching, always calculating. She had a quiet intensity about her, reminding Amber just a little of Lucifer.

The thought sent an unexpected pang through her chest.

Focus.

Together, the three of them entered the academy. The vast halls were lined with flickering torches, the stone walls carved with ancient symbols that pulsed faintly with magic. The academy was unlike anything Amber had ever experienced; it was part school, part fortress, and part testing ground for those training to serve in Hell's many roles.

Today's first class was Psychological Manipulation & Infernal Diplomacy, a class on manipulation, deception, and playing the long game in a realm full of chaos. It also taught them how to negotiate deals, navigate tricky situations, and keep power struggles in check while still making progress.

Amber settled into her seat, gripping her quill as their instructor, Professor Thonth, strode into the room. "Let's begin."

Professor Thonth was an imposing figure, tall and gaunt, his deep crimson robes flowing around him like liquid shadow. His eyes, two pinpricks of burning ember, surveyed the class with an expression that was equal parts disinterest and barely restrained amusement.

"Psychological manipulation," he began, his voice silk-smooth but laced with something unsettling. "The cornerstone of power in Hell. Strength, brutality, and fire may win battles, but the mind, ah, the mind is where true wars are fought and won."

He flicked his wrist, and the massive blackboard behind him came alive with shifting script, the words curling and slithering like living ink.

Lesson One: Perception is Reality.

Amber adjusted in her seat, her quill hovering over her parchment.

"In this realm, perception is more powerful than truth," Thonth continued, pacing slowly and deliberately. "A weak demon who is perceived as formidable will never be challenged. A lie, repeated enough times, becomes a reality. Trust can be manufactured, and fear can be curated."

He turned, eyes locking onto the class. "You will learn to wield these tools as a master craftsman wields his blade."

With a flick of his fingers, the torches in the room dimmed, plunging the chamber into eerie shadows. A moment later, a new figure appeared at the front of the room, a young woman, seemingly human, her face streaked with dirt, her hands trembling. Her eyes darted around the room, wide and fearful.

Amber stiffened. An illusion?

"Tell me," Thonth said, gesturing to the woman. "What do you see?"

Murmurs spread through the class.

"A human," one student said.

"A lost soul," another added.

"A victim," Syn murmured, her voice barely above a whisper.

Thonth smirked. "Are you sure?"

With another flick of his wrist, the woman straightened. The fear in her eyes vanished. Her trembling stopped. Her lips curled into a smirk. And then, her form melted away like ink in water, replaced by something entirely different.

A Crevit.

Not just any Crevit, but one with serrated horns curling back over her head, obsidian skin shimmering in the dim light, and razor-sharp claws flexing at her sides.

The class collectively tensed.

Thonth turned back to them, his grin razor-thin. "What you perceive is what you believe. And what you believe can be controlled. Never trust what is in front of you. Manipulation is not merely about lying but shaping the truth."

Amber's stomach twisted.

Hell wasn't just fire and torment. It was a game, one that required wit as much as strength.

Professor Thonth let the illusion of the demon linger momentarily, her blackened eyes scanning the room as if she could see through them. Then, with a flick of his fingers, she dissolved into nothing but smoke, vanishing like she'd never been there at all.

Amber gripped her quill tighter, her pulse steady but her mind racing.

"Lesson Two," Thonth continued, turning back to the board. The ink slithered and twisted until new words took shape.

The Art of the Long Game: Influence Over Time.

"Anyone can deceive at the moment," he mused, "but true mastery lies in weaving a web so intricate, so carefully placed, that by the time your mark realizes they've been ensnared, it's far too late to escape."

He stepped forward, eyes glinting. "Tell me, what is the most powerful form of manipulation?"

Silence.

Amber's mind sifted through everything she'd learned so far. Lies? No. Fear? No. Those were temporary. But something that could last and change the course of a person's fate without them even realizing...

She hesitated, then said, "Trust."

Professor Thonth turned sharply, his lips curling into a slow, pleased smile. "Precisely."

Amber felt Syn and Lean glance at her, but she kept her gaze locked on Thonth.

"Trust," he repeated, pacing again, "is the single most dangerous weapon in existence. Earn it, and you own someone completely. Break it, and you shatter them beyond repair." He turned his attention to another student, a demon with sharp crimson eyes. "Kyprianos, if I told you I could offer you a power beyond your wildest dreams, would you believe me?"

Kyprianos smirked, leaning back in his chair. "Depends. Do I have to sign anything?"

A few students chuckled.

Thonth let out a dry, humorless laugh. "Smart. And yet, if I spent the next year slowly proving myself to you, guiding you, mentoring you, and rewarding your efforts, you would believe that I had your best interests at heart. And when the time came to offer you that power, you wouldn't hesitate."

The room fell silent again.

"That is influence," Thonth said, his voice dropping lower. "That is power. Not brute strength. Not fleeting deceit. But *time*. A carefully placed word here, a gesture there. You mold someone into what you need them to be without them ever realizing it was *your* hand guiding them all along."

Amber swallowed.

She could feel the weight of his words sinking in, the understanding of just how deep the games in Hell ran.

Thonth surveyed the class. "Now, I want each of you to turn to the person beside you. For the next ten minutes, you will attempt to subtly influence them toward an idea of your choosing, whether it be as simple as convincing them that red Lithebrew is superior to white or as complex as making them believe they were meant for something greater than what they are. Do this without lying outright. Use questions. Suggestions. Appeal to their desires, their doubts. The goal is to make them *think* they came to the conclusion themselves."

The room erupted into quiet murmurs as pairs turned to face each other.

Amber met Syn's steady gaze, already feeling the challenge set between them.

"Alright," Syn said, a slight, knowing smirk on her lips. "Let's see what you've got."

Amber thought momentarily and then said, "Syn, have you ever noticed the beauty that Hell holds?" Syn cocked her head, caught off guard by Ambers's start, "I just mean that before coming here, I expected fire pits and constant screaming, and there's none of that... at least on the mainland."

Syn raised a skeptical brow. "So? What's your point?"

Amber tapped her fingers against the desk, her expression thoughtful. "It just makes me wonder... why Hell has so much beauty? The architecture, the gardens, even the way the sky changes colors, none of it is what I expected."

Syn crossed her arms, clearly unconvinced. "You're avoiding the lesson, Amber. What's your angle?"

Amber gave a small, knowing smile. "No angle. Just an observation. But doesn't it make you wonder? If Hell was meant to be all suffering and punishment, why create anything beautiful?" She leaned in slightly. "Maybe it's not just about punishment. Maybe it's about control."

Syn frowned. "Control?"

Amber nodded. "If Hell was only pain, people would give up before any real torture began. But if you give them glimpses of something more, something worth *wanting*," she gestured vaguely around them, "it keeps them in check. It makes them think they can have more if they just play along."

Syn stared at her, silent for a moment. Then, slowly, she smirked. "You're better at this than I thought."

Amber tilted her head. "I thought we were just having a conversation."

Syn chuckled, shaking her head. "Sure. A conversation."

Across the room, Professor Thonth's lips curled in the faintest trace of a smile. "Interesting approach, Domina Amber," he said smoothly, clasping his hands behind his back. "Offering an idea that makes your target question the world around them. Making them *want* to know more." His dark eyes gleamed with approval. "A classic manipulation tactic disguised as a casual curiosity. Well done."

Amber's pulse quickened at the praise but kept her expression neutral.

Thonth glanced at the rest of the class. "Take note, all of you. True manipulation is never forceful. It's a whisper, a suggestion that buries itself so deep in someone's mind that they believe they thought of it themselves." His gaze flickered back to Amber. "Keep practicing."

Amber swallowed, nodding, but inside, something twisted in her stomach. Had she really been manipulating Syn? Or had she simply been thinking out loud? And if there *was* a difference, did it even matter?

38

The Cost of Nothing

The girls practiced for a little longer, taking turns trying to manipulate each other. Professor Thonth clapped his hands once, and the sharp sound silenced the murmurs of the class. "Now that you've tasted manipulation let's move on to something even more essential: negotiation." His gaze swept the room. "It is the backbone of Hell itself. Every soul that enters, every deal made, every power shift comes down to how well one can negotiate."

Amber straightened in her chair, glancing at Syn, who still wore a smirk from their previous exercise. Two rows down, Lean stretched lazily, looking far too at ease.

Professor Thonth continued, pacing slowly in front of the class. "A successful negotiator understands three things: leverage, perception, and patience. If you lack any one of these, you will fail." He flicked his fingers, and suddenly, the floor beneath them shifted.

Amber's breath hitched as the desks vanished, replaced by an expansive stone hall lined with torches. At its center stood a grand obsidian table, long and polished, reflecting the flickering firelight. The students now sat in high-backed chairs, facing each other.

"This," Thonth gestured around them, "is where real negotiations occur."

The air hummed with power as he took his seat at the head of the table. "You will each take turns striking a deal. Your objective is to get what you want while giving away as little as possible. Fail to do so, and..." His lips curled. "Well, let's just say failure here has consequences."

Amber tensed, her mind already racing through strategies.

Leandros leaned toward her with a cocky grin. "Think he means actual consequences or just academic ones?"

Syn snorted. "It's Hell. What do you think?"

Amber chuckled, but before she could respond, Professor Thonth snapped his fingers, and a card materialized in front of each student. The parchment shimmered faintly with an enchantment, pulsing as if it held a secret.

"In a moment, you will flip your card over and read it silently," Thonth instructed, his gaze sweeping over the class. "You will find something you desire at the top of your card. At the bottom, you will see what you cannot afford to give up." His lips curled into a knowing smirk. "The challenge? Someone in this room has exactly what you need, but to get it, you must negotiate."

Amber exchanged glances with Syn and Lean, the excitement crackling between them.

"The goal," Thonth continued, "is to secure what you want without sacrificing what you cannot lose. This means bartering, deception, persuasion, whatever it takes. Some of you will strike clean deals. Others will find themselves at a disadvantage. And some," his smirk deepened, "may walk away with nothing at all."

He gestured to the cards. "Begin."

Amber flipped hers over and scanned the elegant script.

What you want: A key.

What you can't give up: A promise.

She frowned, mulling over the words. A key could mean anything, a literal key, access to something, even metaphorical freedom. But what kind of promise did she have to safeguard?

Around her, whispers began to fill the air as students leaned toward one another, testing the waters. Some immediately called out their needs, while others sat back, observing.

Amber glanced at Syn. "What did you get?"

Syn's lips quirked up. "Not telling."

Leandros grinned. "Oh, this is going to be fun."

Amber exhaled slowly, straightening her shoulders. *Alright, let's play.*

Amber leaned back in her chair, tapping her card against the table as she surveyed the room. Some students had already begun to haggle, their voices hushed but insistent. She caught snippets of conversations:

"I'll trade you for information."

"I need access. What can you offer me?"

"No deal."

Amber turned back to Syn, narrowing her eyes. "You're not telling me because you think you have something I need, don't you?"

Syn smirked. "Maybe."

Leandros leaned in. "Or maybe she's just watching you squirm."

Amber rolled her eyes but couldn't suppress the grin tugging at her lips. Fine. If Syn wanted to play it that way, she'd have to outmaneuver her.

Instead of pressing Syn for answers, Amber turned to the student beside her, a sharp-eyed demon with curved horns and a calculating expression. "What do you want?" she asked smoothly.

The demon eyed her warily. "What do you have?"

"Ah." Amber leaned forward, feigning nonchalance. "So you're not willing to give something for nothing?"

He snorted. "Obviously."

Amber tilted her head. "But that means I'm already winning."

The demon frowned. "How?"

"Because now I know you have something worth protecting." She grinned. "And I bet someone else in this room wants it."

His frown deepened, but before he could respond, another student approached him, making an offer. Amber smirked. She had no idea what he had, but now he'd be on edge, worried that she was working an angle against him.

Meanwhile, Leandros was deeply conversing with two other students, gesturing wildly. Amber caught pieces of their deal. He was offering something intangible, maybe a favor, in exchange for whatever he needed. It was Classic Lean.

On the other hand, Syn was playing a quieter game, listening more than speaking, her expression unreadable. Amber knew better than to underestimate her.

Amber turned her attention back to her own problem. A key. And she couldn't trade away a promise.

She considered. A key wasn't just a physical object; it could represent access, freedom, and control. Maybe someone in the room had it without realizing it.

Instead of asking outright, she shifted tactics. "Who here has something valuable?" she called out loud enough to draw attention but not enough to sound desperate.

A few students scoffed. Others stayed silent, protective of their cards. But one, a Liberi with sharp, ink-black eyes, raised a brow.

"Depends," he said. "What's valuable to you?"

Amber smiled. *Got you.*

She had no idea if he had what she needed, but if she could make him *think* she wanted something, she might be able to maneuver herself into a winning position.

Amber leaned back, watching the Liberi with ink-black eyes as he studied her, assessing the weight of her words. He was playing it carefully, unwilling to show his hand too soon. *Smart.*

But Amber wasn't about to wait for him to make the first move. She let the silence stretch between them, a trick she'd picked up from watching Professor Thonth. People hated silence; it made them anxious and desperate to fill it. Desperation led to mistakes.

Sure enough, the Liberi finally spoke. "What exactly do you think I have?"

Amber shrugged, twirling the card between her fingers. "I think you *might* have something I need. But I also think you don't realize how much you need something *I* have."

His eyes flickered with interest. "And what's that?"

She smirked. "Leverage."

His expression hardened, but there was intrigue there now. He knew she was bluffing, or at least suspected it, but he wasn't willing to call her out yet. That was the beauty of negotiation: the right words could turn a losing hand into a winning one.

Before he could counter, a commotion erupted on the other side of the room. Leandros laughed as he handed his card to another student, shaking his head. "You got me," he admitted. "Should've known you were setting me up."

Amber turned just in time to see Syn smirking at him, holding up her card in victory. Amber chuckled. *Of course*, Syn had beaten him. She was patient and cunning and never acted before she had all the information.

Professor Thonth clapped his hands, calling the class to order. "Time's up," he announced. "Who managed to get what they wanted?"

A few hands shot up, including Syn's. Leandros groaned dramatically while Amber and the Liberi beside her both hesitated.

Professor Thonth's gaze landed on Amber. "You didn't make a trade?"

Amber tapped her card against the table. "Not yet. But I made my target second-guess himself. And now he will spend the rest of the day wondering if I *actually* had something he wanted."

A slow, approving smile spread across the professor's face. "Interesting strategy, Domina Amber." He looked at the rest of the class. "A deal isn't always about the immediate exchange. Sometimes, it's about planting seeds for the future. A well-placed doubt and a subtle shift in perception can be just as powerful as a signed contract."

Amber caught the Liberi's glance, and he gave her a grudging nod of respect. She grinned.

"Alright," Professor Thonth continued. "Class dismissed. In the next lesson, we'll discuss extraction techniques and how to get what you need when the other party refuses to give it willingly."

A few students exchanged uneasy glances, while others looked intrigued. Amber gathered her things, her mind still repeating everything she'd learned.

She was beginning to realize that Hell wasn't just about brute strength or survival. It was about strategy, patience, and knowing when to strike.

39

The Devil from Her Dreams

Amber had barely made it out of class when Lean, as always, raced over to her and Syn with a glint in his eye. "So, what's the plan for today?" he asked with a mischievous grin.

Syn rolled her eyes, clearly used to his antics. "We're supposed to be learning, remember?"

But Leandros wasn't having any of it. He turned to Amber as if he knew exactly what she needed. "Let's blow off some steam. You know Castellum Umbrae better than anyone. How about we sneak into the kitchen and see what kind of trouble we can stir up?"

"Sneaking into a devil's kitchen. What could possibly go wrong?" she said, already moving.

Syn groaned but couldn't help smiling. "Fine, but I'm not getting blamed if someone catches us."

Amber had spent enough time wandering the halls and exploring Castellum Umbrae to know where things were hidden. It didn't take long before they found their target: a stash of liquor hidden behind the back of a cupboard, far from anyone's eye.

Amber hesitated at first, her fingers brushing the cool glass of the bottle. It wasn't like her to break the rules, but there was something in the air today, a feeling of rebellion, of release, that she couldn't ignore. Her thoughts were still tangled from the class, and Lucifer's absence weighed heavier each minute. A few drinks wouldn't hurt, right?

She grabbed the bottle, pulling it free with a quick tug. She couldn't help but smile as she took a swig, the burn of alcohol immediately warming her insides. The sensation spread like wildfire, loosening the knot forming in her chest for days. Lean and Syn followed suit, both shrugging and laughing.

"Now, this is more like it," Lean said, leaning against the counter with a satisfied smirk.

The three of them fell into a rhythm. The kitchen became their playground, usually a place of mundane preparation and routine. They wandered from one corner to the next, rummaging through cabinets and drawers, finding bits of food to nibble on, all while laughing, teasing, and talking.

Amber drank again, more this time, her fingers trembling slightly as she held the bottle. Her heart started to race with a mix of excitement and frustration, and it wasn't from the alcohol alone. She couldn't help but think about Lucifer. About how they'd been so close, then suddenly so distant. She couldn't seem to make sense of what was happening between them. The anger and confusion all felt so close to the surface now, so raw.

Amber passed the bottle to Lean, who was mid-swallow when footsteps echoed near the kitchen door. The three of them froze, holding their breath, praying the Operario would walk away. But instead, the handle of the kitchen door began to turn.

Amber's eyes widened. "This way!" She motioned urgently to her friends.

Without a second thought, the trio darted toward the back of the kitchen, weaving through shelves of containers and pots. Amber led the way, her heart pounding as she navigated the cluttered space with practiced ease. They rushed toward a back service entrance, the heavy door creaking open just as approaching footsteps grew louder.

They slipped through the door just in time, their breaths coming fast and shallow, the adrenaline coursing through their veins. The dimly lit hallway outside was a welcome escape, and they didn't stop to look back. The last thing they needed was to get caught by an Operario on their tail.

Amber glanced at Syn and Lean, a wild grin on her face. "I told you we'd make it out. Come on, I know where we can go."

She led her friends, their laughter bubbling up between them, their steps a little slow and unsteady from the alcohol to a small room she'd stumbled upon one day, thinking it was just a closet. It turned out to be something far better: a hidden space with a massive bay of windows that overlooked the raging Styx far in the distance.

The trio made their way inside, still laughing and dodging the effects of the booze, to the bean bag-like chairs scattered around the room. They collapsed into them, the cushions soft but unyielding beneath them, as they settled into the quiet of the space.

For a few moments, no one said anything. The bottle passed between them, a comfortable silence falling over the group, broken only by the occasional chuckle or sigh. Amber took a long swig before finally breaking the stillness.

Leandros leaned toward her, his voice low and playful. "Careful, Amber. If you keep drinking like that, I might just fall for you."

Amber smiled automatically, but it didn't reach her eyes. For a flash of a moment, she was back in the garden, in the shadows, with Lucifer's hand curling around her waist, his voice in her ear like a promise.

The memory hit too hard. Too fast.

Her smile dropped. The warmth vanished. The moment soured.

Leandros blinked, clearly noticing the shift, but didn't push.

Shaking off the memory, Amber refocused on her friends: "Your Collocatione Ceremonia can't be far away. Are you nervous?"

Syn shifted, eyes narrowing as she considered the question. Lean, on the other hand, leaned back in his seat, the playful grin on his face fading slightly.

Syn fiddled with the edge of her sleeve, her eyes drifting towards the window. "I guess... a little," she said quietly, her usual confidence flickering momentarily. "There's always pressure, you know? What if I don't live up to expectations?"

Lean snorted, breaking the tension. "Expectations? Please. Who cares about those? You'll crush it, Syn. You've got more smarts than anyone here." He gave her a playful shove, but his smile didn't quite reach his eyes. "Besides, what's the point of being nervous? It's just another day in Hell. We're all gonna end up running things eventually."

Syn rolled her eyes, but Amber could see the glimmer of doubt in her friend's expression. She could relate. She'd spent so many years not knowing where her place was before Hell, and now she was stuck figuring it out.

Amber turned her attention to Lean, who was leaning back, clearly trying to hide his own unease. "And you, Lean?" she asked, keeping her voice light. "Not nervous about your future?"

He let out a slow breath, tapping the bottle against his knee. "Nah, I'm good. I've never really worried about the future. It's all about living in the moment, right?" His voice was too casual, and his eyes darted away from hers as if trying to convince himself more than anyone else.

Amber studied him for a moment, catching the cracks in his usual bravado. But before she could say anything more, the alcohol hit her in full force, and her thoughts began to spin.

Her head felt light, and her words felt a little too loud in her own ears as she spoke again. "I used to think I was only here to survive. You know, to prove I could make it through all of this." She gestured around the room as though Castellum Umbrae itself was part of the puzzle. "But now... I'm starting to think that maybe I'm meant for something more. Maybe we all are."

Lean's smile faltered, and Syn's expression softened. Amber wasn't sure if it was the booze or just the weight of the conversation, but she felt something shift between them.

There was a long silence before Syn finally spoke again, her voice unusually soft. "I think... I think we all have our doubts. But you're right, Amber. We're all here for a reason. And one way or another, we'll figure out what that reason is."

Amber leaned back, her head resting against the beanbag, eyes staring out at The River Styx, which seemed to be in constant turmoil. There was something about that raging water that mirrored the storm inside her. She couldn't help but think of Lucifer, of the things unsaid between them. His absence hung in the air like a thick fog.

She felt something tug at her chest, a longing she couldn't explain, and before she knew it, she was standing up. The sudden movement startled her, and she nearly stumbled, but Lean caught her arm to steady her.

"Where are you going?" he asked, a mix of curiosity and concern in his voice.

Amber gave him a vague smile, feeling the pull of something she couldn't ignore. "To figure out what I'm meant for."

The look on her face must've told them all they needed to know because neither Syn nor Lean stopped her as she approached the door.

Amber's heart raced, each step toward Lucifer's chambers feeling heavier than the last. She wasn't sure what she was going to say when she finally saw him, but she was sure that the silence between them had lasted far too long.

She finally reached his door, her fingers trembling as she knocked. Her heart was racing, not from the alcohol, but from the anticipation of whatever confrontation might come next.

"Lucifer?" her voice came out quieter than she'd meant it to, but she couldn't bring herself to yell as her voice cracked with emotion, the vulnerability beneath the alcohol-fueled anger becoming apparent. The door remained silent, though. No response.

She hesitated for a moment, her breath heavy. With one last push, she flung the door open. The empty room greeted her, the silence oppressive. She felt a pang in her chest, an ache that had nothing to do with the alcohol. The stillness in here was suffocating. He wasn't here.

Amber stumbled inside, her mind still racing. "Lucifer..." she whispered again, softer now, a bit of her earlier bravado slipping away. She looked around the room, expecting to find some trace of him, but the emptiness stretched before her, mocking her.

For a moment, she stood there, alone in the room. Her heart felt heavier than it had in days, and her head swam with the alcohol and her conflicting emotions. The anger, the confusion, and the loneliness all coiled inside her, making her feel more exposed than ever.

She didn't know what she was doing anymore. The alcohol had taken over her senses, but the rawness of everything left her feeling vulnerable and foolish.

A sigh escaped her lips as she sat down heavily on Lucifer's bed. She wasn't sure what she was expecting, but it certainly wasn't this. She wasn't even sure why she was here anymore. She just knew she couldn't be anywhere else.

Behind her, the soft groan of hinges broke the stillness. She turned sharply, her heart lurching, fear coursing through her as uncertainty settled in about what would be creeping in through the window.

But instead, the balcony doors opened on their own, casting the room in Hell's eerie half-light. The shadows shifted, stretching long across the stone floor. And then she saw Lucifer stepping through the doorway as if the night itself had delivered him.

Immediately, his presence overwhelmed the room. But it wasn't just his usual intimidating aura that held her captive; it was the wings. His massive, bat-like wings stretched out behind him with an elegance that made her breath catch. The vein-like strands that ran through them glimmered like shards of midnight, their dark ridges catching the light and casting a shadow over the room. They were like nothing Amber had ever imagined, vast and powerful, and the world seemed to stand still for a moment.

She couldn't tear her eyes away from them. His wings weren't only beautiful in their dark splendor but also a symbol of something deeper, something ancient and untouchable. They seemed to demand reverence, yet there was an unexpected grace to the way they moved as if they were an extension of Lucifer himself.

Her heart raced as she gazed at his wings, the room suddenly feeling small and intimate with the presence of something so extraordinary. Lucifer's form, framed by the dark wings, seemed to loom larger than life, more than just a devil, but something divine, something tragic. His usual confidence and power felt heightened, his essence amplified by his wings. She couldn't help but feel drawn to him in a way she hadn't before, a mix of awe and something deeper stirring inside her.

Lucifer stepped toward her slowly, his gaze intense and unreadable, but she could see the weight in his eyes, as if he, too, were wondering what her reaction would be.

40

Darkness's Smile

"**A**mber?" He questioned, "What are you doing here?"

Amber's heart pounded in her chest, her thoughts swirling. She couldn't find her voice at first, caught off guard by his appearance, his wings, the raw beauty and power they exuded. She was stunned; her breath caught in her throat as she stared at him, trying to compose herself.

"I... I came to talk to you," she finally managed, her words coming out softer than she'd intended. The alcohol still buzzed in her veins, making her feel both bold and unsteady. Her hands trembled slightly, and she clenched them together to steady herself.

Lucifer raised an eyebrow, his gaze flickering over her as if trying to read her thoughts. The room felt charged with tension, his wings barely brushing the edges of the walls as they stretched, as though they were a part of the air between them. His presence was almost too much to handle, and for a moment, Amber forgot why she'd come here.

"You've been avoiding me," she continued, swallowing hard, trying to push past the haze of confusion. "I've been trying to understand what's going on... what this is between us. You can't just shut me out."

Lucifer's expression shifted then, a flicker of something unreadable crossing his face before he masked it with indifference. The wings, though, were still, intensely still, as if they were waiting for his next move.

"I didn't mean to avoid you," he said, his voice a low rumble, as though every word carried more weight than it should. "But you need to understand, Amber, that I can't afford to get too close to you. This... whatever this is... it's not something I can allow."

The words hung in the air, heavy and final. Amber's breath hitched, but the alcohol burning in her veins made her reckless. The walls felt like they were closing in, but she refused to let this moment slip away.

She took an unsteady step toward him, swaying slightly. In a flash, he was in front of her, his hands gripping her shoulders to steady her. His touch was firm and grounding, but it did nothing to stop the dizziness coursing through her.

"Do you think you're drunk?" he asked, amusement lacing his voice, a chuckle slipping past his lips.

Amber tilted her chin up at him, her expression defiant. "I *am* drunk."

Lucifer huffed a quiet laugh, shaking his head as if she'd just said something ridiculous. "You're not... you *can't* get—" He cut himself off, exhaling sharply before muttering a low, knowing laugh under his breath.

Amber didn't care about whatever realization he'd just come to. She was too focused on *him*, on how he stood so close, his broad frame practically swallowing up the space around her. He smelled like smoke and something darker, something more decadent. It was intoxicating.

Slowly, she spoke, her words slightly slurred. "You can't allow *what* to happen?"

Lucifer didn't answer. But his eyes, they burned. A quiet storm brewing beneath the surface, something profound and unreadable, something that made Amber's knees feel weak.

She took a step closer, the space between them shrinking until nothing but a breath of air separated them. "Can't allow yourself to get *this* close?"

His chest rose and fell in sharp, controlled breaths; he didn't need to breathe, yet he was. Amber smirked at the thought, emboldened by it.

"Don't tell me you're scared?" she taunted, her voice barely above a whisper.

She stepped toward him, and he took a step back. A slow, deliberate retreat.

"The great Lucifer," she murmured, tilting her head. "Afraid to get too close?"

Another step. Another backward movement from him.

Then, his legs hit the edge of the bed.

Amber didn't hesitate. She closed the distance, pressing against him, her hands resting lightly against his chest: a challenge. A dare.

And for the first time, Lucifer *couldn't* step away.

They stood like that, locked in a silent battle, neither willing to be the first to break. Amber's hands remained on his chest, his warmth seeping into her skin. She swore she could feel the barely restrained tension in his body as if he were holding himself back by sheer force of will.

Then, his hand moved.

Fingers sliding to her waist, then lower, anchoring at the curve of her ass. He pulled her closer with deliberate pressure, eliminating the last sliver of space between them.

She was entirely against him now, every point of contact igniting with heat and want, with everything neither dared say aloud.

The heat of his body and the firm press of his muscles beneath the thin fabric of his clothes was dizzying. His free hand brushed against her neck, tucking a stray strand of hair behind her ear with an unbearable softness. Then, he leaned in, his breath warm against her skin, sending shivers racing down her spine.

His lips hovered beside her ear as he whispered, "I'm afraid I won't be able to stop."

Amber's breath caught in her throat. A shudder rippled through her, her skin alight with the ghost of his touch. Her knees nearly buckled beneath her, heat pooling low in her stomach as a quiet, unbidden whimper escaped her lips.

Lucifer's grip on her waist tightened, fingers pressing into her skin with a bruising force. Possessive. Restrained. Dangerous.

"Amber..." his voice was low, rough, but before he could finish, the sharp *click* of the door handle turning shattered the moment.

Amber barely had time to register the way Lucifer's expression darkened before reality came crashing back in.

"My Liege, are you ready for me?"

The voice was soft, airy, almost melodic, but it might as well have been a thunderclap.

Lucifer's hands dropped from Amber like she'd burned him.

She took a shaky step back, spinning on her heels to face the intruder.

The door was shut now, and a woman stood inside, framed by the dim candlelight. She was breathtakingly beautiful, her features delicate yet striking. The only thing that gave away what she was were the jet-black wings extending from her back, Angelus Lapsus.

Her brown hair was pulled back into a high ponytail, and her clothing, if it could even be called that, was barely there. Thin strings of leather wrapped around her body in a way that was more suggestive than practical, leaving little to the imagination.

Amber's stomach twisted violently.

There's someone else.

He was waiting for someone else.

The realization hit like a physical blow, knocking the air from her lungs. Had the warmth of his hands on her waist, the heat in his gaze, and the way his breath had shuddered against her skin been meaningless?

Had she been a mistake? A moment of amusement before the one he'd been waiting for arrived?

The sting of it was unbearable.

Amber felt the tears behind her eyes before she could stop them, a burning heat of anger, humiliation, betrayal.

Lucifer, who'd just held her like she was something fragile, something to be cherished, now stood motionless. His face was unreadable, his body rigid.

Amber swallowed past the lump in her throat and turned her gaze back to the woman, forcing herself to breathe evenly.

The Angelus Lapsus tilted her head, dark lashes fluttering as she looked between them. A knowing smirk played at the edges of her lips.

She knows.

She knew exactly what she'd walked in on.

Amber felt something break inside her.

For a moment, neither Lucifer nor the other woman spoke as if waiting for Amber to react. But what was there to say? What could she say?

Amber wasn't his.

She had no claim to him.

She had no right to feel the crushing weight in her chest.

So why did it feel like she was suffocating?

"Right," Amber finally said, forcing a laugh that sounded hollow even to her ears. "I should go."

Lucifer's head snapped toward her, his jaw tightening. "Amber..."

But she was already moving.

Her fingers curled into fists at her sides as she brushed past the other woman, refusing to meet her gaze. The leather strings of the woman's outfit grazed Amber's arm as she moved, and she fought the urge to rip them away.

Lucifer didn't stop her.

Amber didn't look back.

She shoved the door open harder than necessary, letting it slam behind her. The echo followed her down the hall, chasing her as she fled.

41

The Wounded Soul

The Angelus Lapsus merely looked at Lucifer, her expression unreadable, but he knew she understood exactly what she'd just walked in on. She knew her place, knew better than to question him, but she also knew the shift in the air, the crack in his carefully maintained control.

For weeks now, Airlea had warmed his bed. Not because he felt anything for her, she was never meant for that, nor was he capable of it, but because she was a distraction. A substitute for what he truly wanted but could never allow himself to have.

And now, as Amber's scent still lingered in the space between them, as the warmth of her body against his still burned through his skin, Lucifer realized with an unsettling certainty: Airlea was no longer enough. Her skin had been warm, her touch skilled, but none stayed with him. None of it haunted him like Amber's silence did.

Lucifer had spent centuries mastering control. He wasn't a creature swayed by fleeting desire or mortal weakness. And yet, Amber had undone him in ways he'd never anticipated.

It had started subtly, and it was an irritation at first. The way she challenged him and met his gaze without fear, even when she should've been trembling. She'd walked into his world and kingdom, and instead of breaking, she'd adapt. Fought. Survived.

Then came the moments that lingered. The way her laughter, unexpected and rare, had cut through the heavy air of Hell, a sound so foreign it had nearly made him falter. The sight of her with the young demons, teaching them games, scolding them like a mother would. Something had twisted deep inside him then, a realization that he didn't want to name.

And now, here she was. In his chambers. Bold, drunk, fearless. Testing him, taunting him. Closing the distance between them, pressing against him with the kind of reckless abandon that threatened to shatter every barrier he'd spent lifetimes reinforcing.

He'd felt her shiver against him and heard the slight hitch in her breath when he'd whispered against her skin. He'd seen the way her lips parted, the way heat had flared in her eyes, and for one dangerous, fleeting moment, he'd been ready to give in.

All of it, the tension in the room, the ache now spreading through his chest, was a painful reminder of the garden, the pergola, of Amber melting beneath him, his fingers slipping under her nightgown.

He craved to feel her trembling again, her breath unraveling beneath his touch once more. He needed to hear that little sound she'd made when he told her to look at him. It echoed in his thoughts like a record stuck; no one else had ever made that sound.

And he wasn't sure he deserved to hear it again.

But now, as Airlea stood in the doorway, an unspoken question in her gaze, the spell was broken.

Amber had seen her.

And worse, she'd understood exactly what she was looking at.

Lucifer didn't move, but his chest felt tight in a way that had nothing to do with anger. He should've felt relief that Amber would now understand exactly where she stood and why this was a mistake.

But Lucifer felt something else entirely as he watched her shoulders square and saw the flicker of something raw and painful pass through her expression before she masked it with cold indifference.

Regret.

Amber hadn't said a word. She hadn't needed to. The realization in her eyes, the way her lips had pressed into a thin line, spoke volumes.

Lucifer wanted to tell himself that this was for the best. She'd gotten too close and needed to remember what he was. What this place was. What *he* could never allow himself to be.

And yet, when she'd finally met his gaze, something in him clenched, and Lucifer flinched. His wings twitched behind him in a fight-or-flight instinct he couldn't suppress.

She hadn't glared at him. She hadn't spit venom or lashed out. That he could've handled. No, she just... *looked* at him. As if she'd expected this outcome all along as if she'd been foolish to think otherwise.

That was what unsettled him most.

When she went to leave, Lucifer didn't stop her.

He *should* have.

Instead, he clenched his jaw and exhaled sharply, forcing himself to turn back to Airlea.

She tilted her head, watching him closely.

Lucifer's eyes darkened. "Leave."

Airlea arched a brow but didn't argue. She knew better.

Lucifer stood silently as the door clicked shut behind her, running a hand through his hair.

Amber had been in his arms. He'd felt her warmth, her pulse quickening under his touch. And now, he'd let her walk away.

And for the first time in centuries, Lucifer was worried.

Worried that she'd never come back.

42

Whispers and Warnings

Amber woke to a tear-stained pillow, the fabric damp beneath her cheek. She hadn't honestly slept, not for the first time since arriving, but for the first time that it mattered. Physically, she felt fine. Emotionally, she was wrecked.

Slowly, she crawled out of bed, forcing herself to move. She had plenty of time before her first class, but being alone with her thoughts felt unbearable. Dressing mechanically, she avoided the mirror for the first time since she'd arrived, unwilling to face the bloodshot eyes and swollen cheeks she knew she'd see staring back at her.

When she opened the door, bracing herself for the day ahead, she nearly collided with Korinna, who had just been about to enter. The Domina in Exspectatione looked startled to see Amber up and ready, her expression shifting from surprise to something unreadable. Despite herself, Amber let out a small, breathy laugh and waved Korinna off for the morning.

She needed space.

As she walked toward class, her steps fell in line behind two well-dressed demons. Their hurried pace and hushed tones betrayed the weight of their conversation.

"She only has a few months left before she needs to decide," one muttered.

"I'm well aware, Belial," the other responded, voice clipped. "But we can't rush her. She has to decide on her own, with all the information. There are only a few classes left anyway."

Belial let out a sharp breath, shaking his head. "After what we heard about last night, we can kiss this one goodbye."

Amber's stomach twisted. They were talking about *her*.

Amber slowed her steps instinctively, keeping just enough distance to avoid drawing attention but close enough to hear every word. Her heart pounded, drowning out the rhythm of her footsteps.

The other demon, she didn't know his name, sighed. "Lucifer won't be pleased."

"Pleased?" Belial scoffed. "He's already made it clear he doesn't care. That's the problem."

Amber's hands clenched into fists at her sides. Was that true? He didn't care?

The memory of the garden slammed into her without warning: his hand on her thigh, the way his breath had ghosted over her skin as he whispered, "*Open your eyes.*"

Her jaw clenched. She hated that her body remembered, that her skin still burned in the places he touched her. That part of her had wanted him to keep going.

Had he meant it? Any of it?

Or had she just been another soul to test, another to break?

Her mind slid to last night. His hands on her waist, his breath against her skin, the fire in his eyes; it had *felt* like he cared. But then... she thought of the Angelus Lapsus standing in his doorway, her presence slicing through the moment like a blade.

Had she imagined everything?

"If she refuses, it'll cause problems," the nameless demon continued, lowering his voice even further. "It always does when one makes it this far and then decides to leave. She's already integrated. She's already *seen* too much."

Belial let out a dry chuckle. "Then let's hope she isn't as stubborn as she seems."

Amber's breath caught.

She knew she should walk faster, overtake them, pretend she hadn't heard a word. But she didn't. Instead, she let their conversation settle into the marrow of her bones, fueling the quiet storm already raging inside her.

She'd always known she had a decision to make; her own fate had been dangled in front of her since the moment she arrived. But this? This was something else.

They weren't just waiting for her to choose.

They were *betting* on her to break.

Amber forced herself to keep walking, her breath shallow as their words echoed in her head.

"She only has a few months left before she needs to decide."

"After what we heard about last night, we can kiss this one goodbye."

She wasn't just another soul enduring her time in Hell—she was a gamble, a variable they couldn't control. And worse? They thought they already knew the outcome.

Anger simmered beneath her skin, chasing away the ache in her chest. Who were they to decide for her? To assume she was too weak, emotional, or *human* to withstand this place?

Amber's steps quickened, overtaking the demons as she forced herself to school her expression into one of indifference. If they looked at her incorrectly, she wasn't sure she could stop herself from demanding answers.

But she wouldn't give them the satisfaction.

No, she'd walk into class like nothing had happened, like she wasn't unraveling at the seams, like Lucifer's touch from the night before wasn't still burning her skin.

As she reached the lecture hall entrance, she hesitated for the first time.

What if they were right?

What if she wasn't strong enough?

The doubt slithered through her mind, insidious and cruel, but she clenched her jaw and stepped inside.

If they thought she would break, she'd show them just how wrong they were.

43

A Flame Chosen

"Salve." Professor Smeme's voice rang through the classroom as she entered, instantly commanding silence. The students straightened in their seats, their chatter dying off at once.

It had been a while since Amber had seen Smeme, but seeing a familiar face brought relief.

"Welcome," Smeme continued, her sharp gaze sweeping over the class, "to *Forbidden Arts, Dark Magic, and the Art of Eternal Torture.*"

Professor Smeme clasped her hands behind her back, her sharp gaze sweeping across the classroom. "You've all spent time learning about the structure of Hell, its inhabitants, and your place within it," she began, her voice smooth yet commanding. "But knowledge of rank and law is meaningless without power to enforce it. Today, we begin the study of *Forbidden Arts*, the tools that separate the strong from the weak, the rulers from the ruled."

Amber shifted slightly in her seat. The weight of the lesson pressed around her, settling in her bones. This wasn't just another class. This was survival.

"To understand power in Hell, you must first understand the soul," Smeme continued. With a flick of her wrist, dark tendrils of smoke coiled from her fingertips, swirling into the shape of a suspended, glowing orb. "Every soul that passes through these gates carries a history, a life of choices, sins, regrets, and, most importantly, weaknesses."

She turned to the class, her eyes gleaming. "Who can tell me what makes a soul break?"

A few students hesitated before a demon across the room answered, "Pain?"

Smeme smirked. "An elementary response, but not incorrect. Pain is a tool, yes, but a crude one. Tell me, how long can a soul endure pain before it adapts?"

Silence.

"Exactly," she said. "A soul can be tormented indefinitely, yet the truly strong learn to withstand it. That is why the most skilled demons do not rely solely on pain but on the intricate art of *breaking* a soul. And for that, we use more powerful things: doubt, fear, guilt, and hope."

With a flick of her wrist, the glowing orb split into two, flickering like a dying flame. "A soul is strongest when it believes in something. Take that belief away, twist it, corrupt it, strip it bare, and you have something far more useful than suffering. You have *submission*."

Amber swallowed. The lesson had barely begun, and already she felt the implications weighing on her.

Smeme gestured, and the smoke dissolved, reforming into an open book that hovered midair. "We will cover three main elements this cycle: *Forbidden Arts, the Torments of Hell, and the Economy of Souls.* Pay close attention. This knowledge will determine whether you survive or perish."

She turned, eyes narrowing slightly. "Let us begin with spells and dark magic. Who can tell me the difference?"

A demoness with curled horns hesitated before raising her hand. "Spells are structured. They require specific words, gestures, and sometimes materials. Dark magic is... different. It's raw, fueled by willpower and sacrifice."

Smeme's lips curled into a smirk. "Correct. Spells rely on formulas; anyone can learn them with time and discipline. But dark magic? That requires something more. It is not learned. It is *embraced*. Not everyone is strong enough to wield it."

With a flick of her wrist, the torches in the room dimmed, shadows stretching unnaturally, drawn toward her like hungry creatures.

"Spells," Smeme continued, pacing between the rows of students, "are intentional, formulaic, and precise. They require spoken incantations, sigils, or physical components and can be replicated consistently if one follows the correct steps. They can be used for manipulation, enhancement, or specific effects."

She paused, her gaze sharp. "Dark magic, however, is chaotic, consuming, and often irreversible. It's fueled by the wielder's emotions: rage, hatred, desire, suffering, and demands a sacrifice. These sacrifices are no small matter. Dark magic often requires one to surrender power, endure excruciating pain, or even forfeit fragments of their own soul. Worse still, dark magic cannot always be controlled. Once invoked, it takes on a will of its own."

Her voice dropped to a whisper, forcing the class to lean in. "The key distinction is this: a spell is a tool. Dark magic is a force. A spell ends when you stop casting it. Dark magic lingers, shaping you as much as you shape it."

She raised a hand, and symbols formed in the air, glowing with an eerie crimson hue.

"Evil spells are designed for harm. Unlike curses, which are subtle and long-lasting, these spells are immediate, violent, and often destructive. They fall into three main categories: pain and disruption, corruption and influence, and destruction and decay."

She returned to the board. Letters began shifting, twisting into a chant.

"The first group: pain and disruption, designed to weaken, distract, or cause suffering."

The symbols solidified.

"Ignis Venenum," she intoned.

A spark flared in the air before fizzling out. Smeme smiled. "This spell does not burn the flesh but the nerves beneath it, making the target feel as if they are burning from the inside."

A murmur ran through the class.

"Now, you try."

A chorus of "Ignis Venenum" filled the room. A few weak sparks danced in the air, some flickering and dying, others flaring too wildly before vanishing.

"Good," Smeme nodded, though her gaze lingered critically on the weaker attempts. The letters shifted again.

"Fractura Mentis," she recited. "A quick, sharp spell that fractures the target's thoughts, causing momentary disorientation or hysteria."

The students repeated it, their voices blending into an eerie chant.

"The next category is corruption and influence. These spells are subtle, insidious, and powerful."

New symbols burned onto the board.

"Veritas Umbrae," Smeme said smoothly. "A spell that forces a soul to reveal its deepest, most twisted truths."

A ripple of discomfort passed through some of the students.

"Somnus Tenebrarum." Smeme's voice was almost hypnotic. "This spell invades the mind, creating nightmares that blur the line between reality and illusion."

The class attempted it, though a few faltered, stumbling over the words.

"And now, the final group: destruction and decay."

A hush fell over the room.

"Mors Cineris." Smeme's fingers traced through the air, the symbols glowing an eerie, sickly green. "A spell that accelerates decay turning flesh to dust in moments. The caster may decide to affect the entire body... or simply a part."

Several students shifted uncomfortably.

Smeme's smirk deepened. "If that unsettles you, then Nexus Ruina may be beyond your reach."

She moved her hand, and the air itself seemed to tremble.

"Nexus Ruina unleashes raw, unfiltered dark energy, consuming anything in its path, but at great risk to the caster." Her fingers danced through the air, leaving faint trails of energy that flickered and vanished.

"These are spells of ruin. Each has its place, but wield them carelessly, and they will turn on you."

Her gaze swept over the class and seemed to linger on Amber.

"There are many more spells for you to practice and study in your books. For now..." She gestured to the board. "Choose one. *Master it.*"

The lesson had truly begun.

"Now," Smeme said, her gaze sweeping over the class, "let's switch to dark magic."

She stepped forward, her presence suddenly heavier, as if the air bowed to her. A flicker of unease rippled through the students.

"Dark magic is drawn from the raw essence of Hell. It is instinctual. It does not obey the weak."

A few students seemed to shrink at her words. Smeme smirked slightly before continuing.

"There are a few things you must understand before attempting dark magic." Her voice dropped slightly, forcing the class to hang on every word. "First, unlike spells, which follow structure and logic, dark magic *demands* emotion. Rage makes flames burn hotter. Fear makes illusions more convincing. Suffering makes curses stronger."

A wisp of darkness flowed from her, curling through the air like a living thing before dissipating.

"Second," she went on, "every act of dark magic comes with a price. The toll depends on the severity of the magic. It may take a *physical* cost, pain, exhaustion, even injury, or a *spiritual* one, where you risk losing control... or something far worse."

She let the warning settle, watching the growing tension in the room.

"The most important thing to remember," Smeme continued, her voice a deadly whisper, "is that the greater the power, the harder it is to direct."

With a flick of her wrist, a blackened aura spread from her palm, seething with energy. The torches in the room dimmed further.

"This is not something you *learn*; it is something you *become.*"

Her eyes gleamed as she turned back to the class.

"Enough theory. Time for application."

The air shifted, charged with something unseen. A sigil on the floor pulsed, dark energy veins slithering across its surface.

"You will each perform a spell of your choosing." Smeme's smile was razor-sharp. "But be warned, if you lose control, you may not get it back."

The sigil pulsed, casting eerie shadows that flickered along the walls. Amber swallowed hard. The other students were already moving, murmuring incantations, weaving their hands in practiced gestures. The air buzzed with dark energy, a low hum of power pressing against her skin.

She inhaled sharply. *Okay. I can do this.*

She recalled Smeme's words: "Spells are structured. Dark magic is felt."

Amber closed her eyes and focused. She decided on a simple spell, *Ignis Venenum*, the one that burned beneath the skin rather than on it.

Her fingers curled into a controlled motion, attempting to shape the energy around her.

"Ignis Venenum."

Nothing happened.

Amber's chest tightened as a few students glanced her way. Before the silence could stretch too long, Professor Smeme moved to her side, her voice low enough that only Amber could hear.

"Domina Amber," she murmured, her tone measured but firm, "you are not *of* this place, but that does not mean you cannot wield its power. It only means you must try *harder* than the rest of us."

Her gaze was steady, unforgiving, yet not unkind.

Amber swallowed hard, her fingers twitching at her sides. She could feel the weight of the room pressing in, expectant, waiting for her to fail again or to prove them wrong.

Professor Smeme didn't move away. "The forbidden arts don't respond to half-measures," she continued, voice still low. "You *command* the spell, or it will refuse you entirely. Find something within you, pain, anger, desperation. Use it."

Amber closed her eyes, her heartbeat thundering in her ears. She thought of waking up in Hell, of every trial she'd faced, every doubt she'd overcome.

She thought of him.

Of the way Lucifer touched her like he already owned her and then let her go like she meant nothing.

That ache she couldn't shake answered Smeme's command for power louder than anything else.

She clenched her jaw, focused, and tried again.

"Ignis Venenum."

This time, a dark flame flicked around her fingertips, weak but there. A small gasp rippled through the class.

Smeme smirked. "Better. Again."

Amber repeated the spell, "Ignis Venenum."

The flicker grew slightly, burning blue, unstable, twisting in on itself. Amber gritted her teeth, trying to hold it and shape it.

The flame flared suddenly, too fast, too wild. Heat licked up her arm, but it wasn't physical fire but in her nerves, searing through her veins like liquid lightning.

She gasped, stepping back, shaking out her hand as if she could physically shake the pain away.

A few students turned, watching with barely veiled amusement.

Amber clenched her jaw. She knew this would be hard. She wasn't like the demons around her, this wasn't second nature. But she wouldn't let them see her fail.

She forced herself to be steady and focus on the feeling instead of fearing it.

The pain was part of the magic. It was a trade, a cost. She had to *embrace* it, not fight it.

Closing her eyes again, she reached for the power, this time not trying to shape it perfectly, just letting it *exist*.

The fire formed again, but it held its shape this time, a controlled ember dancing in her palm. It was small, but it was *hers*.

Smeme tilted her head, and a glimmer of approval danced over her features.

"Good," Smeme murmured, her voice carrying just enough authority to silence the murmurs in the room. "You've learned the first lesson of the forbidden arts; resistance is weakness. Control does not mean suppression; it means understanding the cost and choosing to pay it."

Amber kept her breathing steady, the ember still flickering in her palm. The pain hadn't faded; it was still there, pulsing under her skin, but she accepted it now. It was part of the magic, part of her.

"Now," Smeme continued, her gaze sweeping over the class, "power is nothing without purpose. Pain for the sake of pain is wasted energy. Tell me, Domina Amber, what would you do with this fire?"

Amber hesitated. She hadn't thought beyond summoning it. She looked at the small flame in her palm, feeling its warmth, its potential.

"Burn something," one of the students muttered, barely hiding their smirk.

Amber ignored them. Fire wasn't just destruction. It was also a transformation.

Instead of answering with words, she moved. She extended her palm and willed the flame to stretch, not destroy, but change. The ember lengthened, shifting, curling around like a wisp of smoke before solidifying into a thin, flickering thread. It hovered above her skin, balanced on the edge of control.

The murmurs in the class shifted from amusement to interest.

Smeme's smirk returned, sharper this time. "Not bad, but tell me, Amber," The professor leaned in slightly. "When the time comes, will you hesitate?"

Amber stared at the fire, then clenched her fist, snuffing it out.

"Not if I have to win."

Smeme's smirk returned. "Good. Take your break, and when we come back, we will go into the depths of the types of torment constructed here in Hell."

Amber stayed still a moment longer. Her hand still tingled where the fire had been, not just from pain, *from want.*

It wasn't power or victory; it was something else entirely.

44

Unbroken

Amber stood in the courtyard, watching the younger Liberi dart around, their laughter filling the air. She smiled as she observed a few of them playing hopscotch, their tiny hooves clicking softly against the stone with each jump.

"Hey."

She didn't turn at Syn's voice, her gaze still on the children. "Hey," she replied.

Syn stepped closer. "Where'd you disappear last night?"

Amber's smile faltered. "Had someone I needed to talk to."

Syn shifted on her feet, clearly debating whether to press further. "How'd it go?"

Amber didn't answer.

"That well, huh?" Syn said, her tone dry. After a pause, she added more softly, "You okay?"

Amber just nodded.

Syn exhaled, watching her carefully. Then her gaze flickered over Amber's shoulder toward something, *someone*, behind her. When she spoke again, her voice had dropped to a whisper.

"I don't know what you said to him... or what happened between you two," she hesitated, "but whatever it was... he *can't* stop looking at you."

Amber had felt it too, the weight of an unshakable gaze burning into her back from above, but she refused to turn toward the balcony.

Instead, she feigned ignorance, "Who?"

Syn gave her a pointed look. "You *know* who." She nudged Amber's arm. "Lucifer."

A quiet laugh escaped Amber's lips, but she didn't deny it.

Syn smirked. "Yeah, that's what I thought."

Amber shook her head, trying to ignore the way her heart pounded harder.

The girls lingered a little longer, chatting idly as they watched the Liberi tackle Leandros to the ground. Their laughter rang through the courtyard as they practiced their physical skills.

Then, Professor Smeme's voice cut through the air, calling everyone back to their classrooms.

Without hesitation, Amber linked arms with Syn and walked inside, never once looking up.

From the balcony above, Lucifer's grip tightened on the stone railing, his blood simmering at her blatant disregard.

He was losing her.

She never looked up. Not once. Even when she knew he was watching.

And that, somehow, hurt more than rage or rejection ever could.

A low growl rumbled in his chest as the stone beneath his hands fractured, thin cracks splintering outward. He exhaled sharply, forcing himself to relax, to push the simmering frustration back beneath his carefully constructed mask.

He wasn't one to give up.

With a final glance at the courtyard below, Lucifer turned on his heel and strode inside.

***

Back inside the classroom, Smeme wasted no time as the students settled into their seats.

"Now," she began, her voice smooth yet laced with something sinister, "we're moving on to something more... practical. The torments of Hell."

The torches dimmed, their flames flickering unnaturally as eerie shadows stretched along the walls. A slow chill slithered through the air.

"Pain is an art form here," Smeme continued, pacing in front of the class. "There are many methods, some physical, others psychological. But tell me, class, what is more effective: endless suffering or the illusion of relief?"

A few murmurs scattered through the room before a student finally spoke. "The illusion of relief?"

Smeme smiled. "Yes. The moment a soul believes the torment is over, only to have it ripped away, is when it truly begins to crack. Predictability is a mercy. Uncertainty is torture."

Amber clenched her fists under the desk.

"You will learn how to inflict both," Smeme said, her tone final.

Smeme turned toward the board, and with a flick of her wrist, words burned into existence in an infernal script.

"There are three fundamental pillars of torment: Physical Pain, Psychological Manipulation, and Existential Despair. Each serves a different purpose, and each leaves its own mark."

She gestured toward the first set of words as they flared brighter.

Physical Pain.

"The simplest, and yet, the least refined," Smeme said. "A blade, fire, the tearing of flesh are crude but effective tools. However, true masters of torment do not simply cause pain. They control it."

She moved toward the edge of the classroom, where a long iron poker materialized in her hand, glowing red-hot at the tip. She trailed it lightly across the air, leaving a faint embered line that lingered before fading.

"Physical pain alone is fleeting. A cut heals. A burn scabs over. The body adapts. But the key to making it last is timing and expectation."

She turned back to the class, her golden eyes gleaming.

"A simple lash across the skin means nothing if the victim knows it's coming. But make them wait, make them anticipate it, and let them tremble in the silence before the strike; that is when pain becomes *effective*. The body can only endure so much before it shuts down... but the mind?" She smiled. "That is where true agony lies."

She raised a hand, and suddenly, a guttural scream echoed through the room, not from any student but from the walls themselves. The sound twisted, morphing into something near-human, full of pleading, choking gasps. The students tensed, some shifting uncomfortably.

Then, as abruptly as it started, it stopped.

"Pain is not just about suffering," Smeme continued, unfazed. "It's about making them *beg for it to stop*. A simple cut is nothing. But stretch it over centuries? Layer it with hope? That is how you turn a soul into dust."

The embers on the board flickered, shifting to the next set of words.

Psychological Manipulation

"This," Smeme said, her voice softer now, more insidious, "is where true artistry begins."

The room's shadows lengthened, creeping up the walls like living things. The torches flickered, casting strange, dancing figures against the stone.

"Hope is the sharpest weapon in Hell. Give a soul a taste of freedom. Let them believe they have escaped. Let them feel *safe*. Give them comfort, let them rebuild themselves... and then, take it away."

A student swallowed hard, but no one spoke.

"The mind is fragile," Smeme continued. "It clings to familiarity, to patterns, to the idea that *this* is the worst it will ever get. Shatter those expectations, and the soul begins to *willingly* unravel."

She took a slow step forward.

"Imagine this: A prisoner trapped in a dark cell for centuries. Then, one day, the door opens. The air smells fresh. They walk free, feeling the warmth of the sun on their skin. They take their first step toward freedom, only for the ground to collapse beneath them, sending them back into darkness."

A cold smile curled her lips.

"The second fall hurts more than the first. Because now, they have been reminded of what they have lost. They felt close to redemption to freedom only to have it slip through their fingers. *That* is devastating."

She let the weight of her words sink in before gesturing to the final set of words.

Existential Despair

"This," Smeme said, her voice dropping to an almost reverent hush, "is the rarest form of torment and the most devastating."

The torches dimmed further, the flames barely flickering, until the room was nearly cloaked in darkness.

"A body can heal. A mind can rebuild. But take away the very foundation of a soul's existence, its *purpose*, and you erase it completely."

Her eyes swept over the students. "What do souls fear more than pain?"

Silence.

Smeme tilted her head. "They fear meaninglessness."

The flames in the torches went out completely, plunging the room into darkness.

"Remove all sense of time. Erase their memories, then give them back in fragments, out of order. Make them question who they are and if they were ever real at all. Let them wake up in a world that doesn't recognize them, where nothing they do matters, where even *they* don't remember what they once were."

A student shifted, uneasy.

"Some souls will scream for mercy or death," Smeme continued. "Others... will forget they were ever alive."

She let the weight of her words settle before straightening, her usual smirk returning. The torches flared back to life, casting warm light that felt almost jarring after the suffocating darkness.

"These methods are the backbone of Hell's torment," Smeme said. "Some of you may find them distasteful. Others may find them *fascinating*." Her gaze flickered toward Amber for the briefest second before moving on.

"In the coming weeks, you will learn how to wield each of these effectively." She turned, flicking her wrist to erase the board.

"But for today..." She lifted a single finger. The air in the room shifted and thickened as an unseen force pressed down on their shoulders. The flickering torches elongated their shadows into something almost sentient.

"You will experience the first lesson for yourselves."

With a flourish, she produced a deck of cards. Then, with a sharp snap of her fingers, the cards took flight, each going to a student at random. The Liberi looked at them with varying degrees of curiosity and apprehension.

"Each of you has been given a card," Smeme explained. "A red card means you are the torturer. A white card means you are the victim. The number on your card determines the category of torment you will practice or endure."

She gestured to the board, where the categories burned into existence:

1 = Physical Pain Ex: simulated burns, pressure, or injury; 2 = Psychological Torment Ex: illusions, false hope, paranoia; 3 = Soul-based Torment Ex: draining energy, exposing fears, emotional suffering.

"You will take turns. Torturers, you will practice your assigned method with your partner. Victims, you will endure and learn how to resist. After one trial, you will switch roles and receive a new number."

A wicked glint danced in Smeme's eyes. "Do not hold back. The true lesson lies in what you *feel*. Begin."

The room buzzed with a nervous energy as pairs formed. Amber glanced down at her card.

White. Victim. Number 2.

Psychological torment.

Across from her, Leandros smirked as he revealed his red card with a matching number 2. "Looks like I get to break you first, princess."

Amber squared her shoulders. "You can try."

The corner of his mouth lifted. "Oh, I intend to."

Smeme clapped her hands. "You may begin."

Leandros took a slow, deliberate step forward. The shadows in the room seemed to stretch, curling unnaturally around them. His voice, when he spoke, was softer than she expected.

"You know," he said, tilting his head, "torment isn't just about pain. It's about truth."

Amber's breath hitched as the space between them seemed to shrink, though neither of them moved.

"It's about finding the thing you don't want to hear, the thing you pretend doesn't exist, and forcing you to face it." He paused, watching her. "I wonder, Amber... what truth are you running from?"

Her mouth went dry.

Leandros stepped even closer, lowering his voice to a near whisper.

"You already know you don't belong here. That's not the part that scares you." He let the words settle before leaning in slightly. "What scares you is that you want to."

Amber's nails dug into her palm.

"That's ridiculous," she said, but her voice wasn't as strong as she wanted it to be.

Leandros smiled. Not his usual teasing smirk, but something sharper. Cruel.

"You're already changing. You're learning our ways. You're good at it. Too good." He tilted his head. "You think Lucifer brought you here as a test? Maybe he's just waiting to see when you'll finally stop fighting it."

Amber clenched her jaw, but the words slid under her skin like barbed wire, prickling with a venom she couldn't shake.

Suddenly, everything shifted. She was no longer in the classroom, no longer talking with Lean. The surroundings blurred, and Amber found herself in a bedroom. Lucifer's bedroom. And Lucifer was there.

"I'm so proud of you," he purred, his voice smooth and dangerously warm. "You're doing so well here."

This isn't real. Amber's heart raced as she took a step back, her breath catching in her throat.

"We're meant to be together. You're meant to stand at my side, my little dove."

Amber froze. The words echoed in her mind, and her chest tightened. *How did Lean know that name? How could he? Was this real?* Was Lucifer really standing before her, speaking to her right now?

Her thoughts spun in a frantic whirl, a battle between confusion and desperation.

Amber's pulse hammered in her ears as she tried to shake the disorienting fog clouding her mind. *This isn't real. This isn't real.* The mantra did little to quell the gnawing sensation growing inside her chest. She wanted to scream and run, but her feet felt frozen. Every part of her body screamed for freedom, for clarity.

Lucifer's smile was twisted, predatory, and knowing, as if he could hear her thoughts. "You can't escape this, Amber. Not me. Not us."

He stepped closer, his presence suffocating. The shadows stretched and writhed around him, responding to his every movement.

"I've seen your heart, your desires," Lucifer continued, his voice like velvet, wrapping around her. "You belong to me. No matter how hard you fight it, this is your place. Your home."

Amber's breath caught, her mind teetering on the edge of reason. The words, their weight, pressed down on her like a physical force.

His eyes gleamed darkly, watching her struggle. "You're nothing without me. Just a lost little girl, wandering through Hell, pretending you're in control. Pretending you matter. But you don't, Amber. Not really."

Something inside Amber snapped at the venom of his words. *No. This isn't him. He'd never say that.*

She forced herself to stand taller. *I matter. I know I do. Lucifer wouldn't have let me walk around free if I didn't.* She refused to let the illusion break her.

"This isn't real," Amber said, her voice quiet but firm.

A cold laugh slipped from Lucifer's lips, but Amber didn't waver this time.

"Let it happen," he coaxed, stepping even closer, his breath hot against her ear. "Give in to the truth. You know it's what you want. The chains, the control, they feel good, don't they?"

Amber shook her head, desperation rising. "This isn't real. You're not real!" she shouted, her voice cutting through the illusion like a blade.

And with those words, the illusion shattered. In the bedroom, Lucifer, everything dissolved into thin air, leaving Amber standing once more in the classroom.

Leandros stood before her, his smirk replaced with a rare, silent glare.

"You can't break me," Amber said, her voice steady despite the lingering tremor inside her.

Smeme approached her expression with rare approval: "Domina Amber, I am extremely impressed. Not many can come out of a full-blown illusion without crumbling. Very well done."

She turned to Leandros, her tone cool but not without a hint of rebuke. "Keep practicing. You'll get there."

Leandros glared at Amber, his frustration barely contained. But Amber's gaze remained unwavering. The remnants of the illusion were still hanging in the air, a ghost she refused to let haunt her.

"It's time to switch!" Professor Smeme announced, her voice sharp and clear. "Please take a look at your cards and check the number."

Amber glanced down at her card, her pulse quickening as she saw it had turned red, the number 3 glaring up at her.

Across from her, Leandros looked slightly pale as he examined his white card, which also bore the number 3.

Amber's lips curled into a sly smirk. "My turn," she said, her voice dripping with newfound confidence.

Leandros shifted, unease flickering across his face. He'd underestimated her. She raised a hand, her fingers trembling with power, as a dark energy began to gather around them.

His breath quickened as Amber's voice lowered, speaking the words that would unleash the torment.

"I'm going to make you face the one thing you can't escape. Yourself."

The shadows around them thickened, the room darkening as if something was smothering the light. Amber's eyes glinted with cold determination.

Leandros's breath caught in his throat as a sudden weight pressed against him. His hands trembled as the torment began, his energy slowly draining away. It felt like his very essence was being sucked out, leaving him weak, vulnerable.

Amber could see it, the flicker of fear in his eyes. He was afraid, not of physical pain, but of what was coming for him. His soul, his very core, was being stripped bare.

"You hide behind that smug exterior," she taunted, watching the terror creep into his expression. "But I can see it. All of it."

A wave of his hidden fears washed over the room, swirling like a storm, and Amber latched onto them. She reached into his mind, pulling his nightmares from the depths and flipping through them like a picture book, each image flashing by with cruel clarity.

She landed on one, a memory, an insecurity, that seemed to glow brighter than the rest.

"Hmm," Amber muttered, intrigued. "What do we have here?"

The image of a demoness flashed before her. She was a Crevit, and the weight of her assignment to the islands pulsed in the air like an unspoken truth. Amber could feel the deep ache of longing Lean felt toward this girl. She could see his desperate desire to be with her, to join the Crevits on the islands, to earn a place beside her. The longing twisted in his chest as he craved to escape his current fate and climb the ranks because the rules of Hell were clear: only those of equal status could fraternize.

"Ahh," Amber said, her voice dripping with malicious satisfaction, "so this is what you've been working so hard for."

Leandros's breath hitched, the weight of the emotion making his chest tighten. Amber didn't let up; she reveled in the slow unraveling of his carefully constructed facade, her power sinking deeper into the core of his vulnerability.

"What happens if I take it all away?" Amber whispered, her voice soft but laced with cold steel.

Leandros's body trembled, and his pulse raced as the crushing weight of his own desires and insecurities bore down on him. Amber crafted a new reality, twisting the very essence of his dream. In this new world, he was never allowed to become a Crevit. The girl, his object of obsession, wasn't his. She was falling for someone else, someone beyond his reach. And Leandros, helpless, had to watch.

He was nothing.

Amber's power pushed him further, pulling him into the depths of his darkest fears. She watched him crumble, gasping for air as his self-worth, his very identity, withered under the torment she inflicted.

Amber's lips curled into a dangerous smile, savoring the moment. She could feel the unraveling of his soul, the desperation, the suffocation.

Her gaze never left him as his once-steady composure faltered, slipping away like sand through his fingers.

"Does it hurt?" she whispered her tone a mix of sweet venom and wicked satisfaction.

"Please," Leandros whimpered, his voice shaky, "make it stop."

Amber didn't hesitate. With a snap of her will, she released her power, and the suffocating weight of the illusion shattered. The classroom snapped back into focus, the air clearing as if it had never been disturbed.

For a brief moment, the two of them simply stared at each other. The silence stretched, heavy and thick, before a slow smile cracked across Leandros's face.

"Damn, girl, you're good," he said, a hint of admiration in his voice.

Amber raised an eyebrow, her lips curling into a smirk. "You're not so bad yourself," she replied. "I'm just stronger." She winked at him, a flash of playful challenge in her eyes.

The two shared a genuine laugh, the tension between them easing as the sound of their amusement filled the air.

But their brief moment of camaraderie was cut short as Professor Smeme's voice rang out, calling their attention back to the front of the room.

45

Tethered

"I am very impressed with the majority of you for not only causing torment but for enduring it, and some of you even overcoming it, but it's time to move on." Professor Smeme said, her voice steady and approving.

A book floated in front of her, its pages flipping rapidly before suddenly stopping. Smeme tapped the open page, and the words began to glow faintly.

"Soul-binding, soul-trading, and soul-restoration are the foundation of power in Hell," she continued. "Deals are made, ownership is claimed, and once you lose a piece of your soul, getting it back is nearly impossible."

Amber felt the weight of those words settle heavily in the air, the gravity of their meaning sinking deep into her chest.

"Power in Hell," Smeme said softly, her tone turning more contemplative, "is not always about force. It's about knowledge, persuasion, and patience. Learn what makes a soul tick, and you will learn how to control it."

Professor Smeme's eyes gleamed with a quiet, knowing satisfaction as she watched the class absorb her words.

"Let's start with soul-binding," she continued, her voice lowering as if the very concept demanded reverence. "It's one of Hell's most powerful and dangerous forms of control. A soul can be tethered to another, but only under strict conditions. Binding yourself to someone more powerful is nearly impossible. The soul resists the imbalance, and the link won't hold."

She began to pace, slow and deliberate.

"Binding to someone *lesser* is far more common. Their soul folds under the weight of the stronger one, becoming an extension of the binder's will. That's where most of the control comes in: domination, obedience, submission."

"And if the souls are equal?" someone from the front asked quietly.

Smeme paused, her eyes darkening.

"Then the bond is... volatile. Equal power creates tension in the link, unpredictable, intimate, and nearly unbreakable. If either tries to sever it, it can destroy them both. The only way to bind two equal souls without mutual destruction is through a specific ritual that requires full consent from both parties. It's rare. Dangerous. And permanent."

Amber's chest tightened. "Permanent?"

"Down to the soul," she confirmed. "You don't just *share power*. You share the pain. Memory. Desire. If one falls, the other will feel it. If one dies..."

Smeme let the silence finish the sentence before gesturing to the book, and a flicker of light danced across the pages.

"Soul-binding is often used in deals," Smeme said, her gaze sweeping across the room, locking onto Amber for a moment before moving on. "A soul can be bound to an object, person, or even place. The possibilities are nearly limitless. But once a soul is bound, it becomes more than just a part of the individual. It's a tool, a weapon, a source of power."

Amber felt a strange chill crawl up her spine as she considered the implications.

"The process itself," Smeme continued, her voice growing more intense, "is both an art and a science. It requires understanding the core of the soul, the essence of someone. And once that is understood, you can forge the bond. The soul may fight at first, but you can make it submit with the right leverage. And once it's bound, you can command it as you would a servant, whether in life or death."

Amber's heart raced at the thought. She knew the stakes were high in Hell, but to truly control someone's essence, what kind of power was that?

"But," Smeme cautioned, her expression darkening slightly, "those who practice soul-binding are often feared and respected in equal measure. It is not a power to be taken lightly."

She paused, letting the weight of her words sink in before adding, "Soul-binding, though, is not just about taking control. Sometimes, it's about giving something back. About forging an alliance with another soul, making it part of your own. But always remember, what is bound can't always be unbound. What is given can't always be taken away."

Professor Smeme's tone shifted subtly as she continued, drawing the class further into the world of soul-binding. The atmosphere grew heavier and more oppressive as if the air was thick with the subject's weight.

"Let's dig deeper," Smeme purred, her fingers gently tracing the glowing pages of the book. "Soul-binding isn't just a transaction or a tool; it's an intimate act. It requires a profound understanding of the soul's essence, deepest desires, and primal fears. The soul is not simply a collection of thoughts or emotions; it is the foundation of who someone is. It holds their memories, will to survive, and sense of purpose."

Amber's pulse quickened. Was there truly a way to manipulate something so... fundamental? To control another being's very sense of self?

"To bind a soul," Smeme continued, her eyes gleaming with an unsettling mix of admiration and cold precision, "you must first learn to strip it down. You tear away the layers, the defenses they've built until you reach the core. Once there, you offer them something, a temptation, a promise, or a threat. The key is to exploit their deepest need. Souls are fragile things. They crave connection, understanding, and security. They'll surrender to the right offer, the right pressure. And when that moment comes..."

She paused, letting the words linger like a sharp edge in the room. The students were rapt, their focus now entirely on the professor and her dark wisdom.

"The bond is formed. You can now command their actions, their thoughts, their very existence. A bound soul will follow your will through a direct command or subtle influence. You can make them forget, fear, or love, depending on the bond you wish to forge."

Amber felt a shudder crawl up her spine. She could hardly imagine the weight of such power.

"But it comes at a price," Smeme said, her voice darkening with a warning. "The soul, once bound, is forever altered. It loses its autonomy. The more powerful the binding, the more the soul erodes. Over time, a bound soul may become nothing more than an empty vessel, a puppet of its master. The individual it once was fades into nothingness, consumed by the bond."

A few students exchanged uneasy glances, but Smeme pressed on. "The strength of the binding depends on the nature of the connection. The stronger the emotional or psychological bond between the binder and the bound, the more lasting and complete the control. It's not just about the power you wield; it's about the emotional leverage you have over them."

"But," Smeme went on, clearly reveling in the darkness of her topic, "if you truly understand a soul, if you know what they desire, what they fear, what they will do to protect themselves, you can bind them in ways that seem like they've freely chosen it. It's a far more dangerous form of manipulation but also the most powerful."

A slow, dangerous smile curled on Smeme's lips as she leaned forward. "And then there is the art of *unbinding*. Unbinding is more difficult, often requiring far more power, sacrifice, or knowledge. To break a bond, you must either overwhelm it with a greater force or destroy the one who bound it. But that, too, comes with a price. Because breaking a bond doesn't always set the soul free. In fact, it can destroy them entirely, leaving them as nothing but a shattered remnant of what they once were."

Amber swallowed hard, feeling the weight of the professor's words. She glanced at the other students, some of them appearing deep in thought, others with a flicker of fear in their eyes.

"The most dangerous bind," Smeme added, her voice taking on a cold finality, "is when one binds a piece of their own soul to another. You risk losing yourself. You risk becoming a part of them and them a part of you. The lines between you blur, and in some cases, you may find yourself unable to distinguish where one soul ends and the other begins. It is the ultimate test of power and the ultimate gamble."

Amber could feel a shiver ripple down her spine. The idea of binding her soul to someone else's and giving up that much control was terrifying. But at the same time, it made the power of soul-binding feel all the more real.

She thought of the deal she'd made with Lucifer. A trade, not a bond. Or... was it?

A sliver of her soul already belonged to him. Was that why she still felt his presence, even in silence? Why did his absence scrape against her skin like a missing limb?

"Remember, my students," Smeme concluded, her voice now softer, almost maternal, "soul-binding is not just about domination. It is about connection. The best binders understand the soul they manipulate, for the understanding of weakness gives them the greatest power."

The room fell into a heavy silence as the class absorbed the lesson, the darkness of the subject hanging in the air like a storm ready to break. Amber's mind raced, the terrifying and intoxicating possibilities spinning wildly in her thoughts.

46

Lashes and Lies

Professor Smeme's voice took on a more measured tone as if shifting gears toward a darker, even more enticing aspect of power.

"Now, let's discuss soul trading, a practice often seen as a form of negotiation, a barter system that has existed since the first soul was claimed in Hell," she said, her eyes gleaming with a cold, calculating light. "Unlike binding, which seeks control, trading seeks exchange. It's a transaction between souls, each offering something of value in return for something desired."

Amber's gaze sharpened as she listened. Trading souls sounded dangerous, but it held an allure, especially if you could get something desperately needed.

"Remember, however," Smeme continued, "a soul is not just an object to be handed over. It's a reflection of one's identity. To trade one is to exchange a piece of yourself...sometimes more than just a piece."

She paused, watching her students carefully. "For a soul to be traded, both parties must agree on the terms. One cannot simply steal another's soul, at least not without a great deal of power and manipulation. But when you can offer something of equal or greater value, the transaction is made."

Amber's mind raced. What would be an equal trade for a soul? What could someone possibly offer in return?

"To offer a soul in exchange for power, a memory, or an ability is common," Smeme explained. "But there are far darker trades as well, some who trade their soul for eternal servitude, others for knowledge or even to erase their very existence."

Amber shuddered at the thought. "To erase one's existence?" she murmured. The implications were staggering.

"Yes," Smeme said, sensing her curiosity. "The concept of erasing one's history, removing oneself from the world entirely, is a rare but potent transaction. For example, someone who wishes to escape their past might trade their soul for a clean slate, their history wiped away as though they never existed. But the price is high, for the very essence of that soul, the memories, the lessons, the experiences, will be lost forever."

Amber's frown deepened as she realized she'd done it. She'd agreed to prove herself to Lucifer in exchange for him making her his partner. She'd soul-traded.

Smeme's lips curled into a smile that was anything but warm, her eyes gleaming as if she could sense Amber's dawning understanding. "When a soul is traded, it is not simply handed over. It's transformed and shifted into something else that can be consumed, absorbed, or used by the one who receives it. The original soul, as it was, is gone. It ceases to exist as the entity it once was. The only exception is if, when the soul is traded, it ends up where it was always meant to be."

Amber's stomach twisted, the implications sinking deep. Was that why Lucifer couldn't simply control her? Because she was meant to be here? Or was he waiting for the right moment to begin shaping her into something else, something he could own?

"And, of course," Smeme added, her voice now colder, "there are *subtle* trades that can be made without a soul being exchanged. This is where manipulation and deceit come into play. Some make deals with their very essence, offering a fragment of their soul in exchange for favors or benefits that seem harmless on the surface. But little by little, those fragments are consumed. They lose pieces of themselves without even realizing it until there is nothing left."

Amber's skin crawled at the thought. To give a piece of yourself away bit by bit and not even notice until you were hollow...

"The most *dangerous* trades," Smeme went on, her voice dropping to a whisper, "are those where souls are traded for *other souls*, whether to bolster one's power or to escape torment. This is often seen among the highest ranks of demons, who trade in souls as though they were mere currency. But remember, every soul traded leaves a gap in the very fabric of who they are. And the deeper the gap, the harder it is to reclaim what is lost."

Amber's heart clenched as Smeme's words painted a grim picture. A soul could be offered in exchange for something material, but what if that something wasn't enough to fill the emptiness that followed? The consequences of such a trade could be far worse than the original loss.

"To add another layer," Smeme said, her tone growing darker, "there's the *twist* of *reciprocal* soul-trading. This is an exchange where both parties agree to trade equal portions of themselves, often a transaction between equals or rivals. But beware, for in some cases, the trade is not equal at all. One party may leave with a more potent soul, while the other loses what makes them truly themselves."

Amber felt her stomach churn at the idea of reciprocal soul-trading. It wasn't just about exchanging items or temporary gains; it was about altering the very core of one's being. The thought was enough to unsettle even the bravest of demons.

Smeme's gaze swept across the class, lingering on Amber for a moment longer. "And there's a final form of trading, the most insidious. The *delayed trade*. This is where a soul is traded with the understanding that the debt will be collected at a later time. The soul is promised, but the final price is not paid until the deal comes to fruition. Some make these trades believing they will never have to pay; others, however, are bound to the *debt* of that trade, and when it is collected, the consequences can be... devastating."

Amber felt her heart drop. A delayed trade could be the perfect trap, where someone wouldn't even know they were in debt until it was far too late. Lucifer had offered her this trade.

Smeme smiled darkly, clearly pleased with the unsettling silence her words had created. "Soul-trading is not a practice for the faint of heart. It is an art, a weapon, and a poison all rolled into one. Master it, and you can bend reality to your will. But understand that each trade leaves its mark on both the soul that is traded and the one who makes the exchange."

She paused, her expression hardening. "And once a trade is made, there is no going back. You may *think* you've gained what you desired, but remember, nothing in Hell is exactly as it seems."

Professor Smeme's gaze floated over the room as she sensed the questions lingering in the air. The darkness in the room seemed to lift as Smeme smiled slightly. The class relaxed a bit as Smeme began the next lesson.

"And now we reach the most elusive and, perhaps, the most desperate form of soul manipulation, *soul restoration*," she said, her voice soft but filled with a weight that made the students sit up a little straighter. "The idea of restoring a soul is powerful, yet it is not without complications. Once broken or traded, souls cannot simply be 'fixed.' No matter how much you might want to put things right, there are limitations."

Amber's brow furrowed. Restoring a soul sounded like something of a paradox in Hell.

"Unlike other practices, soul restoration is not about control or exchange," Smeme continued. "It is, in a sense, an act of *repair*, but only the most skilled and powerful can attempt it, and even then, the cost is often far more than one can bear."

Amber leaned forward slightly. "So, it's possible?" she asked.

Smeme's eyes narrowed. "Oh, it is possible. But most fail to realize that restoring a soul is not simply a process of 'fixing' it. It's about *undoing* the damage; not all damage can be undone." She paused for emphasis, letting her words hang in the air. "For a soul to be restored, it requires immense power. Whether that power comes from another soul, a being of great strength, or even an outside force, it is never truly the same again once the soul has been shattered."

Amber felt a chill creep up her spine. So, even if restoration was possible, the soul would always carry the scars of what had been done to it?

Smeme nodded as though sensing her thoughts. "Yes. A soul, once damaged, whether through torment, trading, or other means, will always bear some form of the wound. Restoration is not about returning it to its *former* state but healing it enough to function again. Think of it like... mending a broken vessel. You can patch it together, but the cracks remain."

"Are there any *true* restorations?" Amber asked, her voice almost a whisper.

Smeme's lips curled into a slight smile, though it was anything but kind. "The only true restoration is when a soul is healed by its own will. When a soul can find its way back to itself without outside intervention, it *may* become whole again, but this is rare. Most souls in Hell are too damaged to restore themselves and will never regain what was lost."

A silence fell over the room as if the weight of Smeme's words pressed down on every student.

"Of course," Smeme added, her voice dropping again to a soft, ominous tone, "there are those who seek *false* restoration. This happens when a soul seeks to regain what was lost, but in doing so, they trade one broken piece for another. They may seek comfort or a sense of normalcy, but they lose even more of themselves in the process. The most common method of this 'false restoration' is through deals, where a soul agrees to offer something else in exchange for the illusion of being whole."

Amber shuddered. The thought of a soul bargaining for false restoration seemed even more terrifying than the soul trading she'd just learned about.

"False restoration can also occur when a soul attempts to regain what was lost without understanding the cost," Smeme continued, her voice smooth and cold. "False restoration is what the Crevits on the islands practice. After tormenting a soul for long enough, the soul will often beg to be put back together. The Crevit will offer the soul false hope, giving it small fragments of itself again, only to rip them away in the next session of torture." She paused, letting its cruelty hang in the air before adding, "The only creatures capable of truly restoring a soul are the Sororibus Anima. But even they only practice this when absolutely necessary."

Smeme's expression grew more serious as she spoke, as though she were about to impart the most important lesson.

"Sometimes, restoration isn't about returning the soul to what it once was. It's about allowing it to *evolve* into something different," she said, her eyes locking with Amber's. "This is the greatest paradox of soul restoration in Hell: the only way for a soul to truly be restored is for it to accept its transformation. The most broken souls often evolve into something entirely new, leaving behind the past to create a new future. But that requires the *soul* to be willing to let go."

Amber's heart beat faster. Could she, too, evolve? Was she already?

"But beware," Smeme warned, her voice turning cold. "The restoration process, whether true or false, is never free from consequences. A soul that seeks restoration without the strength to handle it can burn out, crumble, or turn against itself. Some souls are beyond restoration, and any attempt to heal them will only drive them deeper into despair."

Amber swallowed hard, considering Smeme's words. It was clear that soul restoration wasn't a simple, redemptive process. It was fraught with dangers, traps, and impossible choices. To restore a soul in Hell was to walk a fine line between healing and destruction.

"As you continue your training," Smeme concluded, her gaze sweeping the room. "Remember that knowledge of the soul is power, but knowing when to leave a soul *untouched* is just as important. For some things, once broken, can never truly be repaired. And that is the true nature of power in Hell: not breaking a soul, but knowing exactly how far to bend it before it snaps."

A hush fell over the room.

Then, Professor Smeme broke the tension with a sharp clap of her hands. "Congratulations, students. You have completed your basic knowledge training. Remember to continue practicing your spells and expanding your understanding. As always, I and the other professors are available should you have any questions. But if not," she waved a hand dismissively, "you are free to go."

Chairs scraped against the floor as students began gathering their things, murmuring amongst themselves about the lesson. Amber remained seated for a moment, her mind still turning over everything she'd learned, especially about soul trading.

Leandros nudged her with his elbow. "You look like you just saw a ghost," he teased, though there was a flicker of concern in his eyes.

Amber forced a smirk. "Just thinking."

"Well, don't think too hard. We survived Smeme's class, and that deserves a drink." He slung an arm around her shoulders, steering her toward the door.

As they stepped into the hall, Amber cast one last glance back at the professor, who was watching her with a knowing smile. A shiver ran down her spine.

She had a feeling her lessons were far from over.

That night, she found herself alone in her room, unable to shake the weight of what she'd learned. The silence outside mirrored the silence inside her, and for the first time in weeks, she didn't want company. Just answers.

47

The Eye of the Storm

Amber had been in her room, flipping through a book of spells, her focus half-hearted. The words swam on the page, their meaning slipping through her like water through a sieve. She wasn't avoiding Lucifer, at least, not consciously, but she hadn't sought him out either. The silence between them was its kind of storm, one she had no intention of breaking.

A soft knock pulled her from the page.

When she opened the door, no one was there.

Only a box.

It was small. Black. Unmarked.

Amber hesitated before lifting the lid and froze.

Inside was a single flower.

Not the twisted, sulfur-laced blossoms common in Hell, but something else. Something familiar. Its petals were so dark they were nearly black, but they shimmered with the faintest violet hue in the right light. The petals looked impossibly soft, coiled tight, like they were guarding something secret.

It was from the garden beneath the pergola.

She remembered that night too well. The way he'd looked at her. The way his fingers had brushed down her spine like they had every right to. The garden had smelled like ash and roses. Like him.

She didn't need a note.

She knew who had sent it.

Her fingers hovered above the blossom. She didn't pick it up; she just traced the edge of the box as if it were safer. If not touched, it could keep the memory from blooming again.

But it already had.

Slowly, carefully, she picked it up, letting herself hold it for a breath.

Then, without flinching, she walked to the hearth and threw it into the fire.

The petals hissed as they burned, curling into black smoke.

She didn't look away.

Not until the second knock came.

This time, Korinna was entering immediately.

"Domina Amber," Korinna said, "the liege requests that you dine together tonight."

For a moment, just a heartbeat, she felt the pull again, that maddening warmth that lingered after his touch.

But no.

Not this time.

Amber didn't look up at Korinna. "Please tell our *liege* that I will not be joining him at dinner."

Silence followed. Eventually, Amber glanced up to find Korinna staring at her in stunned disbelief. A look Amber had never seen on her before. She stifled a laugh.

"But..." Korinna started, clearly at a loss for words.

"You can tell him I am not hungry."

The two women locked eyes, the weight of Amber's defiance hanging thick in the air.

"That is all, Korinna. You are dismissed."

***

Lucifer sat in his private dining hall, swirling a glass of deep crimson wine between his fingers, watching the liquid cling to the sides before slipping back down. The room was dim, and candles flickered against the dark stone walls, casting elongated shadows that stretched toward the empty chair across from him.

His jaw ticked.

"She refused?" His voice was smooth, deceptively so. But beneath the surface, something cracked. Something dangerous.

Korinna stood before him, head bowed low. "Yes, my liege. She said she was not hungry."

Lucifer exhaled slowly through his nose, setting the glass down with a deliberate *clink*. Not hungry. The excuse was laughable, but the sheer audacity irritated him more.

Lucifer leaned back in his chair, fingers steepled. "Did she hesitate?"

Korinna shifted slightly. "No, my liege. She did not."

A slow smile curled at the corners of Lucifer's lips, though no amusement existed, "Interesting."

Lucifer dismissed Korinna with a flick of his fingers, watching as she bowed once more before slipping out of the room. The door closed with a dull *thud*, leaving him with the silence.

Amber's defiance intrigued him. It should've angered him; perhaps it did, in some small, simmering way, but more than that, it set his mind ablaze with curiosity.

She was pushing back. Testing him.

Good.

He rose from his seat, driven by impulse and need, but halfway to the door, he stopped.

If she would not come to him, he would not beg.

Instead, he returned to his seat, letting his head fall against the chair and exhaling through his nose. She wasn't avoiding him out of fear. No, if she were afraid, she would've come. She would've sought his favor and played into whatever twisted game she thought he was orchestrating.

But she wasn't playing. She was choosing to keep her distance.

And *that* was what unsettled him.

Lucifer had ruled Hell for millennia. He knew how to command loyalty, break wills, and mold even the most rebellious souls into submission. But Amber was slipping through his fingers like sand.

Lucifer had never been one for regret. It was a mortal affliction, weak and useless. But tonight, it clung to him like smoke. Refusing to lift.

Her scent had lingered. Her warmth had burned against his skin like an unshakable brand; he swore he could still feel it. Her skin had been silk beneath his fingertips, the soft arch of her back pressed to that cold pillar...

He cursed himself for remembering.

Then, in his chambers, she'd been a fire in his hands, dangerous, consuming, impossible to hold without getting burned. And for a fleeting moment, he hadn't cared. He'd let himself touch the flame.

Then, The Angelus Lapsus entered.

Lucifer exhaled sharply, eyes flickering toward the fireplace. The embers glowed dimly, mirroring his chest's slow burn of frustration.

The way Amber had looked at him, like she'd been shattered and was piecing herself back together right before his eyes, had lodged in his mind. A silent accusation.

He hadn't called for the fallen angel, not that night anyway.

That night, he hadn't wanted anyone else.

He'd only wanted her.

And now, she was gone. Not physically. She still walked the halls of his domain, still trained, and still laughed with her newfound companions. But she was distant and guarded.

He'd given her an opening, a glimpse into something neither of them had been ready to acknowledge, and then, with one misstep, he'd slammed the door shut.

Now, she was refusing to open it again. And he couldn't decide if that made her foolish... or the one holding the power.

Lucifer ran a hand through his hair, irritation curling through him like smoke. It wasn't like him to dwell. And yet, as Korinna delivered Amber's refusal to join him for dinner, he didn't feel anger.

He felt the weight of what he'd lost.

Fine.

If she wouldn't come to him, he wouldn't summon her again.

But this distance between them? It was an illusion.

And Lucifer had never been one for pretending.

***

Like ghosts, both Lucifer and Amber haunted Castellum Umbrae, careful to avoid each other at every turn; each determined to keep their distance, each silently daring the other to fold first.

What they didn't know was that Hell had never been theirs to control.

Hell had rules of its own. And it was just about ready to force their hands.

48

The Edge of Control

Amber had never felt anything like it. Earthquake didn't even begin to describe the shaking sensation that had woken her. The rumbling was deep, all-consuming, intense, and violent, yet nothing in the room shifted; nothing seemed disturbed. It was as if the very bones in her body were trembling.

She jolted awake, her heart racing, disoriented, and unsure of what was happening or what she was supposed to do. All she could do was wait, hoping the sensation would eventually subside. And, of course, it did, but as soon as it did, all three of her Dominarum in Exspectatione stormed into her room.

"Domina Amber," the shortest of the three cried, "you must get up!"

Immediately, the demoness yanked Amber's covers off with such force that Amber nearly went with them.

Amber jumped to her feet, anxiety creeping in. "What's going on?" she demanded. "What was that?"

The three demonesses paused, exchanging uneasy glances before Korinna spoke, her tone unusually serious. "That was Vocationem."

"The call? What call? Call for what?" Amber asked, confusion mounting as they quickly ushered her toward the closet.

"Hell has decided it's time for the Collocatione Ceremonia. Everyone must go. No one knows which Liberi will be called upon and moved up in ranking."

Amber's mind raced. She'd known this day could come at any moment, but she wasn't ready to say goodbye to her friends yet. All she could do was hope that Lean and Syn weren't chosen tonight. Her heart clenched at the thought of them being separated and everything changing. She wasn't sure she was ready for what was to come.

Korinna was already in her wardrobe, pulling out a breathtaking gown of deep crimson. The fabric shimmered under the light, soft and luxurious, like the very essence of Hell woven into its fibers. Amber barely had time to process what was happening as Korinna and the others rushed to help her into the gown.

The dress was a marvel, hugging Amber's curves in all the right ways. The intricate black and silver embroidery traced delicate patterns that seemed to shift as she moved. The bodice was tight, the neckline plunging just enough to give it an air of elegance and strength. The skirt flowed like liquid, billowing out as it reached the floor, sweeping over her feet with every step.

The demonesses stepped back to admire their work as they finished, nodding in approval. Amber's reflection in the mirror was stunning, almost unrecognizable in the splendor of the gown. She hardly recognized herself as they swiftly moved to adorn her with makeup fit for a queen. A soft, glowing base and sharp contouring accentuated her features, and dark, dramatic eyes shimmered under the dim light. Her lips were painted a deep, seductive red, adding to the striking transformation.

Amber's hair was quickly whisked into a high, elegant bun, exposing her neck and allowing the dress to take center stage. The intricate gown, with its fluid lines and radiant fabric, now had all the attention it deserved, and she, in this new form, was nothing short of magnificent.

"You look praeclarum, Domina," Korinna said softly, as though the words held more weight than usual.

Amber nodded, still in a daze. The gown was a symbol of power, of change, of whatever the Collocatione Ceremonia would bring. She wasn't sure if she was ready to wear it, but there was no choice now. The time had come.

"Let's go," Amber said quietly, her voice steady despite the storm raging in her chest.

The demonesses moved quickly, leading her out of the room, and as they made their way down the halls, Amber couldn't help but wonder if this would be the moment that changed everything.

As they rushed through the halls, busy Operarios scrambled out of their way, clearing the path for her to pass through. Her heart thumped loudly in her chest, a nervous excitement building as she neared the entrance to Castellum Umbrae. The heavy doors swung wide open for her, but Amber's gaze didn't fall on the waiting chariot; it went directly to the man seated within.

Lucifer.

Her heart skipped a beat, despite herself, at the sight of him. He wore a perfectly tailored black suit with a satin sheen; the jacket was subtly embroidered with dark crimson accents. A deep red pocket square peeked out from his chest pocket, and gold-studded crimson cufflinks adorned his sleeves. Beneath the jacket, he wore a charcoal silk shirt, unbuttoned just enough at the collar to suggest a hint of carelessness, though everything about his ap-

pearance screamed control. His pants were sharply tailored, perfectly matching the jacket's precision. Lucifer's shoes were sleek black leather boots, polished to perfection, minimal in design but radiating sophistication. On his
left wrist, a gold-studded watch gleamed, while his right hand bore a thick,
elegant gold band.

He was breathtaking.

No, Amber scolded herself, demanding her emotions to remain in check.
Although she struggled, she tore her eyes from him.

***

Lucifer, on the other hand, was having an even harder time maintaining his
composure as his gaze locked on Amber. For a moment, the world seemed to
pause around them. His breath hitched imperceptibly.

She was a vision.

The gown shimmered under the dim lighting, its delicate layers hugging
her form in a way that made his chest tighten. Her hair, swept up in a high
bun, only highlighted the grace of her neck and the delicate curve of her
shoulders. His eyes traced the outline of her features as the makeup accentuated her natural beauty, making her look like she'd stepped straight out of
a dream, impossibly perfect.

His hand tightened subtly on the chariot's armrest, his usually composed
demeanor faltering for the briefest moment. The fire in his chest surged, but
he forced himself to rein it in.

"Amber," he said, his voice low but laced with an undercurrent of something deeper, something raw.

He took a moment, his gaze flicking briefly to the Operarios bustling
behind her as if he could shake the effect she had on him. But his eyes returned
to her, unwavering now, filled with something more than simple admiration.
She had his full attention, and she knew it.

Whether he admitted it or not, it was becoming harder to push aside
the thought that she was, in fact, his equal. His counterpart. A queen in her
own right. He hadn't prepared himself for how profoundly seeing her like this
would affect him.

"Stunning," he murmured, more to himself than to her. But the word
hung in the air, thick with an undeniable truth.

For all the power he held in Hell, at that moment, it was as if he had
nothing, nothing but the woman before him.

***

Amber took the hand he held out to her and climbed into the chariot next to him. As soon as she'd settled in, the crack of the whip sounded, and they were off. Amber could feel the wind tugging at her hair, the tension in the air thickening with every passing moment. The city of Hell stretched below them, a place of beauty and torment, its jagged spires casting long shadows across the streets as they made their way through.

Lucifer sat beside her, his presence commanding and palpable, the weight of his gaze settling on her without the need for words. There was a quiet intensity between them as the chariot sped through the darkened sky, a promise of something more, something inevitable. The Equus' wings beat against, echoing their path as they drew closer to the Anulum Pugnatum, its looming gates coming into view.

At one point, Amber felt his hand brush lightly against hers, perhaps accidentally, but he didn't immediately move it away. Neither of them acknowledged the touch, but the silence between them deepened, not cold but charged like two magnets resisting and pulling all at once.

The large gates creaked open as they approached the entrance, revealing the vast arena beyond. The Anulum Pugnatum was full, the stands packed with demons, the air thick with the scent of blood and the sounds of shouting, murmurs of speculation swirling through the crowd. There was an electric charge in the air, a tension that only grew with every inch they gained toward the entrance.

The chariot lowered gracefully and came to a halt at the foot of the front entrance. Lucifer stepped out first, his tall figure silhouetted against the dark sky, a commanding presence in the night. He turned to Amber, offering his hand once more. She hesitated only for a moment before taking it, her fingers curling around his as he helped her down.

She stepped past him, her eyes catching the two Eques who stood waiting. The demons bowed towards them in silent reverence before turning to lead them through the winding tunnels beneath the coliseum. Lucifer's hand rested lightly on the small of her back, and a shiver ran up her spine, and she almost pulled away. Almost. But instead, she let it linger, just long enough to wonder if he meant it as reassurance... or possession.

Together, they ascended the grand stairway leading to the spectator's balcony. Each step they took was slow, deliberate, and regal. Everything about their movements seemed to reaffirm his dominion over this place.

Amber's heart quickened, but she kept her composure, allowing herself to be part of the spectacle.

The crowd's roar reached a deafening crescendo as they emerged into the open. The demons' devotion to Lucifer was evident in the applause that reverberated through the coliseum, a wave of respect that rolled over him like a tide. But as their gaze shifted to Amber, the applause faltered. It dimmed, quieting, until it wavered into an almost uncomfortable silence.

Amber's chest tightened, and she could feel the weight of the eyes on her, but Lucifer didn't seem to notice, or perhaps he simply didn't care. His focus was elsewhere, his gaze fixed ahead as he guided her to their seats.

Perched at the highest point of the coliseum, his throne was an imposing structure of polished black rock adorned with intricate infernal carvings of serpents and flames that flickered as if alive. He settled into it, his posture relaxed but commanding.

Lucifer's gaze flicked to the throne beside him, and he gave a small nod, motioning for Amber to sit.

Amber hesitated for only a moment but knew there was no turning back now. She lowered herself into the seat, the moment's weight pressing down on her. The crowd, still uncertain, began to murmur once more as they, too, took their seats, the nervous anticipation hanging thick in the air.

Amber glanced around, sensing the unease rippling through the demons around them. She could feel the weight of every pair of eyes on her, the whispered doubts that flickered in the crowd, and yet... Lucifer remained unaffected. His focus was on the arena before them, awaiting the start of the ceremony.

The crowd continued to murmur, unsure and hesitant, until the first echoes of the ceremony began to stir.

49

Monsters and Martyrs

One by one, the torches lighting the Anulum Pugnatum flickered and then went out, their flames snuffed as if by an unseen force, an invisible breath sweeping through the air. Darkness crept through the coliseum, swallowing the crowd until only the section where Amber sat with Lucifer remained bathed in light.

The crowd plunged into an unsettling silence, the absence of sound almost deafening.

Amber's heart raced as she looked around, her eyes adjusting to the thickening darkness. The anticipation hung heavy in the air, oppressive in its stillness.

Slowly, Lucifer rose from his seat. His movement was deliberate and measured as he made his way to the edge of the balcony, his silhouette sharp against the remaining light. With a slight clearing of his throat, he addressed the now-silent crowd.

"Grata omnibus ut hac nocte's Collocatione Ceremonia. Incipiamus!"

His voice rang out, deep and commanding, carrying through the darkness. The instant his words hit the air, the crowd erupted into cheers, a chorus of fervent devotion and excitement reverberating through the coliseum.

The ceremony began as the final torch flickered out behind them, leaving only the shadowed expanse of the arena.

Lucifer stood at the balcony's edge, the crowd's cheers filling the air, growing louder with each passing moment. But just as the noise peaked, a hush fell over them like the air had been suspended.

A sudden energy shift surged through the coliseum, and Amber felt it, a pulse that radiated from deep within the pit below them. The lights in the arena, once dim and flickering, flared to life all at once, focusing solely on the Anulum Pugnatum, the ring of battle below.

The darkness above the pit remained absolute, leaving the bleachers and the balconies swallowed in shadow, their occupants barely visible. Still, the light in the pit blazed with an otherworldly intensity. The light revealed seven figures standing in a line, their forms highlighted against the darkness.

The Liberi.

Each stood tall, their faces unreadable but their postures rigid with antic-ipation, like warriors waiting for their fate to be sealed. The air around them crackled with the tension of something monumental about to happen.

Lucifer remained standing, his presence unwavering as his gaze swept across the figures. The crowd around them murmured in dull whispers. Every eye in the coliseum trained on the seven demons.

Amber could feel her heart race, her breath shallow. The Liberi were the future, the next in line, the ones whose choices would echo through Hell, and standing among them were her friends, Efrosyni and Leandros.

The spotlight shifted, accompanied by a whisper of movement.

Lucifer's voice rang out again, commanding and absolute, "Luminus."

A nervous-looking Liberi stepped forward, his gaze fixed downward as if afraid to meet the countless eyes watching him.

"Oratio."

A shorter Liberi followed. She didn't appear nervous, but she didn't exude confidence either. One of her horns was stumped, the other fully grown, giv-ing her an unbalanced look as though she might topple over at any moment.

One by one, the names of the Liberi were called, each stepping forward under the blinding light.

"Lucianus."

The crowd collectively held their breath. He was tall and lean, his features sharp, his jawline cutting like a blade. His cold, calculating eyes flickered under the glow of the spotlight. He was ready.

The light shifted again, landing on a female Liberi with striking silver eyes. Her horns were dark as midnight, and she carried herself with quiet confidence, hands clasped tightly in front of her.

"Selene."

She stepped forward without hesitation, without a glance at anyone, and took her place alongside the others.

"Efrosyni," Lucifer spoke the name without so much as blinking.

Amber's stomach twisted at the sound of Syn's name. Her pulse quick-ened as she watched her friend step forward, not looking at Lucifer but past him. Looking at her.

A lump formed in Amber's throat.

Syn's eyes, warm and steady, locked onto hers. And then, a soft smile. Small, fleeting, but real. Amber exhaled, only then realizing she'd been hold-ing her breath.

From beside her, Lucifer glanced her way. He saw the way her fingers trembled slightly in her lap. He said nothing, but his expression softened for the first time in weeks as he spoke the next name, "Yorgos."

Another familiar name, another classmate, stepped into the light. Amber's fingers curled into fists at her sides. She'd known this was coming, but knowing and feeling were two very different things.

Lucifer's voice rang out again, "And finally, Leandros."

Amber's head snapped toward the spotlight just as he emerged from the shadows. Her heart lurched. Leandros.

He moved forward with that same careless grace he always had, but Amber knew him well enough to see the tension in his shoulders, the way his smirk didn't quite reach his eyes.

A strange mix of emotions crashed over her: relief, pride, anxiety, even something close to dread. She wanted to be happy for them, proud, and she was. But at the same time, an unease settled deep in her chest.

Once all seven stood in line, they lifted their chins and bowed their heads in a single, deliberate motion. Acknowledging their acceptance.

The crowd fell silent.

The spotlight drifted away from the Liberi, hovering now over the center of the Anulum Pugnatum.

Every eye shifted to Lucifer.

Waiting for his words, "Operarios, ready the pit, for we are about to begin."

Lucifer's command rang out, and immediately, the workers below sprang into action, moving swiftly and precisely.

He returned to his seat, turning slightly toward Amber. His hand brushed hers on the armrest as he sat, so brief it could've been an accident, but the burn of it lingered.

"Now," he murmured, his voice smooth, deliberate. "Tonight will go as follows: one by one, in the order I called, the Liberi will enter the center of the Anulum Pugnatum. Five podiums will rise from the ground as they stand in the ring."

Amber's gaze went back to the arena as the earth trembled violently. A deep crack split through the center, and five distinct podiums emerged from it.

The first was a rich teal, its surface wrapped in twisting vines.

The second was bronze, though scorched in places as if it'd been through the fire.

The third was a steel gray, its polished surface glinting faintly under the dim light.

The fourth was a blood-red that almost looked like it was oozing.

And the last was a burnt-sienna, weathered and worn with time.

Lucifer continued, his tone unwavering. "Each of these podiums will bear an object hovering above them."

With a flick of his fingers, the objects materialized.

A scroll unfurled above the teal podium. *Legatus,* Amber thought. *A diplomat.*

A shadow flickered over the bronze one, shifting and twisting. She hesitated, unsure what it meant.

Above the gray podium, a sword gleamed. Eques, the warriors.

Rattling above the blood-red podium, a massive metal hand crushed a snapped chain. Amber recognized the gauntlet; she'd seen it burned onto every Bellator.

And over the final one, a hammer hovered steadily. Operarios, the workers.

Which meant... the shadow belonged to the Crevits.

Lucifer's voice dropped slightly, but it carried all the same. "The Liberi in the center will approach the object that calls to them most. Only they will know where they belong."

Amber inhaled sharply.

"Once they've chosen, they will leave the center, making way for the next. However, there are a few things to note. First, there is a chance that none of the objects will call to a Liberi. This does not mean they have failed. It simply means they are not yet ready to take their place in the ranking order."

The weight of his words settled over her like a thick fog.

"Hell may have called this Collocatione Ceremonia for a single Liberi tonight or for all of them; we will not know until the end of this event."

Amber swallowed. For some, this night would change everything. For others, it'd mean waiting. Watching. Hoping.

Lucifer's eyes darkened slightly as he continued, "The second thing to note is that if a Liberi is claimed by the Crevit category, their skin will change: red, blue, or yellow. The podiums will vanish briefly, then return with six. That signals the Crevit will be placed on one of the Islands."

Amber's eyes widened. She immediately thought of how badly Leandros wanted to be sent there. But something nagged at her.

Slowly, she turned to Lucifer, "Shouldn't there be seven podiums?"

His jaw tightened, his voice dropping into something colder, final. "Only myself, Tisiphone, Timor, and Dolor are allowed on the seventh island. No one gets placed there."

He glanced at her then, briefly but enough to notice the flicker of unease on her face.

"And the same applies to new Operarios," he continued, his tone returning to neutral. "Though their options are far more extensive. They won't receive specific assignments tonight; that decision falls to the Situs Princeps, their site leaders."

Lucifer leaned back in his chair, farther from her this time, as if creating distance would help him stay in control. He could still feel her warmth beside him, a gravitational pull he wasn't ready to name.

With a smirk, he rose to his feet, made his way to the balcony's edge, and spoke the first name.

"Luminus," he called, eyes locking onto the demon below. "You are first. Step into the ring."

50

The Seat Beside the Devil

Cautiously, the nervous-looking Liberi walked toward the center, his gaze lifting toward the podiums before him, though a slight tremble betrayed his hands. The crowd stilled into an almost eerie silence as they watched the young demon take in his surroundings.

The earth beneath him pulsed once, low and deep, before the five podiums shimmered and solidified in front of him: teal, bronze, gray, red, and sienna. The objects above them hovered expectantly, bathed in an eerie glow.

Luminus hesitated, his breath uneven. His tail flicked behind him, a restless movement betraying his nerves. Amber leaned forward slightly, feeling a tension in the air she couldn't quite name.

His gaze swept over the floating objects; the unfurled scroll, the twisting shadow, the gleaming sword, the steady hammer, and the broken chain and gauntlet. For a long moment, he stood frozen, his expression shifting between curiosity and hesitation.

Then, slowly, he moved.

Each step was deliberate as he approached the podiums; his body tensed as if expecting something to pull him back. When he reached the ring's edge, he extended a hand but faltered.

Amber's breath caught in her throat.

The Liberi clenched his fists at his sides before releasing them, taking one last deep inhale. Then, as if something unseen called to him, he lifted his hand again toward the sword.

A sharp, resounding *clang* echoed through the chamber when his fingertips brushed the air beneath it. The steel podium pulsed with light, and the sword flared brightly before vanishing in a burst of silver mist.

The crowd stirred, whispers rippling through the air like a rising tide. The Eques had claimed him.

From a chair next to her, a figure clad in black-plated armor stepped forward on the balcony. His voice rang clear through the chamber. "Luminus," he intoned, his tone both commanding and final. "You have chosen the path of the Eques. Welcome."

"That's Chrysaor," Lucifer said, leaning in, his voice smooth but deliberate. His shoulder brushed Amber's for the briefest moment, but it lingered like static in her blood. She didn't move away as he continued, "The Princeps of the Eques."

Amber followed his gaze to the demon still standing at the edge of the balcony, doing her best to ignore Lucifer's overpowering presence. Chrysaor was a striking figure, his black obsidian-plated armor reflecting the dim light of the chamber. As he turned to return to his seat, she noticed a jagged scar running from his temple to his jaw, a stark contrast against his deep bronze skin. His piercing silver eyes held a quiet intensity, and though he sat still, there was an air of restrained power about him as if he could spring into action at any moment.

Lucifer's gaze shifted past Amber to the right, and she instinctively turned to follow it. Seated slightly behind her, beside Chrysaor, was another figure. "That's Tisiphone," Lucifer continued. "The leader of the Crevits."

Tisiphone was regal in her posture, her presence commanding without effort. Her features were sharp and elegant, her dark eyes unreadable as they flickered over the ceremony with quiet scrutiny. But what caught Amber's attention most was her skin; it shifted in color, flowing seamlessly from deep crimson to cobalt blue, then to a golden yellow, each hue blending like liquid before settling for only moments at a time. Her lips curled ever so slightly as if she was aware of Amber's staring and found it amusing.

"She finds you interesting," Lucifer murmured beside her, a flicker of something unreadable in his tone. "I don't blame her."

Amber's stomach fluttered in a way that irritated her. She tore her gaze away.

Lucifer turned his attention to the other side of his throne. "In the first chair sits Erika, Princeps of the Operarios."

Erika was solidly built, her muscular frame evident beneath her elegant gown. Her horns were dark, auburn, and adorned with tiny metal rings. A thick, worn leather belt was slung across her waist, and pouches and tools strapped securely to it. Her eyes, deep brown and nearly black, held a quiet, assessing sharpness, the look of someone who had built herself from the ground up and expected the same of others.

"And next to her," Lucifer continued, his smirk faint but present, "is Chrysostomos, Princeps of the Legatus."

Chrysostomos exuded an effortless grace, his deep teal robe embroidered with silver filigree. His golden horns stood tall and only seemed to heighten his sharp, symmetrical features. Unlike the others, he carried no weapon or armor, yet there was an unmistakable weight to his presence. His emerald eyes were calculating, yet his expression remained composed, betraying nothing.

"Finally, standing over there in the corner is Ganzorig. Princeps of the Bellatores." Lucifer said, nodding to someone behind her.

Amber shifted her eyes to the back of the balcony. Standing at well over six feet, the demon's size was intimidating. He was a broad-shouldered creature with a physique carved from centuries of battle. Every muscle told a story of war and conquest. His body was marked with deep scars, remnants of past battles, yet he wore them like trophies rather than weaknesses. He looked out across the coliseum, unblinking with a fierce, glowing gaze, like smoldering coals, constantly alight with unyielding intensity. He had razor-sharp horns that jutted out of his head, and his hair was cropped close like a soldier prepared for combat. His armor had to have been forged in Hell's most bottomless pits. It was made of blackened steel laced with veins of dark crimson, pulsating faintly as if alive with the energy of past battles. It was dented and scratched but never broken. A massive, tattered, blood-red cloak draped from his shoulders, heavy with history.

Amber swallowed. Each carried themselves with a distinct power, commanders of their respective roles, rulers in their own right. She'd barely begun to understand the depths of this world, but one thing was clear: these were the demons who shaped Hell.

A second pulse radiated from the ring as Lucifer relaxed back into his chair. Amber watched as the podiums sank back into the ground, leaving only Luminus standing in the silence. The weight of the moment pressed against him, but after a long pause, he inclined his head in a show of acceptance.

Lucifer's gaze remained steady as he lifted a hand. "Step back, Luminus," he commanded, his voice carrying with ease. "Your path begins now."

Luminus exhaled, tension still laced through his shoulders, but he did as instructed, retreating to the edge of the ring. The moment his feet crossed the threshold, the ground rumbled again.

Amber's heart pounded as Lucifer stood from his chair, the familiar smirk returning to his lips. But instead of moving to the edge of the balcony, he remained standing just beside her, the fabric of his sleeve brushing against hers again, intentionally or not, she couldn't tell. She felt the proximity like heat.

He didn't look at her, but his presence spoke volumes.

Then, his voice rang out once more.

"The next name," A beat of silence, a pause heavy with anticipation, "Oratio."

The young demoness stepped forward, her gait steady despite her sharp breath. She was slender but strong, her shoulders squared as she entered the ring. The earth responded instantly, splitting down the center as the five podiums reemerged, bathed in the dim, flickering light of the chamber.

Amber watched closely as Oratio studied each one. The scroll of the Legatus fluttered faintly in an unseen breeze. The hammer of the Operarios hovered in place, steady, unmoving. The twisting shadow of the Crevits slithered restlessly. And the sword, gleaming steel, cold and unwavering, simply waited. The broken chain and gauntlet seemed to glow brighter in the dim light.

Oratio's breathing shallowed. Then, as if drawn by an invisible force, she stepped forward. Each footfall echoed through the still air until she came to a halt before the sword.

A heartbeat passed. Then another.

She lifted her hand, fingers outstretched, and the moment her palm hovered beneath the weapon, the entire ring flared with light. The sword dropped into her grasp, its weight settling into her hand as if it had always belonged to her. A murmur spread through the audience; approval, recognition.

Lucifer nodded, satisfaction glinting in his gaze as Chrysaor stood, returning to the balcony's edge for the second time that night. "Welcome to your future with the Eques, Oratio." His commanding and strong voice echoed around them, and Oratio looked up, smiling. She bowed toward her new leader and exited the center.

51

Blurring Lines

Lucifer's smirk deepened. He didn't wait for the murmurs to settle before calling the next name, "Lucianus."

The broad-shouldered demon strode forward, his expression neutral, though Amber noted how his hands flexed at his sides. As before, the podiums rose, waiting.

Lucianus barely hesitated. He moved directly toward the sword, but it didn't remain within reach.

The blade trembled, almost as if recoiling. Then, without warning, it shot into the air, soaring high above the crowd. Gasps rippled through the chamber as all eyes followed its ascent.

Then, in a swift and merciless movement, the sword turned, dagger-down, and plummeted.

It was headed straight for Lucianus.

The tension in the room snapped taut. A few demons flinched, but Lucianus stood his ground, his fists clenched at his sides.

The blade streaked downward faster than a bolt of lightning.

At the last possible second, it veered, missing his body by mere inches as it buried itself deep into the stone floor between his feet. The impact sent a shockwave through the ground, cracks splintering outward beneath him.

Then, without ceremony, without acknowledgment, the sword vanished.

Amber's breath caught. Lucianus had been rejected.

Beside her, Lucifer shifted slightly in his throne, eyes flicking to Amber. He saw the tension in her jaw, the way her fingers gripped the armrest without realizing it.

He lowered his voice just enough for her to hear, "Even Hell has its own way of saying no."

Amber didn't answer. But she didn't look away either.

Then, turning back to the crowd, Lucifer murmured to himself, "Interesting. I would've chosen him over Luminus."

A murmur swept through the audience, hushed but unmistakable. The podiums remained standing, waiting for him to choose again, but the sword was gone.

Lucifer's expression returned to its natural stoic state, but his following words carried a definitive finality, "Choose again, Lucianus."

The weight of the moment hung heavy in the air.

For the first time, uncertainty flickered across Lucianus's face. His shoulders, once rigid with confidence, now tensed for an entirely different reason. He turned in a slow, deliberate circle, his gaze flickering between the remaining podiums.

Then, the scroll moved.

Not in the way the sword had, not with force or rejection, but with something subtler, something deliberate.

It unfurled, its ancient parchment whispering against itself as unseen hands smoothed its surface. Letters burned into the paper, shifting and reshaping like liquid gold.

Lucianus froze.

Then his expression changed. The hesitation melted, replaced with something steadier, something sure.

Slowly, he stepped forward, extending a hand toward the parchment.

The moment his fingers brushed the edge, a pulse of golden light rippled outward, engulfing him briefly before fading into nothingness.

The chamber thrummed with energy, the decree of his path undeniable.

A knowing smile crossed Chrysostomos' face as he rose from his chair and walked to the balcony's edge, his presence commanding yet welcoming. "Welcome, child, to the ranks of the Legatus."

The crowd erupted in cheers, their voices echoing through the vast chamber. Lucianus, still absorbing the moment, looked up tentatively at his new path leader.

Chrysostomos inclined his head in acknowledgment, his golden eyes gleaming with approval.

Lucianus exhaled, the weight of uncertainty lifting from his shoulders. Steadier now, he turned and stepped away from the ring; his fate was sealed, and his journey had begun.

When Chrysostomos returned to his seat, Lucifer called the next name, "Selene."

A shift rippled through the crowd as a lithe demoness entered the ring. Her horns were twisted and dark, and her golden eyes flickered with something unreadable. She took her time, her gaze sweeping over each podium, lingering on the scroll, then the sword. But then her attention snapped to the shifting shadow.

For a moment, she didn't move. Then, deliberately, she stepped forward, raising her hand toward the dark, twisting form above the podium. The instant her fingers brushed against the swirling black mist, her body stiffened.

A gasp rippled through the onlookers.

Selene seemed to dissolve into shadow for a moment, her form blurring and shifting. Then her skin began to change, rippling in waves of deep red that bled into cobalt blue, which shifted into bright yellow. The colors swirled in an unending cycle, a mesmerizing dance of hues that bled into one another seamlessly. Then, as abruptly as it had begun, the transformation stopped.

She was bright yellow.

The demoness examined her hands, twisting them before her, marveling at the intensity of her new color. An almost menacing smile curled at the corners of Tisiphone's lips as she made her way to the balcony's edge.

"Venenum," Tisiphone hissed, the word dripping with approval as it slid from her tongue. "Well done, my dear Selene. Welcome to the Crevits. Now, let's see where you will be stationed."

With a wave of her hand, the ground beneath Selene began to shake violently, cracks splitting the stone. The five original podiums vanished, only to be replaced by six new ones, all sickly green in color.

On each podium rested a symbol of the islands.

The first was a withered tree, its sparse branches reaching like bony fingers and curling roots that seemed to grip the earth in desperation: Decrepitus Island.

Amber's gaze shifted to the second podium, where a broken hourglass sat, its sand slipping away endlessly yet never fully emptying. Enervated Island.

She immediately recognized the next symbol: a cracked mirror, its shattered fragments reflecting distorted glimpses of what could only be Abominabilis Island.

The fourth podium bore a heavy, tattered cloak, the fabric hanging like a shadow of death. Languorous Island.

Above the following podium hovered a patch of earth, cracked and dried as though long abandoned, the land itself thirsty for something it couldn't have: Pachydermatous Island.

Finally, the sixth podium held a black flame, flickering unnaturally in the darkness: Vehement Island.

Amber refixed her eyes on Selene as she circled the six podiums. The tension in the air was palpable, as though the very stones of the chamber held their breath, waiting for the decision to be made. Amber could feel the heat of the crowd's collective anticipation, the weight of the moment pressing down on everyone present.

Selene's gaze traveled across the podiums, her steps slow and deliberate. Amber watched her fingers curl at her sides, her body tense but purposeful. As Selene passed each podium, something strange seemed to happen. The tree once withered and curling, bloomed. The hourglass, with its sand slipping endlessly, began to fill again. The cracked earth at one podium seemed to moisten as if healing, but there was no such change at the fourth podium.

Amber's eyes followed Selene's gaze, and she saw her stop in front of the podium with the tattered cloak. The moment Selene stepped closer, the fabric stirred, curling and twisting as though it recognized her. Amber's heart skipped a beat as the air grew heavy, a dark hum filling the chamber.

The green hue of the podium deepened, intensifying, as the cloak began to stir more fervently. Amber held her breath, watching as Selene reached out. The cloak seemed to envelop her hand, its weight ancient and unyielding, as if it had waited for her all along. Selene's fingers brushed the fabric, and the cloak surged to life. It moved over her, swirling around her shoulders with a deliberate slowness as though it was both a comfort and a confinement. Selene's form became swallowed by its folds, her movements sluggish as the fabric seemed to weigh down on her very being.

Amber watched in awe as the room seemed to hold its breath, the only sound the faint rustling of the cloak. Tisiphone's voice sliced through the silence. "Languorous Island," she hissed, her voice full of approval. "You will learn what it takes to break a will. Welcome, Selene."

Lucifer's posture shifted as he leaned forward, watching Selene with a frown bordering on something else, worry, perhaps, or memory. The look passed quickly, but Amber caught it.

"What happens to them there?" she asked under her breath.

He didn't answer right away.

When he did finally speak, his voice was quieter than before. "They become tools. Or they become examples."

Amber didn't ask which one he thought Selene would be, but she felt a chill ripple through her as Selene stood there, the cloak now fused with her, its lethargy permeating her every movement. It was as if Selene had been swallowed by time itself, the very essence of it slowing down around her. She blinked slowly, her movements heavy and deliberate. The sensation was almost palpable, as though the air around Selene had thickened.

Selene turned away, the cloak trailing behind her like a shadow, and Amber felt the moment's weight settle over her. The path had been chosen, her future sealed in the weight of the cloak. For Selene, there'd be no turning back. And Amber knew that the same could soon be said for the others who followed.

52

Unspoken Bonds

S eemingly unaffected by the moment, Lucifer didn't pause, "Efrosyni."

Amber's breath hitched as Efrosyni stepped forward, looking every bit the confident and poised leader Amber had always known her to be. The crowd fell silent again, a ripple of recognition passing through them as they watched the young demoness stand at the edge of the circle, her gaze unwavering.

Lucifer's gaze slid sideways, just for a moment. Not to Efrosyni, but to Amber. Watching her chest rise and fall, the flicker of tension in her jaw. He didn't speak, but the look said enough: he saw how this was affecting her, and it mattered for reasons he didn't want to name.

Amber felt a wave of pride surge within her. She'd known this moment was coming, and she knew Efrosyni had the potential to claim her place here in Hell's hierarchy, but it still felt unreal. This would change everything in ways both beautiful and terrible.

Efrosyni's eyes flicked to Amber for a brief moment before she turned her attention back to the podiums. Amber's chest tightened as their eyes met, an unspoken understanding passing between them. They didn't need to say anything to know how much this moment meant. But what would it mean for their friendship once this ceremony was over?

Efrosyni began to move toward the podiums with a grace that was all too familiar, but Amber noticed the subtle shift in her posture; she was more deliberate and determined now. She approached each podium slowly, her fingers brushing against the surface of the objects as if testing them, evaluating them with her sharp eyes. The air around them felt still, as if even time was waiting for Efrosyni to decide.

Amber's heart beat louder in her chest, the silence stretching painfully long. She could see the anticipation building in the crowd, the tension rising as Efrosyni finally stood before the podium with the scroll.

Amber's breath caught as the podium seemed to react to her, the scroll unfurling with recognition. The scroll lifted, hovering above the pedestal, before it shifted mid-air, soaring toward Efrosyni. She stood still, her hands remaining at her sides, and without hesitation, the scroll gently landed in her grip.

The crowd erupted in applause, but Amber couldn't join them. She was frozen in place, her chest tightening as she watched her best friend, her closest ally, claim her place among the Legatus. Efrosyni's eyes met hers again, with a look of quiet triumph mixed with something else, an emotion Amber couldn't quite name. It wasn't just pride, but something deeper. Something that spoke of the future and of the distance that would soon come between them.

Chrysostomos, who had been watching with an inscrutable gaze, stepped forward to the balcony's edge. "Welcome, Efrosyni. You are now among the Legatus. Your path has been set. Congratulations."

Amber's mind whirled, a mixture of emotions colliding. She wanted to be happy for Efrosyni; truly, she did, but a part of her felt a gnawing ache. Things were changing. Their world was changing. And while Efrosyni was rising, Amber was still lost in the shadows of the ceremony, still unsure of what her future would hold. Would she ever belong? Would they remain as close as they had been, or would this divide them in ways she couldn't imagine yet?

Amber watched as her best friend bowed to the man and stepped out of the center, away from her, toward a destiny that would forever change both of them.

The ceremony pressed on.

"Yorgos."

A stocky demon made his way forward, his expression unreadable. The podiums responded, rising to meet him.

Unlike the others before him, when Yorgos stepped into the circle, the hammer didn't wait. It flew from the podium with such force and certainty that it smacked into his palm as if it had been waiting for him all along. A ripple of laughter spread through the crowd at the hammer's boldness, an unspoken acknowledgment that it had chosen its wielder without hesitation.

From the balcony, Erika stirred for the first time that night. Rising with deliberate grace, she approached the edge and looked down at Yorgos, her eyes gleaming with approval.

"You are now an Operario," she declared, her voice carrying effortlessly through the chamber. "It is time for the land to decide your house."

With that, she exhaled light as a whisper yet powerful as a storm. The dust at Yorgos' feet swirled to life, rising and curling around his legs like mist before climbing his body in tight spirals. Amber watched, transfixed, as the swirling ash shifted, *changed, and shaped.*

The crowd hushed as the dust settled into a blacksmith's heavy apron and soot-stained leathers. Then, in a blink, it shifted into sleek robes marked with the ringed crest of the Anulum Pugnatum. A moment later, the high-collared uniform of a Castellum Umbrae worker took form, only to dissolve again.

The dust kept cycling.

Each identity is more fleeting than the last.

Then, suddenly, it stilled.

Gasps rippled through the audience, but Yorgos didn't flinch. He stood firm as the dust wrapped around him, seeping into his skin and staining his veins black for an instant before vanishing.

The fabric that wrapped his body took on a deep, burnt-gold hue. Thick gloves. Polished boots. A high-cinched coat with brass buttons and leather harnesses was strapped across his chest. A whip curled at his hip. It wasn't a soldier's uniform or a scholar's robe. It was a costume. One worn by someone who commanded wild things with nothing but will and illusion.

Amber's breath caught in her throat as the dust shimmered once more before vanishing completely, sealing the uniform in place.

Yorgos exhaled sharply, his hands clenching and unclenching at his sides. When he lifted his head, there was something different in his gaze. Something untamed.

From the balcony, Erika smiled, a knowing, satisfied curve of her lips.

"The Menagerie," she announced, her voice laced with intrigue. "A rare choice. A rarer acceptance." She tilted her head, watching as Yorgos adjusted to the weight of his selection. "You will learn to command the untamable, to master the creatures that do not wish to be mastered. Welcome, Yorgos."

The audience remained silent for a beat longer than usual before a murmur spread through the chamber. The Menagerie wasn't an ordinary placement.

Amber exhaled a breath she hadn't realized she was holding, her hands tightening at her sides. Whatever Yorgos had just bound himself to, it wasn't something easily walked away from.

53

Torn Asunder

Lucifer's gaze darkened slightly as he spoke the final name, "Leandros."

Silence.

Amber's breath hitched as Leandros stepped forward, the absence of his usual smirk striking her harder than she expected. She'd seen him fight with reckless abandon, laugh in the face of danger, and brush off pain like it was nothing more than an inconvenience. But this? This was different.

Just before the name had left Lucifer's lips, his gaze flicked briefly to Amber. Her fingers curled tight in her lap, her jaw clenched with something close to dread. He didn't say anything, but a shadow passed through his expression as if he understood exactly what she was bracing for and hated that it wasn't him she was watching.

Now, the weight of the ceremony settled over Leandros as he walked into the ring. The energy in the chamber felt different. Heavier. More uncertain.

Amber's fingers curled into the folds of her dress, a silent attempt to ground herself. She'd watched every one of her classmates step forward, felt the tension of their choices, and braced herself for the unknown. But with Leandros, it was something else entirely. This wasn't just another Liberi standing in the ring. This was *Leandros,* only mirrored by how she felt when she saw Syn make her choice.

The podiums rose before him, waiting.

Amber swallowed hard as she watched him scan the objects, each one brimming with the promise of a future, of purpose.

But he didn't move.

The others hesitated, some longer than others, but eventually, something called to them. As the seconds stretched into something unbearable, Amber saw it in his eyes.

Nothing was calling to him.

The realization sent a cold shock through her veins.

Lucifer's expression remained unreadable from the balcony, but the longer the silence stretched, the more the tension in the room thickened.

Leandros turned slowly, his brows drawing together. Amber had never seen him like this, uncertain, lost. It was as if, for the first time, he was standing in a moment he couldn't charm his way through or fight his way out of.

The podiums didn't react to him. The objects remained still, unmoving, indifferent.

Amber's heart twisted.

Leandros let out a breath, then, with his chin lifted, he took a step closer. Still, nothing.

The crowd murmured.

Amber could feel the shift in the energy around her, the quiet judgment, the silent questions. The Liberi were meant to be *chosen*. They were meant to *belong* somewhere.

But Leandros didn't.

She saw it in how his hands clenched, his jaw tensed, and his shoulders squared as if preparing for a blow.

Lucifer's voice cut through the silence, "It seems your time has not yet come."

Leandros stilled.

Amber didn't breathe.

As if sensing the finality in Lucifer's words, the podiums slowly sank back into the floor. The ring felt emptier, hollow in a way none of the others had.

Leandros held himself rigid for a moment longer before turning away, his face carefully blank.

Amber's chest ached as she watched him step back and return to the others without a path or direction.

She wanted to reach for him, to say *something*, but what was there to say?

For the first time since she'd known him, Leandros had nothing to hide behind.

Lucifer didn't look at Leandros. He looked at her. The tightness in her throat, the way her breath came slow and uneven, she wasn't gloating at his failure; she was hurting for him. That stirred something in Lucifer he wasn't sure he could name.

With a quiet sigh, Lucifer rose to his full, imposing height, and slowly, the crowd's murmurs faded into silence. The entire arena was plunged into darkness for a moment as the central spotlight flickered out. Then, above where Lucifer stood, a single torch blazed to life, its golden light casting flickering shadows across his sharp features.

"Gratulatur omnibus electis hac nocte!" His voice carried through the chamber like rolling thunder.

The crowd erupted, applause cascading from every level of the arena, a deafening chorus of triumph and expectation. The air thrummed with energy.

Lucifer lifted a single hand, and the noise fell away as swiftly as it had risen.

"You should all be proud of how far you've come," he continued, his voice smooth yet edged with something unyielding. "But understand this: your true work begins now. You will meet with your Situs Princeps to determine your duties and purpose. And for those who were not chosen..." His gaze swept across the room, lingering for the briefest moment on Leandros. "Your time will come."

A beat of silence followed. Then, with a final nod, he declared, "This concludes the Collocatione Ceremonia."

Despite the official end, the weight in the air didn't lift. It remained thick and charged, pressing into Amber's chest.

She curled her fingers into fists.

For some, tonight had been a triumph. A promise of what was to come.

For others, it had been a reminder.

A reminder that in Hell, nothing was guaranteed.

Lucifer turned to Amber, his gaze steady as he extended his hand toward her.

"Come stand next to me," he murmured, his voice meant only for her.

A flicker of hesitation crossed her mind.

Then, quieter, unexpected, almost gentle, he added, "Please."

She looked at him, startled by the softness. Then she placed her hand in his, the warmth of his touch grounding her. As she stepped forward, her magnificent red gown cascaded around her in elegant waves, catching the dim firelight.

"Keep your head high," Lucifer instructed, his eyes fixed on the sea of onlookers below.

It was then that she noticed the other leaders had gathered beside them at the edge of the balcony. The seven stood together, a formidable presence silhouetted against the roaring chamber.

The stands erupted in cheers as they exited, the weight of expectation and power pressing down upon her shoulders.

In front of them, at the base of the stairs, the five section leaders veered off down a narrow hallway, disappearing toward the back of the Anulum Pugnatum.

"Where are they going?" Amber asked, curiosity lacing her tone.

Lucifer's gaze lingered briefly on the retreating figures before shifting forward again. "They're going to collect their new ranks."

Amber took a step closer. "I want to go, I need to talk to Syn and Lean."

Lucifer nodded, but his words didn't match the gesture. "Not tonight. There's too much happening for them right now. But they won't leave for their sites for a few days. You'll get a chance to say goodbye."

Disappointment flickered across Amber's face, her brows pulling together. "What about Lean? What happens to him now?"

"Nothing," Lucifer said simply. "Hell just decided he wasn't ready yet, so he'll keep training and learning until he is."

She exhaled, nodding, relieved that there was no punishment for him.

Together, they walked side by side toward the waiting chariot, though their hands were no longer intertwined.

The chariot awaited them at the base of the grand steps, its obsidian frame gleaming under the dim torchlight. The night air was thick with the lingering energy of the ceremony, the distant murmurs of the dispersing crowd echoing through the coliseum's vast corridors.

Lucifer stepped in first, offering Amber his hand once more. She accepted this time without hesitation, letting him help her into the chariot. The touch was brief but left a strange warmth in her palm.

With a flick of Lucifer's fingers, an Operario cracked the reins, and the chariot lurched forward. The skeletal beasts pulling it spread their enormous wings, and within seconds, they were airborne, soaring over the city's flickering lights below.

Amber inhaled sharply as the wind rushed past her, whipping through the loose strands of her hair. From up here, Hell stretched out before her in a sprawling labyrinth of fire-lit streets, towering structures, and distant islands shrouded in mist.

Lucifer sat beside her, his presence commanding yet oddly quiet. He didn't speak. His eyes flicked to her more than once, but he said nothing. The words churned beneath his surface, praise, apology, something else entirely, but he swallowed them all. She sat beside him, close enough to touch but still so far away.

Amber turned her gaze forward, watching Castellum Umbrae loom in the distance, its dark spires piercing the crimson sky.

The night wasn't over yet, but something had shifted.

The ceremony had changed everything.

54

No More Lies

The chariot touched down at the base of Castellum Umbrae steps, the skeletal beasts huffing out sharp breaths, their wings twitching as they settled. As soon as the chariot stilled, an Operario opened the door, and Amber stepped down, her gown swishing around her ankles as she landed lightly on the stone.

Lucifer stepped down next to her, "Amber, we..."

"Goodnight, Lucifer," she said, cutting him off.

Her voice wasn't cruel; it wasn't even angry. Just... final.

She walked away from him as if stepping back into the coldness between them before the ceremony.

Lucifer remained in place, watching her walk away. He parted his lips as if to call her name and even took half a step forward, but something stopped him. Perhaps it was the tension still lingering from the ceremony, or perhaps it was the way she held herself, composed but on the edge of something unspoken. He could still feel the shape of her hand in his. He could still hear how her breath caught when he whispered, "Please."

Instead of calling out to her, he let her go, watching as she disappeared into the corridors of Castellum Umbrae.

The warmth she left behind clung to his skin like an echo he didn't know how to hold on to. With a grunt, he stalked through the castle, shrugging off his jacket and throwing it at an Operario, who scurried to catch it.

"Scotch. Neat. Now," he commanded to no one in particular, knowing that someone, somewhere, would hear him.

The shadows swallowed his stride as he moved toward his chambers, unbuttoning his shirt. It was off in seconds, crumpled into a pile on the floor. Every movement was precise, fueled by something volatile just under the surface.

It wasn't just frustration. It was want. It was need. It was the unbearable nearness of her on that balcony, the scent of her hair on the wind, the way she'd looked at Leandros like he mattered.

He didn't know what to do with any of it.

"Your scotch, sire," a scrawny demon whimpered from behind him.

Lucifer spun on his heels, nearly ripping the glass from his servant's hands. The creature squeaked in fright as Lucifer swallowed the drink in one gulp.

"I don't understand," he muttered, his voice controlled but edged with barely contained frustration. "How can she be so comfortable next to me one moment and then shut me out the next?"

He wasn't talking to the demon. Not really.

Still, when his question was met with silence, rage lit within him, "Answer me!" he bellowed, his voice reverberating through the chamber.

The scrawny demon shuddered, his bony hands trembling as he wrung them together. "I... I don't know, sire," he stammered, his voice barely above a whisper.

Lucifer roared, hurling his glass toward the wall, missing the servant's head by mere inches. The glass shattered, its fragments falling around him like poisonous snow.

"Useless," he grumbled under his breath. "Get me another drink."

He turned, and the creature scrambled out of the room as quickly as possible, desperate to avoid further wrath.

Lucifer braced his hands on the edge of his desk, muscles taut, jaw clenched, dangerously close to snapping the wood. All he wanted was for her to look at him, not with fear or awe, but with something real.

Soft footsteps echoed behind him. His eyes remained closed as the individual drew nearer. The scent that reached him was warm and comforting, and he rolled his neck as the figure wrapped its hands around his waist.

Hope flickered.

"Amber," he breathed, low and aching.

Hands wrapped around his waist. Fingers slid up his chest, teasing the ridges of muscle. He exhaled through his nose, already leaning back into the touch.

"I'll be whoever you want me to be tonight, baby."

The voice shattered the illusion.

Lucifer's eyes shot open.

He spun, tearing the woman's hands from his body and slamming her against the wall with far more force than necessary.

"What the hell are you doing here, Airlea?" The words dripped with vile hatred, his tone cold and venomous.

Lucifer's grip tightened on her wrists as he loomed over her, his breath heavy, eyes burning with fury. She tried to break free, but the harder she struggled, the more he held her in place, like a predator toying with its prey.

"Did you think you could just waltz in here and get what you want?" he spat, his voice laced with disgust. His gaze flickered over her, a mixture of contempt and disbelief in his eyes. "You're nothing but a shadow, a poor imitation of what *she* could be."

Airlea's eyes narrowed, a slight smirk tugging at her lips despite the intensity of his grip. "I think you're the one who's mistaken," she purred, her voice dripping with false sweetness. "I'm exactly what you need. You know it as well as I do." Her eyes flickered briefly to the space between them, daring him to react.

Lucifer's expression darkened. "You don't know a damn thing about me."

With a swift motion, he shoved her away from the wall, sending her stumbling backward. The force of it knocked her off balance, but she managed to catch herself just in time.

"I know enough," she sneered, her confidence unwavering. "You're lonely. You always have been. That's why I'm here because you want someone who understands."

Lucifer didn't waste a second. He flew toward her, his hands wrapping around her neck as he pinned her harshly against the wall once more.

"You are nothing to me. You have never been, and you will never be. Do you understand that?" His voice was low, dripping with venom.

Her eyes bulged as his fingers pressed tighter. She nodded frantically, fear finally piercing her arrogance. She knew he was the only creature in all of Hell capable of truly killing another, and fear gripped her. She watched in horror as the red in his eyes deepened, glowing like embers, dangerously close to losing control.

Still, Lucifer's grip remained firm, a sick satisfaction curling in his chest as he realized he could release his anger through destruction. But just as his rage seemed to overtake him, a cough came from the doorway.

"Release her, Lucifer," a deep voice drawled from the doorway. "It's not worth your time to kill a whore."

Lucifer snapped out of his daze, his eyes flickering to the figure in the doorway. Mephistopheles, his oldest and most faithful friend, leaned casually against the doorframe, his amusement thinly veiled.

Lucifer dropped Airlea. She collapsed, coughing and gasping for breath.

"Oh, get up," Mephistopheles said, rolling his eyes. "You've overstayed your welcome."

Airlea scrambled to her feet, fear evident in her movements. She darted past the two men, not daring to glance back.

"Well," Mephistopheles chuckled, "she's never going to try that again."

Lucifer shook his head, a slight smile tugging at his lips despite himself. "Not if she knows what's good for her."

Mephistopheles handed him another scotch, then slouched into the armchair by the fire. "You wanna tell me what that was all about?"

"Not really," Lucifer sighed, sinking into the chair beside him. "But I bet you can guess."

Mephistopheles nodded, his gaze focused on the flames.

Lucifer frowned. "What?"

"Oh, nothing," Mephistopheles muttered, taking a slow sip of his whiskey. "It's just... you're the damn king of Hell. If you want to talk to her, then just make her listen. Go find her. You know where she is, so go to her. Put in a little damn effort, Luc."

Lucifer stilled at the use of the name. Only Mephistopheles ever called him that.

And the sting of the words, that's what finally got through.

He swallowed the last of his drink roughly, stood, and crossed the room, grabbing a black t-shirt off the bed.

He pulled it on with quick, determined movements before turning back to Mephistopheles, "I'm going."

Mephistopheles lifted his glass in salute. "About damn time."

Lucifer didn't look back as he left the room.

But as the door shut behind him, the fire in the hearth flickered. And somewhere deep in the castle, something stirred.

***

The door to her room clicked shut behind her, and for a long time, Amber didn't move.

The silence inside Castellum Umbrae felt heavier than the roar of the arena. It pressed in from all sides, muffling her thoughts, her pulse, and the echo of her own footsteps.

She should've felt triumphant; Syn had been chosen, and the others had found their places, but all she could feel was the hollow ache left behind by the way Leandros had stood alone. And the way Lucifer looked at her when he asked her to stand beside him made her feel like her presence still mattered.

She dropped her heels by the door, the gown whispering against the stone floor as she moved to the window.

Outside, the crimson sky pulsed like a heartbeat. Distant torches flickered along the mountain ridges, the dark silhouette of the chariot still barely visible as it circled back toward the castle.

She'd felt his warmth beside her on the ride back. The way he sat too close. The way he didn't speak but kept stealing glances.

And then the way he tried to say something when they landed: "*Amber, we—*"

She'd cut him off without thinking. A reflex. A shield. And now, all she could do was replay it.

Why had she shut him down so quickly?

Because she was afraid of what he might say?

Or afraid of what she might say back?

Amber leaned her forehead against the cool glass. Her reflection stared back, tired eyes, smudged makeup, the red dress still clinging to her like someone else's skin.

For a moment tonight, she could've sworn he'd looked at her like he saw her. Not as a prize. Not as a pawn.

Just... her.

And it was easier to shut the door than admit how much that scared her.

Quietly, she exhaled through her nose and closed her eyes, willing herself not to feel anything.

Not tonight.

Behind her, the candle on the table flickered as if catching some distant shift in the air.

And far below, the echo of a door slamming reverberated through the castle halls.

Amber didn't hear it.

But something in her spine straightened, just the same.

55

Everything He Has, and Everything He Is

L ucifer walked, his every step echoing with determination. The closer he came to her chambers, the clearer his mind became, his thoughts consumed by her. He imagined how she'd feel in his arms, how she'd smell against his skin; the very idea of her was intoxicating.

He took a deep breath as his feet stopped outside her door. Slowly, he creaked it open, a shred of light from the hallway creeping into the room. He glanced at her bed, but it was untouched and empty.

His pulse kicked up.

Stepping fully into the space, his eyes swept over it. Quiet. Still. Then his gaze landed on the open balcony doors, where sheer curtains shifted in the breeze like whispers.

His breath caught.

She stood at the railing, her back to him, golden hair illuminated by the eerie glow of Hell's skyline. She wasn't wearing the magnificent red gown anymore, but somehow, she looked even more stunning. A light pink top hugged her curves, delicate straps tracing over her shoulders. A sliver of skin peaked between the hem and her matching shorts, kissed by the cool breeze.

She looked soft. Unarmored. Like someone he might have known in another life if his fate hadn't damned him.

And still, somehow, she was the most dangerous thing he'd ever seen.

He stepped onto the balcony slowly, quietly. Not wanting to startle her. Not wanting to break this rare, unguarded moment.

"Incredible, isn't it?" he murmured.

Amber jumped slightly, her fingers tightening around the railing. She exhaled when she realized it was him but only spared him a small glance before turning back to the night sky, her gaze lifted to the winged shadows above.

They stood together in silence for a moment, watching the Volaces soar through the blood-red sky.

"What are they doing?" she asked, her voice quieter than usual.

Lucifer didn't answer right away. His eyes were still on her. Then, slowly, he turned toward the sky, placing his hands on the rail next to hers, their pinkies touching just barely, and still heat seared him.

"It depends," he said.

He pointed to a creature bobbing and weaving through the darkness, its bat-like wings flapping furiously against the night sky. "That one, there is a Monstra Parva. A young Angelus Lapsus. That one's still practicing."

Amber followed the creature's path. It wobbled slightly in flight, over-compensating and too eager to climb.

He paused, scanning the sky for something else. "See that group right there?" He said, pointing.

Amber followed his gaze. Their wings glistened in the low light. They barely moved, effortlessly suspended in the sky.

"Those are Eques," he said, "and the others flapping harder are Bellatores. Both are patrolling and practicing war formations. Once a Liberi is chosen by the Bellatures or Eques at their ceremony, they're granted wings. The only demons with them."

She watched one shot straight up into the sky, impossibly fast, like a reverse burst of lightning, disappearing into the void.

"Now, if we're lucky..." His voice trailed off, then his eyes narrowed. "There!"

Amber's eyes widened, and her breath caught.

From the shadows emerged a trio of Angelus Lapsus, their wings rippling like liquid shadow. Each beat sent a cascade of dark shimmer through the sky, like they were stitched from starlight and void.

"They need their wings to leave Hell," Lucifer murmured, "to collect souls. And to return with them."

Amber nodded, captivated by the awe-inspiring creatures. Their wings shifted and morphed, ever-changing, as though made of the darkness they hovered in. She couldn't tear her eyes from the sky as the creatures ducked, dove, spun, and soared; it was chaos and choreography all at once.

Lucifer watched her more than he watched the sky.

"You know," he said quietly, "there's still so much of Hell you haven't seen."

This time, Amber looked at him. The light from the horizon painted her eyes in fire and shadow. Her expression was unreadable, but something in it cracked open: curiosity, maybe, or trust.

Their gazes locked, and an invitation passed between them. An unspoken challenge.

"Do you want to go?" he asked, his voice softer than usual.

She hesitated, her fingers tightening around the balcony rail, but slowly, she nodded.

Lucifer held out his hand and Amber reached for it. As their palms touched, something shifted. Something quiet and ancient. His hand closed around hers, warm and sure.

A slight smirk tugged at the corner of his lips. "Hold on."

And then, without another word, they soared into the night.

Amber barely had time to inhale before the ground beneath her feet disappeared. A rush of wind tore through her hair as Lucifer carried her into the night, the heat of his body pressing against hers. The world blurred below them, Hell's jagged, dark landscape streaking past as they soared higher.

She gripped his shoulders instinctively, her breath catching. She'd flown once before, but the sensation of flying was still unlike anything she'd ever experienced; thrilling, terrifying, exhilarating.

And now, with Lucifer, this was flying without fear. This was letting herself fall and trusting that he'd catch her.

Lucifer didn't look down, didn't look where they were going; he only looked at her. At the way her mouth parted in wonder, the way her eyes danced with the reflection of the lava rivers below, the way she held him like she wanted to.

He could carry her forever if she let him.

His massive and powerful wings stretched wide behind him, slicing through the air with effortless control. Below them, Hell spilled out like a living tapestry, veins of molten fire carving paths through black stone, distant towers flickering with red light.

They dipped low, descending toward a glowing river of lava. A massive bridge carved from shadowed stone arched across it. Nestled along the riverbank was something unexpected: civilization.

Amber's eyes widened as they descended toward what could only be described as a town. Rows of buildings lined the streets, their dark, gothic architecture shaped from obsidian and brimstone. The glow of Hell's fire reflected off iron lanterns hanging from doorways, casting flickering shadows across the cobblestone paths. The air was thick with the scent of smoke and something metallic; iron, perhaps steel.

Lucifer landed gracefully at the entrance of the bridge, setting her down like she was made of glass, breakable. And maybe to him, she was.

Not in body, but in trust.

Amber took a steadying breath, her legs shaky beneath her.

"Welcome to the Nebulonis," Lucifer said, gesturing to the town beyond. "The residency for those who serve Hell."

She looked up at him, blinking. "You mean... like a village? For demons?"

He nodded, "When they're not working, you can find the demons and demonesses here."

Amber's gaze flitted from building to building, taking in the sight of demons walking through the streets, engaged in what seemed like everyday activities. A few figures carried baskets filled with dark, unfamiliar fruit; others bartered at an open-air market where vendors displayed items she couldn't recognize, gleaming weapons, shimmering fabrics, strange glowing stones.

It was nothing like she'd expected and everything she didn't know she needed to see.

Lucifer watched her take it all in.

Not with conquest. Not with desire.

But with the quiet ache of a man with nothing to offer but everything to give.

56

Among Devils

Lucifer led Amber forward, stepping onto the dark cobblestone streets of Nebulonis. The air was thick with the mingling scents of brimstone, iron, and something rich and spiced; *food*, she realized, though not any kind she recognized.

The town bustled with activity. Unlike the torturous landscapes she'd seen so far, this place felt... alive. Vendors called out to passersby, the hum of bartering filling the streets. Lanterns of flickering blue flame hung from wrought-iron posts, casting eerie yet oddly warm light on the figures moving through the town.

Amber's attention snagged on a stall where a demon with curling horns and four arms arranged an array of glowing stones, each pulsing with an inner light. She watched as a customer, a lesser demon with deep violet skin, picked up a shimmering red gem. The stone flared to life in their palm before dimming again. The merchant grinned, sharp teeth flashing.

"Soulstones," Lucifer murmured beside her. "They carry remnants of power. Some hold old magic, others memories, emotions, and echoes of those who lost them. They're useful on the islands especially, a sort of torture used by many."

Amber shivered and moved on.

To the left, a group of demons gathered around a cauldron at a food stall, its contents bubbling with thick, dark liquid. The vendor, a skeletal creature with hollow eyes and long, spindly fingers, ladled portions into obsidian bowls. An Angelus Lapsus with smoke-like wings took a sip, sighing in satisfaction.

"That's an Angelus Lapsus," Amber said breathlessly.

"Of course," Lucifer said, "they live here too."

Amber glanced at Lucifer. "Do I even want to know what they're drinking?"

He smirked. "It's not what you think. That's Lethebrew, a drink made from the Lethe River. It dulls pain and eases the mind. Some of my demons indulge in it after a long day. You've had it, you know."

Amber arched her brow. "I have?"

Lucifer let out a low chuckle. "That night you thought you were drunk? You drank Lethebrew, which has a similar effect as alcohol, without the nasty hangovers."

They walked past a tailor's shop, where shimmering fabrics draped over mannequins shaped like faceless figures. Inside, a seamstress with ink-black skin and glowing golden eyes measured a Bellatores' wingspan, adjusting a flowing coat of deep crimson. The garments ranged from battle-ready leather to regal attire fit for nobility.

Farther down the street, the rhythmic *clang* of metal striking metal rang through the air. They approached a massive forge, the heat rolling off it in waves. Sparks flew as a towering, broad-shouldered demon hammered at a molten blade, carefully shaping it. A set of armor rested nearby, black as night but etched with crimson runes that pulsed faintly.

Lucifer nodded toward the armory. "Every weapon and armor used in Hell is made here. Some hold enchantments, others are tailored to their wielders, and some are simply made of fire itself. If you fight here, you'll eventually wield something from this forge; in fact, you already have when you fought the beast in the Anulum Pugnatum."

Amber swallowed, drawn to the flickering firelight inside. She watched as another demon dunked a newly forged dagger into a vat of dark liquid, steam curling into the air.

"So I've already used one of these?" she asked, nodding toward a glowing blade.

Lucifer's mouth twitched. "Of course. Did you think I'd let you go into the arena unarmed?"

There was something unreadable in his tone, like pride. Or something more dangerous.

Just past the armory, the town began to quiet. The buildings became less like shops and more like homes. They were towering, spire-like structures with jagged edges, some built into the volcanic rock. Wrought-iron balconies overlooked the streets, and strange, spectral creatures slithered along the rooftops, watching from the shadows.

Lucifer gestured toward them. "The Residentiae. This is where demons live when they're not serving a purpose elsewhere. Some have been here for centuries. Others... longer."

Amber exhaled slowly, taking it all in. Nebulonis wasn't just a town; it was a world within Hell, a place where demons lived, worked, and existed beyond the torment and suffering she'd expected.

She turned to Lucifer. "Why are you showing me this?"

His gaze darkened, something unreadable passing through his eyes. "Because you need to understand," he said, voice low, "that Hell is more than what you think. It's not just suffering. It's survival. It's power. And if you're going to make it here, you need to see the full picture."

Amber met his gaze, her heart pounding, not from fear but from the weight of what she was beginning to realize.

Hell wasn't just torment. It was a kingdom. And he was its king.

They kept walking down the curved street. A towering structure loomed before them, its dark, spire-like silhouette cutting against the crimson-tinged sky.

"Do you recognize that building?" Lucifer asked, his voice edged with quiet amusement.

Amber narrowed her eyes, trying to place it. The architecture was familiar; the high, arched windows, the sprawling courtyard beyond the wrought-iron gates, but something felt *off.*

She shook her head. "Should I?"

He nodded. "Well, maybe not from this point of view, but if we were to step inside, I'm sure you would." He paused, watching her closely. "That's the school, little dove."

Amber froze mid-stride. "What? That's not possible." Her stomach twisted. "I never left Castellum Umbrae when I went to school."

"That's the amazing thing about this place." Lucifer gestured around them, his expression unreadable. "Hell is always shifting, always moving."

Amber turned, glancing behind her. Castellum Umbrae wasn't there. Or rather, it *should've* been. She'd stood in the courtyard and *watched* the Liberi wander about; she'd taught them a game. She'd seen Lucifer watching her.

"But... Castellum Umbrae was *right there*," she stammered, her mind scrambling for an explanation. "I saw you. You were looking at me from the balcony."

Lucifer's grin was slow and knowing. "That you did." His eyes gleamed in the dim light. "The school is normally here in Nebulonis, but when you were taking your lessons, Hell decided you weren't ready to learn about this town yet." He tilted his head, watching the realization dawn on her. "So, it *brought* the school to you."

Amber shuddered, glancing at the building again. The realization that Hell itself could bend reality, shifting its foundation to keep her contained, sent a chill down her spine. What else was it keeping from her?

Amber walked beside Lucifer, her mind still turning over the revelation about the school. Hell had hidden an entire town from her, shifting reality to keep her from seeing it until now. What else had it concealed? What else was it capable of?

As they moved through the winding streets, the scent of something warm and sweet drifted through the air. Amber's gaze flickered toward a smaller building nestled between two towering structures. It had an arched doorway carved from obsidian, and its windows were hazy with golden light. Through the open doors, soft murmurs and occasional bursts of laughter carried out into the street.

Curious, Amber stepped closer. Inside, she saw rows of dark wooden cradles, each rocking gently as if guided by unseen hands. Small demons, some with tiny, leathery wings and others with stubby horns barely peeking through their soft hair lay nestled in deep crimson and gold blankets. Along the walls, caregivers moved with practiced ease, tending to the infants. One woman with shimmering black eyes hummed a lullaby in a language Amber didn't understand, her voice low and soothing.

"A nursery," she murmured, barely aware she'd spoken aloud.

Lucifer, standing just behind her, nodded. "I'm sure your lessons have taught you how demons are created here?"

Amber shuddered but nodded.

"The young are raised here until they can fend for themselves, which takes about a month." His gaze swept over the rocking cradles, unreadable. "Most are born of Crevits, but some... some are created by Hell itself." There was a flicker of something in his expression, something she couldn't quite place.

"But that only happens when Hell deems it necessary. If it senses an impending threat, an attack from those who would challenge its rule, or if some great horror unfolds in the Overworld, it prepares." His voice was steady, but there was a weight to his words. "More demons are created to meet the demand, to stand ready for what's to come."

Amber swallowed, glancing back into the nursery, where tiny figures stirred in their blankets. The thought unsettled her: new life was brought forth not by choice, nature, or necessity.

"And the others?" she asked quietly. "The ones that take longer?"

Lucifer's gaze softened as he gestured toward a separate section of the room, where slightly larger cradles rocked independently. "Those are baby Angelus Lapsus. Unlike demons, they require up to six months before they're ready to survive on their own."

Amber's fingers curled into her palms as she watched one of the infants stretch its tiny and translucent wings like ink spreading through water. It was beautiful in a way she hadn't expected, and yet... there was something deeply unsettling about it.

"How does Hell decide?" she asked, barely above a whisper.

Lucifer didn't answer immediately. He just watched the cradles sway, watched one baby cry out as its horns knocked into a cradle rail.

Then, finally, he sighed, "Hell always knows what it needs."

Amber flinched, but a caregiver swept up the baby effortlessly, murmuring something as she rocked it back and forth, soothing it with quiet whispers. The infant sniffled, its tiny claws curling into her robes as it settled against her chest.

Amber's stomach twisted. A strange ache settled in, deep and hollow. The kind that lingers in empty spaces no one else can see.

She'd always imagined this moment differently. A child of her own. Soft fingers in hers. A name whispered with love.

This wasn't that.

This would never be that.

Her throat tightened as she turned away, swallowing the sharp sting behind her ribs. She didn't need to say it aloud; Lucifer already knew.

From the moment she first laid eyes on the nursery, he'd known from the flicker of wonder in her expression that had so quickly crumbled into quiet devastation.

His jaw tensed, but his voice was softer than usual when he finally spoke. He reached for her, his hand hovering... then gently, lightly, he let his palm rest at the small of her back. Not pulling. Not pressing. Just there.

Ready to catch her if she broke.

"Come," he murmured.

She hesitated, her feet feeling heavier than before. But then she felt his hand brush lightly against her back, the barest contact, as though he wasn't sure if she'd accept his comfort.

Lucifer had seen countless souls break in this realm. He'd seen them fight, beg, curse their fates. But this was different. This wasn't anger or defiance.

This was grief.

And for the first time in his existence, he truly *wished* that he could change something. That he could give her something.

But he couldn't.

So, instead, he stood there, watching her swallow down her pain, watching the light in her eyes dim just a little more. And he felt something unfamiliar stir in his chest, something heavy and unbearable.

Something like regret.

Amber turned from the nursery, and he followed, leading them further into town. They passed the market again, the scent of molten metal growing stronger with every step. The ringing of hammers on anvils filled the air as they neared the back of the sprawling forge, its massive stone chimney spitting embers into the sky. Demons worked tirelessly, shaping weapons, armor, and tools. The glow of the molten metal reflected in their eyes as they toiled, crafting pieces that pulsed with an eerie energy.

But Lucifer didn't stop there. He led her past the armory through a quieter street lined with tall, darkened buildings. The air smelled of parchment and aged leather, and Amber saw why as they rounded the corner.

A grand library stretched before them, its towering entrance flanked by statues of winged creatures frozen mid-flight. The doors, crafted from deep mahogany, were engraved with symbols that seemed to shift and change under the dim glow of the lanterns.

Amber stepped closer, unable to resist. She pushed open one of the heavy doors, and the scent of books flooded her senses. Inside, the space was impossibly vast. Shelves climbed so high they disappeared into darkness, filled with books of every shape and size. Some hovered in the air, fluttering their pages as if eager to be read. Others sat locked behind shimmering barriers, pulsing faintly.

"This is the Scientia Locus," Lucifer said, his voice echoing softly. "Every story ever told, every truth and every lie, from every soul that has ever entered Hell, it's all here. Spells and potions, history and achievements, they're all recorded within these pages."

Amber traced her fingers along the spine of a book, feeling the weight of the knowledge within. "This is nothing like the library in Castellum Umbrae."

Lucifer shook his head, "no, those are all replicas. Everything here is first hand."

She was mesmerized; she wanted to stay and lose herself in the endless corridors of words and secrets, but Lucifer was already moving.

"There's more I want to show you," he said.

Reluctantly, Amber followed him back out into the streets. As they climbed a winding path into the hills above Nebulonis, the town began to thin. The buildings here were different, smaller, built high into the jagged cliffs like a network of birdhouses and treehouses suspended in the dark. They seemed to hover just off the ground, suspended in mid-air. Wooden bridges and spiraling staircases connected them, glowing lanterns casting eerie light over the rock face.

"These are the homes of the Angeli Tenebrarum," Lucifer said, gesturing to the structures.

Amber gazed up at the towering dwellings. Some homes were small and isolated, while others clustered together, forming a strange, suspended village above the town. Figures moved among them, their wings constantly shifting. Some were feathered, some leathery, some like the shadows themselves, but each was folded against their backs. They were neither fully demons nor entirely angels, existing somewhere in between.

But at the highest point, perched above all the others, was a structure unlike the rest. It was larger, grander, and its design more intricate. The roof curled upward like the peak of a cathedral, and its windows burned with a dim, golden light.

Amber didn't need to ask to know it was different. "That's Abelia's home, isn't it?"

Lucifer didn't look at the building; he looked at her. "Yes," he said. "The Angel of Death."

As she stared at the terrifyingly beautiful structure, she didn't know what scared her more...the truth that Hell was more than just torment and pain or the way Lucifer looked like he wanted to save her from it.

57

Whispers of the Lost

"Ahh, Lucifer, Amber, how kind of you to drop by."

The voice was airy, familiar, and unmistakably amused. Amber turned just as Lucifer did, her gaze landing on a woman standing behind them.

"Abelia," Lucifer greeted with a smile, though his expression remained unreadable.

The woman bowed in acknowledgment. Lucifer, in turn, gave the most minor dip of his head, the closest thing to a bow Amber had ever seen from him.

"What brings you two to Nebulonis?" Abelia asked, her voice threaded with quiet sincerity.

"I figured it was time to reveal Hell to her," Lucifer answered, his gaze flicking briefly to Amber.

She felt the weight of that look, how it lingered just long enough to say everything he wouldn't. Her stomach fluttered, and she didn't know if it was from the pride in his voice or the ache behind it.

Abelia nodded, her expression thoughtful. "Yes, well, I'm glad you've had the chance to see it, Amber. But you know as well as I do, Lucifer; there's more to Hell than anyone will ever truly know."

Lucifer's lips twitched slightly, a wordless agreement.

A brief silence settled between them before Abelia hesitated, then spoke again. "Lucifer," she said carefully, her gaze darting to Amber as if weighing whether she should hear what came next. "There is an important matter I wish to discuss with you. Do you have a moment?"

Lucifer's expression sharpened slightly. "Now, Abelia?"

"It is rather urgent," she pressed, lowering her voice. "It'll only take a moment."

She turned to Amber then, offering a polite but expectant look. "That is, if you don't mind me stealing him?"

Amber glanced between them, unease curling in her gut. "Of course," she said, though every part of her knew she didn't truly have a say.

Lucifer hesitated. His fingers brushed lightly across hers before letting go, like he was trying to say something he couldn't speak aloud.

Lucifer and Abelia stepped away, speaking in hushed tones, but Amber caught the very beginning of their conversation:

"He's back," Abelia said, urgency laced in her voice.

"It's just rumors," Lucifer countered, his tone unreadable.

"Something about this feels off."

"We'll talk... Castle... Two days' time..."

Then, they were out of earshot.

Amber exhaled slowly, staring after them. Something about the exchange sent a chill through her, the words lingering like a whisper in the back of her mind.

He's back.

Who were they talking about? And why did it feel like something was very, very wrong?

Eventually, Lucifer made his way back to Amber, his expression unreadable, but there was *something* there, something just beneath the surface that she couldn't quite place.

She wanted to ask. The question sat heavily on her tongue, but something stopped her. Maybe it was the way Abelia had looked at her, a flicker of something cautious in her gaze. Or perhaps it was the tight, straight line of Lucifer's mouth, the tension in his jaw.

She didn't ask.

"We're leaving," Lucifer said, his tone final. There was no room for argument.

Abelia nodded in understanding, offering nothing further.

Carefully, Amber reached for Lucifer's hand, and for a heartbeat, when their fingers touched, his grip tightened just enough to make her breath catch.

Then, without another word, he took to the sky, pulling her with him.

They flew in silence, the wind cold against her skin, the weight of unspoken words heavier than the air around them. Lucifer's wings cut through the sky with surgical precision. His body close. His touch was careful.

Amber couldn't help but glance at the furrow in his brow, the distant edge in his stare. She knew that look. It wasn't rage. It wasn't power.

It was fear.

Finally, Amber spoke, "Are we going back?"

"No," Lucifer said at last. "There's one final place I want to show you."

The landscape below began to change. Jagged rock formations gave way to sprawling enclosures, vast and reinforced with dark iron. She caught glimpses of movement, shadows shifting unnaturally, bodies too large to belong to anything human.

Lucifer descended, landing effortlessly at the entrance of what could only be described as a fortress, but not for keeping people out; no, this was for keeping something in. He released her hand as they landed. His touch lingered half a second too long.

"Welcome to the Menagerie," he said, his wings folding behind him.

Amber stepped forward, her breath catching as the guttural sound of a beast's growl echoed through the cavernous space ahead. The air smelled of sulfur, damp earth, and something sharp, like blood on steel.

The entrance was grand, framed by wrought iron fencing and monumental lion-like gargoyles; only these had massive wings and curling horns, their stone eyes seeming to follow her as she moved. Beyond the gate, the cobbled path stretched forward in jagged, uneven stones, fractured as though the very ground had been split apart by the creatures contained within.

From every direction, guttural growls and eerie, high-pitched screeches filled the air, some distant, others unsettlingly close. The sounds varied; some were filled with malice, others with pain or warning. It was a cacophony of untamed fury barely held in check.

Infernal creatures of every shape and size lurked within reinforced pens, some carved directly into the volcanic rock, others lined with ancient sigils that pulsed faintly as if feeding off the energy of those trapped within. Their handlers were Operarios cloaked in dark, reinforced leathers. Each moved carefully between enclosures, with every step deliberate, their weapons always within reach. They cracked glowing whips against the ground, whispering commands in a half-order, half-threat language, ensuring that the creatures didn't turn on their masters.

A massive, reptilian beast with obsidian-black scales and too many eyes to count snarled as one such whip flared against the stone. Its thick, bladed tail swept dangerously close to its handler, forcing him to leap back. Farther down, something once winged but now broken whose tattered remains of flight trailed behind it lurched forward, its skeletal frame barely containing the twisted mass of muscle beneath. When it opened its maw, its jagged teeth jutted at unnatural angles, sharp enough to tear through bone.

Amber swallowed.

"These creatures," she murmured, her voice nearly lost beneath the ceaseless sounds of the Menagerie. Her gaze landed on a horned behemoth, its deep, resonating growl vibrating through the stone beneath her feet. "They're bred here?"

Lucifer nodded. "Bred, trained, and contained." His voice was calm, but there was an edge to it. "Some serve their masters without question. Others..." He glanced toward an enclosure where something enormous prowled just beyond the flickering torchlight. Its shadow stretched unnaturally, shifting as if it knew it was being watched. He stepped closer to her, not touching, but close enough to make her feel it.

His voice was low and measured. "We are waiting for an opportunity."

Amber's gaze swept across the Menagerie, taking in the chaos barely held in check, the raw, unbridled power restrained only by flickering sigils and fraying chains. This was no zoo. No sanctuary. This was a battlefield waiting for the right moment to erupt.

She exhaled slowly, steeling herself. "Why bring me here?"

Lucifer smirked, but there was something dark, something knowing in his expression.

"To show you that in Hell, there is always contrast." His gaze lingered on her for a moment, unreadable. "Places like Nebulonis exist for order. But this? This is where the true monsters are kept."

Amber opened her mouth, a question rising on her tongue, but a voice cut through the quiet before she could speak.

"Lucifer, Domina Amber."

They both turned.

Yorgos stood at the end of the corridor, bowing low. His presence broke the spell of the moment, and Amber blinked, her thoughts scrambling to catch up.

"Yorgos," she said, a grin tugging at her lips. "I'm so glad you're here; I wanted to congratulate you on your placement."

He straightened, offering a soft smile. "Thank you. I would love to show you around. Do you have a moment?"

Amber glanced toward Lucifer, who hadn't moved, though his gaze was still fixed on her.

"Go ahead," he said. "I'll come find you in about an hour."

Their eyes met again. This time, the air between them buzzed with something unspoken.

Just before she turned away, Lucifer added, so quietly it was nearly lost to the wind, "Be careful."

The words brushed the back of her neck like a warning, and though she didn't know why, they made her heart stutter. In return, she offered him a small smile, then followed Yorgos down the corridor.

"I'm glad I ran into you," Amber said as they walked, glancing at the strange, shifting halls around them. "But... why are you here already? Doesn't it usually take time before a Liberi joins their Situs Princeps?"

Yorgos shifted slightly, his steps faltering. "Normally, yes. But this time was... different."

Amber slowed. "Different, how?"

He looked around as if checking for ears, then leaned in. "You haven't heard?"

"Heard what?"

Amber came to a complete stop, forcing him to stop, too. Her expression was sharp now, focused. "Yorgos, what happened?"

He hesitated, then dropped his voice. "Something happened after the ceremony. I don't know all the details; I only know that Lean is mixed up in something seriously dark."

Amber's stomach turned at the mention of his name, "What do you mean?" she repeated, "What happened?"

"No one knows. That's the terrifying thing, after the ceremony, he just... vanished into the shadows. No one's seen him since."

Amber stared at him. That didn't sound like Leandros. He could be reckless, sure, but this?

"The Situs Princeps came to collect us right after," Yorgos continued. "But before they could, a messenger arrived. Said something serious had happened. Everyone was split up and sent to their new posts immediately. No explanations. Just urgency."

Amber's pulse quickened. "Leand wouldn't disappear without a reason."

Yorgos nodded grimly. "Exactly. And that's what's terrifying. He's not easy to lose track of, but he's been... different. Ever since he wasn't placed. Something's changed."

Her mind spun. The pieces didn't fit, but the edges were starting to bleed into each other.

"Do you think it's connected to what Lucifer's keeping from me?" she asked, her voice lower now, wary.

Yorgos tensed. "What's he keeping from you?"

Amber hesitated, then confessed. "I don't know everything, but I overheard him talking to Abelia. She said, 'he's back.'"

Yorgos went still. "Syn said the same thing."

Amber's head snapped up. "What do you mean?"

"She came to see me maybe an hour before you arrived. Asking if I'd seen Lean. She was frantic, talking about some rumor, something dangerous. She said there was going to be a meeting."

"...at Castellum Umbrae," Amber finished, the words sticking to her tongue. "In two days."

They stared at each other.

A chill swept over her. The world she'd stepped into was shifting again, only this time, it wasn't part of a test. It was real. And it was unraveling fast.

"I have to find Syn," she said, suddenly resolute.

Yorgos placed a hand on her arm. "Just be careful. You can't trust anyone right now. Not completely."

Amber nodded, her heart hammering. "I know."

She turned and walked quickly down the corridor, the Menagerie's walls twisting and echoing behind her.

But even as her thoughts raced toward Leandros and Syn and whatever storm was brewing, her mind circled back to Lucifer.

To the look in his eyes, the weight in his voice, and the secrets still left unspoken.

Something was cracking.

And she wasn't going to wait for it to shatter.

58

Broken Restraint

As Amber hurried through the winding corridors, her thoughts racing with the new information she'd just learned, she didn't see Lucifer until she nearly collided with him.

He was standing just ahead, a shadow in the dim light, his posture tense. His gaze flicked to her, eyebrows raised in surprise. "Back so soon?" he asked, his voice a mix of curiosity and something deeper; wariness, maybe.

Amber hesitated momentarily, unsure how to explain her sudden need to leave, but the urgency in her gut pushed her forward. "I need to go back to Castellum Umbrae," she said, trying to sound calm but feeling the heat of anxiety rising in her chest. "There's something I have to check on."

Lucifer's eyes narrowed slightly, his gaze lingering on her. There was a flicker of something in his expression that was almost a mix of concern and something that looked like hesitation. "What's this about?" His voice was quieter now, the weight of his words heavier.

She didn't want to tell him too much, not yet, but she knew he could see through her hesitation. "Nothing," she said, her voice low. "I just... I need to go."

Lucifer studied her for a beat longer before his lips parted like he wanted to say something but wasn't sure if he should. The silence between them stretched out, thick with unspoken words. Finally, he sighed, the tension in his shoulders easing just a fraction.

"Alright," Lucifer said, his voice firm. "Let's get you home." He stretched his hand to her, and with a powerful beat of his wings, they soared into the sky.

The flight back to Castellum Umbrae was quiet between them; the only sound was the rush of wind past their ears. Amber's mind, however, was racing. She couldn't shake the feeling that something was wrong, something big, and she needed answers.

Finally, the questions bubbling inside her became too much to ignore. "Lucifer?" she asked quietly, her voice almost lost in the wind. "Yorgos told me that the ranks joined their Situs Princeps earlier than usual. Do you know why?"

Lucifer glanced at her briefly, his expression unreadable, before returning his gaze to the passing sky. "Sometimes that just happens. Either Hell decides, or the Situs Princeps do."

Amber nodded, not fully accepting his answer but choosing to let it go for the moment. "I didn't get to say goodbye to my friends," she said, her voice tinged with a hint of disappointment.

Lucifer's lips quirked into a small smile, the kind that didn't quite reach his eyes. "Well, then, I have some good news," he said, his tone light, almost teasing. "Syn is stationed at Castellum Umbrae with the rest of the Legatus'. You can have her brought to your chambers in the morning."

Amber's heartbeat quickened at the mention of Syn's name. She'd been hoping to see her friend again, but now there was an undercurrent to that hope, a fierce *need*. Either Lucifer didn't know that Syn had been asking about Leandros, or he didn't think Amber knew. Either way, he wouldn't have allowed her to see Syn if he suspected she knew about Leandros' disappearance.

She glanced at Lucifer, trying to gauge his reaction, but his face remained impassive. His eyes were fixed ahead, and his wings slicked through the air with precision. Amber's stomach twisted. She couldn't help but wonder: What was he hiding? What did he know?

Amber's gaze flicked to the towering spires that loomed against the darkening sky as they neared Castellum Umbrae. The air was cooler here, and the weight of the questions swirling in her mind pressed heavily against her chest.

Lucifer slowed his descent, wings folding neatly as they touched down on Castellum Umbrae, landing with a soft thud. He straightened, his gaze lingering on her face for a moment. "Here we are," he said, his voice low, almost casual.

Amber offered him a slight smile. "Thank you."

He nodded in response as she turned toward the entrance. The large doors creaked open as they stepped inside, the dim glow of torches casting flickering shadows along the walls. Their footsteps echoed in the vast corridor, the silence between them thick but not uncomfortable.

They both stopped when they reached the long hallway leading to Amber's chambers. She turned to him, pressing her lips together in a tight line, but the tension eased when she caught the softness in his gaze.

"Well, it's late. I'll leave you to get some rest."

Amber let out a quiet laugh. "I thought devils didn't need rest?"

The corners of Lucifer's mouth curled up, and he playfully rolled his eyes. But before he could turn to leave, Amber reached out, her fingers closing gently around his arm.

Both of their eyes snapped to the contact. A tingling sensation rippled through them, and actual, flickering sparks danced at the point where their skin met. It didn't burn. If anything, it was warm, like a slow-building fire spreading through her veins.

"Thank you," she whispered, eyes fixed on the tiny, crackling embers between them.

Lucifer didn't move. "For what?" he asked just as quietly.

She finally looked up, meeting his eyes. "For showing me all of that today. For letting me in."

For a long moment, they stood there, caught in something unspoken. Then, with deliberate slowness, Amber rose onto her toes and pressed the lightest kiss to his cheek.

Lucifer stilled. His breath hitched so quick, so subtle that she might have imagined it.

The tension in his body was coiled, restrained, but undeniable. Finally, he pulled back, carefully removing himself from her touch.

For a moment, there was nothing but charged space between them.

Then, he had her backed against the wall with a movement too swift to track. Amber sucked in a sharp breath as he towered over her, the heat of his presence pressing in from all sides. But it wasn't fear that coursed through her veins; no, it was something far more dangerous: excitement. It had her toes curling, chills racing over her skin, and her heart pounding in a rhythm she couldn't control.

"Amber," Lucifer murmured, his breath hot and heavy, laced with nearly tangible desire. "We need to talk about Airlea."

The words hit her like ice water. That wasn't what she'd been expecting.

"Oh." The word came out quiet, more disappointed than she'd intended.

She cast her gaze downward, but before she could retreat into her thoughts, his fingers found her chin, tilting it back up until her eyes locked onto his.

"She means nothing to me," Lucifer said. His tone was resolute, unwavering, like a fact carved into stone, unquestionable, unshakable.

Amber swallowed hard. "Then why was she there?" Her voice wavered just slightly.

Lucifer didn't hesitate. "Because you couldn't be."

Heavy and raw words hung between them, igniting a storm in her chest.

Amber stared at him, looking for a hint that he was lying and teasing her, but there was nothing there. Just the truth, laid bare.

Still, she fought back. "All you've done is push me away. You let me in just enough to make me think that somehow, somewhere, some small part of you cares about me just to slam the door in my face." She shook her head, jerking free from his touch.

Reaching up, she placed a hand on his chest and shoved him back. "It's not fair, Lucifer. I can't keep doing this." Despite herself, a single tear slid down her cheek, but she quickly wiped it away. "I'm done. I've done everything you wanted. I've more than proven myself to you, and still, it's not enough. The truth is, nothing will ever be enough for you, will it?"

She stared at him, daring him to answer, but he said nothing.

Amber let out a low sigh and turned, opening the door to her bedroom.

That was when he snapped.

In an instant, he was on her.

There was no hesitation, no restraint, only raw, unfiltered need. His hands found her wrists, tangled themselves in her hair, and gripped her waist like he was afraid she'd disappear if he let go. The heat between them was unbearable, burning hotter than the flames of Hell itself.

"You don't understand," he ground out, his grip desperate, unyielding. "There were rules I needed to follow."

But Amber didn't back down. "What rules, Lucifer? Talk to me." She met his fire with her own, grabbing his face and forcing him to look at her, "I'm not afraid of you. I never have been. Let me in."

His chest heaved, his pupils blown wide, and red flashed over them as if he was trying to keep himself restrained.

"You needed to want me. This, *we,* couldn't be forced. But Hell, Amber, I've ached for you since the moment I saw you." His voice dropped lower, rough with longing. "When you danced with me in that bar, it was all I could do not to take you then and there."

Amber dragged her nails down his chest, drawing a ragged, animalistic sound from deep in his throat. He pushed her back, slow but deliberate, until the backs of her thighs met the round table in the center of the room.

"And now..." His eyes flashed dangerously. "You need to tell me to stop. Say you don't want this right now. Because if you don't..." His voice broke into something guttural, almost pained. "I won't be able to control myself. I won't be able to stop until I've worshiped every inch of you."

She swallowed hard, but there was no fear.

Only want.

Only him.

"Then don't stop," she whispered. "I want this."

And he didn't.

He kissed her like he'd been dying to.

Like the restraint was finally too much, her mouth was the only thing to save him.

It wasn't rough. Not at first. It was heat restrained, the kind that simmers under the skin until it has no choice but to burn.

Amber melted into him, her hands rising to his chest, fisting the front of his shirt. His arms wrapped around her, pulling her in, anchoring her against the storm building inside them both.

Lucifer lifted her effortlessly, her legs wrapping around his waist, their bodies pressed together so tightly it was impossible to tell where one ended and the other began. His grip turned bruising, possessive, like he needed to memorize her feel, map every place he'd touched and every place that still begged for his attention.

His mouth trailed fire across her jaw, down the column of her throat. He paused at her collarbone, lips brushing where her pulse beat hardest.

"You don't have to—" he started.

But Amber cut him off with another kiss.

"I know," she breathed.

Her fingers clawed into his back, tearing at the fabric of his shirt, needing it to disappear. Sparks, actual, crackling sparks erupted from every place their skin met, racing along her arms and across his back.

And then, Hell reacted.

The torches lining the walls flared violently, their flames stretching high, casting wild shadows that twisted and danced. The very foundations of Castellum Umbrae rumbled as if recognizing that its King had finally found the woman who threatened to change everything.

The temperature spiked, like fire was licking at their skin, and a demonic whisper slithered through the air. Not a word, not a command; just silent, knowing approval.

Lucifer devoured her like she was the only thing keeping him alive. And she let him.

She let him worship her. Let him leave burning trails along her skin as he tore away the layers between them. But Amber wasn't passive. Not now. Not with him.

She dragged her nails down his back, hard enough to leave marks, tearing his shirt over his impossibly broad shoulders.

When the cool air hit his skin, his wings erupted, stretching vast, dark, and shimmering in the firelight.

Lucifer stilled for a fraction of a second, hesitating just long enough to make her whisper his name, "Lucifer."

It wasn't a plea.

It was a command.

And he obeyed.

He groaned, a deep, guttural sound, his grip tightening like he was afraid she'd disappear.

She wouldn't.

She never would.

His wings wrapped around them, encasing them both in darkness.

His voice was a rasp against her skin, "You're mine."

She met his gaze, fierce and unrelenting.

"I always have been."

And then there was nothing left between them but heat, and fire, and the inevitable ruin of them both.

59

Betrayal's Edge

Slowly, still shrouded beneath the darkness of his wings, Lucifer lowered himself to the junction between her thighs.

His tongue entered her first.

Amber's body lurched at the sudden invasion, a gasp tearing from her throat as his hand slid up her torso, fingers pinching and squeezing her breast in all the right places.

His mouth worked her with reverence and hunger as if he were trying to consume something more than just flesh, something more profound. Like he *needed* this. Needed to be as close to her as possible. Needed to prove something he could never say aloud.

He was showing her.

With everything he had, he was showing her.

Amber let out a strangled gasp, her palm flying to the back of his head, pushing him deeper as his tongue found the exact spot that made her vision blur.

He *knew*.

He flicked harder, faster, adding his fingers with devastating precision. His thumb circled her clit in tight, tireless motions while his tongue plunged deeper.

The sensation was overwhelming, and Amber lost all ability to control herself. Her mind blanked, her spine arched, and her eyes rolled back.

"Yes, God, yes!" she moaned, trembling. "Don't stop. Please don't stop."

Lucifer stilled, and Amber immediately whined.

For a moment, the air itself seemed to hold its breath.

Then his low, deadly voice cut through the silence: "Don't bring *Him* into this."

Amber barely had time to blink before he moved.

His hands gripped her thighs tighter, fingers digging in just enough to make her gasp, not in pain, but from the *promise* behind it. And then he was on her again, ruthless, relentless, like her moan had struck something deep and ancient inside him.

"You want to scream someone's name?" he growled against her skin, voice rough with possession. "Then scream *mine*."

He made her. Again and again.

Until the only word on her lips was his.

Her body arched into him, her hips grinding, his tongue and fingers working her with devastating expertise. His hand squeezed her breast just hard enough to make her breath catch.

"I'm gonna come," she gasped, voice breaking.

He didn't stop.

He worked her harder, *hungrier*, driving her to the edge like a man possessed. Her toes curled. Her knees clenched. His head was caught between her thighs, and he didn't even flinch; just *growled* into her, holding her down as she trembled.

Her orgasm ripped through her like lightning.

She cried out, raw and unfiltered, her body convulsing beneath his mouth.

But he didn't stop.

Not until she sagged against the table, limbs twitching, her thighs falling open with a shudder.

Still, he licked, slow and deliberate, like he wasn't done. Like he *couldn't* be.

He wanted more.

When he finally lifted his head, his eyes were dazed, sparkling with mischief and hunger. But behind that: desperation. Need. Possession.

Amber's chest heaved, her breath ragged, as he crawled up over her once more, his torso pinning her down. Her hands tangled in his hair, dragging him to her mouth for a messy, deep kiss full of fire.

"I need more," she whispered against his lips. "I need *all* of you."

Lucifer's gaze burned as his fangs grazed her lip. He tugged, drawing blood, and released it into her mouth like a promise, "I won't be gentle."

"*Good,*" she growled back.

That was all he needed.

The change in him was instant. Something wild flickered across his face. His eyes flashed red. His breath came faster, more ragged.

"I need to be inside you," he whispered, voice hoarse.

She nodded, her heart pounding.

He swallowed her in a kiss, fierce and consuming, then lifted her like she weighed nothing. His hands were careful, almost reverent, despite the chaos burning behind his eyes. He carried her to the bed with surprising gentleness, setting her down like she was something he could break but didn't want to.

Not yet.

He kissed her again, deeper this time, bruising, and with no more warning, he aligned himself against her entrance. Without hesitation, he thrust in, hard and full, making her cry out from the sheer *stretch* of him. He filled her completely, every inch demanding space where there wasn't any.

Just as she began to adjust, he pulled out nearly to the tip, then slammed back into her, deeper than before.

Her hips jerked. Her body strained.

Their moans twisted together like a dark hymn.

He stilled for one heartbeat. One moment to feel her. To memorize the way she clenched around him.

Then he moved.

Slow at first, then faster.

Harder.

They moved together, their bodies perfectly in sync. His hands roamed over her, caressing and exploring as if trying to memorize every inch of her. She wrapped her legs around his waist, pulling him deeper, their connection growing with each thrust.

"You feel so fucking good," he groaned, kissing her, his hands sliding down her waist.

"Don't stop," she panted, nails dragging down his back. "Please, Lucifer. *Don't stop.*"

He didn't.

He couldn't.

He drove them both toward the edge, every sound between them sharp with need. When he reached between them and rubbed her clit, Amber's head snapped back.

She didn't think she had another orgasm in her.

She was wrong.

"Come for me," Lucifer commanded, his voice a snarl against her ear. "Look at me when you do. I want to see you come."

He shifted her legs over his shoulders, angling deeper.

Amber cried out, his length striking something impossibly sensitive, too much, *too good.* Her nerves splintered between agony and bliss.

"Oh—" she gasped, her voice dissolving into a moan.

Lucifer's hand slid to her throat, gripping, not too tight, but enough. Enough to make her pulse flutter. Enough to say *you're mine.*

Amber tore at the seams, shattering around him.

The world around them vanished as her body arched into his. She came with a muffled cry, the sound choked off by the firm hand around her throat.

Her mouth parted as her nails dug into the sheets, desperate for something, *anything*, to ground her. But there was nothing except him.

Her legs tightened around his shoulders, keeping him deep, keeping him exactly where she needed him, where he felt so unbearably good.

Lucifer followed with a guttural moan, burying himself deep, his body shaking as he came hard, grinding into her with a final thrust that stole the air from both of them.

They unraveled together.

Sprawling across the edge of something bigger than either of them.

For a moment, nothing else existed.

No kingdom.

No war.

Just this.

Just *them*.

But then, something shifted.

Lucifer stilled. His arms remained around her, but his muscles tensed, something raw and aching twisting beneath his skin.

Amber felt it before he even moved.

Slowly, he pulled away.

The air between them turned thick, electric, *and devastating*.

She reached for him, "Don't do this."

But he was already stepping back. His hands braced against the stone wall, breath heaving, like he needed to physically steady himself.

"You should get some rest," he said hoarsely.

Amber's heart cracked.

"You're running from me."

He didn't answer.

"You can't take this back," she whispered.

Another silence. His wings twitched, "I'll see you in the morning."

And then he vanished into the shadows, leaving nothing but the lingering scent of embers and the phantom heat of his touch.

Amber lay in the silence, staring up at nothing.

Something had happened that she didn't understand.

And more terrifying than anything?

She wasn't sure she wanted to.

60

The Breaking Point

Morning came far quicker than Amber would've liked.

She stirred at the subtle sounds of Korinna moving about her chambers. Though she'd adjusted to no longer needing sleep, she'd grown fond of the vivid dreams that came when she closed her eyes.

"Salve, Domina Amber." Korinna greeted, glancing to where Amber stretched in bed.

Amber stifled a yawn. "Salve, Korinna."

"You are to take breakfast with Lucifer this morning," Korinna informed her, turning back to the dresser as she pulled out a set of clothing.

A chill ran down Amber's spine.

Last night slammed into her all at once: his touch, his lips, the way he'd unraveled beneath her. The way she'd *let him.*

Her pulse quickened at the thought of seeing him again, of being near him. But then she remembered how quickly he'd turned cold, how effortlessly he'd shut her out.

Dread surged through her, heavy and unrelenting.

But she wasn't going to let this go. She'd see him. She'd *demand* answers.

With quiet resolve, Amber tossed the blankets aside and climbed out of bed, crossing the room to where Korinna stood in silent expectation. Without a word, she let the demoness dress her in the dark leather that had become her daily uniform, though it was slightly different each day.

Today, it felt tighter. Restrictive.

The fitted black leather corset cinched tightly to emphasize the curve of her waist. The material was supple yet firm, embossed with intricate patterns that looked almost like ancient runes, shifting slightly in the dim light of her chambers. Thin straps rested over her shoulders, leaving her collarbones and arms bare, the exposed skin contrasting against the dark, structured fabric.

Carefully, she stepped into the matching leather skirt that fell asymmetrically around her legs, cut high on one side to allow for movement while draping lower on the other in jagged layers. Slits were worked into the design, revealing glimpses of her toned thighs with every step. The edges were charred, as if kissed by Hell's fire, giving the ensemble an untamed, battle-worn appearance.

Over the corset, Korinna draped a cropped, sleeveless jacket made of the same dark leather. Its edges were lined with thin silver embroidery that shimmered faintly in the firelight.

Her boots were sturdy yet sleek, laced up to just below her knees, and the buckles were fashioned into the shape of small, curling horns.

Amber flexed her fingers, rolling her shoulders as she adjusted to the weight of the outfit. It felt heavier today. Or maybe that was just the weight of everything else pressing down on her.

She exhaled, straightened her spine, and met her reflection as Korinna brushed her long hair effortlessly across her shoulder.

"Omnes parata, Domina. Lucifer should already be in the dining room waiting for you. We should go."

Amber nodded and followed the demoness out of her chambers. They walked with a shared confidence, their strides steady, unyielding. Demons scattered out of their path, pressing themselves against the walls as they passed, their eyes filled with wariness and reverence.

When they reached the grand dining hall, two Operarios pushed open the massive doors, revealing the lavish space. Korinna had been right, Lucifer was already sitting at the opposite head of the table. Amber's breath caught in her throat at the sight of him, and she barely registered the sound of the door closing behind her. Korinna left the two of them alone.

His eyes took in her appearance, devouring her like last night hadn't been enough. It would never be enough.

The flicker of red in his irises sent heat curling low in her stomach. His gaze swept over her, lingering on the way the leather clung to her curves, on the dangerously high slit running up her thigh. His hands, resting on the edge of the table, flexed just slightly like he was resisting the urge to reach for her.

Slowly, deliberately, she took her seat.

Lucifer blinked, and the enormous table shrank, condensing until the space between them had vanished. He was right there, mere feet away, close enough that she could feel the tension radiating from him in waves.

Amber refused to react, instead picking up a piece of ripe fruit from the elaborate spread before her. She took a slow, teasing bite, keeping her eyes locked on his.

Juice dripped down the corner of her mouth.

Lucifer moved before she could, reaching across the now-shortened distance to wipe it away with his thumb. The touch was brief, barely there, but it sent a pulse of energy crackling between them.

They sat like that for a long moment, neither speaking, neither moving.

Finally, Amber broke the silence. "It's time you start explaining yourself."

Lucifer leaned back in his chair, exhaling like he'd expected this. His head tilted just slightly, the edges of his mouth curving into something that wasn't quite a smirk.

"I suppose I do owe you that much, don't I?"

Amber nodded, though her pulse thrummed unevenly.

"Alright," he said, crossing his arms and settling in. "I suppose I should start at the beginning."

Lucifer's gaze stayed locked on hers as he spoke.

"When the world was first created, Heaven came into existence alongside it. God, expecting His people to be perfect, didn't create a place of punishment. But, as you well know, with free will comes the capacity for mistakes. The first sin was inevitable. And when it happened, God created Hell, and the sinner was condemned not just to suffer but to rule."

Amber frowned, her fingers tightening around the edge of the table.

"Zagan, the first sinner, became the original ruler of Hell, though not by choice."

Lucifer leaned forward slightly, his voice low and smooth yet edged with something heavier.

"What God didn't foresee was that the first devil would embrace his power. After adapting to his surroundings, he stopped seeing Hell as a punishment and instead as an opportunity. When God realized this, He decreed that a devil could only remain in power if he had an heir. Otherwise, his rule could be challenged at any time."

His eyes flickered with something unreadable before he continued.

"And so, the conditions were set. A devil would need a woman willing to stay in Hell as his partner, but she would need to do so willingly and without coercion, all within the first year of entering Hell. Only after enduring many trials and hardships could she make that choice. If she refused, he would have to release her."

Amber swallowed hard.

"Those are the rules I had to follow," Lucifer said quietly. "*I* couldn't go to you. *You* had to come to me. *You* had to want me."

A sharp, twisting feeling curled in her chest.

She did want him.

That was the problem.

That was why every glance, every touch, every moment where he let his guard slip felt like something dangerous. Something inevitable.

But before she could untangle that mess of emotions, another thought pushed forward, cutting through it.

"What...what about the heir?" she asked, her voice hoarse.

At that, something in Lucifer's face changed.

Something flickered in his eyes, making her stomach tighten in anticipation of an answer she wasn't ready for.

She'd seen him angry. She'd seen him amused, bored, entertained. But this was different. This was something raw. Something aching.

"This is the devastating part," he murmured, almost to himself. "I can never give you what you want."

A cold, sinking feeling formed in Amber's gut.

"What do you mean?" she asked, though part of her already knew.

Lucifer hesitated, his gaze searching hers like he was weighing the damage his following words would cause.

"I've seen how you interact with the young demons," he said softly. "The way you look at them when you think no one's watching. And I know your dreams, Amber. The ones you had when you were human."

Her throat tightened.

"You wanted a family."

It wasn't a question.

It was a truth that wrapped around her like a vice.

She wanted to tell him he was wrong. That she'd never truly let herself believe it was possible. But that would be a lie. Because she'd believed. She'd dreamed. And now, those dreams were unraveling thread by thread.

"God decreed that the only way for a devil to have an heir was if he truly fell in love," Lucifer continued. "But, of course, the Devil is simply a personification of evil. Of humanity's worst. He—*I*," he exhaled sharply, "can never feel love."

Amber flinched like he'd struck her.

"No matter what," he went on, his voice rougher now, "no devil would ever be able to create a successor, keeping his fate uncertain. Having a child would cement his rule over Hell for eternity. And if anyone ever tried to overthrow him, Hell itself would cease to exist, releasing every condemned soul back into the world."

The words echoed in her mind, but all she could focus on was the dull, growing ache in her chest.

I can never give you what you want.

Her stomach turned violently.

She'd known, on some level, that Hell was no place for children. That she could never have the kind of life she once dreamed of. That the warmth of tiny hands, of lullabies, of unconditional love, was something she'd lost the moment she stepped into this world.

But to hear it spoken so plainly. To hear him say it like it was final, like it was impossible, like it had never been an option.

Her vision blurred.

"Why?" she rasped, blinking back a burning sensation in her eyes. "Why would God make it this way? Why all these rules, these loopholes?"

Lucifer's expression darkened.

"Because it was never about benefiting me or any other devil," he said bitterly. "It was about balance. If a devil could never secure an heir, then the throne would always be unstable. Hell would never become too strong. It's a check on my power. A failsafe."

Amber barely heard him.

She was too busy fighting the tremor in her hands.

She could never be a mother.

Never.

The realization was a jagged, gaping wound inside her.

She felt sick to her stomach. But beneath the nausea and heartbreak, something else took root, something more permanent. A quiet, unshakable resolve.

It didn't matter.

She wanted to be a mother. She *would* be a mother.

Maybe not to her own children, not in the way she'd once dreamed. But here, in Hell, among the thousands of Liberi who knew no kindness and had no one to guide them, she could be something to them.

She could find her place here.

She *would* find her place here.

Amber wiped at the tears that had begun to fall freely down her face, barely aware of them until she saw Lucifer watching her.

Not calculating. Not cold.

But watching.

There was something like worry in his expression, something restrained. He didn't reach for her, didn't speak, but the weight of his presence was enough.

She wasn't ready to admit anything to him. Not yet.

There were still too many questions and too much uncertainty.

But one thing had become clear: she wouldn't crumble.

Amber lifted her chin, steeling herself.

"I'm coming up on a year of being here," she said, her voice steadier than expected.

Lucifer nodded the golden ring of his eyes flickering in the dim light. "Yes, you are."

She inhaled slowly. "What does that mean?"

Lucifer leaned back slightly, his gaze never leaving hers. "It means that in two nights, there will be a meeting of all the Legatus. You will announce your decision. Depending on your answer, there will either be a coronation..." he paused, his voice unreadable, "or a farewell."

Amber's heart pounded.

Two nights.

The most significant decision of her life loomed just ahead, and no one could make it for her. No one could guide her.

"What happens if I choose not to stay?" Amber asked tentatively.

Lucifer exhaled, cracking his neck as if he'd been expecting the question.

"I can't tell you that, Amber." His voice was firm. "I can't tell you anything that might influence your decision one way or another."

She studied him, searching for an answer, a hint, *anything*. But his expression was unreadable again, his walls firmly back in place.

Then he added, "There's one more thing. You asked to speak with Efrosyni this morning."

Amber blinked, momentarily thrown off by the shift.

"She's waiting in your chambers for you."

Her breath caught.

Efrosyni.

Amber nodded, pressing her palms against the table as she steadied herself. *Two nights.*

She had two nights to decide the course of her future.

And she had no idea what she was going to do.

61

Heart of Darkness

Amber stood from the table and exited the dining room without so much as a goodbye to Lucifer. Her mind raced with too many thoughts as she returned to her chambers.

Two nights. That was all the time she had left before she had to make a decision. Before, she had to stand before the Legatus and say whether she'd stay in Hell or leave it behind forever.

Her heart felt like it was caught in a vice.

Could she really leave?

Could she really stay?

The doors to her chambers were already open when she arrived. Efrosyni paced near the window, arms crossed, and her nails digging into her skin like she was trying to hold herself together. At the sound of Amber's footsteps, she turned, her green eyes wide and searching.

"You look like you've seen a ghost," Amber remarked, tilting her head.

"Close the door," Syn whispered.

Amber's stomach twisted. "Syn?"

Amber's brows knitted together, but she did as she was told. Syn rushed forward, grabbing Amber's hands when the door clicked shut. Her fingers were ice-cold.

"Something's wrong," she said in a hushed, desperate voice. "Amber, I think...I think Leandros is in real danger."

Amber's heart dropped, "What do you mean? What happened?"

Syn exhaled sharply, looking over her shoulder as if she expected someone to be there, watching, listening.

Her voice shook when she spoke again, "He told me before he left that something wasn't right. That there were things happening in Hell that even Lucifer didn't know about."

Amber felt the air in the room change. The words sank into her skin, cold and suffocating.

That wasn't possible. Lucifer knew everything.

"Syn..." Amber said cautiously. "That doesn't make sense."

Syn let out a humorless, panicked laugh and ran a hand through her hair. "I know! I know it doesn't! But Lean was scared, Amber. He wouldn't tell me much; he just said he was looking into something. Then, the next day, he was gone."

Amber swallowed hard. "Maybe Lucifer—"

"No." Syn cut her off, shaking her head. Her hands trembled. "I talked to the other Legatus, but no one knows anything. Not even Lucifer."

Amber stiffened. That was impossible.

She opened her mouth to argue, but Syn stepped closer, her voice dropping to a whisper, "I heard something else."

Amber shivered. The way Syn said it like, she almost didn't want to say it at all.

"Lean found it. The place in Hell that Professor Solon told us about," Syn continued so quietly Amber had to strain to hear her. "The prison where The First Devil is held."

Amber's blood ran cold, "Zagan?"

Syn licked her lips, glancing at the door again before whispering: "Some say he has him. That Zagan has Lean."

Amber's stomach twisted painfully. Zagan. The First Devil. The one who ruled before Lucifer. The one who had been overthrown and lost everything.

"That's just a story," Amber said, but she could hear the hesitation in her own voice.

Syn shook her head furiously. "Lean didn't think so."

Amber sucked in a breath.

"He thought it was real," Syn continued. "And he was trying to prove it. That's why he's gone."

Silence. The weight of it crushed Amber's chest.

Syn let out a shuddering breath and squeezed Amber's hands. "I shouldn't have told you this," she whispered. "If I disappear next—"

"You won't," Amber said immediately, gripping her back.

Syn gave a weak, almost defeated smile. "Just... be careful, okay? If Lucifer doesn't know about this, then whoever took Lean, whoever's pulling the strings, doesn't want to be found."

Syn walked to the couch in the room and sat down, her foot bouncing like she couldn't stay still. Amber followed quickly, sitting close to her friend, "There's more," Syn said. "I've been researching on my own, digging into Lean's disappearance. I think he found something he's not supposed to."

"Something like what?" Amber asked.

"He was investigating rumors of demons conspiring against Lucifer. Not just petty betrayals but something bigger. I don't know what he found; he disappeared before he told me anything. Amber, it was weird; there was no warning. No sign of a struggle. It was like he was erased."

Amber looked at her friend. She was on the brink of tears when her voice dropped even lower: "You don't understand, Amber. If this is true, we're all already dead."

Amber sat back as fear coursed through her, "There's a meeting tonight."

Syn nodded, "Yes, but only the Archdemons and the highest-ranking Legatus are invited along with Angelus Mortis."

"That doesn't make any sense," Amber said, shaking her head. "All Legatus are supposed to meet at every meeting; that's why your rank is so small." Her heart began to pound, "Do you think it's about Lean?"

Syn exhaled shakily, "If it is, they won't admit it. If Lean discovered something about Zagan, do you really think they'd want us to know?"

Amber's jaw tightened, "Then we need to find out for ourselves."

"Amber, no," Syn said, shaking her head quickly, gripping Amber's hands, her nails digging in. "If they find out we're even asking about this, we'll be next."

Amber set her jaw in a tight line, "Then we don't get caught."

"How do you suppose we do that? Neither one of us is allowed in the meeting." Syn countered, still gripping Amber's hands.

"I know a place," Amber said, determination dripping off her words.

62

Twisted Fate

The hours passed like molasses, or at least that's how it felt. Amber sat on the edge of the bed, fingers curled into the fabric of her leather skirt, her mind racing. The fireplace they'd lit hours ago crackled, its embers slowly dying, casting eerie shadows along the stone walls.

Across the room, Syn paced like a trapped animal, arms crossed tightly, her nails digging into her skin.

"This is insane," Syn muttered for what had to be the tenth time. "We're going to get caught. You know that, right?"

Amber exhaled slowly. "Then don't come."

Syn stopped pacing. Silence. Her green eyes flickered toward Amber, a storm of emotions passing over her face. Fear. Uncertainty. But underneath it all was determination.

She let out a sharp breath. "I'm coming."

Amber nodded, pretending that didn't make her feel relieved.

Korinna had come in and out of Amber's chambers all day, and each time, the girls pretended to be fine, gossiping about random things. Each time, Amber quickly dismissed the demoness. Other than Korinna coming and going, though, the girls hadn't seen anyone else and hadn't left Amber's chambers. All day, they'd set to planning how they were going to gain access to the meeting.

Finally, the clock above the fireplace ticked forward. Midnight. The meeting would begin soon.

Amber stood, shaking out her hands. "Let's go."

Creaking open the heavy bedroom door, the girls snuck into the hallway. It was quieter than usual. There was no laughter, no echoing footsteps of the Operarios, only silence.

Amber led the way, heart pounding, Syn close behind her. Their footsteps barely made a sound against the cold marble floors.

Amber threw out an arm as they rounded a corner, stopping Syn in her tracks.

A figure stood at the end of the corridor.

An Eque.

His horns curved back against his head, his red eyes flickering with torch-light. He wasn't moving, just standing too still. Watching.

Amber's pulse slammed against her ribs. She pulled Syn back into the shadows of an alcove, pressing themselves against the stone.

Seconds stretched.

The demon finally turned, disappearing down another hall.

Amber let out a slow breath. "Come on."

Syn didn't need to be told twice.

Amber guided them through the library toward the bookshelf she'd discovered before.

She ran a hand along the spines of the old books until she found the one she was looking for.

A single red leather tome.

She pulled it. The shelf groaned. The wall behind it shifted.

Syn inhaled sharply as a hidden door creaked open, revealing a dark, narrow passage.

Amber turned to her. "Last chance to back out."

Syn squared her shoulders. "Not a chance."

Amber smirked. *Good.*

They stepped inside, closing the door behind them.

Amber led Syn through the passage's rough, narrow walls and followed the glow to the small, dusty chamber overlooking the Magna Aula.

Through an intricate iron grate, they could see the long table below; the Archdemons Amber had only heard about were seated around it.

Amber's breath caught as her eyes landed on Lucifer.

He sat at the head of the table, posture rigid, eyes dark with something unreadable.

She'd seen him calm. She'd seen him furious. But this?

This was something else.

To Lucifer's right sat Chrysostomos; she'd met him once. To his left, Abelia, her wings tucked neatly around her chair, expression unreadable.

The other demons seated around the table were strangers to her, yet she knew them by reputation alone.

Asmodeus sat beside Abelia, his monstrous form radiating heat, embers flickering off his molten skin. Next to him, Belial hovered, his figure shifting like smoke, dissolving and reforming with every subtle movement of the air.

Across from Asmodeus lounged Mephistopheles, his piercing gaze sharp with amusement or calculation. Beside him sat Bael, his aura heavy and suffocating, as though gravity itself bent in his presence.

Further down, Mammon reclined lazily, but his golden eyes missed nothing, predatory and assessing. Across from him, Beelzebub remained eerily still, his insect-like features glinting in the dim candlelight.

Amber had never seen so many formidable creatures gathered in one place. Power pooled in this room, thick and suffocating.

The tension was thick in the air as Mephistopheles leaned forward, his voice a low growl. "There are whispers," he said. "Whispers that should not exist."

Mammon scoffed. "Rumors are beneath us."

Lucifer's voice was quiet but sharp as a blade. "And yet, they persist."

Amber and Syn exchanged a look.

Abelia leaned forward slightly and spoke, "There have been… disturbances. Places in Hell shifting. Locks breaking." A pause. Then, slowly: "Signs of him."

The air turned frigid.

Amber's hands clenched. *Zagan.*

Asmodeus sneered, "You believe children's stories now?"

Abelia exhaled through her nose. "Leandros did not disappear over a 'story.'"

Amber felt Syn go rigid beside her.

Chrysostomos leaned forward, his voice dropping. "Then tell us, Lucifer… if Zagan truly is stirring, what will you do?"

The room grew even quieter, the tension so thick it seemed to press down on Amber's chest. She felt the cold of the room seep into her bones as Chrysostomos's question hung in the air. All eyes turned to Lucifer, who remained eerily calm, his gaze unwavering.

He was still calculating.

"What will you do about it?" Chrysostomos repeated, his tone tinged with a mixture of respect and challenge.

Lucifer's lips curled into the faintest smirks, but it didn't reach his eyes. His voice was cold, measured, and filled with a dangerous calm. "I will do what is necessary."

Amber felt her pulse quicken. Something in his voice unsettled her, a hint of something darker, a promise not just of action but of destruction.

Abelia tilted her head, her eyes narrowing. "And what does that entail Lucifer?" she asked, the curiosity in her voice thinly veiled with caution.

Lucifer paused. Then, in a voice so quiet it was almost lost among the murmurs, he spoke again. "Zagan's return was always inevitable. The question has never been *if* it's *when.*"

A shiver ran down Amber's spine, and she felt her grip on the edge of the grate tighten. She glanced at Syn, but her friend's eyes were wide, and her face was pale as if hearing those words confirmed all her worst fears.

"And when he does return," Lucifer continued, "I will ensure that his power is sealed. Hell will remain under my rule."

A slight chuckle rumbled from Mephistopheles. "How do you plan on doing that, Lucifer? It's not as if you can just *lock him away*."

Lucifer's gaze flickered to him, and for a moment, there was a chilling silence. "I have once before, haven't I?"

Amber's heart skipped a beat as she felt something shift in the room. A sudden awareness dawned on her, like a terrible truth she'd somehow missed. Lucifer had a plan. A plan to lock away Zagan, but there was something else there, something that hadn't been revealed.

She looked at the faces around the table, each powerful and calculating, but Lucifer's held her attention now. Something in his expression had changed, the lines around his mouth tightening ever so slightly, betraying an emotion he hadn't let slip before.

And then, she understood.

The plan wasn't just about eliminating Zagan's power. Lucifer was preparing for war. But it wasn't just war with Zagan; it was a war to secure his throne *forever*.

Amber's breath hitched. With cold clarity, she realized that Lucifer wasn't merely planning to defend Hell. He was planning to make sure no one could ever rechallenge him.

"What about the clause?" Mephistopheles suddenly asked.

Amber's pulse hammered in her chest.

"You know as well as anyone that you'll never truly be able to secure your role. You'll never be able to create an heir." Chrysostomos stated.

"You can't even force her to stay," Bael added. "And if she doesn't, you'll be weak enough to possibly topple."

If looks could kill Bael, he would've turned to dust under Lucifer's gaze, but his voice was smooth and cold when he spoke. "She's a part of this, too. Her decision will shape the future of Hell. If she chooses to stay..."

"And if she doesn't?" Beelzebub asked.

"Then we'll fight like we did before," Lucifer answered.

Amber swallowed, her throat dry. She realized the weight of the conversation. The decision she needed to make wouldn't only seal her fate but Lucifer's. And Hell's.

He'd already chosen her. She was the key to his future. She could feel it now: He needed her to stay, but more than that, he *wanted* her to stay.

"And what of Lean?" Abelia asked, returning to the conversation at hand.

"We don't even know where he is," Belial said.

"We know he found Zagan," Chrysostomos countered. "He probably collected valuable information about him. Things we might be able to use against him."

Lucifer shook his head, "If he found Zagan it's already too late for him. By now, Lean's soul has been tampered with by him. He's lost."

Silence fell over the room, and Amber turned to Syn, who looked like she might get sick, "We have to do something. Now."

But Amber didn't hear her. Her mind was racing with the new revelation. Lucifer had planned this all along. And she'd never known. The truth about Zagan, the war, and her role in it, *all of it*, was tied to one thing.

Her.

She felt her chest tighten as the realization struck her. If she stayed, it wouldn't just be for her own future but *Hell's* future, too. And Lucifer's.

She knew staying wouldn't secure his reign over Hell. They'd need an heir for that, and that was impossible, but together, they'd be stronger. Amber's thoughts spiraled as she pulled herself away from the grate, clutching the stone walls for support.

Deep down Amber had always known that she was never going to leave Hell, now she was more sure than ever that she was meant to be here. Meant to save her friend. Meant to save Hell.

63

Ash Beneath Their Feet

Amber's hands shook as she left the room, her mind racing with what she'd just learned. If Leandros had truly believed Zagan was stirring, and if he'd disappeared right after, that could only mean one thing: he'd gotten too close to something, something that Lucifer and the others weren't ready for anyone to know. And now, Amber needed to uncover what happened to him.

Amber's gaze flickered over to Syn, her friend's expression clouded with concern.

"What's wrong?" Syn asked, her voice a low murmur, almost as if she already knew the answer.

"I need to find out what happened to Leandros," Amber replied, her voice firm but laced with unease. She wasn't sure whether she was trying to convince Syn or herself, but the decision was made. She couldn't ignore it any longer.

Syn hesitated, "You don't have to do this, Amber. You don't know what you're getting into."

"I know exactly what I'm getting into," Amber said, her eyes hardening with resolve. "I have to know."

"How?" Syn asked, "How do you expect to find a place that Lucifer doesn't even know about?"

"I'll think like Lean." Amber said, "If he could figure it out, so will I."

Syn hesitated, looking intently at her friend. "I know where to start, but we have to be careful."

Amber nodded, her determination unwavering. "I'm ready. Let's go."

Syn gave her a long, searching look as if trying to gauge the weight of Amber's decision. After a long pause, she finally spoke. "Alright. But if things go sideways... promise me you'll stop. Promise me you won't put yourself in danger."

Amber didn't respond right away. Her mind was already racing with the possibilities, the pieces of the puzzle that had yet to fall into place. Finally, she met Syn's gaze. "I promise. I'll be careful. I'll stop if I have to."

Syn nodded, "Alright, we'll leave first thing in the morning."

The girls separated then, but Amber didn't sleep at all. Her mind was wide awake, thinking of Lean and all she'd learned about her role in Hell. At the first shift in color in the sky, Amber was out of bed, and about an hour later, she and Syn found themselves walking through Nebulonis after the chariot ride they had convinced Korinna they didn't need an escort for.

Eventually, they reached the heart of Nebulonis and reached Scientia Locus, a towering edifice of dark stone and impossibly high shelves. The structure loomed before them, its vast doors guarded by a pair of Eques who regarded them with disinterest as they passed. Amber had only been here once, but she'd always been drawn to the world on the shelves.

Inside, the air was cool and thick with the scent of aged parchment. The walls stretched up into infinity. The library was known to hold everything from mundane records of damned souls to the most arcane and forbidden texts in existence. It'd be here if there was any chance of finding something about Leandros.

Amber's heart beat faster with each step she took through the labyrinth of shelves. Syn walked alongside her, her eyes darting nervously, clearly feeling the tension in the air.

"This place isn't safe," Syn whispered. "I don't know if you understand how much danger we're in now."

"I understand," Amber replied, her voice tight. She wasn't sure if she was lying to Syn or if she was lying to herself. "But you were right; this is the only place that might have answers."

They moved deeper into the library, their footsteps muffled by the thick, velvet carpet that covered the floor. Amber's fingers brushed against the spines of ancient tomes, the symbols on their covers seeming to shift and twist as if alive. Her heart pounded as she scanned the rows of books, her mind racing with a single thought: What if the answers were just beyond her reach?

"There has to be something," she murmured to herself, stepping forward.

Syn's eyes narrowed as they approached a section of the library that seemed different from the rest, isolated and hidden. "I know where to look," Syn said, her voice barely above a whisper.

Amber followed her, the tension building between them. Syn's hand hovered over a row of books, her fingers brushing the edges lightly before pulling one free. She glanced at Amber, her expression a mix of caution and resolve.

"This one," she said.

Amber took the book from Syn, but it was heavy in her hands. It was old, the cover worn and tattered, but the symbols etched into its surface seemed to glow faintly in the dim light of the library. Amber flipped it open carefully, her eyes scanning the ancient script.

Together, the girls threw themselves into their search, piecing together fragments of history that had been buried for centuries. They spent hours pouring over the old, dusty books in the town's library, deciphering cryptic references to The First Devil, Zagan, and the terrifying war that had raged long ago. But the deeper she dug, the more elusive the answers became.

It wasn't just about Zagan's return but about something far more dangerous: Lucifer's plan. Amber had always known that Lucifer had his reasons for wanting to keep certain things hidden, but now, she was beginning to understand just how far those reasons went. He was preparing for a war, one not only against Zagan but against anyone who might try to challenge his reign. And it was clear to her now that her role was far more significant than she'd ever been told.

But the more Amber uncovered, the more she realized Leandros had been on the same path. He'd been searching for the truth, which had cost him everything. As Amber dug deeper into Hell's forbidden knowledge, she couldn't help but wonder: Had he found something that even Lucifer had missed?

That night, as the girls continued to sift through the ancient tomes in the library, Amber found something that had eluded her until now: an old, worn book that wasn't cataloged with the rest. It sat inconspicuously on a dusty shelf, waiting for her to discover it.

As her fingers brushed over the cover, a strange chill washed over her. There was something about this book; its aura was different.

Amber carefully opened the book, scanning the delicate, faded pages. She froze. It wasn't a history. It was a map. She'd only seen a map of the islands when flying with Lucifer.

Syn leaned in, her breath catching as she peered over Amber's shoulder. Her eyes widened as she examined the book more closely. Without a word, she reached for another one on the nearby table and carefully placed it on top of the one Amber held.

Amber glanced at the new book, her brow furrowing as she scanned the pages. "This is all about securing the Devil's rule without an heir. I thought that wasn't possible?"

Syn's voice dropped to a hushed whisper. "It shouldn't be. But I think Lean found a loophole." She paused, her fingers trembling slightly as she ran them over the second book's cover. "The only problem is, I think Zagan found out Lean knows."

"Syn, this is it," Amber whispered, her voice trembling as the weight of the discovery settled in. "This is what Lean found." Her stomach twisted, and she felt the blood drain from her face. "That's why Zagan took him. Lucifer doesn't know about this loophole, meaning that if Zagan can defeat Lucifer, he can use the knowledge Lean has to permanently secure his role."

Syn's expression darkened, her eyes narrowing with growing concern. "We need to find out what it is that Lean uncovered."

She didn't add more, but Amber could feel the weight of her words. The gravity of the situation was pressing down on them both.

Amber knew it wasn't just about uncovering a secret anymore; it was about saving Leandros and preventing a shift in the power of Hell that would be impossible to stop. They had to move quickly, but they had to be careful. If Zagan was already after Lean's knowledge, there was no telling how close he was to making his move.

Amber set the books down carefully, her mind racing. "We need to go after him. Find out what Zagan's planning is before he uses it against Lucifer." She looked at Syn, her voice barely more than a whisper but filled with determination. "If we don't stop this now, Hell as we know it will change forever."

Syn's face remained unreadable for a moment, but then she nodded, a resolute spark in her eyes. "Let's find what Lean found. Before it's too late."

64

Dust and Treason

Amber flipped through yet another book, frustration coiling tight in her chest. They had to be missing something. They'd gone through page after page of the books Leandros had looked through, his coded scribbles in the margins, the careful organization of texts that at first had seemed like nothing but now had to mean something.

They were running out of time.

"He was looking for something specific," Amber muttered, scanning the old parchment. "Something that could change everything."

Syn sat across from her, flipping through another one, her usually sharp features tight with concentration. "He wasn't just looking," she corrected. "He found it. That's why he's missing."

Amber didn't argue. She knew Syn was right.

Then, Syn froze.

"Wait." She turned the page carefully, the brittle parchment flaking at the edges. "This... This isn't part of the original text."

Amber looked up. "What do you mean?"

Syn ran her fingers over the words, her dark eyes narrowing. "This is older than the other notes. Someone tried to destroy it." She turned the page toward Amber, revealing a nearly burned-through passage; the ink faded, the words barely legible, but what she could read sent a shiver down her spine:

To rule is to take, but to reign is to be named.
A crown of fire rests uneasily on stolen thrones.
What is given is eternal. What is claimed is fleeting.
A shadow lingers where no light dares to shine.

A long silence stretched between them.

Amber frowned. "What the hell does that mean?"

Syn's fingers tapped against the brittle parchment. "It's talking about... rulership. Power. Look at this part: "What is given is eternal. What is claimed is fleeting.""

Amber exhaled slowly, realization creeping in. "But we know that; we know his reign is vulnerable unless he has an heir."

"I don't know," Syn said, her eyes floating over the words. "I think there's more here. Something about the throne being granted."

Amber's breath hitched, "Granted by who?"

Syn flipped the page and found more notes in the margins. Her movements were quick and almost frantic. "If this is what Leandros was looking into, he must've found a way to secure the throne permanently without an heir or a way someone else could take it from Lucifer."

She stopped flipping pages.

Her expression went blank.

Amber leaned forward. "What?"

Syn's voice was barely above a whisper, "Heaven."

Amber's stomach twisted.

Syn swallowed hard and pointed at another note, scribbled hastily in Leandros' sharp script:

Hell is won. But Heaven may seal it.

Amber felt the weight of the words like a blow.

Lucifer had stolen Hell. He'd ruled it through force, fear, and sheer power.

But he'd never been acknowledged as its rightful ruler.

And if that was true...

Then, someone else still had a claim to the throne.

Syn's voice was clipped, urgent. "This isn't about winning a war. This is about Heaven." She pointed at the passage. "Until Heaven acknowledges him, Lucifer's claim is still... fragile."

Amber shook her head, trying to process it. "But, why would Lucifer care about what Heaven thinks?"

Syn exhaled sharply. "Because if Heaven *refuses* to acknowledge him... someone else can take his place."

Silence.

Amber's heart pounded.

Then, Syn flipped to another section, her hands moving faster now. She pushed aside books, reaching for Leandros' hidden notes.

A tattered, worn page floated to her feet, having fallen out of a book.

It was Lean's handwriting, and it read:

Three impossible conditions to force Heaven's acknowledgment. How to permanently claim the throne.

1. *Worship*

   ○ *Humanity fears Lucifer, but they don't worship him. Without proper, willing devotion, he can't gain the divine acknowledgment needed to secure his rule.*

    ○ *No ruler of Hell has ever been able to turn fear into worship.*

2. *An Angel Kneeling.*

    ○ *Heaven would be forced to acknowledge Hell's ruler if an angel willingly submitted, but no angel, especially not an archangel, would ever bow to Lucifer.*

    ○ *Not unless they were forced to, and Angeli Tenebrarum doesn't count.*

3. *Claiming What Heaven Lost.*

    ○ *Heaven doesn't bargain with Hell. It doesn't negotiate unless something precious to it is in Hell's grasp.*

    ○ *But what could Hell have that Heaven would risk everything to retrieve?*

Amber stared at the list, unease curling around her spine.

This is what Leandros found.

And this was why he was taken.

She looked at Syn. "Zagan is trying to use one of these conditions."

Syn nodded grimly. "And if he succeeds... Lucifer's done."

Amber's fingers clenched the parchment. "We need to find Leandros."

Amber's pulse quickened as she shoved the parchment toward Syn. They needed to move. Whatever Leandros had uncovered, whoever had taken him knew it too.

She turned, searching the chaotic mess of books and scrolls they had spread across the table, flipping through the ones Leandros had marked. There had to be more.

And then, her fingers brushed over the book she'd shown Syn earlier.

Amber froze.

She'd found it before, tucked away in the shadows of the library. It was a book with a map of Hell, unlike anything she'd ever seen. It had been strange and unsettling at the time, but she hadn't understood its importance.

Now, she did.

Amber grabbed it and flipped it open. Syn leaned over her shoulder as the pages shifted beneath their fingers, the ink shifting and crawling as if alive.

"This map," Amber murmured, tracing the worn parchment. "I thought it was just the islands, but... look."

Syn squinted. "What am I looking at?"

Amber pressed her fingers over a part of the map that shouldn't exist.

A place not marked on any of the other books.

A place beneath the Seventh Island.

The ink shimmered, and faintly, almost too faint to read, a name appeared beneath her touch:

Umbra Cavea, The Shadow Cage.

Syn inhaled sharply. "That's not possible."

Amber stared, her throat dry.

But it was.

"This is where they're keeping him."

The girls watched the page as the map ebbed and flowed below her touch.

"The seals holding The First Devil are broken. The same seals Lucifer had worked tirelessly to contain." Amber said so quietly she wasn't sure she'd spoken out loud.

"And if those seals are weakening... if they're about to break, then Hell is on the verge of something far worse than war," Syn added.

The girls didn't have to say anything else; they knew what it meant. They knew that what Lucifer had said was right: Zagan was returning, and that return could unravel everything.

Amber didn't notice that Syn had picked up another book until she started speaking, "According to this, Umbra Cavea is older than the islands, older than Lucifer's reign. It was built for the uncontainable. The beings that even Hell couldn't afford to let roam free..." Syn's voice trailed off.

"What?" Amber asked, "Syn, what else does it say?"

"That no one has ever escaped it." Syn's gaze shifted to Amber, "If this is where Leandros is..."

Amber finished for her, voice steady. "Then there's no way to get him out."

But that wasn't an option.

Amber stared at the map, her thoughts racing. If the Umbra Cavea wasn't accessible normally, then there had to be another way in.

And then, she saw it.

A barely visible, worn-out inscription at the bottom of the page was written in a language she could barely read. But the meaning was clear:

A soul for a soul.

Amber's stomach turned.

The only way in... is to trade.

And before Syn could stop her, Amber already knew what she would do.

A second later, Syn's eyes scanned the same inscription Amber had read, and she realized it was true. She turned to Amber, her expression darkening as she immediately recognized the look on her face.

"No." Syn's voice was sharp, unyielding. "No, Amber, you can't save him. You can't trade your soul for his."

"Syn, I have to."

"No," Syn repeated, stepping closer, her head shaking with growing frustration. "No, I won't let you. It's dangerous and reckless, and for what?"

"He's our friend!" Amber's voice rose, raw and desperate. "You don't understand, Syn. This—this is what I was meant to do. I never knew my purpose in Hell, but now I do. I'm supposed to save Hell."

Syn let out a sharp laugh, but there was no humor in it. "You can't save Hell if you're dead."

Amber held her ground. "I don't have to. If I save Leandros, he can tell Lucifer what Zagan is up to. And together, they can secure his reign."

Syn's jaw tightened. "Why can't we just tell Lucifer ourselves?"

"Because we don't know what Zagan has up his sleeve." Amber took a deep breath, steadying herself. "Syn, I know this is dangerous. I know it's reckless. But I have to do this. I could use your help getting there... but you don't have to be a part of it if you don't want to be."

Syn stared at her for a long moment, her sharp features unreadable. Finally, she exhaled, muttering a curse under her breath.

"I can get you to the island," she said at last. "But the rest is up to you."

Amber nodded. This was it. There was no turning back now.

65

Ash and Bone

Amber and Syn had spent nearly a day and a half buried in the library, chasing down every last piece of Leandros' research. They'd traced his notes, decrypted his codes, and uncovered the impossible truth, one that had changed everything.

Now, they had a plan.

It wasn't a good plan. It wasn't a safe one.

But it was the only one.

By the time they emerged from the library's depths, the weight of their decision pressed down on them like a curse. It settled into Amber's bones, making every movement feel heavy.

This was it.

Syn needed a few hours to arrange the boat so Amber could smuggle herself onto the islands unnoticed. It wasn't an easy task; Hell wasn't kind to stowaways, but if anyone could make it happen, Amber knew Syn could.

Which left Amber with something much more challenging to navigate.

Lucifer.

***

The chariot rattled slightly as Amber dropped Syn off at the edge of the River Styx. Syn barely looked at her as she stepped out, already focused on the next phase of their plan.

She turned back at the last second, hesitation flickering across her sharp features. "You don't have to do this."

Amber forced a smile she didn't feel. "Yeah, I do."

Syn didn't argue. She just nodded once, a barely-there movement, then disappeared into the mist.

The moment the chariot doors shut again, Amber exhaled shakily.

The driver glanced back, awaiting her following command.

She hesitated, fingers tightening over the edges of her seat. She could tell him to take her straight to the docks. To skip this part, to avoid what was coming.

But she couldn't.

She needed to see him.

One last time.

"Back to Castellum Umbrae," she said, barely above a whisper.

The driver nodded, snapping the reins. The chariot surged forward, cutting through the air, the eerie glow of the Underworld casting flickering shadows below.

Castellum Umbrae loomed ahead.

With every inch closer, Amber felt her chest tighten.

This was the last time she'd be here.

She wasn't supposed to think like that, but she knew.

By the time Lucifer realized what she'd done, she'd already be locked away in Umbra Cavea, bound in a prison that no one, not even him, could reach.

And worst of all?

He would hate her for it.

Amber swallowed hard and clenched her fists. "Faster."

***

The halls of Castellum Umbrae were dimly lit, warm with flickering candlelight.

Amber's steps were quieter than usual, her pulse a steady, erratic rhythm in her ears.

She found Lucifer in one of the grand corridors, deep in quiet conversation with Abelia. His stance was relaxed, but his presence, as always, commanded the space.

At the sound of her approaching footsteps, his gaze lifted immediately.

The second their eyes met, Amber felt bare beneath his stare.

Like he could see right through her, past the secrets pressing against her ribs, past the walls she'd hastily put up.

Sensing the shift in energy, Abelia excused herself with a graceful bow and disappeared into the shadows.

Now, it was just the two of them.

Lucifer tilted his head slightly, studying her. "You look troubled, little dove."

Amber forced a smile, but it felt wrong on her face. "Just... a long couple of days."

Lucifer didn't look convinced. "Where have you been?"

Careful.

She'd prepared for this. She had a lie ready, one that was close enough to the truth that he wouldn't question it.

"Syn and I went to Nebulonis," she said smoothly. "Wanted to spend some time together like we used to before everything changed."

Lucifer nodded slowly, but his gaze flickered over her, sharp and assessing. Something in him shifted.

He could tell. He always could.

His fingers lifted, brushing under her chin, tilting her face upward. His touch was light but undeniably firm. "You seem different," he said.

Amber's pulse quickened. "What do you mean?"

Lucifer studied her momentarily, his eyes dark pools of something unreadable. Then, he exhaled through his nose. "You tell me."

A lump formed in her throat.

She wanted to tell him.

Maybe if she did, he'd stop her.

Maybe he'd go after Leandros himself.

Maybe he'd hold onto her, refuse to let her go.

And tonight, he thought she was choosing him.

The thought nearly shattered her.

So, instead, she did the only thing she could.

She leaned into his touch, just slightly, savoring its warmth for as long as she could.

Then, softly, she whispered, "You know... for someone who claims to be all-powerful, you worry too much."

Lucifer arched a brow, amusement flickering across his face. "I have you to keep me on my toes, little dove."

Amber smiled, but it ached.

She reached up, letting her fingers skim the lapel of his coat, an absent gesture that she knew she wouldn't get to do again.

"Tonight's important, isn't it?"

Lucifer's gaze darkened slightly. "It is."

Tonight was supposed to be her decision. Her official commitment to Hell.

The highest-ranking demons would gather, expecting her to stand beside Lucifer to announce that she'd accepted her place in the Underworld.

Of course, she wouldn't be there.

Lucifer had no idea this was the last conversation they'd have before everything fell apart.

He exhaled, stepping back slightly, dropping his hand from her face.

"Speaking of..." His gaze flicked over her shoulder, and his expression shifted slightly. "Korinna's here to take you to get ready."

Amber's breath hitched.

This was it.

She should let him walk away. She should say nothing.

But she couldn't. "Lucifer."

He paused.

Amber swallowed against the lump in her throat. "Thank you."

His brow furrowed slightly. "For what?"

For everything. For pulling her into Hell. Forcing her to fight for herself. For changing her.

For making her fall in love with him.

But she didn't say any of that.

Instead, she just shook her head. "For everything."

Lucifer stared at her for a long moment, something unreadable flickering behind his eyes.

He didn't press her for an answer.

Instead, he simply inclined his head and murmured, "You're a strange little thing."

And with that, he turned and walked away.

Amber watched him go, burning the moment into her memory. Because by the time he realized what she'd done if by some miracle they saw each other again...

He would never look at her the same way again.

66

The Kindness of Chains

The moment Amber stepped into her chambers, she knew she didn't have much time.

Korinna walked in behind her, setting down a collection of silk robes and jewelry on the vanity table. Candles flickered across the room, casting soft, golden light on the grand mirror.

The room was warm and inviting. Candlelight flickered off polished surfaces, painting everything in soft gold and deep amber hues.

It felt safe. Familiar.

And yet, every single thing inside this room, the silken drapes, the velvet-lined chairs, the carefully chosen perfumes resting on the vanity, felt like a trap.

The gemstones on the garments caught the light, twinkling like shackles disguised as finery.

This was her costume for the night.

The ceremony was in a few hours.

Her supposed commitment to Hell.

Her final choice.

It was all here, laid out like a fate she'd already agreed to.

Korinna turned to her, folding her arms. "You should bathe first."

Amber swallowed, nodding absently. Lucifer had probably instructed her to make sure Amber was perfect tonight. Everything about this was crafted, intentional, because he wanted her to feel like she belonged here.

Because he thought she was choosing him.

And she hated what she was about to do to him.

Her throat tightened.

This is the last time you'll ever be here.

She turned to Korinna, forcing a soft smile, pushing the words past the lump in her throat. "Actually... do you mind if I get ready alone tonight?"

Korinna blinked, clearly caught off guard. "Alone?"

Amber nodded, stepping forward and placing a hand on her arm. "Just this once," she said gently. "I want to do this myself."

She didn't miss the flicker of hesitation in Korinna's gaze. Lucifer had clearly given explicit orders about tonight.

But after a long pause, Korinna sighed, exasperated. "Fine. I'll give you an hour, but don't take too long."

Amber smiled, grateful. "I won't."

Korinna gave her a final, assessing look before disappearing through the doors.

The second she was gone, Amber moved.

No hesitation. No second-guessing.

She stepped toward the window, her heart hammering against her ribs, hands already gripping the balcony doors.

She threw them open, and the wind rushed in immediately, thick, hot air rolling over her skin, the scent of fire and ember clinging to the night.

Castellum Umbrae stood high above the shifting landscape of Hell, but far below, she could see it, the water glittering in the dark.

The River Styx cut through the kingdom like a black, glassy vein.

At its edge, she could just barely see the docks where Syn was waiting.

Waiting with the boat. Waiting for her.

Amber's stomach twisted.

This is it. No turning back now.

She grabbed a small blade off a nearby table and slid it into her leg holster. Carefully, she climbed onto the stone railing. Below her, the trellis stretched downward, a climbing lattice of wrought iron and twisting vines.

It would hold.

She took a breath.

And jumped.

Her body twisted mid-air as the impact jarred through her arms, but her fingers found the trellis gripping tight, her muscles burning.

Castellum Umbrae loomed above her now, but she didn't let herself look back.

Hand over hand, she climbed downward, fast and careful. One wrong move, one slip, and she'd fall to the stone path below. Her breathing was sharp and quick, the distant hum of Hell filling her ears, the roar of fire, the whisper of voices.

But no one saw her.

No one stopped her.

By the time her feet hit the ground, her pulse was a wild, erratic thing in her chest.

She took off running.

Every second counted.

By the time she reached the docks, Syn was already waiting. She stood near the edge of the boat, her arms crossed, her expression grim. Amber's breath hitched, her lungs burning, but she didn't slow.

When Amber skitted to a stop next to her, Syn dropped her voice to a whisper, "Do you remember the spell I told you to learn?"

Amber nodded.

"Cast it now," Syn commanded.

Amber took a deep breath, focusing her energy on herself as she quietly chanted, "Muta me esse quod statuo coram me." Amber's eyes flew closed as she spoke the incantation three times.

When she opened her eyes, she looked down at her hands. They were ever-changing from a deep shade of red to a dull yellow, then to an almost midnight blue. She'd done it. She was Tisiphone.

Slowly, she turned her eyes to Syn, who was wiping away tears. "Be careful," Syn whispered as the girls embraced.

Amber nodded and, without a word, boarded the boat. She watched Castellum Umbrae disappear as the vessel slipped away into the black waters.

Lucifer would never forgive her.

But she was doing this for him, for Hell.

The boat cut smoothly through the dark water and thick and humid air.

Amber sat near the edge, watching the shadows ripple beneath the surface.

Her hands were trembling.

She clenched them into fists.

This is the only way.

By the time anyone realized she was gone, by the time Lucifer even suspected, it'd be too late.

She'd chosen her path.

And there was no going back now.

67

Seven-Pointed Thrones

The Magna Aula of Castellum Umbrae wasn't merely a room but a bastion of infernal majesty designed to awe and intimidate. The space, carved from obsidian and brimstone, was adorned with molten gold veins that pulsed faintly, echoing the very heartbeat of Hell. Towering columns, etched with the sagas of Lucifer's conquests, rose to meet the vaulted ceiling where chandeliers, fueled by ethereal flames, cast a ghostly light over all beneath them.

The expansive floor, a dark polished stone canvas, was etched with intricate sigils of dominion and power, so deeply ingrained that not even time could erode their command. At the hall's far end, elevated above all, was the Throne of the Fallen, Thronum Lapsorum, a monument to power wrought from obsidian and the petrified remains of angelic foes. Its imposing structure, crowned with jagged, uneven spires, seemed as though torn right from the heavens in a fit of divine rage.

Upon this throne sat Lucifer, clad not just in his usual attire of dark magnificence but in a garb that whispered of warnings and war. His coat, a rich tapestry of black and gold, bore patterns of an infernal script too deadly for mortal tongues. The high collar framed his stern jaw, the deep cut of his tunic hinting at the sigil of a seven-pointed star seared into his skin, a mark of his unchallenged rule.

His long cloak, lined with the red of Hell's deepest fires, trailed behind him, its folds catching the light with every deliberate step. Golden chains clinked softly at his shoulders, anchoring him to his ancient, undeniable roots. Around his neck hung a shard of Heaven's gates, a dark gemstone rumored to be from the very day The First Devil brokered his rule with God, a relic of his fall and rise.

Lucifer's presence alone dominated the room, his very being the embodiment of Hell's authority, requiring no crown nor armor to affirm his sovereignty.

As the hour approached, the Grand Hall, filled with the elite of Hell's hierarchy, gathered to witness what was to be a pivotal affirmation of loyalty from Amber, the one chosen to stand by Lucifer's side. Among the crowd were the Archdemons: Chrysostomos, the embodiment of pride; Asmodeus, the whisperer of lust; Belial, the master of greed and lawlessness; Mephistopheles, the slow pull of sloth; Bael, the fury of wrath; Mammon, the insatiable glutton; and Beelzebub, the green-eyed envoy of envy.

Mingling with these titans were the remaining Legatus and the Situs Princeps, Hell's sharpest minds and rulers of its vast provinces, all speculating on the implications of Amber's decision for the future.

Yet, as the moment drew near, a palpable tension began to coil within the hall. Lucifer had made his rounds, his demeanor unreadable yet fraught with an uncharacteristic hint of anticipation. He returned to his throne, his gaze occasionally drifting to the grand doors through which Amber was to enter.

But she was late.

This was unlike her. Amber was decisive, known for her resolve, and didn't give second thoughts. Concern flickered in Abelia's golden eyes as she approached the base of the throne, her voice a hushed whisper only for Lucifer, "She should have arrived by now."

Lucifer remained motionless, his voice low and even, "She will."

Amber's absence gnawed at the edge of Lucifer's patience as minutes stretched longer and longer, a taut string ready to snap. The quiet murmur of the gathered crowd began to curdle into whispers thick with concern. He could feel the shift in the air from speculative curiosity to a tensing, palpable worry.

His body tightened, a coil of readiness and restraint. He was on the brink, ready to rise, assert control, and demand answers with his formidable presence when the grand doors crashed open with an echoing boom that silenced the room.

Korinna burst through the threshold, her usually impeccable composure shattered by evident panic. Her pale face and quick breaths were telltale signs of deep distress as she cut a direct path through the sea of bodies to stand at the base of the throne.

"I don't know where she is," she blurted, the words falling like stones into the stillness of the hall.

Lucifer stood slowly, his height casting a long, imposing shadow that stretched across the polished floor. The quiet intensity of his voice belied the rising storm within him. "What do you mean you *don't know*?" The words were soft yet edged with a sharpness that seemed to slice through the thick, charged air.

Korinna's hands trembled slightly, her voice threaded with fear and confusion. "She asked to be left alone to prepare... When I returned, she was gone.

The balcony doors were open..." Her words trailed off, suggesting unspeakable possibilities.

A heavy, suffocating silence engulfed the hall, every attendant holding their breath. The implications of Korinna's report hung over them like a shroud, dark and ominous. The chandelier's flames above flickered erratically as if disturbed by the turn of events, their light casting deep, dancing shadows across Lucifer's face, highlighting the tightening of his jaw and the slight narrowing of his eyes.

When it came, his command was a low growl that vibrated with barely controlled rage, a sound seldom heard and never ignored. "Find her," he ordered, his voice resonating with a fury that made the air in the room seem to tremble.

No one moved; the command hung in the air, a directive that was as much a plea as an order.

Then, as if on cue, the great doors swung open once more. This time, the intruder caught everyone off guard, and Lucifer's heart sank.

68

Caged in Shadows

As the boat sliced through the Styx's murky waters, each chilling wave served as a grim reminder of Amber's daunting fate. A dense mist cloaked the river, wrapping it in secrecy and silence. She stood at the bow, her gaze fixed on the obscured path ahead, though little could be discerned in the oppressive gloom of Hell's waterways.

The grandeur of Castellum Umbrae, with its imposing splendor, had been left far behind. Now, she ventured into the uncertain shadows of the outer realms. Her heart thundered in her chest, a relentless drumbeat warring against the fear seeping into her bones. Gripping the railing, her knuckles turned white against the cold wind that whipped her hair wildly, the chill biting fiercely through her thin garment.

Thoughts of Lucifer, his last look of unknowing expectation, haunted her. She could still feel the weight of his gaze, heavy with a thousand unasked questions. The memory of his voice, low and commanding, echoed hollowly in her ears, a stark contrast to the silent mist that enveloped her now.

The journey felt eternal, time stretching out into an endless thread. With each passing moment, Amber's resolve wavered and then hardened. She'd made her decision in a moment of desperate courage, or perhaps it was a desperate fear, the line between the two blurred in the shadows of her mind.

The boatman, a silent figure shrouded in tattered robes, neither spoke nor acknowledged her presence beyond steering the craft. His face, obscured by the hood, remained a mystery, adding to the surreal quality of the journey. Amber's only company was the soft lapping of the river against the hull and the distant, mournful cries of lost souls echoing across the water.

Amber's heart sank as the silhouette of the Seventh Island began to emerge from the mist. The Pernicious Section was the last place any soul wished to find themselves. Memories of her previous encounters with its keepers, Timor and Dolor, sent shivers down her spine. The island was a notorious prison of endless torment where the condemned faced unimaginable punishments.

The boat slowed as they approached the dock, a rickety structure that looked as though it might collapse at the slightest provocation.

"Tisiphone," the boatman said tentatively, "are you certain you do not wish to wait for Eques to join you on the island?"

Amber spun around, her guise as the fearsome Tisiphone momentarily bolstered her spirit. "What do you take me for? Do you think me weak because I'm a woman?" Her voice was sharp and challenging.

"No, Domina, I meant no offense..." the boatman stammered, shrinking back under her intense glare.

"Shall I demonstrate how powerful I truly am?" Her hand glowed a bright yellow, dripping with something vile.

"Please, no!" The boatman cowered, his fear palpable. "I'm sorry."

Satisfied with his reaction, Amber stepped off the boat, her facade of confidence masking the turmoil within. As soon as her feet touched the soggy ground, the boat retreated hastily into the fog. Alone, she dropped the disguise, returning to her true self.

The island was eerily quiet, except for the unsettling echoes dancing across the barren landscape. Amber knew her task: find the keepers and negotiate her freedom for Leandros'. It was a perilous gamble that risked her soul, but retreat was no longer an option.

With a deep, steadying breath, she began her trek across the desolate island, each step taking her deeper into a realm where hope seemed as distant as the fading world she'd left behind. The ground trembled beneath her feet, a sinister rumble growing with every heartbeat. The island felt alive, watching, hating, recoiling from her presence.

The air thickened, pressing against her lungs like smoke. The agonizing cries of the damned echoed around her endlessly. Still, she pushed forward until the fortress emerged ahead in the distance.

It rose from the earth like a scar, twisting towers of bone and barbed wire, gates built from the shattered remnants of the damned. Nightmarish creatures stood sentinel, their forms constantly shifting, horns becoming wings, claws into chains, eyes multiplying where there'd been none.

Amber swallowed her fear and moved forward.

But before she reached the gates, it hit her.

A force she'd only experienced once before; a tidal wave of despair and terror slammed into her chest, dragging her to her knees. She choked on its weight, her breath coming in short, frantic gasps. Her mind was no longer her own; visions twisted through her skull, memories laced with agony, fears made flesh. Lucifer walking away. Her friends dying. Her soul devoured. Her body was forgotten.

You don't belong here; something seemed to hiss from the shadows. *You think you can bargain with monsters?*

Her hands clawed at the ground, desperate for grounding. Her heart raced. Her thoughts splintered.

Timor. Dolor.

They weren't just next to her. They were *inside* her now, rooting around in her fears and feasting on her regret.

What was I thinking? she thought, teeth chattering. *This was a mistake. I'm going to die before I even see him.*

A sob escaped her throat.

And then suddenly, a voice cut through the chaos. Deep, dry, almost amused.

"Alright, alright. You've had your fun. Off with you."

The pressure vanished in an instant, leaving Amber collapsed on the ground, gasping in the sudden silence. Her body trembled as she forced herself upright, blinking through the veil of pain and confusion.

Lucifer? she thought, dazed. No... it wasn't him.

The figure standing before her was slightly shorter than Lucifer and much less broad, wearing a smile like a knife's edge. He looked as if he'd been waiting there all along. He wore an expectant look that danced with something amused, almost inevitable.

"Zagan," she whispered.

He offered a mock bow, eyes gleaming with cruel delight.

"You're late," he said.

Amber forced herself to meet his gaze without fear, "Why did they listen to you?"

Zagan glanced to where the mythical creatures were floating away, "Lucifer told you they only listen to him, didn't he?" Amber nodded, and Zagan let out a harsh, humorless laugh, "Pathetic. He should have told you that they only listen to *devils*."

Amber inhaled sharply, piecing together the implications. "How are you here on the Seventh Island? Shouldn't you be in Umbra Cavea?"

A smirk crawled across Zagan's aging face, "You already know the answer to that."

"The seals." Amber said in a rush.

"That's right." Zagan smiled, "The seals Lucifer trapped me behind are thinning. Heaven knows Hell has something it desperately wants. But alas, someone didn't realize the importance of what they had standing before them."

"I don't understand," Amber said, quieter than she meant to.

"You will, darling, don't worry." Zagan circled her slowly, predatorily. "But before all that, let's address why you're here. You have something to trade, don't you?"

Summoning her resolve, Amber met his gaze defiantly. "I want to see Leandros first."

Zagan considered her, then snapped his fingers. Immediately, she found herself standing in a dark, wet room, a fortress of bones and barbed wire. Her heart pounded as she crossed the threshold and stepped into the dimly lit chamber. The air here was different, thick with something ancient, something *wrong*. It was more a tomb than a room, echoing with the forlorn breaths of despair. Zagan stood at the far end of the room, the smirk on his face making her skin crawl.

As Amber's eyes adjusted to the lighting, the horrifying sight of Leandros came into focus. Behind Zagan, chained and barely conscious, he hung suspended by chains of shadow, his body limp, his breaths shallow. Alive, but barely. The darkness around them seemed to recoil momentarily at Amber's presence, then greedily closed back in.

"I'll take his place," Amber declared, her voice a beacon of resolve amidst the creeping shadows. "Release him."

Zagan's smirk widened. "So eager to play the martyr."

Zagan snapped his fingers once more, and the chains of darkness around Leandros shattered. His body fell forward, caught by invisible hands that lowered him gently to the ground. He groaned, his eyes flickering open.

Amber exhaled, relief washing over her like a tidal wave, her body shaking from the sheer force of it. She'd done it. The weight that had pressed against her chest for hours, the gnawing fear of failure, the uncertainty, it all began to ease as she watched the shadows release him, lowering him to the ground slowly.

Leandros was free.

She expected him to collapse, to stumble forward exhausted, and to look at her with some form of gratitude or, at the very least, relief.

But he didn't move.

Something was wrong.

Instead of throwing himself toward the exit, instead of reaching for her, instead of reacting at all, he just looked up at her. A shadow passed over his face, not relief, not disbelief, but something far worse.

Fear.

The kind that paralyzes. The kind that makes the blood drain from your face and your breath hitch in your throat. The kind that settles in your bones like a warning.

Amber took a slow step forward, pulse quickening. "Leandros?"

Her voice was cautious, gentle like she might startle him into shattering completely.

He flinched.

A sharp, ragged breath broke from his lips as he stumbled upright, hands shaking violently, his chains lying shattered at his feet. But he wasn't looking at his freedom, he was looking at her.

And he looked horrified.

"No..." His voice was barely a whisper, hoarse and hollow, scraping out of his throat like it had been buried too long. "No, no, no..."

He stumbled back toward the chains, dropping to his knees. His hands, still trembling, scrambled to gather the broken links as if trying to piece them back together, as if he could somehow force himself back into them.

Amber's breath caught in her throat.

"Lean... what are you doing?"

"You weren't supposed to do this," he said, voice shaking. "You weren't supposed to come here, Amber."

He pressed the shattered cuffs against his wrists, trying to make them fit, as if that alone could rewind time. "I was supposed to rot here. That was the point. That was the deal."

"Leandros," she said, stepping closer, "you're free. It's done. I made sure of it."

He froze.

Then his head snapped up, eyes locking onto hers, desperate, raw.

"You don't understand," he breathed. "You've given him everything."

The words were a dagger to her spine.

Amber tried to speak, but her throat closed.

"You shouldn't be here," he said, louder now, ragged. "He's using you; he was always using you. This was never a trade, Amber. It was a trap."

The world tilted around her.

Something dark moved at the edge of her vision, crawling across the floor like smoke. Then, without warning, a violent force coiled around her wrists, yanking her back.

Amber gasped, jerking against the restraint. Shadows surged up her arms, binding her tight, cold, living, sentient. Ancient.

The realization hit like ice water.

This wasn't a sacrifice.

It was a setup.

"Amber!" Leandros lunged forward but was slammed back by an invisible force. His scream was one of pure anguish. "No! Let her go!"

Amber strained against the bonds, heart racing, panic setting in. "It's okay," she managed, voice shaking. "You're free now. Find Lucifer. Tell him everything."

Leandros looked like she'd just asked him to murder her.

His face contorted, grief, guilt, rage, all crashing down on him at once.

"He can't save you," he whispered. "He can't save either of you."

"I know," she whispered, trying to calm him, to make him believe the lie she barely believed herself. "But I'll be okay. I promise."

The words felt like iron shackles around her throat.

Leandros' jaw locked, his hands trembling at his sides, his entire body screaming a warning she couldn't hear. He was trying to tell her something.

Something important.

But she didn't have time to figure out what it was.

Because at that moment, through the thick, suffocating silence, Zagan laughed.

It wasn't cruel.

It wasn't mocking.

It was as if someone had just delivered the punchline to a joke only he found funny.

"Ohhh, bless your brave little heart," Zagan drawled, stepping out from the shadows like he'd been waiting for applause. "That was genuinely touching. Noble. Heart-wrenching, even. I almost cried." He grinned. "And I say *almost* with great restraint."

Amber's eyes snapped to him, fury boiling under her panic, but Zagan only clapped his hands once, like he was announcing a magic trick.

"Behold the great, tragic sacrifice!" he said, gesturing between them. "She gives up her soul, he's traumatized, *I* win."

Leandros surged forward, dropping to his knees in front of Zagan.

"Put me back," he snarled, voice cracking. "You hear me? PUT ME BACK." His eyes were wild and pleading. "Undo it. I didn't ask for this! *She* didn't know what she was giving!"

Amber watched, frozen. Her breath caught. Her pulse thundered.

Zagan blinked, utterly unbothered. "Darling, I just *freed* you. Do you know how difficult that was? Do you have any idea how long it took me to arrange all of this?" He gestured broadly.

Leandros let out a sound between a growl and a sob as he slammed his fist against the stone floor. "You bastard."

"Mmhm," Zagan said brightly. "That's me."

Amber's breathing was uneven, the chains around her wrists biting deeper, and yet Zagan's presence made her feel even more trapped.

"You're sick," she spat.

"Ohhh, please," Zagan rolled his eyes. "You think *I'm* the problem here? You walked into my hellhole with your soul gift wrapped and tied with a bow. I'm not evil; I'm just *efficient*."

"Zagan—" Leandros started, but Zagan cut him off with a raised finger.

"Shh-shh-shhh," he hushed. "No more outbursts. You're ruining my mood. And this is the first time things have fallen perfectly into place in my favor in centuries."

He turned to Amber again, tilting his head with a mock-pitying smile. "Lucifer thought you'd break. That was the plan, of course. But you didn't. You *improvised*. And now here you are, all shackled and glowy and mine." His grin widened. "What *fun* we're going to have."

Amber clenched her jaw. "You'll never win."

Zagan gave an exaggerated gasp, placing a hand on his chest. "Win? *Oh, honey.* This isn't about winning. This is about finally getting to ruin something that matters."

And then, with a devilish twinkle in his eye, he added, "Also, I've been dying to redecorate. You're going to look so *stunning* in chains."

69

Unspoken Truths

Zagan's laughter echoed through the cavernous chamber like a slow-moving storm, curling around the stone like smoke, wrapping its fingers around Amber's spine, and squeezing. The sound wasn't loud; it didn't need to be. It was deliberate. Controlled. A predator enjoying the silence just before the kill.

The shadows around her tightened, their grip like a vice, cold and suffocating. Her pulse thundered, but she forced herself to keep her expression still and keep breathing despite the way the air felt thinner and heavier all at once.

Zagan stepped forward, and the darkness moved with him like a living thing that was obedient, intimate, and wrong.

"Such a waste," he mused, shaking his head in mock pity. "If only you'd been patient, Amber. If only you'd waited."

Amber's fingers twitched against the bonds at her wrists. "Waited for what?"

He smiled, slow and wolfish, and tilted his head like he was correcting a child. Then he began to pace, his steps measured, dragging the moment out like a sharpened knife.

"You were the last variable," he murmured, almost to himself. "The one thing standing in my way."

Amber's brows pulled together. "In your way?"

He let out a cold, breathless chuckle. "Mmm. And yet... all you had to do was wait." He sighed, the sound almost weary. "Just a little longer, and there wouldn't have been a damn thing I could do."

Amber's stomach turned, nausea pressing against her ribs. "What the hell are you talking about?"

He paused directly in front of her, and his gaze flickered down for the briefest second, so fast she might have missed it if she weren't watching him so closely.

But she was.

And something in her mind clicked.

It was a subtle, sickening click, like a lock turning in her chest. Like a door creaking open that she'd been doing everything to ignore.

Zagan didn't need to say the words. He just watched her, lifting a hand coiling the shadows tighter.

Amber gasped as the pressure constricted, painful and oppressive as if she were being swallowed whole.

Zagan leaned in, lowering his voice. "You know, I almost feel sorry for you. You think you did this out of selflessness. That you traded yourself for Leandros because you were meant to save Hell." His lips curled. "But in reality? You just handed it to me on a silver platter."

Amber's body went rigid.

Her mind spun, flipping through every moment leading up to this, trying to understand what he was saying.

And slowly, inch by inch, her world tilted.

The room faded, the cold faded, everything faded except that *one horrifying truth*, slow and irrevocable, unspooling in her mind.

She couldn't breathe.

Zagan's lips curled. "There it is," he whispered. "I was wondering when you'd figure it out."

Amber swallowed, forcing herself not to react.

She couldn't. Not yet.

Amber swallowed hard. Her body swayed, but she forced herself upright. Even as the truth clawed its way through her ribs and settled in her spine, she refused to let him see her break.

"That's impossible," she muttered, voice flat, emotionless.

Zagan's grin only widened, his dark eyes glittering with something that made her skin crawl.

"I thought so too," he admitted, his tone light, almost amused. He *tsked,* shaking his head. "Yet here we are."

The amusement faded, leaving something colder beneath the surface.

Something dangerous.

"You're special, Amber." His voice softened like the words were a truth she should've always known. "Why do you think Heaven is willing to trade for you?"

Her pulse spiked.

She was the trade.

Her mind reeled, flipping through everything she'd uncovered in Leandros' research, everything she'd learned about the balance of Hell and Heaven.

Her mind raced through Leandros' research, every fragment she'd learned about balance, about divine law. There were only a few things Heaven would *bargain* for.

And now she was one of them.

Zagan circled her, slower now, deliberate. "You walked in here believing you were saving someone. But all you did was light the final match. And Hell, darling?" He leaned closer. "Hell is dry kindling."

Amber said nothing. She couldn't.

"Why?" she asked finally, her voice barely above a whisper.

Zagan chuckled. "It doesn't matter now, does it? You won't survive the torment. You'll be lucky if anything survives at all."

The shadows responded, tightening like a muscle around the bone. Amber fought to keep her breath steady, but each inhale felt heavier than the last.

"Oh, Amber." He stepped closer, cocking his head. "You really should have waited."

The words fell like a curse.

And then the darkness slammed into her, and she crumpled to her knees, the air driven from her lungs, her scream caught behind her teeth. The shadows coiled tighter, sinking into her skin like they were rewriting her from the inside out.

There was nothing left for her to do except scream.

And so she did.

Her cry echoed through the chamber, raw and desperate, but it didn't matter. No one was coming. No one would stop this.

Zagan watched.

Smiling.

And as her body was dragged backward into the abyss, the last sound she heard was his voice, low and triumphant, "Goodnight, darling."

70

Beneath the Halo

The Magna Aula pulsed with tension, a living, breathing entity that quaked beneath Lucifer's fury. The air, once electric with the anticipation of Amber's commitment to Hell, had soured into something rank, something oppressive. The gathered demons, the highest ranks of his dominion, stood or sat in eerie silence, their heads turned toward the gaping stone doors that had no right to be open.

Amber should've walked through them; instead, something far worse had.

Lucifer's hands curled into fists, claws digging deep into the palm of his hands, but he didn't notice the pain. He forced himself to remain still, even as something cold and unfamiliar twisted in his gut, a feeling he refused to name. His every muscle coiled with the expectation of battle, of bloodshed. The air thickened, pressing down on his subjects like an unseen force, demanding obedience, demanding submission. But this pressure wasn't his.

It belonged to the creature now standing at the threshold.

A ripple of raw, unchecked power swept through the room, an ancient force that made the torches sputter and the very walls groan. Shadows stretched unnaturally, slithering across the obsidian floors like starving things seeking refuge. The temperature dropped, ice creeping along the edges of Hell's infernal heat.

And then, he stepped forward.

Zagan.

Lucifer had heard the rumors, the whispers in the dark corners of his kingdom that The First Devil still walked, that he was waiting, watching. He'd dismissed them all. He'd killed those rumors. But he'd always known that The First Devil would return.

And there was no mistaking the truth now.

Zagan had returned.

Lucifer barely registered the demons scrambling to clear a path, their eyes wide with something more profound than fear. Not terror, recognition. It was carved into the marrow of every soul forged in Hell's fire. The knowledge that the being before them had been their first master, their original tormentor.

And that he'd come to reclaim what was his.

Still, it wasn't Zagan alone that made Lucifer's rage crack through him like a lightning strike, nor was it the sheer audacity of his presence.

It was the man he dragged behind him.

Leandros.

Bloodied, broken, barely standing, but alive.

Lucifer's vision darkened at the edges, his fury a living, breathing thing clawing to be unleashed as his eyes burned a fiery red. The very foundation of Castellum Umbrae trembled beneath his wrath. His wings unfurled, casting jagged shadows against the walls, and the throne behind him cracked as his power surged.

Yet Zagan walked as if he were unbothered, unchallenged, stepping to the base of the dais like he'd always belonged there. Like Lucifer was the intruder in *his* kingdom.

Lucifer's body moved before thought could intervene, the darkness around him snapping to life, curling into razor-edged tendrils as he prepared to strike.

Then, Zagan spoke.

"I would not be so quick to strike me down, my dear successor." His voice coiled through the room, honeyed poison laced with amusement, sending the gathered demons trembling. His lips curved into a slow, deliberate smirk. "You see, I have something of yours."

Lucifer didn't want to hear it.

He didn't need to.

Before he could stop himself and think, he'd already seen it.

Amber.

Her image flickered before him, a vision conjured by Zagan's will. She was bound, held in some unseen force, trapped in suffocating darkness. She was shivering, her body wracked with a tremor that made his stomach lurch. But she was alive.

The moment stretched, long and suffocating.

Then something in Lucifer snapped.

The room trembled as his fury shattered its confines, bleeding into the air and turning the chamber into a chasm of impending destruction. The very walls screamed beneath the weight of his rage, his power surging outward like a tidal wave of black fire. The demons nearest to him recoiled, some collapsing to their knees, others gasping as the oppressive force stole the breath from their lungs.

He was going to rip Zagan apart.

He was going to burn Heaven and Hell if that was what it took.

But Zagan, *the bastard*, only smiled.

"You have made quite the mess of my kingdom, Lucifer." The amusement in his tone was unbearable. "And while I do find your efforts charming, I think it's time we restored some balance."

Lucifer's eyes burned, the shadows around him coiling with barely contained violence. His mind was a storm, calculating and strategizing. He was already measuring the number of bodies in the way and the chances of tearing Zagan's head from his shoulders before the chamber descended into war.

Zagan tilted his head in a slow, lazy motion. "Oh, don't bother." His voice was silk, drenched in cruelty. "Harm me, and you'll never reach her."

Lucifer's breath came sharp and ragged, his hands twitching as the space between them felt suddenly unbearably vast.

Zagan stepped forward, voice dipping into something almost pitying. "Amber is whole, for now. But she is in a place you cannot even reach." He spread his arms as if welcoming an unseen audience. "You see, I am not looking to barter with Hell. I know what belongs to me." His gaze flicked to Lucifer, too knowing, too pleased. "No, my dear boy, I am here to make an offer to Heaven."

The air in the room shattered.

A collective inhale.

A ripple of disbelief.

Lucifer's chest tightened, the fury in his bones replaced by something colder, sharper. The pieces began to align, the game revealing itself too late.

"I will trade Amber," Zagan said, his voice rich with certainty, "in exchange for Heaven's acknowledgment."

Hell stopped shifting, moving, and changing for the first time in all eternity.

It went completely still.

Lucifer's blood turned to ice.

The words slithered into his mind, wrapping around his throat like a noose. If Heaven acknowledged Zagan as Hell's rightful ruler, if they accepted him as the true heir of damnation, then Lucifer would cease to exist.

He would be erased.

Gone.

As if he'd never ruled at all.

The weight of it settled in his chest, a revelation as brutal as a blade to the gut.

He had been outplayed.

Not just outplayed, blinded.

Zagan had taken Amber not for leverage over Hell but for Heaven. She was the key to forcing their hand, the one soul they might actually bargain for, the one piece that could tilt the scales of power.

Lucifer clenched his jaw so tightly he thought it might break.

"Why Amber?" he forced out, his voice like a growl, his nails drawing blood from his palms, but he barely noticed.

Zagan chuckled, low and dark. "You don't know?" He exhaled, shaking his head as if Lucifer's ignorance truly amused him. "Haven't you felt it? The drain in your power? The shifting of Hell?"

Lucifer stiffened.

Zagan's smirk widened.

"You almost secured your reign, Lucifer." His gaze burned, triumphant. "Now, I'm here to secure mine."

Lucifer's fury roared, and the very walls of the Magna Aula trembled, cracks spider webbing along the obsidian stone as if Hell itself braced for what was to come. He'd played his game well, bending the rules and defying fate itself to cement his reign. And yet, Zagan had been waiting. Watching. Striking the moment, he was vulnerable.

Amber was *his* piece. His claim. His salvation or his damnation.

And now she was gone.

Lucifer took a small step towards Zagan, slow and deliberate, but the power that rippled from him sent every demon in the room recoiling. Even the strongest of them bowed their heads, some dropping to their knees beneath the sheer weight of his rage. Shadows coiled around him, thick and writhing, the air around him warping with hellfire.

And yet, Zagan didn't flinch.

He only smiled.

Lucifer's voice was a razor's edge when he spoke. "You think you can threaten *my* kingdom and walk out of here in one piece?"

The torches along the walls flickered violently, their flames bending inward, their light swallowed whole by the abyss creeping in from the corners of the room. Lucifer's shadows slithered across the floor, reaching coiling as if they were waiting for the order to *devour*.

Zagan's laughter was almost *fond*. "Oh, Lucifer," he sighed, shaking his head, "You were always so predictable." He gestured vaguely to the throne, his fingers trailing through the air as if it bored him. "Threats. Power displays. This is why you will never be anything more than a thief sitting on borrowed power."

Lucifer *moved*.

One second, he stood at the dais; the next, he was in front of Zagan, hand wrapped around his throat.

The hall *shook*.

Demons gasped, some scrambling backward as the weight of Lucifer's power crashed into them like a tidal wave. The shadows in the room *exploded*, slamming into the walls, curling around pillars, devouring all light. Zagan's feet lifted off the floor as Lucifer's grip tightened, the bones in his throat creaking beneath the pressure.

"I *built* this kingdom," Lucifer snarled, voice low and wrathful, the very *voice of Hell itself*. "You were *gone*. *Dead*. No one here belongs to you." His fingers flexed, his grip threatening to crush, to *destroy*. "And Amber is *mine*."

Zagan's lips curled, teeth glinting in the dim light.

And then, he laughed.

Not strained. Not desperate. But soft. *Amused*.

Lucifer barely had time to react before the force hit him.

A shockwave of power burst from Zagan's body, rippling outward, a pressure so immense that the walls *cracked*. The ground beneath them splintered, deep, jagged fissures tearing through the floor as the entire room *lurched*. The demons closest to them were *thrown* backward, colliding with walls and tables, some vanishing into the dark abyss now splitting through the chamber.

Lucifer staggered back just enough for Zagan to land on his feet, brushing himself off as though he hadn't just been seconds from destruction.

Then, he smiled. Slow. Satisfied.

"You have *no idea* what you've taken from me, do you?" Zagan murmured, tilting his head. "You call this place *yours* but have not secured your throne. *She* was securing it for you."

Lucifer's rage simmered beneath his skin, raw and scorching, but something cold slid through his veins at those words.

Zagan's grin sharpened. "Amber was the final thread holding your reign together. Your claim was *almost* complete. She would have chosen you. Would have anchored you to this throne." His voice was thick with mockery. "But now? Now, she is gone. And without her, your rule is *fleeting*." He paused, looking up towards the sky, and began chanting, *calling*, "Lux et tenebrae non sunt miscere, hoc bene novimus, sed habeo aliquid pro vobis, quod nesciatis? Peto age quod tuum est, omne quod peto, tibi quadruplum!"

The weight of those words settled like a stone in Lucifer's chest; Zagan was calling to the Heavens.

Lucifer *felt* it.

He'd dismissed the strange imbalances in Hell as a mere consequence of Amber's trials, as the natural shifting of power as she proved herself. But now, his magic, his very claim to this throne, pulsed with something fragile, something *unsteady*.

And Zagan knew it.

Lucifer's voice was death itself. "Where is she?"

Zagan's smirk remained, but there was something darker behind it now. "Somewhere you cannot follow." He sighed as if discussing a minor inconvenience. "You see, Lucifer, this throne was never *yours* to keep. You fought, you clawed your way to the top, but you *stole* it. And the Divine does not acknowledge thieves."

Lucifer's breathing was slow and measured, even as the foundation of his kingdom trembled beneath him.

Zagan took a step forward. "But if *Heaven* acknowledges me?" His grin was all teeth. "You will cease to exist."

The room *plummeted* into silence.

Lucifer had faced death. He'd faced war. He'd even faced *and beaten* Zagan before.

But never before had he faced erasure.

Never before had he felt the noose tightening around his very existence, pulling taut with each second that Amber remained in Zagan's grasp.

Lucifer had been blind.

Not just to Amber's importance, not just to his own vulnerability.

He'd been blind to the fact that he had *something to lose*.

Amber wasn't just a plaything, not just a pawn in his games. She'd *become* the game. The final piece to cement his reign, the only piece that could unmake him.

She'd changed him, and it was then that he realized he'd fallen for her.

Impossible. And yet there it was, plain as day.

He loved her.

And she was in the one place he couldn't reach.

The air burned with his rage, with the weight of something far more dangerous than fury, *desperation*.

Lucifer's voice was barely above a whisper, but it carried through the room like a promise of destruction. "I will *tear apart* the fabric of this realm to find her."

Zagan only chuckled. "It's too late." He turned toward the doors as if expecting someone to walk through them, the heavy finality of his next words leaving Hell breathless. "Because they're already here."

71

The Heir of Hell

A crack split through the sky.

Not the sky of the mortal world, not the heavy, eternal darkness of Hell, but the very fabric of the realm itself. The ceiling of the Magna Aula didn't just crack; it *shattered*, light pouring through as if the heavens themselves had torn a hole straight through the core of damnation.

Demons recoiled with screams. Some shielded their eyes, others collapsing, clutching their heads as the radiance bore into them like searing blades. The torches that lined the chamber snuffed out, their meager flames swallowed by something purer, something that didn't belong here.

Lucifer didn't flinch.

He *refused* to.

But his body knew what was coming. Knew it on a level so deep, so ingrained in the marrow of his very being, that his fingers curled back into fists, his breath drawing slow and measured through his teeth.

A blinding column of light exploded down into the hall, crashing into the obsidian floor in a burst of divine energy. The ground splintered, sending cracks across the chamber, a jagged divide splitting the space between Lucifer and Zagan.

And then, they stepped through.

First came the wings.

Massive, blinding, unfurling like banners of war. Feathered edges tinged with gold, unfathomable in size and impossibly perfect, they cut through the darkness, turning it to dust.

Then came the figures.

Tall, draped in light, their faces shadowed by the sheer radiance that poured from their forms. Their armor gleamed, forged from celestial fire, and weapons were strapped to their backs.

And then, last of all, *Him*.

The one Lucifer hadn't seen in centuries.

God.

Not a man, not a thing that could be contained in one form, but a force, a presence so absolute that the air around Him was both suffocating and empty all at once.

Lucifer's shadows recoiled. His magic, the very foundation of his power, shrank back, instincts screaming in warning.

He could feel Hell itself pulling away.

His home, his kingdom, *his realm*, bowing under the weight of its Creator.

Lucifer's hands flexed, his throat tight, but he forced himself to meet the presence head-on, to stand firm even as something deep inside him whispered: *this is the end.*

God didn't speak. Not yet.

Instead, the angels stepped forward.

Gold-eyed and draped in celestial war regalia, Michael regarded Lucifer with a burned stare. He hadn't changed, still radiating that same insufferable righteousness. Still looking at Lucifer as if he were nothing more than a mistake.

Gabriel was there, too, his presence lighter but no less powerful. Beside him was Raphael, silent as ever, his gaze unreadable.

They weren't here to debate. Not here to fight.

They were here for Amber.

Zagan smiled as if this were all a pleasant little gathering. He spread his arms, voice thick with victory.

"Well," he mused, glancing toward Lucifer with something dangerously close to pity. "Shall we begin?"

Lucifer felt its full weight now.

The checkmate.

The move he'd never seen coming.

His kingdom trembled beneath his feet.

And for the first time in centuries, he didn't know how to win.

The silence that followed Zagan's words was deafening. Its weight crushed the air, making it heavy with finality.

Lucifer lifted his chin, leveling his gaze at the celestial beings before him. He'd stood before them once before, long ago, when he'd still been something whole. When he'd still believed in the world above, in his place among them.

Now, he stood against them.

Alone.

Raphael moved first, but not towards Lucifer. He turned his gaze to the demons present, "Out."

It was a quiet command, but the creatures wilted under its power. They scrambled over one another, trying to escape the light, until it was only the six of them.

With a flick of his hand, the light around the heavenly creatures dulled slightly, and Michael stepped forward. His presence pressed against the room as if daring Lucifer to falter beneath it. His golden eyes were unreadable, but the disgust and condescension remained just beneath the surface.

It had always been there.

Lucifer saw it now, the way Michael looked at him like a tainted thing, something broken, something not worth saving.

The angel's voice was steady, emotionless. "Where is the girl?"

Lucifer didn't answer. He wouldn't play this game.

Gabriel's voice cut through next, softer but no less weighted. "Give her to us, and we leave."

A cold chuckle slid from Lucifer's lips before he could stop it. "*Give* her to you?" His voice was like smoke, curling, dark and seething. "You think I have her?"

Michael's gaze sharpened. "She was under *your* protection."

Lucifer's jaw tightened.

And there it was; the unspoken accusation.

The realization that Amber had been under *his* claim, *his* rule, and yet she'd still been taken.

His power should've protected her. His throne should've *secured* her.

But he'd failed.

And now, Heaven thought they could simply descend upon his kingdom and steal her away? No.

Lucifer stood against Heaven once before. He wouldn't fall now.

Zagan, the smug bastard, only smiled.

"It's quite unfortunate, isn't it?" he mused, tilting his head. "The girl that Hell and Heaven both want... and yet, she belongs to neither."

Lucifer barely heard him. His focus remained locked on Michael, on the slow, calculated way the angel studied him.

Michael wasn't a fool. He was weighing his options. Measuring just how far Lucifer would go to keep her.

Then, Michael spoke. "You were always just a placeholder, Lucifer."

The words sliced deeper than Lucifer expected. A calculated wound. One that shouldn't have hurt but did.

Michael continued, taking another step forward, his blade gleaming at his side. "Amber's fate is not yours to decide." His voice was a decree. A judgment. "Her soul was never meant to be in your hands."

Lucifer let out a low breath, measured, controlled. The shadows at his feet curled, rising in slow, deliberate waves. His wings stretched slightly, just enough to let them see what coiled beneath his anger.

The depth of his power. The sharp, unrelenting promise of war.

And then, he smiled.

A slow, lethal thing.

"I don't give a damn what was *meant* to be."

Michael stiffened.

Lucifer stepped forward, closing the space between them in a single motion, so close that the divine light scorched the edges of his being. He welcomed the pain and let it settle into his bones because it didn't matter. Not compared to what they were threatening to take.

"She is *mine*." His voice was quiet but echoed through the room like thunder, like a curse that would never be lifted. "And if you think I will let you take her, then you have learned *nothing* in the eons since I left your precious kingdom."

Michael didn't waver. "You have no claim over her."

Lucifer's vision darkened at the edges, his patience unraveling.

"And yet you came all this way to bargain for her," he murmured, tilting his head. "What would Heaven trade, I wonder? What would God Himself sacrifice for a single mortal girl?"

Michael's expression didn't change.

But Zagan laughed. Not the amused, smug chuckle from before, but something harsher, something victorious.

Lucifer turned sharply toward him, shadows twisting as his patience snapped. "What the hell are you laughing at?"

Zagan grinned, his power coiling in lazy tendrils. "Oh, Lucifer," he mused, shaking his head. "You really are centuries behind."

Lucifer's stomach tightened, but he refused to react, refused to let him see the crack that had formed in his understanding.

Zagan only smiled wider. And then, he delivered the final blow.

"You ask what she is to Him?" He gestured toward the divine presence in the room, toward the very force that had shattered Hell's sky just to step foot into his kingdom.

Zagan's grin turned razor-sharp, cutting through the tension like a blade laced with venom. "She is the first soul He has ever come to claim *personally*."

The words struck like thunder, quiet but absolute, and Lucifer's heart stilled, his body frozen not by force but by the weight of something far heavier.

The Magna Aula descended into a silence so profound it didn't feel like the absence of sound but the suffocation of it.

He couldn't move. Couldn't speak. His breath lodged somewhere between his lungs and his disbelief as Zagan's meaning unfurled with cruel, deliberate precision.

God had never intervened in the fate of a single soul.

Not once.

Not in all the time Lucifer had ruled Hell, not in all the ages he had watched the heavens from below.

Until now.

Until *Amber.*

The realization sank into his chest like a falling star, slow, bright, and devastating.

And then suddenly, the light around them began to shift, not fading or dimming but transforming into something new.

What had once been an overwhelming, unfathomable pressure, a force so vast it threatened to rip the realm in two, began to coalesce. The blinding glow that had filled every crevice of the hall softened at the edges, folding inward, condensing into shape.

Divinity, once untouchable, began to take form.

The blinding became bearable.

The formless became familiar.

And Hell, for the first time in its existence, stared directly into the face of its Maker.

Lucifer's breath caught in his throat, his entire being taut with the sheer weight of His presence. It was wrong to see Him like this, to witness divinity take shape in a way that Hell itself could comprehend.

The Archangels bowed in perfect unison.

Lucifer didn't.

He *would not.*

Instead, he stood frozen as God regarded him for a long moment, his gaze unknowable and timeless.

And then, he spoke, "Relax, dear boy."

The voice was calm and steady, but it wasn't the voice of a man; it was power incarnate. It radiated through the hall, seeped into the stone, and filled the very marrow of existence itself.

Lucifer's body braced against it, his every instinct screaming that this wasn't just an enemy, not just an adversary, but the origin. The very thing that had created everything, that had shaped the heavens and the earth.

God's expression didn't waver, "It is not the girl we are truly after," he continued, his tone almost... patient. "She has chosen you. We have seen that. And if she wishes to return to you, she may."

Lucifer's mind went blank. The words didn't make sense. What did he mean?

"I don't..." Lucifer started, voice rough, unsteady.

God raised his hand, not allowing him to finish.

Zagan, however, didn't hide his outrage.

"What do you mean she can return?" he demanded, stepping forward, his power crackling with barely contained fury. "What about the trade?"

God turned his gaze to Zagan. He didn't smite him. Didn't silence him. He simply looked.

And Zagan stilled.

"The girl chose Lucifer, and you cannot trade what does not belong to you." He paused, "what we need, you cannot trade for, as it has not been born yet."

The words echoed like a thunderclap.

Lucifer's breath hitched. His pulse roared in his ears.

God's gaze returned to him.

Not Zagan. Not the angels. Only him.

And then, with a finality that shattered everything Lucifer thought he knew, God spoke, "We never thought it possible, yet you have defied all odds."

The air collapsed around them. The walls creaked, the shadows stilled, and something far more dangerous than war settled between them. "We do not wish to keep Amber from you. We are here for the baby."

Lucifer's world fractured.

72

Shadows Stir

P ain.

It was the first thing Amber registered, sharp and unforgiving, curling through her ribs as she pulled in a breath too quickly. The second was that she was wet. The cloth from her clothes stuck to her, encapsulating her in a mummifying enclosure. Her eyes were open; she knew they were, but everything was dark. Her senses were kicking into high gear, but she could only feel a consistent slow drip on her arm from above.

Goosebumps raced over her body, revealing the fear Amber felt on the inside to the outside world. Her feet sloshed in something ankle-deep that released a putrid odor every time she moved.

Amber's arm met a damp wall of some sort, but it was close to her. Too close. She couldn't fully extend her arm. The wall felt rough and solid beneath her touch. Bubbling with small ridges of some sort, but it continued around her.

Her breath came short and quick, fighting her flight or fight response as there was nowhere to run, no one to fight. She stretched up with her arms, but there was nothing above her. Silently, she prayed that her trembling fingers would graze something resembling anything she could consider a roof. But there was nothing. Her hands met space and the continuous drip directly from above.

Her pulse pounded in her ears, loud enough to drown out the quiet hum of the space around her. Her mind felt sluggish, thoughts slipping like water through trembling fingers as she tried to piece together what had happened.

Zagan. His name slashed through the fog. She remembered him. The trap. The chains. The deal she thought she was making.

And now, she was here.

Wherever *here* was.

Her fingers curled tightly into the wall, pressing hard against the unfamiliar material. It wasn't stone. It wasn't the shifting terrain of Hell. It was something else. Something older. Something *wrong*.

"Hello?" Her voice wavered, cracking against the walls before bouncing back to her. "Is anyone there?"

The silence was deafening.

Her chest seized. Panic clawed its way to her throat, and this time, she didn't fight it. She screamed something raw, wordless, and terrified and beat her fists against the walls until her hands ached. Tears mixed with the foul water at her feet, unnoticed and unimportant. Her throat burned, voice splintering into sobs, until there was nothing left but shaking breath and the echo of her own desperation.

The darkness didn't flinch.

But she felt it around her, watching like something alive, like something hunting her.

Fear threatened to take over, but she shoved it down, biting the inside of her cheek so hard her mouth filled with blood. She couldn't afford to panic.

Not now.

She stretched as best she could, her muscles stiff and sore, her body aching in a way that felt deeper than anything physical. A weight pressed against her chest, and as she pressed a hand to her stomach, an odd sense of unease curled in her gut.

Something was different.

Something was wrong.

But she didn't have time to figure it out.

Amber looked at her feet, shuffling slightly and picking them up. One by one, she watched as shimmering red strings stretched. The smell was suffocating, and the realization of what she was standing in hit her like a truck: blood, too much blood. As she moved, something whispered through the air, a soundless murmur just beneath her ability to understand. It wasn't quite a voice but a vibration curling beneath the skin. Amber froze, breath caught halfway to her lungs.

She wasn't alone.

Something else was here.

She scanned the space around her, heart hammering, eyes straining against the darkness. She could feel it now. A presence. A force pressing in, close enough that the air itself thickened.

Her instincts screamed: *run.*

But there was nowhere to go.

No doors. No light.

Only blackness.

Amber swallowed hard, her mind racing. There had to be a way out. There was *always* a way out. She'd survived Hell, survived Lucifer.

She'd survive this, too.

73

A Voice in the Dark

Amber's breath came in shallow, sharp pulls, her lungs struggling to expand against the weight pressing down from all sides. The silence crawled over her skin, soaked into her bones, and settled deep in the hollow places of her chest like smoke refusing to dissipate. The air pulsed with something sentient, something that felt her fear and savored it.

The presence wasn't waiting anymore. It was creeping closer, slow and deliberate, coiling like a snake around the edges of her consciousness, brushing against her ribs with a coldness that didn't come from temperature. It was anticipation incarnate.

She stepped back instinctively, her boot sloshing through the putrid water below. The sharp scent of copper and rot surged up, thick and nauseating, invading her senses. The sound of movement, so stark in the silence, felt like a betrayal. The air seemed to shudder with her.

Then, a whisper, soft and hollow, like breath sliding over broken glass, "You are not supposed to be here."

Amber's spine locked, her blood plunging into ice. The voice was everywhere, but it wasn't just one voice; it was many, wading through the darkness in a chorus of something ancient and relentless. The words didn't just echo around her; they slipped inside her, brushed against her mind, and threaded through her thoughts.

Amber swallowed, forcing down the panic that clawed at her throat like nails in a coffin. Don't panic. Don't let it see you panic.

She licked her lips, voice rough, raw. "Where is here?"

The whisper rippled as if tasting her words. "Where light comes to die."

Something shifted in the void, a ripple in the shadows. Amber instinctively flinched back, her pulse hammering in her skull.

Another whisper, colder than the first, slipped beneath her skin: "But you are not light." Amber froze. "We devour light, feed off light. You are not light."

The words cascaded into silence, and then, it breathed.

Long. Deep. Drawn from the belly of the dark. It filled the space around her, pressed into her lungs, and invaded her body without permission. Her knees buckled. Her chest seized. Cold fire licked at her insides, spreading from her ribs to her spine, coiling like a second heartbeat.

The darkness was alive, and it was hungry.

"You do not belong."

The words landed at the base of her skull, slithering down her spine. She clenched her fists, needing to feel the shape of herself, something solid. But there was nothing. Her body was no longer her own.

"Then let me out," she said, her voice low, even betraying none of the fear wrapping around her spine like wire.

Laughter answered.

Not cruel. Not mocking but knowing.

"Out?" the voice murmured, crawling through her like smoke curling into untouched corners. "You speak as if this place contains you."

A pause. Then softer, more intimate: "But we are inside you, Amber."

It didn't move through the air; it moved through her, pressing against the walls of her skull. Like fingers slipping beneath bone, it reached down her throat and touched the softest part of her.

Her breath stilled.

"We always have been."

Then it surged.

It didn't step closer. It didn't need to. The darkness moved into her and slid through her skin like oil through cracks. It wasn't a hand. It wasn't a face. It was a will. A force. A drowning.

She gasped, and the air tasted like ash.

She wasn't standing anymore. Though she couldn't remember falling.

The shadows pressed in, wrapped around her ribs, and curled against her spine. Not hurting her. Not yet. Just... claiming her.

Her body responded against her will.

Her arm twitched and wasn't an arm. It was smoke. Her fingers blurred at the edges, dissolving into wisps of shadow. Her skin peeled into vapor, charcoal at the edges, lines smeared and unstable.

"No," she breathed. "No, no, no..."

She fought, thrashed, and screamed, but her limbs wouldn't obey. She was vapor, fog, the edge of a scream that couldn't form.

She was unraveling.

The shadows pressed deeper. Inside her blood, inside her thoughts. Memories loosened their grip, her first kiss, her mother's face, the taste of snow, all of it slipping away.

"Stop," she whispered, but the voice wasn't hers anymore.

And then she understood.

The darkness didn't want to destroy her.

It wanted to claim her.

It was welcoming her home.

"Become." It whispered.

This time, the voice was inside her lungs. Her bones. Her teeth.

She gasped. Her body spasmed.

And the power opened like a door.

It rushed through her, not foreign but terrifyingly familiar. Like it had always been there, coiled and waiting. Her veins burned. Her skin buzzed. Darkness inked across her arms, her nails curling into claws, her limbs stretching in ways that defied understanding. She was becoming two things at once. Amber and not-Amber. Flesh and void. Solid and shadow.

She let it take her.

For a heartbeat, she surrendered.

And when she screamed, the sound that tore from her chest wasn't human. It cracked through the dark like shattering glass. The air warped around her.

And it hurt.

Holy Hell, it hurt.

More than anything ever had. Like her soul was being turned inside out like her bones were softening into smoke, her very essence bleeding into the abyss.

Her vision blurred.

Her self fractured.

Until there was no voice. No body. No girl.

She was nothing; she was *everything*.

She was *darkness*.

And for the first time, the air around her bowed.

74

Styx and Sacrifice

T he shifting ceased, and silence bloomed.

Amber tried to look around, but there was no "her" anymore. No limbs to raise. No chest to rise and fall with breath. She was no longer flesh, no longer blood. She'd become shadow, formless and fluid, a presence suspended in the endless black. She drifted, not with movement, but with will, her consciousness stretching through the void like silk caught on wind.

The whispers that had once tormented her fell still, not out of fear but reverence. The darkness that had wrapped around her now held its distance, obedient. The weight that had once pressed into her ribs now bowed beneath her.

She wasn't mortal.

She wasn't bound.

She was shadow, unmade and remade by the void itself.

Without thought, she ascended. The darkness peeled back before her, not resisting but yielding as though welcoming its rightful queen. She rose through the emptiness, higher, farther until the world around her changed.

Umbra Cavea's top split open, and Amber emerged, a phantom of black mist, a shroud of shadow bleeding into the sky.

For a moment, she hovered, suspended above the Seventh Island, her form shifting like a storm cloud caught in an unnatural, eternal wind. She was neither flesh nor mist, caught in the delicate space between existence and oblivion. Her essence stretched and twisted, pulled by unseen forces, a wraith with no true form.

She felt it before she saw them: a tremor in the dark, a ripple that slid along the edges of her new self. The disturbance wasn't violent but ancient. Familiar. Two forces approached, neither fast nor slow; they simply arrived, folding space around them until they were near.

Timor and Dolor.

They were as they had always been; faceless entities of swirling shadow, their edges undefined, a rippling void in the shape of specters. But something was different.

She didn't flinch at their presence. Didn't kneel or cower.

And for the first time, they spoke. Not in language or words. But in resonance, in pure vibration that sank into her bones, if she still had bones, and echoed in her chest like a name once forgotten.

Angustia.

The name reverberated through her like thunder rolled across silk. It wasn't just given; it was remembered.

She didn't answer with a sound. She didn't need to. Her acknowledgment rippled outward, a pulse of identity and power that matched theirs in depth, if not surpassing theirs in weight.

"We have waited," the feeling said. "We have always waited."

A tremor passed through her essence. Not fear or pain but something else. A distant longing. A pull toward something she couldn't yet name.

"I need to leave," she said, though there were no lips to shape the words. Her will carried the thought outward, crisp and clean in the endless dark.

Timor and Dolor didn't reply. They didn't have to. They turned, slow and weightless, and the world around them obeyed. Reality bent. Space shivered. The island twisted itself open, and Amber followed.

Will alone carried her forward as the landscape peeled back, revealing a path no mortal had ever seen and survived. The terrain twisted, shifting between solid and void, an ever-changing prison for the condemned. The landscape writhed like a living thing, sculpted from the nightmares of the lost. The sky churned above them, black and formless, streaked with veins of something too bright, too unnatural, like the pulse of a dying star. Below them, shadows crawled, whispering prayers that had long been abandoned, their voices blending into the wails of the forsaken.

Yet, nothing touched her. Nothing dared. Because she wasn't a prisoner here. *She* was something to be feared.

The wind howled, but it didn't shift her. It didn't push her back, didn't fight her passing.

It moved around her like it knew her name.

Timor and Dolor moved faster, the world around them blurring, bending, and folding into itself as they broke through the invisible barriers that separated the island from the rest of Hell.

They crossed realms, stepping through unseen thresholds that no living being could ever pass. The world around them flickered, the edges of space and time splitting open like wounds, revealing glimpses of places Amber couldn't name. Then they reached the Styx.

The river churned an endless rush of liquid shadow, its current pulled by the weight of memory and regret. Screams bubbled in its depths. Names long forgotten drifted in its wake. But as Amber approached, the Styx didn't devour her; the waves merely crashed through where her body should've been. There was no impact, only the feeling of something passing through her.

She didn't walk or run.

She drifted, following Timor and Dolor through the dark, the impossible, and the in-between.

And before she knew it, Castellum Umbrae towered before them.

The castle rose like a monument to eternity, its spires cleaving the sky, its walls carved from obsidian so deep they drank the light from the air itself. Clouds swirled above, thick with power and heavy with expectation.

Amber stilled, her essence twisting, coiling, as something inside her whispered.

Home.

Timor and Dolor turned to her, not as guardians or monsters, but as sentinels awaiting command. Their forms curved toward her in silent deference, waiting not for permission but recognition.

Amber lingered for only a moment before willing the shadows forward.

75

When Angels Bleed

T he weight of silence was suffocating.

Lucifer stood at the center of it, his body rigid, his mind warring against the truth that had just shattered everything he thought he knew.

He could still hear the words, hanging in the air like an echo carved into the very walls of his kingdom: "We do not wish to keep Amber from you. We are here for the baby."

The *baby*.

Lucifer had thought himself prepared for anything; every revelation, every trick, every calculated move from Zagan, Heaven, and whatever forces sought to unmake him. He'd spent centuries mastering the art of control, ensuring that nothing could shake him.

But this, this, was something else entirely.

His breath caught, sharp and jagged, his mind slamming against the truth, refusing to process it.

"What... what did you just say?" His voice was low, unsteady, a rare crack in the carefully constructed armor he'd worn for eons.

A soft chuckle reverberated through the air, ancient and absolute, a sound that carried no amusement, only inevitability.

"Amber is carrying your child." The words landed like a death knell, ringing through the Magna Aula with impossible finality.

Lucifer's entire being went still.

He'd withstood the fire of rebellion. Had endured exile, had clawed his way to the throne of Hell, and had watched the weight of eternity crush every other creature who dared to stand in his way.

And yet, nothing had ever felt like this.

His pulse roared in his ears, drowning out the silence.

His hands curled into tight fists, nails cutting into his palms, but the pain barely registered. The space around him throbbed, his shadows twisting at his feet, unraveling because, for the first time in centuries, his control wavered.

His wings flexed, their edges trembling, as if some buried instinct screamed at him to run.

To fight.

To deny.

Lucifer shook his head. One step back, then another. His body moved before his mind could catch up, an unconscious recoil as if distance could sever him from this reality.

"That's impossible," he growled, his voice low but dangerously edged.

God didn't argue. He didn't explain.

He only said, "And yet, it is."

Lucifer's breath stilled in his chest.

The weight of those words crushed into him, deeper than he wanted to admit. The world around him hadn't changed, and yet it felt unfamiliar as if the very foundation of his kingdom had just shifted beneath his feet.

Something cold slid through him, something he didn't want to name.

Not fear. But close.

The firelight flickered, casting shadows across the floor. His shadows. But they were erratic, restless, and uneasy as if they had even recognized the truth before he did.

Because God didn't lie.

Which meant it was true.

Amber carried his child.

And the entire balance of Hell, Heaven, and everything in between was about to change.

He could feel their eyes on him. The Archangels stood unwavering, their expressions unreadable but expectant, watching him as though they were waiting to see the moment realization fully sank in.

But it was Zagan's reaction that drew him back to the present.

The former ruler of Hell had gone deathly still. His usual smirk, which had lingered no matter how dangerous the moment, had vanished. His gaze flickered between Lucifer and the divine figures before him, his mind working frantically, piecing together what this revelation meant.

His lips parted, then closed, as if he were trying to speak but couldn't find the words. And then, slowly, his expression twisted, not into rage, but into something far worse.

Horror.

"You..." Zagan's voice was barely more than a whisper but sharp enough to cut through the silence. "You never wanted her."

The words carried more weight than the accusation they seemed to be.

Heaven had never wanted Amber.

Everything he'd schemed for, believed in, and manipulated into place had been built on a false premise. He'd taken Amber and had planned to use her as a bargaining piece, a trade for Heaven's acknowledgment of his claim over Hell. He'd played his game flawlessly.

But the game had never been his to win.

He'd been doomed from the very beginning.

Michael was the first to speak. "No." The answer was simple, final, and unwavering. "Amber was never ours to take or keep. She went with Lucifer willingly."

Lucifer's jaw clenched. The sheer weight of those words settled into his chest, too heavy, too consuming. His mind raced, trying to process what this meant, not just for Amber but for him.

He felt something dangerously close to uncertainty for the first time in eons.

If Amber was carrying his child, then... what did that mean for his throne? For Hell? For everything?

Zagan took an unsteady step back, his hands clenching at his sides as though trying to grasp something real and solid before he lost it all. When it came again, his voice was hoarse, laced with something close to betrayal.

"I played by the rules," he murmured, shaking his head as if he still couldn't fully comprehend the depth of his failure. "I waited. I planned. And you," His gaze snapped toward Lucifer, burning with a vile hatred that hadn't existed before. "You stole the one thing that was never supposed to be yours."

Lucifer didn't answer. He didn't need to.

Because at that moment, the entirety of Hell shifted.

It was subtle at first. A whisper through the air. A flicker in the torches lining the hall, their flames bending unnaturally, their glow darkening.

But then it became something more.

Lucifer stiffened.

It wasn't Heaven's power this time.

It was Hell's.

A deep, unshakable hum pulsed through the very foundation of his kingdom, ancient and unrelenting like the earth itself had stirred in recognition of something it didn't yet understand.

A shift in the balance.

Something waking.

The angels felt it, too. Michael's expression sharpened, his fingers flexing near the hilt of his blade. Gabriel inhaled slowly, carefully, his usually calm face darkened by something that looked dangerously close to concern. Even

Raphael, silent as ever, turned his gaze toward the unseen force rippling through the chamber.

Lucifer's wings twitched at his back, his instincts coiling, sharpening. Something had changed.

And then, he felt it.

A deep and unshakable pull tied to him like an invisible thread unraveling from his core was leaving him. Traveling away from him.

His brows furrowed as he braced himself against the sensation, trying to grasp what was slipping from his reach. It wasn't weakness, not in the way power was drained, not in the way something was taken. No, this was different. It was his power, but it wasn't *his* anymore.

A sliver of himself had broken off, forging its own path, answering to something else.

Someone else.

Lucifer's head snapped toward the open doors of the hall, his gaze narrowing, focus stretching outward as if he could will himself to see beyond Castellum Umbrae walls. He couldn't place it but somewhere, out there, something had shifted.

No.

Someone had shifted.

Amber.

But not just Amber, his child, *their* child.

His power was spreading to them, changing, evolving, and becoming something new.

The air crackled as if responding to his thoughts, and a second pulse rolled through the hall, heavier this time and stronger.

It was familiar.

His, but changed. It felt older than him, wilder, unshaped by restraint, untamed in a way he'd never known. Raw. Ancient. And it belonged to her. Lucifer wasn't the only one who noticed.

Zagan's breath hitched, his gaze flickering with realization. And dread.

He understood but it was too late.

Lucifer's grip on control frayed. His shadows surged at his feet, curling outward, growing with each passing second. His mind roared with questions, but only one truly mattered now: "Where is she?"

Silence answered him.

But Lucifer knew she was coming.

And the entire balance of Hell was about to change.

76

Hellbound Queen

C astellum Umbrae trembled, not with sound, but with something deeper, something ancient. A pulse rolled through the obsidian walls, subtle at first, like a murmur rising from the bones of Hell itself. Most wouldn't have noticed. But Lucifer did.

He straightened, his wings flexing instinctively, shadows curling around him and skittering up the walls in response to the unseen force slithering through his domain. The torches flickered violently, their flames stretching unnaturally before snuffing out one by one. The hall grew dimmer and darker, not the comforting kind of dark that had always bent to his will, but something different.

Something opposing him.

Lucifer clenched his jaw.

This wasn't Heaven's doing.

This was Hell turning against him.

The realization sent a slow, simmering rage through his veins. He'd spent centuries breaking this kingdom into submission, molding it into his image, forcing every stone, every shadow, every piece of this wretched realm to bow to his power.

And now it was resisting him.

Lucifer lifted a hand, willing the flames to return, commanding the darkness to settle. Castellum Umbrae had always answered him. Hell had always answered him.

But nothing happened.

For the first time ever, the darkness didn't obey.

The chamber grew colder. The air thickened like oil in his lungs. Darkness bled across the floor in long, jagged tendrils, stretching from the far hall like veins of ink, pulsing, twisting, alive.

Lucifer clenched his jaw, unease creeping beneath his skin like frost. Something was coming.

Michael shifted at his side, one hand resting on the hilt of his blade. Gabriel's wings flared slightly, tension rippling through him like a static charge. Even Zagan, usually a beacon of smug detachment, had gone quiet.

They all felt it.

The air grew thick, pressing against Lucifer's skin like a living thing. The stone beneath his feet felt less stable as if the very foundation of Hell was reconsidering who it truly belonged to.

His eyes narrowed.

"Show yourself," he commanded, his voice low, edged with enough force to shake the room.

Silence answered him.

But something moved.

A shadow slithered from the distant corridor, inching forward, not like mist but like an insect skittering in and out of view. The torches that still burned struggled against their weight, their flames bending toward the encroaching darkness as though drawn to something greater.

Everyone tensed.

It wasn't a demon's shadow. Not one of his own creatures. Not anything born of Hell's depths.

This was something else.

Lucifer *hated* that he didn't recognize it.

The Magna Aula's massive doors creaked on ancient hinges, the groan sounding more like a warning than an opening. A rush of icy wind surged inward, sharp enough to bite flesh from bone. And through that wind came a figure. Something weightless, shapeless, moving with the slow, deliberate certainty of a force that had no need to rush.

Lucifer's pulse thundered in his ears.

It was neither demon nor angel, neither flesh nor mist. A shifting void, flickering between form and formlessness, something unfinished yet whole, as if Hell itself hasn't decided what to make of it.

It had no face or shape; it was only a shadow.

A cold dread curled through Lucifer's chest because he didn't know what he was looking at. And that was what truly unsettled him.

Michael stiffened beside him. Zagan remained unnervingly still. The weight of something unspoken pressed against the hall, heavy and waiting.

And then the shadow expanded.

It wasn't alone.

Two more figures emerged from the darkness, flanking it like sentinels.

Lucifer's breath slowed, his wings twitching involuntarily. His gaze snapped between them and the central shadow, this being that moved with no hesitation, no fear, no allegiance to anything he knew.

And then the truth began to sink in.

Timor and Dolor didn't flank demons.

They obeyed only devils.

And yet, they stood beside the first shadow.

Not as captors or hunters but as something else entirely.

Lucifer's throat tightened.

This wasn't an intruder, an enemy at Hell's gates.

This was something that had come home.

Lucifer inhaled slowly, watching, waiting. His mind roared with possibilities, trying to place this *thing*, this presence, this being that had entered his kingdom and dared to shift the balance of his rule.

And then, it spoke.

The voice came from nowhere and everywhere, layered and raw, slipping into the cracks of the chamber like a liquid shadow. "I am home."

Lucifer's entire body locked.

The voice was distorted, inhuman.

But something in it, something beneath it, was familiar.

A flicker of recognition, so faint it nearly slipped through his fingers.

And then the mist said his name. "Lucifer."

And in that moment, his world shattered.

Because he knew.

He knew exactly what had returned to him.

Not a stranger.

Not an enemy.

Not a shadow crawling from the depths.

It was Amber.

But not the one he'd touched, kissed, burned for.

This was something else entirely, something that was never meant to exist.

For all his fury, power, and pride, Lucifer now understood that Amber had never been and would never be his to command.

77

The Angels and the Abomination

A stunned silence fell over the Magna Aula.

The torches that still burned flickered weakly, their light swallowed by the thick presence of shadow curling through the room. The ground beneath them had stilled, but the weight of what had just entered was undeniable.

No one spoke because no one knew what to say.

Lucifer was still staring, his expression unreadable, his body taut with something unfamiliar, not fear, not anger, but something close to both.

Amber floated there, or what was left of her. But it wasn't Lucifer who reacted first; it was Zagan. His breath was uneven, his hands trembling at his sides, not in rage, but in something closer to disbelief. His golden eyes flickered with the dull glow of the torches, his sharp mind racing to piece together what he saw.

This wasn't possible.

It wasn't possible.

Amber had been a pawn, a tool, a body to be traded, broken, and used as leverage. She was supposed to have been a means to an end.

She was never supposed to be this.

A mistake. A miscalculation. An anomaly.

His throat worked, but he had no words for the first time in millennia.

Timor and Dolor stood at her side, their presence undeniable, unwavering. Not chained. Not bound. Not waiting for orders by anyone but her.

They were *hers* now.

Zagan's fingers curled into fists. His breath hitched, fury and realization battling in his chest as he turned his gaze toward the Heavenly creatures.

Michael's grip on his sword was tight, and the tension in his stance was a visible sign of restraint. Gabriel's expression had darkened the flicker of something troubled beneath his golden eyes. Even Raphael had gone unnaturally still, his hands clasped together, but not in prayer.

They hadn't expected this.

Zagan's lips curled into something sharp and bitter. "You knew." His voice was rough and low, a whisper edged with something dangerous. He turned toward God, who had yet to speak since the shadow Amber had entered. "You knew this was a possibility."

Michael shifted, the slightest flicker of hesitation crossing his face before replacing it with the same unwavering control he always carried. God didn't answer.

Raphael spoke instead, "We feared it."

A heavyweight dropped into the silence.

Zagan's mouth parted slightly before he let out a sharp breath, half a laugh, half a snarl. "Feared?" He shook his head, a humorless sound escaping his throat. "You fear many things, angels. But you do nothing to stop them." His eyes burned. "You could have stopped this before it began. And yet, you watched. You let it happen."

His hands trembled as his voice rose, bitter and wild with the realization of it all.

"Was that your plan all along?" He turned his gaze back to God, his power crackling at his fingertips, desperate for something to hold onto. "To see if she would survive? To see if she would become *this*?"

God was silent.

And that was the answer.

Zagan stepped back, his jaw clenching, his fury coiling like a snake inside his chest. "You never wanted Amber," he murmured, shaking his head as if he still couldn't comprehend the depth of his failure. His voice turned hoarse, almost broken, "You wanted to see if Lucifer could do what even you could not."

The words landed like a strike of lightning through the hall.

Lucifer's head snapped toward Zagan, his eyes narrowing, but he didn't speak.

Because there was truth in the accusation.

A truth no one had ever considered.

Michael exhaled through his nose, his grip tightening on his sword. "We didn't plan this," he said, his voice even, but there was an edge to it.

"But you let it happen," Zagan spat. "Because you wanted to know if a devil could create an heir."

Gabriel flinched. A slight movement, nearly imperceptible.

But Lucifer saw it, and so did Zagan.

A sharp, bitter laugh left him as he threw his head back, exhaling like something inside of him had finally unraveled. "That's it, isn't it?" His eyes were wild now, filled with something unhinged, something broken and triumphant all at once. "You feared it. You let it happen to see if it could be done." He turned to Lucifer now, the madness in his gaze sharpening to something wicked. "And now, you have your answer."

He gestured toward Amber, toward whatever she'd become.

Hell had never had an heir because no devil had ever been able to create one. And now, standing before them was the first impossible thing. Not just Amber. But the child she carried.

Lucifer's grip tightened at his sides. His power throbbed through the room, shadows curling outward in warning.

But Zagan only grinned.

"Tell me, angels." His voice dropped lower, mocking, taunting. "What do you do with an anomaly? What do you do with something that was never meant to exist?"

Michael's expression was stone.

Gabriel didn't answer.

Raphael lowered his gaze, but not out of subservience, out of uncertainty.

Zagan let out another laugh, shaking his head. "You don't know." His voice was full of something almost gleeful. "For the first time in eternity, you don't know what to do."

He turned to Lucifer now, the weight of the revelation settling between them like a final nail in a coffin. "You don't know what to do either."

The words landed sharper than any blade.

Because he was right.

Lucifer stood before Amber, before the thing she'd become, before the power that had never existed.

And for the first time in centuries, Lucifer had no idea what to do.

78

Heaven's Hounds

Amber stood at the center, still shifting, a being of shadow and form, flickering between existence and something more.

Gabriel took a slow step forward, his presence calm but unwavering. The offer was simple: "Amber, come with us. We can care for you and your child. This is not a demand," he said, his voice steady and measured. Kind but firm, this is protection."

The Magna Aula had grown eerily quiet. The flames of the torches flickered, their glow barely touching the darkness that curled at Amber's feet, deep and endless.

Amber's head tilted slightly, her form still flickering, unstable, caught between a formless shadow and something solid.

"You expect me to believe that?" Her voice didn't come from anywhere in particular. It came from everywhere. It seeped through the cracks in the walls, slid beneath the throne, coiled around the edges of the Archangels' armor like whispering fingers.

The shadows stirred, thickening.

Raphael moved next. Slowly. Carefully. Like one would approach something unpredictable. "Wouldn't a child be better off above than below?" His voice carried no malice, only certainty. "Wouldn't you? You don't have to reject the light, Amber. You can choose to leave."

Something shifted.

Not in Amber, in Hell itself.

A ripple of energy passed through the hall, unseen but undeniable, as if the very realm was reacting to his words.

But Amber didn't move. She didn't reach for them. Didn't reach for anyone. Because she already knew the answer.

She'd chosen.

The moment she'd stepped willingly into Hell, clawed through the trials and survived.

She'd never belonged to Heaven.

Gabriel sighed as if he already knew her answer as if he'd hoped for something else.

And finally, God spoke.

"Amber." His voice wasn't cruel. Not forceful. But it was absolute. "You do not belong here. You will come with us."

A ripple tore through Hell.

The air shook, and the very foundation of the Magna Aula trembled as if even this realm couldn't defy Him.

The weight of His words pressed into Amber's very being, wrapping around her like unseen chains, like a force much more significant than herself.

For the briefest moment, it seemed as if Heaven's will was absolute.

Amber's breath hitched.

She could feel a pull, an unraveling like something was reaching through her, weaving into her shadows, fraying the edges of what she'd become as if the fabric of her being had already begun to obey.

She wavered, and the shadows around her shrank just slightly, and Timor and Dolor shifted a microstep away.

But Michael saw it.

And that was all he needed.

The Archangel lifted his hand, his movements controlled, practiced, as if he'd done this before.

"No—" she breathed, but the light struck instantly.

An impossibly bright beam extended from Michael's hand, a golden, burning ray of divinity stretching toward her, calling to her.

It wasn't violent or cruel.

It was final.

Amber choked on a gasp as the light wrapped around her, into her, through her, tearing at the fabric of her existence.

It was pulling her apart.

Piece by piece.

Severing her from this place, from this power, from everything she'd fought to claim.

The pull was relentless.

Timor and Dolor flinched.

She was being taken.

And for the first time, she had no shape to fight it.

She stumbled, gasping, but there was nothing to grab onto.

No ground.

No walls.

No body.

Only the pull.

Only the light.

Only—

"ENOUGH."

The word cracked through the air like thunder, Lucifer's voice sharp and unrelenting.

Amber couldn't see him, but she felt him. Felt his power surge forward like a tidal wave of shadow.

He wasn't letting her go.

Not to them. Not to anyone.

The light wavered for the first time, flickering at its edges as Lucifer's presence collided with it.

But still, it held her.

Still, it tried to pull her.

And Amber, heart racing, soul fraying, understood.

Lucifer couldn't stop this alone.

It had to be her.

She didn't want Heaven.

She didn't want their light, their promises, their control.

She wanted Hell.

And so, she fought.

With everything inside her, she closed the shadows tighter, wrapping them around herself, sealing off every crack the light tried to enter. She wasn't light. She wasn't theirs.

She was something else.

Lucifer's shadows surged again, not to shield her but to join her, intertwining with her own and amplifying what she had begun.

His power became hers.

Not a rescue.

A reckoning.

Together, their shadows rose, coiling like living tendrils around the golden light, absorbing it, consuming it, and changing it.

For the first time in eons, Michael's power faltered.

His stance braced. His breath caught.

The glow meant to reclaim her flickered and bent, twisting into something it had never been before.

Something unclaimed.

Something unstoppable.

Amber's breath steadied. Her grip tightened.

And when Michael reached for her, desperate and defiant, she didn't flinch.

The golden glow cracked at the edges, black veins spidering through its core.

Amber met his eyes and whispered, "I don't belong to you."

Michael stepped back.

Heaven had no answer for this.

The Archangel took a deliberate step forward. The tension between everyone thickened, manifesting as a battle of wills in the air around them.

"You cannot take her." Lucifer said, his voice low, lethal, unwavering. His wings stretched behind him, his presence commanding, unyielding. "She belongs here."

Michael didn't waver. "She belongs where the child inside her will not be tainted by Hell's corruption."

The words were measured, yet they struck like a hammer, rippling through the chamber like an unavoidable truth.

Lucifer's fingers twitched at his sides. "That child is mine," he growled, his power flaring, dark and commanding. "And per the clause that governs my reign, if I bear an heir, my claim to this throne is irrefutable."

The words echoed through the Magna Aula.

Every one of them knew what that meant.

Heaven's grip over Hell would be broken.

Lucifer's rule would, *could*, never be rechallenged.

The ancient law was undeniable.

Michael's expression didn't change, but the air around him grew colder, heavier, a pressure that threatened to swallow the space between them.

"You are not wrong," the Archangel admitted. "But you are not right either."

Lucifer's eyes narrowed.

Gabriel took a step forward now, his golden gaze unreadable. "Your claim is only cemented if she declares herself yours, verbally and willingly. The clause does not apply until Amber swears herself to your side."

Lucifer stilled.

The weight of those words crashed through him like a storm.

Amber hadn't done so.

She'd never spoken the words, never solidified what had been written in the ancient laws. And because of that, Heaven still had the right to take her.

The realization clawed through him like slow-burning agony.

Michael's wings stretched slightly, the light around him bending, his presence almost glowing in certainty.

"She missed the ceremony," he said, finality in his tone. "She has not claimed her place. So she does not yet belong here. And until she does, we will take her and the child."

The weight of the decree slammed through the hall, crashing like a bell tolling in the distance. Lucifer's wings flared, his body tensed, his power surging outward in a silent, violent protest. And Hell trembled. The temperature dropped, shadows stretched violently, and the stone beneath their feet splintered.

But before anyone else could move, Amber began to change.

The flickering, shifting shadow form that had carried her through the Seventh Island and to Castellum Umbrae began to solidify, twisting and warping as the weight of her power unfurled around her. Lucifer turned sharply, his breath caught in his throat as he felt the pull, the change, the inevitable coronation of something beyond mortal understanding.

And to everyone's disbelief, Timor and Dolor knelt.

Not to Lucifer or Zagan.

Not to Michael or any of the Heavenly creatures.

To *her*.

A slow breath escaped Amber's lips, but it didn't belong to the girl who'd once been mortal.

This was something else.

Something final.

The shadows around her thickened, molding, sharpening, the very fabric of her being burning into something undeniable, unshakable. Amber's form shifted, her body no longer flickering like a wavering storm but becoming defined, shaped, whole. Her eyes burned red-ringed black, the red pulsing with the darkness, a war of her true self existing within her irises. Her skin was laced with faint markings of something ancient, something that had been waiting to exist. It was smooth but not human, kissed by Hell's fire and the void's embrace, shimmering with subtle darkness that seemed to drink in the light around her rather than reflect it.

Her wings unfurled slowly, stretching wide and endless. They were not of flesh or bone but of woven shadows, thick and curling like tendrils of the void. They shifted with her breath, alive, the edges lined with faint, glowing golden veins of divine power she'd stolen from Heaven's reach.

Her hair, long and weightless, moved as if caught in an invisible current, flowing with the slow, hypnotic grace of something untouchable, something beyond the reach of time. It was no longer just blonde; it was stolen sunlight. Divine and damned, chaos and creation, balanced and broken all at once.

Her horns, which appeared as she rolled her neck out, rose from her temples. Sleek and sharp, they curved like the celestial crescents that had once belonged only to the divine. They pulsed faintly with power as if they'd grown not from corruption but from ascension.

She was no longer bound by fire, light, or shadow; she'd become something more.

The gown she wore was woven from the fabric of Hell itself, shifting between armor and elegance, the material glistening with dark embroidery that flickered and moved like living ink. It coiled around her like a whisper, cinching at the waist but flowing outward, pooling at her feet like a shadow that bled into the floor.

She lifted her head, and her voice carried through the hall like a force of nature, "I do not need a ceremony."

She wasn't just choosing Hell.

She was becoming part of it.

The walls shook, and Amber's body solidified, raw power lacing through her very existence. The transformation wasn't forced; it was claimed.

And then, she smiled.

A slow, knowing thing filled with the weight of her undeniable truth, "I am Hell's. And I am his."

The words rippled outward, binding, final, as power crashed through the room. Lucifer inhaled sharply as he felt it happen.

The clause was sealed.

Heaven couldn't take her.

The baby would be born in Hell.

His reign was cemented.

Michael's expression darkened, his jaw tensing, his wings flaring as if to brace against the weight of what had just transpired. Gabriel exhaled, his golden gaze flickering with something deep and troubled. Raphael exhaled softly as if he'd known this would happen all along. And Zagan stumbled back as the full realization struck him all at once.

Lucifer stepped forward, his gaze locked onto Amber's, and for the first time in all of Hell's existence, there was no question.

No hesitation.

No uncertainty.

Only the undeniable truth.

She was his She-Devil.

And she'd chosen her place.

Forever.

79

The Fading Light

T he air in the Magna Aula was thick with power, Hell's fire clashing against Heaven's light, the echoes of Amber's declaration still trembling through the stone.

She stood at the center of it all: The She-Devil.

Hell's ruler and Lucifer's Queen.

For a moment, no one spoke.

As she turned to look at him, the darkness at her back moved. It wasn't just her shadow any more. It was Hell's. The night that had once been untamed, that had once obeyed only the will of Lucifer, now curled at her feet. They answered to her now. When she breathed, Hell breathed with her.

She wasn't just a ruler.

Not just a She-Devil.

She was Angustia.

Hell's balance and Hell's most dangerous creation.

As Lucifer approached, he extended his hand toward her, and she took it gently, her fingers curling effortlessly into his. His gaze lingered on the point of contact, watching as his power unfurled across her skin like delicate spiderwebs cascading up her arms in intricate, pulsing threads. But that wasn't what stunned him.

What stole the breath from his lungs was the way her power surged in return.

It spread over his unmarred skin like smoke curling from a cigarette, ghosting along his arms with an electric hum. He felt it slither and coil, not in resistance, but in recognition, until it reached the sigil of the seven-pointed star branded upon his chest. Lucifer inhaled sharply as her power wove itself into the mark, the ancient symbol glowing a deep crimson before dulling into a subdued thrum beneath his skin.

His gaze snapped to Amber, expecting shock, but she was transfixed, still watching as his power finished its ascent, reaching the center of her chest. Then, in a single, searing pulse, the power that had wrapped around his sigil snapped back to her, their energies entwining in a final, irrevocable claim.

Amber gasped as fire licked across her collarbone, her skin burning as if seared by something beyond mortal comprehension. Together, they watched as the seven-pointed star, the very sigil that had marked Lucifer as ruler of Hell for centuries, etched itself into her flesh.

It didn't shimmer with light nor flicker like flames. It pulsed a slow, rhythmic surge of power, ancient and absolute, an equilibrium of darkness and something more. Something that had always been a part of her.

Slowly, Lucifer lifted his gaze, and Amber did the same. Their eyes met, and at that moment, there was no longer any doubt.

Amber hadn't merely chosen Hell; Hell had chosen her.

She wasn't just his Queen; she was its Queen.

And now, there was nothing Heaven could do to take her back, or so they thought.

The silence was palpable until a low, knowing chuckle filled the space.

Lucifer looked around for the source of the sound, but Michael and Gabriel remained stoic. Even Zagan was silent as he looked around. Only Raphael stepped aside, allowing God to step past him; he was the source of the chuckling.

"Darling," the word dripped with something infuriatingly soft as he looked at Amber, its warmth masking the sheer weight of its finality.

God's presence had been quiet throughout the exchange, His power lingering but restrained. Now, it filled the room, pressing into the very bones of every being present, "Although your proclamations are divinely sweet, the rules were clear." Amber's breath stilled. "You needed the ceremony."

The shadows around her rippled, uneasy, like they didn't know if they should attack or run away. Lucifer stiffened, his wings flaring, his stance bracing for something unseen.

God exhaled as if He were amused as if this was a conversation rather than a declaration of war, "We simply cannot allow this child to be born in Hell." The words hit like a stone dropping into a still lake, the impact unseen but felt everywhere.

Amber's fingers twitched, power curling at her sides, a silent protest already forming.

God's gaze flickered toward her, and for the first time, she felt something reaching for her, something inevitable. "I was giving you an option to come with us, but the truth is..." The world stilled. "You don't have one."

The silence was deafening.

Michael's eyes widened.

Gabriel stiffened.

Even Raphael, who was always so composed, lifted his head in something close to regretful knowing.

Lucifer took a sharp step forward, his voice a warning, a threat, and a promise all at once, "Don't—"

But it was too late.

The light came instantly.

A blinding flash, pure and all-consuming, exploded through the Magna Aula with a force that sent Lucifer and Zagan staggering backward.

By the time the light had dulled and Lucifer could open his eyes again, Amber was gone.

The angels had vanished with her, their forms swallowed by the sheer divinity of the moment, leaving nothing but the heavy stillness of Hell behind.

There hadn't been a fight or a choice.

And now there was just absence.

Lucifer's shadows roared outward, colliding violently against the remnants of the fading light, but it was too late.

Hell had just lost its Queen.

For a moment, there was nothing but crushing silence. The air in the Magna stilled, thick with an unbearable pressure, as if the entire realm of Hell held its breath. Lucifer's shadows, ever restless, froze in place. And then, The Magna Aula trembled.

Columns didn't simply splinter; they exploded, fractures spiderwebbing through their ancient stone before they collapsed into ruin. Shadows writhed violently, twisting and thrashing like living things caught in a tempest. The air, thick with sulfur and smoke, curdled into something unrecognizable.

The walls buckled. The foundations groaned. The very essence of his domain shrank away from him.

Lucifer stood at the center of the destruction, his breaths shallow and controlled, but his hands trembled at his sides, but not from weakness, never from weakness.

From rage.

No one took what was his.

Not God. Not Heaven. Not the celestial forces who'd already stripped him of everything once before. He'd suffered exile, waged war, crushed rebellion after rebellion with fire and fury, reducing would-be usurpers to ash at his feet. But this, this was an abomination. A direct affront to his rule, claim, and very existence.

This was unforgivable.

His fury erupted.

The Thronum Lapsorum, his throne, the seat of his dominion, cracked beneath the sheer weight of his power. Its obsidian frame split with a deafening shatter, exploding outward like a dying star. Shards of black stone, pulsing with the remnants of his infernal magic, ricocheted through the chamber, embedding themselves into the walls, the floors, and anything unfortunate to still stand.

Hellfire surged.

Crimson veins of raw, unbridled destruction tore through the floor, searing everything in their wake. The heat was unbearable, suffocating, but Lucifer felt none of it. The Magna Aula itself bent under his wrath, the infernal architecture groaning as if Hell feared it wouldn't survive its own king.

The grand iron chandeliers, suspended by chains as old as time, snapped from above, plummeting into the inferno below. Smoke choked the air. The sound of splitting stone and roaring flames consumed the chamber, but there was something far more terrifying beneath it.

Silence.

Lucifer stopped.

In an instant, all movement ceased. The fires burned, the ruins smoked, but Lucifer himself was still. His body was rigid, his hands curled into fists so tight that his bones would've snapped beneath the pressure if he were mortal.

His usual golden eyes now glowed molten-red with fury, burned through the haze. His shadows remained deathly still, awaiting his command.

A plan was already forming.

He exhaled, slow and steady, the sound almost *dangerous* in its restraint. His mind, a storm of calculation and vengeance, narrowed in on the next step as he forced the rage into something sharper, something lethal. There'd be no hesitation.

His voice, when it came, was calm. Too calm.

"Abelia." The name was spoken like a death sentence.

She was already there, lingering in the ruined threshold, carefully maintaining distance, as if she feared he might turn his wrath upon her next. *Smart girl.*

Lucifer didn't turn to face her. His gaze remained fixed on the remnants of his shattered throne.

"Summon the Legatus," he ordered his voice smooth but carrying a razor's edge. "Now."

A sharp nod. A flicker of movement, and she vanished.

Lucifer rolled his shoulders, forcing the last traces of unchecked fury to settle, but the anger remained cold and lethal, coiled like a serpent in his chest. His forces would be gathered, and every weapon in his arsenal would be prepared.

But there was one problem.

He couldn't reach Heaven.

The realization sent a fresh wave of loathing through him. The celestial realm remained beyond his reach, untouchable, shielded by divine law. He couldn't storm its gates the way he'd once stormed the halls of Hell. He'd spent centuries ensuring no celestial influence could touch Hell, but the same barriers worked both ways; he couldn't reach the kingdom of light any more than they could reach his without consequence. The only way he knew of was the same way God had been able to reach Hell just moments ago. A resident needed to call upon them, asking them to enter, using the chant Zagan had used.

The only problem was that no one would call Lucifer to Heaven.

He needed a way in.

And he needed it *now*.

A low, slow chuckle echoed through the broken chamber.

Lucifer's jaw tightened. He didn't need to turn to know who it was.

"You need something," Zagan drawled, leaning lazily against the fractured remains of a column, his arms crossed, amusement flickering in his dark eyes. "And lucky for you, I have exactly what you're looking for."

Lucifer's expression didn't shift. His fury had settled into something far more dangerous than rage: purpose.

His gaze, molten and unwavering, finally met Zagan's, "Then start talking."

"You see, I would, but what do I get out of this?" Zagan's arrogance rippled through the room, hitting Lucifer like poison in his veins.

Lucifer moved without thought.

One second, Zagan was lounging against a fractured column, that insufferable smirk still lingering at the edges of his mouth. The next, Lucifer had him by the throat.

The chamber shook as he slammed Zagan into the broken remains of a wall. Stone cracked, the impact sending a shockwave through the ground. Shadows lashed out violently in response, wrapping around Zagan's arms and legs, curling like tendrils of ink tightening around prey.

Lucifer's grip was crushing. Unrelenting.

"Tell me," he said, his voice lethal, barely above a whisper. The kind of quiet that came before an execution.

Zagan's hands grasped Lucifer's wrist, his nails digging into his skin, but the Devil didn't move.

He only squeezed harder.

Zagan's smirk faltered. "You, *kff*, kill me; you'll never get her back."

Lucifer slammed him into the wall again. Harder.

The stones shattered, raining like acid around them.

A deep, guttural growl ripped through Lucifer's chest. His patience was gone. His restraint was thin. His vision swam red with the need to destroy.

"You called them here." The words were sharp, *deadly*, edged with something raw and unforgiving.

Zagan coughed, his breath ragged. "You're going to have to be more specific."

Lucifer's shadows lashed like whips, slicing deep into Zagan's skin. Blackened veins of infernal energy spread from the wounds, searing through his flesh painfully slow, not enough to destroy, but enough to make him suffer.

Zagan gritted his teeth, a short, breathless laugh escaping him. "I didn't *give* her to them," he rasped, voice strained. "I only set the bait. I didn't think they'd actually..."

Lucifer's grip tightened.

The Magna Aula rumbled, the very air becoming suffocating under the weight of his fury. Everything inside him screamed for blood.

"I could end you." The words weren't a threat. They were a fact.

Zagan knew it, too. He had always known Lucifer was more powerful than he was. Lucifer had spared him once; at the time, maybe he wasn't powerful enough, but now? Now, Lucifer could blink, and Zagan would be nothing more than a cautionary tale. Lucifer could crush him here and now, burn his essence from existence, rip him apart piece by piece until there was nothing left to remember him by.

But he didn't.

Because despite everything, despite the unforgivable betrayal, Lucifer needed him.

Damn it all.

A long, seething breath hissed through Lucifer's teeth. His grip loosened, but only slightly. "You will fix this."

Zagan coughed, inhaling sharply as the shadows loosened their vice-like grip. His throat was raw, and his usual bravado weakened but not gone. He lifted his gaze, dark eyes gleaming with something dangerously close to amusement.

"Well," he rasped, rubbing his bruised throat. "If you'd rather throw me through a few more walls, I'd understand."

Lucifer nearly did.

Instead, he released him, stepping back as the air in the Magna Aula crackled around him. His control was razor-thin.

Zagan rolled his shoulders, wincing as he worked out the damage. "I'll take that as a *no*." He sighed, tilting his head, assessing Lucifer like he was enjoying this too much. "You *really* don't like it when something gets taken from you, huh?"

Lucifer's jaw locked.

He didn't answer.

Didn't need to.

Instead, he turned sharply, his pace quick and determined, and strode toward the center of the ruined throne room. His wings twitched, and shadows curled beneath his feet like storm clouds ready to burst.

"I don't care what it takes," he said, voice dark and merciless. "You will get me into Heaven."

Zagan let out a low whistle. "That's a tall order."

Lucifer stopped.

His head turned slightly, golden eyes burning, "I wasn't asking."

The temperature in the room dropped. Zagan exhaled, tilting his head with a smirk that was far more cautious than before.

"Well then," he murmured. "Let's get to work."

80

A Prison Without Walls

N othing.

At first, that was all there was.

An endless expanse of white, stretching in every direction, swallowing everything in its immensity. There were no walls. No ceiling. No floor she could truly feel beneath her. It was like floating, like being suspended in an empty eternity, weightless and disconnected from anything real.

Then, the pain came.

A dull ache spread through her limbs, but it wasn't like any pain she'd felt before. This was a weakness. The sensation of something gnawing at her, leeching at the fire that had burned so fiercely in her veins since arriving in Hell.

Her fingers twitched, but something stopped them from moving.

Amber inhaled sharply. Light wrapped around her wrists and ankles, and very form, golden chains that were warm, not searing, but inescapable. Not metal. Not magic. Something more. Something that made her stomach twist with a deep, primal unease.

She tried to pull free.

Nothing.

Tried again, harder.

Still nothing.

Her power crackled beneath her skin, a familiar fury building inside her, but the moment she tried to summon it, the light tightened, draining it from her like a parasite sucking marrow from bone.

Amber's breath hitched.

Her gaze snapped downward, to her chest, to the sigil.

The seven-pointed star, Lucifer's mark. Her mark. Hell's claim on her.

It was fading.

The edges, once solid and unmovable, had begun to blur as if something was trying to erase it from her flesh, from her very soul.

Panic surged through her veins, mixing with rage.

No.

No, no, no—

"Relax, child," a voice murmured.

Amber's head snapped up.

They were watching her.

Figures in white and gold, silhouettes of celestial brilliance, angels with faces too perfect and untouched by anything real, as if they were carved from the concept of purity itself.

Her lip curled. *Disgusting.*

Amber pulled against the restraints again, harder this time, her teeth clenched. "Let me go."

One of the angels tilted their head slightly, almost as if they pitied her.

"You do not belong there," the angel said, her voice like chimes in a winter breeze. "You were stolen. Claimed by something that was never meant to have you."

Amber let out a sharp, humorless laugh despite the exhaustion coiling in her bones. "That's where you're wrong. *I chose Hell.*"

"You were deceived."

She snarled. "You don't know a damn thing about me."

The angels didn't react. Their presence was calm, suffocatingly, and their patience unshaken, which only made her angrier.

One of them, taller than the others, stepped forward. "You will only be held here until the child is born."

The words hit her like ice water.

The fight in her stilled, just for a moment, "What?"

The angel's expression didn't change. "You are carrying something sacred. Something we cannot allow to be born, unless born as an angel here in Heaven. Once the child is born, you will be free to choose your fate."

Her stomach tightened as the angel stepped aside.

And Amber saw her.

A small child stood at the edge of the nothingness. *Human.* Young. Innocent.

Her heart lurched.

No.

This wasn't real. This was a trick, an illusion. But, when the little girl's eyes met hers...Amber froze.

Her chest tightened as something cold and unbearable curled in her gut. She recognized that face.

The golden curls. The soft, round cheeks.

It was the same child from the vision that Lucifer had shown her all that time ago. From the dream life, he'd promised her in exchange for her soul.

She was real.

Amber's breath came in sharp, uneven pulls. The air in the vast white expanse felt too thin, sterile, and *wrong*. Her pulse roared in her ears, drowning out the suffocating silence of Heaven. But she couldn't take her eyes off the little girl, standing at the edge of the nothingness, soft, untouched, impossibly absolute. But it wasn't possible. It couldn't be possible.

And yet, she knew.

Deep in her bones, in the marrow of her very being, she knew exactly who that little girl was: her child.

Amber's pulse roared in her ears, her entire body rigid as she stared into the girl's innocent blue eyes, but they held no recognition or awareness of who Amber was.

Because she'd never been born.

A cold, unbearable weight pressed down on Amber's chest. Her fingers twitched at her sides, aching to reach out, to touch, but she couldn't. Her chains held firm, their golden light burning into her wrists.

One of the angels spoke softly, almost gently, "This was meant to be your daughter." Amber's stomach twisted. "She would've lived a full life," the angel continued, "free of pain. Loved. Protected. She would've had your kindness. Your humanity."

The words wrapped around her like a noose.

This is a lie.

Her mind screamed it, but her body betrayed her; her breath hitched, her throat burned, and something deep inside her ached. But she'd chosen a different path. She'd chosen Hell.

But in doing so, had she truly killed this child before she could ever exist? The thought gutted her.

She gritted her teeth, forcing her voice to steady. They were manipulating her. She wouldn't break.

Amber lifted her chin, forcing steel into her voice. "That life was a lie."

The angel blinked, unbothered by her response. "It was what you wanted."

Amber's eyes burned, but she didn't falter. She refused. "It's not what I chose."

The angel sighed as if disappointed. "And yet, you still grieve her."

Amber's breath caught.

For a fleeting second, she hated how much those words rang true. But she didn't let them see it. She clenched her jaw, forcing down the ache, smothering the rising wave of doubt. They wanted her to hesitate. To question herself. To regret.

She wouldn't give them that.

Her lips curled in defiance. "She never existed."

A long silence followed before another angel stepped aside. And Amber saw the second child.

Her stomach plummeted.

This time, the weight of pure, unshakable terror crashed down on her. Because the child before her wasn't human.

It was real.

Amber's pulse stopped.

The baby cradled in an angel's arms was so small, but it was undeniably Amber's. She knew it in her bones, in her blood.

Soft white wings curled at its small shoulders, shifting as it moved. A faint, angelic glow pulsed around it as if Heaven had already claimed its soul.

Amber's veins turned to ice.

No.

NO.

"She is yours," the angel murmured, "but she belongs to Heaven now."

The words shattered something inside her.

"You planned this," Amber said, voice low, shaking with something close to rage. "*You knew.*"

The taller angel didn't flinch. Didn't waver.

"It is the only way," she said, as though stating some universal truth. "If born in Heaven, the child will be cleansed. It will belong to the light. Lucifer's reign will not be sealed. Hell will remain unstable, vulnerable to—"

Amber lunged or tried to. The chains tightened, yanking her backward, searing into her skin, draining what little power she had left. She gasped as something sharp and searing ripped through her, a force she couldn't shake, couldn't fight. The golden restraints pulsed, siphoning her strength, fury, and essence. She sagged forward, panting, her vision darkening at the edges. She let out a raw, furious snarl, but it didn't matter. She was trapped. Helpless.

The angels watched impassively.

"The baby will never know suffering," the angel continued, unmoved by Amber's struggle. "It will never know, Hell. It will never be claimed by darkness."

Amber's vision blurred, her mind spinning, her pulse wild with desperation.

They were taking it.

Her child.

Lucifer's child.

If it was born in Heaven, his rule would never be cemented. But more than that, Lucifer's hold on Amber would be broken, and their child would never be his.

Her stomach twisted.

She couldn't let that happen.

"Stop fighting," the shortest one said. "This is what is best for the child. For you. The darkness in you will fade, and you will be as you were always meant to be."

Amber laughed.

It was raw, breathless, bitter beyond words.

"*As I was meant to be?*" she spat, lifting her head to glare at them. Her limbs trembled under the force of the restraints, but she forced herself to stand taller. "You think you can cleanse me? You think you can turn my child into some hollow, winged puppet?"

The angel's face remained blank. "You are still connected to Hell. But in time, that will fade."

Amber's heart slammed against her ribs.

Her hand twitched against the restraints, fighting to move, fighting to touch the sigil on her chest. Hell's claim would vanish if they kept her here long enough if they drained enough of her power.

Amber took a slow, steady breath, forcing herself to ignore the unbearable pull of weakness clawing at her. She had to think. Had to figure out how to get out of this.

She tore her gaze from the child and back to the angels. "You think you're protecting something sacred." She let the words drip with venom. "You think you're saving a piece of Heaven, bringing an heir of Hell into your little prison of purity, and washing it clean."

The tallest angel didn't confirm nor deny.

Amber narrowed her eyes. "But you're afraid, aren't you?"

That got a reaction. A subtle one. Barely there. A flicker in the angel's expression, gone as fast as it had come.

Amber's lips curled.

Good.

"You wouldn't be doing this if you weren't afraid of what this child means," she said, voice sharpening. "If you weren't afraid of me."

The angel studied her for a long moment. Then: "We do not fear you."

Amber smiled. A slow, dangerous thing despite the weight pressing down on her. "Then why am I chained?"

Silence.

A long, heavy pause stretched between them.

Then, the angels stepped back as one single organism. "You will come to understand in time. You will see the truth."

Amber's head snapped up, eyes blazing with hate.

"The only truth," she growled, "is that I will burn this place to the ground before I let you take my baby."

An angel sighed.

"As expected," she murmured, then turned away. "We will give you time to accept your fate."

Amber kept her smirk in place, but her panic only deepened inside. The baby cooed slightly in the angel's arms, and Amber's heart sank because it sounded like a bell. Soft and pure and light. Amber's breathing came sharp, ragged, her body shaking under the strain of her fury. She wouldn't let this happen.

Even if it killed her.

"You can fight," the last angel said before following the rest, "but this is already happening. The longer you stay, the more Hell's claim on you will fade. And once it does, you will see the truth."

The chains tightened, and the child, *her child*, was pulled away into the light.

Amber screamed.

She fought harder than she ever had. She pulled, she writhed, she raged against the restraints, her power burning against them, but it was no use.

The child disappeared into the blinding abyss.

Amber was left alone.

And she'd never been more afraid.

81

The Devil who Loved

Lucifer stormed out of The Magna Aula, leaving ruin in his wake. The air was thick with the scent of fire and destruction; the shattered remains of his throne scattered like broken bones across the floor. But he paid it no mind.

His rage burned too hot.

His strides were measured, but the air around him warped, twisting with barely contained fury as he made his way to The Bellum Locus, his war room.

Behind him, his shadows dragged Zagan across the scorched marble floor. The First Devil struggled, grumbling between pained curses. "I can walk, you overdramatic bastard."

The shadows tightened.

Zagan huffed, giving up. His body thudded against the stone as he was pulled along like discarded prey.

The doors to The Bellum Locus flew open before Lucifer even reached them, slamming against the walls with a reverberating crack. His rage was no longer the wildfire that had nearly leveled The Magna Aula. That had been raw. Unrestrained. Destructive. This? This was something worse. This was controlled.

Poised.

Lethal.

He strode to the head of the long, obsidian table and sat heavily, his presence suffocating as the room seemed to shrink around him.

A single tap, just once, against the armrest of his chair.

The only sound in the room.

His shadows restrained Zagan to a chair in the corner, curling around his mouth like iron chains, cutting off his incessant complaints.

Abelia had gathered his Legatus, and they now stood at the edges of the space, their expressions unreadable. No one spoke.

Only Abelia stepped forward. She kept her head high, but there was an unease in her step, something almost hesitant, and that alone told Lucifer what he needed to know: she had answers, and he wasn't going to like them.

Lucifer didn't rise. Didn't move.

But the temperature in the room plummeted.

"Speak," his voice was quiet, eerily quiet.

Abelia inhaled, slow and steady, "Heaven has already begun the process of claiming Amber."

The air in the chamber cracked as the shadows not holding Zagan lurched, and the walls shuddered as if Hell was bracing for the coming storm.

Lucifer still didn't move.

He didn't breathe.

Didn't even blink.

His voice was calm when it came, "Clarify."

Abelia hesitated, just barely.

"They've restrained Amber," she said carefully. "They're severing her connection to Hell." She exhaled, the weight of the words sinking into the room like a death sentence.

A long, horrific silence followed.

Then, to everyone's surprise, Lucifer laughed.

It was soft at first. A low, dark sound. One that made the shadows on the walls twitch and curl made the very floor beneath them tremble.

The Legatus shifted where they stood, some casting wary glances at one another, but no dared to speak. Because the last time Lucifer laughed like that, cities burned.

The sound faded almost as quickly as it came.

And when he finally looked up, Abelia flinched.

Because his golden eyes burned like the heart of a collapsing star.

"They would dare find a loophole?" he murmured, voice barely above a whisper. "They would steal what is mine?"

The words weren't questions.

They were promises.

Zagan, who'd finally shaken the shadows just enough to open his mouth, blew a slow whistle. "Well," he mused, "this just got interesting."

Lucifer slammed his palm against the table, and the obsidian shattered. Large, jagged fractures spidered out from the impact, the glow of Hellfire seeping through the cracks. The Bellum Locus groaned, walls threatening to collapse inward, shadows writhing in agony, yet Lucifer's expression never wavered.

"We go to war," one of the Legatus said as if it were the only logical conclusion. "We'll summon the Bellatores."

"No," Lucifer's voice cut through the chaos, smooth and dangerous.

A war would take too long. Heaven would've time to prepare, to fortify itself. Or, worse yet, the child would already be born. No, he wouldn't give them the luxury of preparation. He'd take back what was his. Personally.

The Legatus remained silent, waiting for his order.

Lucifer turned to Abelia, his gaze razor-sharp. "You still have connections in Heaven."

Abelia nodded. "I do."

Lucifer took a step toward her. "Then you're going to tell me exactly how I get in."

She stiffened. "Lucifer."

"I don't want a way in through war." His voice dropped lower. Darker. "I don't want a passage through some diplomatic loophole."

He moved closer, towering over her now, and though Abelia was strong, though she'd stood against horrors that would break lesser beings, she couldn't hold his gaze.

"I want the way in that no one is watching," he said, voice smooth as silk. "The one they do not expect."

Abelia faltered. For the first time in centuries, she faltered.

Lucifer saw the hesitation, the uncertainty flickering in her usually composed features, and his golden eyes narrowed.

She had no answer.

She didn't know.

"I..." She swallowed. "I don't know of one."

The words rang hollow in the vast, smoldering chamber. Lucifer's jaw ticked. His fingers curled, slow and deliberate, at his sides. Hell had never been able to reach Heaven. The balance had been enforced, etched into the very fabric of existence.

Then, like a knife through butter, a low, amused chuckle broke the silence. Lucifer's golden eyes slid toward Zagan.

Leaning lazily against his restraints, dark eyes glinting with amusement.

"Well, well," he drawled, "it seems you need me after all."

Lucifer turned fully toward him, shadows curling at his feet.

"Speak carefully." His voice was lethal.

"See, I would, but..." he drawled, shifting in his restraints. "I think we both know that if you expect me to help, I should at least get a seat at the damn table."

Lucifer didn't react.

Zagan sighed dramatically. "Unless, of course, you'd rather try figuring out the Veil on your own. I'll even sit here quietly and watch while you fail." He smirked, but his eyes were calculating.

The room waited.

Lucifer didn't speak.

But after a moment, the shadows binding Zagan loosened. Though, not entirely, just enough for him to move, enough for him to stand, but not without reminding him who was in control. Zagan stretched leisurely, rolling his shoulders as he sauntered toward an open seat at the table. The shadows followed, curling around his wrists like shackles.

He didn't complain.

But Lucifer saw how his fingers twitched at his sides and how his smirk flickered, if only for a second.

Noted.

Lucifer exhaled slowly. His golden gaze swept across the table.

"Tell me," he said, his voice smooth and composed. Lethal. "How do I get in?"

Zagan's lips curled into a slow, deliberate smirk, "Like I said, that's tricky."

"It's impossible!" Abelia said sharply in her head, snapping toward him.

Zagan grinned. "Is it?"

Lucifer's patience thinned. "Explain."

Zagan let the silence stretch a little longer, just to test him. Then, finally, he sighed, shaking his head.

"There's a passage," he admitted. "One that doesn't belong to Heaven or Hell. A space between. A place where the rules bend just enough to let something... slip through."

Lucifer's eyes darkened.

"The Veil," he murmured.

Zagan snapped his fingers. "Bingo."

The room went still.

Abelia paled. "You can't be serious. That place is unstable, Lucifer; even if you make it through, you could be lost in it. the Veil isn't just a passage, it's a—"

"A graveyard," Lucifer finished. "A place for the things that don't belong."

"Exactly," Zagan said with a menacing smile. "No one is immortal in there. Time doesn't work as it does here or even in Heaven." He flicked a glance at Abelia. "The longer you stay, the faster it unravels you. And if you're there too long?" He made a slicing motion across his throat. "Poof. You'll age out of existence. No throne, no Hell, no dramatic exit. Just gone."

Lucifer glanced between Zagan and Abelia as they stared each other down. "Speak," he said pointedly to Abelia.

Abelia set her jaw before she spoke, her voice tight with something unspoken. "It's worse than that."

All eyes turned to her.

She lifted her chin, steadying herself. "Heaven can manipulate time."

A ripple of silence spread through the room.

Zagan's cocky posture stiffened just slightly.

Lucifer's gaze sharpened. "Explain."

Abelia's throat bobbed before she continued. "They can accelerate it. Bend it. Slow it if they want to, but they'll likely speed it up."

Lucifer said nothing, but the shadows around his chair thickened like a second skin.

Abelia kept going, unaware of the landmine she was walking toward. "If they want to sever her connection to Hell, to strip the sigil off her body, they'll need to weaken her. Fast. Rip her open in every way. And the easiest way to do that?"

She hesitated, "They'll collapse time around her."

Lucifer's grip on the table didn't change. Not visibly. But Zagan noticed it, the slightest twitch in his knuckles. His expression didn't break, but something behind his eyes did.

Abelia continued, oblivious. "If she's been there long enough already, we don't know what state she's in. For all we know, they're preparing to cut the last ties and rewrite her completely. And once that happens..."

Lucifer stood.

The scrape of his chair silenced the room. His shadows slithered out like vines, curling through the stone beneath them, and his golden eyes cut through the tension like flame through parchment.

"Then we're already late," he said, his voice low, steady, and terrifying.

Abelia stiffened, but she didn't speak again.

Zagan, now dead silent, didn't smirk. He *watched*. Because whatever Abelia had stumbled into, she hadn't known how close to the truth she'd come.

82

A Name Worth Losing Himself

"I don't care how long they think they have," he murmured. "I'm taking her back,"

Abelia said nothing.

Lucifer's golden eyes burned as he turned back to Zagan. "How do I get in?"

Zagan's grin stretched wider.

"That," he said, "is where it gets... tricky."

Lucifer waited.

Zagan took a slow, exaggerated breath. "Without being summoned," he gave a pointed look to Abelia, "The Veil is extremely unstable. Not only do you have to sacrifice something of grave importance just to open it. You can't enter it alone. The Veil doesn't work like that. You need something to anchor you to this realm; otherwise..."

He trailed off, flashing a sharp grin. "Otherwise, it'll swallow you whole."

Lucifer's fingers twitched. "And what do you suggest?"

Zagan hesitated, just for a second. Barely a flicker. But Lucifer caught it.

Zagan's grin wavered. His eyes darkened. "You have to soul-bind to someone willing to go in with you."

The world around them seemed to still, holding its breath, waiting to see how Lucifer would react. Soul-binding was dangerous. Seldom used by anyone. And for a lord to link his life, his very existence, to someone lesser? To tether his immortality to another?

Unheard of.

But to everyone's shock, Lucifer...smiled.

But it wasn't kind.

Lucifer turned his focus back to Zagan. "How do we open The Veil?"

Zagan tilted his head, watching him too carefully now. Then he exhaled dramatically. "Oh, this is the best part."

Lucifer didn't react. He simply waited.

Zagan leaned forward slightly, resting his arms on the table. His smirk sharpened, "The Veil requires an offering. Something permanent. Something irreplaceable. You don't just walk into The Veil. It doesn't want you there. And if it swallows us, we don't come back."

Lucifer's patience thinned. "Be specific; how do we open it?"

Zagan's grin stretched wider, savoring the moment, "Ritu Bestiae."

The chamber gasped. That ritual hadn't been performed in eons; it was too dangerous and unpredictable.

But Zagain only continued, his gaze locked on Lucifer, "The moment you step through, the Veil will take a memory of Amber."

The room stilled.

Abelia's eyes widened, and a small breath escaped.

Lucifer's grip tightened, "That's not an offer." He said through gritted teeth.

Zagan let out a light laugh, "It is to The Veil. Your memories and anything else it deems worth taking is seen as an offer as soon as you enter." He paused, and his voice turned light, too light. "And if you stay too long? Well... you might forget her entirely."

Lucifer's grip on the table tightened just slightly.

No one moved.

No one spoke.

His mind flickered to quick, sharp memories: Amber's voice. The way she laughed when she thought no one was watching. The look in her eyes when she'd chosen him.

Gone.

He could lose her. Before he even reached her.

He didn't realize his fingers had curled into fists.

The room waited.

Then, finally, Lucifer exhaled. Slowly, controlled, and dangerous, and loosened his grip on the table. "Then I won't stay long."

His voice didn't waver, but Syn's expression shattered for half a second.

Zagan chuckled, "Oh, brave words." He said, but he wasn't smiling anymore. "But let's be real. You won't have control over how long you're in there. Not really."

Lucifer didn't look at him, but his shadows grew darker. Zagan noticed, leaning too casually back in his chair. "What if you forget the way out?" Zagan continued, still testing. "What if you forget why you're even in there?"

Lucifer was silent for a long, long moment. Then, softly, "I suppose you should try your very best to remind me because, remember, if I go down, you're coming with me."

Zagan's smirk faltered.

Not enough for most to see. But Lucifer saw it. And for the first time, Zagan had nothing to say.

"Lucifer," Abelia spoke tentatively. Not afraid, but aware. Aware of just how close to the edge he already was.

Lucifer didn't look at her.

"Even if you make it through," she pressed, "Heaven is still fortified. This only gets you to the doorstep. How do you suppose to enter Heaven?"

"I will enter," he said, his voice smooth, absolute.

Abelia stared at him, "That's not an answer."

Lucifer didn't repeat himself; he didn't need to; he was going to get in, one way or another.

But she wasn't finished, "And the bond," Abelia said carefully, "Once you're tied to Zagan, how do you plan to break it?"

Zagan perked up slightly at that, tilting his head.

Lucifer remained silent for a moment before standing sharply, the shadows around him coiled instantly, thick and smoky, twisting through the air like a storm waiting to break.

His voice was quiet as he finally looked at her, "One problem at a time."

The Legatus fell silent as the reality of what was about to transpire sank in.

Then, to everyone's terror, Lucifer turned to Zagan with a smile. "I suppose you should start preparing." He said, his smirk only widening as he looked at Zagan.

Zagan's cocky grin faltered completely. "Oh, no, no, absolutely not. That's not what I meant."

Lucifer was already moving.

Shadows surged forward, curling around Zagan's wrists like ink, yanking him forward until they were nose to nose.

"I wasn't asking," Lucifer murmured.

Zagan's mouth opened, but before he could argue, Lucifer snapped his fingers.

The shadows tightened, and Zagan could no longer speak, only stare wide-eyed at Lucifer's unrelenting, merciless grin.

Finally, Lucifer pulled away, slow and final, as he turned from the table, "Prepare the ritual." And with that, he stormed out of the room, and no one dared to stop him. But just before disappearing, he spoke again, "We leave at nightfall."

And just like that, the conversation was over.

83

Decree of Fire

Amber didn't know how long she'd been alone.

Seconds. Hours. A lifetime.

Time didn't feel real here; nothing did.

The endless white pressed around her like a suffocating fog, still and unyielding, stretching into infinity. Her chains hadn't loosened, but the angels had left, taking her child with them.

Her child.

Her body convulsed with rage, but she had no outlet. Her fingers trembled at her sides, too weak, too drained, as black shadows sputtered into nothingness from the tips of her fingers. The golden restraints still burned, siphoning what was left of her power. Every time she pulled, they tightened, latching onto her like a parasite.

She gritted her teeth, inhaling through the ache, trying to steady herself and think when suddenly she knew something was wrong.

Her stomach twisted, a deep, sickening pull that spread from her core and curled around her ribs. A sharp, nauseating wave rolled through her, and her breath hitched as bile rose in her throat.

Amber barely had time to turn her head before she vomited.

Her knees buckled, but the chains held her upright, forcing her to remain exposed and vulnerable. Her body trembled violently, her breath coming in ragged, uneven pulls. The acrid taste burned her throat, and still, the sickness didn't stop.

Her stomach clenched again.

A second wave crashed through her, but it wasn't just nausea this time. It was something deeper. Something unnatural.

She gasped, her pulse roaring in her ears.

Her hands twitched toward her stomach.

A sinking feeling, like something shifting beneath her skin.

Amber's breath stilled.

Slowly, her fingers brushed against her lower abdomen, and she froze.

Too soon.

She'd barely known she was pregnant. Had barely even processed the fact that this impossibility was her reality. She couldn't be showing already.

But she was.

The realization sent a bolt of pure, unfiltered terror through her chest.

Her stomach wasn't flat anymore.

It had changed. Rounded, subtly, but undeniably.

Amber's fingers jerked away as if burned. Her mind screamed at her that this was wrong. That this was unnatural.

This wasn't supposed to be happening so fast. The angels had said nothing about this. Had they known?

Her stomach twisted again, and Amber bit back a cry. The chains kept her upright, kept her exposed, her body betraying her while she remained powerless to stop it.

Footsteps echoed.

She snapped her head up, panting, shaking, but glaring as the angels returned.

One of them, the tall, ethereal being with an expression carved from stone from before, paused before her.

Her gaze flickered down, landing on her stomach, and Amber watched in horror as a small smile crept across her face. It was soft and serene, but Amber's skin still crawled.

"Good," the angel murmured. "It's progressing more rapidly than we anticipated."

The words hit her like ice.

Amber's vision darkened at the edges, a combination of exhaustion, nausea, and unshakable horror.

They *knew*. They'd planned this. They were *controlling* this.

Her pulse pounded violently against her skull, her breathing too shallow, too sharp. Her hands clenched into fists, but she couldn't move, couldn't fight.

The angel tilted its head, regarding her like one might a work of art.

"This is a blessing," she said, like a whisper of wind. "You were never meant for Hell. Soon, you will understand."

Amber let out a low, shuddering laugh. It was raw. Breathless and spiteful.

"As soon as I get out of here," she rasped, "I'm going to rip your wings off one by one."

The angel didn't react. Instead, she simply turned and began to walk away, the others following in her silent, unsettling grace.

Amber jerked against the restraints again, harder this time, desperate, furious.

"Let me go, you sanctimonious cowards!" she snarled, thrashing despite the excruciating pull of her chains.

No one turned back; no one even looked at her.

Again, she was left alone.

Her breath trembled as she stared at the endless white, at the place where the angels had vanished.

Her pulse was erratic. Her thoughts were racing.

She had to escape and find a way out of this place, out of this prison, before it was too late. Before Heaven erased her entirely. Before they turned her child into something she'd no longer recognize. Before, she lost herself forever.

Amber clenched her jaw, steeling herself, when suddenly, as if ice water had been poured over a scorching fire, a searing pain shattered through her chest. It was blinding. Overwhelming. A raw, merciless force that tore through her like jagged glass.

Amber screamed.

The sound was wretched, ripped from her throat as she arched against the chains, her body convulsing under the crushing weight of it. She felt as though she were burning from the inside out as if something deep inside her was being forcibly severed.

Tears spilled from the corners of her eyes as she fought to keep herself conscious, to keep herself present, when just as suddenly as it had started, it stopped.

Amber gasped for air, her breath ragged, uneven. Every muscle trembled, a cold sweat breaking across her skin.

She barely had the strength to lower her gaze, but when she did, her stomach plummeted.

The sigil on her chest was down to six points, not seven.

Her breath hitched, her pulse pounding violently in her ears.

They were erasing her, piece by piece.

84

A Damned Choice

The sky above Castellum Umbrae burned with the fading hues of twilight. The first dark coils of night began piercing through the smoldering reds. The air was thick with the scent of sulfur and something sharper: anticipation. Every demon in the fortress could feel the shift, the ripple of power rolling off their king in waves.

Lucifer stood in the highest tower, staring out over his domain. Below, preparations were underway. Zagan was bound to a ritual post in the courtyard, his wrists and ankles wrapped in icy tendrils conjured by a blue-skinned demon. The runes carved into the black stone beneath him pulsed with a sickly light, flickering like a dying heartbeat.

Abelia had disappeared into the castle's depths, no doubt ensuring that every necessary precaution was taken. She knew this was a gamble of cosmic proportions, but she also knew Lucifer well enough to understand that once his mind was set, there was no stopping him. The tension in the air was palpable, the unspoken weight of what was to come pressing down on all of the cives inferni.

One problem at a time.

He repeated the words in his mind, clenching his fists at his sides. He didn't have the luxury of entertaining doubt. The moment he stepped onto the threshold of Heaven, the entire balance of the universe would shift. He couldn't afford to fail.

But the moment Amber had been taken, the moment he'd felt the bond between them sever like a blade to his spine, there'd been no other choice.

He was going to get her back.

No matter what it cost.

Behind him, the door creaked open.

"You're brooding," Mephistopheles said, his voice quiet but dry. He stepped into the room without waiting for permission, his arms crossed. "That never leads anywhere good."

Lucifer didn't turn. "You're far from where you're needed."

Mephistopheles walked to his side, his gaze flicking toward the ritual circle below. "No, I'm exactly where I should be. This is far too reckless, even for you."

Lucifer remained silent. "Luc," Mephistopheles tried again, "This is the first time in centuries. I'm not sure you'll come back from something."

Lucifer turned slightly, just enough to glance at him. "Don't be dramatic."

"I'm not." Mephistopheles' voice was flat. "You're about to walk into Heaven. Bound to Zagan, of all creatures. You're gambling with Amber's life. With your own. With the very structure of Hell."

Lucifer's gaze returned to the window. Below, the ritual circle flickered, still alive with binding threads. The plan was madness, but it was the only one he had.

"I have a plan."

Mephistopheles exhaled slowly. "Let me guess. Trade Zagan for Amber. A soul for a soul. It's poetic. Tragic. Completely suicidal."

Lucifer's jaw clenched.

"Only one slight problem," Mephistopheles added, "you'll be bound to the very soul you're trying to trade."

Lucifer finally looked at him. "I'll break the bond."

Meph's eyes narrowed. "Before or after you tear your soul in half?"

Lucifer didn't answer.

Mephistopheles shook his head, "You *think* you will. You *hope* you will. But if you're wrong, and you hand Zagan over while tethered to him? You'll be giving Heaven not just your enemy, but *you.*"

Lucifer didn't respond.

Mephistopheles' voice dropped. "Lucifer, if you're bound to him and you die up there if *either* of you is taken, consumed, or torn apart, Hell will have no ruler. No heir. No fallback."

Lucifer's wings shifted, tension rippling through every inch of him. "I'm aware."

"Then act like it," Mephistopheles snapped. "You've always taken risks, but this? This isn't just a risk. This is annihilation."

"I will get her back."

"And at what cost?" Mephistopheles pressed. "What if you succeed, but she comes back twisted, broken? What if *you* come back that way?"

Lucifer turned sharply now, shadows flaring at his feet. "Then we rebuild. As we always do."

Mephistopheles stared at him. "*We?* There might not be a *we* if you fail. If you and Zagan are both lost, there will be no one left strong enough to hold this realm. The other Archdemons will tear each other apart trying to seize the throne, and Heaven will watch it all burn."

Lucifer's mouth tightened, but his silence was telling.

Mephistopheles lowered his voice, the sarcasm stripped away now. "I've followed you into darkness before. I've backed every war you waged. But this..."

He stepped closer, his voice quieter, rawer. "I'm scared, Lucifer. Not just for her. For you. For *us*. If you go in unprepared or fail, we don't just lose Amber. We lose *you*. We lose *Hell*."

Lucifer turned fully, the fire behind his eyes burning low and dangerous.

"I don't care what I lose," he said, voice cold as ice. "I only care what I refuse to leave behind."

"Why?" Mephistopheles snapped, his frustration finally boiling over. "Why do you care so much about some damn soul? Just let her go, Luc. This isn't worth it!"

Lucifer turned on him so fast the air itself seemed to twist.

His eyes burned, not with fire, but with something older. Darker. A storm on the edge of breaking.

"Because she's carrying my child," he hissed, voice low but lethal.

The words rang out like a curse, quiet but catastrophic.

Mephistopheles froze.

Lucifer stepped forward, shadows flaring around his boots like cracks spreading across stone. "That's why, Meph. That's why I can't let her go. That's why I will burn Heaven to the ground if they don't give her back."

Mephistopheles's lips parted, but no words came. His face had gone pale.

"She's carrying my heir," Lucifer repeated, barely above a whisper now but no less searing. "So you ask me why I'm reckless? Why I'm willing to risk everything? It's because I *already have*."

The air trembled around them, thick with restrained power. The shadows in the corners of the chamber curled inward, reacting to the truth now bared.

Silence fell like a guillotine.

Mephistopheles's throat bobbed. "That... that's not possible."

Lucifer's voice dropped, sharp and deadly. "I didn't think so either."

He turned his back again, pacing like a caged beast. "But it's real. She's already changed. I felt it. God said so. He was afraid, Meph—He was afraid. And that's why they took her. That's why they're trying to erase her."

Mephistopheles finally found his voice shaky and hoarse. "Lucifer, if they know, if they know what she carries..."

"They'll destroy her," Lucifer growled. "They'll do what they've always done: rip away the thing they fear most."

He slammed his fist into the edge of the stone railing, cracks spidering out from the impact. "But not this time. I won't let them."

"You can't go alone," Mephistopheles said, stunned. "You can't fight them like this—not bound to Zagan, not without—"

"I don't care," Lucifer snarled, whirling back toward him. "I will tear the gates off their hinges if I have to. I will drag Heaven down by its roots. I will shatter every law that's ever been written. Do you hear me? I will become everything they've always feared and worse."

His chest rose and fell, each breath like bellows feeding the forge inside him.

"I am the Devil," he spat, voice venomous. "And they've taken what's *mine*."

Mephistopheles could only stare at him, this ancient, furious god of wrath and love, and realize that the war was already underway.

Lucifer turned away again, jaw clenched, shoulders tense. "You're the only one who knows. And you'll keep it that way."

Mephistopheles spoke, though it was rough, shaken. "Then we can't lose you. Either of you."

Lucifer's voice came like a vow. "We won't."

"I'm with you, Lucifer. You know I am. Let me help you," he said, soft but firm. "Let me be your anchor. Your way back."

Lucifer didn't look at him but said, "Call me back. Every hour on the hour. Summon me to Hell. When I break the bond and have Amber, I'll answer."

Mephistopheles nodded slowly, the weight of what he now carried settling in his bones. "I can do that."

For the first time in centuries, Mephistopheles wasn't just afraid for his king.

He was afraid for his friend.

And the child who could remake Hell.

***

Nightfall came swiftly, swallowing the sky in an inky void. The usual crimson glow of Hell's horizon dimmed beneath the weight of what was about to transpire. In the courtyard below, the ritual had already begun. Candles, their eerie, unnatural blue flames, flickered as if caught in breathless anticipation. The symbols carved into the black stone pulsed with raw energy, veins of molten gold weaving through their intricate patterns, alive with magic older than Hell itself.

Zagan stood at the center, still bound to the post, his ever-knowing grin stretched across his face. His wrists and ankles were still held fast by the same icy tendrils that had shackled him earlier, yet there was no struggle, no tension in his posture. He was waiting. *Patient. Pleased.*

Slowly, Lucifer descended the steps with measured, deliberate movements. His presence alone sent a ripple of silence through those gathered. The murmurs died. The air thickened. Every eye turned toward him, but none dared to meet his gaze.

He stepped into the circle. And the world seemed to *exhale.*

Hesitantly, two red-colored demons stepped forward, their clawed hands flexing as they shifted, clearly reluctant to approach. Even with all their power, they knew what it meant to bind Lucifer. To try and contain him, even for a moment, was an act of near-suicidal courage.

Lucifer gave them a slight nod, wordless permission. Without hesitation, he strode to a post across from where Zagan was bound. The moment he positioned himself, the demons moved.

Flames erupted.

Coils of fire, deep, scorching red with veins of molten gold, snaked around his wrists and ankles, hissing as they latched onto him, searing into his skin. The fire didn't consume, but it *held.* The weight of the restraint pulled against him, ancient magic forcing compliance where none should've been possible.

He didn't resist, yet the demons struggled. Their bodies trembled with the strain, and their eyes glowed like embers as they fought to keep their king against the post. It took *everything they had.*

Lucifer almost smirked at their desperation. Almost.

Across from him, Zagan let out a slow, pleased breath. The grin on his lips deepened, his teeth flashing in the eerie glow of the ritual circle. He was smug, expectant, and dangerous.

"Ready to be bound to me, old friend?" Zagan drawled, voice thick with amusement.

Lucifer didn't answer him. Instead, he met Abelia's gaze, unflinching. "Do it."

She nodded once.

Abelia was cloaked in something ancient and dark. Her robes flowed like liquid shadows and red and gold soul stones were woven into intricate chains around her wrists and throat. They pulsed with energy, *with sacrifice.* This ritual would take more than power. It demanded blood.

Slowly, Mammon stepped forward, but it wasn't the powerful Archdemon that sent a ripple of silence through the gathered crowd.

It was the Goliath he towed behind him.

The creature loomed over them all, towering well past seven feet; its beady yellow eyes scanned the courtyard with a cold, calculating hunger. Despite its sheer size, it followed Mammon with deliberate, measured steps, its massive talons clicking against the stone with unnatural precision.

It was leashed if the thin, fraying rope wrapped around its thick, muscled neck could even be called that. A mockery of control. Everyone knew if it wanted to run, to strike, to kill, nothing would stop it.

Its back was a grotesque blend of scales and fur, thick and bristling, a testament to its unnatural origins. A forked tongue flicked from its muzzled mouth, tasting the air as though savoring what was to come.

The surrounding demons instinctively recoiled. Even those who'd seen war, who'd faced punishment, who'd walked through the horrors of Hell itself took a step back. Those who worked in the Menagerie and knew this creature well retreated the furthest; they knew its true power and were *terrified*. The path cleared without a single command as Mammon and the beast passed through.

Lucifer had known this was coming.

He'd known that for the ritual to work, one of his own creations would have to sink its fangs into his flesh, ripping an opening for the spell to take hold. The magic needed a conduit, and there was no stronger one than blood.

But that didn't mean he was looking forward to it.

The actual danger wasn't the pain.

It was how much the beast would take.

Too much, and Lucifer wouldn't have the strength to withstand the ritual. Too much, and Zagan would collapse before the bond could fully seal.

The creature couldn't kill Lucifer.

But it could leave him too weak to hold the spell's power.

And if that happened, the ritual would consume them both.

85

Blood on the Trellis

Mammon halted, giving a sharp tug on the rope. The goliath barely reacted, only tilting its monstrous head to the side, its forked tongue flicking out again as if tasting the power thickening the air.

The courtyard was deathly silent.

Mammon turned toward Lucifer, his expression unreadable.

"It's ready." There was something almost mocking in his tone, but Lucifer didn't react.

He simply inclined his chin, "Unmuzzle it."

A ripple of unease spread through the gathered demons. Even Mammon hesitated. His gaze flicked from Lucifer to the beast as if considering whether or not to question the order. But in the end, he obeyed.

With slow, deliberate movements, Mammon reached up and unlatched the steel-plated muzzle.

The moment it fell away, the beast growled.

Low. Deep. Guttural.

The sound slithered through the air like a warning, vibrating through the stone beneath them. The gathered demons tensed. A few took instinctive steps backward, but there was nowhere to run.

Lucifer's gaze remained steady.

The goliath turned toward him, its beady yellow eyes locking onto his throat, his pulse.

It knew.

It knew who he was, what he was, and hesitated. But Lucifer offered no struggle, no challenge. He merely tilted his head, baring his forearm in a silent command. The creature sniffed the air, its tongue flicking out again, tasting him.

And then, it struck.

Faster than a creature of its size should've been able to. Faster than the eye could track, its fangs plunged deep into Lucifer's arm.

A brutal, tearing pain shot through him as the creature's teeth dug past muscle, past resistance, down to the very marrow. The sound of his own flesh giving way was drowned beneath the collective gasp from the demons around them.

Lucifer didn't move. Didn't react.

His grip tightened against the bindings at his wrists, but he refused to give the creature, or anyone else watching, the satisfaction of a flinch.

The beast growled, low and pleased, its thick, forked tongue flicking against the wound as it drank. Not greedily, not yet. But testing. Tasting.

After a few agonizing seconds, the creature released its grip on Lucifer's arm and slowly turned.

Zagan barely had time to swear before the fangs sank into him with a sharp, wet tear of skin breaking.

He jerked against the post, his muscles locking as the beast latched onto his shoulder. His smirk, the ever-present amusement he carried, faltered.

The beast's growl deepened. Its talons flexed into the ground, its massive frame hunching lower, tighter, more possessive.

And then, something shifted.

The creature's grip tightened, sinking its fangs deeper.

Zagan let out a sharp, snarling breath, his body tensing against the restraints as the creature's feeding turned ravenous.

Lucifer watched, his eyes narrowing.

This was wrong.

The beast was taking too much.

A violent snarl tore from its throat as it latched on, its forked tongue flicking wildly, its pupils blown wide as the taste of Zagan's blood drove it into a frenzy. It wasn't letting go.

For a split second, there was only chaos as a dozen demons rushed forward at once. Shouts erupted as the beast thrashed against the post, its claws raking into the stone, trying to rip more from Zagan's body.

"Get it off him!" Someone shouted.

The first demon reached for the rope too slowly.

The beast swung a mangled, clawed hand at him, nearly taking off his head.

Zagan let out a ragged hiss, his body arching violently as the creature's fangs dug deeper, its entire form shuddering with hunger.

More demons piled in.

One grabbed its back legs. Another wrenched at its head, trying to pry its jaws open.

Nothing.

It wouldn't let go.

Lucifer exhaled, slow and measured, before his voice cut through the madness, "Enough."

The word was quiet, but the air shook with it.

For a split second, everyone froze.

Then, Lucifer moved.

Bound or not, he jerked his wrist, letting his own blood drip to the ground, letting the scent cut through the frenzy like a blade.

The beast's head snapped toward him, its teeth still deep beneath Zagan's skin, but for a moment, it hesitated. Then, with a final, bone-tearing rip, it tore itself from Zagan, a fresh chunk of flesh in its teeth. Zagan cursed viciously, his body slumping slightly, blood spilling freely down his side. The beast panted, its entire form trembling, but it turned back to Lucifer.

Waiting.

Wanting.

Lucifer lifted his gaze to Mammon.

"Control it," he said. "Now."

For a moment, everything was still.

The only sound was the creature's labored breathing, its forked tongue flicking out, tasting the air still thick with blood.

Zagan slumped against the post, his chest rising and falling in shallow, uneven breaths. His usual smugness was gone, replaced by something darker. His head tilted slightly, his eyes unfocused as fresh blood seeped down his shoulder, pooling at his hip.

Lucifer observed him. But it wasn't out of concern; it was out of calculation.

"Too much?" He finally asked with a slight smirk.

Zagan let out a ragged breath, his lips twitching toward something resembling a smirk. But it was weaker than before. His skin looked paler, and his muscles were slacker.

He wouldn't admit it.

Wouldn't say the words aloud.

But Lucifer could see it.

The beast had taken more than it should have. And that meant Zagan wasn't as strong as he needed to be.

Around them, the demons were regrouping, some pulling back while others still hovered in uncertainty. No one dared move toward the beast just yet, not while it twitched with hunger, its claws digging into the stone, its tail flicking like a restless predator.

Mammon was the first to step forward, and with one sharp whistle, the beast's ears twitched. He whistled again, and the beast's shoulders tensed, its golden eyes narrowing.

Mammon yanked the rope hard, his body still relaxed, but there was an edge to it now. "That's enough," he muttered, voice clipped. "You got your fill."

For a long moment, the creature didn't move.

Lucifer could see it, the hesitation.

The choice.

Would it submit? Or would it challenge?

Lucifer narrowed his eyes. *Choose wisely.*

The beast let out a low, rumbling growl, but then, at last, it stepped back, allowing Mammon to lead it away.

The tension in the courtyard fractured just slightly.

Lucifer turned his gaze back to Zagan, still watching, measuring.

"Will you hold?" he asked, voice devoid of anything but cold expectation.

Zagan gave a sharp, bitter chuckle.

He rolled his neck, wincing slightly but forcing himself upright. "I'm still standing, aren't I?"

Lucifer said nothing; he knew the truth. Zagan was weaker now, and in the coming moments, that might matter.

Abelia, who'd been silent until now, finally spoke.

"The ritual will take more from you than the beast has," she warned. "If you're already—"

"I said," Zagan interrupted, his teeth bared in something too sharp to be a grin, "I'm still standing."

Lucifer let his gaze linger a moment longer.

Then, finally, he nodded. "Then we begin."

86

The Binding

A belia took a breath and began to chant:

"Te nunc invocamus, te laudamus, Sanctissima.
Voces nostras audi, et has necessitudines crea.
Has duas animas te rogamus assumere, et antiquorum verbis alligare.
Animas suas alligant in magica antiquitatis, ut semper tamen tragica conjungantur.
Te rogamus antiquos, exaudi preces nostras, sicut es clavem desiderantis."

As the incantation wove through the air, deep and commanding, the symbols on the ground ignited, burning with crimson and gold. The flames seared into the ground, marking the path of fate. Shadows twisted and curled from the edges of the circle, slithering inward like starving creatures drawn to a feast.

Then, they fought back.

The darkness was resisting.

It lashed out violently, writhing against the spell, pushing against the summoning. The shadows surged like a living tide, battering against the protective wall the soul stones had created around Abelia. The demons holding Lucifer and Zagan staggered, struggling.

Panic flickered across their faces. The shadows were too strong.

The darkness was fighting back because it knew what this was. It knew what binding a devil truly meant, but blind two devils to each other? Insanity.

One of the demons holding Lucifer snarled, his claws digging into the ground for support. "We need more!"

More demons rushed forward, throwing everything they had into holding the spell together. The ritual's pull grew heavier. Lucifer could feel it in his chest, pressing, sinking, and twisting into his bones.

Abelia's lips moved faster, her voice sharpening, commanding. Unrelenting.

She wouldn't let the magic disobey her.

The shadows had no choice but to yield.

Lucifer felt it before he saw it: *the chain.*

It lashed out from the burning sigils, striking through the air like a living thing, a serpent of molten energy and endless void. It wrapped around Zagan's throat first, spiraling down his chest, digging into his being.

The moment it touched him, he buckled.

The force of it wrenched his body against the post. His head snapped back, his teeth clenched so tightly his jaw trembled. The magic hit him like a wildfire tearing through dry earth.

Lucifer watched, his golden eyes narrowing.

Zagan wasn't strong enough for this.

His fingers curled against the restraints, nails breaking under its force. His body shook, not with power, but with strain.

Lucifer felt its resistance as if the bond itself was rejecting his counterpart. The spell was trying to tear Zagan apart before it even reached Lucifer.

Zagan let out a sharp, guttural breath. His body arched violently against the post, his smirk from earlier wholly gone.

He wasn't controlling this.

He wasn't winning.

It was breaking him.

Lucifer finally spoke.

"Balance it." His voice was low, steady, but absolute.

Abelia's focus snapped to him. She saw what he saw: if the spell continued like this, Zagan wouldn't survive it.

She nodded toward a group of gathered Angelus Lapsus, not stopping her chanting, and Cadeyrn stepped forward.

He knew what to do, and his words cut like a blade: "Iubeo te divider. Nunc."

The spell obeyed.

A second chain lashed out, dividing the weight as it struck Lucifer.

The moment it wrapped around his arm, the balance shifted.

Zagan's body slumped slightly, the unbearable force easing off him. But the damage had been done. His body still shuddered from the strain, his breathing ragged and shallow. His skin was paler than it should've been, his muscles barely holding.

The chain coiled up his arm, winding through his torso, tightening, binding. Weaving through them both, threading through their existence like a needle stitching two souls into one.

And Lucifer absorbed the weight.

And then, the pain began.

It was like being torn apart and remade in the same instant. A searing force laced through him, burning flesh and bone and carving itself into his essence. It was fire and shadow, light and void.

Still, Lucifer didn't falter.

His wings snapped out violently, the power coursing through him. The flames in the courtyard burned higher, hotter, and wilder, reaching for the sky. The ritual torches exploded, their blue fire surging like a storm.

The demons holding the chains nearly collapsed, straining, breaking.

Zagan's head tilted back, his breath unsteady, his body barely upright. Lucifer turned his head slightly, his gaze cutting through the flickering light.

Zagan's hands trembled.

It was slight, almost imperceptible.

But Lucifer saw it.

Zagan had barely survived this.

And they hadn't even reached Heaven yet.

The ritual was over. The bond had taken hold.

Zagan let out a slow, uneven breath, forcing his usual mocking tone.

"There," he mused, rolling his shoulders, though his movements were sluggish, unsteady. "That wasn't so bad, was it?"

With that, the demons released Zagan and Lucifer, utterly exhausted as they crumbled.

Lucifer's head lifted, his eyes burning with golden fire. He could feel the bond now. Tied to him. Threaded through him, and he had no idea how to break it.

His voice was quiet but absolute. "We leave. Now."

Zagan's smirk remained, but it was weaker. He could feel it, just as Lucifer could. The weight of what they'd done. The uncertainty of what was to come.

"Eager, aren't we?" Zagan hummed, but even he couldn't mask the rough edge in his voice.

Lucifer didn't answer. He turned toward Abelia, "Open The Veil."

Abelia hesitated only a moment before she spoke, quieter this time, "Ligaverunt animas suas, dedit tibi quod rogasti. Nunc te revela iam non palliatus es."

For a heartbeat, nothing happened, and red flashed through Lucifer's gaze. When suddenly, the ground trembled. A tremor deep, ancient, reverberating through the stone. It deepened slowly, spreading like a shockwave through the ground beneath them. The sigils, still glowing with molten gold and searing crimson, flickered wildly, their power straining under the weight of what they'd just summoned.

The very fabric of Hell's reality ripped.

A howling wind erupted from the courtyard's center, laced with whispers that scraped against the skin, voices that spoke in no language known to anyone. They were old, ancient, unrelenting. A chorus of those who'd tried to cross the threshold before and failed.

Abelia stepped back instinctively, her hands still raised, her breath uneven as the air shuddered.

Then, the sky tore apart.

The darkness above them fractured, splitting open as a jagged wound carved itself into existence. A gateway. A passage. A violent rupture between two realms that should never touch.

The air around them turned heavy and thick with the pressure of something unnatural. The torches lining the courtyard snuffed out, plunging the space into eerie half-darkness. Shadows twisted unnaturally. The flickering sigils on the stone flared one last time before collapsing into silence.

The Veil was open.

At first, it was nothing but a swirling void, black upon black, emptier than anything in existence. It stretched forward, hollow and hungry, warping the space around it like a gaping wound that refused to heal. The edges shimmered like broken glass, shifting between forms, struggling to decide if it was meant to exist at all.

And then, the color changed.

The void swirled.

Darkness gave way to a pulse of light, not warm, not divine, but something colder: silver, ashen, and hollow. The threshold between Hell and Heaven was never meant to be seen, but here it was, raw and exposed.

Lucifer's eyes burned as he stared into the nothingness beyond, but he knew the boundary had been breached.

"It's done." Abelia's voice was hoarse as if the ritual had drained her.

Lucifer didn't hesitate.

He stepped forward.

The moment his foot crossed the edge of the circle, the wind howled, the Veil reacting violently to his presence. It didn't want him. It rejected him. The very nature of it screamed against him, clawing at his being.

But Lucifer didn't stop.

Zagan's smirk had faded. He could feel it too. The weight, the pressure, the force trying to repel them.

"Hell cannot pass through," Zagan said, but his voice was strained as if it had taken all his effort to speak against the darkness.

Lucifer bared his teeth. "Then we break through."

He pushed forward and stepped completely into The Veil.

Behind him, the world he knew, the kingdom he ruled, shattered. And he and Zagan were plunged into an all-consuming darkness.

87

Chains and Choice

The Veil wrapped around them instantly, violently. It hated them, *rejected* them. The force of it crashed against Lucifer's body like an unseen tide, trying to rip him backward, pull him under, and consume him whole.

A high and unnatural howl slithered through the air, a sound that came from everywhere and nowhere. The Veil screeched as their presence forced it to bend, its resistance sharpening into a pressure that pressed against their skin, into their bones, beneath their very existence.

Lucifer pushed forward, unrelenting. He knew what would happen if they hesitated. Time moved differently here. It'd take everything from them if they gave it a chance, and Zagan was already faltering.

Lucifer didn't need to look back to know. He couldn't see through the darkness even if he wanted to, but he could hear it in Zagan's breathing, ragged and unsteady. He could feel it in the way Zagan's presence behind him wavered and flickered.

"Keep moving." Lucifer said, keeping his voice low, steady, and commanding.

Zagan exhaled sharply but didn't argue, and together, they walked.

The ground beneath them was unforgiving, shifting. Each step felt unsteady, like walking across the surface of something that wasn't meant to be stood on. The space around them warped, twisting corridors of endless black, bottomless drops that appeared without warning. Things they only realized when they walked into walls or one of their feet dropped out from below them.

The Veil was a labyrinth without logic, and they were already running out of time.

Lucifer stumbled, tripping over something he couldn't see as the first toll was taken from him.

It happened fast. It was a flash of pain. A pull of something. A sensation like something being torn from him, something profound, something vital was just gone.

He inhaled sharply, his vision blurring for a split second. His balance wavered, his steps faltering, but he recovered. The pain vanished, but something felt different. Something was wrong.

His hands curled into fists as he tried to grasp it; what had been taken?

He knew it was important. He knew it had mattered.

And yet, he couldn't name it.

Couldn't picture it.

It was just...gone.

Zagan swore viciously behind him, staggering.

Lucifer turned but could only see Zagan's glowing eyes squint slightly, his body shuddering. His head was bowed, his breath shallow.

Lucifer narrowed his eyes. "What did it take?"

Zagan lifted his head.

His eyes were dull, unreadable.

And for the first time since stepping into The Veil, he didn't smirk.

"I don't know." He snarled.

Lucifer exhaled slowly, turning back toward the shifting abyss ahead.

"We keep moving." he said.

The Veil was just getting started.

As they walked, the Veil shifted, but not like a place, like a living thing.

Lucifer didn't hear it move; he felt it. The way the space around them flexed and rippled, stretching in places and collapsing in others. The ground beneath their feet pulsed like a dying heartbeat, steady one second and treacherous the next.

There was no path forward, no sky, and no landmarks to mark their progress. Just blackness, hollow and endless, stretched in every direction.

Lucifer walked anyway.

Zagan followed, but barely.

His steps were uneven, his breathing shallow and too fast. Lucifer could feel the weight of his presence flickering and thinning.

The Veil was already unraveling him.

Lucifer didn't look back. Didn't check. Didn't ask.

He couldn't afford to.

Because the moment he did, the moment he hesitated, he knew the Veil would take more.

They walked silently, each step uncertain, each movement feeling like it took too much effort.

And then, it happened again, the Veil took its second toll.

It came without warning.

A sudden, violent pull.

Lucifer's chest tightened. His vision blurred again.

He staggered, catching himself with one foot before he collapsed forward. The sensation was worse than before, a hollowing, a carving, a piece of him being torn out at the root.

This time, he heard Zagan choke.

Lucifer turned his head sharply.

Zagan was on one knee. His fingers dug into the ground, but there was nothing there to hold onto. His entire body was trembling, and his breath was ragged.

Lucifer stared at him.

Zagan's hands lifted slightly, his fingers twitching as if trying to grasp something that should be there but wasn't.

Lucifer felt it, too.

Something was missing.

He clenched his fists, searching his mind to grasp what was gone.

But that was the problem: there was nothing to grasp.

Whatever it was, it was like it had never existed.

His mind continued forward as if nothing had changed, but his body, his soul, they knew.

Something had been taken.

More of himself. More of Zagan.

And it'd keep happening.

Lucifer inhaled slowly, forcing himself to steady.

Zagan let out a sharp, broken laugh. It wasn't amusement; it was disbelief. He lifted his head, eyes ablaze with golden hate, but they were unfocused. He was lost.

"How much longer before we don't remember why we're here?"

Lucifer didn't answer because, for the first time, he didn't know.

Suddenly, the ground moved.

Not in a tremor. Not as a shift.

It simply ceased to exist.

Lucifer's feet came out from under him.

He reacted instantly, his wings snapping open, his body twisting as his claws dug into the nearest surface. His grip held. Just barely. His legs dangled over an abyss, nothing beneath him but endless black.

A second later, Zagan fell past him.

Lucifer shot out a hand, gripping his wrist at the last possible moment.

Zagan's full weight yanked downward, dragging against Lucifer's fragile grip. The strain burned his arms, and the pull of the abyss felt like an unseen force trying to rip them both down.

Zagan released a low, shaky breath, "Well, this is unfortunate."

Lucifer's claws dug deeper into the rock.

The Veil was fighting back.

And this time, it wasn't just taking pieces of them.

It was trying to swallow them whole.

On instinct, Lucifer moved to beat his wings, expecting to lift them both to safety, but nothing happened.

His body remained pinned against the edge of the abyss, unmoving. The weight of the fall still dragged at him, his talons digging into the crumbling ledge as they began to slip.

Confusion flickered through him. He tried again, a powerful beat of his wings, and still nothing. No resistance. No force.

It was as if they didn't exist at all.

Zagan noticed first.

He saw the tension in Lucifer's shoulders, the way his jaw locked, the sharp flicker of something close to unease in his expression.

"Something wrong?" Zagan taunted, his voice edged with amusement despite his worsening grip.

Lucifer didn't answer.

But the weight of both of them dragging downwards increased as they slipped another fraction lower. Only this time, the Veil was waiting to take them.

Before Lucifer could react, the surface he clung to began to disintegrate. The rock beneath his claws crumbled into dust.

There was nothing left to hold on to, and together, they fell.

But it wasn't just a drop.

It was a severing.

The abyss was swallowing them whole.

The moment his body plunged into the endless void, everything felt wrong. The sensation wasn't just falling; it was like being pulled apart. His limbs felt like they were stretching too far, too thin as if the Veil itself was trying to strip him down to nothing.

The air was thick and suffocating. It dragged against his skin, slowing him and pressing into him like a weighted tide. Every inch they dropped felt like it took an eternity to arrive.

And then came the first ripple of pain.

Lucifer's breath hitched. His body seized.

Something was happening, something *inside* him.

A sharp, unnatural ache tore through his bones, muscles, and essence. His body began to ache, but it wasn't from exhaustion; it was from something deeper, something irreversible.

Then he saw it.

His hands, *his own hands*, were different.

Older.

His skin, ordinarily flawless, eternal, unmarred by time, was changing.

Faint, nearly invisible lines traced over his knuckles, the subtlest sign of age creeping in. He could feel the slow, terrible drag of time that had never once touched him until now.

The Veil was aging them.

Lucifer's stomach twisted, but it wasn't just him. Sharply, he turned his head toward a screaming Zagan. Lucifer had never heard him cry before, and when he looked, it wasn't pain that was etched across Zagan's face. It was terror.

Zagan's body was withering. His skin dulled and grayed slightly as if something had drained its vitality. The normally faint scars across his torso were deepening. His once firm and sculpted muscles were losing their shape and beginning to collapse inward.

He wasn't just aging.

He was decaying.

Lucifer gritted his teeth, forcing himself to focus. They had to stop this. They had to...

Before he could finish his thought, they slammed into something solid.

For a moment, both of them lay there panting. Their body ached against the impact in a sensation of fatigue and pain they weren't used to. With a shutter, Lucifer rolled to his side and noticed the ripple of something unnatural beneath him. The surface wasn't still. It moved. The second they made impact, the floor tilted and rotated beneath them as if alive.

The wind howled one last time before cutting out completely, leaving only dead silence. Lucifer couldn't hear anything for the first time since stepping into The Veil.

No murmurs. No voices.

No Zagan.

Lucifer's pulse spiked; he actually had one now, a beating heart, but that wasn't what terrified him most. What did terrify him was the realization that he was alone. The Veil had separated them. One second, they were next to each other; the next, Zagan was gone.

Lucifer staggered as he pushed himself up, the impact of their fall still rattling through his bones. Pain. *Real pain.* It sat like lead in his limbs, something he hadn't felt in eons. He exhaled sharply, his lungs burning as if the air in this place was poisoning him.

Slowly, he climbed to his feet, turning his golden eyes to the void. The walls, if they could even be called that, shifted, stretched, curved. The Veil was no longer just a passageway between worlds.

It was a thing. A living thing.

Lucifer clenched his jaw. He didn't care if the bastard got himself lost in here, or at least he wouldn't care had they not been tied together, but they were, and he needed him to complete the trade. If Zagan died, the entire plan unraveled.

A sound rippled through the air, but it wasn't a voice or words; it was something else.

Lucifer's gaze snapped up, and though he couldn't see anything, he knew there was something here with him.

88

The Crown of Fire

Z agan was dying.

Or at least, he felt like he was.

His hands shook violently as he pressed them against the wall of the shifting corridor, trying to keep himself upright. His entire body felt wrong. Weak and heavy, his bones ached, and his breath came in shallow gasps. He gritted his teeth, dragging himself forward despite the unnatural weight pulling at him.

The Veil was rotting him from the inside out.

He stumbled forward, blinking rapidly, trying to steady himself when suddenly, he saw it.

Just ahead, a figure stood eerily still. He didn't know who it was, but somewhere deep inside, he knew he recognized the figure. As he clamored forward, his mind reeled as realization dawned on him.

Zagan's lips parted slightly, a ragged breath escaping him as the shape moved closer, his cape catching in the dim, silver light.

No. No, he couldn't be here.

But there, standing in front of him, draped in fire and darkness, stood the first ruler of Hell.

Him.

Or at least the version of him that mattered.

The figure stood at the end of the corridor, watching him. He looked exactly as Zagan remembered himself at the height of his rule: untouchable, unstoppable, powerful beyond reckoning.

Not this weakened, decaying shell.

Zagan's pulse thundered. The moment his gaze locked onto him, his mind fractured.

It wasn't real. He knew that. He had to know that.

But the Veil was pressing down on him, his memories slipping through his fingers like sand. His past was collapsing, his body withering, his mind fraying.

The past version of himself studied him, expression unreadable. Then, slowly, he smirked, "Look at you."

Zagan froze.

His past self's eyes burned molten gold, brighter than Lucifer's, sharper, crueler. They swept over him, not with fear, not with hatred.

With disgust.

"You're pathetic." The former version of himself said, tilting his head slightly, his eyes glinting like something inhuman.

Zagan staggered backward. His breathing was ragged and uneven. The shadows around his old self stretched longer, curling toward him.

The figure took a step forward.

"This is what you've become?" The voice slithered through the air, coated in something venomous. "A dying wretch, stumbling through The Veil, clinging to the scraps of a life you lost centuries ago?"

Zagan's jaw locked. His claws curled so tightly his nails bit into his palms, "You're not real."

The version of him from his past chuckled. "I am. I am the only thing that's real. The only part of you worth remembering."

Zagan's vision wavered, but the shadows struck before he could react.

"You had it all," the words twisted around him like chains. "The power. The Dominion. The *fear*." His past self leaned forward, grinning. "And you let Lucifer take it from you."

Zagan's breath came faster.

The walls were closer now, suffocating.

His former self loomed over him, impossibly massive, a symbol of everything he'd lost. "He didn't even have to try."

The words carved like a blade.

Zagan's entire body locked up because it was true.

Lucifer hadn't needed to fight him.

Lucifer had just been better.

And Zagan had lost.

He'd always known it.

But he'd never let himself feel it until now.

His past self stepped closer. His presence commanded the room the way it used to, the way it should. "You know what happens now." Zagan's throat went dry, and his past self smiled, "You bow."

Zagan lashed out violently, but his movements were too slow. Too weak. The Veil broke him down, unraveling him into something less than himself.

The thing in front of him wasn't his former self. It never had been.

It was something else.

Something that wore his face.

And it wasn't alone.

A whispering chorus rose behind his former self, more figures crawling from the blackness, all wearing faces he once knew.

All smiling.

All saying the same thing: "You are nothing."

***

Lucifer moved forward heavily. Ahead of him, the corridor twisted, shifting with no sense of direction and no way to navigate. His breath came harder. The exhaustion was creeping deeper into him, curling like something poisonous.

He was trying to ignore it when he heard the voice. It was familiar and soft like a warm blanket, "Lucifer."

He froze.

Amber.

His pulse spiked violently. He turned sharply, scanning the darkness, searching. But no one was there.

The corridor was empty.

Then he heard it again. Closer, "You forgot me."

Lucifer exhaled sharply and shook his head. The Veil was toying with him. Tearing at what little remained of his memories.

"You forgot me." The whisper curled against his ear again, even closer than before.

His jaw clenched.

It was a trap, and he wouldn't fall for it. But suddenly, there was a breath of movement behind him.

Lucifer spun, reacting on instinct, just as the air around him *twisted*, not a thing, but the space itself folding inward like reality had lost its grip.

The pressure hit him like a wave: crushing, unnatural, alive.

The corridor groaned around him, the walls pulsing as if they were breathing, closing in.

He braced against the force, but it wasn't enough.

With a soundless crack, the world ruptured.

Reality split open like tearing fabric, and the Veil vanished.

In the blink of an eye, the corridor, the darkness, and the very plane he stood on were gone, and Lucifer was somewhere else entirely.

Blinking slowly, Lucifer found himself standing in a room he knew, though he couldn't place how. It was like his essence knew it even when his body didn't.

The air was warm, gentle, and alive. It breathed around him, soft and honeyed, nothing like Hell's dry, electric burn. The scent of lavender and vanilla wrapped around him like a memory, and beyond the window, sunlight filtered through gauzy curtains, casting golden beams across the polished floor.

And sitting just across the room, mere feet away, was Amber. She sat at a vanity, brushing her long blonde hair, the strands catching the light like fire. She looked alive, untouched by the torment of Hell. She looked safe.

Lucifer's chest constricted. His breath stilled, his power curling in on itself as his traitorous and aching heart swelled at the sight of her.

She looked like she belonged here. Not in Hell. Not beside him.

Here.

He knew it wasn't real. Of course, it wasn't. But it didn't matter; his feet moved before his mind could convince them otherwise. He took one step, then another. His fingers twitched, reaching for her, something raw rising in his throat, something he didn't want to name. Not hope. Not love. Something *older*. Something *holy* in its desperation.

"Amber," he whispered.

She turned at the sound slowly and gracefully and smiled radiantly. His heart swelled for a fraction of a second.

But her eyes slid right past him, freezing Lucifer mid-step.

She didn't see him.

Didn't *recognize* him.

She looked *through* him like he wasn't there at all.

His breath caught, shattered.

Gracefully, she stood, smoothing the fabric of her dress, moving with purpose, as her gown flowed around her like liquid sunlight. She crossed the room but not toward him. She passed him like he wasn't there and reached the door. It was then that another figure entered.

A man.

Tall, golden, and familiar.

Michael.

Lucifer's blood turned to ice.

But Amber's face lit up with a softness he had never seen. A tenderness so open, so complete, it hollowed him out. She moved into Michael's arms like she'd done it a thousand times before. Like she'd *always* belonged there.

Lucifer's hands curled into fists at his sides, his shadows shrinking, wilting against the warmth of the light. His body locked up, a tension so unnatural and deeply ingrained into him that he felt sick for the first time in centuries.

He'd never seen her look at him like that because she never had. Or at least, he had no memory of it.

"You forgot me." The whisper came from nowhere, and then suddenly, from *everywhere*.

Lucifer turned sharply.

Amber was staring at him now.

But her eyes weren't soft. They were empty. Cold. A bottomless chasm.

"So I forgot you too."

Lucifer staggered back as the words hit him like a blade to the chest. His lips parted, but nothing came out. He couldn't move. Couldn't breathe.

And then, from the corner of the room, a sound echoed.

A small voice. High and soft.

He didn't recognize it.

But it ignited something in him, something primal. His chest burned, aching so suddenly it stole his breath like his soul had reached out before his body could follow. His eyes snapped toward the sound, hunting for the source with rising urgency.

And there, stumbling out of the darkness, came a small child.

Lucifer's breath hitched.

Golden curls framed their face, bright like Amber's but wavy and wild in a way that echoed his. Their eyes were wide and curious, with a hint of glowing gold in the irises, *his* gold. Bare feet padded softly against the sunlight-soaked floor, small toes sinking into the plush carpet as if they belonged there.

He didn't need a name. A sign. A word.

He *knew*.

This was his child.

His.

There wasn't a sliver of doubt; he felt it in his blood, in the marrow of his bones, and in the way his magic stirred, reaching for something familiar.

But as the child came fully into view, Lucifer gasped because tucked neatly against their back were a pair of wings.

Only they weren't dark like his; they were pure white, radiant, and Heavenly. Feathers shimmered like glass kissed by sunlight, each movement trailing faint threads of divine light. They weren't just angelic; they were *pure*. Claimed.

Lucifer took a step forward, unable to hold himself back, and a need poured through him. Need to pull his child into him to return them to Hell where they belonged. The child giggled and reached up with tiny, eager hands.

But not toward him.

Toward Michael.

"Daddy!" the child squealed, delight bursting from their voice as Michael bent to scoop them up in one smooth, practiced motion.

Lucifer went still, his entire body locking.

Every nerve screamed. Every cell burned.

The child was *his*. He knew it from the cadence of their laugh, the echo of his blood, the mark of his magic etched into their being like a brand.

But Heaven had taken it.

He was too late.

Too late to claim. Too late to fight. Too late to save.

He could only watch in frozen horror as Amber wrapped her arms around Michael and the child, beaming as she kissed the baby's brow like it was *natural*. Like it was *home*.

Lucifer watched as her expression softened, not with recognition of him or with mourning but with peace.

Like this was the life she'd always wanted.

Like Hell had been the lie.

Like *he* had been the mistake.

Lucifer stumbled back, pain flaring through his chest, not sharp, but *crushing*. Like he was folding inward. Like he was vanishing.

Michael turned then, still holding the child easily in one arm, the other resting at Amber's waist. He looked at Lucifer, not with cruelty or anger, but with a gentle, measured pity that made Lucifer want to tear the world in half.

"This is peace," Michael said, smiling quietly. "*Real* peace. Born of grace. Of obedience. Of surrender."

He paused, his eyes meeting Lucifer's, ancient and knowing, full of something colder than divinity. "And you, brother...You were made to *break it*."

Lucifer's throat clenched. His shadows recoiled. His breath came ragged, too loud in a room that suddenly felt too still.

Michael tilted his head, voice softening to a whisper that carried like judgment written in stone. "You were never meant to have this. You were only ever meant to *watch it slip away*."

Lucifer's lips parted. He tried to speak. To scream. To *move*.

But before he could do anything, he was yanked backward.

The floor ripped away.

The air vanished.

The warmth *snapped* into cold.

And Lucifer was falling.

Around him, there was no wind, no sky, no gravity, only emptiness. The warmth from Amber's smile, the weight of the child in Michael's arms, and the scent of lavender and sunlight were all gone and in their place: *nothing*.

A silence so absolute it made his ears ring.

Lucifer tumbled through the dark, not screaming, not breathing, not thinking, just falling through the echo of every mistake he'd ever made. Amber's voice haunted the edges of his mind. The child's laughter still rang in his ears.

Michael's voice whispered like venom along his spine, *"You were never meant to have this."*

His body twitched, flinching as the realization hit him: he wasn't in control. Not anymore. The Veil had him now.

And that should have been the end, but something shifted.

It started as a flicker, a pulse.

Like a heartbeat, only it wasn't his own.

It came from below.

No, further. It came from beneath the beneath. From the place, even the Veil couldn't reach.

The darkness trembled, and Lucifer's body stilled mid-fall. The weightless void cracked beneath his feet, though there *was* no floor. No gravity. Only... defiance.

A single strand of gold light bloomed along his skin, pulsing outward like molten lightning.

When suddenly, the mark on his chest flared to life, searing through his shirt and flesh. An illusion, glowing brightly as a star.

Hell was fighting The Veil.

The air warped, the illusion twisted, and the silence cracked open with a low, bone-deep groan, not of pain but of *warning*.

Lucifer's eyes snapped open.

Red.

Burning.

Alive.

The child's laughter fractured like glass. The scent of lavender curdled into smoke. The room he'd been trapped in began to peel back, edges fraying into shadow and ash.

The Veil tried to hold him. It failed.

A roar burst from Lucifer's chest, not as a scream of rage or grief, but a *summoning*, a call to everything that still obeyed him.

Hell rose to answer.

Shadows erupted around him like wings made of wildfire, stretching in every direction and splitting through the false sky. The Veil shrieked in resistance, but it was too late. He wasn't a man in love anymore.

He was the Devil, and he had been provoked.

The ground beneath his feet formed out of nothing, forged by will alone. His power surged outward in a violent wave, reality buckling around him. The Veil released him as fire licked through its seams, devouring everything it had used to torment him.

He stepped forward.

Each stride cracked the illusion further; walls falling, light dimming, Heaven's false warmth *dying* in his wake.

And then he heard it: someone else screaming.

Zagan.

89

One Step from Oblivion

Elsewhere in the maze, Zagan's body shook violently. His fingers trembled against the shifting ground, his mind fractured between the real and the unreal.

"You are nothing." The figures stepped closer. Their features distorted, twisting in and out of focus. Their mouths moved, but their voices weren't right.

The Veil was dragging him into something deeper.

No longer showing him memories; it was creating them.

"No," Zagan rasped, trying to hold onto his thoughts. "This isn't real."

A hand grasped his wrist.

Zagan flinched violently, his entire body recoiling as ice shot through his veins. The figure's fingers were thin, corpse-like, brittle as old parchment.

His breath hitched.

The hands were wrong, and as he stared at them, he realized they weren't hands at all.

They were bones.

The things around him weren't people anymore.

They were skeletal figures draped in shadows. Their skulls were cracked, and their spines twisted unnaturally. They had no eyes, just empty sockets filled with writhing darkness.

And they were still speaking in his voice, "You are nothing."

The figures lunged.

Zagan moved on instinct. His claws ripped through the first one, splitting bone and sinew like wet paper, and the creature collapsed into dust at his feet. But it didn't matter. Another surged forward. Then another. And another.

A whispering, crawling tide of dead things, all his past, failures, regrets, wearing his own face, his voice.

His claws were slick now. His breathing was erratic. His vision *fractured*.

When suddenly, a new voice rang through the chaos, only this one was real. "Zagan!"

The shriek of his name snapped through the air like the crack of a whip, and the swarm faltered for a moment.

Zagan staggered back, chest heaving, as a new figure crashed into the corridor; Lucifer, wild-eyed, golden irises burning with fury and fear. His clothes were torn, blood dripping down one arm, and shadows writhing around him like living smoke.

He was powerful. Terrifying. *Real.*

But to Zagan, he looked *wrong.* His limbs were bent in unnatural configurations, his face twisted at the edges, his aura stained. The Veil hadn't released its grip; it had only changed the illusion.

And in one horrifying moment, Zagan's perception snapped.

Lucifer blurred, becoming the enemy, and Zagan roared.

He lunged with lethal force, claws outstretched, and Lucifer barely had time to brace before Zagan slammed into him with bone-rattling weight. They hit the wall hard, the stone warping and flexing beneath them like breathing flesh. Zagan snarled like a feral beast, his claws at Lucifer's throat, eyes wide and gleaming with madness.

He wasn't just attacking.

He was trying to kill him.

Lucifer ducked a strike, barely avoiding a slash across his face, but the second swipe caught his shoulder, slicing deep. Fabric tore. Flesh opened. Blood bloomed in a hot, sudden burst.

Pain flared white-hot up his arm, but Lucifer didn't flinch because this wasn't Zagan. This was The Veil, wearing Zagan like a mask. It had twisted his senses, poisoned his instincts, and now it was dragging him under.

"You are nothing." The voices were louder now. Echoing from every wall, every shadow. Multiplied. Warped. Layered. Like a chorus of nightmares all speaking through his skin.

And Zagan was falling deeper.

Lucifer could see the shimmer of hallucination crawling through Zagan's pupils. The man wasn't in the corridor anymore; he was somewhere else, *dying.*

Lucifer gritted his teeth, but the next time Zagan swung, Lucifer didn't dodge. He caught his wrist, cutting off his movements. His hand closed around Zagan's wrist like iron. Zagan thrashed, snarling, spitting rage, but Lucifer didn't let go. Instead, he pulled *hard*, using the momentum to turn, slamming Zagan down onto the twisting, breathing floor with brutal finality.

Zagan hit hard. The wind tore from his lungs in a wheeze of pain. But Lucifer was already on him, pinning him down, knee against his ribs, one arm wrenched behind his back.

Beneath him, Zagan bucked, violent and desperate, foam clinging to the corners of his mouth. He growled something low and inhuman as if speaking was beneath him now.

Lucifer leaned in close, lips nearly to his ear, voice like thunder pressed into stone, "Zagan. Stop."

But Zagan only fought harder.

Lucifer shifted and pressed his knee deeper into his ribs, locking him in place. "*Look at me.*" The words cracked like a command layered with ancient power.

Zagan's struggles slowed, but his body still shook violently. His breath was labored, shallow. His pulse was too fast, so Lucifer didn't let go.

"You're in The Veil," Lucifer said, voice sharper now, cutting through the layers of illusion. "It's not real. None of it's real."

Zagan's body stilled, and finally, his eyes flickered with recognition.

Lucifer felt a drop in pressure, like air, returning to a room that had long been choking. The hallucination was slipping, not broken, but beginning to crack.

And that was enough to keep him from being swallowed whole.

Zagan exhaled shakily, his body finally slackening beneath Lucifer's grip. His muscles still trembled, but his mind was returning, piece by piece. Lucifer waited until he was sure Zagan was truly back before letting him up. Zagan rolled onto his back, staring at the shifting ceiling above them, chest heaving.

For a long moment, neither of them spoke.

Then, Zagan let out a weak, bitter laugh, "That was embarrassing."

Lucifer's expression didn't change, "It'll happen again if we don't keep moving."

Zagan's smirk wavered, and for the first time, Lucifer could see the real damage in him. His body was still decaying, and his movements were slower and weaker. The Veil was killing him faster than it was killing Lucifer.

They were running out of time.

Lucifer pushed himself up, offering no help as Zagan slowly dragged himself to his feet.

Without looking back, Lucifer turned toward the corridor ahead, toward the only way forward.

"Come on," he called over his shoulder.

Zagan exhaled sharply, shaking off the last remnants of the hallucination, but he followed.

Turning his walk to a run, Lucifer felt the sting of where Zagan's claws had dug into his shoulder, the shallow wounds aching in a way they shouldn't. He was healing, but he was healing too slowly.

The Veil was draining them, pulling at their strength, at their time, at their very existence.

Zagan ran a few feet behind, breathing hard. The hallucination had shattered, but the damage remained. There was a limp to his run, and his skin was paler than before and thinner. He looked like he'd aged another decade in just the past few minutes.

Lucifer was doing better, but not by much.

A strange sense, like something was watching them, washed over Lucifer as they ran. It was an eerie feeling that made his stomach churn. He couldn't see anything as he scanned around them, but he knew, in his bones, something was hunting them.

Every move they made, the Veil made one too. The corridor lurched, twisting on itself, warping in unnatural, impossible angles. The walls curved inward, then snapped back, like the jaws of a great beast, testing how close it could come before swallowing them whole.

Zagan stumbled slightly, catching himself.

He gritted his teeth and shouted to Lucifer in front of him, "What now?"

Lucifer didn't answer. His focus was ahead as the corridor they were running down changed yet again. The darkness that stretched in front of them had always been deep, endless, and unnatural. But now it was deeper, and it wasn't just empty.

It was watching.

Lucifer exhaled sharply, his muscles tightening.

They had to move faster.

"This way," he shouted as he picked up his pace.

Zagan didn't argue.

They moved forward, their steps echoing unnaturally, The Veil's silence pressing down on them. The path ahead was shifting as they ran, doors appearing and disappearing, openings collapsing into walls of solid nothing.

The Veil was herding them.

And Lucifer didn't like being herded.

Sounds echoed around them as they sprinted. They weren't loud, but they were wrong. Sounds that dragged past their ears slowly and deliberately, like something was moving just behind them but never quite touching the ground. Like it was always next to them no matter how fast their feet went.

Lucifer's jaw locked, but he refused to turn around. Refused to acknowledge the pressure building at his back, the way the shadows seemed to breathe.

But Zagan did.

He turned, just a glance, and froze.

His entire body went rigid, breath catching like something had seized it mid-air.

Lucifer sensed it before he saw it. "Don't stop," he growled, his voice sharp, commanding. "Zagan, *keep moving.*"

But Zagan didn't.

His eyes were wide now, locked onto whatever was behind them. Whatever was following them. His feet kept moving, but slower. Like gravity had changed for him. Like he wasn't sure if he was running from something or being pulled toward it.

Skitting to a stop, Lucifer took a deep breath and slowly turned. At first, there was nothing. Then, out of the darkness, a shape appeared. It was half-formed. Flickering. Shifting. Unstable.

A shadow of something that had once been alive.

Its limbs were too long, its movements unnatural. It had no face, just a void where its features should've been.

But it was watching them.

Lucifer knew it.

And it was smiling.

As the devils stared at the creature, the sensation of being watched grew as they realized there wasn't just one.

Lucifer could feel them now.

More figures, barely visible in the shifting corridors, crawling forward, moving along the walls and ceiling.

They weren't moving fast, but they were closing in.

Zagan swallowed, his body tensing. "I hate this place."

Lucifer exhaled, slow and sharp. "Run."

90

A Perfect Flaw

Lucifer and Zagan ran.

The Veil was collapsing around them, shifting violently and twisting into tighter, more unstable corridors. Every turn they took, the walls moved with them, closing off paths and forcing them deeper into its grip.

The creatures followed.

They didn't rush; they didn't have to. They were part of this place.

Lucifer could hear their whispers slithering through the air, weaving into the very fabric of the Veil itself. Words he couldn't understand, or worse, words he did.

"You are lost."

"You don't belong anywhere."

"You will never leave."

Zagan was falling behind.

Lucifer could feel his presence flickering, *fading*. The Veil was sinking its teeth into him, trying to finish what it started. But Lucifer didn't stop; he couldn't.

Stopping meant death.

Stopping meant losing.

His body ached as he sprinted, and his movements slowed, becoming heavy and tired. He looked at his hands; they were nearly skeletal as his breathing became labored. His lungs were screaming at him to stop, but he refused to give in; refused to let the Veil win. And just when it was becoming too much, when he thought his body would give out no matter what his mind said, a light appeared before him.

It wasn't warm or divine. It was *different*.

Ahead, at the end of the shifting corridors, was the boundary.

A wound carved into the darkness, jagged and pulsing with something colder than the Veil itself.

Lucifer didn't hesitate.

With all his strength, he grabbed Zagan by the arm and shoved him forward. Together, they burst through, and the Veil shattered behind them.

The moment they crossed the threshold, the air shifted.

Lucifer felt it first, a lightness creeping into his bones, undoing the weight that had settled over him. The exhaustion that had coiled around his limbs, the ache that had seeped into his very core, began to fade. His skin, lined with subtle, unnatural traces of age, smoothed. The sharpness of his features dulled ever so slightly as the Veil released its grip .

The damage was reversing.

The Veil had no hold here.

Behind him, Zagan let out a low, unsteady breath.

Lucifer turned just in time to see The First Devil stagger slightly, bracing himself against the jagged remnants of the broken path behind them. His fingers curled into the dirt, his body shaking.

For a moment, Zagan didn't move.

Then, ever so sharply, he inhaled. The color began returning to his skin, and the frailness that had settled into his form began to dissolve. The hollowness beneath his eyes, the weight of his limbs, and the unnatural thinness of his frame all began to unravel.

Zagan lifted his hand, turning it over as if testing reality. His lips parted slightly as if about to say something, but then, he just let out a breathless, bitter laugh. "Well. That was unpleasant."

Lucifer shook his head as a small chuckle escaped him, but he didn't offer more of an answer. He turned his gaze forward, toward the horizon, toward the towering golden gates in the distance.

They were close.

But not close enough.

Lucifer ran a hand through his hair, rolling his shoulders, testing his strength. It was returning faster than he expected. But that meant Heaven's influence was already touching them.

They didn't have long.

He turned to Zagan. "We don't rush in blind."

Zagan exhaled through his nose, amused despite everything. "Since when do you plan ahead?"

Lucifer shot him a sharp look, "Since we're about to walk into the gates of Heaven."

That, at least, wiped the amusement from Zagan's face.

Lucifer crouched low, scanning the terrain. The land leading up to the gates was unforgiving, with sharp cliffs and jagged peaks leading toward a narrow passage. It was designed to be a killing ground, *not* a battlefield.

It was a perfectly laid trap. There was no cover, no shadows, and no escape.

Lucifer curled his fingers into his palm.

He knew they couldn't just walk through the front door. Not without a distraction.

He glanced back at Zagan. "We need a way inside that doesn't end with both of us cut down before we get near the gates."

Zagan arched a brow, rolling his shoulders as the last traces of weakness drained from him. "And here I thought you were invincible."

Lucifer's expression didn't change. "Neither one of us is. Not here."

The words hung between them.

Zagan cracked his neck, considering. Finally, his smirk returned, sharper now, as if he'd fully returned to himself, "Then we better find a way to knock."

Together, they inched closer to the towering white gates but stopped two hundred yards from the entrance, crouched behind a jagged outcropping of stone.

The air was different here. Lighter. Almost weightless. It brushed against Lucifer's skin like a whisper, unfamiliar, unwelcome.

Heaven had a way of making things feel clean. Untouched.

Lucifer hated it.

"How the Hell do you expect us to get inside?" Zagan said from next to him.

Lucifer didn't answer because, honestly, he didn't know. The two devils sat for a while, crouched behind the rocks, watching the gates that never seemed to open.

But then, out of the corner of his eye, Lucifer saw it: movement. He snapped his head to the far right side of the towering wall, but again, there was nothing but stillness. Then, almost like a shimmer against the golden structure, there was a ripple of movement too soft to be seen unless one was looking for it. A small door was opened.

There was a secondary entrance seamlessly hidden in the vast golden walls.

Lucifer watched carefully as two figures stepped into view, one angel guiding a slow-moving line of souls.

They marched like shadows, translucent, their forms barely tethered to the ground beneath them. The angel in front carried a staff, its tip glowing faintly as it waved them forward. Another angel stood beside the entrance. And with a slow, effortless motion, he reached toward the heavy golden doors and pulled them open.

Lucifer's eyes narrowed.

This was it. This was their way in.

91

Shadows in the Light

Lucifer smirked slightly to himself. He'd seen this before. Hell had its own soul passage, a back door, an entryway that wasn't made for creatures like him. But it existed for the same reason this one did.

The afterlife was a machine, and souls were the fuel.

Every kingdom needed a way to move them.

Hell's soul passage was rarely spoken of, but every high-ranking devil knew it existed. A place where the weight of judgment pressed down, determining whether a soul was to be broken, shaped, or discarded altogether.

Zagan must have realized it, too. He let out a low chuckle.

"Of course, they have one." He shook his head. "And here I thought Heaven was supposed to be fair. Turns out they just take the Almighty through the front door and funnel the rest through the back like livestock."

Lucifer's jaw tightened.

This could work, but the problem wasn't just getting through; the issue was being seen.

They weren't souls. They weren't supposed to be here.

Zagan sighed, stretching out his arms. "Well, I hope you've got a plan because unless you're suggesting we kill an angel and walk in wearing his skin, I don't see how we—"

Lucifer cut him a sharp look. "A disguise."

Zagan rolled his shoulders as he leaned back against the stone. "Well, now that you mention it, I know a spell."

Lucifer turned his head slightly. "Of course you do."

Zagan flashed a sharp grin. "You think I made it through centuries of ruling Hell without knowing how to get through locked doors?"

Lucifer didn't argue. Of course, Zagan knew a way in. Still, Lucifer eyed him carefully. "Does it work?"

Zagan snorted. "You doubt me?"

Lucifer didn't answer.

Zagan rolled his eyes. "It's not permanent. And it won't make us angels, obviously. But it'll mask what we are. To Heaven, we'll be nothing more than two souls, freshly passed over, looking for entry."

Lucifer considered this. It was risky, but it was their best shot. "Do it."

Zagan exhaled, closing his eyes, "Muta me esse quod ante me video. Tantum nunc peto, o veteres, ut plus videat quam per me permittas. Libera animam meam."

His fingers moved through the air, his lips murmuring the incantation low and slowly. The air around them shuddered, bending beneath the weight of the dark magic.

Lucifer felt it immediately.

His power folded inward, buried beneath something thinner, lighter. His presence was being smothered beneath a false identity.

Lucifer hated it.

As Lucifer watched, Zagan's form began to change too. His usual sharp, imposing presence dulled. The heavy weight of his aura faded into something weaker, something lost.

Slowly, Lucifer dropped his gaze to himself.

His shadows were gone.

His wings were gone.

He felt weightless like he could float away at the slightest breeze, and as he brought his hand in front of his face, an eerie realization struck him; he could see Zagan *through* his hand. It wasn't a clear picture; it was dull, like someone had sucked all the color out of the world and covered it in a sheet of parchment paper.

They looked like souls.

Stripped of identity. Wandering. Lost.

Lucifer rolled his shoulders, testing the spell. It held for now.

Zagan smirked. "Not my best work, but I think I captured the 'tragic lost soul' look well enough."

Lucifer turned back toward the passageway where the line of souls was still moving forward, and the doors were still open.

Now, they just had to fool Heaven itself.

Standing, Lucifer took a deep breath, "Let's go."

Zagan clamored to his feet next to him and nudged him slightly, his grin now plastered back on his face. "Try to look more lost."

Lucifer shot him a warning look.

And then, together, they stepped forward toward Heaven's backdoor.

"By the way," Zagan whispered as they walked, "if this gets us killed, I'm haunting you."

Despite himself, Lucifer smirked. "You can try."

They walked silently for a moment as Lucifer took in the world around them. He'd expected smooth stone, perfect and polished like the Heaven he once knew. But here, on the outskirts, the terrain was pale, almost colorless, stretching in vast, endless plains that seemed to shimmer and shift as though it wasn't entirely solid.

Each step felt too light. The weight of his body, of existence itself, felt wrong.

Even the air was different.

It wasn't just clean; it was thin, weightless, and pressing without touching. The scent of it curled inside his lungs like something soft and sweet, an intoxicating purity meant to lull a soul into submission.

Lucifer knew what this was.

Heaven didn't just expect souls to come.

It made them want to stay.

It was all a trick. A pull. A gentle, insidious tether.

Lucifer gritted his teeth. He knew it wouldn't work on him, but Zagan was struggling. He didn't dare turn around and face Zagan or comment on it, but he could hear it: the way Zagan's breath came too fast, the way his steps dragged, his body trembling just slightly. The spell pulled too much power from him to hide it.

Lucifer winced slightly as Zagan exhaled sharply, shifting his weight as they moved, his movements looser than usual, not in a controlled way, not like a demon who didn't care, more like someone who didn't trust his own footing.

Lucifer didn't offer a hand; Zagan would refuse it anyway. Instead, he focused ahead, watching the only movement in this lifeless, perfect expanse. The seemingly endless line of souls.

"You ready for this?" Lucifer whispered to Zagan as they neared the edge of the line.

"As I'll ever be." Zagan said, passing by Lucifer and merging into the mash of wandering figures.

Taking a deep breath, Lucifer joined Zagan in line, keeping his head down. Around them, the souls were faint, shifting between transparency and form, all moving in the same direction. Some drifted listlessly, their shapes flickering like candlelight, uncertain, unknowing. Others moved with more awareness, though their steps were hesitant and reluctant. Some souls clung to one another, holding hands, linking arms, desperate not to be separated.

From the corner of his eye, Lucifer saw one figure whispering prayers to itself, clutching at its chest as if trying to remember the feeling of breath.

What was most unsettling to him wasn't the endless number of them; it was the fact that none of them resisted, none of them fought.

This was a stark contrast to the soul passage to Hell. Their souls were dragged, screaming, clawing, refusing the foreign land.

Here, they went willingly. Mindlessly herded like sheep to the slaughter.

His stomach curled with something dark and irritated, but he kept walking, moving as souls moved: hollow, quiet, and resigned. Zagan walked beside him, head lowered, steps careful. He was doing what Lucifer was doing, mimicking the lost.

But Lucifer knew him too well.

Beneath the facade, Zagan's muscles were too tight. His fingers kept twitching and flexing, eager to curl into fists.

This wasn't his Hell.

But it wasn't Lucifer's either.

And Zagan hated it.

Lucifer could feel the tension rising in him, a slow, growing storm, an unspoken defiance held back by sheer will. He leaned in slightly as they walked, his voice low, "Don't break now."

Zagan's shoulders stiffened.

For a moment, he didn't respond. Then, without looking, he muttered under his breath, "I've got this."

Lucifer didn't push, keeping his gaze forward, unyielding.

They were close now.

The gates were ahead.

And the Videntes were waiting, but before they reached the door, a shuddering inhale came from next to him.

At first, he didn't pay much attention, but then he heard it whisper, "No."

Lucifer snapped his gaze sideways. His eyes met a soul that had gone rigid. Its shape, faint and formless, quivered violently as if in distress. His stomach tightened. The soul wasn't just reacting to being in Heaven.

It had recognized something.

"They don't belong," the voice was a sharp, broken breath.

Then, suddenly, it began to panic. The soul lashed out, clawing at nothing, its body convulsing as if trying to warn the others.

"They don't belong!" it yelled over and over again.

Lucifer moved instantly, snapping his hand out and gripping the soul by the wrist. His hold wasn't tight or violent, but enough to anchor it and silence it. The form in his grasp wasn't real, not in the way demons or mortals were. But it felt real.

The shape shivered violently beneath his grip.

Leaning in, he lowered his voice and laced it with a quiet command, "You're mistaken."

But the soul staggered, shaking its head, its translucent face twisting, "No...no, I know, I know—"

Lucifer tightened his fingers around the shape, "You don't."

The soul wavered, and Lucifer could see the uncertainty crawling in. Its fractured memories blurred and overlapped, confused by its own panic.

The longer he held it, the more it wavered, doubted.

Next to him, Zagan shifted uneasily, and the spell around him flickered for just a second, the form of his disguise glitching.

Lucifer saw it.

And he was terrified the Videntes, who were now paying them far too much attention, did too.

As subtle as he could, Lucifer released the soul and returned his gaze to the ground, nudging Zagan, who quickly did the same. They reached the door, and in front of them, the celestial presence stirred. It wasn't a warrior; it didn't carry a weapon because it didn't need one.

The Vidente turned its gaze toward them, its white eyes cast over them, and for a moment, it felt like Lucifer was falling into them. Like he was being pulled into an endless pit of white made to unravel him, unmake him, into nothingness.

The Vidente wasn't a being of action nor of brute force; it was a being of knowing.

Its eyes were white voids, seeing through layers of existence. Not just flesh or spirit, but truth. And in response, Lucifer's entire body locked down, bracing against the force of its gaze.

The Vidente tilted its head.

"This one," it said. "He is not as he seems."

The line of souls stilled.

Zagan barely held himself together beside him. Lucifer could feel him failing, and he knew their disguise was slipping.

Without thinking, he lowered his head and kept his voice careful, measured, and fractured just enough to sound weak: "I...I don't remember who I am."

The words drifted into the space between them, uncertain, longing, and hollow.

The Vidente's head tilted again.

Closing his eyes briefly, Lucifer forced himself to take a step forward. Not aggressively. Not with defiance but with confusion.

"I don't remember..." He let his words fray, shatter slightly, the way a soul should sound when pulled from existence.

The Vidente watched him, then it turned to Zagan, and Lucifer's breath hitched.

Zagan wasn't responding.

Lucifer could feel the struggle inside him, the way his body wanted to buckle, the way his form flickered just slightly beneath the disguise.

So, he did the only thing he could.

Taking a slow, steady breath, he turned inward, searching. At first, he found nothing but the normal makings of his soul and body. But then, his mind traced the length of his spine, and there, buried deep, woven between each vertebra, sunk into the very marrow of his bones, he found it.

The chain.

A sharp inhale caught in his throat. The intensity of its grip was suffocating. It wasn't just wound around him; it had *become* him, threading itself into his very essence like a second spine, a new lifeline.

For a moment, he steadied himself, forcing himself to focus. Then, ever so carefully, he pulsed.

No one noticed.

The transfer of power was seamless, undetectable to all but one.

Zagan felt it instantly.

Like a drained battery snapping back to life, a spark, a jolt. His entire body reacted, his form jerking subtly before he fell perfectly into character. His movements turned sluggish, disoriented. His head drooped, his steps faltering, confusion clouding his features as if he were lost.

The Vidente watched him, unmoving.

A long pause stretched between them.

Then, slowly, the seer's gaze sharpened, cold and assessing, as if peeling back the layers of deception, searching for something beneath the surface.

Lucifer didn't breathe.

He watched in silence as the Vidente blinked once. Then again. Then, it stepped aside.

He didn't hesitate as he grabbed Zagan tightly and led him forward.

They'd made it inside, and the moment the golden doors sealed behind them, the air changed. It became lighter and more structured.

Slowly, Lucifer turned in a tight circle, taking in his surroundings. They were surrounded by souls in every direction, another waiting cell. The air echoed with whispers and soft murmurs, all sounds of waiting.

He had no idea where they were or which way to go. All he knew was Amber wasn't here, and they were running out of time.

92

Ashes

A shuddering breath wrenched through Amber's chest, sharp and uneven, dragging against the rawness in her throat. She'd almost gotten used to the pain, almost. But no matter how often it scorched through her, she'd never grow accustomed to the damage.

Her body was failing.

She could feel it in the hollow ache nestled between her ribs, in the way her limbs trembled with a weakness that wasn't just exhaustion but something more profound. Something stolen. Her sigil had once burned beneath her skin, bright with defiance, a brand of her choice. Now, only three dim points remained, flickering like dying embers.

A slow, creeping horror curled through her: she was disappearing.

Piece by piece, Heaven was erasing her. They weren't doing it violently; they were taking their time. Moving insidiously and subtly. Layer by layer, they were stripping her of herself until there'd be nothing left but what they wanted her to be.

She curled her fingers into fists, vowing to herself that she wouldn't let them, but even as the thought crossed her mind, a weight settled over her body, thick and suffocating. Her limbs felt foreign, unresponsive like her own muscles were betraying her.

A single tear slipped free, rolling down her cheek before splattering onto the white floor beneath her.

She wanted to fight. Wanted to scream. Wanted to claw her way out of these golden chains, to tear apart the angels who dared to do this to her. But she couldn't.

She could barely lift her head.

This wasn't what she'd expected. She'd known they'd weaken her. That much was inevitable. But she hadn't realized how much they'd take. The restraints around her wrists glowed faintly, their burn no longer searing but insidious, constantly siphoning away what little strength she had left. The more she fought, the tighter they wound, latching onto her like a sycophant.

That, she'd expected.

But the child, her breath caught, her fingers twitching as she lowered a trembling hand to her stomach; it was growing too fast. She could feel it shifting beneath her skin, a presence undeniable and hungry. She should've felt joy. She should've been overcome with joy at realizing she would be a mother. But instead, all she felt was fear.

She hadn't been showing when they brought her here. But now, as she pressed a weak palm against herself, her stomach was full. Heavy. At least seven and a half months along, if not more.

Impossible, and yet it was happening.

She'd thought Heaven had taken her to punish her. To purify her, but no, they'd taken her because they were afraid.

Not of her, of the child.

And yet, something was wrong. The sterile, suffocating light warped it, twisting it into something unnatural, killing her in the process. She knew they didn't care.

No matter how many times they spoke in hushed tones, their voices gentle, their words coated in poisoned honey, saying things like:

"You were never meant for Hell, Amber."

"That place twisted you. Broke you."

"But you are healing now."

She knew they didn't care, and she laughed bitterly the first time they said it. The second time, she'd spat blood at their feet, and the third time, she'd stayed silent.

Not because she was breaking but because she was tired. Their voices didn't hurt her. Their empty reassurances, their quiet, patient smiles meant nothing.

But time did, and they were using it as a weapon.

The more they spoke, the more the whispers of Hell began to fade. Her memories were slipping. Not all at once, but she could feel small things vanishing, dissolving like mist.

She'd once known the sound of screaming flames, the weight of shadows curling against her skin, and the scent of ash and blood and something darker, something forbidden, but now, they were harder to hold onto. As hard as she tried to remind herself that Hell was real, that she'd chosen it, every time she tried to picture the one who had brought her there, the one who had stood before her, bathed in fire and power, smiling with something too sharp to be gentle, but too real to be cruel, the image blurred.

Biting back a scream, Amber dug her fingernails into her palms.

No, she wouldn't forget. She wouldn't. She refused to give Heaven the satisfaction, but her body was failing.

Her mind was slipping.

He will find me, find us. She repeated the words over and over again in her head. She couldn't picture him fully anymore, but she knew, deep in her bones, in her very being, that he'd do whatever it took to rescue her.

As she repeated the words, the soft sound of calm footsteps cut through her thoughts. Despite herself, Amber went rigid.

They were back.

The light in front of her shifted, bending, forming into something solid as an angel stepped forward, her robes flowing like liquid silver, her face serene, untouched. The chains around Amber's wrists burned, tightening slightly, not as a punishment, but as a reminder.

She was still bound.

Still *theirs*.

The angel's gaze swept over her, lingering on her stomach. A slight, satisfied nod, "You're progressing well."

Amber's jaw locked, but the angel ignored her silence. Instead, she took another slow step forward, her expression unreadable, her voice soft. "You should rest, Amber. There is no reason to hold on to what no longer exists."

Amber's fingers twitched, and something in the angel's tone made her chest tighten. She had to fight to keep her face carefully blank. Still, the angel studied her as if measuring something unseen.

And then, the angel spoke again, "Lucifer is gone."

The fight left Amber, and her entire body froze. Her breath stalled, and her pulse thundered against her ribs. The words should've meant nothing. But the moment she heard them, something inside her *cracked*.

Before her, the angel's expression didn't change.

"The Veil swallowed him." A pause. Then, softer, gentler. "There is nothing left of him. It was a gallant effort, really. He thought he could save you. But no one uninvited gets through the Veil and *lives* to tell about it."

Amber's stomach lurched.

Lies.

They were lying.

They *had* to be.

Lucifer was...

Her mind reeled, grasping, desperate, clawing for any trace of him. Firelight against gold. Shadows curling at his feet. A smirk, dangerous and certain.

Slipping.

Fading.

No. No, she *wouldn't forget...*

The angel stepped closer, lowered herself slightly, and tilted her head as if she were speaking to a wounded thing: "You don't have to hold onto the past, Amber."

Then, to Amber's disgusted shock, the angel reached out. Slowly, carefully, as if approaching a skittish animal, she pressed a hand to Amber's forehead.

Amber flinched, recoiling as much as she could. The touch was cool. Not cruel or burning, but soft. The feeling was so light and delicate that it sank into her skin like poison. She wanted to tear this thing apart with her bare hands. But she was so, so tired.

Her limbs felt even weaker. Her thoughts were even slower.

And Lucifer's face...

Lucifer's name...

She clenched her jaw, trying to fight against the haze creeping into her mind. Around her, the angel's voice wrapped like silk: "It's time to let go."

Amber squeezed her eyes shut, trying to drown out the angel, to remember Lucifer or Hell, but she couldn't. Then, from the corner of her consciousness, blinding light swam towards her, and before she could react, before she could even scream, the searing pain returned.

93

The Storm Crowned

The air was too light, not just in weight but in presence and meaning.

Carefully, Lucifer stepped forward, mimicking the uncertain shuffle of the souls around him. His breath was steady, but he could feel it, the wrongness. Heaven wasn't rejecting him outright. No, it was watching.

Testing.

The walls pulsed with awareness, as though the light could see. The ground beneath him didn't reject his steps but *noticed them like* Heaven was waiting for something.

And Lucifer knew precisely what it was waiting for: a mistake. A flicker. A break in the illusion, but he was determined not to give in.

He kept his head slightly bowed, forcing his hands to remain slack at his sides. Souls didn't move with purpose. They drifted, uncertain, lost. If he acted like one of them, perhaps Heaven would hesitate a little longer before tearing him apart.

But it wasn't just him at risk.

Beside him, Zagan moved, his usual confidence buried beneath careful restraint. Unlike Lucifer, he wasn't struggling against Heaven's weight; there was no slow, crushing force pressing him onto the floor and no unbearable burn clawing at his essence.

Instead, there was nothing.

He saw it in the way Zagan's eyes flickered as he looked around, expecting something but finding only absence.

The light didn't push against him.

The air didn't ripple at his presence.

Heaven wasn't testing him; it was ignoring him.

And Lucifer knew that cut Zagan deeper than he'd ever admit.

Still, they moved through the space in practiced silence, their steps measured, carefully unremarkable. Their bodies adjusted to the slow, meandering pace of the lost, mimicking the vacant hesitance of souls who had nowhere to be.

Lucifer kept his gaze lowered, but his senses stretched outward, reading the space and its weight.

The hall where they were kept was vast, stretching into eternity, its height swallowed by a soft, unnatural glow that pulsed like something alive. Pillars of white stone curved into delicate arches overhead, each one carved with seraphic scripture, the letters shimmering faintly with celestial power. The floor beneath them was too smooth and polished as if nothing had ever touched it.

It was pristine. Unblemished. A place that didn't tolerate imperfection.

Around them, souls drifted.

Some knelt, their hands clasped in silent devotion, mouths moving soundlessly in prayers no one answered. Others simply floated, weightless, their faces blank, their eyes fixed on nothing.

There was no weeping here. No screams. No struggle.

Only waiting.

It was wrong. All of it.

Lucifer could feel it coiled beneath the surface like a whisper of something unspeakable. This wasn't a sanctuary. It was a holding place, a realm where lost things remained until they were deemed worthy or discarded.

Zagan let out a slow breath beside him, his voice nothing more than a ripple in the silence.

"At least we're not standing out," he muttered under his breath.

Lucifer didn't answer. He didn't need to.

Because something ahead had shifted, a ripple in the air, subtle but unmistakable. Heaven was always still, always calm until something disrupted it. And just ahead, near the far end of the hall, a cluster of angels had gathered. Their presence was a break in the illusion of peace.

They stood in a loose circle, their backs impossibly straight, their hands folded before them, their eyes sharp. Though they spoke in hushed tones, their voices carried, effortlessly woven into the air.

Lucifer exhaled slowly, carefully, his voice barely a breath, "Stay close."

And then, they moved, inching their way closer to the group of angels. Their steps slowed instinctively, bodies adjusting to the faintest shift in their surroundings. The glow of the walls felt brighter as they closed the distance between them and the angels, hotter, as if some unseen force was testing the weight of his disguise.

Zagan, beside him, barely moved. But Lucifer could feel the way his breathing had changed and the almost imperceptible tension in his muscles.

The angels hadn't noticed them, but the light had.

It pulsed just once. A quiet, waiting thing.

A warning.

Still, they crept closer, keeping their heads down until they were within earshot of the angels. They spoke softly, their voices like a hum that blended into the stillness.

Lucifer focused, letting the words slip through the meaningless droning of prayers and whispered confessions.

"...the abomination..."

His hands curled into fists, but Zagan nudged him quickly, reminding him to remain in character, and he unfurled his fingers.

"The cleansing is nearly finished. It won't be much longer now."

He forced his breath to stay even, but the weight behind it shifted.

"Have you seen her?" one asked.

"No," A tall, lengthy angel said, "only the higher-ups are allowed to. But I heard she's being kept in Turris Purgationis."

Lucifer's eyes widened as fear washed over him, but he forced his head to remain down.

"I thought...I thought they didn't use that tower anymore?" One asked with a hint of a tremor in his voice.

"They don't, save for very special guests, "the tall one said without emotion. "She'll be gone before the next cycle."

A faint tremor rippled beneath his skin. The disguise held, but it was straining; he was straining.

Zagan's eyes flicked to him, reading the tension in his posture. His voice was barely audible, a breath of sound. "We need to move."

But Lucifer didn't respond. Not yet.

"What of Lucifer?" Another voice, softer, curious.

"What of him?" The first voice responded.

"You don't think he'll come to try to rescue her?" The softer voice asked.

A huff of a laugh came from one, "that would be a suicide mission."

"I heard he tried," a different, slightly deeper voice chimed in. "The fool tried to breach The Veil. He was erased."

There was silence for a minute, then the first said calmly, flatly, "See, suicide mission."

Something sharp lodged itself beneath Lucifer's ribs at the sound of his own death, but what pained him more was the realization that Amber must've heard that, too. For days, maybe weeks, she must've believed it.

He forced himself to breathe, to keep his steps even and his form steady, but his mind reeled with the implications.

If they'd told her he was gone, if they'd repeated it, day after day, pressing the lie into her mind like a brand, what'd be left when he found her?

Would she even recognize him?

He swallowed the thought and turned his focus inward. Thinking like that would get them killed.

They had what they needed.

Amber was being held in Turris Purgationis. Only Archangels and select warriors had access, which meant more barriers, restrictions, and less time. But Lucifer had one advantage the angels didn't account for.

He could find her.

Heaven was built on purity and order. Everything here was pristine, which meant that if there was a disturbance, Lucifer might be able to sense it.

His focus stretched outward, not as a net, cast wide and thin, but as shadows, creeping slowly and deliberately through every crevice of Heaven. They didn't rush or fumble.

They crawled.

The sterile brightness of Heaven resisted him, its light pressing against the edges of his reach, trying to force him out, to erase the wrongness of him. But his shadows were patient. They didn't demand space. They claimed it, inch by inch, slipping into places light had forgotten to fill.

Lucifer didn't search for Hellfire; he knew there wouldn't be any. He knew there wouldn't be flames, screaming embers, or blistering scars of darkness cutting through Heaven's glow. That would be too easy; Heaven wouldn't allow such chaos.

Instead, he searched for the quiet thing. The thing Heaven tried to smother before it took root: pain.

It was never loud in Heaven. Not like in Hell, where agony lived in the very bones of the realm, where suffering was written into the stones, into the breath of every soul trapped beneath its dominion.

Here, pain was buried. Hidden beneath prayers and hymns, beneath soft words and empty reassurances.

Lucifer slipped past them, past the veils of peace stretched over the realm like a thin sheet trying to conceal something broken underneath.

He let the shadows of his mind crawl deeper.

They didn't move as a single entity but as many.

A thousand tiny threads of darkness wove their way through the fabric of this place, threading beneath the marble floors, slipping through cracks invisible to the eye, curling up the towering spires of white stone.

They reached places where the angels didn't look.

Where light didn't linger.

Where something was *wrong*.

And then he felt it: a pulse.

It was faint but undeniable.

His breath hitched.

There was a disturbance in the pattern. Something frayed, something unraveling. He pressed deeper, following its thread, letting the shadows twist and tighten around the source: Amber.

She wasn't screaming or fighting.

Her pain was too deep for that now, but it was fading.

Not naturally. Something was taking it from her.

No, Lucifer's shadows recoiled for a second before shooting forward again, not just her pain; her.

Piece by piece, they were erasing *her*.

His grip on his form tightened, his disguise flickering briefly before he forced himself to breathe.

He had her.

He *had her*.

But she was slipping fast.

And if he didn't move *now*, there'd be nothing left to find.

Quickly, Lucifer reigned in his shadows, calling them back to his sides.

Zagan must have sensed the shift in him because he tensed. "You saw her."

Lucifer didn't hesitate. "Yes."

Zagan exhaled. "She's alive?"

Lucifer's voice was steady, cold, but determined, "For now."

And then they moved.

94

Heaven Holds Its Breath

L ucifer moved with purpose. Slow, calculated, deliberate.

Lost souls were everywhere. Drifting, kneeling, whispering prayers that no one was answering. Their presence stretched in every direction, a sea of hollow faces and unfocused eyes, and for the first time, he was glad that it was so crowded. It was easy to disappear here, maybe easier than it should've been.

But he knew Heaven was still watching. He felt it with every step. The pressure hadn't lifted. The air still hummed with something too aware. But the angels didn't move toward them. Not yet.

It made sense; after all, lost souls didn't need to be watched; they'd already been judged.

Lucifer adjusted his posture, loosening his stance, letting his movements blend into the aimless shuffle of the damned. He let his hands stay slightly open at his sides as if he were waiting, hoping, for guidance.

Zagan mimicked him, but not perfectly. Lucifer could sense the tension in him. The rigid control.

The lost didn't hold tension. They yielded. They waited.

Lucifer murmured just loud enough for Zagan to hear, "Soften your step."

Zagan exhaled through his nose, adjusting just enough, and together, they drifted deeper into the tide of lost souls.

The air was thick with murmured prayers, the same hushed phrases repeating over and over:

"I am ready."

"I will be cleansed."

"Let me be remade."

Lucifer forced himself to keep moving.

Some souls had collapsed to their knees, their bodies folded inward, clutching at their chests as if something unseen was pressing into them. Others simply wandered, their gazes flickering, lost in some internal struggle only they could feel.

The weight of waiting was suffocating.

Lucifer caught a glimpse of an elderly man, his eyes vacant. He whispered words into his cupped hands like he was afraid they'd be stolen. A woman stood motionless, her fingers curled into the fabric of her gown, trembling.

These weren't souls that had been condemned.

They were the ones who hadn't yet been chosen.

Neither pure enough to rise nor wicked enough to fall.

Lucifer resisted the urge to look at their faces. To acknowledge them, to acknowledge what'd been taken from them.

They weren't here to be saved.

They were here to be forgotten.

As they shuffled their way toward the far edge of the hall, Lucifer allowed himself a single glance at the angels standing there. They were positioned like statues: tall, motionless figures woven into the fabric of the hall itself. Their robes flowed seamlessly into the marble like they'd been carved from the same material. Their eyes didn't move.

They didn't need to.

Lucifer forced his shoulders to relax. He knew souls didn't fear angels; they longed for them.

A soul who'd truly surrendered wouldn't hesitate. Wouldn't falter at their presence.

He let himself breathe slower, his pace even, reverent.

Zagan did the same.

The angels didn't react, but Heaven did.

The pressure curled around the edges of his being, testing.

Keeping his hands loose and his expression passive, he moved carefully. One wrong move and the light would strip him bare.

Suddenly, a voice sounded, "It is not yet time."

Lucifer's spine locked, but he relaxed slightly when he realized the voice wasn't directed at him. It had come from an angel, its tone smooth, calm, unshaken, but it was talking to a woman, one of the lost, who'd fallen at its feet, weeping.

Her hands were clasped in desperate prayer, her forehead pressed against the marble, "Please, please, I am ready—"

The angel didn't move. Instead, it simply repeated, "It is not yet time."

The woman let out a choked sob, but still, she didn't rise.

Without looking back, Lucifer kept walking.

The further they moved, the thinner the crowd became.

The lost souls faded as they crossed the room's threshold, leaving them in emptier halls and quieter spaces.

The air was denser now. Not heavy like Hell, but structured, as if the very walls knew who was meant to be here and who wasn't.

Zagan exhaled softly, shaking off the last traces of tension. He'd felt it, too.

Lucifer spoke under his breath. "We're past them."

Zagan nodded. "Now what?"

Lucifer glanced ahead, his gaze locking onto the looming structure beyond.

The Sanctum.

Where Amber was and where the real challenge began.

They'd passed unnoticed, but Heaven knew they were here, and soon, it would act.

"Now we find her." Lucifer said, turning and starting down the narrow hall.

As they walked, the walls curved inward, subtly at first, then more deliberately, like a throat slowly closing in around what didn't belong.

But Lucifer didn't slow.

The light was pulling at the edges of his form, pressing against his skin like hungry fingers, trying to peel him apart. He exhaled through his nose, forcing his disguise to hold.

Every angel they passed seemed to pay them no mind; they didn't need to. Heaven didn't grant passage to intruders. It didn't allow the unworthy to wander its halls, not without consequence.

And yet, Lucifer and Zagan passed without challenge.

It had unsettled him before; now, it unraveled something colder inside him.

Had Heaven let them come this far because it had already decided the outcome?

His fingers curled at his sides, pulse steady despite the unease crawling along his spine.

The temple that towered before them didn't look like a prison. The walls stretched impossibly high, smooth and flawless, untouched by time. The entrance stood before them, its doors woven from pure light, shifting in and out of solidity like something beyond comprehension. It wasn't a barrier or a guarded threshold.

It was a verdict.

Nothing entered unless Heaven allowed it, and still, Lucifer pressed forward.

The four angels guarding it stood in perfect stillness, their forms wrapped in flowing silver, their faces serene, unburdened by expression. Their wings were vast, gilded, seamless in purity, and remained half-folded at their backs as if they'd never needed to move because nothing entered here that wasn't permitted.

Lucifer slowed, calculating, and Zagan took a slow breath beside him.

"We need a distraction," Zagan murmured.

Lucifer's gaze flicked to him, but Zagan's face remained neutral and unreadable. His eyes stayed fixed ahead, locked onto the gate as if he were already planning his next move.

"I can pull them away," Zagan continued. "Long enough for you to get inside."

For a fraction of a second, Lucifer hesitated.

There was something wrong.

Zagan's voice was too carefully measured. His posture was too controlled.

Lucifer almost questioned it. Almost.

But Amber was slipping.

He had no time.

Lucifer nodded once. "Make it fast."

Zagan exhaled sharply, almost relieved, then turned and vanished into the shifting light.

Lucifer didn't watch him go. Instead, he inched closer to the threshold, every muscle in his body tense.

And then he felt it: the shift.

At first, it was subtle, just a ripple in the air, like a held breath just before exhaling; then, it was absolute chaos.

A loud and sudden crack split through the stillness like a jagged tear in silk. Light flared somewhere behind him, followed by another, then another. All around him, angels moved.

Lucifer barely turned his head, just enough to see the unfolding disturbance, a brilliant flare of celestial light bursting outward, washing over the sea of souls like an eruption of judgment.

Zagan had drawn their attention.

He could hear the rising murmurs, the movement, and the shuffling of bodies as the air became tense with an unseen presence.

And then, the first guardian angel stepped forward. The movement was slight, a single shift of their robes, a fraction of space surrendered.

But it was enough.

The second angel followed, then the third, and Lucifer felt his breath slow. Their movements were unhurried but absolute. They were being pulled away, drawn toward the flare of light, toward the unnatural break in Heaven's order.

Toward Zagan.

Only the fourth angel remained, unmoving and unblinking, simply waiting.

Lucifer forced his pulse to steady, but the angel had noticed him. He knew it; he could feel the weight of its presence pressed against him, like a palm against his chest, unseen but crushing. It hadn't yet called him out, hadn't yet spoken.

But it knew.

Keeping his body loose and his expression carefully composed, he stepped forward. His movements were slow and fluid, shifting into the calm reverence of the lost.

At first, the angel didn't react, didn't even move to stop him; it only stared.

He carefully adjusted his posture further, with a slight downward tilt of his head, a breath held just too long, and his steps quiet and careful.

Slowly, he found himself standing in front of the angel. For a moment, there was nothing but silence between them, and then the angel spoke, "Are you ready?"

Lucifer forced his pulse to remain steady. The voice had been smooth and unshaken, neither warm nor cold. It wasn't asking him a question; it was a confirmation.

Slightly, Lucifer lifted his gaze to meet the angel's face. It was untouched, unburdened by expression. It had no need for emotions.

It didn't ask because it cared but because it already knew the answer.

Lucifer's fingers curled slightly at his sides before he spoke, "I am."

The words left his lips without hesitation, smooth, quiet, almost reverent, and the angel tilted its head.

For a moment, there was nothing but stiff, dead silence. Heaven was waiting, testing, deciding. So, Lucifer forced his shoulders to loosen further, his breath to remain steady while the angel studied him.

Then, slowly, it turned its head toward the disturbance behind them.

Lucifer didn't move; didn't breathe.

The angel stepped away, and the weight around them lifted just slightly. Forcing himself not to react or to look at the angel, who was once again motionless, Lucifer stepped forward, passing through the veil of light.

95

Forgotten but Not Gone

His disguise dropped as soon as he passed into the eerily quiet chamber.

It wasn't peaceful but sterile, the kind of silence after something had been carved away, leaving behind only the shape of what used to be. It was a small space but the white seemed to go on forever and there in the middle of it all, Lucifer found her.

She sat curled against the cold stone, her fingers tracing invisible patterns against the ground. Her body was small, and her skin, once flushed with life, was too pale. Her form was thinner, almost frail. The golden chains binding her wrists pulsed softly as if they were breathing with her, feeding off what little she had left. She should've looked up, should've felt him, but she didn't.

Her eyes, once sharp, once defiant, were distant now. Dazed.

Slowly, he stepped forward, swallowing the space between them, but still, she didn't flinch.

"Amber." His voice came out quiet but carried, curling around them like smoke. A command. A plea.

She lifted her head slowly, her brow furrowing, not as if the word meant something but as if it *should* mean something. Her gaze settled on him, and for a brief, fleeting moment, he *hoped* she knew.

But then, her expression smoothed, going blank, as if someone had reset her, and Lucifer's chest tightened.

"Oh," she breathed, tilting her head the way one does when observing something distant, something unreachable. "You shouldn't be here."

His muscles flexed. "Amber—"

"You died." She spoke like she was recalling a story, like it had been whispered to her in quiet, unyielding repetition. A truth carved into her bones. "In the Veil."

Lucifer's fingers curled into fists. His breath felt thick in his throat, his fury an ember threatening to ignite.

Lies.

They'd fed her *lies*.

"Amber," he tried again, more forceful this time, stepping closer. Close enough to reach her, to pull her to him, to remind her.

But she only blinked, confusion flashing across her face, a momentary crack in her serenity before she shook her head, her hands rising slowly and delicately.

A gesture of comfort, of pity.

"I know what you are," she said, her voice soft, reverent. "You're an angel."

Lucifer stilled, and his heart, his wicked, ancient heart, lurched.

She didn't recognize him.

Not as her captor. Not as her devil. Not as the man she'd once dared to challenge, to defy, to—

His throat burned.

"I'm not..." He exhaled sharply, willing the rage to settle. It wouldn't help. Not now. "It's me, Amber."

She frowned. Something flickered across her face, a shadow of uncertainty, of something long buried trying to resurface. Her fingers twitched. Her breath hitched. But then, just as quickly, it was gone.

"No," she murmured, shaking her head, the warmth in her eyes dimming into something like sorrow. "Lucifer is dead."

And with those words, she turned away. Leaving him standing there, hollow, unrecognized, a stranger to the only soul that had ever made him feel like something more than the monster he was supposed to be.

Lucifer didn't move; he couldn't.

Amber had turned away from him, dismissing him like a phantom, like an illusion conjured from her unraveling mind.

But then he saw it.

The shift in her weight as she adjusted her position, the way her hand drifted, unthinking and instinctual, down to her stomach, and his breath caught.

For the first time in his eternal existence, time stilled.

Amber's gown, tattered at the edges, stretched over the very swollen curve of her belly. It wasn't just a trick of the dim light or a hallucination. No, this was real.

His child.

His.

And by the looks of it, she was *almost due.*

Something inside him cracked wide open, splitting through bone, through centuries of control. He stared, unable to tear his eyes away. She was heavy with his child, her body unmistakably shaped by its weight. *Their* child. *His* heir. She was too far along for this place, too far along to be here, where the air reeked of sanctity and lies, where her body had been forced to endure without protection, *without him.*

The breath left his lungs in a sharp, ragged exhale.

How had he not known? How had they hidden this from him?

Amber curled further into herself, arms tightening around herself, protective. A mother's instinct, one he'd no claim to. She didn't recognize him, didn't trust him.

Didn't know *him.*

Lucifer swallowed the acid rising in his throat. There was no time to process. No time to be paralyzed by the gut-wrenching truth that he'd lost more than just months with her; he'd lost *her* when, suddenly, the ground beneath them trembled in warning.

The angels were coming.

He needed to get them out of here before she was too far gone to save.

Lucifer's voice came out hoarse. "Amber."

She flinched.

That hurt more than it should've.

"I don't have time to explain," he forced out, trying to keep his voice steady. "But you need to come with me."

Amber shook her head violently. "No." Her breath hitched, her chest rising and falling too fast. "I—I *won't.*"

Lucifer's legs twitched. He could hear the faint shift of energy in the air, the slow, creeping hum of something gathering strength. They were coming.

No.

His heart pounded as he moved closer, but she clamored to her feet, off-balance from the weight of her belly. Lucifer caught her, instinct, pure instinct, and the moment his hands touched her arms, a shudder ran through her.

A memory. A crack in the foundation of whatever they'd done to her.

Her lips parted, her pupils blown wide as she looked up at him, really *looked.*

Lucifer held his breath.

For a moment, just a moment, he saw something flicker in her expression. Recognition? Fear? *Trust?* But just as quickly as the moment had come, it vanished. Forcefully, she tore away from him, pressing herself against the cold stone wall. Her hands cradled her belly, her breathing sharp and shallow.

"I won't let you take my baby," she whispered.

Lucifer's lungs clenched.

His baby.

His child.

A part of him was inside of her, alive, growing, thriving despite everything. A flicker of something unfamiliar, something *dangerous*, rippled through his chest.

Mine.

A roaring, possessive need to protect, *claim* what was his, and burn the world down before letting anything touch them.

He forced it down. He couldn't afford to lose control. Not now.

"Amber," he said again, his voice rough, "I swear to you, I will not harm you. I will not take your child from you. But if we don't leave *now,* you won't get the chance to raise them."

Her fingers pressed harder into the fabric of her dress, over the curve of her stomach.

Lucifer took a step closer, slow, deliberate. "You don't have to trust me," he murmured. "But trust yourself. Do you feel safe here?"

She wavered.

He could see it: doubt began to seep in. The air in this place felt heavier and colder, and she was *listening.*

Ever so slowly, she shook her head, "This is a trick."

He clenched his fists, his nails biting into his palms. His rage was a living thing, slithering up his spine, coiling around his ribs like a vice.

He would burn Heaven to the ground for this.

Lucifer moved closer, careful now. Measured. She wasn't the woman who'd spat at him, who'd fought him with sharp words and sharper glares. She was slipping. Fractured. He had to be careful, or he'd lose her entirely.

"They lied to you," he said, voice low, coaxing. "I'm alive, Amber. Look at me."

She shook her head. "You're not real."

His patience frayed. He stepped in front of her and dropped to one knee, his voice dropping to something lower, softer, as he forced her to see him, to *really* see him.

Amber sucked in a sharp breath, eyes widening because up close, she couldn't deny it anymore. Her lips parted. Her body swayed.

Lucifer reached for her, his hand hovering just above her arm. "It's me, little dove."

Something flickered in her eyes. A spark. A memory trying to claw its way to the surface. A tremor ran through her, her fingers twitching slightly against the chains.

Then, her gaze dropped to his chest, his arms, his hands, and the raw power vibrating off him, dark and consuming, nothing like the angels she'd come to trust.

Her breathing quickened, so Lucifer leaned closer, "You chose me."

Her breath shook.

Lucifer's voice lowered, steady and grounding. "And I will never let you go."

For a moment, just a moment, her eyes flickered in recognition, disbelief, something too raw to name.

But before she could say anything, the doors behind him slammed open, and a presence filled the space.

Lucifer didn't turn; he didn't have to, he knew.

Zagan.

And with him, the Archangels.

96

Heaven's Favorite Traitor

Amber flinched at the sudden force of power that entered the room, but Lucifer didn't move. Didn't turn. His shoulders squared, his body shielding Amber instinctively as the weight of celestial power flooded the room. It was suffocating, thick with divinity, pressing against his skin like molten iron.

He knew who it was before he even heard the voice.

"Lucifer." Michael's voice was coated with finality, laced with the smug certainty of a man who'd already won.

Lucifer exhaled slowly through his nose. *Breathe.* Stay *still.* Stay *calm.*

But then Amber whimpered. A slight, unsteady sound, half pain, half fear, as she shrank further behind him.

And that, *that*, ignited something ancient and unholy inside him.

His head turned just enough to catch sight of Zagan, standing at the forefront of the Archangels. His expression was impassive, but his eyes were cold and calculating.

The bastard *knew.*

Knew exactly what he'd done.

Lucifer's stomach twisted, rage pooling in his throat like bile. "So," he said, his voice deceptively smooth, "this is how you do it? A knife to the back?"

Zagan didn't flinch. "I did what had to be done."

Lucifer let out a short, humorless laugh. "Had to be done," he echoed. "That's what you're calling it?" His voice darkened, something sharp and cruel slipping in. "Cowardice?"

Zagan's jaw clenched.

The Archangels stood motionless behind him, silent, waiting, not out of deference but because they had already won.

Lucifer's gaze flickered to Amber, her breath uneven, her arms curled around her belly in a protective grip. She was too far along. Too weak.

Lucifer turned back to Zagan, his stance easy, almost relaxed. "I should've seen this coming," he murmured. "You've always been afraid, haven't you?"

Zagan's eyes flashed. "I'm not afraid."

Lucifer arched his brow. "Then why are you standing with *them?*"

Something flickered in Zagan's gaze, but he crushed it down before it could take shape. "You're going to lose, Lucifer."

Lucifer just smiled. "You think Heaven will let you keep your power?" He tilted his head slightly. "Or is it my child you want?"

Amber sucked in a breath.

Zagan didn't respond, didn't *deny it*. Instead, he simply turned to Michael beside him, his voice void of remorse. "Do what you have to do to get rid of the girl. Then sever the tie between me and Lucifer."

Lucifer looked between them for a second as he realized why Zagan had betrayed him, but his amusement drained instantly and was replaced by something cold, something lethal. His fingers twitched at his sides, his magic coiled in his palms, blacker than the void, hungering for release, but the Archangels moved first.

Light exploded outward, divine power streaking through the chamber in blinding arcs. Lucifer barely had time to react before a force slammed into his chest, sending him skidding backward, boots scraping against the stone.

Amber *screamed*.

His head snapped toward her just as the golden light wrapped around her wrists, ankles, and stomach began to glow brighter. The sigil carved into her skin *burned*, glowing white-hot.

Lucifer lunged. "No—!"

But the moment he reached for her, the air *shattered*. A pulse of holy power detonated through the chamber, and Amber's scream twisted into something *agonized*.

The sigil burned brighter, searing through her skin, her body convulsing as an unbearable crackle of energy coursed through her, and she collapsed.

Lucifer *felt* it. The shift. The loss.

Another sigil point gone.

She had *one left*.

The reality of it slammed into him harder than any divine force Heaven could conjure. His hands shook as he fell to his knees beside her, cupping her face, his touch careful, *too careful*, as if she'd break apart beneath his fingers. Her body twitched with the aftershock, her lips parted in a silent cry, her breath shallow, ragged.

She was slipping, breaking, running out of time.

Lucifer's vision blurred, not with grief but with rage. It curled inside him, thick as smoke and heavy as war. He rose to his feet, slow and deliberate.

The air trembled.

A low hum built in the stone beneath them, reverberating outward in steady, deadly waves. Lucifer's rage had weight. It had teeth.

It was *alive*.

And yet, when he finally spoke, his voice was calm. *Too calm,* "You made the wrong choice, Zagan."

The air between them thickened, a slow, simmering heat crackling at the edges of Lucifer's control. He stepped forward, shadows twisting at his feet like hungry things, curling and coiling with every step.

Zagan's body tensed, but he held his ground. "Don't look at me like that," he muttered, lifting his chin. "You brought this on yourself."

Lucifer didn't stop, and Zagan's fingers twitched at his sides, his power curling and preparing.

The Archangels didn't move. They stood still, watching, waiting, silent judges at the end of a trial, their verdict already decided. They weren't going to interfere, at least, not yet. They wanted to see what would happen first. Lucifer could *feel* their amusement, their patience.

It made his blood boil.

But his focus was singular. One more step, and he was close enough to feel the heat of Zagan's skin, the tension rolling off him. Close enough to strike.

Zagan took a slow breath, clenching his jaw.

Lucifer saw the moment hesitation flickered through him.

A muscle in his cheek jumped. "What?" Zagan scoffed, forcing a smirk that didn't quite reach his eyes. "Not going to say something poetic before you try to kill me?"

Lucifer tilted his head, expression unreadable.

"No," he said simply.

And then he *moved.*

Faster than lightning, his fist connected with Zagan's ribs, sending him staggering back, his feet scraping against the stone. But Lucifer wasn't done. He lunged, power crackling, shadows surging around him like living things, coiling up his arms, lashing out.

Zagan twisted, dodging at the last second, barely managing to plant his feet before retaliating. Hellfire erupted from his palms, scorching the air as he struck.

Lucifer didn't flinch. He took the blast straight to the chest, barely staggering. The flames flickered and died the moment they touched him, swallowed whole by the endless darkness unraveling at his feet.

Zagan swore under his breath.

Lucifer's eyes gleamed bright and burning.

"You thought you could play both sides," he murmured, advancing again.

Zagan backpedaled, magic coiling in his fists. "I *had* to."

Lucifer's lips curled, amusement flickering at the edges of his fury. "Had to?" He tilted his head. "Or were you just waiting for an excuse?"

Zagan's eyes flashed, his control fraying. "*Fuck you!*" he snarled, throwing his power forward.

Their magic collided.

Shadow against flame. Chaos against control.

Lucifer caught his strike, twisting Zagan's arm behind him, slamming him down to his knees with enough force to crack the stone beneath them.

Zagan gasped, the sound ragged, but he didn't yield. His breath hitched, his muscles tensed, and then he *grinned*.

Lucifer saw it too late.

Zagan twisted hard, throwing Lucifer off balance just enough to rip free. His fist came up, but Lucifer caught it.

And *crushed* it.

A sharp, brittle crack split the air as Zagan screamed.

His wrist was broken.

Lucifer wrenched his arm further, twisting until Zagan's body buckled beneath the weight of the pain until he was forced to his knees, gasping, struggling, *losing*.

The Archangels still didn't move; they were waiting.

Zagan coughed, his breath shuddering. His free hand pressed against the ground, trying to push himself up, but Lucifer's grip tightened.

"You never had the stomach for war," Lucifer said, his voice quiet, almost thoughtful. "Did you really think you'd survive playing *both* sides? I've beaten you once. Did you really think I wouldn't beat you again?"

Zagan's shoulders heaved. He was breathing too fast. Too wild. His gaze darted to the Archangels. Still, they stood there, watching.

He wet his lips, voice uneven. "Aren't you going to help me out here?"

Silence.

Zagan's breath caught. His eyes flickered with something, *fear*, as the truth sank in.

They weren't going to help him.

And then, Raphael finally spoke, "You made the wrong choice, Zagan."

Zagan barely had time to react before Michael's smooth and measured voice cut through the chaos like a blade, "You really thought we would reward you, Zagan?"

Lucifer didn't loosen his grip, but he did smile.

Slow. Cruel.

Because he'd already *known*.

Of course.

"You are filth," Raphael continued, his voice ringing with quiet disgust. "A creature of the Pit." His gaze swept over Zagan, detached, dismissive.

Zagan's brows furrowed, confusion flickering behind his eyes, but Raphael wasn't finished. His gaze swept over him, detached. Dismissive. "Do not mistake our tolerance for mercy."

Zagan's lips parted slightly, his breath unsteady. "But you said—" He faltered, then forced the words out. "You said you'd cut the soul chain if I told you where Lucifer was. You'd bow to me."

Raphael tilted his head slightly. Then, without looking away, he glanced toward the others.

Gabriel smirked. "As if we would ever do such a thing."

Michael shook his head, the amusement in his expression light, almost *bored*.

And then, they laughed. Soft, at first, then it grew, rolling over each other like the toll of a bell. Not cruel. Not mocking,

Dismissive.

Zagan was *nothing* to them.

Lucifer saw the moment it sank in. A flicker in Zagan's expression, the smallest shift, the kind that only came when a man realized he'd sold his soul for nothing.

"You've never been enough on your own," Lucifer murmured.

It wasn't an insult. Just the truth.

But it wasn't his words that broke Zagan.

It was *hers*.

Still on the ground, trembling from the sigil's burn, Amber looked up at Zagan, not with rage or even fear.

With *pity*.

Then, she let out a soft, bitter laugh.

"Of course," she breathed. "I should've known."

Zagan stiffened.

"You've *always* been a coward." A statement of fact. Nothing more.

But Lucifer saw it, saw the way Zagan *felt* it, deep inside, in a place he'd ignored for centuries.

He'd never fought for anything. Never *stood* for anything, always following the strongest side.

And now, he had no side at all.

The Archangels moved again, their power coiling around Amber like a noose, divine fire licking at the edges of her skin. She let out a strangled gasp, her back arching when suddenly Zagan felt it.

A pulse.

Faint but undeniable.

Zagan flinched. He thought, for a second, that it came from Lucifer. Or maybe Amber.

But no.

The pull, the *recognition*, came from somewhere else.

Came from the child.

A flicker of something foreign rippled through Zagan's being, a whisper of magic brushing against his soul. Not from Heaven. Not from Hell, from something deeper.

The baby had reached for him, not as an enemy or a betrayer, but as one of their own.

Zagan's stomach twisted. A foreign, sick feeling clawed up his spine because suddenly, he *saw*.

The Archangels weren't just here for Amber.

They weren't just here for Lucifer.

They wanted the child gone.

Purged.

Erased from existence.

Lucifer's voice cut through the air, rough with fury. "You *chose* them, Zagan."

Zagan barely heard him. His mind was spinning, the cold weight of realization sinking into his bones because he knew Heaven.

He knew what they did to things that didn't belong.

And the child, Lucifer's child, was something new. Something they deemed *dangerous* because it was something that should never have existed.

He looked at Amber again, at the way she gritted her teeth against the pain, her body curling protectively around the life inside her.

And Zagan realized he couldn't let them do it.

He couldn't let them take the child.

He'd made a mistake.

And now, he had to fix it.

97

The Unborn War

"Honestly, Zagan, just sit down. You've done your part." Michael said dismissively, barely sparing Zagan a glance as he waved a hand in his direction.

Then, with a slow, measured turn, his attention settled fully on Lucifer. His lips curved, but there was no warmth, only the sharp edge of amusement laced with contempt.

"Lucifer," he drawled, the name curling off his tongue like something unpleasant he had to taste. "What a... pleasant surprise."

Lucifer didn't respond with words. He bared his teeth instead, the gold in his eyes flickering dangerously, power coiling under his skin, ready to strike.

"You didn't think I'd come?" he asked, voice low and venom-laced.

Michael tilted his head as he stepped forward, calm and composed, as if this moment had been rehearsed centuries ago. "Oh, we knew you would."

His tone was patient, almost *pitying*, and that made it worse.

He continued, stepping into the flickering half-light of the chamber. "You really believed you'd gone unseen? That the whispers, the flickers in the air, the sudden stillnesses were just Heaven responding to your... aura?"

A pause. Then, with a cold smile: "We let you through."

Lucifer's breath hitched, just for a second, but they all saw it.

Michael's eyes gleamed. "How else do you think you passed through the halls unnoticed?" he said softly, mockingly. "Did you truly believe you'd bested us? That you outwitted *Heaven*?"

Gabriel stepped forward, shrugging lazily, his grin curling. "Every moment you thought the air shifted because it sensed you..." He shook his head slowly, lips parting in a cruel smile. "That wasn't the air."

"It was *us*," Raphael added, his voice soft and cutting, like a blade wrapped in silk. "We watched you every step."

Lucifer's wings flinched, shadows crawling around his feet like fire without flame.

Gabriel's smirk widened as his gaze turned toward Amber, who was trembling and bleeding magic, her arms cradling her swollen stomach protectively even as pain etched lines into her face.

"You were never a threat, Lucifer," Gabriel said, eyes glinting. "You were the audience."

Lucifer stepped forward, fury rolling off him like a Stormfront, but Gabriel only laughed under his breath.

"She's just about due, wouldn't you say?" he mused, head tilting as his gaze raked over Amber. "But judging from the look of her..."

Amber's breathing came in sharp, shallow pants. Her skin was pale, nearly gray, sweat gleaming at her hairline. Her arms curled tighter around her stomach like she could shield what little time she had left.

Gabriel took another step, his voice dropping to something almost reverent. "She won't survive the birth."

Lucifer surged forward, but Michael blocked him with a simple hand raise. The force of it froze him mid-step, power meeting power.

Gabriel's smile stretched wider. "Let alone the final sigil removal."

Amber's breath caught, and Lucifer stilled.

"You knew what we were doing," Gabriel continued, his voice almost soothing now, a priest performing the last rites. "But you didn't know what it meant. The seals, the markings... they were never about protection. They were transformation. Ascension."

He turned back to Amber.

"You think we'd allow the child of Hell to be born in its image?" he asked, voice sharp now, bright with the brilliance of righteous cruelty. "No. If it lives, it lives as *ours*. Washed clean. Made holy. Made useful."

Amber's eyes were filled with tears, but not of fear of *rage*. Her hand found Lucifer's. Her grip was shaky but defiant.

Gabriel's voice dropped to a whisper.

"And if the birth kills her..." He exhaled slowly. "All the better."

Lucifer's power flared in a sudden wave of heat.

But before he could speak, Raphael did, stepping forward at last, his voice quiet and measured. Almost bored.

"We told you," he murmured, looking at Lucifer. "Heaven doesn't make mistakes."

A pause. A breath.

Then, without blinking: "It remakes them."

The words sliced through the air like a blade, sharp and deliberate.

Lucifer *felt* Amber stiffen beside him, her breath hitching, her fingers curling tighter around the swell of her stomach. His rage surged, an inferno barely restrained, crackling beneath his skin like a caged storm.

Gabriel's smirk deepened, eyes gleaming with something wicked, something *certain.*

"You can feel it, can't you?" he tilted his head. "She's unraveling. One more sigil and she'll be gone. Or..." His gaze flicked lower to the weight of life pressing against Amber's frame. "Maybe she won't even make it that far."

Lucifer moved. He didn't think. Didn't hesitate, just *moved.*

In an instant, he was there, his hand wrapped around Gabriel's throat, his grip tightening, dark power pulsing against the radiant glow of the Archangel's skin. The room shook with the force of his fury.

Gabriel's smirk faltered just slightly.

Michael sighed. "Oh, come now, Lucifer." He didn't sound concerned. If anything, he sounded bored. "Is this really how you want to spend her last moments? Bickering?"

Lucifer's grip tightened. Shadows curled around his wrist, seething, hungry. "I should rip your tongues out," he growled. "See how you speak in riddles then."

Michael chuckled. "And what? You think that will change anything?"

Lucifer didn't answer. He could feel Amber's heartbeat behind him, *too fast,* the tremor in her limbs growing stronger. He was running out of time.

Gabriel exhaled sharply, his expression strained but still laced with amusement. "That temper of yours," he rasped, voice slightly hoarse from the pressure on his throat, "has always been your greatest flaw."

Lucifer barely resisted the urge to *break* him.

Behind him, Amber shifted, her breath shallow. "Lucifer..."

His rage *flared* at the sound of her voice, at the weakness in it.

Michael clasped his hands behind his back as if discussing the weather. "You could surrender," he suggested lightly. "Lay down your weapons. Hand over the girl and the child. We'll make it quick."

Lucifer let out a slow, deadly laugh. "You must take me for a fool."

Michael sighed, tilting his head. "I was hoping you'd see reason."

Lucifer shoved Gabriel away, sending the Archangel staggering back. Gabriel wiped his throat, exhaling a small *tsk* before straightening his robes, unconcerned.

Michael took another step forward, eyes glinting. "You know this is inevitable, don't you?"

Lucifer bared his teeth. "You think I'd let you have them?"

"I think," Michael said smoothly, "you don't have a choice."

The air shifted.

Amber gasped as light crackled across the chamber, the sigil on her skin pulsing violently.

Lucifer's vision darkened.

They were starting the final removal.

Michael smiled. "Shall we begin?"

The chamber began to tremble when suddenly Zagan acted. He didn't think. Didn't plan. His body moved before his mind could catch up. For one second, he stood paralyzed by realization, guilt, and the sheer weight of his mistake. And the next, he *lunged*.

Not at Lucifer.

Not at the Archangels.

At Amber.

His arms wrapped around her, his body forming a barrier between her and the burning light closing in. A shield. A decision. A *choice*.

Lucifer's world tilted. For a second, a single breath, he didn't understand what he was seeing. Zagan, a traitor, wasn't standing with Heaven.

Lucifer moved on instinct, his shadows flaring, his magic screaming for release, ready to tear Zagan apart until he realized Zagan wasn't attacking.

He was shielding her.

The brilliant golden light surged toward them, Heaven's judgment coalescing into something sharp, something final, something meant to *erase*.

And Zagan took it.

His back arched, his mouth parting in a silent gasp as the force struck him instead of Amber. It seared into his skin, cutting deep, burning, but he didn't move. Didn't let go.

Lucifer's rage morphed into something sharper, colder.

"*Get off of her!*" he snarled, his voice raw with fury.

Zagan gritted his teeth, barely breathing, barely standing, but his grip only tightened.

"You don't get to die for her," Lucifer spat. His shadows writhed, deadly. "Not after what you've done."

Zagan exhaled, ragged, his voice hoarse. "They're not just after Amber. They're after the child."

Lucifer froze. Then his head tilted just slightly, his expression sharpening into something lethal. "You think I don't know that?" His voice was quieter now. More dangerous.

Zagan swallowed. "I *felt* it. The child... it reached for me."

Lucifer's eyes darkened, his wings shifting behind him like a coming storm. Amber let out a strangled noise beneath them, her body convulsing as the sigil pulsed against her skin, the last remnants of it struggling to hold on.

Lucifer snapped his head toward Michael, but the Archangel's expression remained *placid and* indifferent as if watching a predictable outcome unfold.

"Strange, isn't it?" Michael mused. "For all your talk of war, of power... it always comes down to this." His gaze flickered toward Zagan. "Demons groveling for scraps of salvation."

Zagan shook. Not from pain. From something deeper. Something Lucifer recognized.

Michael's lip curled. "Disgusting."

Zagan let out a shuddering breath. His grip on Amber faltered for a fraction of a second, and Lucifer moved. He shoved Zagan back hard, sending him crashing against the floor. Before Zagan could react, Lucifer crouched low, his arms sliding beneath Amber's trembling form, lifting her effortlessly.

"Lucifer," she choked, barely conscious.

His grip tightened. *No.*

He lifted his head toward Michael, his expression empty, cold.

Michael sighed, watching them with thinly veiled amusement. "You're running out of time, Morningstar."

Lucifer exhaled. Steady.

His wings flared, power curling around his body, but the moment he moved, the sigil flared, sending a violent pulse through Amber's body.

She screamed.

Lucifer *froze.* His entire being seized at the sound, at the sheer agony in her voice.

The sigil's last point was breaking.

If it shattered completely, she would...*no.*

He wouldn't let that happen.

Clenching his jaw, he pressed his palm to the sigil mark, focusing his power. His vision blurred, and the room around him faded.

"Take me," he said.

98

A Knife in the Flame

For a moment, there was nothing but silence, and then slowly, Michael exhaled, shaking his head as if disappointed. He took a measured step forward, hands clasped behind his back. "How gallant," he murmured. How noble." He stepped closer, tilting his head slightly. But there's just one problem."

Lucifer didn't move or even blink as Michael smiled, something slow and cold.

"You're tied to Zagan," Michael said smoothly, his voice maddeningly calm. "And cutting the soul-tie will kill both of you."

Lucifer's arm tightened around Amber like steel, but he didn't flinch or hesitate.

But Amber *did*.

Her fingers latched onto him, weak and trembling but driven by something primal: panic, desperation, *love*.

"No," she whispered, her head shaking once, then again, faster. "No, no, no, please no..."

She could *feel* it, *feel* the choice forming in him, feel his magic beginning to shift, sharpening like a blade. He'd already decided.

Lucifer, the one who'd held her when she was breaking, the one who'd burned for her, who'd walked the line between tormentor and savior, was going to die.

Or worse, he was going to be ripped from her forever.

The realization hit like a blade to the chest, splintering her breath. Her heart pounded out of rhythm, her lungs seized, her whole body shaking as if trying to tear free from the reality forming around her.

"You don't have to do this," she gasped, her voice high and splintered, raw with disbelief. Her hands clung to him like lifelines, even as another wave of pain wracked her body. "Lucifer, please...please..."

But he didn't look at her.

Didn't argue.

Because, in his mind, the decision had already been made.

Across the room, Zagan pushed himself up on shaky elbows, blood smeared down his chin. He stared in absolute silence as he watched Amber unravel in Lucifer's arms. Her hands trembling. Her voice breaking. Her tears fell without restraint.

And for some reason, it made his stomach twist, but he couldn't look away.

Lucifer was really going to do it.

Not for Hell. Not for power, reputation, or revenge.

He was going to die for *her*.

For *the child*.

For something so far outside his usual orbit of cruelty and control that it made Zagan feel ill.

He looked at Lucifer again, and in that unflinching, unreadable face, he saw it: peace. Resignation. *Readiness.*

Zagan swallowed hard, his mouth dry as he realized the Archangels were right. If Lucifer died, so did he.

But for the first time in his long, miserable existence, Zagan looked at the destruction around them, at Amber sobbing brokenly against Lucifer's shoulder, and thought: *maybe I deserve to go first.*

His voice came rough, sharp, like stone ground against stone. "Cut mine," he said. He didn't look at Amber, he looked at Michael. "Take him."

Lucifer's head whipped around, and Amber *screamed*.

It wasn't loud or elegant.

It was hoarse, raw, and *shattered*, a sound born of too many broken things happening simultaneously.

Her entire body jerked, her back arching as her breath caught in her throat and her vision blurred with white-hot panic. "No don't...you can't...Zagan, you can't..."

But he could.

And he *would*.

A heavy, unnatural stillness swept through the chamber, and for a heartbeat, no one spoke.

Then Gabriel let out a soft, dry chuckle. "Well. *That* was unexpected."

Michael tilted his head, studying Zagan like something half-interesting beneath a microscope. "An interesting offer," he murmured. "And a tempting one." His eyes slid toward Lucifer, cold and calculating. "Keep the Morningstar and let you die in his place? It certainly solves several problems."

Amber choked on a sob, her body *trembling* so violently now it looked like she might come apart at the seams.

Lucifer and Zagan were both willing to die.

And it was going to happen right in front of her.

Her pulse screamed against her ribs. Her lungs refused to fill.

"No," she croaked, the word barely audible. "No, no, stop...please, just stop..." Her voice was a shredded sound, cracking under the weight of everything. She clutched at Lucifer like she could anchor herself to him, like if she held on tight enough, the rest of the world would have to stay still.

Lucifer's jaw clenched, and Zagan's fists curled.

And then, for the briefest moment, Lucifer looked down at her.

Not at her hands. Not at her tears. *At her.*

And in his eyes, she saw it.

Goodbye.

Her breath stopped.

"No..." she whispered her voice broken glass in her throat. "Lucifer, please...don't you dare..."

But before she could speak again, Raphael's voice sliced through the room with clinical precision.

"This is all well and good," he said, glancing between the men like they were papers on a desk. "But what about the child?"

Amber stilled.

Her body was locked up with dread as Raphael's calm, cold eyes flicked toward her. "We can't simply allow it to be born in Hell."

Lucifer's head snapped toward him. His voice came low, steady, *lethal.* "Yes, you can."

Everything in the room stilled.

Lucifer stepped forward, his shadows curling beneath his feet like smoke, his presence suddenly vast, too large for this space, too powerful for this moment. His wings flared slightly behind him, not in threat but in undeniable truth.

"Without me," he said, his voice like thunder behind a closed door, "there's no one for the child to cement into power, no throne to inherit, no realm to anchor it."

He paused, and the weight of his words settled like gravity over the room.

"Without me, it's just a baby."

The Archangels hesitated. That wasn't something they were used to doing. They didn't *waver,* not in Hell, and certainly not in Heaven.

But Lucifer had struck something real. Something undeniable.

Amber could feel it, that shift, the sliver of uncertainty sneaking in beneath their polished armor. *Lucifer was right.*

Without him, there was no heir.

No queen.

No legacy.

Only a choice.

Michael's face remained unreadable, but the flicker of uncertainty in his gaze betrayed his unease. Raphael looked away slowly, his jaw tightening. And Gabriel sighed as if this was all too exhausting to be worthwhile.

Finally, Michael spoke, his voice low and flat. "You're asking us to ignore what this child represents."

Lucifer didn't blink. "I'm asking you to acknowledge the truth." His wings shifted again, his voice deepening. "Without me, there is no threat. Unless you *make* it one."

Silence.

The air in the room was heavier than ever, as if every breath taken cost something.

Amber gripped Lucifer's sleeve, knuckles white, pulse fluttering. She didn't speak. Couldn't. Her throat was too tight, her soul stretched too thin. She felt like she was holding onto the last thread in a fraying universe.

Michael stared at Lucifer for a long time. Then, finally, he nodded.

It was small but deliberate.

And it broke the hold over them like shattering glass.

Lucifer and Amber both exhaled in unison, breaths sharp and shaking as if only now realizing how long they'd held them in.

But before the moment could settle, Lucifer turned to Zagan, and their eyes met.

No words passed between them; they didn't need them.

There were no more bargains or schemes, only resound understanding.

Lucifer lifted his chin. "Come on, then."

Zagan swallowed, a flicker of wariness crossing his face, but he nodded. He dragged himself to his feet, muttering, "Just so you know, what I said before still holds true: when I die, I'm haunting you."

Lucifer smirked faintly. "You already do."

Together, they turned to face Michael, and the Archangel's lips curled into a dry, amused, and deadly smile.

"Oh, this," he said, "should be *very* interesting."

99

Shattered Bonds

With a sigh, Lucifer turned inward, reaching for the tether that had bound him to Zagan. His breath caught the instant his consciousness brushed against it.

His entire body locked.

The soul-tie wasn't a spell. It wasn't a simple bridge of energy or intention. It was ancient, brutal, and alive.

It was bone-deep, stitched into the marrow of their spines, woven through muscle and nerve, a second nervous system formed of pact and punishment, legacy and power. It wasn't a thread to be cut. It was an organ.

And now, Lucifer was tearing it out.

The moment he pulled, it fought him *hard*.

Zagan gasped, his eyes wide as the bond's first layer began to peel away from his spine like a molten wire being unraveled from the inside out. The magic clung, refused to release, and screamed as it was torn free.

A brutal wrench dragged down through his back, each vertebra igniting with pain, like claws were raking through his insides, dragging something sacred and corrupted from his flesh.

Lucifer felt it, too.

The identical invisible coils, cold as iron but hot as hellfire, wrapped around his vertebrae, his back bowing involuntarily as the pressure mounted. It felt like the chains were *inside* him, strangling his nerves, suffocating his power.

A violent shudder passed through him, and for a moment, they couldn't move. The bond had seized them, locking them in place, resisting, fighting, *begging* not to be undone.

Lucifer gritted his teeth until his jaw ached. His fists were clenched so tight that blood welled from the creases in his palms. His wings jerked behind him, spasming with each pulse of rejection.

He forced the next pull, and pain, unlike anything he'd ever endured, shot through his spine, up into the base of his skull, white-hot and searing, like his body was rejecting itself. Like he was being hollowed out.

Zagan cried out in a ragged, furious scream that echoed through the chamber. His back arched so violently it looked like it might break. Magic bled from his skin in rivulets of light and shadow, the power inside him turning against him, trying to root itself deeper, to hold on.

It didn't want to leave.

It didn't want to die.

Lucifer's breath came ragged and uneven as he pushed harder. Magic burned in his palms, veins glowing gold beneath his skin, and each strand of the bond began to loosen in slow, screaming threads of history and pain coming undone one after the other.

He could feel it *peeling him apart*, layer by layer, a sensation that didn't stop at flesh. It burrowed deeper through sinew, soul, and memory. Each unraveling thread dragged part of him with it. A name. A thought. A piece of who he used to be.

His vision blurred. Blood dripped from his nose.

Still, he *didn't stop*.

The pain surged again, this time marrow-deep like someone was scraping the inside of his bones with a blade forged from lightning. Zagan's body convulsed beside him, limbs twitching uncontrollably, fingers clawing at the stone floor as if trying to root himself in the only reality left.

Lucifer's magic flickered.

Then, with one final wrench that tore the breath from both their lungs, the last tether snapped.

Its force tore through the chamber like a shockwave, but there was no sound. No explosion. Just the raw, echoing sensation of something ancient being *undone*. A silence so profound it rang in the bones like a scream left unvoiced.

Lucifer collapsed first.

His knees hit the stone, his body sagging forward like all his strength had been stolen instantly. His wings drooped, limp and trembling, dragging behind him like the broken limbs of some tremendous fallen beast.

Zagan followed seconds later, his body convulsing once before he hit the ground facedown, blood seeping from his mouth as he lay still.

And then there was nothing.

No movement.

No breath.

No magic.

Only stillness.

The chamber, once ablaze with tension and divine fire, now held the hush of a tomb. The kind of silence that made even gods uncomfortable.

All Amber could do was stare; she was frozen.

It didn't register at first; her mind refused to process what her eyes were seeing. One heartbeat passed. Then another. Then a third, longer and quieter than it had any right to be. And still, Lucifer didn't move.

He was always moving. Always burning with purpose or fury or control.

But now he was still.

"Lucifer?" Her voice cracked, barely a whisper, a child calling into the dark.

Nothing.

Her chest seized, and her vision swam. She tried to sit up, but her body was too weak, too wrung out, so all she could do was drag herself across the stone, trembling, breathless, her hands scraping raw against the floor.

"No. No, no, no..." The words spilled from her in a desperate, uneven rhythm. "Lucifer, look at me. Please..."

He didn't.

Her hand reached out, trembling, and landed against his face, her fingers brushing the cooled gold of his skin.

He felt like marble.

She pressed harder, her breath now ragged sobs.

"You promised me," she whispered, forehead pressing against his temple. "You chose me for eternity. You said you'd never leave me."

Tears streamed down her face unchecked, soaking into his hair, her body shaking with grief she had no strength to hide.

And still, he didn't move.

Behind her, the Archangels stood in expectant silence, their expressions a study in contrast, as if they'd known this would be the outcome.

Gabriel's arms crossed, jaw set, the tight lines around his eyes betraying a bitter satisfaction.

"Well," he muttered coldly. "It was bound to happen eventually. He made his choice."

His voice was quiet but sharp enough to cut through bone.

Amber turned, her eyes blazing with disbelief.

"You think this is a *win*?" she spat, voice cracking. "You think this is *justice*?"

Gabriel didn't answer; he didn't need to.

Raphael stood a few feet away, silent and unmoving, his hands folded neatly. He looked upon the scene with the strange serenity of someone who'd already seen it all play out. His expression held neither surprise nor sorrow.

"I told you," he said simply, his voice the barest breath of wind. "You can't sever something like that and walk away unchanged."

Michael exhaled slowly, eyes narrowing, lips pursed, not in grief, but in thought. His gaze swept over Lucifer's collapsed form, then Zagan's twitching frame, and finally landed on Amber, on the slow shatter of her composure as she curled around Lucifer's unmoving body.

"Well," Michael said softly, his voice like the closing of a book. "That was... dramatic."

He stepped forward, boots clicking softly across the stone.

"Now then," he continued, businesslike, brushing dust from his coat. "Someone should tend to the girl. And the child."

Amber's head snapped up, something wild in her eyes. "You *touch* my baby..."

Michael held up a hand, calm as a priest. "Easy. I'm not here to take. Just to ensure the *aftermath* is... manageable."

But before he could take another step, a sound broke the silence.

A gasp.

A breath.

Amber froze, her heart stumbling in her chest.

Lucifer's fingers twitched.

She stared, unable to move or speak, as his shoulders lifted with the smallest, shallowest inhale. Another followed. Then another. His lashes fluttered against his cheeks, slow and heavy, like it hurt to return.

Amber's hand flew to her mouth.

He was breathing.

He was alive.

Barely. But alive.

And as she collapsed against him in relief, sobbing anew, the Archangels watched in stunned silence.

Gabriel said nothing, though his glare deepened.

Raphael bowed his head faintly, unsurprised.

With a tilt of his head, Michael merely sighed and said, "Well. That complicates things."

Amber barely heard Michael as she held Lucifer's face in her hands, trembling fingers brushing the soot and blood from his skin, her tears dripping down to mingle with the ash along his jaw. He was breathing, slow and shallow, but his eyes remained closed, his body limp in her arms like a statue not yet returned to life.

For a moment, nothing happened, then finally, his eyes cracked open, unfocused and faintly glowing gold, as though even his power was exhausted. He blinked slowly as if time had thickened around him. His gaze shifted to her face, and something warm flickered through the haze, a recognition, a tether, a promise.

Amber let out a sound, half-sob, half-laugh, and buried her face in the crook of his neck, relief shaking through her in waves.

And then, "Holy Hell, that hurt."

The voice behind them came loud, nasal, and *deeply* annoyed.

Amber's head snapped up.

Zagan rolled onto his side before sitting up too quickly and immediately wincing. "Gods, it's like someone unzipped my spine and poured salt inside."

Amber rolled her eyes and retook Lucifer's face in her hands. She leaned in, her lips brushing against his ear, her voice barely audible, as if saying it too loud might break the spell, "Don't ever leave me again."

100

Fissures and Fury

A hush fell over the chamber.

The moment the soul-tie snapped, the celestial energy in the air stilled. The golden glow of the Archangels' presence flickered, dimming for just a breath as if even Heaven hadn't foreseen this outcome.

Lucifer panted, his hands pressing into the cold stone beneath him, his body wrecked from the violent severing. Beside him, Zagan shuddered, still shaking from the force of the break, his breathing uneven.

Michael's expression remained unreadable, his celestial glow flickering slightly as he took a slow step forward. He studied them as one might a shattered relic, something that shouldn't exist anymore yet somehow still did.

Raphael exhaled sharply, adjusting the cuffs of his robes. "Huh," he mused, tone light, almost thoughtful. "That wasn't supposed to happen."

Gabriel tilted his head, unimpressed. "And yet, here we are."

None of them moved.

None of them interfered.

They were waiting, watching, as if trying to decide whether to finish this themselves.

Michael's gaze swept over Lucifer, then Zagan. Slowly, his lips curved into something like mild amusement. "Well," he said finally, voice smooth as ever. "That's... inconvenient."

Lucifer barely lifted his head, his breath still ragged, but the corner of his mouth twitched slightly. "For you?" he rasped, voice raw. "I'd imagine so."

Michael chuckled under his breath. "Oh, Lucifer," he murmured, shaking his head. "Even now, you don't understand what you've done."

Lucifer's spine stiffened.

Gabriel sighed, stretching his shoulders as if this ordeal had been nothing more than an inconvenience. "And now," he drawled, "we're right back where we started."

Amber shifted behind Lucifer. Weak. Barely holding herself up.

Michael's gaze flicked to her, then to the full curve of her stomach.

Lucifer's entire body went still.

"Ah," Michael murmured. "That's right." His eyes gleamed. "The child."

Amber's breath hitched.

Raphael hummed, tilting his head. "Lucifer," he said, his voice lighter now, patient. Dangerous. "You know we can't allow this child to be born in Hell."

Lucifer's vision sharpened, his exhaustion momentarily drowned by the sheer threat laced in those words, and slowly, he rose. His body ached, his spine still searing from losing the soul tie, but his magic stirred, clawing back to the surface. His wings flared, his shadows curling like a storm at his feet.

Michael didn't move. He didn't need to. He only smiled.

Amber stiffened.

Lucifer's golden eyes burned. "You have no say in that."

Michael hummed. "Don't we?" He gestured to the three of them, the divine authority in this room. "We control the balance, Morningstar."

Then, Lucifer felt the shift: they weren't trying to trap him anymore but deciding whether to kill the baby.

Amber sucked in a breath, instinctively curling her arms around her stomach, her expression twisted in fear, and Lucifer's rage boiled over. Shadows snapped up from the floor, coiling around him, seething in dark tendrils as his power crashed through the room like a tidal wave.

Michael remained unmoved.

"The deal can still stand," Lucifer snarled. "Take me in their place."

Michael's lips twitched, "We were hoping you'd say that."

But just as the angels moved forward, their steps echoing through the charged stillness of the chamber, Amber's body arched suddenly, *violently*, as a sharp, consuming pain tore through her, stealing the breath from her lungs and replacing it with nothing but fire.

The sound that ripped from her throat wasn't a scream or a cry but something far more raw; a fractured, guttural moan that seemed to claw its way out of her chest, as if her body was trying to purge something it could no longer hold.

Her hands shot out blindly, and her fingers found Lucifer's arm. They clamped down with a force that startled even him, her nails slicing through his skin without hesitation, without awareness, only need. She clung to him not out of fear but from something more profound and far more ancient. A visceral instinct to hold on to the one fixed point in a world spinning out of control.

Lucifer's stomach turned to lead.

There was a moment, one single heartbeat, where he could only stare, frozen, watching Amber contort in agony, her mouth parted, her eyes wide and unfocused as another wave of pain surged through her with the merciless precision of a blade.

"Amber?" His voice was hoarse, ragged, barely more than a breath.

She didn't answer. She couldn't breathe, and he could feel her panic thrumming against him, in every shudder of her limbs, every ragged pull of air that never seemed to reach her lungs. Her whole body trembled, not in fear, but in the helpless, convulsive way that comes when pain becomes too much to hold inside.

A contraction hit, deep, brutal, and unrelenting, as it twisted through her abdomen with such intensity that her spine bowed, her muscles locking as her body fought against itself, against time, against the inevitable.

Her breath came in sharp and shallow gasps as if the air around her had thickened, refusing to enter her lungs. Her vision went white. Her pulse thundered in her ears. Her entire world narrowed into a single, suffocating point of pain.

Lucifer's name escaped her lips again, though it was broken this time, barely more than a ghost of sound, but it was enough to shatter him.

She was going into labor.

And he couldn't stop it.

His hand moved instinctively to support her back as her knees buckled. Her grip on his arm was unrelenting, her fingers digging into bone now as she clung to him like he was the only thing anchoring her to this world. He caught her fully, cradling her against his chest, one hand in her hair, the other pressed to the curve of her spine. His voice was low and shaking as he whispered her name again and again, as though speaking it could keep her here.

But her eyes weren't focused anymore, her mouth was slack, and her body had become a vessel for something more significant than her, something she could no longer contain.

And all around them, the room changed.

The shadows that once curled so loyally around Lucifer began to falter, shrinking back from the swirling storm of energy that now built around her. The chamber walls seemed to hold their breath as the air thickened, charged, and oppressive as if the realm had begun to tilt on its axis.

And still, Lucifer didn't move.

He couldn't.

His magic sparked weakly at his fingertips as if trying to form something, to reach for a spell, a tether, *anything*, but it was useless, meaningless, against the storm that had already begun to rage within her.

Across the room, the angels hesitated.

Michael's expression shifted like the mask of certainty he wore had cracked. Gabriel's steps faltered, his gaze flickering toward Amber with something that almost resembled fear. Even Raphael took a slow, uncertain step backward, his hands twitching at his sides.

They all understood now: this wasn't just a pregnancy. This wasn't a warning, a bargaining chip, or a future threat.

This was a birth.

And it had begun.

Amber's body lurched again as another contraction ripped through her, more forceful than the last, a full-body quake that sent a choked cry bursting from her lips. Blood bloomed beneath her, fast and bright, splashing across the stone like the realm had been wounded.

Lucifer could do nothing but hold her tighter, burying his face against her hair as his entire being shook with a terror he had no name for.

She was breaking in his arms, unraveling before his eyes.

For the first time since the creation of life, there was nothing Heaven or Hell could do.

Lucifer's instincts screamed. They had to get out. They had to leave. Now. NOW.

But the Archangels were already moving again. Light gathered, golden and lethal, burning brighter and brighter, their divine energy coiling, preparing to strike, when suddenly everything went black.

Not the absence of light or dimming of the chamber; this was true, absolute, suffocating darkness.

The kind that erased existence itself.

Lucifer's wings snapped open. His magic rushed outward, but this wasn't his doing. His head whipped to the side just as a familiar figure rose from the shadows, standing between them and Heaven's fury.

Zagan.

His body was wrecked, his breath shallow, his hands shaking from exhaustion, but his eyes were burning with something fierce, something defiant. Lucifer could barely make out his shape, the sheer void swallowing everything in its wake.

Lucifer understood in an instant as he heard the confused shouts of the Archangels as their magic reacted instantly, their power rising, colliding, burning against the onslaught, but for one moment. One brief, critical moment, they couldn't see.

This wasn't an attack or a fight; it was a sacrifice.

Zagan was giving himself over for *them*. For Lucifer. For Amber. For the baby.

Lucifer's jaw clenched, his magic clawing to push forward, to drag Zagan out of this.

"Zagan..." his voice cracked as it left his throat.

Zagan just shook his head.

"Funny, isn't it?" He rasped, voice weak but steady. "I spent centuries trying to reclaim Hell..." His lips curled, something like a smirk flashing through the dark. "And now, I'm being used to save it."

Lucifer's throat tightened. He didn't know what to say, but with a single sharp look from Zagan, he knew nothing was left to say.

Go.

Lucifer swore under his breath but didn't argue; he didn't have time to.

Amber let out another sharp cry, her body convulsing in his arms, and that was all the confirmation he needed. Lucifer grabbed her, pulled her close, wrapped his arms around her tight, and with a single, powerful beat, he vanished into the dark.

Leaving Zagan behind.

101

Neither Mortal nor Monster

They crashed into Hell like a falling star.

Lucifer's knees slammed into the obsidian ground with a force that cracked the stone beneath them, his wings snapping open too late to slow their descent. His arms locked around Amber, shielding her, taking the full impact as they hit the ground.

A tremor ripped through the Underworld and the air thickened, heavy and charged, an unseen force pressing in from all sides, as if Hell was hesitating.

As if the realm didn't know what to do.

The walls of the realm groaned, warping like living things trying to shift away from her presence. Shadows surged forward, thick, writhing tendrils creeping toward her, uncertain.

The air crackled, heat swelling in waves as Hell tried to decide what she was.

Lucifer had never felt Hell react like this to him, but he couldn't question it for long as Amber convulsed in his grasp, her spine bowing, a choked, guttural scream ripping from her throat.

Lucifer's stomach dropped.

She was burning up, searing hot one second, deathly cold the next. Her breath hitched, her body locking up, her pulse hammering against his skin.

Then she started changing.

Her skin flickered violently, one moment soft and human, the next darkening, hardening, shifting into something hellish.

Then back, again, and again.

Lucifer's wings flared, his power curling around her, desperate to stabilize her, but this wasn't just labor.

Hell was fighting her.

The realm, this place that had broken, reshaped and swallowed so many souls, didn't know what to make of Amber, the first devil to give birth.

Lucifer's claws dug into her skin, grounding her, holding her together. "Amber," he snarled, his voice rough, commanding. "Stay with me."

She couldn't answer.

Her fingers curled against his chest, clutching at him, grounding herself in the only thing she still recognized when suddenly her body arched violently, her fingers clawing at the stone beneath her as another contraction ripped through her.

Lucifer swore under his breath, his mind racing.

It was brutal. Not natural. Not normal.

She let out a sound that wasn't just pain; it was raw, soul-deep torment.

Her legs kicked out, her body twisting in his grasp as if something inside her was trying to break free too soon.

Her nails dragged against his skin, deep enough to draw blood, but she wasn't even aware of it.

And Lucifer felt it now; this wasn't just a fight against her own body; this was Hell trying to unmake her, to return her to what she once was, to force her back into humanity.

Or rip her entirely into something else.

Her body wasn't just rejecting the process; it was being pulled in two directions.

A war of creation versus destruction.

And it was killing her.

Lucifer's eyes burned gold, his jaw locking as he tightened his hold on her, shielding her from the darkness slithering closer. "You are mine, Amber," he growled. "Not theirs. Not Heaven's. Not Hell's. Mine."

Her body shook violently, her chest rising and falling in jagged, shallow gasps, when suddenly horns began to push through her skull.

Lucifer barely held in a snarl, rage flaring through his blood.

In Heaven, she'd been her human self, a weaker version, but human. Now, in Hell, it was trying to change her back into the She-Devil, a form Lucifer was just now realizing she couldn't give birth in.

No. No, no, no.

The pain was too much, too wrong.

Amber threw her head back, her entire body locking up, her mouth opening in a silent scream, and around them, the ground shattered, cracks ripping outward in jagged patterns, the weight of Hell itself pressing down.

Without thinking, Lucifer opened his wings and took flight, headed toward the castle. He flew hard and fast, but Amber was slipping. Her fingers dug into his biceps, weak but unrelenting, her grip the only thing grounding her to this world.

Her breath came in short, broken gasps, her body wracked with violent tremors, her skin flickering between forms. One moment soft and human, the next dark and shifting, her horns half-formed, curling before vanishing again.

Hell is rejecting this.

Lucifer's wings beat furiously, but his mind raced.

This isn't just labor. This isn't just a child being born.

"Lucifer..." Her voice was barely there, a fractured whisper, a thread of sound stretched too thin.

Her head lolled against his shoulder, her lips parting in agony, "I can't..."

Lucifer's entire body tensed.

No. No, no, no—

"You will," he snarled, his grip tightening, his magic coiling around her, holding her together. "Do you hear me, Amber?"

Her body jerked violently, her back bowing as another contraction tore through her, and around them, the air itself howled. A deep, eerie keening sound rippled through Hell, echoing from the depths of the realm.

Lucifer felt it.

Hell was reacting to her labor, *fighting* it.

The temperature plummeted.

The ever-burning rivers of fire dimmed, flickering as though something greater was pulling the heat from them. The wails of the damned rose in pitch, their screams twisting into something warped, agonized, feral.

Lucifer cursed under his breath.

This wasn't supposed to happen.

He should've known this wouldn't be normal.

Devils don't create life. They were never meant to.

Amber let out a strangled, broken sob, her fingers clawing weakly at his chest.

Lucifer clenched his jaw, pushing forward. The castle was ahead, its towers dark against the blood-red sky, its walls trembling. Lucifer's power usually bent the realm to his will. But now, it wasn't obeying him.

It was reacting to her, to what was happening inside her.

It didn't know if it should accept or reject this new being.

It didn't know if this child was a devil, a ruler, or something else entirely.

And that terrified Lucifer more than anything.

He landed hard at the castle gates, his boots scraping against the stone as his wings folded back. He didn't stop moving, didn't hesitate as Amber gasped sharply, her body arching against him as another contraction wracked through her.

The doors before him slammed open.

Abelia and Syn were already there, running toward him, but they skidded to a stop at the sight of Amber limp in Lucifer's arms.

Their eyes went wide.

The sight of her, barely conscious, flickering between human and something darker, writhing in his grasp, paralyzed them.

"What the hell is happening?" Abelia's voice was sharp, horrified.

Lucifer didn't slow. "She's in labor."

Silence.

Absolute. Horrified. Silence.

Syn was the first to move, but her expression was unreadable, somewhere between shock and sheer disbelief. "What?"

For a moment, the demonesses stared at Amber with confusion and fear written on their faces.

"That... that isn't supposed to be possible; Hell's rejecting it," Syn said her words barely a breath.

Lucifer snarled. "No shit."

Abelia moved closer, reaching out as if afraid to touch Amber, afraid she might unravel completely.

Her voice dropped. "How do we stop it from killing her?"

Lucifer's grip on Amber tightened as the shadows lashed against the walls, the air thick with magic, the storm of Hell's resistance building.

He had no answer.

But he knew one thing.

He wasn't going to lose her.

Not now.

Not ever.

102

The Blade and the Bell

A s he strode through the castle halls with Abelia and Syn in tow, his wings flared wide, and Amber cradled against his chest, her body burning like fire in his arms.

The castle was alive with movement.

Demons stopped and stared. The walls writhed, reacting to the unnatural energy spilling from Amber's body.

Lucifer's steps only picked up in pace as she let out a choked sound, another contraction wracking through her, her body twisting painfully.

Lucifer snarled. "Move!"

The gathered demons scattered.

He didn't hesitate as he took her deeper into the castle, crashing the doors to the lower chambers open, revealing the Sanctum.

It was one of the few places in Hell designed to repair instead of destroy. A circular chamber, ancient sigils carved into the stone, golden and dark magic coiled together, opposing forces locked in balance.

Torches flared violently as Lucifer entered, the entire room reacting to Amber's presence. Still, Lucifer didn't stop. He moved to the center of the room, his shadows reaching out, forming a bed of darkness, and for the first time since escaping Heaven, he put Amber down.

Her body arched, her back bowing as another contraction tore through her. She wasn't breathing right. Her skin flickered between mortal softness and demonic hardness, unable to settle.

Abelia rushed to her side.

"This—" Her voice faltered, pure horror spreading across her face. "This isn't normal."

"No," Lucifer snarled. "It's not."

Syn pressed two fingers to Amber's pulse. Her brows furrowed. "Her heartbeat is..." She shook her head, the uncertainty in her face infuriating Lucifer. "It's not staying consistent. It keeps changing."

Amber let out another cry, her hands gripping the solidified shadows, her claws dragging deep gashes through it.

Her body didn't know what it was anymore.

Lucifer's chest tightened. "Fix this."

Silence.

Abelia and Syn exchanged a glance, the kind that meant they had nothing. The kind that meant they didn't know what to do.

Lucifer's rage crashed into the room like a storm. "FIX IT."

"She's not just giving birth, Lucifer," Abelia snapped. "She's being rewritten. By Hell itself."

Lucifer froze.

His wings stilled.

Syn hesitated before speaking. "Her body is being pulled in two directions. One side is trying to make her human again; the other is trying to keep her as the She-Devil." Her eyes lifted uneasily to Lucifer's.

His mind went blank as Amber let out a broken sob, her arms wrapping around herself, her body curling inward, instinctively protecting the life inside her.

Lucifer couldn't breathe.

"You need to do something," Abelia whispered.

Lucifer barely heard her; his golden eyes were locked onto Amber.

She was breaking.

And he couldn't stop it.

A strange feeling pressed against his chest, something cold: fear.

Not just the kind that came with losing a battle, the kind that came with losing *everything*.

"Get the Sororibus Anima." Lucifer said, his rage seconds from boiling over.

Abelia stilled; even Syn's usually unreadable expression flickered with something uncertain.

"The Sororibus Anima?" Abelia echoed, her voice laced with something dangerously close to doubt.

Lucifer's golden eyes snapped to her, burning with barely contained rage, "Now."

She didn't argue. Instead, she turned on her heel and vanished into the dark, her form melting into the shadows. Lucifer didn't spare her retreating figure a glance.

Amber's body arched violently, another contraction hitting her with a force so strong the floor cracked beneath her and her skin flickered again. One moment, she was soft, warm, and human, and the next, she was dark, shifting into pure, uncontained power rippling beneath the surface.

Lucifer held her down, pressing his palm against her chest, trying to anchor her, force her to stay, force her to remain in Hell's grasp.

But the war inside her wasn't stopping.

Lucifer's jaw locked, his entire body coiled so tight he thought he might snap. Then, the room shifted, and a presence filled the space, pressing against every inch of the air. Still, he didn't turn as the Sororibus Anima appeared.

Sana, Subsidio, and Pax appeared through the threshold as one, their forms drifting like smoke, but there was no mistaking the divine power woven between them. Their robes floated behind them, pale as bone, yet they carried an aura of something unnatural. Something older than Hell.

Sana led, her piercing silver eyes locking onto Lucifer. They didn't breathe or speak, but Lucifer heard them, not as words but as a feeling, a pulse of sound that slipped beneath his skin, curling around his mind like tendrils of smoke.

A whisper that didn't come from their lips but from the space between realms.

"This summons was not made lightly," Sana said, her voice ringing in his bones, carrying an echo of something beyond this place.

Lucifer barely restrained a snarl; his thoughts became angry. "I wouldn't have called you if I had another option."

Her eyes flickered downward, and for the first time, she saw Amber, the tremors in her limbs. The way her body was trying to unmake itself, something passed across Sana's face, an emotion too fleeting to name.

"Help her," Lucifer commanded. "Now."

Sana didn't hesitate. She lowered herself gracefully, kneeling beside Amber, her hands hovering over the broken woman's body.

Subsidio followed, her pale hands outstretched, golden energy blooming at her fingertips.

Pax remained the furthest back, her expression unreadable. She was always the quietest. The last to act.

Lucifer barely noticed the movement as the sisters' power spilled into the air, curling around Amber like a gentle, unseen thread.

He felt the shift instantly as the air grew lighter. The unbearable weight pressing against Amber's form receded, if only slightly.

The air shifted around Subsidio as if she'd let out a soft breath, her magic pulsing faintly, "She is in pain." Her voice slid into his thoughts, cold and ancient.

His voice, raw and burning, answered them, "I am aware."

Subsidio's brow furrowed as she placed her hands on Amber's wrists, sending waves of relief through her body, and to Lucifer's relief Amber's body stopped trembling, her pain momentarily receding. And for a moment, just a moment, he thought it might work, but as the thought crossed his mind, Amber's body seized.

Her eyes flew open, glowing pure gold before turning black, and her breath ripped from her lungs as if something inside her had turned against itself.

Her body rejected their magic.

Lucifer moved instantly, grabbing her shoulders and holding her down. The sisters stilled. Even Sana looked... concerned.

Lucifer's heart pounded, his mind racing.

"What are you waiting for?" he sent, his thoughts clawing against their minds.

Sana's silver eyes met his, and she hesitated for the first time in her existence.

"Lucifer," she hesitated. "This... is beyond us."

His world stopped.

"What?" His thought came low, dangerous.

Sana's hand hovered over Amber's stomach. The magic there wasn't something they could touch.

"I can heal wounds. I can mend flesh," Sana admitted, "But this is not an injury."

Subsidio's hands trembled as she pulled back. "Her body is rejecting the pain relief."

Pax, who had been silent until now, let out a quiet breath, her head tilted toward Amber, listening.

"She does not need peace." Her voice didn't come as speech but as a feeling, an absence of pain, a moment of stillness, a single heartbeat suspended in time.

Lucifer's blood turned to ice because Pax's gift, her ability to grant peace to any suffering soul, had no effect.

None.

Amber was beyond their reach.

Lucifer's claws dug into the shadows, his entire body shaking with fury. He'd summoned the greatest healers Hell had to offer, and they were powerless.

Sana met his gaze again, and in her silver eyes, he saw something he'd never seen before: regret.

"I am sorry, Lucifer." Her thought came like a last breath.

Lucifer closed his eyes as his wings flared wide, his power crackling through the room like a violent storm. His rage was absolute, and his fear was suffocating.

No one could save her.

Amber let out another shaking, pained breath, her fingers curling toward him. She was fading.

Lucifer clenched his jaw so hard it ached.

No, he wouldn't allow this.

Sharply, he turned to the sisters, his voice dangerously low, "Leave."

Sana hesitated, but he didn't give them another chance. His shadows surged, pushing them, and everyone else, back, banishing all from the room.

The Sororibus Anima vanished like mist.

He was alone with Amber once more. His breath came sharp and fast, his golden eyes wild as he sank down beside her, hands shaking as he brushed his fingers over her cheek.

She was barely conscious now, her breaths shallow and uneven, but with what seemed like the last ounce of strength she had left, she turned her head to him, and Lucifer froze.

A ghost of a smile, so soft, so faint, brushed against her lips, and then, in a voice so small, so cracked it nearly broke him, she whispered, "Lucifer."

His name, barely a breath.

Her fingers twitched as if reaching for him, as if trying to hold onto something, onto him, before she slipped too far.

"I would've walked through Hell for you," she murmured, her words fragile but unshaken. Then, with what little strength she had left, she corrected herself, "No... I would've fought Heaven for you."

Her lips trembled, her lashes fluttered, and her golden eyes, so dim now and so tired, still looked at him like he was her entire world. "I would have always chosen you," she said, her voice like shattered glass. "Because I love you."

Lucifer leaned in, his hand cupping her face, fingers trembling as if sheer touch could hold her together.

And then, just as he opened his mouth to speak, she whispered, "If it comes down to me or the baby..."

Her voice broke. Her gaze didn't.

"Amber..." Lucifer's voice caught, smaller than he meant it to be. "No."

"Save the baby."

Lucifer froze.

The words hit him like a curse, like a prophecy. Like the cruelest mercy he'd ever been given.

Before he could respond, before he could beg her to take it back, her body seized. Her back arched violently, a contraction ripping through her like a tidal wave.

Lucifer caught her wrists, frantic now, golden eyes wide with panic.

But there was nothing he could do; she crashed back down.

Perfectly still.

103

Hell's True Face

He couldn't breathe.

The silence around them rang louder than any scream. He reached for her face again, his fingers trembling as they ghosted along her cheek, soft, reverent, and desperate. As if gentleness could undo what had just happened. As if stillness could rewrite fate.

She was warm, but not warm enough.

And that look in her eyes... that final look... it wasn't fading fast enough to make this real.

Something inside him cracked.

Something deep.

Something ancient.

"No..." The word tore from his throat like it had claws, raw and strangled. "No. No...Amber."

His hands slid to her shoulders, shaking her now, gently at first, then rougher, panic bleeding into every motion. Her head lolled slightly with the movement, her hair falling across her face like a curtain between them.

He shoved it back.

"Don't do this," he rasped, his voice breaking. "Don't... don't leave me."

She didn't move.

"No," he growled, voice rising. "No, no, no!"

He gathered her into his arms, cradling her like she might come back if he held her tighter, keeping her anchored to the world by force of will alone. His claws dragged against her skin, his magic pulsing wildly, uncontrolled and unstable.

"Souls don't die," he choked, shaking his head. "They don't...they don't die twice. That's not how this works, that's not..."

His breath hitched.

She wasn't fading.

She wasn't turning to ash. There was no flicker of release, no sign of her crossing realms. She just... *stopped*.

And the realm around them, *his* realm, did nothing.

Hell didn't claim her.

Heaven didn't reach for her.

His golden eyes went wide, wild, as the truth struck him like a blade to the ribs.

She wasn't dying. She was being erased.

And he didn't know how to stop it.

Lucifer's head dropped as a broken, ragged sob escaped him, one he didn't recognize as his own. The sound of a creature *mourning*, not commanding. Of a man brought to his knees by something he'd never learned to fight.

Not even when he fell.

Not even when he rose again.

But this *devastation* was different.

"Amber," he whispered, his voice shattered glass. "Please..."

His hand curled around hers, forcing her fingers into his palm. "I've never begged before. Not once. Not for Heaven. Not for the throne. But I will beg for you. I will beg..."

His voice cracked and cut off as a sob tore loose from his chest, animal and violent. He crushed her to him, holding her like if he let go, she'd disappear entirely.

His magic snapped.

It didn't just pulse this time; it *erupted*.

A shockwave exploded outward from his body, tearing through the chamber like a storm, slamming into the walls of Hell. Torches blew out. Stone cracked. Shadows screamed.

And still, Lucifer held her. Still, he shook with every breath.

"I can't fix this," he whispered, eyes squeezed shut, tears running freely. "I can fix *everything*. I can *change* everything. But not this. Not you."

He pressed his forehead to hers, voice barely audible. "I don't know how to let you go."

Still in his arms, Amber didn't stir.

He clutched her tighter, claws slicing through fabric and skin.

"This realm is *mine*," he snarled. "And it will not take her from me."

Lucifer rose to his feet in a single, violent motion. He turned his face to the darkened sky above the castle and *screamed*.

A raw, animal, godless scream. One that shook the bones of Hell itself.

"You obey *me*! Do you hear me?" His voice boomed like thunder across the realm, echoing through every chasm, every furnace, every cursed island.

Magic exploded from his body in every direction, searing against the stone, ripping torches from the walls, and reducing iron to molten slag.

"I made you!" he roared, arms thrown wide as the wind around him swirled with fire and ash. "You exist because *I* do! You breathe because I command it!"

The skies above Hell split open, a web of red lightning tearing across the horizon. Mountains cracked. The seas of flame trembled.

And still, Amber didn't stir.

His magic coiled around her now, frantic, desperate, trying to knit her back together, to restart what had stilled. But nothing worked.

"You bend to my will," he bellowed at the realm. "And I will tear you apart if you don't answer me now!"

The floor beneath him split open. Geysers of fire erupted around him like volcanic rage. The very stones of Castellum Umbrae shuddered beneath his feet.

"You are *mine!* She is *mine!*"

Lucifer thrust both hands toward the ground, fingers clawed, blood dripping from his palms, and commanded the very fabric of Hell:

"You will not take her from me.

You will not reject what I love.

You will bring her back."

A silence fell.

And then Hell screamed back.

The skies howled. The castle groaned as if in pain. Red light poured from every crack in the stone. Power surged beneath Lucifer's feet, rising like a tidal wave, ancient, volatile, but obedient.

He let out a harsh, ragged breath as his body locked up, and something deep inside him shifted: a pulse, a presence.

Something old that Heaven feared and Hell had never been able to contain.

Exhaling sharply, he opened his eyes, only they weren't golden anymore.

The torches exploded, black flames spiraling violently around him. The shadows at his feet grew in darkness and size as they snapped outward, twisting, curling, and coiling as his body began to change.

His wings grew darker, shifting to something monstrous, shadows instead of patagium, serrated at the edges. His skin darkened, his veins pulsing like molten lava beneath the surface, and his horns curved sharper, taller, ancient, and terrifying. His power cracked through the air like a living thing, warping the space around him. And his eyes burned hellfire red.

And in the center of it all, Amber's chest shuddered.

Once.

Then again.

She drew in a breath, ragged and shallow but real.

His gaze snapped down to her, and something deep inside him snarled.

Mine.

His wings flared wide and with a single, final roar...Hell bowed.

The very foundation of the realm bent to his command, and the castle walls shook. The magic of Hell lashed out before collapsing in submission, and the creatures of Hell fell silent.

And for the first time in eternity, Lucifer had truly become what Hell feared most.

Not just the Devil.

Not just the ruler of the damned.

Something beyond even that.

His rule had been cemented.

He *was* Hell.

104

Born in Rage, Crowned in Flame

S ilence.

Not just in the chamber, not just in the castle, but across all of Hell.

A silence so deep, so unnatural, it felt like the realm was holding its breath, and at the center of it all, Lucifer stood, his body burning with power, his newly awakened form still pulsing with molten rage.

Against him, Amber lay still, her body unmoving, barely holding on, but his arms were unshaken, unyielding, unrelenting.

The tension thickened, pressing in, smothering, and a sound broke through the stillness.

A single, piercing cry.

The sound shattered the air, ripped through the realm, echoing in the farthest depths of the Pit, and Lucifer stopped breathing, because in his hands the first child of Hell had been born.

For the first time in his immortal existence, Lucifer Morningstar felt true stillness. His burning red eyes flickered downward. And there, resting in his hands, small, fragile, impossibly real, was the child that shouldn't exist.

A child born in fire and shadow, war and defiance, love and blood. A child that no god, no realm, no force had ever foreseen.

Amber barely moved, but Lucifer could hear her breathing, faint and unsteady, her body too weak to do anything but exist. But she was alive.

They both were.

And in his arms, small, fragile, and impossibly real, was their daughter. The first heir of Hell.

Lucifer had faced gods and won. He'd defied Heaven, shattered Hell, and rewritten the very laws of the Underworld, but he'd never been more terrified than he was at this moment.

A deep, unfamiliar weight settled in his chest as he stared down at the child cradled in his arms. Something deeper than power, more profound than rage, deeper than anything he'd ever known. Something he couldn't command or bend to his will.

Something he could only hold and love.

Amber stirred, and Lucifer's head snapped down immediately, his grip on the child tightening instinctively. Her lashes fluttered, her breath coming in shaky gasps, but her golden eyes opened, and she saw them.

Lucifer didn't speak or breathe as Amber's gaze landed on the baby in his arms, and a slow, disbelieving smile curved her lips.

Soft, small, but utterly, completely real.

Her eyes filled with something he'd never seen before, and his chest tightened painfully because he'd almost lost her. Almost lost them both.

His power meant nothing at that moment. His rule, his kingdom, his fury, none of it would have mattered if she'd died.

For the first time in eternity, Lucifer realized they were the only things he couldn't afford to lose.

And now?

Now, they were his to protect.

Forever.

Around them, the castle shook, not in rejection but in acknowledgment. The creatures of the Underworld, the beasts that had known nothing but chaos and carnage for eternity, bowed.

One by one, the demons, the rulers, the damned all bowed their heads.

The shadows in the walls curled in submission, and the flames in the pits lowered briefly as if exhaling. Lucifer felt the shift in his bones, in the marrow of the Underworld itself.

This child belonged to Hell, and with it, Lucifer's rule was eternal, but for the first time in all existence, he didn't care that he was a ruler, a king, the Devil.

He only cared that he was a father.

His entire body trembled from what he'd just done, what he'd just become.

Amber's eyes met his, and he felt exposed for a single, shattering second because she saw it too. She saw the awe, the fear, the realization. She saw Lucifer Morningstar, the most feared being in existence, brought to his knees by something as small and fragile as a child.

A child he'd burn the world for.

A child he already loved in a way he couldn't understand.

Slowly, Lucifer exhaled, letting the truth settle into his bones as he lowered his gaze to Amber, still weak in his arms. Her golden eyes barely stayed open, but he saw it.

The truth that had been written into her bones the moment she stepped into his kingdom: she belonged here, with him, with their child.

For eternity.

Lucifer's fingers brushed against her cheek, his grip still firm but gentler now. And then, with a slow, rare smile, he bent down and pressed a kiss to her forehead.

A simple touch, but it carried the weight of something deeper, something he'd never dared to name before because, for the first time, he knew what that feeling curling inside him was.

And he whispered to her, "I love you."

105

A Father's Vow

Far above Hell, light fractured. The celestial realm trembled as an unseen force rippled through its endless golden halls.

The Archangels felt it.

Michael stilled, his jaw tightening. Gabriel exhaled sharply, his wings tensing at his sides, and Raphael lowered his head.

Then, a single bell tolled in warning. The sound echoed through the golden expanse, vibrating through the very foundations of Heaven.

No one said anything; they didn't have to; they all knew the impossible had happened.

A new power had been born.

One that didn't belong to Heaven.

One that shouldn't exist.

The Archangels had failed; Lucifer hadn't just survived; he'd won.

And from behind them, locked in a cage deep within Heaven, a slow, curling laugh rose from the shadows.

Zagan.

His voice slithered through the stillness, wrapping around the Archangels like snakes, "Incredible."

***

Far below, Lucifer lifted his head. His burning red eyes flickered toward the sky, toward the light that had fractured far above Hell's abyss.

His expression turned cold. Calculating.

He knew Heaven wasn't done.

They'd come for this child.

They'd come for Amber.

The only difference? This time, Lucifer would be ready.

His voice, low and unrelenting, carried through the halls of Hell, through the endless fire and shadow, through the very fabric of existence, "Let them try."

Latin Translations

"Spectaculum finit. Redeat unusquisque ad operandum. Solus qui ad disciplinam attinent vel adsunt mundare possunt manere, secus exitus. Nunc."

"The show is over. Let everyone return to work. Only those who are involved in the discipline or are present to clean up may remain, otherwise exit. Now."

"Grata omnibus ut hac nocte's Collocatione Ceremonia. Incipiamus!"

"Welcome, everyone, to tonight's inauguration ceremony! Let's begin!"

"Gratulatur omnibus electis hac nocte!"

"Congratulations to all those selected tonight!"

"Muta me esse quod statuo coram me."

"Change me to be what I see before me."

"Lux et tenebrae non sunt miscere, hoc bene novimus, sed habeo aliquid pro vobis, quod nesciatis? Peto age quod tuum est, omne quod peto, tibi quadruplum!"

"Light and darkness do not mix, we know this well, but I have something for you, can you not tell? Come, take what is yours, all I ask in return is that you fall to all fours!"

"Te nunc invocamus, te laudamus, Sanctissima. Voces nostras audi, et has necessitudines crea. Has duas animas te rogamus assumere, et antiquorum verbis alligare. Animas suas alligant in magica antiquitatis, ut semper tamen tragica conjungantur. Te rogamus antiquos, exaudi preces nostras, sicut es clavem desiderantis."

"We invoke you now, we praise you, Most Holy One. Hear our voices, and create these connections. We ask you to take these two souls and bind them with the words of the ancients. Let them bind their souls in the magic of antiquity, so that they may always be joined in tragedy. We ask you, ancients, to hear our prayers, as you are the key to the longing."

"Ligaverunt animas suas, dedit tibi quod rogasti. Nunc te revela iam non palliatus es."

"They have given you what you asked, now reveal yourself, you are no longer masked."

"Muta me esse quod ante me video. Tantum nunc peto, o veteres, ut plus videat quam per me permittas. Libera animam meam."

"Change me to be what I see before me. Only now I ask, oh ancient ones, to be more than one can see as you let light pass through me. Set my soul free."

INSIGNIA

"Et lux in tenebris non lucet. Umbra regnat in perpetuum."

"And the light shineth not in darkness. Shadow Reigns Eternal."

www.ingramcontent.com/pod-product-compliance
Lightning Source LLC
Chambersburg PA
CBHW020645110726
47901CB00001B/66